I0818007

MUSKERRY CRITICAL EDITIONS

Vol. 1

NIAMH
(a new edition in modern spelling)

ón Athair
Peadar Ua Laoghaire
Canónach, S.P.

edited by David Webb

ISBN: 978-1-7398872-0-9

An Clár

NIAMH

Preface

Niamh is a historical novel based on the events leading up to the Battle of Clontarf in AD 1014. Published in 1907, *Niamh* did not have the positive reception of the earlier novel published by Peadar Ua Laoghaire (hereinafter, PUL), *Séadna*, although in many ways it is a more serious and more interesting work. The book was criticised early on as a historical novel that betrayed the author's ignorance of the social realities of tenth- and eleventh-century Ireland. The high king of Ireland, Brian Bóruma (the historical form of his name, edited as Brian Bórú in this work), is mythologised by PUL as a patriot who waged war on his enemies in defence of Ireland and the Catholic faith. Historical myths are the stuff of national identity in the present, and such a take on Brian Bórú, while anachronistic, is essentially no different from national myths in other lands. *Niamh* contains a sheaf of anachronisms largely because PUL reads history backwards and sees in Brian Bórú the type of patriotic leader an independent Ireland could have had; such a view was the product of cultural and political currents in Ireland in the immediate pre-independence period.

In her book *An tAthair Peadar Ó Laoghaire agus a Shaothar*, the nun Sister Mary Vincent (an admirer of PUL who wrote under the name Maol Muire) explained:

> Ach bhí An tAthair Peadar ag dul tar a chómhacht nuair a thug sé fé sgéal startha do sgríobhadh. An buadh is mó a bhí aige—fír-eolas ar shaoghal na Gaedhealtachta, agus comhacht chun pictiúirí an tsaoghail sin a léiriú—níor chabhruigh sé leis insan iarracht san. Dá thoisc sin, isé an sgéal so "Niamh" an ceann is luige 'na chuid saothair. Leabhar iseadh é atá lán d'aistí breaghtha, ach ní ró-mhaith a dhein an tAthair Peadar na haistí sin do cheangal dá chéile chun sgéal do dhéanamh dhíobh. Ní raibh aon eolas puinn ag an Athair Peadar ar stair na haoise sin ...

> Níl aon ní sa sgéal a chuirfeadh i n-úil do dhuine gur bhain sé le haois imigéineamhail na Lochlannach; táid na daoine go léir ró-ghar don aois seo; níl blas na firinne ar an slighe n-a labhraid; níl aon fhírinneamhlacht ag baint le n-a ngníomharthaibh; níl suidheamh an sgéil go nádúrtha. [pp64, 66.]

Interestingly, PUL's interest in tenth-century Ireland, despite his lack of adequate knowledge of the period, had earlier contributed to a falling out with Eóin Mac Néill, the editor of *Irisleabhar na Gaedhilge* (see the discussion in Philip O'Leary's *The Prose Literature of the Gaelic Revival*, p182, and in Fr. Shán Ó Cuív's essay, "Caradas nár Mhair: Peadar Ua Laoghaire agus Eóin Mac Néill", pp59-63, where it is explained that the two men parted ways over PUL's eccentric plan to extend the story of *Séadna* back to the time when Ireland's high kings were based in Teamhair na Rí).

Maol Muire criticised the depiction in *Niamh* of Ireland under Brian Bórú before the Battle of Clontarf as a united realm that he could rally as a nation against the Norse, whereas in fact Brian Bórú's authority was patchy, wars were being conducted in various places, and he was only able to rally the Munstermen and armies from two small states in Southern Connacht to his side in advance of the Battle of Clontarf (*An tAthair Peadar Ó Laoghaire agus a Shaothar*, pp70-71). To understand the Ireland of ten centuries ago, it is necessary to realise that the country, while having a high king, had no real central authority, being ruled by scores of hereditary kings who held the real power in their own territories. While Brian Bórú came closer than previous high kings to establishing the authority of the high king, he still had the provincial kings to contend with. PUL refers to the provincial kings (*ríthe cúige* here) as being *fé smacht an Árdrí*, but it is doubtful that this was really fully the case. Brian finally subdued the last of the kingdoms opposing him in AD 1011, but Donncha Ó Corráin explains the situation in the following way:

> By this time, Brian had enforced authority of a sort over the whole country and could claim with some basis in truth, as he did in 1005, to be king of Ireland. However, it is to be doubted if his authority was much greater than the greatest of the Uí Néill kings in the previous three centuries ... He did not create a national monarchy or the institutions of such a monarchy, but he did contribute greatly to advancing the idea of a kingship of the whole island. [*Ireland before the Normans*, p125.]

PUL seems to overemphasise his view that Ireland was a basically peaceful country, governed by the rule of law. By viewing the tenth century through the prism of a man in 1907 who wished to see an end to English rule, he manages to imagine that Brian Bórú was kind enough to spare the life of the high king he ejected from the position, Máel Sechnaill mac Dómnaill (referred to as M'leachlainn here), simply because Ireland was a gentler and less violent country than England. In point of fact, Brian Bórú waged war against many kings, but had to work within the framework of a fragmented country, and found it convenient at the time to allow M'leachlainn to remain as king of Meath.

An error even more glaring was PUL's presentation of Clontarf as *an cath san idir Ghaelaibh Éireann agus Lochlannaigh an domhain*. He portrays the Vikings of Denmark and Norway as preparing in large numbers to join the Battle of Clontarf, and yet the army opposing Brian Bórú at Clontarf was largely comprised of Leinstermen, with a small Norse contingent, and in any case the Norse kingdom of Dublin had nothing to do with the Danes (see *An tAthair Peadair Ó Laoghaire*, p71). The Norse kingdom of Dublin did receive help from the Norse of the Orkneys and the Isle of Man, but not from the wider Viking world. Later accounts enlarged on the events of 1014. "The list of combatants was swelled by numerous additions and the contingents from the Isles and from Man became the forces of the whole Viking world. Brian himself became in story what he never was in fact: the sovereign of Ireland who led the forces of the nation to victory over the foreigners" (*Ireland before the Normans*, p131). As Maol Muire points out, Clontarf was not a battle to defend Catholicism, and many of the Norse-Gaels Brian fought against had themselves adopted Christianity:

> *"Na fir a thuit sa chath so is ar son Creidimh Chríost do thuiteadar".* Is truagh baint ó bhrígh na cainnte uaisle sin, ach mar sin féin, ní féadfí gan cuimhneamh air seo: gur Chaitilicigh, leis, furmhór na slóighte a bhí i gcoinnibh Bhriain idir Ghaedhil agus Lochlannaigh dóibh. [*An tAthair Peadar Ó Laoghaire agus a Shaothar*, pp71-72.]

Some of the historical events referred to in this book appear to have been drawn from earlier works, such as the seventeenth-century *Foras Feasa ar Éirinn* (FFÉ) and *Annála Ríoghachta Éireann* (ARÉ), both of which were based on earlier sources, and a much earlier work, *Cogad Gáedel re Gallaib* (CGG). He appears not to realise, however, that there are many question marks over the details of early Irish history, and in particular there are differing accounts in the various annals. CGG is a southern work that attempts to give a good account of Brian Bórú, even claiming (incredibly) that Brian Bórú gave M'leachlainn a month's notice, and then a year's notice, in advance, of the need to prepare his troops to defend his title as high king. Such details are not given in ARÉ, a northern work, less inclined to flatter the Dalcassian dynasty that hailed originally from County Clare. Many asides in *Niamh* discuss events in the Ulster cycle of myths or the Fenian cycle of myths, or refer to early mythological or legendary high kings of Ireland with no apparent awareness that none of these events or persons is historically attested.

PUL's attitude towards the Catholic church also betrays a lack of basic knowledge of the time period. The Irish church was an independent church based on a monastic framework, not integrated into the wider Western church based in Rome, and there was no Papal legate to Ireland at the time. Only in the twelfth century, after Brian Bórú's time, did the Irish church begin to come under the control of Rome. The notion in this book that priests could not marry also shows a woeful ignorance of the mores of the time: priests and bishops were free to marry during the time under discussion, and it was not until the fourteenth century that clerical celibacy was enforced in Ireland.

This lack of historical truth was criticised in an unbylined article in *An Claidheamh Soluis* that Maol Muire states was penned by Pádraig Mac Piarais:

> As a historical romance, it has the cardinal fault of being untrue—not merely to history, which is a small matter—but to historical vraisemblance. A novelist owes no respect to history, but he owes every respect to the verisimilitude of things. He may play fast and loose with the mere events recorded by annalists,but he should not give a false picture of the life of an historical epoch. He should not make men and women of the tenth century think and talk and act like men and women of the seventeenth century. We quarrel less with the unwarranted apotheosising of Brian, the refusal to do justice to Maelsheachlainn, the failure to appreciate at their true worth those great nation-builders, the Norsemen, the introduction of the Papal Legate, and the rest, than with the air of modernity which pervades the descriptions of life throughout the book. ["History and Romance", *An Claidheamh Soluis*, September 7th, 1907, p8.]

The character of Niamh in this book does not have the ring of truth about it. She is presented as impossibly pure and holy; indeed, one could argue that one of PUL's aims in this book was to encourage vocations among the women of Ireland to enter religious orders. The character of Queen Gormfhlaith, by contrast, has a greater feel of truth about it: she is shown as a scheming individual, but this is mitigated by her love for her son, Amhlaoibh (see *An tAthair Peadar Ó Laoghaire*, pp75-77). The description of Brian Bórú is absurdly complimentary at each turn; arguably PUL was trying to use this novel in order to advance his view of what leaders of an independent Catholic Ireland should be like.

None of this is to say that *Niamh* is devoid of literary value. Pádraig Mac Piarais praised the vivid and descriptive language of *Niamh*, particularly when describing people, something that is seen more generally as one of PUL's strong points. The description of the love between Niamh and Amhlaoibh, and Amhlaoibh's betrayal of her and his other Gaelic friends in order to steal a golden chalice leaves one interested to see how the story develops. The plot advances a little woodenly, as it seems it should have been obvious from the outset to Brian Bórú and the monks of Scattery Island who had stolen the chalice. Nevertheless, some individual vignettes are very well written, including the description of Brian's army as a *sí gaoithe* in chapter 28, the passage in chapter 42 where Murchadh exposes Gormfhlaith's treachery and that in chapter 55 where Amhlaoibh deals Niamh's brother a non-fatal blow, only to look up and see Niamh, with whom he had once had an unstated romantic connection of some kind, witness the deed.

PUL uses this book (as he does his other works) to comment freely on issues of interest to him. He presents the Irishman in constant asides as upright and decent in a way that was, according to him, rare in the rest of Christendom—and, especially, England. The reception of the Norse pupils in monastic schools was *rud a chuireann iúnadh anois ar dhaoine ná tuigeann i gceart an mhór-aigne atá san Éireannach.* The Irish of a divided country were apparently unusually law-abiding: *bhí a leithéid d'urraim i gcónaí riamh ag an nGael do dhlí na ríochta nár ghá a dhéanamh ach a chur in úil do go raibh an dlí ann chun a chur ' fhiachaibh air an dlí do chómhlíonadh.* He was writing at a time (in the pre-Great War period) when a simple, unnuanced kind of nationalism was not unusual in the countries of Europe, and later writers might be more inclined to accept that the Irish were no more likely to show magnanimity of character than members of other nations. A lengthy and absurd aside on the wearing of hats shows the quirkiness of PUL's views: hats were a dreadful import from England, and the wearing of them had led to the spread of baldness in Ireland.

Despite the anachronisms in the text and free comment on extraneous issues, it is undoubtedly the case that the book has much to interest Irish people in the modern day and much of a more general human interest. The time period covered is fascinating, as, regardless of the historicity of every event in this book, Brian Bórú is a provocative character, raising questions as to whether Ireland could have found its way early on to becoming a stable, united and independent country had history adopted only a slightly different path back in the 11th century. An interesting question readers might like to consider is to what extent the Vikings, the builders of Ireland's earliest cities, contributed to the forging of the Irish nation as Mac Piarais states and to what extent they inhibited it. Whatever its literary and historical merits and flaws, Pádraig Mac Suibhne reviewed the book in *An Claidheamh Soluis*, arguing that the beauty of the Irish alone meant that the book ought to be committed to memory, albeit unreliable in terms of historical truth:

> Ní dócha gur breacadh páipéar riamh le Gaedhilg chómh bog binn milis agus atá sí ag an Athair Peadar ins an leabhar nua, "Niamh". Beifear dá léigheamh agus dá ath-léigheamh ar fuaid na hÉireann, agus tá daoine agus beidh sé de ghlan-mheabhair aca ar ball. Is féidir Gaedhilg d'fhoghluim anois gan aon nídh a dhéanamh acht sgríbhinní an Athar Peadar do léigheamh agus duine éigin ó Mhúsgraidhe do sholáthar chun na bhfuaimeanna do mhúineadh. Tá Dia beag déanta ag an Athair Peadar, agus ag "Sgeilg", agus ag "Conán Maol" de Bhrian Bóirimhe. Ní ghéillim i n-éan chor go raibh sé 'n-a dhuine de'n tsórt a cheapann siad-san agus tá mórán im'

> dhála. Cé chuirfidh an taobh eile de'n sgéal os ár gcomhair? Ní mór do dhuine éigin é dhéanamh. ["Ó Chúige Mumhan", *An Claidheamh Soluis*, September 7th, 1907, p1.]

Pádraig Mac Piarais also commented on the linguistic style and usages found in *Niamh* in *An Claidheamh Soluis*:

> The obvious, natural, spontaneous word or phrase which would be used in ordinary conversation by a good Irish speaker is the one invariably chosen—even though the word may be plainly a borrowed one or the idiom may translate directly into King's English. An tAthair Peadar has not the squeamishness about Béarlachas which some younger writers have or affect. He does not hesitate to write in his very first sentence: *"Do thóg Brian Boramha Luimneach ó-s na Lochlanaigh"*, and in his second: *"An meid des na Lochlanaigh nár tógadh 'n-a bprísúnachaibh". "Níor fhágadar aon nídh i bhfuirm leabhar"* (p. 9); *"bheadh an sgéal go holc ... ag gach nídh i bhfuirm léighinn agus eóluis agus nósmhaireachta ar fuid na Críostaidheachta"* (p. 33) are other expressions which a tyro would hesitate to use. It is certain that Cormas mac Cuileannain would not have written these things, but it is equally certain that good Irish speakers of the present day agree to use them; and correctness in language is, after all, a matter of usage among good speakers. ["History and Romance", *An Claidheamh Soluis*, September 7th, 1907, p8; all the vowel lengthmarks were missing in the original in this paragraph and have been supplied here.]

This is an important point at a time when learners of the *Caighdeán Oifigiúil* (CO) seem to have access to an Irish word for everything—including words and concepts not found in the Gaeltacht, where native speakers are happy to use a sprinkling of English words. PUL's *Niamh* shows that words such as *deacon*, *sacraistí* and *conbhint* were preferred by him to *deagánach*, *eardhamh* and *clochar*. Because, as

Mac Piarais states here, correctness in language is determined by the usages of the best speakers, borrowed words used in the Gaeltacht are correctly so used in Irish, and revived or concocted Irish words are only good Irish if they have entered native Gaeltacht speech. Similarly, phrases that translate directly into English are good Irish if they would be used by the strongest Irish speakers, and cannot be compared to the Béarlachas of learners or to words and phrases not found in native Gaeltacht speech invented by learners in the Galltacht (including the learners of Irish staffing the Coiste Téarmaíochta).

It is important to note that the form of Irish referred to as the CO would properly be termed Standardised Irish, and not Standard Irish. This is because it was not a codification of literary usages found before its introduction, as one would expect of a "standard", but an artificial attempt to create a cross-dialectal standard that did not reflect historical literary norms. The mid-twentieth-century script reform, which had the effect of driving all previous literary works, including *Niamh*, out of print, and thus removing out of the way the Irish canon of literature, gave the government a free hand to standardise the language artificially. As the CO properly refers to a specific document codifying grammar, where the Irish taught in Ireland today is being referred to in a wider sense, including lexical forms found in Standardised dictionaries not officially part of the CO document, it will be referred to here as GCh, standing for *Gaelainn Chaighdeánaithe*.

The linguistic value of *Niamh* lies in the fact that it was written in traditional modern Irish, and not in GCh. Consequently, an attempt here has been made to fully preserve all dialectal forms, while modernising the spelling where possible. The overriding assumption here is that PUL wrote West Muskerry (WM) Irish. However, a caveat is in order, owing to the long years that PUL spent away from Muskerry, and, in particular, in Anglophone Ireland. It is for this reason that numerous grammatical solecisms in PUL's *Séadna* were identified by the editor of *An Músgraigheach*, a quarterly magazine published in the 1940s:

> Bheadh breall ar éinne a shamlóchadh gur caighdeán fíor-bheacht ar fad é le cainnt na sean-daoine i Músgraighe. Ní healadha dhúinn a dhearmhad ná raibh an tAthair Peadair ach 'na gharsún óg nuair fhág sé an baile agus gur chaith sé an chuid is mó dá shaoghal i dtaobh amuigh dá dhúthaigh. Ar a chuimhne is mó a bhraitheadh sé nuair a bhíodh an Ghaeluinn aige á sgríobh, agus bhíodh Gaeluinn na leabhar a bhí léighte aige agus Gaeluinn na ndúthaí do shiúbhluigh sé ag teacht i gcoinnibh na cuimhne. Iongna shaoghail is eadh a fheabhas do chimeád sé greim ar a Ghaeluinn féin i n-aimhdheoin na mbarraí sin. Rud eile: sgríobhaidhe neamh-chríochnamhail ab eadh é riamh. Ba chuma leis ach bheith ag sgríobh roimis, gan puinn suime chur sa litriú, agus is annamh i n-aon chor do cheartuigheadh sé an méid a bhíodh sgríobhtha aige. ["Séadna", *An Músgraigheach*, Uimhir 2, Fóghmhar 1943, p7.]

It seems therefore that there are minor differences between PUL's written Irish and the Irish of good native speakers who spent their lives in West Muskerry, and yet it would not be correct to attempt to iron out all such differences in a way that appeared to misrepresent the original work here (see, for example, the note in the *Glossary* on PUL's feminine *an tsí gaoithe*, found here, but rejected by *An Músgraigheach*). Before explaining the spelling system that has been adopted here, it would be apposite to briefly outline the sources available for the study of WM Irish that have been relied upon to determine the correct dialectal forms and the problems they present.

1. As the most extensive writer of the WM dialect, PUL's own works have to be seen as the key source of information on the dialect. However, his early works contain a large number of typographical errors, and the spelling system he later adopted

was only haphazardly implemented in his works, with the result that the original spelling of his works comprises a confusion of classical norms (*coimeád* and *buidhchas* being frequently found in his works, despite being words whose dialectal forms are well-established as *cimeád* and *baochas*, which forms are also found in his works) and spellings that aim to clarify the WM dialectal pronunciation. In the preface to the 1898 edition of Part II of *Séadna* (piii), PUL explained that he had never heard words such as *buailfear*, *bainfear* and *chídhfear*, as he had only ever heard *buailfar*, *bainfar* and *chídhfar*, yet in the complete editions of *Séadna* published in 1904 and 1910, spellings such as *bainfear* made a comeback. Many of the spellings in PUL's published works may reflect the hand of editors and may therefore not reliably give his own pronunciation.

2. Some more carefully edited editions of PUL's works were produced in the 1920s and 1930s, including *Sgéalaidheachta as an mBíobla Naomhtha*, edited by Risteárd Pléimeann in 1922-25; *Críost Mac Dé*, edited by Risteárd Pléimeann in 1924-25; and *Aesop a Tháinig go h-Éirinn* (series I and II in one volume), edited by Dómhnall Ó Mathghamhna in 1931. These are relatively free from typographical errors and show a more concerted attempt to give the correct forms. Both Pléimeann and Ó Mathghamhna were trusted acolytes of PUL.

3. PUL himself made extensive comments on Irish words, many of them in the *Cork Weekly Examiner*, being collated by Dómhnall Ó Mathghamhna in 1926 in *Notes on Irish Words and Usages* (NIWU). For example, PUL's statement that the genitive of *seilbh*, *sealbha*, was pronounced *sealú* (NIWU, p94) has to be considered of greater authority, at least as far as identifying PUL's own pronunciation, than Shán Ó Cuív's decision to transcribe *sealbha* in *Letiriú Shímplí* (LS) as *shealava* (see *Shiàna*, p66). Shán Ó Cuív's LS edition of *Séadna*

transcribes *éasga* as *iàsga* (*Shiàna*, p12), although PUL wrote in NIWU (p43) that a better spelling for this word would be *aosga*, showing that he had /e:skə/ in this word. (*Iàsga* would be a good transcription of *iasga*, a variant of the plural *éisc* found in some of PUL's works.)

4. Given that direct evidence of PUL's pronunciation of most words is lacking, it seems logical to take the Irish of Amhlaoibh Ó Loinsigh (AÓL), a native of West Muskerry 33 years the Canon's junior, as a starting point. More has been written academically about AÓL's pronunciation than about that of any other speaker of WM Irish. AÓL is the key source used by Brian Ó Cuív in his 1943 work *The Irish of West Muskerry* (IWM) and also provided the bulk of the pronunciations indicated in Brian Ó Cuív's 1947 edition of Mícheál Ó Briain's *Cnósach Focal ó Bhaile Bhúirne* (CFBB). Altogether, between the two works, AÓL's pronunciations of around 5,000 words were compiled by Brian Ó Cuív in phonetic transcription and the phonological system set out in IWM provides a basis for determining the pronunciation of many words not separately transcribed therein. Donncha Ó Cróinín also used a semi-phonetic transcription to show AÓL's pronunciation in *Scéalaíocht Amhlaoibh Í Luínse* and *Seanachas Amhlaoibh Í Luínse*. There are occasions where IWM conflicts with statements made by PUL—for example, PUL stated explicitly that he had a slender *-tear* in present-tense autonomous forms such as *buailtear*, yet IWM shows such forms to have a broad *t*. PUL also stated he had three syllables, with a short vowel in each, in the word *forlamhas/fórlámhas*, i.e. /forləvəs/, where AÓL had /fo:r'lɑ:s/, probably because this is a literary word unlikely to have been found in PUL's spoken Irish.

5. While it is difficult to believe that common words such as *cimeád* were pronounced by PUL any differently to other

speakers of the WM dialect, there seems to be some justification for accepting PUL's authority in the spelling of less common words. For example, PUL writes *braighdineas*, with a slender *n*, and while IWM shows AÓL had a broad *n* in this word (*braighdeanas*), it is easy to imagine that PUL might have had a slender *n* in a word like this, which does not form part of the core vocabulary of the spoken language. Similarly, the spelling *deifrígheacht* was used in the original text here, contrasting with the spelling *defearaíocht* used in CFBB, showing a broad *r*. To intrude the spelling *deifearaíocht* would require a greater level of certainty over PUL's pronunciation, and so the spelling adopted in the editing here is *deifríocht*.

6. The spellings used throughout CFBB by Brian Ó Cuív are reasonably authoritative for WM Irish. The spellings adopted by Shán Ó Cuív, Osborn Bergin and Risteárd Pléimeann in their LS editions of PUL's works also point to many of the correct dialectal pronunciations. However, LS transcriptions are internally inconsistent and less reliable than those given in IWM and CFBB.

An example of the difficulties thrown up by the gross frequency of typographical errors in PUL's published works is *deimhne ceart* here. As Ó Dónaill's *Foclóir Gaeilge-Béarla* (FGB) shows *deimhne* to be feminine, without strong evidence that this word was definitely masculine in WM Irish it would be advisable to have the feminine gender here. PUL's *deimhne ceart* could therefore be seen as a typographical error, for *deimhne cheart*, and yet the phrase occurs twice here, and there is a further example cited in the *Glossary* here of a masculine *deimhne* in PUL's works, and so it seems this word was masculine in PUL's Irish. This seems to reflect an uncertainty among native speakers in the treatment of rarer abstract nouns. It is likely, however, that contexts that reveal the gender of this word are rarely found, in any form of Irish.

As far as pronunciation is concerned—and therefore the spelling used in this edition—combining the evidence of the various sources of information on WM Irish outlined above, it is possible to draw conclusions as to the correct pronunciation of Irish words in the WM dialect, and then to use that knowledge to devise an approach to the editing of PUL's works. The style of editing, a kind of Muskerry House Style (MHS), needs to be one that can be applied to all of PUL's works, despite the variation in spellings between his works. The principles of MHS are set out as follows.

Vowel length is shown, in a departure from the conventions that obtain in GCh. For example, *eo* is usually pronounced *eó*, but not all words observe this rule (cf. *leogaim*, etc), and so *eó* is preserved where the vowel is long. This is frequently indicated in the original text of *Niamh*, but the original text had numerous orthographical inconsistencies, and so *eó* is also adopted where the pronunciation requires it where the original text had *eo*. A similar situation applies to lengthened vowels before *r*: *ard* is given as *árd*, the spelling used by PUL that gives the correct pronunciation in WM Irish. Complex rules on vowels in position before nasal sounds are discussed in IWM (§401). Given their complexity, it has been thought better to spell the word that was traditionally *sinnsear* and that appears in GCh as *sinsear* as *sínsear*. *Cinn* becomes *cínn* and *tuillte* becomes *tuíllte*. That *dinnéir* is pronounced *dínnéir* is not clear from the rules, but the length is clarified by the spelling used here (which happens to be identical in this case to the spelling used in the original edition of *Niamh*). Readers will know that *ann* is pronounced /aun/; this reflects a principle of broader application, and a double *n* or *l* is used here to indicate a diphthong, as in *cainnt*, *splanncracha* and *canncar*. A rule applies whereby an *ll* or *nn* is dropped in pronunciation before *r* leaving the diphthong, and so the (traditionally correct) spelling *deallramh* (*dealramh* in GCh) is adopted here, indicating the pronunciation /d′aurəv/. *Banríon* is pronounced /bau'ri:n′/ and edited as *bannrín* here. Notes in the appended *Glossary* discuss the deletion of the *l*- and *n*-sounds in these words. Close familiarity with IWM is recommended in any case. Long *i* and *u* vowels are indicated in words such as *ríghneas*, *Múmhain* and *úrnaithe*, a usage found inconsistently in the original. It is generally the case that marking a long vowel before digraphs such as *bh*, *gh* and *mh* implies deletion of the digraph in the pronunciation, but counterexamples, such as *scríbhinn* exist. *Aoi* is generally pronounced /i:/ in the dialect, but the spelling changes of the 1950s have created a large number of words that violate this rule. An example is the deletion of *-gh-* in *saoghail*, producing *saoil*, which is pronounced /se:l'/; this word has therefore been edited in the genitive as as *saeil*. An additional point is that where the GCh spelling is adequate it should be retained. For example, the genitive of *réidh* ("moorland") was given in PUL's *Mo Sgéal Féin* as *réidhe*, but the GCh *ré* can be accepted for the genitive of this word, although not for the nominative.

On occasion, a spelling at variance with both the original text and the GCh form is preferred. An example is *coimeád*, edited as *cimeád*, as discussed above, but this principle also concerns *leigim*, a spelling influenced by classical norms, where *ligim* is found in GCh. This has been adjusted to *leogaim*, in line with WM pronunciation. Similarly, *druidim* in the original text has been edited here as *dridim*. These adjustments are supported by the use of *cimeád*, *leogaint* and *dridim* in some of PUL's published works. More problematic are words such as *taispeánann* and *muineál*, which are spelt with a broad *t* and broad *m* respectively in the original text. An editorial decision has been adopted to impose a slender *t* and *m*, as the LS editions of PUL's works show a pronunciation identical to that of AÓL given in IWM. PUL wrote *dó* for the prepositional pronoun pronounced /do/ (with a short vowel). As the assumption here is that PUL's pronunciation was broadly the same as that of AÓL, *do* is used in the editing here. Another example is *adhsáideach* for the original *eidhsáideach*. This is because *adhsáideach* is listed as a variant of *aosáideach* in FGB, one that yields the correct WM pronunciation, whereas *eidhsáideach* was an idiosyncratic spelling choice. *Comairce* in the original becomes *coimirce* here and *deacair* becomes *deocair*; such spellings are not found in PUL's works, but the form *comairce* is not accepted in GCh in any case, and *deacair* is relatively distant from the desired pronunciation. By contrast, a similar adjustment cannot be made where extraneous morphological forms are employed. *Fé* occurs once as *faoi* and *ins gach* is found as *i ngach* a number of times in this work, and these forms are retained as given to avoid giving the impression that PUL never used extraneous dialectal forms.

PUL's haphazard use of spellings that clarified epenthetic vowels, e.g. *ainim* for *ainm*, *fiacala* for *fiacla* and *osgaladh* for *oscladh*, is not adopted here. This decision also applies to dative plural forms such as *focalaibh* and *pobalaibh*, which are edited here as *foclaibh* and *poblaibh*. PUL was not consistent in the spelling out of epenthetic vowels, and a decision to spell them all out as a global change would require a very large number of spelling changes. In consonant clusters such as *rth*, where it is unclear whether an epenthetic vowel is required, a different approach is required: *seirbhthean* is edited here as *seirithean* to show the additional vowel; *beirthe*, the past participle of *beirim*, is edited here as *bertha* (thus clarifying the distinction between *beirthe* and *beirithe*). In the opposite case, the dative plural spellings *namhdaibh* and *deamhnaibh* rather than *namhadaibh* or *deamhanaibh* have been preferred. The additional vowel would be purely orthographic, and it was traditionally correct to omit it. Orthographic vowels in verbal endings, such as *rabhadar* and *gheibhimís*, for *rabhdar* and *gheibhmís*, are retained, because such usage has been standardised on in GCh (e.g. *faighimid*). PUL also spells *oi* as *ui* where the pronunciation is /i/, e.g. *guid* for *goid*; his usage in this respect is not consistent across all words, but where his spelling is more or less consistent in the case of a particular word and better represents WM dialectal pronunciation, it is retained. A final point on the spelling of vowels relates to the plural of nouns derived from verbal nouns in *-ú*: while there are no instances in *Niamh*, words such as *órduighthe* are found in PUL's other works, and this word should become *órdaithe* (*na hórdaithe*) in MHS. While GCh uses *ordaithe* in the genitive and *orduithe* in the plural, there is no learning or scholarship to back up such an arbitrary distinction: both *ordaighthe* and *orduighthe* are correct traditional spellings for both the genitive singular and the nominative plural, and no distinction in number or case can correctly be inferred therefrom.

As far as the spelling of consonants (and their broad/slender quality) in verb conjugations is concerned, in the classical orthography, and also in the spelling adopted in GCh, the *caol le caol, leathan le leathan* spelling rule is adhered to in the autonomous form of the verb. However, PUL told Gerald O'Nolan, "I have never heard, e.g., *buailfear.* What I have heard is *buailfar,* with the *l* slender and the *f* as broad as it is in *ólfar.* But I have always heard *buailtear.* I dare say some people have heard *buailtar.* If they have, then they ought to write *buailtar,* and then we should know that they have heard it" [*Beatha Dhuine a Thoil,* pp137-138]. For this reason, and regardless of the spellings found in the original text of *Niamh,* the spellings *-tear* and *-far* are used in this edition with slender stems in the present and future autonomous. As far as the imperfect and conditional autonomous forms are concerned, the inconsistent spelling found in PUL's works appears to indicate that he uniformly pronounced the autonomous endings *-taí/-tí* or *-faí/-fí* with a slender *t* and *f,* which accords with their general pronunciation in WM Irish. For this reason, the spellings *-tí* and *-fí* are used with broad stems here. The autonomous forms of the verb *cuirim* are consistently edited as *curtar, curfar, curfí* and *curtí* in this edition, as PUL seemed generally consistent in his use of *cur-* (although counterexamples of spellings such as *cuirtear* were also found in the original text of *Niamh*). Similarly, the second-person singular of all verbs is edited uniformly with a broad *-fá* in the conditional tense here. PUL's spelling was inconsistent on this point, but there are enough examples of *-fá* appended to a slender stem to be sure his pronunciation was broad, as it would be in modern-day WM Irish. Thus PUL has *churfá* (*dá gcurfá* here) in the conditional, where *chuirfá* would be found today. The modern convention whereby verb forms have *-igh* rather than *-idh* (for example, *chuaigh* for *chuaidh*), has been adhered to, although this "rule" does not appear to be based on anything substantial. Conversely, PUL's *diaigh* has been edited here as *diaidh*, to avoid needlessly diverging from modern spelling conventions where the generally accepted spelling produces the correct pronunciation in any case.

Where PUL had *cosmhail* in the original, this has been retained to show an /sv/ pronunciation. (Had the original text had *cosamhail*, this would have been edited as *cosúil* here, and *cosamhlacht* is edited as *cosúlacht* here for this reason.) PUL also shows the broad/slender quality of an initial *r*, sometimes writing *ramhar* (*bhíodh suas le trí mhíle bó ann de bhuaibh ramhara*) and sometimes *reamhar* (*trí chéad bó reamhar*), and sometimes writing *ruith* and sometimes writing *rith*. This has not been retained here, as there is no likelihood that PUL was consistent in using such spellings (compare *a rí* and *do rug* here, where IWM §404 shows AÓL had a broad and slender *r* respectively). PUL's spellings of these words have, instead, been discussed in the *Glossary*.

It should be added that PUL's use of proper names often appears to be based on Middle or Early Modern Irish texts, and so *Tonn Clíodhna* and *Giolla Pádraig* and many others did not contain the expected lenition in the original text. These have been edited as *Tonn Chlíona* and *Giolla Phádraig*, etc. Names beginning with *Maol-* are especially problematic in this respect (in the original text some have lenition of the second part of the compound, where others do not; some have *Maoil-* in the genitive, where others do not). PUL may have been attempting to give the text an 'authentic' or archaising tone by the (haphazard) use of forms he encountered in older Irish texts. I felt that retaining *Maolmuaidh*, rather than respelling it *Maolmhuaidh*, would be incorrect. I believe the English version "Molloy" gives a good indication as to the (modern) pronunciation, /me:l 'uəg′/or possibly /mə 'luəg′/, which could even have justified a spelling *M'luaidh*. It may be that PUL's reluctance to reach for *Maoilmhuaidh* in the genitive with a slender *l* reflected his awareness that the pronunciation was /mə 'lˠuəg′/, and so intruding a slender *l* in the genitive would be unjustified. For this reason, *Maolmhuaidh* is used in this edition in both nominative and genitive. The original text repeatedly has *Oileán Mhanain*, "the Isle of Man", although the genitive and dative should be *Manann* and *Manainn* respectively. I have used *Oileán Mhanann* here. *Cluain Tairbh*, "Clontarf", for what is usually given as *Cluain Tarbh*, was also noteworthy. I have searched PUL's writings, and cannot find a single instance of *Cluain Tarbh*, and so I think it is likely that he was more familiar with the English version of this placename. It is a shame that the original manuscript is not extant, and so the accuracy of the published text cannot be assessed. Further discussion of all proper names can be found in the backmatter.

PUL used *dá dhéanamh* to mean "being done" and *'ghá dhéanamh* to mean "doing it"; these are both normally pronounced *á* in modern Cork Irish. However, PUL was very insistent on this point (see, for example, his comments in NIWU, p131). For this reason, *dá* is retained as *dá*, *'ghá* is given as *dhá* and *'á* becomes *á* here. The particle governing the verbal noun is shown by an apostrophe where missing in the original (*é ' chur*). The use of the apostrophe is grammatically clear and editing such phrases as *é a chur* would be misleading in terms of the pronunciation. *A* and *do* are both accepted here as relative particles. A relative particle that is dropped in the original is also shown by an apostrophe here (as in *chómh maith agus ' bhí...*). *Dh'* alone as a relative has been edited to produce *' dh'* for grammatical clarity's sake. The various relative forms of the verb *deirim* have been edited as a single word, as in *adúradh*, as the *a* was originally part of the verb; this reflects the same principle that lies behind the universal use of *atá* for the relative form of the verb *táim*. An apostrophe in lieu of a relative particle is used between interrogatives such as *cé* and *cad* on the one hand and present-tense forms of the verb *táim*, giving *cad 'tá* (*cé atá* is retained once here, in chapter 42, because the relative particle, although not audible in pronunciation, was given in the original). Similarly, relative forms of *deirim* after *cé* and *cad* take an apostrophe, as in *cad 'deirir?*

The dropping of the *n* of the interrogative particle occasionally found in the text has been retained, as in *a' bhfuil* for *an bhfuil*, but not imposed where it was not found in the original. The apostrophe in *uair a' chloig* is left untouched, although this phrase is edited here as *uair a' chluig*. Where grammatically required h-prefixation is not given before the autonomous form of verb (as in *nár aithníodh* for *nár haithníodh*), the original form is retained, as h-prefixation often seems hit and miss in PUL's published works and manuscripts, and this may be a detail of interest in academic treatment of his Irish. An adjustment is made for *go raibh Brian ar dhuine de sna trí hÁrdríthibh*, where h-prefixation before *Árdríthibh* is added here. In a number of cases, an unpronounced letter is replaced by an apostrophe, regardless of the spelling of the original, as in *dó'* for *dóich*, *lasmu'* for *lasmuich*, *amu'* for *amuich*—it is likely that PUL used *-ch-* in these words rather than writing *dóigh*, *lasmuigh* and *amuigh* in order to indicate that the pronuncation was not with /gʹ/—and a silent digraph is omitted in *scríodar*, for *sgríobhadar*. The verbal nouns *sgríobhadh* and *léigheadh* (=*léamh* in GCh) are here rendered *scrí'* and *lé'*.

PUL frequently spelt *de* as *do*. *De* as a simple preposition (as opposed to the prepositional pronoun *de*) is pronounced /də/, in other words, pronounced identically to *do*, in the local dialect, and PUL is on record insisting on spellings such as *do réir*. He consistently used the spellings *do ghnáth* and *do phreib* and *macshamail don eochair* in the original text. He may have believed that some of these were derived from an original *do*. PUL's views on the matter are given in *Mion-chaint Cuid a III* (p18):

> *Tháinig sé thar abhainn do chosaibh tirme.* He came across the river on dry legs. *Ghabhas do láimh é.* I took the matter in hands. *Ghabhas do dhóirnibh air.* I (did) beat him with (my) fists. *Ghabhas de dhóirnibh air.* I (did) beat him with (my) fists.

> Here the thought has either of two modes. If I use *do*, I tell the manner in which I beat him. If I use *de*, I tell the instruments with which I beat him. The use of *do* or of *de* entirely depends on the state of the speaker's mind. He can choose.

There are many examples of erratic usage in the original text of *Niamh*, including both *gabháil de chosaibh* and *gabháil do chosaibh*. It has been thought best to edit all instances of the simple prepositions *de* and *do* in line with the (presumed) historically correct prepositions, which is also the usage preferred in GCh. Abbreviated words that give the correct pronunciation, as in *pé'r domhan é* for an underlying *pé ar domhan é*, are retained, although where *an domhan* stood in the original for *den domhan*, it has been thought best to edit this as *'en domhan*, for clarity's sake. *Pé'cu* has been edited as *peocu* and *cé'cu* as *ceocu*. *Agá* is occasionally found in the original and has been edited as *ag á*. *A fhios*, which variously appears as *fhios*, *a fhios* and *'fhios* in the original, is uniformly edited as *' fhios*, in line with the pronunciation. *A'* for *as*, "from", has been edited as *a*; despite some loss of clarity, *a* as a variant form of *as* is given in FGB, which does not list *a'* or *à*, as it has sometimes been written, as headwords. Occasional use of *-t* in a combined prepositional form, the only examples of which found here are *dot chuid* for *dod chuid* and *ageat shlóitibh* for *agead shlóitibh* (spelt *do t' chuid* and *agat' shlóightibh* in the original), has been accepted as it seems likely the following consonant would devoice a preceding *-d*; however, use of these follows the original, and similar usages have not been inserted where the original did not so indicate such a devoicing. The second-person singular possessive is rendered as *t'* before a vowel here, although both *t'* and *d'* are found in apparent haphazard distribution in the original. Similarly, the combined pronoun *ad'* where found before a vowel in the original has been edited here as *i t'*. (All four such instances are of *ad' aigne*, but *at' aigne* was also found twice in the original, as well as *at' aonar* and other analogous examples.) *Tu* and *thu* are accepted as the disjunct forms of the second-person singular pronoun and *me* as the disjunct form of the first-person singular pronoun. This usage was haphazard in the original, but standardised on throughout here. The prepositions *tré* and *thré* have been edited as *trí* and *thrí* in line with the pronunciation of WM Irish. Where declined forms of the noun *slua* have an *-ó-* in the spelling in the original, e.g. *slóighte*, this is retained (as *slóite*).

The combined prepositional form usually found as *'n-a* has been spelt *'na*, without a hyphen, including the single instance in chapter 2 where the original text had *iona* (*súil iona raibh fíor uaisleacht*) and eight instances where *i n-a* was found in the original (by contrast, *'n-a* and *n-a* were found more than 600 times in the original). There are very few examples in the original texts of PUL's works of phrases such as *ina raibh* and *ina bhfuil*, which give the wrong pronunciation for what are in fluent speech *'na raibh* /nə rev′/ and *'na bhfuil* /nə vil′/. Before a vowel *ina* has been edited as *in'*, producing *in' aonar* with the masculine possessive, and *'na haonar* and *'na n-aonar* with the feminine and plural possessives; this is generally how such forms stood in the original here and in PUL's other works. The prepositional form *inár* is edited as *'nár* throughout and the single instance of *i nbhúr* has been edited as *'núr* (reflecting similar choices made in the LS versions of PUL's works where *inár* or *i nbhúr* stood in the *gnáth-leitriú*). A similar approach is also followed in indirect relative clauses, as in *fear 'narbh ainm do* for *fear n-ar bh'ainim dó*. Just as the indirect relative particle *gur* no longer has any connection with the preposition *ag* that it derives from, the indirect relative particle *'nar* no longer has anything to do with the preposition *i*, and it would be a glaring grammatical mistake to edit such sentences as **fear inarbh ainm do* (for the same reason that *fear gurbh ainm do* cannot be edited as **fear ag arbh ainm do*). Prepositional pronouns spelt *-u* in GCh are so spelt here too, including words such as *rómpu* and *eatarthu* where the final vowel is a neutral vowel /ə/ in WM Irish. This is to avoid the very frequent use of words spelt differently from GCh that would not add much to the reader's understanding of the *differentia specifica* of WM Irish. Verbal forms such as *feacaigh* (from *feaca* and *feacaidh* in the original), where the final *-igh* is not heard before a third-person pronoun, are consistently spelt in full to avoid requiring extensive changes in the spelling of preterites. In present subjunctive forms such as *go gcuiridh*, where the final consonant is not always heard, the spelling of the original (generally with *-idh*) is retained. The Irish surname *Ó Ceallaigh* is spelt in line with the pronunciation in the original, i.e. as *Ó Cealla*, and this is retained. Finally, some words are spelt in a manner that poorly illustrates the pronunciation, e.g. *inniu* for /i'n'uv/, but it has been thought better to retain the spelling rather than generate innovative spellings (*iniubh?*) never in general use.

PUL's punctuation often diverged from modern norms. I have not retained his frequent use of two or three consecutive dashes, and have often added in commas not given in the original text. I have tried to adopt a standardised approach, and decided that adverbial phrases such as *Nuair a tháinig sé* at the beginning of the sentence would always be set off by commas, unless particularly short, such as *fé dheireadh*. I did not accept the way a short adverbial phrase with *go* was often appended with a comma: *arsa Amhlaoibh, go símplí* loses its comma here. I have preferred to use a comma in phrases like *óig-fhear chómh breá, chómh dathúil*, where *chómh* is used, although a succession of adjectives is usually given in PUL's works without commas. I have added in commas in phrases such as this: *na fir ba thréine a bhí ar chlannaibh Lochlann, bhíodar sa chath san*. My approach may be debatable, but the result should be a punctuated text that can be read with less confusion.

Apparent grammatical irregularities that do not seem be typographical errors, such as *dhá bhuíon* for *dhá bhuín*, are left unamended, as it seems likely that use of the dual number was patchy even in PUL's writings. Another example of such irregularities in usage is the use of forms such as *eaglaisíbh* and *eagailsíbh* in this work; they have been left as they appeared in the original, as both forms may be found. Dative plurals are unstable in this work:

gnóthaíbh and *gnóthaibh* are both found, and numerous analogous examples can be adduced, but these are also left as they stood.

An attempt has been made to adopt a standardised approach to hyphenation in this text, although the approach varies from that adopted in GCh. Compounds where the components are still felt to be separate words and compounds where the pronunciation is influenced by the fact that the word is a compound are hyphenated here. An example is *óig-fhear*, where the pronunciation is /o:g′ar/ and the second element does not contain the neutral vowel.

No attempt has been made to note all the numerous typographical errors in the early editions of *Niamh*, which would run into the many hundreds. The second edition (that of 1910) contained a number of corrections (adding in some instances of lenition where the 1907 edition omitted it and correcting some instances of dative usage), and so the text here has been compared in detail with that more correct edition. As far as obvious errors are concerned, it seems clear that the presence or absence of lenition is the key type of typographical error found in PUL's works. In a letter to Risteárd Pléimeann dated February 6th 1918, PUL admitted that his manuscripts were littered with many such errors:

> D'fheuchainn tré gach aon chaibidiol fé mar a bhíodh sé críochnuighthe agam, chun na marcana do chur síos. Tá eagal orm go mb' fhéidir gur chuaidh cuid acu uaim gan cur síos. Ach beidh tú féin ábalta ar iad do chur síos. Is dóich liom gur géire do shúil chun na h-oibre sin 'ná mo shúil-se. Ní bhíon aon ghá agamsa leó ar mo shon féinig, agus mar gheall ar sin sleamhnuíghid siad orm. Uaireanta, féuch, cuirim síos iad a ganfhios dom féin, sa n-éagcóir. Bhíos ag féuchaint anois ar an ait [*sic*] ud 'n-ar chuir an Samaritánach fóghanta an duine créachtnuighthe "ar muin a bheithíg féin". Agus cad a bhéadh curtha síos agam ach "ar mhuin"! rud nár airígheas riamh;

> agus rud a cheartuígheas do dhaoínibh eile "chómh minic agus tá méireana orm"!

The types of errors found throughout the original text here include the following (with page numbers referring to the 1910 edition):

ríoga 'n-a cruith agus 'n-a phearsain [p11]	edited as	*ríoga 'na chruith agus 'na phearsain*
a mic [in the vocative; p12]		*a mhic*
ar ceathramhain an fhir bhréige [p14]		*ar cheathrúin an fhir bhréige*
d'aon guth [p48]		*d'aon ghuth*
longphort Thaidhg Móir uí Chealla [p76]		*longphort Thaidhg Mhóir Uí Chealla*
tugadh an mí do M'lsheachlainn [p82]		*tugadh an mí do Mh'leachlainn*
duais saidhbhir [p100]		*duais shaibhir*
trí caoghaid [p117]		*trí caogaid*
an géire inntleachta [p119]		*an ghéire íntleachta*
dúbhrais [contrasting with *dúbhraís* elsewhere in the text; pp123, 291]		*dúraís*
laeth láidir [pp158-159]		*leath láidir*
do cuirfeadh [p162]		*do chuirfeadh*
iad do breith [p162]		*iad do bhreith*
ní feadaraís a leath [p167]		*ní fheadraís a leath*
chómh ghleusta [p177]		*chómh gléasta*
níor bh'fhéidir aon bhob a bualadh ar Bhrian [p177]		*níorbh fhéidir aon bhob a bhualadh ar Bhrian*
aire maith [p180]		*aire mhaith*
sa bhfear a geóbhaidh sgoluigheacht [p180]		*sa bhfear a gheóbhaidh scolaíocht*
buail sí [p208]		*bhuail sí*

Niamh a caitheadh na ceisteana go léir a fhreagairt dó [p278]		*Niamh a chaitheadh na ceisteanna go léir a fhreagairt do*
mac Cuinn Chéadchathaigh [p279]		*mac Chuínn Chéad-chathaigh*
chun an chatha mhór do throid [p281]		*chun an chatha mhóir do throid*
a bheithigh allta! [in the vocative; p287]		*a bheithígh allta!*
caithfidh tu labhairt [p281]		*caithfidh tú labhairt*
siúbhluigh sé [p300]		*shiúlaigh sé*
Danmarg [contrasting with a previous *Danmharg* in the original text; p320]		*Danmharg*
fanaidis [p321]		*fanaidís*
athair Caoilte [p342]		*athair Chaoilte*

Where the original editions enumerated chapters separately in each of three "books", the chapters are numbered successively from 1 to 59 in this edition. Endnotes are appended to the text, explaining various grammatical points and commenting on the relationship of the text to annalistic records of the period (the presence of an endnote is indicated by a raised asterisk in the text and crossreferenced back by page number in the *Notes* section), but most notes on people and placenames appearing in the text have been included in the *Index of Personal Names* and the *Index of Placenames and Population Groups*. The extensive *Glossary* attached here comments on the meaning and pronunciation of many words and phrases, and explains their relationship to the words standardised on today in GCh. The aim is that any words not found in FGB will be given in the *Glossary*, but an attempt has also been made to note all words with epenthetic vowels or other pronunciation peculiarities. This means that even some common words are given in the *Glossary* if I felt the stress needed to be commented on, or the presence of an epenthetic vowel, or the meaning of a phrase noted. **The specific aim and point of the *Glossary* is that learners of Munster Irish adopt PUL's**

vocabulary and not that of the standardisers and dictionaries such as FGB. Useful information contained in the backmatter appended to the 1910 edition has been integrated into the backmatter appended to this edition. Where the pronunciation is indicated, the system used in IWM has been largely followed here, with one exception. Brian Ó Cuív stated in IWM that voiced *b*, *d* and *g* are used after *s* in WM Irish, in words such as *scéal* (see §335). While PUL did use the traditionally correct *sg* spelling where *sc* is found today, it seems Ó Cuív would have been on firmer ground had he said that unvoiced but unaspirated *p*, *t* and *k* are used (i.e. they are not followed by a puff of breath as would be the case where they did not follow an *s*), and so words and phrases such as *bun-os-cionn* and *tispeáint*, the pronunciation of which is given here in the *Glossary*, are better transcribed /bin′iʃ 'k′u:n/ and /t′is'p′a:nt′/ than /bin′iʃ 'g′u:n/ and /t′is'b′a:nt′/. As modernised editions of older works generally reprint the original preface, it is worth stating that neither the 1907 nor the 1910 edition contained a preface.

Finally, I am a self-taught learner of Cork Irish and have spent around five weeks in Ireland. I have never attended any classes or any *ciorcal cómhrá*, and so I have broadly studied Irish in the same way in which Latin or Ancient Greek are studied. Many people have helped me over the years, including during my initial reading of *Niamh*. After my initial transcription of the book, Ailín Ó Súilleabháin and Aonghus Ó hAlmháin took a great deal of time to answer my questions on passages then opaque to me in the book. Darran McManus provided me with many scans of LS works and PUL's correspondence held in the National Library of Ireland. Eilís Ní Mhearraí at the Royal Irish Academy arranged for me to receive copies of the RIA's digital transcriptions of many of PUL's works, which considerably facilitated searches of PUL's Irish while preparing the detailed *Glossary* here. My queries specifically on Cork Irish, which have over the years numbered probably a couple of thousand, were directed towards Dr Seán Ua Súilleabháin at the University College Cork, who is also the leading member of the Coiste Litríochta

Mhúscraí. Without his patient help, it would have been impossible to complete this modernisation of PUL's *Niamh* and to provide the wealth of detail in the *Glossary*. I will be satisfied that I have done a good job here only if Dr Ua Súilleabháin is happy with the result. I hope I do not let him down. In any case, any errors (typographical and otherwise) in the text are mine, and can be notified to me at foghlamoir@gmail.com.

David Webb

Lincolnshire

November 2024

Abbreviations

AÓL: Amhlaoibh Ó Loingsigh.
ARÉ: *Annála Ríoghachta Éireann.*
CFBB: *Cnósach Focal ó Bhaile Bhúirne.*
CGG: *Cogadh Gaedhel re Gallaibh.*
CO: An Caighdeán Oifigiúil.
FFÉ: *Foras Feasa ar Éirinn.*
FGB: *Foclóir Gaeilge-Béarla.*
GCD: *Gaeilge Chorca Dhuibhne.*
GCh: Gaelainn Chaighdeánaithe (the general form of Irish taught in Ireland today, defined more widely than the CO as such).
IWM: *The Irish of West Muskerry.*
LASID: *Linguistic Atlas and Survey of Irish Dialects*, Volume II.
LS: An Letiriú Shímplí (Simplified Spelling).
MHS: Muskerry House Style.
NIWU: *Notes on Irish Words and Usages.*
PSD: *Foclóir Gaedhilge agus Béarla*; Patrick S. Dinneen.
PUL: Peadar Ua Laoghaire.
WM: West Muskerry.

References

"An Choróinn Mhuire", in *An Músgraigheach: bulletín do cháirde Mhúsgraighe*, Uimhir 6, Fóghmhar 1944.

"Filí agus Filíocht Mhúsgraighe", in *An Músgraigheach: bulletín do cháirde Mhúsgraighe*, Uimhir 2, Fóghmhar 1943.

Preface

"Maol Muire" (Sister Mary Vincent). *An tAthair Peadar Ó Laoghaire agus a Shaothar*, Baile Átha Cliath: Brún agus Ó Nualláin, 1939.

"Seachain!", in *An Músgraigheach: bulletín do cháirde Mhúsgraighe*, Uimhir 1, Meitheamh 1943.

"Séadna", in *An Músgraigheach: bulletín do cháirde Mhúsgraighe*, Uimhir 2, Fóghmhar 1943.

"Séadna", in *An Músgraigheach: bulletín do cháirde Mhúsgraighe*, Uimhir 3, Nodlaig 1943.

Céitinn, Seathrún. *Foras Feasa ar Éirinn*, translated by Edward Comyn and Patrick S. Dinneen as *The History of Ireland*, London: The Irish Texts Society, 1902-1914.

Dasent, George W. (tr.) *The Story of Burnt Njal* (abridged), London: Grant Richards, 1900.

Dinneen, Patrick S. *Foclóir Gaedhilge agus Béarla*, Dublin: The Irish Texts Society, 1927.

Gwynn, Stephen Lucius. *Thomas Moore*, London: Macmillan, 1905.

Mac Suibhne, Pádraig, "Ó Cúige Mumhan", and Mac Piarais, Pádraig, "History and Romance", in *An Claidheamh Soluis*, Dublin, September 7th, 1907.

Marstrander, Carl J. S. *et al. Dictionary of the Irish Language*, Dublin: Royal Irish Academy, 1913-76.

Ó Briain, Mícheál. *Cnósach Focal ó Bhaile Bhúirne*, Baile Átha Cliath: Institiúid Árd-léighinn Bhaile Átha Cliath, 1947.

Ó Céileachair, Donchadh. *Nótaí do 'Scéal mo bheatha'*, an unpublished M.A. thesis held at University College Cork, 1950.

Ó Corráin, Donncha. *Ireland before the Normans*, Dublin: Gill and Macmillan, 1972.

Ó Cróinín, Donncha, "Scéalaíocht Amhlaoibh Í Luínse", in *Béaloideas*, Vol 35/36, 1967/1968.

Ó Cuív, Brian, "An t-Athair Peadar Ua Laoghaire's translation of the Old Testament", in *Zeitschrift für celtische Philologie*, Vol 49–50 (1997), pp. 643–652.

Ó Cuív, Brian. *The Irish of West Muskerry, Co. Cork*, Dublin: The Dublin Institute for Advanced Studies, 1944.

Ó Cuív, Shán (Fr), "Materials for a Bibliography of the Very Reverend Peter Canon O'Leary 1839-1920", in *Celtica*, Vol II, Part 2, 1954.

Ó Cuív, Shán, "Caradas nár Mhair: Peadar Ua Laoghaire agus Eóin Mac Néill", in Martin, Francis X. (ed.), *The scholar revolutionary: Eoin MacNeill, 1867-1945, and the making of the new Ireland*, Shannon: Irish University Press, 1973, pp49-73.

Ó Dónaill, Niall. *Foclóir Gaeilge-Béarla*, Baile Átha Cliath: An Gúm, 1977.

Ó Laeri, Peaduir, *An Teagasc Crísdy*, Dublin: Browne and Nolan, 1922.

Ó Laeri, Peaduir. *Catilína: cúntas ar choga Chatilína*, Bleáclieh: Muíntir na Leour Gäluingi, 1913.

Ó Laeri, Peaduir. *Don Cíchóté*, Bleáclieh: Brún agus Ó Nóláin, 1921.

Ó Laeri, Peaduir. *Eshirt*, Bleáclieh: Muíntir na Leour Gäluingi, 1913.

Ó Laeri, Peaduir. *Mo shgiàl fén: Cuid a hän*, Bleáclieh: Brún agus Nólán, 1915.

Ó Laeri, Peaduir. *Shiàna*, Bleáclieh: Muíntir na Leour Gäluingi, 1914.

Ó Luínse, Amhlaoibh. *Seanachas Amhlaoibh Í Luínse*, Dublin: Comhairle Bhéaloideas Éireann, 1980.

Ó Nualláin, Gearóid. *Beatha Dhuine a Thoil*, Baile Átha Cliath: Oifig an tSoláthair, 1950.

Ó Sé, Diarmuid, "Contributions to the Study of Word Stress in Irish", in *Ériu*, Vol 40, 1989.

Ó Sé, Diarmuid. *Gaeilge Chorca Dhuibhne*, Dublin: Institiúid Teangeolaíochta Éireann, 2000.

O'Donovan, John (ed. and tr.). *Annála Rioghachta Eireann. Annals of the Kingdom of Ireland by the Four Masters, from the earliest period to the year 1616*, Volume II. Dublin: Hodges, Smith & Co, 1856.

O'Leary, Peter and Borthwick, Norma. *Foclóir do Shéadna*, Baile Átha Cliath: Irish Book Company, 1909.

O'Leary, Peter, "Dr. Sheehan's *Gabha na Coille*", in *The Freeman's Journal*, Dublin, March 17th 1915, p7.

O'Leary, Peter. *Ésop a háinig go Héring*, Dublin: Irish Book Company, 1911.

O'Leary, Peter. *Papers on Irish Idiom*, Dublin: Browne and Nolan, 1929.

O'Leary, Philip. *The Prose Literature of the Gaelic Revival*, Pennsylvania: The Pennsylvania State University Press, 1994.

O'Nolan, Gerald. *A Key to the Exercises in Studies in Modern Irish (Part I)*, Dublin: Educational Co. of Ireland, 1920.

O'Nolan, Gerald. *Studies in Modern Irish: Part I*, Dublin: Educational Co. of Ireland, 1919.

O'Nolan, Gerald. *The New Era Grammar of Modern Irish*, Dublin, Cork: Education Co. of Ireland, 1934.

Pléimeann, Risteárd, letter dated December 19th, 1917, Gaelic manuscript collection G 1,277 (1) comprising correspondence of An tAthair Peadar Ua Laoghaire of Castlelyons (Caisleán Ua Liatháin), Co. Cork, with An tAthair Risteárd Pléimeann (Fr Richard Fleming), Shán Ó Cuív Papers, National Library of Ireland, Dublin. PUL's replies to various points raised in the letter are written directly on this letter from Pléimeann.

Pléimeann, Risteárd, letter dated January 4th, 1918, Gaelic manuscript collection G 1,277 (1) comprising correspondence of An tAthair Peadar Ua Laoghaire of Castlelyons (Caisleán Ua Liatháin), Co. Cork, with An tAthair Risteárd Pléimeann (Fr Richard Fleming), Shán Ó Cuív Papers, National Library of Ireland, Dublin. PUL's replies to various points raised in the letter are written directly on this letter from Pléimeann.

Todd, James H. (tr.) *Cogadh Gaedhel re Gallaibh: the War of the Gaedhil with the Gaill*, London: Longmans, Green, Reader and Dyer, 1867.

Ua Laoghaire, Diarmuid. *An Bhruinneall Bhán*, Baile Átha Cliath: Oifig Díolta Foillseacháin Rialtais, 1934.

Ua Laoghaire, Diarmuid. *Cogar mogar*, Baile Átha Cliath :Muintir na Leabhar Gaedhilge, The Irish book company, 1909.

Ua Laoghaire, Peadar (ed.) and Ua Cathain, Uilliam. *An Teagasg Críosdaidhe*, Baile Átha Cliath: Brún agus Ó Nóláin, 1920.

Ua Laoghaire, Peadar, "Rosg Catha Bhriain i gCluain Tairbh", in *An tAithriseóir: An Chéad Chuid*, Baile Átha Cliath: Connradh na Gaedhilge, 1900.

Ua Laoghaire, Peadar, "Rosg Catha Bhriain i gCluain Tairbh", in *Staraidheacht: Pieces for Recitation in Irish*, Baile Átha Cliath: Muinntir na Leabhar Gaedhilge, 1905.

Ua Laoghaire, Peadar, letter dated December 21st, 1917, Gaelic manuscript collection G 1,277 (1) comprising correspondence of An tAthair Peadar Ua Laoghaire of Castlelyons (Caisleán Ua Liatháin), Co. Cork, with An tAthair Risteárd Pléimeann (Fr Richard Fleming), Shán Ó Cuív Papers, National Library of Ireland, Dublin.

Ua Laoghaire, Peadar, letter dated December 3rd, 1919, Gaelic manuscript collection G 1,277 (1) comprising correspondence of An tAthair Peadar Ua Laoghaire of Castlelyons (Caisleán Ua Liatháin), Co. Cork, with An tAthair Risteárd Pléimeann (Fr Richard Fleming), Shán Ó Cuív Papers, National Library of Ireland, Dublin.

Ua Laoghaire, Peadar, letter dated February 27th, 1918, Gaelic manuscript collection G 1,277 (1) comprising correspondence of An tAthair Peadar Ua Laoghaire of Castlelyons (Caisleán Ua Liatháin), Co. Cork, with An tAthair Risteárd Pléimeann (Fr Richard Fleming), Shán Ó Cuív Papers, National Library of Ireland, Dublin.

Ua Laoghaire, Peadar, letter dated February 6th, 1918, Gaelic manuscript collection G 1,277 (1) comprising correspondence of An tAthair Peadar Ua Laoghaire of Castlelyons (Caisleán Ua Liatháin), Co. Cork, with An tAthair Risteárd Pléimeann (Fr Richard Fleming), Shán Ó Cuív Papers, National Library of Ireland, Dublin.

Ua Laoghaire, Peadar, undated, Gaelic manuscript collection G 1,276 comprising correspondence of An tAthair Peadar Ua Laoghaire of Castlelyons (Caisleán Ua Liatháin), Co. Cork, with Shán Ó Cuív, Shán Ó Cuív Papers, National Library of Ireland, Dublin.

Ua Laoghaire, Peadar. *Aesop a Tháinig go h-Éirinn*, Dublin: Brún agus Ó Nóláin, 1909.

Ua Laoghaire, Peadar. *Aithris ar Chríost*, Baile Átha Cliath: Muintir na Leabhar Gaedhilge, 1914.

Ua Laoghaire, Peadar. *Aithris ar Chríost, Leabhar a hAon*, Baile Átha Cliath: Brún agus Ó Nóláin, 1930. Note: this edition gives Simplified Spelling opposite the normal spelling.

Ua Laoghaire, Peadar. *An Choróinn Mhuire*, Baile Átha Cliath: Muintir na Leabhar Gaedhilge & Brún agus Ó Nualláin, 1917. Note: Simplified Spelling is given opposite the normal spelling.

Ua Laoghaire, Peadar. *An Cleasaidhe*, Baile Átha Cliath: Brún agus Ó Nuallain, 1913.

Ua Laoghaire, Peadar. *An Craos-Deamhan*, Baile Átha Cliath: Muintir na Leabhar Gaedhilge, 1905.

Ua Laoghaire, Peadar. *Ár nDóithin Araon*, Baile Átha Cliath: Brún agus Nuallán, 1919.

Ua Laoghaire, Peadar. *Bricriu: nó "is fearr an t-imreas 'ná an t-uaigneas"*, Baile Átha Cliath: Muintir na Leabhar Gaedhilge, 1915.

Ua Laoghaire, Peadar. *Cath Ruis na Rí for Bóinn*, Baile Átha Cliath: Brún agus Ó Nualláin, 1922.

Ua Laoghaire, Peadar. *Catilína: Cúntas ar Chogadh Chatilína*, Baile Átha Cliath: Brún agus Ó Nóláin, 1914?

Ua Laoghaire, Peadar. *Cómhairle Ár Leasa*, Baile Átha Cliath: Brún agus Ó Nóláin, 1923.

Ua Laoghaire, Peadar. *Críost Mac Dé*, Baile Átha Cliath: Brún agus Ó Nóláin, in three volumes, 1923-1925.

Ua Laoghaire, Peadar. *Don Cíochótė*, Baile Átha Cliath: Brún agus Ó Nóláin, 1921.

Ua Laoghaire, Peadar. *Eisirt*, Baile Átha Cliath: Muintir na Leabhar Gaedhilge, 1909.

Ua Laoghaire, Peadar. *Gníomhartha na n-Aspol*, Baile Átha Cliath: Brún agus Ó Nóláin, 1921.

Ua Laoghaire, Peadar. *Guaire*, Baile Átha Cliath: Muintir na Leabhar Gaedhilge, in two volumes, 1915.

Ua Laoghaire, Peadar. *Irish numerals and how to use them*, Dublin: Browne and Nolan, 1922.

Ua Laoghaire, Peadar. Letter dated March 10th, 1918, Gaelic manuscript collection G 1,277 (1) comprising correspondence of An tAthair Peadar Ua Laoghaire of Castlelyons (Caisleán Ua Liatháin), Co. Cork, with An tAthair Risteárd Pléimeann (Fr Richard Fleming), Shán Ó Cuív Papers, National Library of Ireland, Dublin.

Ua Laoghaire, Peadar. Letter dated November 29th, 1917, Gaelic manuscript collection G 1,277 (1) comprising correspondence of An tAthair Peadar Ua Laoghaire of Castlelyons (Caisleán Ua Liatháin), Co. Cork, with An tAthair Risteárd Pléimeann (Fr Richard Fleming), Shán Ó Cuív Papers, National Library of Ireland, Dublin.

Ua Laoghaire, Peadar. *Lúcián*, Baile Átha Cliath: Brún agus Ó Nóláin, 1924.

Ua Laoghaire, Peadar. *Lughaidh Mac Con*, Baile Átha Cliath: Muintir na Leabhar Gaedhilge, 1914.

Ua Laoghaire, Peadar. *Mion-chaint, Cuid a III*, Dublin: The Irish Book Company, 1903.

Ua Laoghaire, Peadar. *Mo Sgéal Féin*, Baile Átha Cliath: Brún agus Ó Nualláin, 1915.

Ua Laoghaire, Peadar. *Na Cheithre Soisgéil*, Baile Átha Cliath: Brún agus Ó Nualláin, 1915.

Ua Laoghaire, Peadar. *Niamh*, Baile Átha Cliath: Muintir na Leabhar Gaedhilge, 1907 and 1910.

Ua Laoghaire, Peadar. *Notes on Irish Words and Usages*, Dublin: Browne and Nolan, 1926.

Ua Laoghaire, Peadar. *Séadna*, Baile Átha Cliath: The Irish Book Company, 1904.

Ua Laoghaire, Peadar. *Séadna: an dara cuid*, Dublin: Gaelic League, 1898.

Ua Laoghaire, Peadar. *Seanmóin is Trí Fichid*, Baile Átha Cliath: Muinntir na Leabhar Gaedhilge, in two volumes, 1909.

Ua Laoghaire, Peadar. *Sgéalaidheacht na Macabéach*, Baile Átha Cliath: Brún agus Ó Nóláin, in two volumes, 1926.

Ua Laoghaire, Peadar. *Sgéalaidheachta as an mBíobla Naomhtha*, Baile Átha Cliath: Brún agus Ó Nóláin, in seven volumes, 1922-1925.

Ua Laoghaire, Peadar. *Sgothbhualadh*, Baile Átha Cliath: Brún agus Ó Nóláin, 1904.

Ua Laoghaire, Peadar. *Táin Bó Cuailnge 'na dhráma*, Baile Átha Cliath: Muintir na Leabhar Gaedhilge, 1915.

Ua Siochfhradha, Pádraig. "Mairbhne Eithne Nó Mairbhne Phádraig" in *Béaloideas*, Volume 4, No. 3: An Cumann Le Béaloideas Éireann/Folklore of Ireland Society, 1934.

Ua Súilleabháin, Seán, "Comhfhreagras idir an Athair Peadair agus an tAimhirgíneach", in *Celtica*, Vol 24, 2003.

Ua Súilleabháin, Seán, "Gaeilge na Mumhan", in McCone, Kim (ed.) *et al*, *Stair na Gaeilge*, Maigh Nuad: Roinn na Sean-Ghaeilge, Coláiste Phádraig, 1994.

Wagner, Heinrich. *Linguistic Atlas and Survey of Irish Dialects: Volume II. The Dialects of Munster*, 1964, Dublin: Dublin Institute for Advanced Studies, (Reprint) 1982.

Leabhar a hAon

Caibideal 1: Imirt Anama

Sa bhliain d'aois an Tiarna naoi gcéad cheithre fichid a ceathair do thóg Brian Bórú Luimneach ó sna Lochlannaigh. Do loisc sé an chathair, agus an méid de sna Lochlannaigh nár maraíodh agus nár tógadh 'na bpríosúnachaibh, b'éigean dóibh teitheadh lena n-anam as an áit. Chuaigh cuid acu síos go hInis Cathaigh. Bhí seilbh ag Lochlannaigh in Inis Cathaigh an uair sin agus ar feadh mórán aimsire roimis sin. Bhíodar tar éis na manach a dhíbirt as an oileán agus iad féin do dhaingniú ann, agus bhí an áit caothúil adhsáideach acrach acu, lámh le farraige agus lámh le tír. An sochar agus an saibhreas a bheiridís leó as an dtír mórthímpall, le guid agus le fuadach agus le creachadh, chimeádaidís ar an oileán é go dtí go dtagadh na luingeas agus go bhféadaidís é ' chur soir abhaile nú é ' dhíol, nú é ' mhalairtiú ar bhia nú ar éadach nú ar arm, nú ar pé nithe eile a bhíodh ag teastabháil uathu.

Nuair a tháinig an lucht teithe anuas ó Luimneach agus nuair a dh'ínseadar do Lochlannaigh Ínse Cathaigh cad a bhí déanta ag Brian, go raibh an chathair 'na luaithrigh agus a raibh de dhaoine inti marbh nú tógtha nú imithe gan tuairisc, shocraíodar go léir ar an oileán do chur i dtreó chosanta chómh maith agus dob fhéidir é, agus ar iad féin a chosaint go himirt anama. Tháinig triúr curaí anuas ón gcathair in éineacht leis an lucht teithe. Íomhar agus Amhlaoibh agus Duíbhgeann an triúr san.

Chuireadar an t-oileán i dtreó chosanta. Níorbh fhada go raibh Brian anuas 'na ndiaidh. Do bhris sé féin agus a shlua isteach chúthu ar an oileán. Do troideadh go dian ó gach taobh. Imirt anama dáiríribh ab ea é do sna Lochlannaigh. Do briseadh agus do brúdh agus do buadh orthu. Do thiteadar 'na gcéadtaibh. Do fágadh a bhformhór marbh ar an oileán agus do tógadh an triúr, Íomhar agus Amhlaoibh agus

Duíbhgeann. D'fhág san Luimneach agus oileán Ínse Cathaigh folamh ó Lochlannachaibh, agus gan aon tsúil go dtiocfadh a thuilleadh acu chun na háite sin, an fhaid a bheadh Brian beó pé'n Éirinn é.

Nuair a tuigeadh an ní sin, tháinig na manaigh chun an oileáin arís. Tháinig duine ana-naofa 'narbh ainm do Colla, agus bhí sé in' Ab ar an mainistir, agus chuir sé gach gnó Creidimh ar siúl arís ann, fé choimirce Sheanáin Naofa. Na manaigh agus na sagairt a dhíbir na Lochlannaigh as an áit, thánadar arís, an méid a bhí beó acu, agus do luíodar isteach san obair bheannaithe mar ba ghnáth roimis sin. Bhí gach aon rud loitithe briste scartálta i ndiaidh na Lochlannach. Do dhein Colla na háiteanna a bhí beannaithe do choisreacan arís, agus do chuir Brian chuige síos adhmad agus clocha agus aol agus saoir agus lucht ceárd, agus gach aon chóir a bhí riachtanach chun gach díobhála dár dhein na Lochlannaigh do leigheas, agus chun gach ar bhriseadar do dheisiú, i dtreó, ar ball, go raibh an áit níos feárr agus níos uaisle agus níos órnáidí agus níos oiriúnaí chun gnóthaí Creidimh agus chun onóra ' thabhairt do Dhia ann, ná mar a bhí sé, adéarfadh duine, sara dtáinig aon Lochlannach riamh isteach ann.

Fé mar a bhí na manaigh ag teacht thar n-ais ann, bhí na daoine, sa chómharsanacht mórthímpall, chómh fada siar le Léim Chúchulainn agus chómh fada ó thuaidh le Cíll Chaoi, ag cur arbhair agus éadaigh agus abhar tine, agus nithe den tsórd san, isteach chúthu ar an oileán. Do chuir Brian féin chúthu a lán nithe a bhí ag teastabháil uathu agus nárbh fhéidir dóibh a dh'fháil ó sna daoine. Chuir sé chúthu, mar bharra ar gach bronntanas eile, cailís óir a bhí tar éis teacht chuige féin ón Róimh, ón bPápa, dhá chur in úil do cad é an baochas a bhí ag an bPápa air mar gheall ar a mhór-ghníomhartha i gcoinnibh na Lochlannach, i gcoinnibh namhad an Chreidimh*. Ba mhór ab fhiú an chailís sin. Ór ar fad ab ea í, agus bhí sí téagartha, trom, agus má ba mhór ab fhiú an méid óir a bhí inti, ba mhó ná san ab fhiú an gréas órnáide a bhí geárrtha uirthi, chómh healaíonta agus chómh ceárdúil agus chómh greanta. Ach bhí ní uirthi a bhí ní ba dhaoire go mór ná an t-ór agus an órnáid in éineacht. Bhí ag bun an chupáin uirthi, mórthímpall, san áit 'na raibh an cupán suite ar an gcois, crios de chlochaibh lómhara go raibh, ba dhó' leat, fuascailt mic rí a braighdineas ins gach cloch díobh*. Thug Brian an chailís sin do Cholla agus do mhainistir Ínse Cathaigh, in onóir do Dhia agus do Sheanán Naofa, agus ba mhór ag Colla agus ag na manaigh go léir, agus ag cléir na tíre go léir sa tímpall, an chailís sin, agus ba mhór é a mbaochas ar Bhrian dá bárr.

Chómh luath agus ' bhí na manaigh tagaithe, tháinig na mic léinn. Chómh luath agus ' tháinig na mic léinn, do cuireadh na scoileanna ar siúl.

Nuair a tháinig na Lochlannaigh, níor fhágadar aon ní i bhfuirm leabhair, dár tháinig féna súilibh, gan cur sa tine nú san uisce, agus ba mhar a chéile do leabhraibh na haimsire sin tine nú uisce, mar is ar chroiceann a deintí an scríbhinn agus do bhaineadh an t-uisce an scríbhinn den chroiceann chómh luath agus do fliuchtí é. Ach níorbh fhada go raibh leabhair a ndóthain arís acu, mar, an mhuíntir a bhí ag teacht, do thugadar leabhair leó ar iasacht agus ansan do scríodar macshamhla, a ndóthain díobh, sarar chuireadar abhaile na hiasachtaí.

Níorbh fhada gur leath an scéal ar fuid na hÉireann go raibh na scoileanna ar siúl arís in Inis Cathaigh. Tháinig na hógánaigh ó gach aon pháirt d'Éirinn chun na scolaíochta ' dh'fháil. Bhí ainm Cholla i mbéalaibh daoine ar fuid na hÉireann, agus lasmu' d'oileán na hÉireann, le méid an eólais a bhí aige agus le doimhneacht a thuisceana agus le feabhas an teagaisc a thugadh sé do sna hógánaigh. Ba gheárr go raibh na hógánaigh ag teacht anall ón oileán ar a dtugtar Sasana anois, agus aduaidh ó Albain, agus aneas ón bhFrainnc agus ón Almáinn. Clann na ríthe agus na n-uasal is iad a thagadh. Do gheibhidís scolaíocht agus bia agus deoch agus díon, agus gach cimeád suas eile a theastaíodh uathu, saor in aisce, gan aon tsaghas díolaíochta, i scolaibh* na hÉireann an uair sin. Níorbh aon iúnadh go dtagaidís 'na gcéadtaibh agus 'na míltibh.

Caibideal 2: Tadhg agus Amhlaoibh

Tímpall na haimsire sin bhí cuid de sna Lochlannaigh féin ag tosnú ar an gCreideamh a ghlacadh, go mór mór an chuid acu a bhí tar éis cur fúthu in Éirinn agus cónaí a dhéanamh dóibh féin ann, agus tar éis cleamhnaisí ' dhéanamh le mnáibh Éireannacha. D'éirigh an cóngas, agus ansan an gaol, idir iad féin agus na cómharsain a bhí 'na dtímpall. As san amach do thosnaíodar ar nósaibh na hÉireann do ghlacadh. Chuaigh eólas ar an gCreideamh i bhfeidhm orthu i ndiaidh ar ndiaidh, agus thosnaíodar ar an gCreideamh do ghlacadh. Chun iad féin d'ollmhú i gceart i gcómhair an Chreidimh thosnaíodar ar dhul isteach insna scoileannaibh chómh maith le cách, agus rud a chuireann iúnadh anois ar dhaoine ná tuigeann i gceart an mhór-aigne atá san Éireannach, bhí fáilte rómpu insna scoileannaibh chómh maith agus a bhí roim chách.

Lá, agus an obair ar siúl i scolaibh na mainistreach, tháinig ógánach uasal chun an oileáin. Bhí folt fionn air, ag titim go trom anuas ar a ghuaillibh agus ar a shlinneánaibh. Bhí clóca, nú brat, aniar ar a shlinneánaibh mar ba cheart a bheith ar mhac rí, agus bhí sé ríoga 'na chruith agus 'na phearsain. Go mór mór, bhí an tsúil ríoga ag taithneamh 'na cheann, súil 'na raibh fíor-uaisleacht, gan uabhar, úmhlaíocht gan cheann-ísleacht, fírinne aigne gan nochtadh aigne. Tháinig sé go doras na mainistreach. Tháinig an dóirseóir chuige.

"D'oirfeadh dom, led thoil, an tAb a dh'fheiscint", ar seisean leis an ndóirseóir.

"Tá go maith, a rí", arsan dóirseóir. "Buail mar seo, led thoil".

Do rugadh i láthair Cholla é.

"Cad é seo atá uait, a mhic?", arsan tAb leis.

Caibideal 2: Tadhg agus Amhlaoibh

"Tá, a Athair", ar seisean, "gur mhaith liom, dá mb'é do thoil é, roinnt aimsire ' chaitheamh sa mhainistir seo ag déanamh foghlama".

"Cé hé thu, led thoil?", arsan tAb.

"Tadhg Ó Cealla is ainm dom, a Athair", arsan t-ógánach, "agus aduaidh ó Uíbh Máine do thánag".

"Airiú", arsan tAb, "an mac do Thadhg Mhór Ó Chealla* thu?"

"Is ea, a Athair", arsan t-ógánach.

Do cuireadh isteach láithreach é sa scoil a bhí oiriúnach do. Bhí an Tadhg Ó Cealla san ocht mbliana déag d'aois an uair sin.

Cúpla lá i ndiaidh an lae a tháinig Tadhg Ó Cealla tháinig ógánach eile isteach sa mhainistir. Lochlannach ab ea é, agus ba léir gur mhac rí é. Bhí folt gruaige air a bhí chómh dubh le gual, agus bhí a chroiceann chómh geal leis an sneachta. Bhí luisne chraidhreac 'na dhá leacain, agus bhí geal-gháire 'na dhá shúil agus 'na bhéal i dtreó go raibh báidh ag gach éinne leis ar an gcéad amharc.

Do tugadh i láthair Cholla é.

"Cad é an ainm atá ort-sa, a mhic?", arsa Colla leis, "agus cá mbíonn cónaí ort nuair a bhíonn tú sa bhaile?"

"Lochlannach is ea me, a Athair", arsan t-ógánach, "agus Amhlaoibh is ainm dom. Amhlaoibh Óg a tugtar orm, mar Amhlaoibh is ainm do m'athair leis. Thánag anso chun scolaíochta ' dh'fháil, mar deir gach éinne gur anso atá an scolaíocht is feárr le fáil".

"Tá go maith", arsan tAb. "Is dócha nách dár gCreideamh tu, ach ní dheineann san deifríocht ar bith. Tabharthas ó Dhia is ea an Creideamh. Múinfar duit anso pé léann nú pé eólas atá uait, agus ní baol duit go ndéanfaidh éinne aon chur isteach ort mar gheall ar chreideamh".

"Táim dhá chuímhneamh le fada, a Athair", arsan t-ógánach, "gur mhaith an rud dom eólas éigin do chur ar úr gCreideamh. Ní féidir do dhuine creideamh do ghlacadh gan eólas a chur ar dtúis air. Má chím ón eólas gur ní fónta é, ba chóir gur mhaith an rud dom é ' ghlacadh. Peocu ' ghlacfad é nú ná glacfad, cad é an díobháil a dhéanfaidh sé dhom eólas do chur air?"

"Tá go maith, a mhic ó", arsan tAb. "Lean do thoil agus do thuiscint féin sa ní sin. Go dtugaidh Dia agus Seanán Naofa dhuit an t-eólas atá uait!"

Do cuireadh Amhlaoibh Óg isteach sa scoil do ceapadh a bhí oiriúnach do, agus cá gcurfí é ach isteach sa scoil chéanna 'nar cuireadh Tadhg Ó Cealla.

Níorbh fhada gur chuir an bheirt aithne mhaith ar a chéile. Níorbh fhada gur éirigh caradas mór eatarthu. Bhíodar araon go hana-mhaith chun an léinn a thógaint, agus ba dheocair d'éinne a dh'ínsint ceocu ab fheárr chuige. Ins gach ní a bhain le neart géag agus le cleasaibh lúth dob é an scéal céanna é. Ní raibh aon bhreith ag éinne den bheirt ar bhuachtaint i gceart ar an bhfear eile. Ach bhí so le feiscint soiléir go leór. Ní raibh aon fhear eile insna scolaibh sin a dh'fhéadfadh cimilt le héinne den bheirt in aon rud a bhain le neart cuirp ná le cleasaibh lúth.

Ní raibh Tadhg Óg Ó Cealla i bhfad in Inis Cathaigh nuair a rugadh soir go Ceann Cora é, go rí-theaghlach Bhriain féin. Bhí aithne mhaith agus cion mór ag Brian ar athair an fhir óig sin, ar Thadhg Mhór Ó Chealla. Ní haon iúnadh nár fágadh Tadhg Óg i bhfad gan breith soir go Ceann Cora.

Caibideal 2: Tadhg agus Amhlaoibh

Agus, dar ndó', nuair a hiarradh ar Thadhg dul soir níorbh fhéidir a chara agus a chómhalta, Amhlaoibh, a dh'fhágáilt 'na dhiaidh sa mhainistir. B'éigean dóibh araon dul soir. Chómh luath agus do cuireadh aithne thoir orthu, ba dhó' leat gur anuas as an spéir a thiteadar, tháinig a leithéid sin d'urraim ag gach éinne dhóibh agus a leithéid sin de chion ag gach éinne orthu.

Bhí ' fhios ag gach éinne gur mhac rí Tadhg Óg Ó Cealla, agus is é rud adeireadh na daoine a chíodh é ná, "An té ná déanfadh ach féachaint air, gan aon phioc dá fhios a bheith aige cé hé féin, d'aithneódh sé gur mac rí é!" Bhí an urraim ag ár sínsear riamh don rí agus do mhac an rí. Nílimíd féin ró-shaor ón ngalar gcéanna[*].

Bhí tuairim láidir ag daoine gur mhac rí Amhlaoibh, leis, bíodh ná duairt sé féin, luath ná mall, gurbh ea. Níor admhaigh sé gurbh ea agus ní lú ná mar a shéan sé gurbh ea.

Áit chun an uile shaghas cleasaíochta, idir rith agus léim agus iomrascáil agus caitheamh cloch araige agus tógaint ualaí troma, ab ea Ceann Cora an uair sin, agus bhí fir óga ann nárbh fhuiriste buachtaint orthu insna gníomharthaibh sin. Bhí an bheirt a tháinig aniar ó Inis Cathaigh maith a ndóthain don chuid ab fheárr acu, 'sé sin dá gcómhnaoisibh. Ní raibh aon bhreith acu, áfach, ar aon chimilt a dhéanamh leis na fearaibh stálaithe crua a bhí ann.

In éaghmais na lúth-chleas, bhíodh cleasa agus gleacaíocht ar na hairm acu. Bhíodh airm éadroma ann do sna buachaillíbh chun bheith ag déanamh taithí dhíobh. D'imir gach duine den bheirt cluiche ar gach arm de sna hairm sin leis na buachaillíbh ab fheárr a bhí ar theaghlach Bhriain, agus chuireadar iúnadh ar gach éinne. Bhíodh capall bata acu ann agus marcach bréige in áirde air agus éide ar an marcach, agus gníomh fir ab ea rith chun an mharcaigh sin agus buille ' thuaigh[*] a thabhairt do sa cheathrúin agus idir éide agus ceathrú do ghearradh leis an mbuille sin i dtreó go dtitfeadh an chos ar thaobh den chapall agus an marcach ar an dtaobh eile.

Duairt Amhlaoibh gur dhó' leis go ndéanfadh sé an gníomh san. Do tugadh tua Mhurchadh mhic Bhriain chuige. Bhí sí ró-throm do. Do tugadh tua ná raibh chómh trom chuige. Do cuireadh in áirde an fear bréige ar an gcapall bréige. Do chas Amhlaoibh an tua agus do rith sé chun an mharcaigh agus do bhuail sé a bhuille. Chuir an buille stangadh san éide a bhí ar cheathrúin an fhir bhréige. Sin ar chuir[*].

Do cuireadh suas an fear bréige arís agus éide shlán air. Do rug Tadhg Óg Ó Cealla ar thuaigh eile. Do thoibh sé féin an tua. Bhain sé casadh as an dtuaigh agus do rith sé chun an mharcaigh bhréige. Tháinig an tua anuas ar an gceathrúin. Do thit an chos ar thaobh den chapall agus an fear ar an dtaobh eile.

Do leath a dhá shúil ar Amhlaoibh.

"Ó!", ar seisean, "agus níor chuiris leath do nirt leis an mbuille!"

"Do chuireas", arsa Tadhg, "ach níor dhó' leat gur chuireas. Cleas is ea é. Chuiris-se oiread nirt leis an mbuille agus ' chuireas-sa leis, ach níor thugais a cheart féin don fhaobhar. Níl ann ar fad ach cleas, agus taithí ar an gcleas".

"B'fhéidir é", arsa Amhlaoibh, "ach mo thrua-sa an fear go n-imreófá-sa an cleas san air i láthair catha".

Do rug Amhlaoibh ar bhogha Mhurchadh. Mheas sé an bogha do lúbadh. Do theip air.

"Ba mhaith liom aon urchar amháin a dh'fheiscint uait, a rí", ar seisean le Murchadh.

"Chífir agus fáilte, a mhic ó", arsa Murchadh. Do rug Murchadh ar an mbogha agus do lúb sé é agus chuir sé an tsrang air mar ba chóir chun lámhaigh. Ansan do rug sé ar shaíghid agus chuir sé an saíghead leis an sraíng. Bhí an bogha dhá shlait ar faid. Chuir sé an lámh chlé 'na lár. Tharraig sé an tsrang leis an láimh dheis go dtí gur dhó' le duine ná raibh dhá throigh idir dhá cheann an bhogha. Thug sé aghaidh ar an dtaobh thall den ghleann. Do thárla éan farraige ' bheith ag gluaiseacht fan an ghleanna thall, lasmu', dar lena raibh láithreach, de raon aon urchair. Do sheinn an tsrang. Do ghluais an saíghead. Bhí súil gach éinne ar an saíghead agus ar an éan. Chonacadar ag teacht chun a chéile iad. Do chuaigh an saíghead tríd an éan agus thiteadar araon chun tailimh thall ar thaobh an ghleanna. Do rith buachaill anonn agus thug sé leis anall iad. Bhí iúnadh agus alltacht ar Amhlaoibh nuair a thuig sé in' aigne cad é an neart nárbh fholáir a bheith sa bhfear a chaith an t-urchar san.

Caibideal 3: Íntinn Bhriain

Do caitheadh an lá ar an gcuma san, go suairc agus go soilbhir agus go muínteartha. Ansan do shuigh cuideachta mhaith uasal chun dínnéir, agus do tispeánadh urraim agus onóir don dá mhac rí sin agus d'uaislibh eile a tháinig an lá san go rí-theaghlach Bhriain ar ghnóthaíbh a bhain leó féin.

Bhí aghaidh na hÉireann go léir an uair sin ar Bhrian agus ar Cheann Cora agus ar Dhál gCais. Bhí sé daingean in aigne gach éinne, idir Ghael agus Lochlannach, nár mhaith an bhail ar chine Ghaelach ná ar chine Lochlannach Brian agus Clann Chais a bheith 'na namhdaibh acu, agus gurbh é a leas, thar gach ní, Brian agus Clann Chais a bheith 'na gcáirdibh acu. Gach aon chine, dá bhrí sin, ar fuid na hÉireann, agus go mór mór ar fuid na Múmhan, a bheartaigh go bhféadfaidís caradas Bhriain do chimeád, má bhí sé acu, bhídís ag teacht go Ceann Cora agus ag tabhairt cíosa nú bronntanas leó; agus an mhuíntir a bhíodh a d'iarraidh an charadais sin a dh'fháil dóibh féin, mura raibh sé cheana acu, bhídís ag teacht ar an gcuma gcéanna a d'iarraidh é ' thuilleamh.

Do thuig Brian iad go léir go hálainn. Fear ana-dhoimhinn ab ea é. Bhí beartaithe in' aigne aige, agus bhí an machnamh in' aigne le fada dh'aimsir, neart na hÉireann go léir do chnósach agus do chur le chéile i gcoinnibh na Lochlannach, agus i gcoinnibh gach namhad iasachta. Deireadh ' chur leis an obair a bhí ar siúl in Éirinn ar feadh cúpla céad blian an uair sin, nuair a bhíodh eaglaisí agus mainistreacha agus scoileanna dá gcur suas le neart Creidimh agus dúil i léann agus in eólas, agus ansan nár thúisce a bhídís thuas ná mar a bhíodh na Lochlannaigh ag preabadh isteach agus á scartáil, dhá loscadh agus ag loscadh na leabhar a bhíodh iontu agus ag marú na manach. Do thuig Brian in' aigne, nuair a dheineadh cléir agus daoine naofa na hÉireann, agus lucht léinn na hÉireann, na heaglaisí agus na mainistreacha agus na scoileanna do chur suas agus an obair do chur ar siúl, gurbh é ba lú ba ghann do ríthibh Éireann*, agus d'fhearaibh Éireann, Éire agus an obair, agus an mhuíntir a bhí ag déanamh na hoibre, do chosaint ar namhdaibh iasachta. Chonaic sé conas a bhí an scéal ag Éire ocht gcéad blian nú míle blian roimis sin, nuair a bhí Fionn agus Fiann Éireann* beó, nú le línn Chonchúir agus Chúchulainn. Bhí a leithéid sin de scannradh an uair sin ar dhúthaíbh iasachta roim fhearaibh Éireann agus roim chómhacht na hÉireann nár leómhaigh aon chómhacht iasachta aon chur isteach a dhéanamh orthu. Dá mb'iad na Rómhánaigh féin iad, do chuireadar an domhan go léir féna smacht ach Éire amháin. "Ach!", adéarfaidh duine, b'fhéidir, "níorbh fhiú leó teacht ag cur isteach ar oileán na hÉireann. Bhí Éire ró-shuarach, dar leó, agus ró-imigéiniúil".

Nách maith ná raibh Ínsí hOrc ró-imigéiniúil. Chuir na Rómhánaigh Sasana féna smacht, agus chuireadar mórán de chrích Alban féna smacht. Agus chuadar ní ba shia ó thuaidh agus chuireadar Ínsí hOrc féna smacht, dá fhaid ó thuaidh iad, agus dá shuaraí le rá iad an uair sin.

Bhí ' fhios acu go dian-mhaith gurbh fhiú dhóibh Éire ' thabhairt féna smacht, dá bhféadaidís é. Bhí aithne mhaith acu ar an oileán, ach bhí ' fhios acu go maith, leis, cad é an saghas daoine a bhí 'na gcónaí ar an oileán. Níor thánadar ag cur isteach orthu. Níor dhein cómhacht na Rómha riamh oiread agus sméideadh ar oileán na hÉireann.

Do thuig Brian, an rud a deineadh cheana go bhféadfí é ' dhéanamh arís. Go bhféadfí cómhacht na hÉireann do chur le chéile, agus do tháthú 'na chéile, agus do dhlúthú 'na chéile arís, agus neart fear Éireann do ghléasadh agus do chórú, mar a ghléas Fionn é*. Ansan nár bhaol ná go bhfanfadh na Lochlannaigh amach, nú, dá dtagaidís, gur theacht gan imeacht dóibh é.

Is léir d'aon duine a dh'fhéachann isteach sa scéal go raibh an machnamh san agus an beartú san agus an íntinn sin istigh i gcroí Bhriain ón gcéad uair a thosnaigh sé ar dhroch-obair na Lochlannach do thuiscint i gceart. Níorbh fhuiriste dho, áfach, a bheartú do chur i ngníomh mar bhí ríthe Gael ar bheagán meabhrach agus ar bheagán tuisceana an uair chéanna. Níor tháinig aon phioc dá chuímhneamh chun éinne acu go raibh aon bhaol go bhféadfadh Lochlannaigh, ná aon allúraigh eile, Éire do chur féna smacht go hiomlán choíche. Do thuig Brian go raibh an baol ann, agus gur mhóide an baol a laíghead a tuigeadh é. Thuig sé, leis, go mbeadh an baol ann an fhaid a bheadh ríthe Éireann ag gabháil i gcoinnibh a chéile, agus ag troid lena chéile, agus ag lagú a chéile mar a bhíodar. Dá bhrí sin, chómh luath agus ' thosnaigh a chómhacht ar dhul i méid, do thosnaigh sé ar na ríthibh eile do thabhairt féna smacht féin, agus ar a chur ' fhéachaint orthu oibriú a lámhaibh a chéile i gcoinnibh na Lochlannach. Níorbh é sin féin ach, fé mar a fuair sé an chaoi air, do ghlac sé isteach 'na shlóitibh armála na Lochlannaigh a bhí dílis do, chun cogaidh a dhéanamh i gcoinnibh na Lochlannach eile. Bhí cuid acu ní ba dhílse dho ná mar a bhí cuid de sna hÉireannaigh.

Caibideal 4: Ó Bhealach Leachta go Gleann Mháma

Bhí cómhacht Bhriain ag méadú agus ag neartú agus ag leathadh go dtí go raibh sé 'na rí ar leath na hÉireann, ar Leath Mhogha, ar an leath theas den oileán. Ní gan mórán trioblóide agus mórán cogaidh a chuir sé an méid sin de thír na hÉireann fé smacht a lámha. Bhí a dhriotháir, Mathúin mac Cinéide, 'na rí ar an Múmhain roimis. Rí cróga, cómhachtach, mór-aigeanta ab ea an Mathúin sin. Chonaic ríthe agus tiarnaí eile na Múmhan go raibh Dál gCais agus clann Chinéide ag dul i neartmhaire, agus tháinig éad agus eagla orthu.

Chonaic Lochlannaigh na Múmhan, leis, mura gcurfí cosc éigin leis an mbeirt driothár, le Mathúin agus le Brian, ná fágfaidís Lochlannach beó sa Mhúmhain. Dheineadar eatarthu, na Lochlannaigh agus na hÉireannaigh 'na raibh an t-eagal orthu, feall gránna ar Mhathúin. Mharaíodar é in áit ar a dtugtí Bealach Leachta. Deir cuid den tseanchas gur in aice Magh Chromtha atá an áit. Tá cloch mhór, i bhfuirm galláin, 'na seasamh ar bhruach an tSoláin, ar an ínse, in aice na háite 'na dtagann an Leamhain isteach sa tSolán, agus de réir gach deallraimh tá an chloch san 'na seasamh ar uaigh Mhathúna mhic Cinéide, rí Múmhan.

B'fhearra go mór, áfach, do lucht an éada agus an eagla ná déanfaidís an gníomh san. Íomhar, rí Lochlannach Luimní, agus Maolmhuaidh, rí Deas-Mhúmhan, agus Donnabhán, rí Fighinti, is iad a dhein an gníomh. Do las fearg Bhriain nuair a fuair sé cad a bhí déanta. Do chruinnigh sé a neart. Sin é an uair a scrios sé na Lochlannaigh a Luimneach agus a hInis Cathaigh. Do bhris sé cath ar Dhonnabhán agus mhairbh sé é. Do lean sé Maolmhuaidh go Bealach Leachta, an áit 'nar maraíodh Mathúin. Bhí Maolmhuaidh ann agus slua líonmhar láidir aige, de Ghaelaibh agus de Lochlannachaibh. Do bhuaigh Brian orthu, agus do thit Maolmhuaidh sa chath. Deir an seanchas go raibh Murchadh, mac Bhriain, sa chath san agus gan é ach chúig* bhliana déag, agus gur lena láimh a thit Maolmhuaidh.

Nuair ' airigh Dónall Ó Faoláin, rí na nDéiseach, cad a bhí imithe ar Mhaolmhuaidh agus ar a shlua, d'éirigh sé agus chruinnigh sé slóite a thíre go léir, agus tháinig Lochlannaigh Phort Láirge ag cabhrú leis. Siúd chúthu Brian. Do bhris sé cath fuilteach orthu in áit ar a dtugtí Fán Chonradh*. Do theitheadar, idir Ghaeil agus Lochlannaigh, isteach go Port Láirge. Do lean Brian iad agus dhein sé éirleach orthu agus do loisc sé an chathair. Do thit Dónall san éirleach.

Caibideal 4: Ó Bhealach Leachta go Gleann Mháma

Bhí an Mhúmhain fé smacht Bhriain ansan. Níor ghéill a namhaid go léir do, áfach. Bhí ' fhios acu ná géillfeadh Cúige Laighean go ró-bhog do. D'imíodar ó thuaidh. D'éirigh na Laighnigh leó. Do cruinníodh slua ana-mhór, Lochlannaigh agus Éireannaigh ón Múmhain, agus Lochlannaigh ó Áth Cliath, agus iomláine cómhachta na Laighneach, idir Lochlannaigh agus Éireannaigh. Cheapadar, anois nú riamh, go gcuirfidís neart Bhriain ar neamhní. Thuig na hÉireannaigh a bhí ann go ndéanfaidís díoltas ar Bhrian agus ar Chlaínn Chais fé dheireadh thiar thall. Thuig na Lochlannaigh dá mbeadh Brian agus Clann Chais ar neamhní nár ró-fhada go mbeadh Luimneach, agus Inis Cathaigh, agus an Mhúmhain, agus b'fhéidir Éire go léir, acu féin arís. Níor thug Brian puínn aimsire dhóibh chun machnaimh a dhéanamh. Siúd chúthu isteach i gCúige Laighean é féin agus a shlua. Ar Gleann Mháma is ea ' tháinig sé suas leó. Siúd chun a chéile an dá shlua go fíochmhar agus go mallaithe. Do throid na Laighnigh agus na Lochlannaigh agus a lucht cabhartha go léir go cróga agus go seasmhach, an fear* ag titim agus fear eile in' inead láithreach, gan staonadh gan géilleadh, gan suím i mbás ná i mbeatha. Níorbh aon mhaith dhóibh é. Do bhrúigh Brian agus Murchadh agus Clann Chais isteach trína lár. Do leagadh agus do maraíodh iad 'na sraitheannaibh. Fé dheireadh do ruagadh chun siúil an méid nár leagadh díobh. Do leanadh iad ins gach treó baill 'nar theitheadar. Do cuireadh an mhór-shlua ar neamhní glan. Do thit sa chath san chúig mhíle fear de Lochlannachaibh agus de Laighneachaibh.

D'fhág san Leath Mhogha ar fad fé smacht Bhriain, agus thug sé le tuiscint go soiléir do sna Lochlannaigh ná raibh aon bhreith acu go deó arís ar oileán na hÉireann do thabhairt féna smacht. Ansan is ea ' bhí ríthe agus uaisle agus tiarnaí tíre ag teacht as gach áird go Ceann Cora ag tabhairt cíosa agus tabharthaistí agus bronntanas ag triall ar Bhrian agus ag snadhmadh caradais leis.

Cuid de sna huaislibh sin is ea ' bhí tagaithe ann an oíche a bhí an bheirt bhuachaillí ó mhainistir Ínse Cathaigh ann. Chuir an mhuíntir a tháinig aithne láithreach ar Thadhg Óg Ó Chealla. Níor fhéad éinne puínn aithne ' chur ar an mbuachaill eile, ar Amhlaoibh. Ní raibh ' fhios acu cérbh é ná cé 'ra* díobh é, ach gurbh ógánach uasal é a tháinig anall ó chrích Lochlann go mainistir Ínse Cathaigh ag déanamh foghlama. Do caitheadh an oíche go suairc agus, bíodh ná raibh aon aithne cheart ar an Lochlannach óg, bhí gach éinne ag déanamh cúraim de agus ag tispeáint bá dho, díreach fé mar ba mhaith leó a chur in úil do, dá mba Lochlannach féin é ná raibh aon doicheall acu roimis.

Tá an tréith sin san Éireannach fós go láidir. Má bhímíd muínteartha le duine iasachta, is minic gur mó go mór a thispeánaimíd ár muíntearthas do ná mar a thispeánaimíd é dár nduine féin. Chonac go minic a leithéid.

Tháinig an mhaidean. Bhí na huaisle a tháinig ag dul abhaile. Má thugadar tabharthaistí leó ag triall ar Bhrian, do thug Brian tabharthaistí móra maithe dhóibh nuair a bhíodar ag imeacht. Bhí brí leis na tabharthaistíbh sin, áfach. An priúnsa do ghlac tabharthas mar sin ó Bhrian, d'admhaigh sé Brian a bheith 'na rí os a chionn, agus bhí ceangailte air as san amach an admháil sin do sheasamh. Thuigeadar go léir an ní sin go maith agus ní raibh aon chur 'na choinnibh acu. Is amhlaidh a bhí áthas mór orthu fear a bheith os a gcionn a bheadh ábalta ar iad do smachtú dá mba ghá é*.

Tháinig an bheirt bhuachaillí abhaile chun na mainistreach agus chun na leabhar agus chun an léinn.

Bhí Brian pósta an tarna huair an uair sin. Gormfhlaith ab ainm don tarna mnaoi. Bhí sí 'na bainntrigh nuair a phós Brian í. Drifiúr ab ea í do Mhaolmhórdha, an rí a tháinig ar Laighnibh nuair a ghéilleadar do Bhrian. Bhí sí pósta ar dtúis ag rí de ríthibh Lochlannach Átha Cliath. Amhlaoibh ab ainm don rí sin. Bhí mac aici leis an Amhlaoibh sin agus Sitric ab ainm do, agus bhí sé 'na rí ar Lochlannaigh Átha Cliath nuair a bhí sise pósta ag Brian i gCeann Cora.

Caibideal 4: Ó Bhealach Leachta go Gleann Mháma

De réir gach seanchais dá mbaineann leis an aimsir sin, ní raibh an uair sin ar mhnáibh an domhain bean eile a bhí in aon ghaobhar do bheith chómh breá leis an mnaoi sin. Ach tá ní eile, leis, le feiscint sa tseanchas. Ní raibh bean ar bith a bhí chómh breá léi. Ní lú ná mar a bhí bean ar bith a bhí chómh holc léi. Nuair a phós Brian í, ní raibh ' fhios aige cad é an saghas í. Bhí beartaithe in' aigne aige, ní hamháin Gaeil Éireann do dhlúthú lena chéile i dtreó gur mhóide a neart é in aghaidh namhad iasachta, ach, dá mb'fhéidir é, na Lochlannaigh a bhí socair chun cónaithe in Éirinn do tháthú leis na cineachaibh Gaelacha, agus aon neart amháin a dhéanamh díobh go léir. Thuig sé gur mhaith an cúnamh do chuige sin máthair an rí a bhí ar Lochlannaigh Átha Cliath a bheith pósta aige; go dtabharfadh an cleamhnas san páirt di-se 'na chómhacht féin agus páirt do féin i gcómhacht a mic. Do neartaigh sé an pháirt sin a bheadh aige féin i gcómhacht a mic le cleamhnas eile. Thug sé a iníon féin* le pósadh do Shitric, do rí Lochlannach Átha Cliath.

Bhí gaol agus cóngas achomair go leór ansan idir é agus rí Laighean agus idir é agus Lochlannaigh Átha Cliath, agus bhí gach aon deallramh go ndéanfadh aimsir agus foighne agus faidearaí agus dea-chómharsanacht caradas do dhlúthú agus do bhuanú idir é agus iad go léir, go mór mór ó bhí san agus a mbuac féin ag teacht isteach lena chéile. Bhí gach aon deallramh, leis, dá leanadh an caradas san agus an dea-chómharsanacht san go sroisfeadh Brian Árdríocht na hÉireann agus go leanfadh sliocht Bhriain in Árdríocht na hÉireann, ó ghlúin go glúin, ar feadh mórán aimsire, agus go gcuirfeadh san rath agus séan go saibhir agus go marthanach ar Éirinn agus ar Chlannaibh Gael, agus ar an gCreideamh in Éirinn.

Ach bhí a mhalairt sin ar fad de mhachnamh in aigne na Bannríne, in aigne Ghormfhlaith. Ní har Bhrian ná ar a shliocht a bhí sí ag cuímhneamh, i gcómhair Árdríochta na hÉireann, san aimsir a bhí le teacht, ach ar a mac féin, ar Shitric, rí Lochlannach Átha Cliath. Bhí Brian aosta. Ní raibh, agus a dhícheall a dhéanamh, puínn eile aimsire aige le caitheamh ar an saol so. B'fhéarr léi í féin a bhá* ná Murchadh

' dh'fheiscint in' Árdrí. Níorbh fholáir, dar léi, rud éigin a dhéanamh a chimeádfadh Murchadh as an Árdríocht. Chuir sí an scéal i gcómhairle a mic. Do socraíodh eatarthu ar nimh a thabhairt do Bhrian. Dá mbeadh Brian as an slí, do thitfeadh a chómhacht as a chéile. Ansan níor ró-dheocair di cómhacht na Lochlannach do chruinniú agus oileán na hÉireann do chur féna smacht féin, agus Árdrí a dhéanamh dá mac, de Shitric. Bhí an t-uisce-fé-thalamh san ar siúl idir Cheann Cora agus Áth Cliath ar feadh i bhfad. Bhí sé ar siúl, i ganfhios don tsaol, le línn na haimsire 'na raibh an bheirt bhuachaillí úd ag déanamh a bhfoghlama i mainistir Ínse Cathaigh.

Caibideal 5: Creideamh á Ghlacadh

Tar éis suím aimsire tháinig an bheirt arís go Ceann Cora agus bhí lá gleacaíochta eile acu agus oíche shuairc 'na dhiaidh. Níorbh fhada gur dheineadar taithí de bheith ag teacht, agus bhíodh súil leó agus fáilte rómpu ag gach éinne sa teaghlach. Bhíodh gach éinne mór leó, agus gach éinne ag déanamh cúraim díobh, agus ní raibh éinne ba mhó a dheineadh cúram díobh ná an Bhannrín. Dheineadh sí ana-chúram den bheirt, ach nuair a chuadar i dtaithí bheith ag teacht do thárla go mbíodh Amhlaoibh agus í féin go minic ag cainnt agus ag cogarnaigh* fé leith. Níor dhein éinne aon iúnadh dhe sin. Lochlannach ab ea é, agus mac rí ab ea é, agus níorbh aon iúnadh mórán a bheith aici le rá leis an mbuachaill i dtaobh a thíre féin agus i dtaobh a mhuíntire.

Nuair a tháinig an t-am 'nar mhithid do Thadhg Ó Chealla cuaird a thabhairt ó thuaidh go hUíbh Máine, ag féachaint a mhuíntire féin, ní shásódh aon rud é gan Amhlaoibh do dhul ó thuaidh in éineacht leis. Chuaigh an bheirt ó thuaidh. Má ba mhór an fháilte a bhíodh roimis an mbeirt i gCeann Cora, agus má ba mhór an cúram a deintí dhíobh ann, ba mhó ná san an fháilte a bhí rómpu thuaidh, agus ba ghrámhaire, agus ba mhó an cúram a deineadh díobh ann. Bhí Tadhg Óg Ó Cealla i dteaghlach a athar féin nuair a chuaigh sé ó thuaidh go hUíbh Máine, agus is mó rud ' fhéadfadh sé a dhéanamh ann chun cúraim a dhéanamh de charaid ná féadfadh sé a dhéanamh i rí-theaghlach Bhriain i gCeann Cora. Do dhein sé gach aon rud fé mar a thaithn leis chun a thispeáint cad é an cion a bhí aige ar a chomrádaí. Nuair a chonaic an t-athair, Tadhg Mór féin, an cúram go léir á dhéanamh den ógánach Lochlannach, do dhein sé féin cúram de, chun a mhic do shásamh. Ansan do dhein an mháthair, agus an chuid eile den chlaínn, an cúram céanna dhe, chun Taidhg Óig do shásamh. Níor dheocair dóibh sin, mar, chómh luath agus ' tháinig sé 'na measc, agus chómh luath agus do chonacadar é agus do labhradar leis, tháinig báidh chómh mór san acu féin leis go mbeadh fáilte acu roimis agus go ndéanfaidís cúram de ar a shon féin dá mba ná beadh Tadhg Óg in aon chor ann. Bhí saol maith aige an fhaid a bhí sé thuaidh.

Do críochnaíodh an chuaird agus tháinig an bheirt thar n-ais go hInis Cathaigh.

Do ghluais roinnt aimsire. Bhí Amhlaoibh ag déanamh na foghlama go tiubh. Lá dá raibh an bheirt i bhfochair a chéile ar imeall an oileáin, ar bruach na farraige, do labhair Amhlaoibh. Duairt sé gur mhaith leis an Creideamh a ghlacadh. Bhí áthas mór ar Thadhg.

"Is feárr labhairt leis an Ab", ar seisean.

Do labhradar leis an Ab.

"Tá go maith", arsan tAb. "Ní foláir an Creideamh a mhúineadh dhuit ar dtúis".

Do ceapadh sagart chun an Chreidimh a mhúineadh dho. Do glacadh an scéal go réidh. Do tugadh a dhóthain aimsire dho chun an Chreidimh a dh'fhoghlaim. Do tugadh ní ba mhó ná a dhóthain aimsire dho. Fear eagnaí ab ea Colla. Thuig sé gurbh "fheárr féachaint roime dhuine ná dhá fhéachaint 'na dhiaidh", gurbh fheárr deimhne ' dhéanamh sara ndéanfí dithneas. Gurbh fheárr "bheith díomhaoin ná droch-ghnóthach". Ach do múineadh an Creideamh d'Amhlaoibh, agus do chuir sé an ríghneas go léir de go breá réidh foighneach. Ba léir do gach éinne go raibh sé dílis, dáiríribh. Do baisteadh é. Tar éis roinnt eile aimsire do dhein sé faoistin agus do cuireadh fé láimh Easpaig é. Ansan, tar éis tuilleadh aimsire dhein sé faoistin agus ghlac sé Comaoine. Bhí áthas mór sa mhainistir agus baochas mór á thabhairt do Dhia mar gheall ar a thabarthaistí.

Tháinig an t-am don bheirt chun dul soir go Ceann Cora ar chuaird. Chuadar soir. Bhí míle fáilte rómpu mar ba ghnáth. Ach bhí rud éigin tagaithe sa bhfáilte ná bíodh ann roimis sin. Bhí an oscailt croí ann a bhaineann leis an gCreideamh. Ní haithnítear cad a bhaineann leis an oscailt croí sin go dtí go mothaítear beó é. Ní raibh aon phioc dá fhios ag Amhlaoibh cad a bhain leis go dtí gur mhothaigh sé beó é. An cion a gheibheadh sé i gCeann Cora agus in Uíbh Máine sarar ghlac sé an Creideamh, níor thug sé fé ndeara go raibh aon rud in easnamh air. Bhíodh gach éinne geal do. Níor mheas sé go bhféadfaidís bheith ní ba ghile dho. Nuair a tháinig sé, tar éis an Chreidimh a ghlacadh dho, ansan is ea ' thuig sé cad a bhain leis an oscailt croí. Do chonaic sé ansan go soiléir nárbh é an duine céanna in aon chor acu é, agus nárbh é an cion céanna in aon chor a tispeánadh do. Gur hoscladh do, i gcroíthibh na ndaoine, seómra éigin a bhí, ní hamháin dúnta uaidh roimis sin, ach a bhí ann i ganfhios do agus ná raibh aon phioc dá fhios aige é ' bheith ann in aon chor.

Bhí áthas ana-mhór ar mhuíntir Thaidhg Óig Uí Chealla nuair a tháinig an bheirt chúthu agus Amhlaoibh tar éis an Chreidimh a ghlacadh. Dá mba bhuachaill Tadhg go bhféadfí éad a chur air, do bheadh éad a dhóthain air, do dheineadh a mhuíntir a leithéid de chúram d'Amhlaoibh.

Bhí drifiúr ag Tadhg. Mórling ab ainm di. Bhí sí fionn ar nós a driothár. Cailín ana-dhathúil ab ea í. Bhí a gruaig ar dhath an óir. Bhí idir ghruaig agus dath chómh saibhir sin gur tugadh "Niamh Chínn Óir" mar ainm cheana uirthi nuair a bhí sí 'na leanbh beag. D'oir an ainm chómh maith san di gur lean sé dhi. Ansan do thug daoine mar bhéas dóibh féin an cóngar a ghlacadh ar an ainm agus gan a thabhairt uirthi ach Niamh. San am 'na mbíodh a driotháir agus Amhlaoibh ag teacht ó mhainistir Ínse Cathaigh go tigh a hathar bhí sí seacht mbliana déag, agus deirtí go dtógfadh sé an ceó de chroí dhuine féachaint uirthi, bhí a scéimh chómh hálainn sin. Deirtí gur dhó' le duine go mbíodh mar a bheadh scáil éigin solais 'na tímpall, i dtreó, nuair a thagadh sí isteach i gcuideachtain, gur chuma é nú ga gréine do theacht isteach ann. Bhí a lán d'uaislibh óga na tíre agus ba ró mhaith leó bheith 'na cuideachtain agus bheith go mór léi, ach bhí dhá shúil ghorma, sholasmhara, ríoga 'na ceann, agus ní raibh aon duine de sna huaislibh óga san a dh'fhéadfadh an fhéachaint a bhí insna súilibh sin do sheasamh dá dtugadh a shúile féin, 'na gcoinnibh, aon fhéachaint nár cheart. Bhí an fhuil uasal inti, an fhuil ríoga. D'inis a dhá súil duit, ar an gcéad amharc, gurbh í iníon Thaidhg Mhóir Uí Chealla a bhí agat, agus peocu ab í nú nárbh í, gurbh é do bhuac bheith chómh múinte, chómh béasach agus d'fhéadfá ' bheith.

I dtaobh an óig-fhir, áfach, a thagadh in éineacht lena driotháir aneas ó mhainistir Ínse Cathaigh, chonaic sí an ghruaig chiardhubh air, an t-ualach gruaige go raibh dóthain trír ann, agus é ag titim síos leis na huiseannaibh a bhí ar dhath an tsneachtaidh; ar na slinneánaibh breátha láidre leathana; síos go caol an droma, caol droma a bhí chómh seang le caol droma an chapaill ráis, agus go raibh neart suite ann mar a bheadh i ndrom an chapaill ráis. Chonaic sí an dá shúil a bhí 'na cheann agus iad chómh dubh leis an sméarabhán, agus, nuair a gháireadh sé, an tine chreasa ag teacht as na súilibh sin le neart suilt agus dea-mhéinne, ba dhó' leat. Chonaic sí na nithe sin go léir an chéad lá a tháinig an tAmhlaoibh sin go hUíbh Máine, agus má chonaic do thug sí grá agus taithneamh a croí agus a haigne dho go hiomlán agus go beacht, láithreach bonn, gan aon dá chuid a dhéanamh díobh. Do thuig Amhlaoibh gur thug, agus do thuig sise gur tugadh an grá agus an taithneamh céanna dhi, agus bhí a haigne sásta. Níor labhair éinne den bheirt aon fhocal. Ní raibh gá le cainnt. Bhí an scéal go léir socair eatarthu ar an gcéad fhéachaint. Dheineadar an chainnt a dhein an chuid eile a bhí láithreach, agus níor tugadh aon phioc dá fhios d'éinne dá raibh láithreach go raibh an scéal san socair eatarthu.

Caibideal 6: Abhar an tSagairt

Nuair a tháinig an scéal nua go raibh Amhlaoibh ag glacadh an Chreidimh, bhí áthas mór ar gach éinne i gCeann Cora agus ar gach éinne in Uíbh Máine, agus ní raibh duine i gCeann Cora ná in Uíbh Máine ba mhó áthas* ná Niamh. Nuair a tháinig Amhlaoibh go hUíbh Máine agus é tar éis an Chreidimh a ghlacadh, do fuair sé an oscailt croí ó gach éinne, ach ní raibh éinne ba mhó a thug oscailt croí do ná mar a thug Niamh. Ach más ea níor leog sí uirthi gur thug. Bhí sí díreach mar a bhí an chuid eile den teaghlach, chómh fada agus a dh'fhéad éinne a thuiscint.

Do lean an scéal ar an gcuma san. Tar éis suím aimsire do labhair Amhlaoibh arís lena chara*, le Tadhg Óg Ó Cealla.

"Táim á chuímhneamh, a Thaidhg", ar seisean, "gur mhaith liom bheith im shagart".

"Labhair le Colla mar gheall air sin", arsa Tadhg.

Do labhair.

"B'fhéidir, a mhic ó", arsa Colla, "ná fuil fios t'aigne féin i gceart agat i dtaobh na híntinne sin. Is feárr machnamh a dhéanamh ar an scéal. Imigh leat agus tabhair aire dot chuid léinn, agus tar chúm arís mí ó 'nniu más maith leat é, agus i gcaitheamh an mhí bí dhá iarraidh ar Dhia, trí ímpí Sheanáin, tu ' sheóladh ar do leas".

D'imigh an mí. Tháinig Amhlaoibh arís ag triall ar Cholla.

"Tá sé socair i m'aigne, a Athair", ar seisean, "gur im shagart is ceart dom mo shaol do chaitheamh".

Caibideal 6: Abhar an tSagairt

"Tá go maith, a mhic ó", arsa Colla.

Do cuireadh isteach é i measc na mac léinn a bhí dá n-ollmhú d'Órd Bheannaithe. Níorbh fhada gur hairíodh i gCeann Cora agus in Uíbh Máine gur deineadh. Duairt a lán daoine gur mhaith é. Duairt a lán eile gur mhór an trua sagart a dhéanamh d'óig-fhear chómh breá, chómh dathúil. D'airigh Niamh é. D'airigh sí daoine dhá rá gurbh álainn an sagart a dhéanfadh sé. D'airigh sí daoine dhá rá gur mhór an trua sagart a dhéanamh de. Bhí lán a croí d'iúnadh agus d'alltacht istigh 'na haigne féin, ach ní baol gur leog sí amach aon phioc den iúnadh. Níor dhó' le héinne beó uirthi go raibh sí ag cuímhneamh in aon chor air féin ná ar conas ba mhaith leis a bheatha do chaitheamh. Ach do bhí. Bhí dhá mhachnamh 'na haigne 'na thaobh agus bhí sé ag teip uirthi glan an dá mhachnamh a thabhairt dá chéile,—an grá úd a thispeáin sé a bheith aige dhi féin ón gcéad lá do chonaic sí é, agus an socrú so a bhí déanta anois aige ar bheith 'na shagart. Gan amhras dob fhíor nár labhair sé aon fhocal riamh léi dhá ínsint di go raibh an grá san aige dhi, ach níor dhein san blúire deifríochta sa scéal. Rud ab ea é nár ghá labhairt 'na thaobh. Bhí stoirm 'na haigne, ach do chimeád sí istigh é. Bhí sí chómh séimh, chómh solasmhar, chómh geal-gháiriteach agus ba ghnáth léi ' bheith. B'í an ga gréine céanna í ag teacht i gcuideachtain. Do tugadh fé ndeara, áfach, gur bhánaigh a haghaidh. Ach is mó trúig a dh'fhéadfadh ' bheith leis sin, agus níor chuir éinne aon tsuím ann nuair nár thispeáin sí aon easpa sláinte.

Nuair a bhí roinnt aimsire caite ag Amhlaoibh ag déanamh na foghlama i gcómhair na nÓrd, do thug sé féin agus a chomrádaí cuaird soir go Ceann Cora. Bhí áthas mór ar gach éinne agus gach aon tsaghas urrama agus onóra acu á thabhairt* d'abhar an tsagairt, agus ba mhó an t-áthas a bhí ar an mBannrín, ar Ghormfhlaith, ná ar éinne. Thug sí féin agus é féin ana-chuid den lá i bhfochair a chéile. Níorbh aon iúnadh é sin. Bhí a lán nithe aici le hínsint do i dtaobh a mhuíntire féin, lastoir i gcríochaibh Lochlann, agus a lán cainnte acu araon le déanamh 'na dtaobh, ní nárbh iúnadh.

Thug an bheirt, Tadhg Óg agus Amhlaoibh, cuaird ó thuaidh go hUíbh Máine. Bhí an fháilte ba ghnáth rómpu, agus bhí an fháilte fé leith roim abhar an tsagairt, agus an onóir fé leith á tabhairt do, agus an urraim fé leith. Thug Niamh an onóir do a thug gach éinne eile dho. Bhí a haigne smachtaithe aici um an dtaca san, agus bhí socair aici, i láthair Dé, go raibh ceangailte uirthi féin gan teacht, ar aon tsaghas cuma, idir é agus an ghairm bheannaithe a bhí, dar léi, ceapaithe ag Dia dho. Ach bhí an t-aon mhearathall amháin úd os cómhair a haigne. Cad chuige gur thispeáin sé an grá úd di an chéad lá má bhí aon chuímhneamh aige ar bheith 'na shagart?[*] Má bhí grá aige dhi de réir mar a thispeáin sé a bheith, conas ' fhéad sé a aigne d'athrú? Níor réitigh an chuaird an mearathall. An suím laethanta a bhí le caitheamh in Uíbh Máine do caitheadh iad, agus d'imigh an bheirt abhaile go hInis Cathaigh, agus bhí an meascán mearaí ar a haigne ag Niamh nuair a bhíodar imithe, chómh mór díreach agus ' bhí sé ar a haigne aici sara dtánadar ar an gcuaird sin. Níor dhein sí ach a toil do chur le toil Dé, agus bheith á iarraidh ar Dhia agus ar Mhuire Mháthair agus ar Sheanán í ' chur ar a leas.

Nuair a tháinig an t-am chuige do cuireadh Amhlaoibh insna mion-órdaibh. Do deineadh *deacon** de. Ansan, an *deacon* go raibh cúram an *érdaim*[1]* air go dtí san, do críochnaíodh 'na shagart é, agus do cuireadh go dtí an Róimh é ar ghnó éigin, agus do cuireadh cúram an *érdaim* in Inis Cathaigh ar Amhlaoibh. Bhí sé ag déanamh an ghnótha san go maith agus go cruínn agus go slachtmhar, agus bhí na sagairt go léir ana-shásta leis. Bhí gach ní in' áit féin aige agus an glanachar ins gach aon bhall aige.

Caibideal 7: An Leagáid

[*]Do ghluais suím aimsire. Tháinig easpag ón Róimh go hÉirinn. Go hInis Cathaigh a thug sé aghaidh ar dtúis. Do cuireadh scéala soir go Ceann Cora dhá ínsint don rí, do Bhrian, go raibh sé tagaithe ann. Bhí cómhairle agus teachtaireacht ón bPápa aige do Bhrian i dtaobh a lán

---

1 PUL: níl aon fhocal nua-Ghaelainne againn ar '*érdam*' ach '*sacraistí*'.

nithe a bhí ag baint leis an Eaglais agus le gnó na hEagailse in Éirinn an uair sin. Bhí gach aon rud a bhain le gnóthaíbh Creidimh briste, stollta, stracaithe as a chéile, ag na Lochlannaigh leis an ndroch-obair a bhí acu á dhéanamh in Éirinn ar feadh breis agus cúpla céad blian roimis sin. Bhí Brian ag déanamh a dhíchill chun na díobhála do leigheas. Níorbh fhéidir do an leigheas a dhéanamh sa cheart agus é ' dhéanamh de réir dlí na hEagailse ar gach aon tsaghas cuma, mar ba chóir, gan cómhairle agus teagasc agus stiúrú a bheith aige ó cheann an Teampaill, ó Fhear Inid Íosa Críost*.

Chómh luath agus d'airigh Brian an tEaspag a bheith tagaithe ón Róimh go hInis Cathaigh, tháinig sé féin agus uaisle a theaghlaigh anoir ó Cheann Cora chun na mainistreach chun teachtaire an Phápa do ghlacadh mar ba chóir. Tháinig Brian um thráthnóna. Fuair sé féin agus na huaisle a tháinig in éineacht leis beannacht an Phápa ón Easpag. Ansan thug sé féin agus an tEaspag mórán aimsire i bhfochair a chéile, agus thug Brian cúntas cruínn don Easpag, le breith thar n-ais chun na Rómha ag triall ar an bPápa, ar an gcuma 'na raibh an Creideamh in Éirinn an uair sin, ar an léirscrios a bhí déanta ag na Lochlannaigh ar eaglaisíbh agus ar mhainistríbh agus ar scoileannaibh, agus do léirigh sé dho an obair mhór nárbh fholáir a dhéanamh chun na díobhála do leigheas, agus conas mar ná raibh aon bhreith ar an ndíobháil do leigheas go hiomlán, mar nárbh fhéidir na mairbh a thabhairt thar n-ais as an gcré. D'inis an tEaspag don rí, do Bhrian, cad é an grá a bhí ag an bPápa dho, agus méid na hurrama a bhí ag an uile dhuine íseal agus uasal do ar fuid na hIúróipe go léir; ná raibh i mbéalaibh ríthe agus daoine ar fuid na Críostaíochta ach na gníomhartha iúntacha a bhí ag Brian á dhéanamh in Éirinn i gcoinnibh na Lochlannach, i gcoinnibh na slua págánach* a bhí tar éis gabháil de chosaibh um an dtaca san i Sasana agus in Albain, agus a bhí ag súil le brú ó dheas ar mhághaibh míne na Frainnce agus na hIodáile, fé mar a dhein a sínsear na céadta blian roimis sin.

"Tuigeann an Pápa, a rí", arsan tEaspag, "agus tuigid na daoine go léir, mura mbeadh an cosc atá agat-sa agus ageat shlóitibh Gael á chur le cómhacht na nDanar anso in Éirinn go mbeidís chúinn ó dheas fadó ag marú agus ag loscadh agus ag creachadh. Níor mhaith leó aghaidh a thabhairt ó dheas go dtí go mbeadh greim i gceart acu ar Éirinn, agus a gcómhacht suite daingean acu san oileán. Dá mbeadh Sasana agus Alba agus Éire acu féna lán-smacht do bheadh caoi acu go hálainn ar a gcómhacht do leathadh ó dheas ar an Iúróip, i ndiaidh ar ndiaidh, agus bheadh na hoileáin seo acu mar chúl dín agus mar bhun-áit chun ollmhúcháin. Mura mbeadh tusa, a rí, do bheadh an greim a bhí uathu acu ar oileán na hÉireann um an dtaca so, fé mar atá acu ar Shasana*. Ní hea ach i bhfad roimis an dtaca so. Ansan is ea ' bheadh an scéal go holc ag an gCreideamh agus ag gach ní i bhfuirm léinn agus eólais agus nósmhaireachta ar fuid na Críostaíochta. Tá an saol go léir baoch díot, a rí, agus tá gach éinne ag guí go cruaidh chun Dé ar do shon, dhá iarraidh ar Dhia neart cuirp agus neart aigne do bhronnadh ort agus faid saeil a thabhairt duit, chun na hoibre atá agat á dhéanamh do chríochnú go beacht".

"Cuireann sé áthas mór orm, a Thiarna Easpaig", arsa Brian, "' fhios a bheith agam go dtuigeann an Pápa chómh maith san an obair seo atá againn á dhéanamh anso in Éirinn. Is trua chráite ná tuigid ár ndaoine féin, leath chómh maith, brí agus bunús an scéil. Dá gcuirimís go léir le chéile, d'fhéadfaimís a bhfuil de Dhanaraibh in Éirinn do mharú nú do dhíbirt in aon cheithre huaire fichead amháin. Níl aon ní is deocra ' chur isteach in aigne na nGael, cuid acu pé'r domhan é, ná aon bhaol a bheith go bhféadfaidh Lochlannaigh choíche greim daingean a dh'fháil ar an oileán so na hÉireann. Níl rí cúige againn ná measann go bhféadfadh sé féin a bhfuil de Dhanaraibh in Éirinn do mharú nú do dhíbirt amáireach, dá mba mhaith leis é, gan cabhair ná cúnamh ó aon rí cúige eile. Sin é atá ag briseadh mo chroí ionam, a Thiarna Easpaig. Ní fhéadaim choíche a chur ' fhiachaibh ar aon rí cúige cabhrú liom i gcoinnibh na Lochlannach gan gabháil go maith ar an rí cúige sin féin ar dtúis. B'éigean dom gabháil ar Mhaolmhuaidh, ar rí Ó nEachach*. Ansan b'éigean dom gabháil ar Dhónall, rí na nDéise. Ansan b'éigean dom éirleach uathásach a dhéanamh ar Lochlannachaibh Átha Cliath agus ar Ghaelaibh Laighean, agus ar chuid de Ghaelaibh Múmhan leó, i nGleann Mháma. Tá Leath Mhogha fém láimh anois agam, idir Ghaelaibh agus Lochlannaigh. Tá an méid sin de thír na hÉireann sámh síochánta socair. An Eaglais ar a suaimhneas. Na scoileanna ar siúl. An talamh dá shaothrú. Lucht ceárd agus ealaíon ag obair gan eagla. Lucht foghla iompaithe ar mhacántacht mar go dtuigid siad 'na n-aigne gurb í an mhacántacht is feárr agus is torthúla agus is rafaire. Ach féach, a Thiarna Easpaig. Níl ann go léir ach mar a bheadh lá breá samhraidh ansan a bheadh go hálainn agus go grianmhar agus go brothallach agus ná feadair éinne cad é an neómat a dh'iompódh sé chun splanncracha agus chun tóirthní agus chun éirligh. Ní thuigid na daoine an scéal. Tuigim-se é. Is cuma leó, na daoine bochta, ach an tsíocháin agus an suaimhneas do shealbhú go sámh an fhaid a fágfar acu an tsíocháin agus an suaimhneas".

"Nách mór an trua, a rí", arsan tEaspag, "gan rud éigin a dhéanamh do thabharfadh síocháin sheasmhach do sna daoine? Dá dtuigeadh daoine i gceart tairbhe na síochána, ba chóir go ndéarfaidís leó féin go gcuirfidís in áirithe dhóibh féin í ar ais nú ar éigin. Tá síocháin curtha i bhfeidhm agats-a anois, a rí, sa taobh so theas d'oileán na hÉireann. Nár chóir go ndéanfadh an tÁrdrí an tsíocháin chéanna do chur i bhfeidhm sa taobh thuaidh den oileán?"

"Ba chóir, a Thiarna Easpaig", arsa Brian. "Fear maith is ea M'leachlainn. Fear tréan cuthaigh is ea é. Ach ní dó' liom go bhfuil aon ghrá ró-mhór aige dhómh-sa. Is maith leis cúnamh a dh'fháil ó Dhál gCais nuair a bhíd na Lochlannaigh ag brú ró-dhian air, ach tá ' fhios agam go maith gurbh fheárr leis go mór iad do chur fé chois le neart a lámha féin, dá bhféadadh sé é, ná aon chúnamh ' fháil uaim-se".

"Ba dhó' liom, dá dtuigeadh sé a dhualgas Árdrí i gceart, gurb amhlaidh a dh'iarrfadh sé an cúnamh ort agus go dtabharfadh sé le tuiscint duit gurbh é a cheart an cúnamh a dh'fháil. Ba dhó' liom gurb é ceart an Árdrí a bheith ar a chumas glaoch chuige ar a bhfuil de neart san oileán go léir, agus an neart go léir do ghléasadh agus do stiúrú in aghaidh namhad iasachta", arsan tEaspag.

"Sin é adéarfadh fir Éireann, a Thiarna Easpaig. Sin é adéarfadh éinne a dhéanfadh machnamh ar an scéal. Is eagal liom ná tuigeann an tÁrdrí an ní sin i gceart. Sin é fé ndeara dhom an tsíocháin seo atá anois againn i Leat Mhogha do chur i gcúmparáid le lá breá gréine ná feadair éinne cathain a dh'iompódh sé chun tóirthní agus chun éirligh. Dá dtagadh aon neart mór de sna Lochlannaigh seo isteach chúinn agus go mbeadh M'leachlainn a d'iarraidh iad do chloí le neart a theaghlaigh féin in inead neart na hÉireann go léir do chruinniú agus do ghléasadh 'na gcoinnibh, do bhuafaidís ar Mh'leachlainn. Ansan do bhuafaidís ar Éirinn go léir i ndiaidh ' chéile, mar ní bheadh éinne chun nirt na hÉireann do chruinniú agus do ghléasadh agus do stiúrú 'na gcoinnibh".

"Ba dhó' liom, a rí", arsan tEaspag, "gurb in rud agus gur cheart d'fhearaibh Éireann féachaint chuige in am. Ba cheart a chur ar a shúilibh don Árdrí gurb é a leas, agus leas na tíre go léir, gan bheith ag feitheamh le namhaid iasachta do theacht chuige thar farraige sara ndéanfadh sé é féin d'ollmhú dhóibh. An tÁrdrí ná hollmhóidh é féin roim ré, ach a bheidh ag feitheamh go dtagaidh an namhaid, tiocfaidh an namhaid air agus ní bheidh sé ollamh".

"Is fíor san, a Thiarna Easpaig", arsa Brian. "Ba cheart d'Árdrí Éireann neart na hÉireann a bheith gléasta i gcónaí aige, in aghaidh namhad na hÉireann, fé mar a bhí an Fhiann ag Fionn, nú fé mar a bhí curaí na Craoibh-rua ag Conchúr. Dá mbeadh san amhlaidh, d'fhanfadh Lochlannaigh amach anois fé mar a dh'fhan slóite na Rómha amach an uair sin".

Caibideal 8: An Bosca

Chomáineadar leó ar an gcuma san ag cainnt agus ag cur thrí chéile go dtí go dtáinig aimsir codlata. Nuair a bhíodar go léir imithe a chodladh, chuir an tAb fios ar Amhlaoibh. Tháinig Amhlaoibh.

"Seo, a mhic", arsan tAb, "eochair an chóthra iarainn atá san *érdam* duit, agus tabhair chúm anso an bosca iarainn atá istigh sa chóthra. Istigh sa bhosca iarainn sin is ea 'tá an chailís óir úd a thug Brian dúinn. Déarfaidh an tEaspag so a tháinig ón Róimh Aifreann Árd anso amáireach dúinn i láthair an rí, agus ní mór an chailís óir sin a thabhairt do chun an Aifrinn sin do rá".

D'imigh Amhlaoibh agus do rug sé an eochair leis. Níorbh fhada gur tháinig sé agus an bosca iarainn aige.

"Cuir ansan ar an gclár é, a mhic", arsan tAb.

Do chuir. Do thug an tAb leis eochair eile. D'oscail sé an bosca. D'fhéach sé isteach ann. Chuir sé a lámh isteach ann. Do lúb a chosa fé, agus bhí sé i riocht titim ach gur rug Amhlaoibh air.

"Cad a tháinig ort, a Athair?", arsa Amhlaoibh.

Níor labhair sé. Shín sé a mhéar chun an bhosca. D'fhéach Amhlaoibh isteach sa bhosca. Bhí an bosca folamh!

Do stad an bheirt ar feadh tamaill mhaith agus iad ag féachaint ar an mbosca. D'fhéach an tAb isteach ann cúpla uair. Ba dhó' le duine air gurbh amhlaidh nár fhéad sé radharc a shúl féin do chreidiúint. Ansan do dhún sé an bosca arís, agus chuir sé an eochair 'na phóca.

"Beir leat é, a Amhlaoibh", ar seisean, "agus cuir isteach arís é sa chóthra iarainn, díreach san áit 'na bhfuarais é, agus cuir an glas ar an gcóthra agus tabhair chúm an eochair. Agus féach. Ná labhair amach as do bhéal le héinne beó ar an scéal. Tá an chailís imithe. Níorbh fhéidir í ' ghuid as an mbosca san gan an dá eochair a dh'fháil, eochair an chóthra agus eochair an bhosca san. Ón lá ' chuireas an chailís isteach sa bhosca san, agus an bosca isteach sa chóthra, tá an dá eochair agam féin. Níor scaras le haon eochair acu go dtí gur thugas duit-se eochair an chóthra ó chiainibh, agus an uair úd a fuaramair an íomhá ó Ghormfhlaith. Níor scaras in aon chor le heochair an bhosca. Ní féidir liom an scéal a thuiscint. Ná labhair le héinne 'na thaobh. Cuir amach an chailís óir eile atá againn, i gcómhair an Aifrinn amáireach".

D'imigh Amhlaoibh agus dhein sé mar adúradh leis. Chuir sé an bosca folamh, agus an glas air, isteach sa chóthra láidir iarainn mar a raibh sé cheana, agus thug sé eochair an chóthra thar n-ais ag triall ar an Ab.

Ar maidin amáireach a bhí chúinn do cuireadh gach aon rud i dtreó i gcómhair an Aifrinn Aoird. Do ghluais an tuairisc, um thráthnóna an lae roimis sin, go raibh Leagáid an Phápa tagaithe go hInis Cathaigh agus go raibh Brian agus a theaghlach tagaithe ann ag cur fáilte roimis an Leagáid, agus go raibh an tAifreann Árd le rá, agus beannacht an Phápa le tabhairt don rí agus do sna manaigh agus don phobal. I bhfad sara dtáinig am an Aifrinn, bhí na daoine cruinnithe isteach ar an oileán ón dtír mórthímpall i dtreó gur dhó' leat go raibh an t-oileán clúdaithe acu.

Dúradh an tAifreann. Do tugadh beannacht an Phápa don phobal agus don rí, agus do thug Colla seanmóin álainn uaidh. Fear ana-léannta, ana-dhea-labhartha, ab ea é. Bhí rith cainnte aige agus uchtach láidir ceólmhar bínn, agus, dá mbeadh sé ag cainnt go hoíche, ba bhreá leis an bpobal bheith ag éisteacht leis. D'inis sé dhóibh conas mar a tháinig an tEaspag san ón Róimh, ón bPápa, agus conas mar a chuir an Pápa a bheannacht ó chroí ar Bhrian agus ar a shlóitibh agus ar Chlannaibh Gael go léir mar gheall ar na gníomhartha móra a bhí acu á dhéanamh in aghaidh namhad an Chreidimh. D'inis sé conas mar a bhí aithne an uair sin ar Bhrian, ní hamháin ar fuid na hÉireann go léir ach ar fuid na hIúróipe go léir, mar go raibh gníomhartha Bhriain i gcoinnibh na Lochlannach ag sábháil na hIúróipe ó léirscrios de shaghas an léirscriosa úd a tháinig uirthi nuair a tháinig na gínte fiaine aduaidh agus ghabhadar de chosaibh i gcómhacht agus i ngradam agus i nósmhaireacht ímpireachta na Rómhánach. Duairt sé, mura mbeadh Brian, go mbeadh Éire ag na Lochlannaigh um an dtaca san mar áit bhunaidh chun a neart do chruinniú agus do ghléasadh, i dtreó go bhféadfaidís a gcómhacht do leathadh ó dheas ar chríochaibh na hIúróipe ar fad, agus ná raibh theas ná thuaidh san Iúróip an uair sin aon tsaghas cómhachta a dh'fhéadfadh cosc do chur leó, murarbh ionann is sé chéad blian roimis sin nuair a bhí cómhacht na Rómhánach ann chun seasaimh éigin a dhéanamh in aghaidh na ngínte fiaine. Duairt sé gur thuig muíntir na hIúróipe go léir an ní sin, agus go rabhadar ag faire ar Bhrian agus ar an obair a bhí aige á dhéanamh, agus gur mhór acu Brian agus gur mhór acu an obair.

Nuair a bhí a chainnt ráite ag an Ab agus gach gnó creidimh déanta, do rugadh an Leagáid mórthímpall an oileáin agus do tispeánadh do gach aon rud ab fhiú a dh'fheiscint ann, go mór mór gach ní go raibh aon bhaint ag ainm ná ag beatha Sheanáin naofa leis. Ansan do tispeánadh do gach lot agus gach réabadh-reilige dár dhein na Lochlannaigh an fhaid a bhíodar ann, agus gach ní dá raibh déanta ag Brian agus ag muíntir na tíre agus ag an Ab agus ag na manaigh chun gach díobhála do leigheas.

An fhaid a bhíothas ag gabháil tímpall ar an gcuma san, ag tispeáint agus ag feiscint, bhí rud age sna manaigh á dhéanamh sa tseómra mhór, seómra an bhídh. Bhí dínnéar acu dá ollmhú, dínnéar don Leagáid agus don rí, agus do sna maithibh móra tuatha agus eagailse a bhí in éineacht leó. Ar ball, nuair a bhí an dínnéar ollamh, chuaigh Amhlaoibh amach agus do thug sé cogar don Ab. Do labhair an tAb leis an rí agus leis an Leagáid, agus tháinig* an chuideachta go léir isteach sa tseómra mhór. Bhí an seómra gléasta riartha go hálainn, fé bhórdaibh fada, agus bia agus deoch go flúirseach ar na bórdaibh sin. Do shuigh Brian sa chathaoir ríoga. Do shuigh an Leagáid ar dheis an rí. Do shuigh Murchadh, an rí-dhamhna, ar ghualainn chlé an rí. Do shuigh an chuid eile de sna huaislibh, de réir a ndán agus a n-uaisleachta, de réir na nós agus na rial a bhí i bhfeidhm in Éirinn riamh roimis sin. Bhí ' fhios ag gach duine den chuideachtain cá raibh a inead féin chun suite, agus chuaigh sé agus shuigh sé san inead san.

Bhí an tráthnóna go suairc acu go léir. Bhí a lán-ndóthain* bídh agus dí acu. Nuair ' airigh muíntir na tíre mórthímpall, ar gach taobh den abhainn, an Leagáid agus an rí agus na maithe móra go léir a bheith ag teacht chun na mainistreach, thosnaigh na báid ar theacht chun an oileáin agus fáltas feóla, agus aráin, agus ime, agus uachtair, agus b'fhéidir fáltas fíona, ar gach bád acu. Ní raibh aon angar sa tseómra mhór. Níor ghá do Cholla aon eagla ' bheith air go raghadh dá chuid lóin bídh ná dí, pé tarrac a déanfí orthu.

Bhí an chuideachta go soilbhir agus go séimh. Dheineadar a lán cainnte agus a lán suilt i gcaitheamh an tráthnóna i dteannta a ndóthain a dh'ithe agus a dh'ól. Do tráchtadh arís, fé mar a tráchtaithí i gcónaí an uair sin ins gach cruinniú den tsórd, ar na cathannaibh móra a bhí buaite ag Brian agus ag Dál gCais i gcoinnibh na Lochlannach. Éinne go raibh aon rud le rá aige i dtaobh na gcathanna san, ba mhaith leis labhairt an uair sin ó bhí Leagáid an Phápa ag éisteacht leis. Do hínseadh don Leagáid conas mar a cuireadh teitheadh ar na Lochlannaigh ar an Móin Móir. Conas mar a chuir Mathúin, driotháir Bhriain, an ruag orthu ag Loch Guir. Conas mar a chuir an bheirt driothár, Mathúin agus Brian, ár agus dearg-ruathar orthu sa chath a buaileadh ag Solchaid*, mar ar maraíodh trí mhíle acu, agus conas mar a leanadh isteach go cathair Luimní an méid acu nár thit sa chath, agus conas mar a tógadh an chathair agus mar a scártáladh agus do loisceadh í. Do hínseadh do conas mar a tháinig Maghnas mac Arailt* agus slóite móra Lochlannach aige, agus conas mar a dhein sé mainistir Ínse Cathaigh do robáil agus do loscadh.

Caibideal 8: An Bosca

Ansan do hínseadh do conas mar a bhí daingean láidir déanta dhóibh féin ag na Lochlannaigh sa mhainistir sin 'na raibh an chuideachta 'na suí an uair sin, agus conas mar a tháinig Brian agus Dál gCais agus conas mar a bhriseadar an daingean agus chuireadar na Lochlannaigh chun báis, agus conas mar a thit an Maghnas mac Arailt úd sa chath. Ansan do tugadh cúntas do ar chath Bhealaigh Leachta; agus ar an gcath ag Fán Chonradh; agus ar an gcath mór fíochmhar fuilteach a troideadh i nGleann Mháma, mar ar thit chúig mhíle fear de sna fearaibh ba thréine ar shlóitibh Lochlann; agus gurbh é an cath san Ghleanna Mháma do mhíll ar fad cómhacht Lochlannach in Éirinn agus do chuir Leath Mhogha, gan chosnamh, fé láimh Bhriain.

Do tugadh an uile shaghas cúntais ar na gníomharthaibh móra san don Leagáid, agus bhí a lán daoine ag cainnt ag tabhairt na gcúntaisí dho. An rud nár chuímhin le duine, ba chuímhin le duine eile é, agus an rud a théadh amú ar dhuine, thugadh duine eile sa cheart leis é.

Do tugadh an méid seo fé ndeara, áfach. Na fir ba thréine gníomh i ngach* cath de sna cathannaibh úd, níorbh iad ab aoirde glór san ínsint. Is ar éigin a labhair Brian ná Murchadh aon fhocal san ínsint. Do thuig an Leagáid an ní sin. Fear géar-chúiseach ab ea é.

Bhí na manaigh ag friothálamh ar na huaislibh, agus bhí an *deacon*, Amhlaoibh, an Lochlannach óg, ins gach aon chúinne ag freagairt do na manachaibh fé mar a ghlaeidís, agus ag déanamh gach aon tsaghas friothála fé mar a hórdaítí dho. Bhí sé ag éisteacht leis an gcainnt go léir i dtaobh na gcathanna móra, agus ní fhéadfadh éinne a dh'ínsint óna chúntanós ceocu ' thuig sé an chainnt nú nár thuig, nú ceocu ba Lochlannach é nú nárbh ea. Dhein sé an gnó a bhí idir lámhaibh aige agus dhein sé go maith é, agus bhí a aigne chómh daingean ar an ngnó san go ndéarfadh duine ná raibh blúire suime aige sa chainnt a bhí ar siúl. Bhí Tadhg Óg Ó Cealla ag déanamh an fhriothála, leis, agus bhí sé ag éisteacht leis an gcainnt a bhí ar siúl. Nuair ' airíodh sé an chainnt, b'fheárr leis go mór gan Amhlaoibh a bheith ag éisteacht léi. Ach nuair ' fhéachadh sé ar Amhlaoibh agus nuair a chíodh sé an neamh-shuím, dar leis, bhíodh a aigne sásta. Thuigeadh sé ná bíodh aon chorrabhuais ag an gcainnt á chur ar Amhlaoibh. Ansan arís, ní ró-mhaith a thaithneadh an neamh-shuímh sin leis. Thuigeadh sé in' aigne, dá mba Lochlannach é féin agus go mbeadh cainnt den tsórd san ar siúl 'na láthair, ná féadfadh sé fulag léi pé dícheall a dhéanfadh sé air. Do thaithn leis nár ghoíll an chainnt ar Amhlaoibh, ach 'na thaobh san ba mhó an meas a bheadh aige ar a charaid, ba dhó' leis, dá ngoilleadh an chainnt air agus dá gcuireadh sí fearg air. Níor ghoíll, agus níor chuir.

Caibideal 9: "Is Éagsamhlach na Daoine Iad!"

Ach do críochnaíodh an dínnéar agus tháinig deireadh na cainnte agus d'éirigh an chuideachta. D'iarr Brian ar an Leagáid teacht ag triall air féin go Ceann Cora ar chuaird chómh luath agus ' thiocfadh san isteach lena chaothúlacht. Duairt an Leagáid go n-oirfeadh do roinnt laethanta ' thabhairt sa mhainistir, i bhfochair Cholla, ag socrú agus ag léiriú a lán nithe a bhain le gnóthaíbh Eagailse agus le gnóthaíbh Creidimh, ní hamháin sa mhainistir sin Ínse Cathaigh ach i mainistribh agus in eaglaisibh na Múmhan go léir. Go mbeadh an chuid ba bhruidiúla de ghnó Ínse Cathaigh déanta aige laistigh de sheachtain. Ansan, dá mb'é toil an rí é, go dtabharfadh sé cuaird go Ceann Cora. Do socraíodh ar sheachtain ón lá san do chun na cuairde sin do thabhairt. Ansan d'imigh Brian agus a chuallacht abhaile agus d'fhan an Leagáid sa mhainistir, é féin agus an chuallacht bheag a tháinig leis ón Róimh.

Ar ball, nuair a bhí Colla agus an Leagáid i bhfochair a chéile 'na n-aonar, do ghlaeigh Colla ar Amhlaoibh.

Tháinig Amhlaoibh.

Caibideal 9: "Is Éagsamhlach na Daoine Iad!"

"Seo, a Amhlaoibh", arsa Colla, ag síneadh na heochrach chuige, "imigh agus tabhair chúinn anso an bosca iarainn úd 'na raibh an chailís óir ann*".

D'imigh Amhlaoibh agus thug sé leis an bosca, agus chuir sé ar an mbórd é i bhfianaise na beirte.

"Imigh-se a chodladh anois, a mhic ó", arsa Colla leis. "Ní foláir nú tá codladh ort agus tuirse tar éis an lae".

Ansan d'oscail Colla an bosca iarainn agus thispeáin sé don Leagáid é, agus d'inis sé dho cúrsaí na cailíse.

"Is cuímhin liom an chailís sin go hálainn", arsan Leagáid. "Bhí sí im láimh agam go minic. Cailís ana-dhaor ab ea í. Anoir ó Chathair Chonstantín a cuireadh ar dtúis í ón Ímpire, mar bhronntanas chun an Phápa. Mise aduairt* gur cheart í ' chur anso go hÉirinn ag triall ar Bhrian. Is mór an trua í ' bheith imithe".

Ansan do cheistigh sé Colla go dlúth i dtaobh na n-eochrach, agus conas a bhí cimeád orthu, agus cérbh é an gabha a dhein iad, agus cérbh é an gabha a dhein an bosca iarainn. D'imigh sé féin amach chun an *érdaim* go bhfeicfeadh sé an cóthra daingean 'na raibh an bosca iarainn fé ghlas istigh ann. Nuair a bhí gach aon rud feicithe, trialta, iniúchta go maith aige tháinig sé thar n-ais agus do shuigh sé agus dhein sé a mhachnamh. Nuair a bhí a mhachnamh déanta aige, do labhair sé.

"Inis dom, a Cholla", ar seisean, "cá raibh an chailís sarar tugadh don mhainistir seo í".

"Bhí sí thoir i gCeann Cora, gan amhras", arsa Colla.

"Cé aige go raibh sí i gcimeád i gCeann Cora?", arsan Leagáid.

Caibideal 9: "Is Éagsamhlach na Daoine Iad!"

"Is dócha go raibh sí i gcimeád ag an mBannrín, a Thiarna Easpaig", arsa Colla.

Do stad an Leagáid agus dhein sé machnamh eile. Do labhair sé arís.

"Ca bhfuil an gabha a dhein na heochracha so?", ar seisean.

"Tá sé thuas i Luimneach, a Thiarna Easpaig", arsa Colla. "Is é ' dhein an dá eochair sin dom, agus is é ' dhein an bosca iarainn dom. Ceárdaí ana-shlachtmhar, an-eólgaiseach, is ea é. Tá íntleacht aige nách gnáth a bheith ag ceárdaithibh dá shórd. Bíonn sé ag obair do Bhrian ag déanamh arm do, agus deirtear gur feárr leis na fir na hairm a dheineann sé ná na hairm a dheineann aon cheárdaí eile dá bhfuil ag obair ag Brian. Cruann sé an faobhar ar chuma éigin nách eól d'éinne ach do féin, agus gléasann sé na hairm i dtreó gur feárr a féadtar iad do bheartú agus úsáid a dhéanamh díobh ná mar a féadtar an mheáchaint chéanna iarainn agus adhmaid do bheartú chun gnímh insna hairm a dheineann aon ghabha eile, agus gur feárr a chimeádaid siad an faobhar ná mar a chimeádaid aon airm eile é".

"Is dócha", arsan Leagáid, "ó tá an bua san aige ar na gaibhníbh eile, gur fear saibhir é".

"Is ea, a Thiarna Easpaig", arsa Colla. "Fear ana-shaibhir is ea é. Nuair a fuair Brian amach an t-eólas go léir a bheith aige ar dhéanamh na n-arm, thug sé fearann tailimh saor do lasmu' den chathair, ar bruach na Sionainne, ar choinníoll ná déanfadh sé aon arm d'aon rí eile ach do Bhrian féin".

"Cad é an ainm atá air, a Cholla?", arsan Leagáid.

"Níor airíos riamh an ainm a tugadh air nuair a baisteadh é. Níl ag an bpoiblíocht air ach leas-ainm. 'Meargach na Lann' a tugtar air, mar gheall, is dócha, ar fheabhas na n-arm a dheineann sé. Tugtar

'Meargach Gabha' air, leis, agus 'Meargach Maol', agus 'Meargach Dubh', agus 'Meargach', gan aon rud a chur leis".

Dheineadar roinnt eile cainnte ar ghnó na mainistreach, agus ansan chuadar a chodladh.

D'imigh an tseachtain. Do ghluais an Leagáid agus a chuallacht soir go Ceann Cora. Chuaigh Colla agus Tadhg Óg Ó Cealla agus Amhlaoibh soir in éineacht leó. Bhí cuideachta mhór cruinnithe rómpu thoir. Bhí a lán de ríogra agus d'uaislibh Múmhan agus Laighean ann. Bhí Tadhg Mór Ó Cealla ann agus cuid de ríogra Connacht lena chois. Bhí Niamh ann. An áit 'na mbíodh Tadhg Mór Ó Cealla, ba ghnáth go mbíodh a iníon ann. Bhí tréithe móra maithe sa ríogan* óg san agus ba mhór é urraim na ndaoine go léir di mar gheall ar na tréithibh sin. Bhí sé i mbéalaibh daoine gurbh í an Bhannrín, Gormfhlaith, an bhean dob áille ar bith an uair sin, ach, fé mar a bhí Niamh ag éirí suas, bhí daoine dhá rá go mbuafadh a háilleacht ar áilleacht Ghormfhlaith féin um an dtaca 'na mbeadh sí ag imeacht as na déagaibh. Bhí sí i ngar do bheith ag imeacht astu le línn na haimsire sin 'nar tháinig sí féin agus a hathair go Ceann Cora, go rí-theaghlach Bhriain, chun Leagáid an Phápa ' dh'fheiscint. In éaghmais a háilleachta, bhí mórán de thréithibh maithe eile inti. Bhí an Creideamh ana-láidir istigh 'na croí. Bhí grá aici don Chreideamh agus do gach ní a bhain leis an gCreideamh, agus do ghealadh a croí i gcónaí do sna daoine a bhíodh dílis don Chreideamh, agus do thispeánadh sí é nuair ba cheart é ' thispeáint. Bhí na daoine bochta go léir baoch di, agus do tugtí fé ndeara go mbíodh sí chómh fial sa déirc leis an Lochlannach a bheadh 'na ghátar agus ' bhíodh sí, nách mór, leis an Éireannach a bheadh 'na ghátar. Bhí a ciall agus a tuiscint chómh géar-chúiseach san gurbh ar éigin a bhíodh aon rud ar aigne a hathar ná hínseadh sé dhi agus ná cuireadh sé 'na cómhairle. Ach bhí aon tréith amháin inti do tharraig urraim na ndaoine chúithi thar gach tréith eile dá raibh inti. B'é tréith é sin ná an cion a bhí aici ar a hathair. Dar léi, ní raibh fear eile beó in Éirinn a bhí chómh maith leis, ná chómh huasal leis, ná chómh ríoga leis, ná chómh fial leis, ná chómh mór-chroíoch leis, ná chómh breá d'fhear leis.

Bhí féasta mór i gCeann Cora an lá san. Bhí cuideachta ríoga bailithe ann, agus bhí dóthain na cuideachtan de rí i mBrian. Do thuig gach éinne go raibh, agus bhí daoine ann adéarfadh nách i gCeann Cora ba cheart an chuideachta san a bheith i bhfochair a chéile an uair sin ach thíos i dTeamhair, agus nách ar Leath Mhogha ba cheart Brian a bheith 'na rí ach gur in' Árdrí ar Éirinn ba cheart é ' bheith. Do hairíodh cogarnach den tsórd san ar siúl go minic i gcaitheamh an tráthnóna agus i gcaitheamh na hoíche. D'airigh Brian an chogarnach, ach níor leog sé air gur airigh. D'airigh Murchadh an chogarnach, agus duairt sé leis an bhfear a labhair ciall a bheith aige. D'airigh Gormfhlaith an chogarnach. Do chruaigh a gnúis agus do las solas 'na súilibh, agus níor sholas fónta é.

Bhí cogarnach eile, leis, ar siúl. Bhí Niamh agus a hathair 'na suí in aice ' chéile, agus is ar éigin ' fheádadh an chuideachta gan bheith ag féachaint orthu. Is beag ná go mbuadh an iúnadh ar na béasaibh acu, agus ná go bhféachaidís ní ba mhó ná mar ba cheart i dtreó na beirte, bhí a leithéid sin de sholas áilleachta in aghaidh na hiníne. Ansan do fuaradar go léir amach, sa chogarnach dóibh, gur Mórling ab ainm di agus gurbh amhlaidh a tugadh Niamh Chínn Óir mar leas-ainm uirthi nuair a bhí sí 'na leanbh. Thuigeadar go léir 'na n-aigne nárbh aon iúnadh in aon chor gur tugadh an leas-ainm sin uirthi, mar gurbh í an "Niamh Chínn Óir" i gceart í.

In éaghmais na cogarnaí, bhí gleó cainnte sa chuideachtain a bhí árd go leór. Do cíoradh agus do slámadh agus do cuireadh trí chéile arís gach gníomh de sna gníomharthaibh móra a deineadh insna cathannaibh úd, ó chath Bhealaigh Leachta go cath Ghleanna Mháma. Na fir, sa chuideachtain, ná raibh i gcath acu, bhíodar i gcath éigin eile acu, agus an té ná féadadh tuairisc a thabhairt ar chath acu, thugadh sé tuairisc ar chath eile acu, agus uaireanta d'éiríodh argóint the idir bheirt a bhí san aon chath amháin, duine acu dhá áiteamh gur 'na leithéid seo ' chuma* do buadh an cath, agus an duine eile dhá áiteamh nárbh ea ach 'na leithéid siúd eile de chuma. Ansan b'fhéidir go labharfadh an tríú duine agus go ndéarfadh sé go raibh an éagóir ag an mbeirt, agus go dtabharfadh sé a mhalairt ar fad de thuairisc ar an gcuma 'nar buadh an cath. Bhí oiread san nithe titithe amach sa Mhúmhain i gcaitheamh beagán blianta roimis sin nár bhaol don chuideachtain aon tocht a theacht orthu le heaspa abhar cainnte. Níor tháinig aon tocht orthu. Bhí gleó agus argóint agus áiteamh agus aighneas acu go tiubh, agus má bhí ní baol ná go raibh sult agus greann agus gáirí go tiubh acu, leis, agus iad ag maíomh go hárd agus go suairc agus go mór-aigeanta mar gheall ar an gcuma 'na raibh Clanna Gael in uachtar agus Lochlannaigh ar lár.

Fé mar a tháinig a ndóthain a bheith ite agus ólta ag an gcuideachtain, bhí an chainnt agus an sult agus an gleó ag dul in aoirde. Fé dheireadh do bhuail Brian an cluigín. Do stad an gleó. Bhí gach éinne ciúin. Do labhair Brian. D'iarr sé ar an gcuideachtain sláinte an Phápa ' dh'ól. Do mhol sé an Creideamh agus do mhol sé Ceann So-fheicse* an Chreidimh, agus do gheall sé, uaidh féin, agus thar cheann a raibh láithreach d'uaislibh Gael, agus tar cheann a raibh beó de shíolrach Gael, go mbeadh sliocht Gael dílis don Chreideamh, le cúnamh Dé, an fhaid a bheadh grian ar spéir agus daoine ar talamh.

Do hóladh sláinte an Phápa agus do guíodh faid saeil chuige. Ansan do labhair an Leagáid. Duairt sé arís os cómhair na cuideachtan san an chainnt aduairt sé thíos in Inis Cathaigh. D'inis sé conas mar a bhí an Iúróip go léir ag faire an uair sin ar Bhrian agus ar Ghaelaibh agus ar an ngleic uathásach a bhí acu á dhéanamh le cómhachtaibh Lochlann; gurbh í an ghleic uathásach san a bhí ag sábháil na hIúróipe agus ag sábháil na hEagailse ar fuid na hIúróipe, ón leirscrios a dhéanfadh na Lochlannaigh orthu mura mbeadh an cosc a bhí dá chur lena réim agus lena neart anso in Éirinn. Duairt sé go mbeadh an Pápa agus cléir na Rómha agus an Eaglais ar fuid na hIúróipe ag guí chun Dé de ghnáth dhá iarraidh ar Dhia na Glóire cabhrú go láidir leis na Gaelaibh agus le Brian sa ghleic sin, agus an bua a bhí acu dá thuilleamh chómh maith do thabhairt dóibh sa deireadh go hiomlán.

Do thug an chuideachta trí gártha molta don Phápa. Ansan do thugadar trí gártha molta do Bhrian. Ansan d'iarradar d'aon ghuth ar an Leagáid an bheannacht a thabhairt arís dóibh. Bhí iúnadh air nuair a hiarradh san air, ach nuair a chonaic sé Brian agus Murchadh agus an chuideachta go léir ar a nglúinibh, thug sé dhóibh an bheannacht. Duairt sé in' aigne féin áfach: "Is éagsamhlach na daoine iad! Gleó agus aighneas agus glór árd agus éirleach cainnte—agus ansan—beannacht an Phápa! Is éagsamhlach na daoine iad!"

Caibideal 10: Dúlainn Óg

Tháinig an t-am chun dul isteach i halla an rínce. D'iarr Brian ar an Leagáid altú. Do dhein. D'fhreagair an chuideachta go léir. Ansan d'éirigh an rí agus an chuideachta agus chuadar go dtí an halla mór, halla an rínce. Tháinig an t-aos ceóil. Do spreagadh suas an ceól. Do leath an chuideachta iad féin mórthímpall an halla. Ba gheárr go raibh na daoine óga ag rínce agus na seandaoine ag cainnt 'na mbuínibh beaga anso agus ansúd. Bhí Brian agus an Leagáid in aice ' chéile agus iad ag cainnt ar a lán nithe a bhain le gnóthaíbh ríochta na hÉireann agus le gnóthaíbh Creidimh in Éirinn. Bhí Gormfhlaith agus Colla agus Tadhg Mór Ó Cealla in aice ' chéile agus iad ag trácht ar a lán nithe nár chuir éinne acu puínn suime iontu. Tháinig Dúlainn Óg ag triall orthu agus níorbh fhada go raibh cainnt a ndóthain ag an gceathrar san, Dúlainn ag áireamh na ngníomhartha a dhein Brian agus na ngníomhartha a dhein Murchadh ar na Lochlannaigh i gcath Ghleanna Mháma, agus Colla ag ceistiúchán air. Bhíodh Dúlainn in aice Mhurchadh i gcónaí insna cathannaibh, agus nuair ' bhíodh an namhaid 'na dtímpall, thugaidís a dhá ndrom lena chéile agus chosnaidís iad féin go dtí go dtagadh cúnamh chúthu. Ní har a ghníomharthaibh féin, áfach, a dheineadh Dúlainn puínn cainnte. Ar ghníomharthaibh Mhurchadh ba mhaith leis bheith ag cainnt.

Caibideal 10: Dúlainn Óg

"Lá uathásach ab ea an lá san Ghleanna Mháma", ar seisean. "Na fir ba thréine a bhí ar chlannaibh Lochlann, bhíodar sa chath san. Bhíodar lán-deimhnitheach go mbuafaidís. Bhíodar socair air. Bhíodar ceapaithe air. Bhí a n-aigne socair go daingean acu ar bhuachtaint nú ar thitim. Ní fheaca riamh a leithéid de neamh-shuím i mbás agus ' chonac 'nár namhaid an lá san. Chómh tiubh agus ' thiteadh an fear, bhíodh fear in' inead. Tá an méid seo agam-sa le rá, agus deirim é mar do chonaic mo dhá shúil é. Mura mbeadh Murchadh, bhí* Gleann Mháma ag na Lochlannaigh".

"Is mór an focal é sin, a Dhúlainn", arsa Gormfhlaith.

"Is mór an focal é, a ríogan, agus is fíor é. D'admhaigh na Lochlannaigh féin é, an méid a bhí beó dhíobh tar éis an chatha. Bhí an cath ar siúl ar feadh cúpla uair a' chluig nú mar sin. Bhíomair ag brú orthu agus bhíodar san ag brú orainn, agus bhí sé ag teip ar aon taobh an taobh eile do chur oiread agus órlach i ndiaidh a gcúil. Bhí na fir ag titim ar gach taobh. Ní buailtí buille ná titeadh fear leis, ba dhó' leat. Do shocraigh Brian agus Murchadh agus tuilleadh againn ar bhriseadh isteach trína lár. Do dhúnamair chun a chéile agus bhrúmair isteach. Do leagamair roinnt acu agus bhriseamair beárna iontu, agus bhíomair ag brú amach tríd an mbeárnain. Lena línn sin, cad a chífinn tamall beag uaim ar ár láimh chlé ach Lochlannach mór mileata agus beárna briste amach aige trínár slua féin, agus é féin agus na Lochlannaigh a bhí in' aice ag gabháil amach go tiubh ann, agus iad ag leagadh ár ndaoine rómpu agus ar gach taobh díobh. Bhí an Lochlannach ní b'aoirde go mór ná aon fhear eile a bhí in' aice, de Ghael ná de Lochlannach. Gach aon uair a thaghadh a chlaíomh anuas, do thiteadh fear. Ní raibh éinne ábalta ar sheasamh 'na láthair. Chonaic Murchadh é. Do léim sé siar as an mbeárnain a bhí déanta againn-na, agus siúd fé dhéin an fhir mhóir é. Do leanas féin é. Bhí an dá chlaíomh aige 'na dhá láimh. Thug sé aghaidh ar an bhfear mór. Do thóg an fear mór a chlaíomh agus tharraig sé a bhuille. Do ghoibh Murchadh an buille ar an gclaíomh a bhí sa láimh chlé aige, agus san am gcéanna díreach do chuaigh claíomh na lámha deise trí chroí an fhir mhóir. Ní fheaca riamh gníomh chómh deas. Aon ghníomh amháin ab ea an dá ghníomh, an chosaint leis an láimh chlé agus an sá leis an láimh ndeis. Dá bhfeicfá an fear mór, déarfá gurbh uathásach an neart nárbh fholáir a bheith sa chuislinn a ghlac an buille agus nár lúb fén mbuille. Déarfá gur mhór an gníomh a dhein an fear a chosain an buille sin. Ach dhein sé an gníomh eile le línn an ghnímh sin a dhéanamh. Chuir sé an claíomh eile trí chroí an fhir mhóir. Ní raibh aon choinne in aon chor ag an bhfear mór go dtiocfadh an chosaint agus an sá in éineacht air. Ní raibh aon choinne aige go raibh sé i gcuislinn an fhir a bhí os a chómhair an chosaint a dhéanamh, gan bac d'aon tsá ' dhéanamh. Chuir an chosaint iúnadh air, agus chuir an sá alltacht ar fad air. Ní raibh uain aige, sarar imigh an t-anam as, ach ar a rá, 'Is tu an fear is feárr a bhuail riamh umam!' Chuir an gníomh dúbalta san scannradh ar na Lochlannaigh eile a bhí ar an láthair. Do tharraigeadar siar. Tháinig buile misnigh ar ár bhfearaibh féin agus bhrúdar amach. Bhriseamair an tarna beárna rómhainn amach. Cad a chífinn ansan ach ár neart féin ag géilleadh do neart na Lochlannach, tamall soir ó dheas ar ár ndeis. Siúd siar Murchadh agus me féin arís agus soir ó dheas chun na háite 'na raibh na Gaeil ag dul i ndiaidh a gcúil. Chómh luath agus ' chonacadar ag teacht sinn, tháinig náire orthu agus sheasaíodar an fód. Um an dtaca 'nar shroiseamair iad, is ag brú amach a bhíodar in inead bheith ag dul i ndiaidh a gcúil. Bhíodar ar buile chúthu féin a rá go bhfeacaigh Murchadh ag dul i ndiaidh a gcúil iad. Tháinig, ba dhó' leat, dúbailt nirt iontu. Bhrúdar rómpu an namhaid, agus ba dheocair é. Bhí na fir ag titim chómh tiubh le grean ar gach taobh. Bhí na cuirp 'na gcruachaibh in áirde ar a chéile. Is in áirde ar na cruachaibh sin a chaitheamair seasamh agus sinn ag brú ar an namhaid agus dhá leagadh. Bhrúmair rómhainn iad. Chuireamair cruach dínn. Ansan chuireamair cruach eile dhínn. Mheasas go gcaithfimís iad go léir a mharú sara n-iompóidís uainn. Fé dheireadh d'iompaíodar. Do theitheadar, agus do leanadh iad agus do maraíodh oiread acu sa ruagairt agus do maraíodh sa chath. Mura mbeadh Murchadh, bheadh a mhalairt de scéal againn. Mura mbeadh Murchadh, do rithfeadh leis an bhfear mór úd. D'iompódh na Lochlannaigh isteach laistiar dínn nuair a bheimís imithe amach tríd an mbeárnain úd. Bheadh an ruag ar ár muíntir féin ar thaobh na lámha deise agus ar thaobh na lámha clé. Ansan d'iompódh neart ár namhad go léir orainn agus ní thiocfadh duine againn beó as an gcath. Ansan bheadh seilbh ag Lochlannachaibh in Éirinn agus bheadh sé fuar ag M'leachlainn bheith ag cur 'na gcoinnibh. Mura mbeadh Murchadh, bheadh Éire ag Lochlannachaibh anois! Deirim leat go mbeadh. Agus deirim rud eile. Tá sé buailte isteach i m'aigne agus deirim go láidir é. Ní bheidh Éire ó bhaol i gceart go dtí go mbeidh Brian in' Árdrí!"

"Ochón, a Dhúlainn", arsa Gormfhlaith, "measaim gur maith an bhail ort gan M'leachlainn a bheith ag éisteacht leat".

"Ba chuma liom 'en tsaol, a ríogan", arsa Dúlainn, "ach go bhfeicfinn tu féin thíos i dTeamhair i t'Árdríogain ar Éirinn go léir ó Dhonncha Dí go Tigh Mháire![*]"

Caibideal 11: Ceann Leóin

Scian trí chroí Ghormfhlaith ab ea an uile fhocal den chainnt sin a labhair Dúlainn an fhaid a bhí an cúntas san aige á thabhairt ar chath Ghleanna Mháma. Ba mhaith léi, gan amhras, bheith 'na hÁrdríogain ar Éirinn, ach más ea ní raibh aon lorg aici ar Bhrian a bheith in' Árdrí. Bhí ' fhios aici, dá dtagadh Brian chun na hÁrdríochta, nár ró-fhada 'na dhiaidh san go dtí go mbeadh Murchadh in' Árdrí. Bhí a leithéid sin d'fhuath aici do Mhurchadh gur thúisce léi í féin agus ar bhain léi ' bheith sínte fén bhfód ná é ' dh'fheiscint in' Árdrí. Bhí gach aon tsúil aici go dtitfeadh sé féin agus Brian i gcath Ghleanna Mháma agus go mbeadh bua ag na Lochlannaigh ann. Ansan, dar léi, d'iompódh cómhacht Lochlann 'na lán-neart ar Mh'leachlainn. Ní bheadh aon bhreith aige ar sheasamh 'na gcoinnibh. Ní fhéadfadh sé neart fear Éireann do chur le chéile 'na gcoinnibh. Do buafí air. Do buafí ar ríthibh Éireann 'na nduine is 'na nduine, fé mar a buadh orthu cheana. Ansan do bheadh an lámh uachtair ag Lochlannaigh agus bheadh mac Ghormfhlaith in' Árdrí ar Éirinn. Sin é a bhí uaithi.

Caibideal 11: Ceann Leóin

Chuir cath Ghleanna Mhámа an méid sin go léir ar neamhní, agus má b'fhíor cainnt Dhúlainn b'é Murchadh fé ndeár san. Má bhí fuath aici do Mhurchadh roimis sin, do mhéadaigh an chainnt sin an fuath. Scian trína croí ab ea an uile fhocal den chainnt.

Is ró-bheag dá chuímhneamh, áfach, a bhí ag Dúlainn féin ná ag éinne den mhuíntir a bhí ag éisteacht leis an gcainnt go raibh an chainnt ag gearradh an chroí aici ar an gcuma san. Bhí a gnúis chómh séimh, chómh glan, chómh ríoga, chómh solasmhar, chómh caoin, chómh cneasta san aici gur dhó' le duine uirthi ná raibh aon ní ar an dtalamh so ba mhó ' thug de shásamh aigne dhi ná mar a thug an cath san Ghleanna Mhámа dhi.

Ach dá mhéid gearradh a dhein an cúntas ar a croí, bhí aon ní amháin ag baint leis an gcath agus ' thug sé roinnt sóláis di. Má deineadh uisce-fé-thalamh riamh do dhein sí é chun cómhacht na Lochlannach do neartú i gcómhair an chatha san. Ach do dhein sí an t-uisce-fe-thalamh chómh cliste sin nár tháinig aon phioc dá eólas chun Briain ná chun Murchadh, ná chun éinne a thabharfadh dóibh aon chogar de. Bhí iúnadh ar gach éinne neart na Lochlannach a bheith chómh mór sa chath agus é ' bheith gléasta chómh maith, agus an oiread san d'fhearaibh cróga mileata ' bheith tagaithe ann ó dhúthaíbh iasachta a bhí i bhfad ón áit agus i bhfad ó chéile, ach níor chuímhnigh éinne, lasmu' den mhuíntir a bhí 'na cómhairle agus ag déanamh a hoibre, go raibh aon bhaint ag Gormfhlaith leis an ní sin.

"Is eagal liom, a rí", ar sise le Dúlainn, "go bhfuil an iomad de chreidiúint an lae sin agat dá thabhairt do Mhurchadh, agus go bhfuil éagóir agat dá dheanamh ort féin sa scéal. Dá mb'iad na Lochlannaigh féin iad, déarfaidís, dá labhraidís, ná fuil fear ar shlóitibh Bhriain is truime buille i gcath ná Dúlainn Óg. Tá aithne mhaith acu ort, a rí, agus déarfadh cuid acu gur feárr d'fhear thu ná Murchadh féin, agus gur maith an bhail ar Mhurchadh go minic tusa ' bheith in' aice sa spéirling".

Caibideal 11: Ceann Leóin

"Na daoine do labharfadh ar an gcuma san, a ríogan", arsa Dúlainn, "daoine is ea iad nár theangmhaigh riamh i gcath le Murchadh agus nár mhothaigh a neart. Na daoine do theangmhaigh leis agus do mhothaigh an neart atá 'na chuislinn ní puínn acu a tháinig uaidh chun an scéil a dh'ínsint. Gan amhras do dheineas mo ghníomh agus bhuaileas mo bhuille nuair a bhí namhaid ar m'aghaidh amach, ach níl aon chomórtas idir mo bhuille agus buille Mhurchadh".

Níorbh aon iúnadh go nduairt Gormfhlaith an chainnt aduairt sí i dtaobh an fhir a bhí os a cómhair an uair sin. Fear córach, dea-chúmtha ab ea é. Bhí ualach trom gruaige ar a cheann agus í ag titim anuas ar a shlinneánaibh. Gruaig chiardhubh ab ea í, agus bhíodh sí ag crith agus ag taithneamh sa tsolas le gach focal dá labhradh sé. Bhí dhá mhalainn throma dhúbha os cionn a dhá shúl agus bhí an dá shúil sin suite 'na cheann, gan iad ró-mhór ná ró-bheag, agus an té a dh'fhéachfadh díreach 'na gcoinnibh, níor mhaith leis fearg a dh'fheiscint iontu. Ba dhó' leat go mbíodh scáil éigin, agus solas éigin, coitianta ag lasadh agus ag athrú iontu, fé mar a bheadh gaoth agus scamaill agus solas, lá cruaidh Márta. Bhí fáibre doimhinn idir an dá mhalainn fé mar a bheadh in éadan leóin, agus srón mhór fhada sheabhcaí chaol-dromach anuas ón bhfáibre, agus béal láidir daingean laistíos den tsróin sin, béal a bhí lán d'fhiaclaibh breátha geala a bhí de réir a chéile go cruínn, agus gur dhó' leat go ndeinidís solas uathu féin nuair a gháireadh sé. Bhí an croiméal trom ciardhubh os cionn an bhéil agus an fhéasóg throm chiardhubh chas laistíos den bhéal. Idir ghruaig agus mailí agus fáibre éadain agus súile agus srón agus croiméal agus béal agus fiacla agus féasóg agus ceann ar fad, bhí rud éigin sa bhfear san a chuir in úil duit, ar an gcéad amharc, gur mhaith an bhail ort é ' bheith 'na charaid agat, agus dá mbeadh sé 'na namhaid agat gur mhaith an bhail ort bheith i bhfad uaidh. Bhí cosúlacht mhór idir a cheann agus ceann leóin, agus ansan, ba léir go raibh cruadas agus anam agus neart agus fuinneamh an leóin 'na chabhail agus 'na ghéagaibh, agus dá mba namhaid é go mbeadh sé chómh tapaidh agus chómh maraitheach leis an león. Bhí aithne mhaith ag na Lochlannaigh air agus sin í aithne a bhí acu air, go raibh sé chómh tapaidh agus chómh maraitheach leis an león.

Ní gá léiriú cruínn a dhéanamh ar na huaislibh eile a bhí ag cainnt agus ag cómhrá anso agus ansúd ar fuid an halla mhóir. Bhí an folt mór fada trom ar gach éinne, ag titim siar síos ar a shlinneánaibh. Thug san féachaint an-uasal do sna fearaibh. Bhí cuid de sna foltaibh odhar agus bhí cuid acu liath, agus cuid acu, ar na fearaibh críonna, chómh geal le mustairt, ach ní raibh éinne maol. Chimeádaidís an ghruaig go dtéidís sa chré, mar ní chaithidís choíche hata ná caipín ná aon chlúdach eile ar a gceann. Is iad na hataí seo a caitear anois a bhaineann an ghruaig de dhaoine. Dá dtugtí mar thaithí do cheann an duine ó thosach a óige imeacht gan aon chlúdach ach an ghruaig a chuir Dia air, d'fhásfadh an ghruaig láidir trom agus chimeádfadh sí a greim an fhaid a mhairfeadh an duine. Sin mar a deintí in Éirinn fadó. Níor chuir daoine hataí ná caipíní orthu go dtí gur thosnaigh nósa Shasana ar theacht chúinn anall. Is mó droch-nós nách hataí ná caipíní a thug muíntir Shasana chúinn.

Dá bhféadadh duine againn-na dul isteach an oíche úd sa halla mór úd Bhriain, i rí-theaghlach Cheann Cora, chuirfeadh na foilt mhóra throma úd iúnadh orainn ar an gcéad amharc. Ach ar an dtarna hamharc d'admhóimís ó chroí gur deineadh éagóir ana-throm ar cheann an Éireannaigh nuair a baineadh de an folt álainn uasal a chuir Dia ag fás air. Dá bhféadadh Dúlainn Óg teacht ar an saol arís agus féachaint ar na plaoiscíní beárrtha atá orainn-na, ar na cluasaibh gan scáth agus ar an mbaic miníl gan díon ón bhfuacht, agus ar an rud i bhfuirm canna stáin, ach é ' bheith dubh, atá thuas ar an gcloigeann mar hata, cad é an seirithean a chuirfidís air! "Ó!", adéarfadh sé, "cad 'tá imithe ar ár sliocht! An iad so na daoine a tháinig uainn-na! Nú an daor-aicme éigin iad a dh'fhás in Éirinn 'nár ndiaidh! Séanaim iad! Ní linn in aon chor iad!"

Dá bhféadadh Niamh, nú Gormfhlaith, nú éinne eile de sna ríoganaibh uaisle a bhí sa halla mór úd Bhriain an oíche úd, teacht ar an saol arís agus féachaint ar na mnáibh atá anois againn, ar na sciathógaibh móra leathana a bhíonn ar mhullach a gcínn acu, agus ar na cleitíbh a bhíonn sáite insna sciathógaibh sin, agus ar na ribíníbh a bhíonn astu, cad 'déarfaidís? Déarfaidís an rud úd aduairt Cathal leis an gcleasaí. "Airiú, a mhic léinn", arsa Cathal, "cad fé ndeara dhuit bheith as do mheabhair?"*

Dá dtagadh Gormfhlaith nú Niamh chúinn cheithre fichid blian ó shin, ní bheadh an scéal chómh holc agus 'tá sé anois. Chífidís an uair sin na clócaí breátha fada dúbha ar na mnáibh, agus na caipíní deasa sásta maisiúla ar na clócaíbh sin, i dtreó dá mb'ar óinsigh féin a bheadh clóca acu, agus an caipín ar a ceann aici, gur dhó' leat gur bhean chiallmhar í. Ach anois, nuair a chífidís na sciathóga agus na cleití agus na ribíní, agus an ghluaiseacht éaganta, cad a bheadh le rá acu? "Ó!", adéarfaidís, "nách mór an trua na mná san go léir a bheith as a meabhair! Cad fé ndeara iad a bheith ar an gcuma san?" Ansan, nuair adéarfí leó, "Ní has a meabhair atáid siad in aon chor. Níl aon easpa meabhrach orthu. Níl insna sciathógaibh sin ach nós a bhaineann leis an aimsir seo", déarfaidís "Mo thrua na fir! Agus mo thrua an chlann!"

Ansan dá n-abradh duine leó, "Is iad na fir féin fé ndeár é. Ní labharfadh aon fhear acu le cailín mura bhfeicfeadh sé an sciathóg san ar a ceann!", ní dhéanfaidís ach a rá "Tá an saol ar buile!" agus imeacht.

Ach ní feárr bheith ag cainnt air. Ní baol go dtiocfaid siad. Ní har nithibh den tsórd san a bhí an bheirt ag cuímhneamh an oíche úd. Bhí a mhalairt de chúram orthu. Bhí Gormfhlaith ag cuímhneamh ar Árdríocht na hÉireann, agus ar Bhrian, agus ar Mhurchadh, agus ar a mac féin, agus ar conas a thiocfadh sí ar Mhurchadh do chur ón Árdríocht agus ar an Árdríocht do chur in áirithe dá mac féin. Bhí Niamh agus a driotháir agus an chuid eile de sna mnáibh óga agus de sna fearaibh óga ag rínce, agus an ceól dá spreagadh dhóibh, agus gur dhó' le duine orthu ná raibh aon ní fé bhun Dé ar an dtalamh so ag déanamh aon chúraim dóibh ach an ceól agus an rínce agus an t-aoibhneas a bhí ansúd 'na dtímpall. Ach bhí. Bhí Niamh ag rínce lena driotháir ar feadh tamaill, agus le Murchadh ar feadh tamaill. Agus bhí sí ag rínce le hAmhlaoibh, le habhar an tsagairt, ar feadh tamaill. Bhí sí chómh séimh, chómh geal-gháiriteach le hAmhlaoibh agus a bhí sí le héinne de sna huaislibh óga a bhí ag rínce léi. Ach an dá mhachnamh úd, dá mhéid a dhein sí breithniú orthu is ea ba ghlaine a theip uirthi iad do thabhairt dá chéile. Agus bíodh gur chimeád sí a haigne aici féin go beacht, bhí daoine láithreach, agus níor bheagán daoine é, a chuímhnigh 'na n-aigne, nuair a chonacadar an bheirt agus iad araon chómh dathúil, chómh séimh, chómh huasal ar gach aon tsaghas cuma, gurbh álainn ar fad an lánú a dhéanfaidís, agus gur mhór go léir an trua sagart a dhéanamh d'Amhlaoibh. Bhí daoine ann, áfach, aduairt a mhalairt sin. Bhí fir óga ann agus, nuair a chonacadar é féin agus Niamh ag rínce, dúradar dá luathacht a críochnófí 'na shagart é gurbh ea ab fheárr é. Bheadh sé as an slí ansan. Agus bhí cailíní óga uaisle ann agus bíodh go ndúradar 'na n-aigne féin gur mhór an trua sagart a dhéanamh de, b'fheárr leó seacht n-uaire é ' dh'fheiscint 'na shagart ná é ' dh'fheiscint ag Niamh.

Chómh fada agus a théann scéal den tsórd san, ní hé mo thuairim go bhfuil aon athrú tagaithe ar Ghaelaibh Éireann. Fé sna foltaibh breátha fada troma, nú fé sna hataíbh ar na cloigeannaibh beárrtha agus fé sna sciathógaibh agus na cleití, tá an nádúr céanna díreach ionainn chómh fada agus a théann scéal den tsórd san.

Ach do ghluais an oíche, ar cos in áirde, díreach fé mar a ghluaiseódh oíche den tsórd anois. Tháinig an lá agus do scaip an chuideachta, gach éinne fé dhéin a thí féin. Thug Tadhg Mór Ó Cealla agus Niamh aghaidh siar ó thuaidh ar Uíbh Máine. Bhí, mar adúradh, teipithe glan ar Niamh an dá mhachnamh úd a thabhairt dá chéile. Is é rud a dhein sí ná iad araon do dhíbirt ar fad as a haigne agus as a croí, agus í féin do thabairt suas do Dhia.

"Is cuma liom 'en domhan", ar sise 'na haigne féin agus í ag socrú a hathar agus dhá ollmhú i gcómhair an bhóthair. "Is cuma liom 'en domhan ó tá m'athair agam. Ní fhéadfaidh sagart ná bráthair m'athair a bhaint díom. Is feárr d'fhear é ná éinne acu, íseal ná uasal. Is measa liom a lúidín ná dá n-imíodh sé siúd, agus an chuid eile acu, le fánaidh na habhann! Cad é sin dómh-sa cad é an cor a thabharfaidh sé siúd do féin! Má deintear sagart de, tá súil agam go ndéanfaidh sé sagart maith. Ní baol do go ndéanfad-sa aon chur isteach air ná go dtiocfad idir é agus Dia. Ní ró-mhaith a thaithneann an scéal in aon chor liom. Dá mbeinn i gcás Cholla, ba dhó' liom gurbh fheárr liom a chúram a bheith ar dhuine éigin eile.—Go gcuiridh Dia ar ár leas sinn go léir!"

Caibideal 12: Diabhal Coímhdeachta

Thug Colla agus an Leagáid agus Tadhg Óg Ó Cealla agus Amhlaoibh aghaidh siar ar Inis Cathaigh. Ar loíng is ea ' chuadar síos ó Luimneach. An fhaid a bhíodar ar an slí, bhí an bheirt ógánach thuas ar bórd agus bhí Colla agus an tEaspag thíos i seómra leó féin. Bhíodar ag cainnt.

"Ní maith a thaithneann an Bhannrín liom, a Cholla", arsan Leagáid. "Cuireann sí i gcuímhne dhom focal aduairt duine dúr naoimh".

"Má chuir sí cainnt naoimh i gcuímhne dhuit, a Athair", arsa Colla, "nár chóir go dtaithnfeadh sí leat?"

"'S dó', is é rud aduairt an naomh ná gur 'mairg a dh'fhéachfadh go dlúth in aghaidh mná le heagla go bhfeicfeadh sé a diabhal coímhdeachta*'. Tá 'diabhal coímhdeachta' ag Gormfhlaith. Chonac é go minic i gcaitheamh na hoíche aréir. Tá eagal orm go bhfuil ' fhios aici go bhfeaca é. An airíonn tú leat me, a Cholla", ar seisean. "Tabharfaidh an bhean san nimh do Bhrian nú do Mhurchadh nú dóibh araon mura ndéanfar iad do chosaint go maith uirthi!"

Caibideal 12: Diabhal Coímhdeachta

"Ní fheicim conas a bheadh aon tairbhe ag teacht chúithi óna mbás san, a Athair", arsa Colla.

"B'fhéidir", arsan Leagáid, "go bhfeiceann sí féin é, nú b'fhéidir gur dó' léi go bhfeiceann. Ba cheart rud éigin a dhéanamh a chuirfeadh as a cumas aon díobháil a dhéanamh don rí. Bheadh an scéal go holc ag Éire* agus ag an Eaglais in Éirinn anois dá n-imíodh aon rud ar Bhrian, go ceann tamaill eile pé'n Éirinn é".

"Cad is dó' leat ba cheart a dhéanamh, a Thiarna Easpaig?", arsa Colla.

"Ná féadfí gan leogaint do Bhrian bia ná deoch do ghlacadh a láimh éinne ach duine áirithe éigin go mbeadh iúntaoibh as?"

"Is dócha go bhféadfí", arsa Colla.

"Deintear san láithreach. Ní gá aon droch-amhras a chur ar éinne. Níl aon rí ná deineann a leithéid. Tá mná ann, a Cholla, agus tá eólas acu ar conas duine ' chur chun báis le nimh ar chuma ná fágfadh aon chaoi ar thrúig bháis an duine sin a dh'fháil amach go deó. Do chonac-sa cuid de sna mnáibh sin. Chonac an diabhal coímhdeachta a bhíodh acu, díreach mar a chonac diabhal coímhdeachta Ghormfhlaith aréir. Chonac an duine ar a raibh an paor. Níor ró-fhada an aimsir 'na dhiaidh san go dtí go raibh an duine sin as an slí. Ná dein aon ríghneas".

"Ní dhéanfad, a Athair", arsa Colla. "Raghad soir go Ceann Cora amáireach agus labharfad le Murchadh. Ar mhiste dhom a rá, a Athair, gur tusa ' thug an foláramh dom?"

"Ní miste", arsan Leagáid, "ach dein mar seo é. Abair go nduart ná fuil aon rí ná deineann beart mar adeirim chun é féin a chosaint ar nimh".

Caibideal 12: Diabhal Coímhdeachta

"Tá go maith, a Athair", arsa Colla. "Conas a thaithn an chuid eile den chuideachtain leat, a Athair?", ar seisean.

"Go maith", arsan Leagáid. "Tá nósa agus béasa agus slithe agaibh ná fuil taithí agam-sa ar a sórd. Ach measaim, dá mbeadh taithí agam orthu ná faighinn aon locht orthu. Bainid siad geit a duine nuair a chíonn sé iad an chéad uair. Níor chuir aon rud riamh oiread iúnadh orm agus do chuiriúir go léir orm i dtosach na hoíche aréir. Is dó' liom go rabhúir go léir ar leath-mheisce. Bhí teinneas im cheann ón ngleó agus ón bhfothram a bhí ar siúl. Ansan, ar leagadh na súl bhíúir go léir ar úr nglúinibh chun beannacht an Phápa ' dh'fháil uaim arís! Mura mbeadh feabhas na haithne atá agam oraibh, déarfainn gur ag magadh fúm a bhíúir".

"Bhíomair lom dáiríribh, a Athair", arsa Colla. "Neart ár gCreidimh a chuir ' fhiachaibh orainn é sin a dhéanamh".

"Is fíor san", arsan Leagáid. "Tuigim anois go maith é. Ag machnamh dom ar an scéal, is é rud adeirim liom féin ná gur mhaith an bhail ar chuid againn theas dá mbeadh cuid dúr bhfothram againn agus cuid de neart úr gCreidimh, ar scáth an fhothraim".

Thánadar chun na mainistreach. D'éirigh Colla go moch ar maidin amáireach a bhí chúinn chun dul thar n-ais arís láithreach go Ceann Cora.

"Raghad-sa leat chómh fada le Luimneach, a Cholla", arsan Leagáid. "Tá roinnt gnótha agam le déanamh ann i measc na sagart atá ann. Tabhair dhom an eochair úd an bhosca iarainn 'na raibh an chailís agat ann".

Thug Colla an eochair do agus do ghluaiseadar. D'fhan an Leagáid i Luimneach agus tháinig Colla go Ceann Cora. Dhein an Leagáid an gnó a bhí le déanamh aige i measc na sagart. Ansan chuir sé tuairisc Mheargaigh, an gabha a bhíodh ag déanamh na n-arm do Bhrian. Do stiúraíodh é chun na háite 'na raibh a cheárta ag an ngabha. Ní ceárta a bhí aige ach fiche ceárta, agus gaibhní ag obair agus builg dá séideadh agus iarann dá loscadh agus dá léasadh le hórdaibh agus le casúraibh ins gach aon chúinne. Bhí claimhte agus tuanna agus pící agus sleánna agus clogaid, agus gach aon tsaghas gléas cogaidh, caite anso agus ansúd, cuid de sna nithibh sin geall le bheith críochnaithe, agus gan cuid acu ach ar éigin tosnaithe. Bhí Meargach Gabha ag imeacht anonn 's anall i measc an lucht oibre agus a shúil ar gach aon rud agus é ag órdúchán agus ag stiúrúchán, ag moladh agus ag cáineadh, fé mar a deintí an obair chun a thoile nú ar a mhalairt de chuma.

Tháinig an Leagáid chun cainnte leis.

"Tá obair mhór á déanamh anso, a dhuin' uasail", arsan Leagáid.

"Tá fáltas oibre á dhéanamh ann, a Thiarna Easpaig", arsa Meargach.

Ansan do rug sé an Leagáid mórthímpall tríd an obair agus bhí sé ag tispeáint gach aon rud do agus ag míniú gach aon rud do. Fé dheireadh do tharraig an Leagáid an eochair as a phóca agus thispeáin sé dho í.

"Féach, a dhuin' uasail", ar seisean, "b'fhéidir go bhféadfá macshamhail den eochair sin a dhéanamh dom".

"Ambasa ach féadfad agus fáilte, a Thiarna Easpaig", arsan gabha. "Tá aithne mhaith agam ar an eochair sin. Is me a dhein an eochair sin do Cholla. Fuair sé cailís ana-dhaor ó Bhrian, agus d'iarr sé orm-sa bosca iarainn a dhéanamh don chailís, agus glas a chur ar an mbosca nárbh fhéidir a dh'oscailt ach leis an aon eochair amháin a dhéanfainn féin don ghlas. Ach mheasas gur chuaigh an eochair sin amú, a Thiarna Easpaig", ar seisean. "Tháinig teachtaire anso chúm, tá suím aimsire ó shin ann, ó Cholla féin, agus duairt sé liom gur cailleadh an eochair agus ná féadfí an bosca ' dh'oscailt, agus d'fhiafraigh sé dhíom an bhféadfainn, óm chuímhne, macshamhail a dhéanamh den eochair. Duart go bhféadfainn agus do dheineas".

"Cérbh é an teachtaire?", arsan Leagáid.

"Duine de sna manaigh, a Thiarna Easpaig", arsan gabha.

"Buail anso i leith, a dhuin' uasail, i dtreó ná haireóidh éinne sinn".

Dhrideadar i leataoibh.

"Níor cailleadh an eochair in aon chor, a dhuin' uasail", arsan Leagáid, "agus níor chuir Colla aon teachtaire chút-sa dhá iarraidh ort macshamhail a dhéanamh den eochair. An té a tháinig chút, bithiúnach ab ea é. Tá an chailís imithe".

"An chailís imithe!", arsan gabha.

"Tá sí imithe", arsan Leagáid. Agus d'inis sé tríd síos do conas mar a bhí an chailís le tabhairt do féin chun an Aifrinn Aoird do rá os cómhair Bhriain agus na n-uasal, agus conas mar a fuaradh an bosca iarainn folamh nuair a hoscladh é.

Do stad an gabha. Níor fhan focal ann. Thuig sé láithreach gur dhein sé árd-dearúd nuair a dhein sé an mhacshamhail den eochair gan dul síos agus labhairt ar dtúis le Colla féin. Thug an bheirt roinnt aimsire gan labhairt. Do labhair an Leagáid.

"An aithneófá an teachtaire, an dó' leat?", ar seisean.

"'Sé mo thuairim go n-aithneóinn, a Thiarna Easpaig", arsan gabha. "Duine de sna manaigh ab ea é".

"Téanam ort síos anois agus gheóbhaimíd radharc ar na manaigh go léir. Buailfimíd eatarthu agus iad ag déanamh a ngnótha. Ní neósfaimíd d'éinne cad 'tá uainn. Ní haon iúnadh mise agus tusa ' bheith ag gabháil tríd an mainistir. Déarfar gur gnó éigin a bhaineann led chéird a bheidh agam á thabhairt duit le déanamh".

Chuir an gabha fear eile os cionn na hoibre, agus do ghluais sé féin agus an Leagáid síos go hInis Cathaigh. Bhuaileadar tríd an mainistir. Bhíodar ag féachaint ar dhóirsibh agus ar ghlasaibh agus ar bhacánaibh agus ar thuisleannaibh. Bhí an Leagáid ag cur fios ar an manach so agus ar an manach úd agus é ag déanamh gach aon tsaghas ceistiúcháin orthu, agus bhí an gabha ag faire chuige. Thánadar chun an *érdaim.* Do glaodh ar an *ndeacon.* Ní raibh sé ann. Do rith teachtaire anso is teachtaire ansúd ar a lorg. Ní raibh sé le fáil. Do glaodh ar Thadhg Óg Ó Chealla. Tháinig sé. Do fiafraíodh de cá raibh a chomrádaí.

"Duairt sé go raibh sé ag dul suas go Luimneach in éineacht leat-sa, a Thiarna Easpaig", arsa Tadhg. "Ní fheaca-sa ó shin é. An amhlaidh nár tháinig sé anuas in éineacht libh?", ar seisean.

"Níor tháinig", arsan Leagáid, "nú má tháinig ní fheacamair-na ag teacht é".

Lena línn sin, tháinig Colla. Do fiafraíodh de an bhfeacaigh sé Amhlaoibh in aon bhall.

"Nuair a shroiseas Ceann Cora", arsa Colla, "bhí sé ann rómham. Duairt sé go raibh teachtaireacht éigin aige á bhreith uait-se, ag triall ar an rí, a Thiarna Easpaig. Is dócha go mbeidh sé anso sara fada".

"Is dócha é", arsan Leagáid. Ní duairt sé a thuilleadh. Bhí ' fhios aige go nduairt Amhlaoibh bréag i dtaobh na teachtaireachta; nár thug sé féin aon teachtaireacht do le breith ag triall ar an rí.

"Tá gnóthaí móra ar siúl thoir i gCeann Cora", arsa Colla.

Caibideal 12: Diabhal Coímhdeachta

"Cad iad na gnóthaí iad, a Athair?", arsan Leagáid, agus chuir gach éinne a bhí láithreach cluas air féin.

"Tá*", arsa Colla, "maithe móra a bheith tagaithe ann ó Leath Chuínn agus iad a bheith dhá iarraidh ar Bhrian an Árdríocht do ghlacadh".

"An amhlaidh atá M'leachlainn tar éis bháis?", arsan Leagáid.

"Ní hamhlaidh, a Thiarna Easpaig", arsa Colla, "ach deir an mhuíntir a tháinig go bhfuil Leath Chuínn go léir cortha de Mh'leachlainn agus nách foláir é ' chur i leataoibh agus Árdrí ' dhéanamh de Bhrian".

"Is olc agus is dian-olc an scéal é sin", arsan Leagáid. "Éireóidh cogadh fuilteach as san má ghéilleann Brian dóibh. Cad 'deir Murchadh?"

"Ní deir sé puínn", arsa Colla. "Deir sé nách ceart géilleadh in aon chor dóibh ach ar aon choinníoll amháin".

"'Ar aon choinníoll amháin'. Cad chuige an coinníoll? Cad é an coinníoll é? Conas ' fhéadfadh aon choinníoll ceart a thabhairt do Bhrian chun na hÁrdríochta?", arsan Leagáid.

"Deir Murchadh", arsa Colla, "nách ceart do Bhrian toiliú in aon chor chun na hÁrdríochta do ghlacadh mura n-iarraidh Leath Chuínn agus Éire go léir d'aon ghuth air í ' ghlacadh. Agus deir Gormfhlaith go bhfuil an ceart aige".

"Tá, an ceart aige", arsan Leagáid. "Ach conas a gheófar amach an t-aon ghuth san? Má thugann Brian aon chluas do chómhairle na n-uasal san, aireófar láithreach é ar fuaid na hÉireann go léir. Glacfaid* cáirde Mh'leachlainn arm. Glacfaid cáirde Bhriain arm. Beidh sé 'na chogadh dhearg againn. Ní mór dom dul chun cainnte le Brian agus le Murchadh. Téanam ort arís, a Cholla. Go gcuiridh Dia ár ríthe ar a leas!"

Caibideal 13: Fágtar Fúm-sa Féin É

Níor cuímhníodh a thuilleadh ar Amhlaoibh ná ar an mbréig a bhí ínste aige, ná ar an eochair. Do ghluais an Leagáid agus Colla agus an gabha, chómh tiubh agus d'fhéadadar cóir iompair a dh'fháil, soir arís go Ceann Cora. Fuaradar Brian agus Murchadh agus Dúlainn Óg agus Gormfhlaith i gcómhairle, istigh i seómra leó féin, agus na hUltaigh i seómra eile ag feitheamh le freagra. Chómh luath agus ' tháinig an Leagáid isteach, do chuir Brian fáilte roimis agus d'inis sé bunús an scéil do agus d'iarr sé cómhairle air.

"Níl agam le tabhairt duit, a rí", arsan Leagáid, "ach an t-aon chómhairle amháin. Is é M'leachlainn an tÁrdrí. Is é Árdrí Éireann é i láthair na huaire seo 'na bhfuilimíd ag cainnt anso. Beart éagóra is ea é ' chur as an Árdríocht. Gabhann an éagóir sin i gcoinnibh dlí Dé. Má tá Leath Chuínn cortha de Mh'leachlainn, cuireadh Leath Chuínn féin as an Árdríocht é. Ansan más toil le fearaibh Éireann Árdrí a dhéanamh de Bhrian, deinidís é. Ní bheidh Brian ag déanamh éagóra ar éinne an uair sin má ghlacann sé an Árdríocht. Má géilltear anois do sna maithibh seo atá tagaithe anso ó Chúig' Uladh, raghaid siad abhaile agus neósfaid siad do gach éinne gur géilleadh dóibh. Beidh sé i mbéal gach éinne go bhfuil Brian le bheith in' Árdrí. Pé áit 'na bhfuil cáirde Mh'leachlainn ar fuaid na hÉireann, glacfaid siad arm láithreach, agus glacfaid cáirde Bhriain arm láithreach. Beid fir Éireann 'na dhá gcamtha agus iad ag marú a chéile. Loitfar agus leighfar in aon lá amháin a bhfuil de thairbhe déanta ag Brian in Éirinn ón gcéad lá a thóg sé claíomh".

Do labhair Dúlainn.

"Is maith í do chainnt, a Thiarna Easpaig", ar seisean, "agus is eagnaí, ach tá cúpla rud agus níor thugais aghaidh orthu. Má curtar abhaile na daoine seo atá tagaithe anso ó Chúig' Uladh chúinn, gan aon tsásamh in aon chor a thabhairt dóibh, cad is dó' leat a dhéanfaid na daoine a chuir anso iad? Is dó' liom-sa go bhfuil ' fhios agam cad a dhéanfaid siad. Raghaid siad i gcómhairle. Neósfar dóibh ná glacfadh Brian an Árdríocht. Déarfaid siad san: 'Tá go maith. Níl againn ach Árdrí éigin eile do sholáthar. Ní chimeádfaimíd M'leachlainn a thuilleadh, pé cuma 'na mbeidh an scéal againn'. Curfar na teachtairí céanna so ag triall ar fhear éigin eile, ar fhear éigin ná fuil ábalta ar Ghaelaibh Éireann do ghléasadh fé aon smacht amháin chómh maith agus 'tá Brian ábalta air. Ansan is ea ' bheidh meascán mearaí i gceart agat ar fhearaibh Éireann. Ansan, ní 'na dhá gcuid a bheid fir Éireann agat ach 'na dtrí codaibh, 'na gceithre codaibh, agus iad ag marú a chéile, agus ní fios cathain a déanfar aon neart amháin arís díobh. I dtaobh éagóra: ní héagóir ar rí ná ar Árdrí más toil lena dhaoine féin é ' chur i leataoibh toisc gan an gnó a thugadar le déanamh do a bheith aige á dhéanamh dóibh de réir a dtoile. Mura héagóir* dá dhaoine féin M'leachlainn do chur as an Árdríocht, ní héagóir do Bhrian an Árdríocht do ghlacadh".

Do stad sé agus do shuigh sé. Chuaigh a chainnt i bhfeidhm go hanadhaingean ar a raibh ag éisteacht leis. Níor chuímhnigh éinne acu, go dtí gur labhair sé, ar cad a thitfeadh amach dá n-iarrtí ar dhuine éigin eile teacht san Árdríocht in inead Mh'leachlainn.

"B'fhéidir", arsa Murchadh, "gur mhaith an rud glaoch isteach anso ar na teachtairíbh seo agus a rá leó a dh'ínsint dúinn go hiomlán cad 'tá uathu. D'ínseadar cheana é, ach is ní é seo nách miste mórán cainnte ' dhéanamh 'na thaobh. Anois an t-am chun na cainnte ' dhéanamh. Is feárr féachaint ar an uile thaobh den scéal anois ná b'fhéidir dearúd a dhéanamh nárbh fhéidir a leigheas ar ball".

Do glaodh isteach orthu.

"Ba mhaith linn, a uaisle", arsa Brian, "go neósfadh sibh anso arís, i láthair an Easpaig, an toisc a thug sibh, agus na cúiseanna a bhí ag an muíntir a chuir chúinn sibh le sibh a chur chúinn".

Caibideal 13: Fágtar Fúm-sa Féin É

D'ínseadar arís cad a thug iad. Go raibh sé buailte isteach in aigne na poiblíochta go léir lastuaidh ná beadh rath ná séan ar Éirinn go dtí go mbeadh Brian in' Árdrí ar Éirinn. Go raibh M'leachlainn maith go leór mar rí cúige, ach gur léir do gach éinne ná raibh an acfuinn aigne ann, ná an éirim aigne, ná an cumas gnímh, ba cheart a bheith in Árdrí Éireann. Ná raibh aon fhear beó go raibh na tréithe sin ann an uair sin chómh láidir agus ' bhíodar i mBrian. Dá bhrí sin, gurbh éagóir ar Éirinn gan Brian a bheith in' Árdrí uirthi. Go raibh fir Éireann ceapaithe ar Bhrian do chur san Árdríocht dá dtoilíodh Brian féin chuige.

Ansan d'áiríodar na cineacha agus na tuatha agus na treabhchasaí, ní hamháin i Leath Chuínn ach ar fuaid na hÉireann go léir, a bhí ar an aigne sin.

Nuair a bhí deireadh ráite ag na teachtairíbh, do labhair Brian.

"Beiridh libh abhaile, a uaisle", ar seisean, "ag triall ar an muíntir a chuir anso sibh, an freagra so. Glacfad-sa an Árdríocht má thoilíonn M'leachlainn chuige, agus is me féin a raghaidh síos ag triall air agus a chuirfidh chuige an cheist. Socrófar an scéal idir mise agus M'leachlainn agus ní gá d'éinne eile beó a thuilleadh cainnte ' dhéanamh 'na thaobh".

Níor labhair éinne eile. Do hollmhaíodh dínnéar mór do sna teachtairíbh agus do deineadh cúram mór díobh ar feadh trí lá agus trí oíche, agus ansan d'fhágadar slán agus beannacht ag Brian agus ag á theaghlach, agus d'imíodar ó thuaidh abhaile.

Nuair a bhíodar ar an slí ag dul abhaile, bhíodar ag machnamh ar an bhfreagra a bhí fálta acu ó Bhrian, ach dá mbeidís ag machnamh go ceann bliana air, ní fhéadfaidís aon tuairim a thabhairt do cad a thiocfadh as, agus 'na theannta san is eile níorbh fhéidir dóibh aon locht ' fháil air. Ní lú ná mar ' fhéadfadh an Leagáid aon locht ' fháil air. Ní lú ná mar a dh'fhéadfadh M'leachlainn féin aon locht a dh'fháil ar an bhfreagra dá n-airíodh sé é, agus is dócha gur airigh. Do ghlacfadh Brian an Árdríocht—ach ní ghlacfadh sé í i gcoinnibh toile Mh'leachlainn féin. Cad é an locht a bhí le fáil ag éinne air sin?

Chuir an freagra san cosc láithreach leis an bhformad ar ar thrácht* an Leagáid. Ní raibh aon ní chun carad Mh'leachlainn agus cáirde Bhriain do chur i gcoinnibh a chéile, mar do chimeád an freagra an gnó go léir idir Bhrian agus M'leachlainn féin. Ní raibh aon bhaol go raghadh éinne ag tairiscint na hÁrdríochta d'aon fhear eile, mar ní duairt Brian lom díreach ná glacfadh sé féin í. Ní raibh ag daoine ar gach taobh le déanamh ach a suaimhneas a cheapadh agus fanúint go bhfeicfidís cad a dhéanfadh Brian.

D'imigh Colla agus an Leagáid siar go hInis Cathaigh. D'fhiafraíodar cá raibh Amhlaoibh. Ní raibh aon tuairisc air. D'imigh lá agus d'imigh dhá lá, agus níor tháinig sé. D'imigh seachtain agus níor tháinig sé. Do cuireadh teachtaire soir go Ceann Cora, féachaint a' raibh sé ann. Ní raibh. Do ghluais tuilleadh aimsire agus níor tháinig sé. Ansan tháinig nithe eile agus gnóthaí eile crosta ar an mainistir agus ar na manaigh, agus d'imigh Amhlaoibh as a gceann. Ní raibh aon fhios acu ar ghuid na cailíse. Níorbh aon iúnadh ró-mhór leó ógánach a dh'imeacht mar sin leis féin as an mainistir. Ní ab ea é do thiteadh amach anois is arís. Nuair a thiteadh sé amach, ní bhíodh cathú ró-mhór orthu 'na thaobh. Dar leó "b'fheárr teitheadh maith ná droch-sheasamh". Agus dá luathacht a deintí an teitheadh ab ea ab fheárr é, dar leó, ó bhí sé le déanamh in aon chor. Dar leó, ba thrua nár theith Amhlaoibh sarar deineadh *deacon* de.

Níor ghlac Tadhg Óg Ó Cealla an scéal chómh neamh-chorrabhuaiseach san. Ní raibh aon fhios aige ar ghuid na cailíse ach chómh beag le héinne de sna manaigh, ach ní áiteódh an saol air gurbh amhlaidh a theith Amhlaoibh. Dar leis, má bhí Amhlaoibh beó, thiocfadh sé thar n-ais chun na mainistreach mura mbeadh go raibh rud éigin á chosc ar theacht thar n-ais. Thoir i gCeann Cora do chonacthas go déanach é.

Caibideal 13: Fágtar Fúm-sa Féin É

"Raghad soir", ar seisean, "agus labharfad leis an mBannrín agus má tháinig aon tuairisc óna mhuíntir a chuir ' fhiachaibh air cuaird a thabhairt abhaile, neósfaidh sí dhom é. Bhí sí ana-mhór leis. Má tá aon droch-ní imithe air, ní fheadar cad a dhéanfad".

Is ar éigin ' fhéadadh sé aon bhlúire bídh a chaitheamh ná aon néal den oíche do chodladh. D'imigh sé soir. Fuair sé caoi ar chainnt le Gormfhlaith. Bhí sí go hana-shéimh leis, agus bhí sí go hana-bhuartha mar gheall ar gan aon tuairisc a bheith aige ar Amhlaoibh. Ní raibh aon tuairisc in aon chor aici féin air. Mheas sí, ní nárbh iúnadh, go raibh sé thiar sa mhainistir. Chuir sí a lán ceisteanna chun Taidhg 'na thaobh. Ar thug sé fé ndeara le déanaí go raibh aon ní ag déanamh aon bhuartha dho? An raibh aon trioblóid idir é féin agus Colla mar gheall ar aon rud? Ar tugadh aon mhilleán do mar gheall ar aon ní? Chuir sí a lán ceisteanna den tsórd san chuige, agus thug sé fé ndeara go bhféachadh sí ana-ghéar air le línn gach ceiste ' chur.

Bhí an chuaird sin in aistear. Níor fhéad Gormfhlaith aon tsásamh aigne ' thabhairt do. Siúd ó thuaidh go hUíbh Máine é féachaint a' bhfaigheadh sé aon tuairisc ann. Chómh luath agus ' chonaic Niamh é, ba bheag nár thit sí i laige, bhí sé ag féachaint chómh holc san.

"Airiú, a Thaidhg", ar sise, "cad d'imigh ort?"

D'inis sé dhi.

"Is dócha", ar seisean, "gurb amhlaidh atá sé marbh, agus cad a dhéanfad!", agus siúd caise deór anuas óna shúilibh.

Do leog sí dho ar feadh tamaill, agus ní tirim a bhí a súile féin. Fé dheireadh do labhair sí.

"Má tá sé beó, a Thaidhg", ar sise, "agus má tá cion chómh mór san agat air, ní mar sin is ceart duit an cion a thispeáint".

"Agus cad 'tá le déanamh agam, a Niamh?", ar seisean.

"Cuir daoine amach ar a thuairisc", ar sise, "agus geall luacht saothair maith don té a thabharfaidh tuairisc chút air. Ní hé mo thuairim féin go bhfuil aon droch-ní tar éis imeacht air. Fear ró-ghasta is ea é. Ní dó' liom go bhfuil aon namhaid aige".

"Ní fheadar 'en tsaol", arsa Tadhg, "cad é an gnó a bhí soir go Ceann Cora aige an lá a chuaigh Colla agus an tEaspag soir ann. Chonaic Colla ann é ach ní fheacaigh éinne ag dul ann é ná ag teacht as".

"Cuir t'aigne chun suaimhnis, a Thaidhg", ar sise. "Níl baol air. Tá fios a ghnótha féin aige. Má tá oiread ceana aige ort agus 'tá agat air, tiocfaidh sé thar n-ais chút chómh luath in Éirinn agus d'fhéadfaidh sé teacht".

Chuir Tadhg amach an lucht cuardaigh agus gheall sé an luacht saothair dóibh, ach níor tháinig aon tuairisc ar Amhlaoibh. Ach tháinig tuairisc nárbh é. Tháinig tuairisc ó Cheann Cora, agus chuir an tuairisc sin gach aon rud eile soir siar.

Caibideal 14: Giollaí Turais

Bhí Tadhg Óg Ó Cealla tagaithe thar n-ais go mainistir Ínse Cathaigh chun a chuid léinn do chríochnú, agus bhí sé ag faire chuige gach lá, féachaint an aireódh sé tásc nú tuairisc ar Amhlaoibh. Lá dá raibh sé ar an gcuma san, tímpall mí nú chúig sheachtaine tar éis na dteachtairí ó Leath Chuínn a bheith i gCeann Cora, tháinig teachtaireacht ó Uíbh Máine ag triall air dhá rá leis dul ó thuaidh abhaile láithreach, go raibh teachtairí Bhriain tar éis dul mórthímpall chun uaisle na tíre go léir, dhá rá leó bheith i gCeann Cora lá áirithe, iad féin agus a gcúnamh fear, agus do hainmníodh an lá. D'imigh sé abhaile. Do ghléas sé féin agus a athair oiread nirt agus d'fhéadadar, agus thánadar go Ceann Cora. Bhíodar ann i gcómhair an lae a bhí ceapaithe. Níorbh fhada go raibh mór-shlua láidir uasal cruinnithe ann. Ní raibh ' fhios acu cad é an gnó a bhí dhíobh, ach ba chuma leó. Bhí ' fhios acu go raibh gnó ag Brian díobh agus gurbh é a ngnó féin é. Nár bhaol go dtabharfadh Brian ón mbaile iad mura mbeadh cúis mhaith a bheith aige chuige, agus gurbh iad féin a bheadh bertha* ar ball le pé gnó a bhí le déanamh aige.

Na Lochlannaigh a bhí socair chun cónaithe in Éirinn agus tar éis géilleadh do Bhrian agus dá dhlithibh, bhíodar ann chómh maith leis na Gaelaibh, agus ba mhór an bhreis iad ar neart sló Bhriain, agus ba mhaith.

Bhí teachtairí maithe ag Brian. Giollaí turais a tugtí orthu. Fir óga luatha láidre ab ea iad agus bhí ana-chuisíocht ag gach teachtaire acu. Fir thofa ab ea iad. Mar gheall ar fheabhas a gcuisíochta a deintí iad do thoghadh. 'Na gcuis is ea ' théidís ar theachtaireacht. Nuair a bhíodh scéala ag Brian le cur go hobann ag triall ar rí éigin de ríthibh Éireann nú ar dhuin' uasal éigin, ní dheineadh sé ach duine de sna teachtairíbh sin a chomáint uaidh ag triall ar an rí sin, nú ag triall ar an nduin' uasal san, leis an dteachtaireacht. Ghluaiseódh an teachtaire sin 'na chuis, agus níorbh fhada go mbeadh an teachtaireacht tagaithe chun cínn.

'Na chuis is ea ' dh'imíodh an teachtaire, ach más ea ba luaithe 'na chuis é ná fear eile ar muin capaill. Nuair a théadh na giollaí turais sin i dtaithí reatha ba luaithe iad ná aon fhear capaill, agus ba bhuaine. Ní sheasódh capall in aon chor le duine acu. B'fhéidir go mbeadh an capall níos géire ná an cuisí i dtosach an chúrsa, ach sara mbeadh fiche míle curtha dhíobh acu, bheadh an capall buailte amach. Ansan is ea ' bheadh a chuisíocht ag teacht i gceart don ghiolla turais, agus bheadh trí fichid míle curtha dhe aige sara mbeadh aon bhlúire tuirse ag teacht air. Ansan féin níor ghá dho ach sodar réidh a dhéanamh ar feadh tamaill bhig agus bheadh anál agus misneach agus a lán-rith arís aige. Ní raibh aon mhaith i gcapaillibh 'na n-aice siúd.

Dá éaghmais sin, ní raibh coíll ná cnuc, gleann ná portach ná abha in Éirinn ná raibh aithne acu orthu go léir, agus ghabhaidís gach aon chóngar, i dtreó gur mhinic ná bíodh míle ' shlí[*] acu le gabháil nuair nárbh fholáir d'fhear capaill gabháil, b'fhéidir, deich míle de thímpall. Ansan, is mó rud a chuirfeadh ríghneas ar fhear capaill ná cuireadh aon ríghneas orthu súd. Bhíodh balcaisí éadroma orthu, agus bróga éadroma, agus is minic ná bíodh aon bhróga orthu. Bhíodh aithne ins gach aon bhall orthu, agus chómh luath agus ' thiocfadh tart nú ocras orthu, ní bhíodh acu ach aghaidh a thabhairt ar an gcéad tigh a bhuailfeadh úmpu agus gheóbhaidís a ndóthain bídh agus dí. Dá mbeadh orthu gabháil trí dhúthaigh namhad, bheadh arm acu, arm éigin ná beadh ró-throm. Nuair a neartaigh cómhacht Bhriain, ní bhíodh aon ghá le harm acu. Bhí ' fhios ag gach éinne gurbh iad teachtairí Bhriain iad. Níor bheag san. Is amhlaidh a bhíodh gach éinne ag cabhrú leó in inead aon cheataí ' dhéanamh dóibh. Do tugtí bia agus deoch agus onóir agus urraim dóibh mar gheall ar Bhrian, agus ní baol go dtugaidís aon chúis d'éinne chun aon ghearáin a chur isteach orthu, bhí a leithéid sin de smacht ag Brian orthu.

Bhíodh cuid de sna huaisle ab aoirde in Éirinn sa ghnó san. Thugadh an gnó eólas dóibh ar an dtír agus ar na daoine, ní b'fheárr ná mar a dh'fhéadfaidís a dh'fháil ar aon chuma eile. Bhíodh fo-dhuine d'ríogra Éireann féin sa ghnó. Do thárla, an uair seo ar a bhfuilimíd ag trácht, go raibh duine de ríogra Éireann sa ghnó. Fé cheilt, áfach, is ea ' bhí sé sa ghnó. Donn ab ainm do, Donn mac Beathach. Ón dtaobh thiar theas den Mhúmhain ab ea é agus mac rí ab ea é. Ó bhí sé deich mbliana d'aois, do tugadh fé ndeara go raibh cuisíocht uathásach aige. Nuair a bhí sé cheithre bliana déag, do bheireadh sé ar na giorraithibh ar thaobh an ghleanna, ag rith 'na ndiaidh agus dhá gcasadh mar a dhéanfadh cú. Mar gheall ar an gcuisíocht san a bhí aige, do tugadh "Caoilte" mar leas-ainm air. Tháinig sé ag triall ar Bhrian chun go nglacfí i measc na ngiollaí turais é. Do glacadh láithreach é chómh luath agus do chonacthas an rith uathásach a bhí aige. Ní raibh aon fhear ann a dh'fhéadfadh cimeád in aice leis in aon chor i gcúrsa reatha. Nuair a fiafraíodh a ainm, duairt sé gur Caoilte ab ainm do.

Caibideal 14: Giollaí Turais

Bhí tuairim acu go léir gurbh ainm bréige an ainm sin do, ach ba chuma leó. Bhí ' fhios acu, gan ach féachaint air, go raibh fuil uasal ann.

Bhí sé chómh maith sa ghleacaíocht agus ar na harmaibh gaisce agus ' bhí éinne dá lucht cómhnaoise. Fear breá córach cumasach ab ea é. Má bhí aon locht air, b'é seo é. Déarfadh duine go raibh a chosa, ó chrománaibh go talamh, beagáinín ró-fhada agus ró-láidir i gcúmparáid lena chabhail. Ach bhíodar téagartha thuas agus caol thíos, agus bhí an dá throigh ana-bheag, ana-theann, i dtreó go raibh neart mór agus meáchaint bheag iontu. Bhí an léim aige chómh maith agus ' bhí an rith aige. An falla a bheadh chómh hárd leis féin, do raghadh sé de léim thairis gan lámh ná cos a chur ann. Do rithfeadh sé in aice capaill agus do raghadh sé de léim i ndrom an chapaill sin agus an capall ar cos in áirde.

Ní raibh sé ró-fhada i gCeann Cora i measc na ngiollaí turais nuair a cuireadh amach an teachtaireacht úd. Cé ' curfí siar go hUíbh Máine ag triall ar Thadhg Mhór Ó Chealla ach Caoilte.

Chuaigh sé siar agus thug sé a theachtaireacht. Chonaic sé Tadhg Mór, agus chonaic sé teaghlach Thaidhg Mhóir. Agus féach. Chonaic sé an ríogan óg. Chonaic sé Niamh. Ba bheag ná gur baineadh a mheabhair shaolta dhe glan chómh luath agus ' chonaic sé í. Chonaic sé áilleacht agus uaisleacht go minic roimis sin, i mnáibh a dhútha féin, agus i mnáibh eile i ndúthaíbh eile. Ní fheacaigh sé riamh roimis sin in aon mhnaoi, uasal ná íseal, aon ní a dh'fhéadfadh sé ' chur i gcúmparáid leis an solas áilleachta a tháinig os cómhair a shúl chómh luath agus ' tháinig Niamh os cómhair a shúl. Chómh luath agus d'fhéach sé uirthi, do leath a dhá shúil air agus ba bheag ná gur leath a bhéal air, agus níor fhéad sé a shúile ' bhogadh dhi. D'fhéach sise air, agus má fhéach ní baol ná gur bhog sé dhi láithreach iad. D'fhéach sé síos ar an dtalamh, agus do las sé go bun na gcluas nuair a thuig sé an tuathal a bhí déanta aige. Do labhair sise go breá neamh-iúntach neamh-thuairimeach, agus chuir sí roinnt ceisteanna chuige i dtaobh Bhriain agus i dtaobh na hoibre a bhí ar siúl, agus i dtaobh na ríthe agus na n-uasal eile a bhí ag teacht go Ceann Cora. Do labhair sí chómh cneasta leis agus chómh réasúnta gur chuir sí a aigne chun suaimhnis i dtaobh an tuathail a bhí déanta aige.

Is é ' chuaigh ó dheas go hInis Cathaigh ó Uíbh Máine chun an scéil a dh'ínsint do Thadhg Óg. Tháinig sé féin agus Tadhg, agus tuilleadh de sna huaislibh óga a bhí ar scoil na mainistreach ó Chúige Connacht, thánadar abhaile le cois a chéile. Do ghléasadar go léir iad féin in arm 's in éide agus thugadar aghaidh ar Cheann Cora. Chuaigh Niamh go Ceann Cora in éineacht lena hathair. Chuaigh a lán eile de mhnáibh uaisle na háite ann, leis, in éineacht lena muíntir féin. Do rith an giolla turais rómpu chun a dh'ínsint go rabhadar ag teacht agus chun áite do cheapadh agus do chimeád dóibh 'na bhféadfaidís longphort a chur suas dóibh féin. Ní baol ná go raibh sé ann sara dtáinig puínn eile, agus ná gur shocraigh sé ar áit dheas oiriúnach do longphort Thaidhg Mhóir Uí Chealla. Níorbh fhada go dtáinig Tadhg Mór féin agus Niamh agus an teaghlach go léir, agus thug daoine fé ndeara go raibh an giolla turais ana-chúramach i dtaobh longphuirt Thaidhg Mhóir.

Bhí longphort rí Connacht eile in aice na háite 'na raibh longphort Thaidhg Mhóir Uí Chealla. Bhí cuid de ríogra Connacht a thug fé ndeara go raibh an giolla turais ana-thiúnsclach ag cur gach aon ní in' áit féin i longphort Thaidhg Mhóir Uí Chealla, agus bhí roinnt iúnadh orthu.

Níor fágadh an giolla turais i bhfad ag déanamh an tiúnscail, áfach. Do comáineadh chun siúil é ar theachtaireacht eile. Is air a glaeití i gcónaí nuair a bhíodh gá le dithneas agus le cruinneas agus le géar-chúis. Chuir duine éigin de sna huaislibh leathscéal éigin uaidh dhá rá ná féadfadh sé teacht. B'éigin do Chaoilte dul ag triall air agus a thispeáint do gur cheart do teacht, go mbeadh sé ag déanamh díobhála dho féin mura dtagadh sé agus a thispeáint do sna huaislibh eile go raibh sé chómh maith le héinne acu chun dualgais fir do chómhlíonadh.

Nuair a bhí na huaisle go léir cruinnithe, bhí mór-shlua álainn uasal acfuinneach ag Brian. Níor mhiste "gasra nár dhó'" a thabhairt ar an mór-shlua san, mar a tugtar sa tsean-amhrán*. Ó thosnaíodar ar theacht, bhí Meargach Gabha agus a raibh de cheártanaibh 'en tsaol aige ag obair go dian ag déanamh arm agus ag deisiú arm. Tháinig gaibhní in éineacht leis an muíntir a tháinig. Mura mbeadh san, níorbh fhéidir do Mheargach teacht ar an obair. Na gaibhní a tháinig, áfach, is amhlaidh a luíodar isteach san obair a bhí ar siúl, i dteannta na ngaibhní a bhí ann rómpu, agus do stiúraigh Meargach an obair go léir. B'in mar ba thúisce a bhí an obair go léir críochnaithe. Do críochnaíodh an obair go léir fé dheireadh agus do scuireadh na longphuirt agus do ghluais an mhór-shlua chun bóthair.

Caibideal 15: Fir Éireann

Ba mhór an radharc an mhór-shlua san. Bhí seacht cathanna ann agus bhí os cionn trí mhíle fear ins gach cath acu san. Bhí gach cath féna ríogra féin.

Bhí Cian mac Maolmhuaidh ann, ó Uíbh Eachach Múmhan, agus Dónall mac Duibh, agus bhí trí mhíle fear acu. Bhí rí na nDéiseach ann, Mothla mac Faoláin, agus trí mhíle fear aige. Bhí Loíngseach mac Dúlainn ann, rí Uíbh Chonaill Ghabhra, agus trí mhíle fear aige. Bhí Mac Beathach, rí Chiarraí Luachra ann agus trí mhíle fear aige. Bhí Tadhg Mór Ó Cealla ann ó Uíbh Máine agus trí mhíle fear aige. Bhí na ríthe agus na huaisle ann ó gach aon pháirt de Leath Mhogha, na ríthe agus na huaisle a bhíodh ag cur cogaidh ar a chéile agus ag marú a chéile agus ag dísciú a chéile ar gach aon tsaghas cuma go dtí gur chuir Brian smacht orthu, agus gur chuir sé ' fhiachaibh orthu, dá lom deiridh ainneóna, a leas a dhéanamh agus leas a ndaoine do dhéanamh agus cur le chéile in aghaidh namhad iasachta.

Caibideal 15: Fir Éireann

Dob álainn an radharc iad, ag gluaiseacht soir ó thuaidh fé dhéin na Teamhrach. Dob uasal an radharc iad. Ba chómhachtach an radharc iad.

Thánadar i gcóngar na Teamhrach. Chuir Brian teachtairí ag triall ar Mh'leachlainn, dhá rá gurbh é toil fear Éireann go ndéanfadh M'leachlainn scarúint leis an Árdríocht i dtreó go dtabharfí do Bhrian í. Gurbh é cúis a bhí ag fearaibh Éireann leis sin ná a laíghead a bhí déanta ag M'leachlainn, i gcaitheamh na haimsire a bhí sé in' Árdrí, chun na Lochlannach a dhíbirt a hÉirinn agus chun cómhacht na hÉireann do chur le chéile 'na gcoinnibh. Go raibh Brian tar éis cómhacht na Lochlannach do chur ar neamhní i Leath Mhogha. Dá mbeadh sé in' Árdrí ar Éirinn an fhaid a bhí sé 'na rí ar Leath Mhogha, go mbeadh cómhacht na Lochlannach curtha ar neamhní aige ar fuaid na hÉireann go léir. Dá luathacht a tabharfí Árdríocht na hÉireann do anois gurbh ea ba luaithe a bheadh cómhacht na Lochlannach ar neamhní. Dá bhrí sin, nárbh fholáir do Mh'leachlainn scarúint leis an Árdríocht i dtreó go dtabharfí do Bhrian í. Dá mba rud é ná toileódh M'leachlainn chuige sin nárbh fholáir d'fhearaibh Éireann a iarraidh ar Bhrian an Árdríocht a thógaint de thoradh catha.

Thug M'leachlainn freagra ar na teachtairíbh.

"Is liom-sa an Árdríocht", ar seisean, "agus cimeádfad í. Nílim ollamh anois láithreach chun catha agus crua-chómhraic a dhéanamh chun í ' chimeád. Tháinig Brian anso agus mór-shlua aige. Thóg sé a aimsir féin chun é féin d'ollmhú agus do chur i dtreó. Tugtar dómh-sa mí ón lá inniu chun mo nirt do chruinniú. Má fhéadaim mo neart do chruinniú, tabharfad cath do Bhrian agus dá mhór-shlua. Má theipeann orm an neart a dh'oirfeadh dom do chruinniú, tabharfad an Árdríocht do Bhrian. Má thoilíonn Brian chuige sin, iarrtar air fanúint i dTeamhair agus a shlóite do chosc ar chreachadh ná ar argain a dhéanamh ar an dtír mórthímpall".

Caibideal 15: Fir Éireann

Thoiligh Brian agus d'órdaigh sé na slóite do chosc ar aon díobháil a dhéanamh don chómharsanacht.

Chuir M'leachlainn a theachtairí ag triall ar ríthibh agus ar uaislibh Leath Chuínn dhá iarraidh orthu teacht agus Árdrí Éireann do chosaint i gcoinnibh Bhriain. Thugadar go léir cainnt bhreá bhog réidh do sna teachtairíbh, ach níor ghealladar aon chúnamh a thabhairt. Duairt cuid acu nár mhór dóibh aimsir a thógaint chun an scéil a bhreithniú. Duairt cuid acu go gcaithfí a leathscéal a ghabháil mar ná raibh ar a gcumas teacht an uair sin le haon chúnamh. Dá nglaeití bliain roimis sin orthu, nú i gceann bliana 'na dhiaidh san, go mb'fhéidir go bhféadfaidís rud éigin fónta ' dhéanamh. Ach an uair sin, dá mbeadh ' fhios ag M'leachlainn féin conas a bhí an scéal acu ná cuímhneódh sé ar a iarraidh orthu teacht ag triall air.

Nuair a hiarradh ar Aodh Ó Néill teacht, duairt sé go tur, nuair a bhíodh Teamhair agus Árdríocht Éireann ag á thaobh féin de shliocht Néill, go ndeinidís Teamhair agus Árdríocht Éireann do chosaint ar namhdaibh iasachta agus ar Leath Mhogha Nuat. Dá mbeadh an Árdríocht acu anois go ndéanfaidís an chosaint chéanna. B'é sin le rá, mura raibh M'leachlainn ábalta ar an Árdríocht do chosaint, nárbh fhearra dho rud a dhéanfadh sé ná í ' thabhairt don fhear a chosnódh í, nú í ' thabhairt do Bhrian.

Nuair a fuair M'leachlainn nárbh aon mhaith dho bheith ag brath ar chúnamh ó sna ríthibh thuaidh, is é rud a dhein sé ná dírim beag marcach a thabhairt leis agus teacht chun cainnte le Brian. Do ghlac Brian é le hurraim agus le mór-chroí. D'inis sé do Bhrian conas a bhí caillte air ag ríthibh Leath Chuínn agus an easonóir a bhí tabhartha ag Ó Néill do.

"Ní foláir dom géilleadh dhuit, a Bhriain", ar seisean, "nuair ná fuil ar mo chumas cur id choinnibh".

Do stad Brian agus dhein sé a mhachnamh.

"A Árdrí", ar seisean, "ní healaí dhómh-sa aon éagóir a dhéanamh ort. Más toil le fearaibh Éireann an Árdríocht so ' thabhairt dómh-sa is é a gceart í ' thabhairt dom. Más é a dtoil í ' chimeád agat-sa is é a gceart í ' chimeád agat. B'fhéidir ná fuil fios aigne fear Éireann fós agat-sa ná agam-sa sa scéal. I dtreó nách féidir choíche a rá gur dheineas éagóir ort, socraímís mar seo é. Bíodh bliain agat chun do nirt a chruinniú agus chun tu féin a chur i dtreó. Ansan, má bhíonn tú ábalta air, cosain tu féin orm".

Bhí iúnadh a chroí ar Mh'leachlainn nuair ' airigh sé an chainnt sin*.

"Tá go maith, a rí", ar seisean. "Is fial an socrú é!", ar seisean. "Mura mbead-sa ábalta an uair sin ar me féin a chosaint ort-sa, tabharfad an Árdríocht duit gan chosnamh, agus tabharfad géill* anois duit go seasód an socrú san".

"Ní iarrfad-sa aon gheall ort", arsa Brian, "ach do bhriathar rí".

Ansan do bhronn Brian dhá chéad agus daichead capall, de sna capaillibh ab fheárr a bhí aige, ar Mh'leachlainn, agus thug sé seóid éigin uasal do gach fear de sna fearaibh a bhí in' fhochair, agus do scaradar, agus tháinig Brian agus a mhór-shlua abhaile go Ceann Cora.

Tá abhar machnaimh sa méid sin gnótha agus is fiú an gnó machnamh a dhéanamh air. Bhí mór-shlua ag Brian. Ní raibh aon neart sló ag M'leachlainn. Cad 'na thaobh nár dhein Brian príosúnach de Mh'leachlainn láithreach bonn, agus an Árdríocht do thógaint chuige féin? Cad a déanfí thall i Sasana aon lá le hocht gcéad blian dá mba thall i Sasana ' bheadh an t-imreas ar siúl? Cad a dhein an ceathrú Hamhrí, an fear ar a dtugtí Bolingbroke*, nuair a bhain sé ríocht Shasana den tarna Risteárd? Dhein sé príosúnach láithreach den tarna Risteárd agus ansan níorbh fhada gur mhairbh sé é. Ní fhéadfadh sé a thuiscint in' aigne go raibh sé féin ó bhaol ná go raibh greim ceart ar an ríocht aige go dtí go raibh Risteárd curtha chun báis aige. Féach ar an dtríú Risteárd, thall i Sasana. Chun teacht ar ríocht Shasana agus chun na ríochta ' chimeád do féin, do mhairbh sé a ghaolta go léir díreach mar a mharódh búistéir muca!* Féach siar orthu go léir, ón lá a tháinig Uilliam agus a shlua Nórmánach isteach*, go dtí gur bhain na daoine an chómhacht as a lámhaibh ar fad nách mór, agus nár fágadh acu ach ainm na cómhachta. Cad a bhí acu á dhéanamh i gcaitheamh na haimsire go léir ach ag sá a chéile agus ag tachtadh a chéile ag baint na ríochta dá chéile!

Cad 'déarfadh duine acu súd dá n-airíodh sé an chainnt úd a thárla an lá úd, idir Bhrian agus M'leachlainn? "Nílim ollamh anois chun catha ' thabhairt duit, a Bhriain", arsa M'leachlainn. "Tabhair mí dhom chun mo nirt do chruinniú agus ansan tabharfaidh mé cath dhuit chun na hÁrdríochta do chosaint ort".

Cad 'déarfadh Bolingbroke dá n-abradh an tarna Risteárd an chainnt sin leis? "Nílim ollamh anois, a Bholingbroke, chun catha ' thabhairt duit. Tá mo neart scaipithe uaim. Nílim ach tagaithe i leith ó Éirinn* mar a rabhas a d'iarraidh smacht a chur ar mhuíntir na hÉireann. Tabhair mí dhom chun mo nirt do chruinniú. Ansan tabharfaidh mé cath dhuit chun mo ríochta do chosaint ort". Cad é an sceartadh gáire a dhéanfadh Bolingbroke dá n-airíodh sé cainnt den tsórd san ó Risteárd! Ba dhó' liom, áfach, go ndéanfadh Risteárd féin sceartadh gáire ba mhó ná é dá n-airíodh sé an chainnt eile úd ó Bholingbroke: "Ní hea, a Risteáird, ach tabharfaidh mé bliain duit chun do nirt a chruinniú!"

Ach sin í díreach an saghas cainnte do thárla idir Bhrian agus M'leachlainn i dtaobh Árdríochta na hÉireann, agus níor chuir an chainnt iúnadh ar éinne den bheirt, ná ar éinne de ríthibh ná d'uaislibh na hÉireann a bhí ag éisteacht leis an gcainnt.

Níor thárla an chainnt sin ná aon chainnt dá sórd, idir Bholingbroke agus Risteárd. Murar thárla, do thárla gur thóg Bolingbroke chuige ríocht Shasana, agus gur chuir sé Risteárd chun báis le heagla go mb'fhéidir go dtiocfadh le Risteárd a neart do chruinniú agus an ríocht a bhaint de arís.

Do thárla an chainnt idir Bhrian agus M'leachlainn. Má thárla do thárla gur tugadh an mí do Mh'leachlainn. Níor fhéad sé aon neart do chruinniú i gcaitheamh an mhí. Ansan do tugadh an bhliain do. Níor fhéad sé aon neart do chruinniú i gcaitheamh na bliana ach chómh beag agus d'fhéad sé é ' chruinniú i gcaitheamh an mhí.

Ansan do tugadh an Árdríocht do Bhrian—agus níor chuir Brian M'leachlainn chun báis. Níor chuir, ach más ea do deineadh rí cúige de Mh'leachlainn, agus bhí sé chómh maith, chómh dílis de rí cúige le haon rí eile cúige dá raibh in Éirinn. Bhí an Árdríocht ag Brian agus níor mhairbh sé éinne chun í ' fháil ná chun í ' chimeád*.

Míle blian sarar thárla an méid sin cainnte agus an méid sin gnótha idir Bhrian agus M'leachlainn do thárla cainnt den tsaghas chéanna agus gnó den tsaghas chéanna idir dhá rí eile a bhí in Éirinn an uair sin. B'iad dhá rí iad san ná Conchúr mac Neasa agus Feargas mac Róigh. Bhí Feargas mac Róigh 'na rí ar Chúig' Uladh*. Do chuir Conchúr mac Neasa Feargas as an ríocht, agus dhein sé rí ar Chúig' Uladh dhe féin. Ansan féach cad a thit amach. Ar chuir Conchúr Feargas chun báis le heagla go n-éireódh sé 'na choinnibh agus go gcuirfeadh sé as an ríocht arís é? Níor chuir. A mhalairt sin ar fad is ea do thit amach. D'fhan Conchúr suite go daingean sa ríocht agus bhí caradas dlúth idir é agus Feargas, agus ní raibh aon chómhairleach aige ba ghiorra dhá chroí ná Feargas, ná ba dhílse dho ná Feargas, go dtí gur dhein sé féin an feall mór ar chlaínn Uisnigh.

Cad 'na thaobh gur fhéad an dá ní sin titim amach ar an aon chuma amháin sin in Éirinn fadó agus an míle blian san eatarthu? Níl ach aon fhreagra amháin le tabhairt ar an gceist sin. Sid é an freagra. Bhí in Éirinn, i gcaitheamh an mhíle blian san, cómhacht éigin a bhí ní ba threise ná na ríthe. Chuir an chómhacht san ' fhiachaibh ar Fheargas luí isteach i ngnó na ríochta fé smacht Chonchúir, agus chuir sí ' fhiachaibh ar Chonchúr gan aon éagóir a dhéanamh ar Fheargas. Chuir an chómhacht san ' fhiachaibh ar an mbeirt ceart a chéile ' dh'admháil agus beart a dhéanamh de réir chirt a chéile. Thug san deimhne do Chonchúr nár bhaol do Feargas, agus thug san deimhne d'Fheargas nár bhaol do Conchúr. Ónár n-aithne ar Chonchúr is deimhin dúinn, mura mbeadh ' fhios a bheith aige nár bhaol do Feargas, agus mura mbeadh nárbh fhéidir do gabháil i gcoinnibh na cómhachta a thug an deimhne sin do, go gcuirfeadh sé Feargas chun báis tapaidh go leór.

Cad í an chómhacht í sin a chuir an smacht uathásach san ar an dá rí sin an uair sin, in Éirinn, agus do chuir an smacht céanna ar an dá rí eile, ar Bhrian agus ar Mh'leachlainn, míle blian 'na dhiaidh san? Ainmníthear an chómhacht san go minic i seanchas na hÉireann. "Firu Éireann*" a tugtar ar an gcómhacht san i seanchas na hÉireann. "Aigne na ndaoine" nú "an aigne phoiblí" a tugtar i mBéarla anois ar an gcómhacht san.

Nuair a bhíonn ag an bpoiblíocht eólas agus tuiscint agus éirim aigne, agus nósa láidre daingeana cúmtha as an eólas san agus as an dtuiscint sin agus as an éirim aigne sin le taithí agus le himeacht aimsire, ní bhíonn sé ar chumas aon duine, dá mbeadh sé 'na rí seacht n-uaire, gabháil i gcoinnibh aigne agus toile na poiblíochta san, go mór mór insna nithibh ar a mbíonn aigne na poiblíochta socair. Dá mhéid iad an t-eólas agus an tuiscint agus an éirim aigne, sa phoiblíocht, is ea is treise agus is ea is uaisle an chómhacht, agus is ea is iomláine a théann an chómhacht i bhfeidhm.

Bhí an chómhacht san i bhfeidhm in Éirinn in aimsir Chonchúir mhic Neasa. Bhí sí i bhfeidhm in Éirinn in aimsir Bhriain agus Mh'leachlainn. Do chothaigh na ríthe féin an chómhacht san in Éirinn mar bhí ' fhios acu gurbh é a mbuac í ' chothú agus í ' chimeád neartmhar. Bhí ' fhios acu, bíodh nárbh fholáir dóibh bheith úmhal di i nithibh áirithe, ná raibh ní ar bith ab fheárr ná í chun a n-údaráis féin do chur i bhfeidhm, ar gach aon tsaghas cuma 'narbh é a leas a n-údarás do dhul i bhfeidhm.

Tispeánann an méid sin go léir go raibh in Éirinn fadó, ó aimsir Chonchúir mhic Neasa go dtí aimsir Bhriain, uaisleacht phoiblí, agus úmhlaíocht phoiblí do dhlithibh agus do nósaibh maithe uaisle, nách ró-fhuiriste a leithéid a dh'fheiscint anois in aon treabhchas daoine dá bhfuil suas.

Ná ropairí Gallda so a mheasfadh a chur 'na luí ar dhaoinibh anois ná raibh in Éirinn fadó ach daoine fiaine, deinidís machnamh ar an méid sin. Agus an chuid dár ndaoine féin nár chuid ba lú ná a fhonn a bheadh orthu géilleadh d'éitheach na ropairí sin, deinidís machnamh ar an méid sin.

Caibideal 16: Fear na gCos

An fhaid a bhí an mhór-shlua ag dul ó Cheann Cora soir ó thuaidh go Teamhair, bhí Meargach agus na gaibhní ab fheárr a bhí aige i bhfochair an tslóigh. Bhí seacht cínn de cheártanaibh aige agus iad ar rothannaibh agus na gaibhní ag obair iontu. Ceárta acu ag gabháil le gach cath de sna seacht cathannaibh. Tháinig gaibhní ón mbaile le cuid de sna cathannaibh, ach nuair a tháinig na cathanna go léir i bhfochair a chéile, do cuireadh na gaibhní go léir fé smacht Mheargaigh. Bhí siúinéirí, leis, ann chun pé obair adhmaid a bheadh riachtanach do dhéanamh. Agus bhí mná uaisle ann, mná agus driféaracha agus iníona na ríthe agus na dtaoiseach a bhí ar na cathannaibh. Bhí ana-thuiscint ag na mnáibh uaisle sin ins gach ní a bhain le haireachas a thabhairt do dhaoine gunta, agus thugadar leó ón mbaile na córacha a bhí riachtanach dóibh chun na hoibre sin. Thug gach bean uasal díobh léi, leis, roinnt ban eile mar sheirbhíseacha agus bhí na mná go léir, idir sheirbhíseacha agus mná uaisle, ana-thuisceanach sa ghnó a bhí le déanamh acu. Measaim, nuair a bhíodh cath ar siúl, gurbh fheárr an t-aireachas a thugadh na mná san an uair sin do sna fearaibh gunta ná mar a tugtar anois dóibh nuair a bhíonn cath ar siúl. Is dó' le liagaibh agus le dochtúiribh na haimsire seo gur mó agus gur feárr go mór an t-eólas atá acu féin ná mar a bhí ag éinne sa tsean-aimsir. Tá dearúd mór orthu. Imeóidh garsún anois agus foghlamóidh sé roinnt bheag Laidne. Ansan imeóidh sé isteach i gcoláiste éigin. Tabharfaidh sé formhór na haimsire sa choláiste sin ag imirt chártaí agus ag cuideachtanas agus ag ól. Déanfaidh sé iarracht ar cheisteannaibh áirithe do thógaint agus ar iad do fhreagairt. Ansan tiocfaidh sé chúinn amach agus é 'na dhochtúir! Ansan beidh ár n-anam i láimh an dochtúra san! Bhí níos mó eólais ag cuid de mhnáibh na sean-aimsire ná mar atá ag formhór na ndochtúirí seo anois againn. Eólas as leabhraibh atá acu so. Eólas as an obair a bhí acu súd. Do fuaradh an t-eólas as an obair. Chimeád na mná é agus thugadar dá n-iníonaibh é, agus bhí an obair agus an taithí dhá chur i méid agus i gcruinneas ó shliocht go sliocht. In éaghmais an eólais a bheith ag na mnáibh, bhí deimhne eile ag fearaibh gunta insna seana-chogaíbh úd ar aireachas maith a dh'fháil. Na mná a bhíodh ag tabhairt an aireachais dóibh, b'iad a ngaolta féin iad, a mná pósta nú a ndriféaracha.

Bhíodh na giollaí turais go líonmhar i gcónaí in armáil Bhriain. Bhídís ag gluaiseacht ar an uile shaghas teachtaireachta ó Bhrian chun na mbuíon eile den tslua nú chun na n-uasal a bhíodh sa chómharsanacht. Bhídís roimis an slua amach ag réiteach na mbóithre nú ag déanamh an eólais, dhá dhéanamh amach ceocu bóthar ab fheárr nú ba ré nú ba chóngaraí. Mar sin ní bhídís choíche daingean in aon áit amháin den tslua. Bheireadh a ngnó sa tímpall iad i dtreó go mbídís tamall ins gach aon bhuín.

Níorbh fhada gur tugadh fé ndeara go mbíodh Caoilte i mbuín Thaidhg Mhóir Uí Chealla, ní ba mhinicí go mór ná mar a bhíodh sé in aon bhuín eile, pé cúis a bhí aige leis. Bhíodh daoine dhá fhiafraí dá chéile cad iad na teachtaireachtaí móra a bhíodh ag Brian le cur, chómh minic sin, ag triall ar Thadhg Mhór Ó Chealla seochas aon rí eile dá raibh ar an slua. Ansan do tugtí mar fhreagra ar fhiafraí den tsórd san: "Nách mó gnó a bheadh ag giolla turais i mbuín Thaidhg Mhóir Uí Chealla in éaghmais aon teachtaireacht a thabhairt ón rí?"

Ansan déarfadh duine eile: "Bíonn daoine nách giollaí turais ag teacht chun buíne Thaidhg Mhóir Uí Chealla".

"Bíonn go díreach", adéarfadh duine eile, "agus ní ró-mhór an fháilte a bhíonn ag uaislibh buíne Thaidhg rómpu".

"Cad é an chúis ná beadh fáilte ag uaislibh buíne Thaidhg rómpu, airiú?", adéarfadh áilteóir a bheadh dhá leogaint air nár thuig sé an scéal.

"A dhe, nách neamh-thuisceanach an duine thu!", adéarfadh duine eile. "Ná fuil ' fhios agat go maith conas mar atá an scéal ag uaislibh óga Connacht i dtaobh iníne Thaidhg? Go bhfuil gach éinne acu ag cailliúint a mheabhrach a d'iarraidh go bhfaigheadh sé féin í le pósadh. Táid siad i reachtaibh an anama* ' bhaint as a chéile mar gheall uirthi, ach nuair a thagann aon fhear iasachta isteach sa bhuín, bíd siad go léir in éineacht i reachtaibh an anama ' bhaint as san".

"Agus, ar ndó', tá ' fhios ag an saol", adéarfadh duine eile as a mhachnamh, "nách í Niamh atá ag tarrac Chaoilte chun buíne Thaidhg Mhóir".

"Dar fia", adéarfadh duine eile, "ach má thuigid uaisle óga Connacht agus na huaisle óga eile gur mar gheall ar Niamh atá Caoilte ag dul chómh minic chun na buíne sin, beidh an scéal go holc aige sara gcuirfidh sé puínn eile aimsire dhe".

"Tá an scéal go háiféiseach* acu go léir", adéarfadh duine eile. "Níl blúire binne ag Niamh ar éinne acu, amu' ná i mbaile. Is measa léi a hathair ná aon fhear beó, uasal ná íseal".

Caibideal 16: Fear na gCos

Sin mar a bhídís ag cainnt agus ag cur thrí chéile. An fhaid a bhí an mhór-shlua ag gabháil ó thuaidh ó Cheann Cora go Teamhair, ní ró-mhór an suím a curtí sa chainnt. Bhí tuairim ag na fearaibh go mb'fhéidir go raibh obair throm rómpu, cathanna fuilteacha, b'fhéidir. Nuair a bhí an chuaird tabhartha agus an tsíocháin déanta agus an mhór-shlua ag filleadh go Ceann Cora, bhí aigne gach éinne saor ó bhuaireamh agus bhí gach éinne ní ba thugtha do shult ná do ghruaim. Do thuig na ríthe agus na taoisigh, ó bhí san mar sin, gur cheart spórt agus caitheamh aimsire ' chur ar bun, i dtreó, nuair a stadfí i gcómhair na hoíche i gcónaí, go mbeadh rud éigin chun daoine ' chimeád go suairc agus go sultmhar. Do cuireadh a lán nithe ar siúl. An ghleacaíocht úd a bhíodh i gCeann Cora, do cuireadh ar siúl roinnt di. Bhíodh rith agus léimreach agus iomrascáil ar siúl, agus caitheamh cloch araige, agus a lán cleasaíochta a thispeánfadh neart agus fuinneamh. Bhíodh uasal agus íseal meascaithe ar a chéile sa ghleacaíocht. Uaireanta bhíodh bua ag an uasal agus uaireanta bhíodh bua ag an íseal.

Bhí ógánach uasal ar theaghlach Thaidhg Mhóir Uí Chealla agus Conn ab ainm do. Thug sé fé ndeara Caoilte ag teacht chómh minic chun teaghlaigh Thaidhg Mhóir. Níor thaithn san leis. Ní leogfadh sé air, áfach, gurbh aon éad a bhí air. Is amhlaidh a bheifí ag magadh faoi* dá leogadh. Níor fhág san é gan a thispeáint nár thaithn an giolla turais leis. Thug sé leas-ainm air, "Cosa Buí Árda".

"Féach", adeireadh sé, "tá Cosa Buí Árda chúinn". Thugadh sé "Caoilte Cosach", leis, air, agus "Fear na gCos".

Mac ab ea an Conn san do Mhaolruanaidh na Paidre, rí Ó bhFiachrach Áidhne, agus ógánach ana-chróga ab ea é. Bhí sé go maith ar an uile shaghas gnímh, ach bhí sé thar bárr i ngníomh reatha nú i ngníomh iomrascála.

Caibideal 17: "Bíodh Ciall Agat"

Do cuireadh rásanna ar bun. Na giollaí turais is iad ba mhó a chuaigh ag rith na rás. Cheap Conn go mbainfeadh sé cuid den mhóráil d' "Fhear na gCos", dar leis. Chuaigh sé isteach ar na rásannaibh. Níor chuaigh Caoilte isteach orthu i dtosach. D'fhág sé ag na giollaíbh eile iad. Níor dhein Conn a dhícheall i dtosach. Do leog sé bárr le duine de sna giollaíbh. Ar ball do deineadh tathant ar Chaoilte dul isteach. Do chuaigh. Do rith Conn i dtreó gur chimeád sé suas le Caoilte, le "Fear na gCos", dar leis. Níorbh fhada gur fhág an bheirt na giollaí laistiar díobh ar fad. Do ghéaraigh Conn. Má ghéaraigh do chimeád Caoilte suas leis. Do ghéaraigh sé tuilleadh. Má ghéaraigh do chimeád Caoilte suas leis. Do ghéaraigh sé go dtí ná raibh ann géarú a thuilleadh. Chimeád Caoilte suas leis. Ansan, d'fháisc Caoilte chun an reatha agus do ghluais sé amach ó Chonn i dtreó gur dhó' leis na daoine ná raibh Conn ag rith in aon chor! Do stad Conn. D'éirigh an liú óna raibh ag féachaint orthu i dtreó gur chrith an talamh fé chosaibh na ndaoine go léir. Ní de Chaoilte a baineadh an mhóráil ach de Chonn, agus do baineadh an mhóráil i gceart de.

"'Sea!", adeireadh na huaisle eile leis agus iad ag gáirí, "sin é 'Fear na gCos' agat! Sin iad na cosa buí árda agat! Má táid siad fada, tá fuinneamh iontu. Is uathásach an rith atá aige. Ní fheaca a leithéid de chuisíocht i gcosaibh duine riamh".

Do críochnaíodh an spórt. Bhí Conn agus na huaisle eile a bhain le teaghlach Thaidhg Mhóir Uí Chealla ag cainnt agus ag trácht ar an ngníomh uathásach reatha a dhein Caoilte. Cé ' chífí ag teacht féna ndéin ach Caoilte féin. Do bheannaigh sé dhóibh. Bheannaíodar do. Dheineadar roinnt cainnte. Níor labhair Conn sa chainnt. Bhí sé gruama, do-thíosach go maith. Fé dheireadh do labhair sé as a mhachnamh féin, agus ní ró-chneasta an focal aduairt sé.

Caibideal 17: "Bíodh Ciall Agat"

"Má tá teachtaireacht agat ó Bhrian, a ghiolla", ar seisean, "b'fhearra dhuit imeacht agus an teachtaireacht a thabhairt. Ní maith an teachtaire teachtaire ríghin".

"Níl aon teachtaireacht agam ó Bhrian, a rí", arsa Caoilte.

"Ó, an ea?", arsa Conn. "Níor mheasas go bhféadfadh aon ghnó eile thu ' thabhairt anso ach teachtaireacht éigin a bheith agat á thabhairt ó Bhrian ag triall ar Thadhg Mhór Ó Chealla".

"Tá faobhar ar do ghuth, a rí", arsa Caoilte. "Níl aon ghá leis an bhfaobhar. Má bhuas ort, ba chóir go bhféadfá é ' dh'fhulag mar a dhéanfadh fear. Ní dócha gurb amhlaidh a mheasfá dhom gan mo dhícheall a dhéanamh".

"Ní tu ' bhuachtaint orm sa rith atá ag déanamh aon bhuartha dhom, a ghiolla", arsa Conn. "Ní raibh aon cheart agam dul sa rith in aon chor. Ní ró-mhaith a dheineas é agus me féin a chur i gcúmparáid le giolla turais".

B'fhuiriste ' aithint air go raibh árdfhearg air. Bhí an chainnt dhá thachtadh, ba dhó' leat. Chaitheadh sé stad idir gach aon dó nú trí ' fhoclaibh* le tocht feirge.

"Tá fearg ort, a rí", arsa Caoilte. "Ní fheicim cad ' fhéadfadh an fhearg a chur ort ach mise do bhuachtaint ort sa rith. Ní bhuafainn ort mura mbeadh tu ' theacht im choinnibh sa rith. B'fhéidir nárbh fhearra dhúinn rud a dhéanfaimís ná sinn féin a thriail i ngníomh éigin eile. B'fhéidir dá dtrialaimís sinn féin i ngníomh éigin eile go bhfaighfá an lámh uachtair orm agus ansan go n-imeódh an fhearg díot".

Níor fhéad na huaisle eile gan sceartadh gáire ' dhéanamh, do labhair Caoilte chómh réidh sin agus an fhearg chómh fíochmhar san ar an bhfear eile.

Caibideal 17: "Bíodh Ciall Agat"

"Dá mba mhac rí thu", arsa Conn, "níor mhiste dhuit labhairt ar an gcuma san. Agus dá mba mhac rí thu, níor mhiste dhuit, b'fhéidir, bheith ag teacht anso ar an ngnó a thugann ann tu. Ach giolla turais!"

Níor thug Caoilte freagra ar an gcainnt sin. D'iompaigh dath bán ar a ghnúis. D'fhéach sé 'na thímpall ar na huaislibh eile. Bhí Niamh agus a hathair ag éisteacht leis an gcainnt. Ní fheidir sé cad ba mhaith dho a rá ná cad ba mhaith dho a dhéanamh. Bhuail Niamh chúthu anall go breá réidh. Bhíodar go léir ag úmhlú dhi láithreach.

"A Chuínn", ar sise le Conn, "tá gnó éigin ag Brian díot-sa. Oireann dómh-sa leis dul chun cainnte leis. Fan liom ansan tamall beag agus beidh mé in éineacht leat ag dul ag triall air. Tar-sa i leith anso go fóill, a ghiolla", ar sise le Caoilte. "Tá teachtaireacht agam le tabhairt duit".

Nuair a bhí sí féin agus Caoilte a raon na gcluas, do labhair sí.

"A Chaoilte", ar sise, "tabhair aire agus ná leog ort go gcuirfidh an ní atá agam le rá leat aon iúnadh ort. Táid na huaisle sin go léir ag faire orainn. Tá ' fhios agam-sa cad a thugann anso thu. Agus tá ' fhios ag Conn cad a thugann anso thu. An ní céanna a thugann anso é féin, agus tuilleadh acu. Mheasas go dtiocfadh liom a chur 'na luí ar a n-aigne, gan a bheith orm labhairt, gur gnó gan éifeacht an gnó atá dhá dtabhairt anso. Táim-se ceapaithe, a Chaoilte, ar mo shaol do chaitheamh ag tabhairt aire do m'athair an fhaid is toil le Dia é féin agus mise ' dh'fhágaint ar an saol. Más ar m'athair is túisce a ghlaofaidh Dia, fanfad singil ar an saol so go leanad é. Imigh anois, a Chaoilte, agus bíodh mo bheannacht agat, agus más maith leat pósadh, cuímhnigh ar mhnaoi éigin eile. Imigh leat láithreach, i dtreó go measfar gur 'od chur ar theachtaireacht atáim".

D'imigh Caoilte.

D'fhíll Niamh ag triall ar na huaislibh a bhí ag feitheamh léi.

Caibideal 17: "Bíodh Ciall Agat"

"Téanam, a Chuínn", ar sise le Conn. Thugadar aghaidh ar phuball Bhriain.

Mac driothár céile do Bhrian ab ea Conn. Drifiúr do Mhaolruanaidh na Paidre*, do rí Ó bhFiachrach Áidhne, ab ea an chéad bhean a bhí pósta ag Brian. B'í sin máthair Mhurchadh, agus ba léi tuilleadh de chlaínn Bhriain, leis.

Nuair a thánadar chun cábáin Bhriain, chonacadar Murchadh agus beirt nú triúr d'uaislibh Dál gCais 'na seasamh lasmu' den chábán.

"D'oirfeadh dúinn labhairt leis an rí, a Mhurchadh", arsa Niamh.

"Anois díreach a thánamair uaidh, a ríogan", arsa Murchadh. "Dé bheatha-sa, a Chuínn", ar seisean. "Raghad isteach, a ríogan", ar seisean le Niamh, "agus neósfad do thu ' bheith anso. Níl éinne in' fhochair istigh ach Maolshuathain, an sagart".

B'é Maolshuathain anamchara Bhriain. Anamchara a tugtí an uair sin ar oide faoistine.

Chuaigh Murchadh isteach. Níorbh fhada gur fhíll sé amach.

"Téanam, a ríogan", ar seisean le Niamh.

Chuaigh Niamh isteach agus do fágadh Conn amu'. D'úmhlaigh sí do Bhrian mar ba cheart, agus d'úmhlaigh sí do Mhaolshuathain. Ansan do labhair sí.

"Thánag ag triall ort, a rí", ar sise le Brian, "chun go n-iarrfainn ort cúnamh a thabhairt dom, féachaint a' bhféadfainn a chur ' fhiachaibh ar chuid dár n-uaislibh óga bheith síochánta lena chéile".

Caibideal 17: "Bíodh Ciall Agat"

"Ba chóir, a 'níon ó", arsa Brian, "nár bheag dóibh na Lochlannaigh a bheith le troid acu agus gan bheith ag troid eatarthu féin. Cad é an cúnamh is dó' leat a dh'fhéadfainn a thabhairt duit, a Niamh?"

"Ní ró-fhuiriste dhom ainm a chur ar an gcúnamh, a rí", arsa Niamh, "ach táim dhá thabhairt fé ndeara go bhfuil cuid acu go fíochmhar agus go feargach lena chéile, agus measaim gur mise fé ndeár é".

"Ó, tuigim", arsa Brian. "Éad atá orthu. Measann gach fear acu gur aige féin is ceart tu ' bheith mar mhnaoi, agus tá sé i reachtaibh an anama ' bhaint as aon fhear eile a dhéanfadh oiread agus féachaint ort".

"Cúis gháire chúinn, a rí", arsa Niamh, agus do gháir sí féin, "is cruínn díreach a buailis do mhéar air!"

"Ba dhó' liom, a Niamh", arsa Brian, "ná fuil éinne chun an scéil sin do shocrú ach tusa féin, agus dá laíghead baint a bheidh agam-sa ná ag éinne eile leis an scéal gurb ea is feárr a dhéanfair é ' shocrú. Inis dóibh lom díreach ceocu dhíobh a phósfair. Gabhaim-se orm go gcuirfidh san deireadh leis an imreasán".

"Do chuirfeadh gan amhras, a rí, san deireadh leis an imreasán", ar sise, "ach ní féidir dom san a dh'ínsint dóibh, mar ní phósfad éinne acu. Tá m'aigne socair, a rí", ar sise, "ar gan pósadh choíche".

Do stad sí. Níor labhair éinne ar feadh tamaill. Ansan do labhair Brian.

"Déanfad-sa aon ní is maith leath, a ríogan", ar seisean.

"Tá duine acu anso amu', a rí", ar sise, "agus dá mb'áil leat glaoch isteach air agus a rá leis ciall a bheith aige. Gaol duit féin is ea é. Mac do rí Ó bhFiachrach Áidhne is ea é. Do labhair sé go han-fheargach ó chiainibh le duine eile".

Caibideal 17: “Bíodh Ciall Agat”

Do glaodh isteach ar Chonn. Nuair a tháinig sé isteach, do labhair Brian leis.

“A Chuínn, a mhic ó”, ar seisean, “mheasas go raibh ciall agat-sa”.

Ní fheidir Conn ’en tsaol cad é an bun a bhí leis an gcainnt. Níor labhair sé.

“Do hiarradh orm labhairt leat agus a rá leat ciall a bheith agat”, arsa Brian agus é ag gáirí.

Níor labhair Conn focal. Ní fheidir sé cad ba cheart do a rá, agus cheap sé gurbh fheárr éisteacht.

Do labhair an sagart.

“B’fhéidir nárbh fheárr rud a déanfí ná an ceann a bhaint den scéal duit, a Chuínn”, ar seisean.

“Leog dómh-sa imeacht, a rí”, arsa Niamh.

Chrom Brian a cheann chúithi, agus d’imigh sí amach.

“Do labhrais go feargach ó chiainibh, a Chuínn”, arsan sagart. “Is dócha go bhfuil ’ fhios agat féin cad é an chúis a bhí agat leis an bhfeirg. Níl agam-sa le rá leat ach an méid seo. Tá socair ’na haigne féin ag inín Thaidhg Mhóir Uí Chealla gan pósadh choíche”.

“Sin é cúis, a Chuínn”, arsa Brian, “gur hiarradh orm-sa labhairt leat-sa agus a rá leat ciall a bheith agat”.

“Agus, a Chuínn”, arsan sagart, “féadfair-se a dh’ínsint dá thuilleadh, fé mar a thuigfir féin gur gá é, ná fuil aon bhreith ag aon fhear go deó ar inín Thaidhg Mhóir a dh’fháil le pósadh”.

Caibideal 17: "Bíodh Ciall Agat"

"Imigh leat anois, a mhic ó", arsa Brian, "agus bíodh ciall agat".

D'imigh Conn gan labhairt. Bhí sé ag dul ó dhearg go bán agus ó bhán go dearg an fhaid a bhí sé ag éisteacht leó, agus ansan d'imigh sé gan labhairt.

Dhein sé an rud adúradh leis, áfach. D'inis sé an rud a hínseadh do. As san amach níor deineadh a thuilleadh éada mar gheall ar Niamh. Más ea, níor laígheadaigh san an urraim a bhí acu go léir di. Ba dhó' leat gur mhéadaigh sé an urraim. Má bhíodar úmhal di roimis sin, ba dhó' leat gur mhéadaigh ar an úmhlaíocht acu 'na dhiaidh san. Má bhíodar ollamh roimis sin ar gach aon ní a dhéanamh ar an gcuma ba dhó' leó dob fheárr a thaithnfeadh léi, bhíodar ní ba thugtha 'na dhiaidh san chuige, agus rud ab fheárr ná gach ní eile, ní raibh scamall an éada ag dorchú gach maitheasa acu agus ag séideadh mioscaise suas eatarthu.

Ba ró-mhaith an bhail orthu féin an scéal a bheith mar sin acu. Bhí a tuiscint chómh haibidh sin ag Niamh, agus a heólas orthu chómh cruínn sin, nár thúisce a bhíodh gá ag duine acu le cómhairle a leasa ná mar a thuigeadh sise an gá. Ansan, ní túisce a thuigeadh sí an gá ná mar a thugadh sí an chómhairle. Bhí sí chómh doimhinn, chómh gasta san go dtugadh sí an chómhairle ar shlí nár bhaol aon ghortú ' dhéanamh. Bhí sí ana-chneasta leó, an-aicillí, ana-shéimh. An t-aimhleas 'na mbeadh duine acu lán-cheapaithe ar é ' dhéanamh, bheadh sé curtha dhe aici sara mbeadh ' fhios aige go raibh sí dhá chur de in aon chor, agus an gníomh fónta 'na mbeadh duine acu lán-cheapaithe ar gan é ' dhéanamh, bheadh sé meallta aici chun an ghnímh sin a dhéanamh sara mbeadh ' fhios i gceart aige cad a bheadh ar siúl aici.

Is mó tairbhe a dhein sí, ar an gcuma san, do Bhrian. Do thuig Brian féin a lán den tairbhe sin, ach bhí mórán de ná raibh aon phioc eólais aige air. Bhíodh cosc curtha aici le droch-obair go minic sara mbíodh uain ag an ndroch-obair ar theacht, agus an droch-obair a bhíodh tagaithe, is minic a bhíodh sé* curtha ar neamhní aici, curtha soir siar aici, sara mbíodh uain aige ar aon díobháil a dhéanamh, nú sara mbíodh uain aige ar phuínn díobhála ' dhéanamh.

Bhí urraim thar bárr ag Brian di, agus ag an ríogra go léir di. Ach bhí fuath nímhneach ag Gormfhlaith dhi.

Caibideal 18: Ráflaí

An fhaid a bhí mór-shlua Bhriain ag teacht abhaile ó Theamhair go Ceann Cora an uair sin, ní raibh aon lá gan an uile shaghas ráflaí ag gluaiseacht i measc na bhfear ar na nithibh iúntacha a bhí, dar le daoine, ar siúl lastuaidh i Leath Chuínn. Bhí mór-shlua uathásach ag M'leachlainn á chruinniú, adeirthí. Clanna Néill go léir ag cruinniú as gach áird agus a gcáirde leó. Lochlannaigh ag dul amach ó Bhaile Átha Cliath ag cabhrú le M'leachlainn i gcoinnibh Bhriain. Lochlannaigh ag dul ó thuaidh ón Múmhain chun díoltais a dhéanamh ar Bhrian agus ar Leath Mhogha. Slóite Lochlannach ag teacht anall thar farraige ag cabhrú le Lochlannaigh na hÉireann i gcoinnibh Bhriain, i gcoinnibh an aon fhir amháin a bhí tar éis cómhacht Lochlannach do chur ar neamhní in Éirinn. Dar le lucht na ráflaí, dhein Brian botún uathásach nuair a thug sé an bhliain do Mh'leachlainn chun a nirt a chruinniú agus chun é féin do chur i dtreó i gcómhair an chatha mhóir a troidfí nuair a bheadh an bhliain istigh.

Duairt daoine ná raibh aon bhrí leis na ráflaibh sin. Duairt daoine eile go raibh agus gach aon bhrí leó, agus go neósfadh an aimsir go raibh brí leó.

D'airigh Brian agus a lucht cómhairle na ráflaí go léir. Níor chuir sé aon tsuím iontu. Ní duairt sé 'sea ná ní hea leó. Níor ghá dho é. Ní raibh aon pháirt de Leath Chuínn ná raibh a theachtairí aige ann agus cúntas cruínn aige dá fháil uathu ar gach aon rud a bhí ag titim amach lastuaidh. Is é Caoilte a bhí 'na cheann ar na teachtairíbh sin.

Caibideal 18: Ráflaí

Chuireadh sé duine acu ó dheas in aghaidh an lae nách mór, le blúire éigin eólais, ag triall ar Bhrian.

Bhí ' fhios ag Niamh agus ag á driotháir Caoilte ' bheith ag déanamh na hoibre sin. Bhí ní ar a n-aigne féin a bhí ag déanamh buartha dhóibh. B'é ní é sin ná cad a bhí imithe ar Amhlaoibh nú ceocu beó nú marbh a bhí sé. Bhí an ní sin ag déanamh buartha do Thadhg, mar ní áiteódh an saol air ná gur deineadh éagóir throm éigin ar Amhlaoibh. Go dtiocfadh sé thar n-ais gan teip mura mbeadh nár fágadh ar a chumas teacht. Bhí an ní sin ag déanamh buartha do Niamh, ach más ea ní buairt den tsaghas chéanna a bhí aige á dhéanamh di. Bhí an dá mhachnamh úd 'na haigne aici mar gheall air, agus gan ar a cumas an dá mhachnamh a thabhairt dá chéile.

Duairt Tadhg gur dhó' leis gur mhaith an rud teachtaire ' chur ó thuaidh ag triall ar Chaoilte dhá rá leis bheith ar thuairisc an té a bhí uathu. Go mb'fhéidir go dtiocfí suas le tuairisc éigin air lastuaidh, go mór mór i measc Lochlannach Bhaile Átha Cliath. Do socraíodh air sin. Do soláthraíodh an teachtaire. Do scríodh leitir fhada agus do tugadh do í le breith ag triall ar Chaoilte. Do cuireadh síos sa leitir sin an uile bhlúire eólais dá raibh ag an mbeirt ar Amhlaoibh. Do cuireadh síos a chómharthaí go léir inti, a dhriuch agus a dheallramh, a aos de réir tuairim', a théagar agus a aoirde agus dath a ghruaige. Ní baol ná gur mhol Tadhg a phearsa agus a thréithe. D'imigh an teachtaire agus do rug sé leis an leitir. Tar éis roinnt aimsire, tháinig sé suas le Caoilte agus thug sé dho í. Do léigh Caoilte an leitir. Má léigh ba chuímhin leis láithreach an t-ógánach Lochlannach a bhí ar iarraidh. Bhí aithne mhaith aige air, ach ní raibh, dar leis, aithne ag Amhlaoibh air sin. Chuir sé leitir thar n-ais ag triall ar Niamh agus ar Thadhg dhá ínsint dóibh go raibh aithne aige ar Amhlaoibh, agus go ndéanfadh sé a dhícheall ar a dh' fháil amach cá raibh sé, nú an raibh sé beó.

Bíodh nár chuir Brian suím insna ráflaíbh, mar nár ghá dho é, do dhein sé an uile shaghas díchill ar a shlóitibh do mhéadú agus do neartú agus do chur i dtreó i gcómhair na hoibre a bhí roimis ar theacht na haifliana. Chuir sé tuilleadh fear isteach ins gach buín dá shlua, agus dhein sé buíona eile i dteannta na mbuíon a bhí aige. Chruinnigh sé ualaí móra éadaigh agus ualaí móra arbhair ó gach aon pháirt den Mhúmhain agus dá raibh d'oileán na hÉireann féna smacht. Tháinig ualaí móra iarainn go Ceann Cora ó gach áit 'na raibh iarann á thógaint as an dtalamh, agus b'éigin do Mheargach oiread eile gaibhní ' chur ag obair agus ' bhí ag obair cheana aige, i dtreó go raibh na hairm dá ndéanamh níos tiúbha ar dúbailt ná mar a deintí roimis sin iad. Nuair a chonaic lucht na ráflaí an t-éirleach oibre ar fad ar siúl: "Ach!", adeiridís, "buafaidh Brian ar Mh'leachlainn agus ar a bhfuil de Lochlannachaibh fé luí na gréine!"

Do fuaradh amach lastuaidh, i gcaitheamh na bliana, cad é an t-éirleach ollmhúcháin a bhí ar siúl i gCeann Cora. Má fuaradh is é rud a dhein gach rí de sna ríthibh thuaidh ná cúbadh chuige agus M'leachlainn a dh'fhágáilt gan chabhair gan chúnamh. Thugadar cómhairle chóngarach neamh-chúntach do. Dúradar leis, nuair ná raibh ar a chumas an Árdríocht do chosaint ar Bhrian nárbh fhearra dho rud a dhéanfadh sé ná an Árdríocht a thabhairt do Bhrian agus luí isteach fé Bhrian 'na rí cúige. Dúradar leis nárbh aon mhaith dhóibh féin dul i gcoinnibh Bhriain agus Dhál gCais. Ná géillfeadh Dál gCais an fhaid a bheadh duine acu beó, agus ná fágfaidís namhaid beó 'na ndiaidh. Ná géillfeadh ríogra Uladh ach chómh beag. Gurbh amhlaidh a dhéanfadh an dá shlua a chéile do dhísciú. Ansan nárbh fhios cé aige go mbeadh Éire, ná cé aige go mbeadh Árdríocht na hÉireann. Gurbh fheárr an tsíocháin agus géilleadh do Bhrian.

B'éigean do Mh'leachlainn bheith sásta. Tháinig deireadh na bliana. Do ghluais Brian agus a mhór-shlua ó thuaidh arís go Teamhair. Tháinig M'leachlainn ag triall air agus thug sé dho an Árdríocht agus do luigh sé féin isteach 'na rí cúige fé Bhrian. Ar Chúige na Mí* is ea ' dh'fhág Brian 'na rí é.

Caibideal 18: Ráflaí

Bhí a lán daoine sásta go maith. Bhí a lán daoine agus ba chuma leó. Agus bhí roinnt daoine agus bhíodar ana-mhí-shásta. Bhí Gormfhlaith ar an roinnt sin.

Caibideal 19: Cogarnach

Is dócha gur mithid tuairisc éigin a thabhairt ar cad d'imigh ar Amhlaoibh. Tá ínste cheana conas mar a bhí sé féin agus Gormfhlaith ana-mhór lena chéile go luath tar éis iad do chur aithne ar a chéile i gCeann Cora. Ón gcéad lá a chonaic Gormfhlaith é, do chrom sí ar ana-chúram a dhéanamh de i gcónaí. Sa chainnt dóibh do chuir Gormfhlaith isteach in aigne an ógánaigh na smaointe céanna a bhí 'na haigne féin i dtaobh Bhriain agus i dtaobh Mhurchadh agus i dtaobh Árdríochta na hÉireann. Dhein sí an obair sin, i ndiaidh ar ndiaidh, go hana-réidh agus go hana-ghasta. Chuir sí isteach in' aigne, i ganfhios do nách mór, an fuath agus an mhioscais chéanna a bhí 'na croí féin i gcoinnibh Bhriain agus i gcoinnibh Mhurchadh. Dhein sí rud eile. Do mhúin sí dho—níor dheocair di é, áfach—conas an fuath do chimeád istigh agus an geal-gháire do thispeáint lasmu'.

Lá dá raibh sé féin agus Tadhg Óg Ó Cealla i gCeann Cora, bhí sé féin agus Gormfhlaith in áit fé leith agus iad ag cainnt, agus gan aon choinne ag Tadhg ná ag éinne eile nách ag trácht a bhíodar ar mhuíntir Amhlaoibh a bhí thoir sa bhaile. Ní har aon ní dhá shórd san a bhíodar ag cainnt. Bhí Gormfhlaith ag cur síos d'Amhlaoibh ar Bhrian agus ar Mhurchadh, agus ar an gcuma 'na raibh an uile shaghas éagóra ag an mbeirt á dhéanamh uirthi féin. Ní raibh seóid ná duais shaibhir* riamh aici nár tógadh uaithi chun é ' bhronnadh ar rí éigin nú ar phriúnsa éigin, i dtreó go mbeadh sé baoch de Bhrian.

"Nár chóir, a ríogan", arsa Amhlaoibh, "go dtuigfeadh sé in' aigne nár bheag do a chuid féin do bhronnadh agus gan cuid duine eile do bhronnadh".

"Is cuma leis, a mhic ó", ar sise. "Aon rud uasal 'na gcuirfidh sé a shúil agus a lámh air, ní bheidh suaimhneas ná sástacht aigne air go dtí go mbeidh an rud san tabhartha uaidh aige do rí éigin nú d'uasal éigin. Do chuir an Pápa chúinn anall anso ón Róimh seóid ana-shaibhir, cailís óir a bhí chómh trom san gurbh ar éigin ' fhéadfá í ' dh'iompar id láimh. Bhí muiríon mo dhá lámh féin inti. Dob fhiú saibhreas mór í mar gheall ar a raibh d'ór inti agus gan trácht ar a thuilleadh. Ach an órnáid oibre a bhí geárrtha uirthi, ba mhó ab fhiú an órnáid ealaíonta san ná an t-ór féin. Agus dá éaghmais sin go léir, bhí crios uirthi de chlochaibh lómhara agus cheannódh gach cloch díobh leath na Múmhan duit! Ní thabharfainn an chailís sin ar shaibhreas na Múmhan. Ní thabharfainn go deimhin. Ba liom-sa an chailís sin má ba le Brian í. Cad a dhein sé? Chómh luath agus ' tháinig Colla agus na manaigh sin thíos go hInis Cathaigh do rug sé leis síos an chailís uasal san agus thug sé do Cholla í, gan oiread agus a fhiafraí dhíom-sa ar mhaith liom é nú arbh oth liom é! Cad 'deirir leis sin, a Amhlaoibh? Ná déanfadh cailís ba lú ab fhiú ná an chailís sin an gnó do mhainistir Ínse Cathaigh?"

An fhaid a bhí an méid sin cainnte ag Gormfhlaith á rá níor labhair Amhlaoibh. Nuair a bhí an chainnt ráite aici, níor labhair sé puínn. An méid cainnte do labhair sé, ní har an gcailís a labhair sé í. Níorbh fhada go ndeigh sé ag triall ar an gcuid eile den teaghlach mar a raibh Tadhg. Chríochnaíodar an chuaird agus tháinig an bheirt abhaile go hInis Cathaigh.

Tamall 'na dhiaidh san is ea ' tháinig an fonn ar Amhlaoibh chun an Chreidimh a ghlacadh. Níorbh fhada a bhí an Creideamh glacaithe aige nuair aduairt sé gur mhaith leis bheith 'na shagart. Chuir Colla an mí teástála air, mar adúradh. D'imigh an mí agus do hollmhaíodh é agus do cuireadh insna mion-órdaibh é. Do deineadh *deacon* de agus do cuireadh isteach san *érdam* é. Istigh san *érdam* san a bhí an cóthra láidir, agus istigh sa chóthra san a bhí an bosca iarainn agus an chailís uasal istigh sa bhosca.

Caibideal 19: Cogarnach

An fear 'na raibh cúram an *érdaim* air roime Amhlaoibh bhí sé, mar adúradh, imithe anonn go dtí an Róimh. D'fhan culaith éadaigh leis, culaith manaigh, 'na dhiaidh san *érdam.* Fuair Amhlaoibh an chulaith, idir aibíd agus cochall. Chuir sé an chulaith i gcimeád. Bhí gnó aige dhi. Ansan do leog sé air le Colla go raibh gnó ag an mBannrín de agus gur mhaith leis cead ' fháil chun dul go Ceann Cora. Fuair sé an cead. D'imigh sé suas. Níorbh fhada gur iarr sé arís an cead céanna. Má iarr do fuair. Nuair a bhí taithí déanta aige ar an gcead san d'iarraidh agus d'fháil, dhein sé rud eile. Do thóg se leis aibíd agus cochall an mhanaigh a bhí roimis san *érdam* chun a sheómra codlata agus chuir sé uime iad. D'fhíll sé a ghruaig fhada dhubh fén gcochall agus dhún sé an aibíd tímpall a mhiníl agus d'fhéach sé sa scáthán.

"Déanfair an gnó!", ar seisean in' aigne féin.

Cúpla lá 'na dhiaidh san, tháinig sé ag triall ar Cholla agus d'iarr sé cead dul suas go Ceann Cora.

"Tá, a Athair", ar seisean, "bád ag dul suas ar éirí lae ar maidin. Raghaidh mé suas ar an mbád san agus ansan féadfad, b'fhéidir, bheith anuas níos tráthúla".

"Tá go maith, a mhic ó", arsa Colla.

Ní har éirí lae a bhí an bád san ag dul suas go Luimneach ach uair a' chluig roim lá. D'éirigh Amhlaoibh uair go leith a' chluig roim lá agus chuir sé uime culaith an mhanaigh agus d'fhíll sé a ghruaig fén gcochall, agus siúd chun an bháid é. Bhí an doircheacht ann agus níor chuir éinne aon speic air. Dhíol sé an t-éileamh agus chuaigh sé isteach. Nuair a shrois sé Luimneach is ar cheártain Mheargaigh a thug sé aghaidh. Chonaic sé Meargach.

"Duairt Colla liom, a dhuin' uasail", ar seisean, "a fhiafraí dhíot a' bhféadfá macshamhail a dhéanamh den eochair úd a dheinis do chun na cailíse ' chur fé ghlas".

Caibideal 19: Cogarnach

“Cad d’imigh ar an eochair a dheineas do?”, arsa Meargach.

“Níor inis sé dhom, a dhuin’ uasail, cad d’imigh uirthi ná ar imigh aon rud uirthi”, arsa Amhlaoibh go símplí.

“Tá go maith”, arsa Meargach. “Is cuímhin liom an eochair. Ní bheidh mé neómat á déanamh duit. Suigh ansan. Ní fiú dhuit imeacht. Tabharfaidh mé dhuit í láithreach”.

B’fhíor dho. Cúpla buille ’ chasúr[*] agus cúpla scríob barra ciomalta agus bhí an eochair déanta.

“Seo”, arsa Meargach. “Sin í agat í. Seachain agus ná caill í mar a cailleadh an ceann eile”.

“Go ra’ maith agat, a dhuin’ uasail”, arsan manach bréige.

Tháinig Amhlaoibh amach as an gceártain agus an eochair aige. Bhí scannradh air an fhaid a bhí sé istigh le heagla go ndéarfadh Meargach, “Raghad féin síos ag triall ar Cholla leis an eochair seo”. Ní duairt. Thug sé an eochair don mhanach, dar leis, agus bhí Amhlaoibh sásta.

Chómh luath agus ’ bhí sé ar an dtaobh amu’ den cheártain, d’imigh sé in áit chaothúil éigin agus bhain sé dhe an aibíd agus an cochall agus bhí sé ’na riocht féin. Dhein sé ceirtlín bheag chruaidh den aibíd agus den chochall agus chuir sé fén’ oscaill an cheirtlín, agus d’imigh sé suas go Ceann Cora. Chonaic sé Gormfhlaith. D’inis sé dhi cad a bhí déanta aige, agus thispeáin sé an eochair di.

“Nuair ’ ínsis dom, a ríogan”, ar seisean, “conas a tógadh uait an chailís sin, bheartaíos i m’aigne go dtabharfainn chút thar n-ais í nú go gcaillfinn an t-anam. Tá an eochair seo agam anois, agus féadfad an chailís a thabhairt liom agus an bosca ’ dh’fhágáilt im dhiaidh agus an glas air, agus ní aithneóidh éinne an chailís a bheith imithe ní fios cathain. Tá cailís eile ann agus is í a tógtar amach nuair a bhíonn aon ócáid áirithe ann. Ní tógtar amach an chailís dhaor choíche. Tá aon chúntúirt amháin sa scéal, áfach. Dá ráineódh Meargach agus Colla ' bheith ag cainnt agus go bhfiafródh Meargach de Cholla, 'Ar dhein an eochair nua úd a dheineas duit an gnó?', nú rud éigin den tsórd san, bhí an scéal amu' orm. Ní mór dhom an chailís a thabhairt chút, a ríogan, chómh luath agus d'fhéadfad é, agus ansan bheith ag faire chúm".

Bhí áthas an domhain ar Ghormfhlaith. Ní raibh aon chuímhneamh aici go ndéanfadh an buachaill sin a leithéid de ghníomh, agus é ' dhéanamh chómh ciúin, chómh gasta. Do mhol sí é agus do mhol sí arís é. Do rug sí air agus chrom sí ar é ' phógadh. Do phóg sí go dlúth é, arís agus arís eile, agus "Mo ghrá mo leanbh!" ar sise leis, in aghaidh gach póige dár thug sí dho. Ansan do chrom sí ar ghol. Ansan d'áirimh sí arís do na héagórtha troma crua a bhí dá ndéanamh uirthi, Brian á ndéanamh uirthi agus Murchadh ag séideadh fé.

Ar ball do chuaigh sí chun suaimhnis, agus thriomaigh sí a súile, agus tháinig a snua féin agus a gnaoi féin di. D'fhéach Amhlaoibh uirthi agus thuig sé in' aigne gur mhór an tíoránach Brian agus gurbh é rud Murchadh ná annscian diablaí, agus an té a chuirfeadh as an saol an bheirt go mbeadh comaoine mhór curtha ar an saol aige.

"Suigh ansan go fóill, a lao", ar sise. "Beidh mé thar n-ais chút láithreach".

D'imigh sí. Níorbh fhada gur fhíll sí, agus rud éigin aici 'na láimh, fíllte in éadach. D'oscail sí an t-éadach. Íomhá den Mhaighdin Mhuire is ea ' bhí aici, íomhá airgid. An té a dhein an íomhá san, dhein sé go maith í. Bhí sí tímpall sé hórla ar aoirde agus bhí sí cúmtha ana-chruínn den réir sin, agus í fírinneach 'na déanamh de réir mar ba cheart cló duine a bheith. Ach bhí ní thairis sin inti. Tháinig leis an gceárdaí, pérbh é féin, scáil gnaoi éigin do chur san aghaidh i dtreó gur dhó' leat nuair ' fhéachfá ar an aghaidh gurbh í aghaidh na Maighdine féin a bheadh ann. D'fhéach Amhlaoibh ar an íomhá, agus má fhéach do mhothaigh sé ag teacht 'na chroí, don íomhá san, urraim nár mhothaigh sé a leithéid riamh roimis sin 'na chroí.

"Is álainn an íomhá í sin, a ríogan!", ar seisean.

"Seo, a mhic ó", arsa Gormfhlaith, "beir leat síos go dtí an mhainistir í sin, agus tabhair do Cholla í, agus abair leis gur mise ' chuir chuige í, agus gurb in é gnó* a bhí agam díot-sa inniu, chun na híomhá san a bhreith síos ag triall air agus í ' bhronnadh air. Íomhá dheas is ea í. Ní thabharfainn-se, áfach, an chailís úd ar mhíle, ní hea, ach ar deich míle, dá sórd. Beidh áthas mór ar Cholla nuair a gheóbhaidh sé an íomhá san. Cuirfidh an t-áthas san é ó aon chuímhneamh in aon chor a bheith aige go bhféadfá-sa aon ghnó eile ' bheith anso aníos inniu agat ach chun í sin a bhreith síos ag triall air. Déanfaidh an t-áthas rud eile. Nuair ' iarrfair-se ar Cholla cead teacht aníos arís amáireach, tabharfaidh sé dhuit an cead gan cheistiúchán".

"Tuigim thu, a ríogan", arsa Amhlaoibh.

Bhí sé ag imeacht agus an íomhá aige, agus an cheirtlín fén' oscaill aige. Do labhair Gormfhlaith arís agus na deóracha lena súilibh.

"Tabhair aire mhaith dhuit féin, a lao", ar sise. "Beart ana-chúntúrthach is ea an bheart atá idir lámhaibh agat. Ní tusa amháin atá sa chúntúirt feasta. Táim-se anois chómh fada isteach sa chúntúirt agus ataoi-se*. Tabhair aire mhaith dhuit féin".

"Ná bíodh eagal ort, a ríogan", ar seisean, agus d'imigh sé.

Tháinig sé chun na mainistreach. Chuaigh sé chun an *érdaim*. D'oscail sé an cheirtlín agus chuir sé an cochall agus an aibíd san áit 'na bhfuair sé ar dtúis iad. Siúd ag triall ar Cholla ansan é.

“Seo, a Athair”, ar seisean, “rud a chuir an Bhannrín anuas chút-sa. Sin é gnó a bhí aici dhíom inniu, chun go dtabharfainn chút anuas é sin”.

D’fhéach Colla ar an íomhá. Do stad sé ar feadh tamaill agus é ag féachaint uirthi.

“Ó”, ar seisean, “is álainn an íomhá í sin! Is beannaithe an íomhá í. Ní fhéadaim gan grá don Mhaighdin Mhuire do mhothú ag lasadh istigh im chroí nuair ’ fhéachaim ar an íomhá sin! Abradh an saol a rogha rud”, ar seisean, “bean mhaith is ea Gormfhlaith! Mura mbeadh gur bhean mhaith í, ní bhronnfadh sí an íomhá so orainn. Mura mbeadh gur bhean mhaith í, ní bheadh a leithéid in aon chor aici”.

“Duairt sí liom dul suas arís amáireach, a Athair”, arsa Amhlaoibh, “go raibh gnó éigin eile aici dhíom”.

“Tá go maith, a mhic ó. Comáin leat”, arsa Colla.

Caibideal 20: Bithiúntas

D’imigh Amhlaoibh agus thug sé cuaird ar an *érdam* ag cur gach aon rud i dtreó ann. Thug sé an tráthnóna ag ní agus ag glanadh agus ag sciomar agus ag slachtú go dtí go raibh gach aon rud ar áilleacht aige. Fuair sé eochair an chóthra dhaingin ó Cholla chun na n-árthaí airgid agus óir a bhí istigh ann do thógaint amach agus do ghlanadh. Nuair a bhíodar glan aige, chuir sé isteach arís iad. Bhí an oíche ann sara raibh an obair go léir déanta aige.

Nuair a bhí an doircheacht aige, tharraig sé amach an mhacshamhail eochrach a bhí aige féin. D’oscail sé an bosca ’na raibh an chailís dhaor. Thóg sé amach an chailís. Chuir sé i bhfolach san *érdam* í. Chuir sé an glas ar an mbosca arís, agus shocraigh sé é díreach ar an ndul ’na raibh sé cheana. Dhún sé an cóthra daingean, agus do rug sé eochair an chóthra ag triall ar Cholla agus thug sé dho í. D’imigh sé a chodladh. Shín sé ar an leabaidh, ach má shín níor thit aon néal codlata air. D'éirigh sé tímpall na haimsire céanna 'nar éirigh sé an mhaidean roimis sin. Thug sé aghaidh ar an mbád gcéanna. Bhí ceirtlín fén' oscaill aige. Thug sé an díolaíocht uaidh agus níor cuireadh aon speic air. Tháinig sé go Ceann Cora. Bhí Gormfhlaith ag faire agus í ag feitheamh leis. Chómh luath agus adúradh léi go raibh sé ann, tháinig sí chuige. Do rug sí léi isteach é i seómra uaigneach. D'oscail sé an cheirtlín agus shín sé chúithi an chailís. Ansan is ea ' bhí an mhóráil uirthi! Ní fheidir sí conas a thispeánfadh sí dho méid an bhaochais a bhí aici air.

Níorbh aon iúnadh í ' bheith baoch de. Dob álainn an tseóid an chailís sin. Dar leis an mbeirt, ní raibh seóid eile mar í le fáil sa domhan an uair sin.

Nuair a bhí tamall beag caite acu ag féachaint uirthi agus ag déanamh iúnadh dhi, do thóg Gormfhlaith léi í agus chuir sí i gcimeád í.

"Agus", ar sise, "beidh an tseamróg ag an té a gheóbhaidh amach as mo láimh-se arís í!"

D'órdaigh sí chúig dosaein fíona, d'fhíon altórach, do chur i gciseán agus é ' thabhairt d'Amhlaoibh le breith síos go hInis Cathaigh agus le cur isteach san *érdam*, i gcómhair na sagart. Do cuireadh capall agus carbad leis féin agus leis an gciseán fíona síos go dtí an bád. Nuair a shrois sé an mhainistir, do tógadh an ciseán agus do cuireadh isteach san *érdam* é, agus bhí Colla agus na sagairt go léir baoch den Bhannrín. Agus ní baol ná gur tugadh d'Amhlaoibh a chion den bhaochas.

Nuair a bhí an méid sin déanta, chuaigh gach aon rud chun suaimhnis. Do ghluais obair na mainistreach agus obair an rí-theaghlaigh i gCeann Cora, ag dul ar aghaidh go breá réidh gan chosc gan cheataí, go dtí gur tháinig an Leagáid anall ón Róimh.

Caibideal 20: Bithiúntas

Ansan do fuaradh amach, mar a hínseadh thuas, go raibh an chailís imithe.

An lá ' bhí an Leagáid i Luimneach ag cainnt le Meargach, bhí ' fhios ag Amhlaoibh go raibh sé ann agus bhí ' fhios aige cad a bhí uaidh. Bhí ' fhios aige go maith go neósfadh Meargach don Leagáid gur dhein sé an mhacshamhail den eochair. Níor fhan sé lena thuilleadh. D'éalaigh sé amach as an mainistir agus phreab sé suas go Ceann Cora. D'inis sé do Ghormfhlaith cad a bhí ar siúl. Chonaic Colla i gCeann Cora é, ach níor dhein Colla aon iúnadh dhe sin. Cheap sé go mb'fhéidir gur chiseán eile fíona a bhí ag dul síos.

Chuir Gormfhlaith Amhlaoibh i bhfolach go dtí go dtáinig an oíche. Ansan do ghuid sí amach é i lár na hoíche agus chuir sí chun siúil é i riocht giolla turais, agus chuir sí in éineacht leis giolla turais eile go raibh iúntaoibh mhaith aici as. Bhí dhá chapall mhaithe ag an mbeirt, agus bhíodar tamall maith den tslí ar bhóthar Bhaile Átha Cliath sara dtáinig an lá orthu. Nuair a tháinig an lá, do chonaic na daoine iad ach níor dheineadar aon iúnadh de bheirt ghiollaí turais. Shroiseadar Baile Átha Cliath. Bhí leitir ó Ghormfhlaith ag Amhlaoibh do Shitric, do rí Lochlannach Átha Cliath. Thispeáin sé an leitir. D'inis an leitir do Shitric gach aon rud. Níorbh fhada go raibh Amhlaoibh ar bórd luinge agus é ag dul soir abhaile go crích Lochlann.

Bhí sé thoir sa bhaile, slán folláin, saor ó bhaol, gan bheann ar Cholla ná ar an Leagáid, ar Mhurchadh ná ar Bhrian, agus Tadhg Óg Ó Cealla ag briseadh a chroí ag gol 'na dhiaidh agus ag cuardach na ndúthaí dho.

Dá mbeadh ' fhios ag Tadhg cad a bhí déanta aige, bheadh sé ag cuardach na ndúthaí dho agus ní har mhaithe leis é. Dá mbeadh ' fhios ag Niamh cad a bhí déanta aige, níorbh fhada an mhoíll uirthi dhá thaobh an scéil úd do thabhairt dá chéile. Fuaradar araon amach 'na dhiaidh san cad a bhí déanta aige.

Caibideal 21: Droch-amhras

Níorbh fhada go raibh Amhlaoibh imithe as aigne agus a cuímhne gach éinne in Inis Cathaigh agus i gCeann Cora, lasmu' de Thadhg Óg Ó Chealla. Bhíodh Colla agus an Leagáid ag cuímhneamh go minic ar an gcailís a guideadh, ach níor chuímhníodar in aon chor ar Amhlaoibh 'na taobh. Agus ar ndóin, ní nárbh iúnadh, níorbh fhéidir dóibh cuímhneamh ar Ghormfhlaith. Chuímhníodh an Leagáid uaireanta ar Ghormfhlaith, ach do dhíbreadh sé an smaoineamh as a chroí. Is aici a bhí an chailís sarar thug Brian do Cholla í. Ach conas ' fhéadfadh an ríogan san, dar leis, a bhí chómh huasal, chómh fial, leis an mainistir agus leis na manaigh, ag bronnadh fíona agus gach ní eile dá fheabhas orthu, an ríogan a bhronn an íomhá san na Maighdine Muire ar Cholla, conas ' fhéadfadh sí aon lámh a bheith aici i nguid na cailíse? Gan amhras, dar leis, ba mhó ab fhiú an chailís, naoi n-uaire, ná a raibh tabhartha dhóibh aici, agus ná a bhféadfadh sí a thabhairt dóibh i gcaitheamh a saeil. Ach ní chuirfeadh san ' fhiachaibh ar mhnaoi dhá sórd an chailís do ghuid. Níor dhiabhal gadaíochta an diabhal coímhdeachta a bhí aici.

Chuímhnigh an Leagáid ar an sagart a cuireadh anonn go dtí an Róimh. Is air a bhí cúram an *érdaim* sarar críochnaíodh 'na shagart é. Arbh fhéidir go mbeadh sé de mhí-fhoirtiún air go spriocfadh an t-áirseóir é agus go ndéanfadh se a leithéid de ghníomh? Cérbh é an manach a chuaigh suas go Luimneach agus d'inis an bhréag do Mheargach agus do fuair an eochair uaidh? Pérbh é féin, ní raibh sé i measc na manach a bhí sa mhainistir an lá a tháinig Meargach anuas chun iad go léir a dh'fheiscint. B'é an sagart a bhí imithe chun na Rómha an t-éinne amháin ná feacaigh Meargach an lá san.

Ní fheacaigh Meargach Amhlaoibh an lá san, ach níor chuímhnigh an Leagáid in aon chor ar Amhlaoibh. Ní chuímhneódh éinne ar Amhlaoibh sa scéal. Ní chuímhneódh éinne go ndéanfadh Amhlaoibh a leithéid de ghníomh. Bhí sé ró-oscailte, ró-gheal-gháiriteach, ró-mhacánta in' fhéachaint.

Caibideal 21: Droch-amhras

De réir gach deallraimh ní raibh éinne chun na cailíse ' ghuid ach an sagart a bhí imithe chun na Rómha. Bhí buairt agus doilíos ar an mbeirt, ar Cholla agus ar an Leagáid fé mar a bhí an méid sin ag dul 'na luí ar a n-aigne. Bhí sé ag brú isteach agus ag dul 'na luí ar aigne gach duine acu i bhfad sarar thráchtadar lena chéile air. Nuair a thráctadar air, ní puínn cainnte a dheineadar air.

Art ab ainm don tsagart, Art mac Duibh. Aneas ó Mhúscraí ab ea é. Daoine ana-chreidiúnacha ab ea a mhuíntir. Bhí a lán acu in armáil Bhriain. Bhí ana-chion ag Colla air.

"Má dhein sé an gníomh san", arsa Colla, agus an bheirt ag tagairt don ghnó, "ní cuid ba lú ná a fhonn a bheadh orm a rá gur trua nár ghlaeigh Dia as an saol me sarar deineadh an gníomh!"

"Ní fada gur mithid do bheith ag teacht thar n-ais ón Róimh", arsan Leagáid. "Má dhein sé an gníomh, ní dócha go dtiocfaidh sé thar n-ais anso".

"Ó, a Thiarna Easpaig", arsa Colla, "is fíor dhuit é! Níor chuímhníos riamh air sin. Má dhein sé an gníomh, ní thiocfaidh sé thar n-ais. Má thagann sé thar n-ais, tispeánfaidh san go soiléir nár dhein sé riamh é!"

Níor dhó' leis an Leagáid go dtispeánfadh a theacht thar n-ais nár dhein sé an gníomh, ach ní duairt sé aon rud. Do leog sé do Cholla an méid sin sóláis a bheith aige.

Suím laethanta 'na dhiaidh san do tháinig Art. Thug sé a lán teachtaireachtaí ón Róimh leis, teachtaireachtaí ag triall ar Cholla, agus ag triall ar an Leagáid, agus ag triall ar Bhrian. Thug sé leitir ón bPápa ag triall ar an Leagáid. Thug sé a lán rudaí beannaithe leis ag triall ar an mainistir, taise naomh agus íomhánna agus nithe den tsórd san. Agus thug sé leabhar Aifrinn leis don mhainistir, agus leabhar Soíscéal a bhí scríofa i Laidin. Ach ní raibh aon ní dár thug sé leis ba mhó gur deineadh iúnadh dhe ná éide Aifrinn a bhí déanta d'éadach snáth óir agus gur dhó' le duine gurbh ór ar fad í, bhí sí chómh greanta san.

Ní raibh aon tseó ach ar dhein na manaigh go léir de chúram den tsagart óg. Agus ní raibh aon teóra leis an áthas a bhí orthu nuair a chonacadar sa bhaile acu féin arís é. Bhíodh sé ag déanamh a dhíchill ar na ceisteanna d'fhreagairt a bhíodh ag teacht ón uile thaobh air agus iad go léir 'na thímpall.

"Cad é an fhaid a bhís ar uisce?"

"A' raibh droch-aimsir agaibh, a Airt?"

"Cad é an saghas daoine na Rómhánaigh, a Airt?"

"A' dtuigfidís aon fhocal Gaelainne ó dhuine, a Airt?"

"A' bhfuil siad chómh buí agus adeirtear iad a bheith?"

"An daoine fónta iad?"

"A' bhfuil Creideamh acu, a Airt?"

"Is dócha gur Laidean ab éigean duit a labhairt leó i gcónaí, a Airt?"

"Is dócha, a Airt, gur fear breá naofa an Pápa".

"An cathair ana-mhór cathair na Rómha, a Airt?"

Chomáineadar leó ar an gcuma san. Bhí Colla agus an Leagáid ag féachaint orthu agus ag féachaint ar Art. Ar ball do dhrid an bheirt i leataoibh.

Caibideal 21: Droch-amhras

"Chíonn tú féin anois, a Thiarna Easpaig", arsa Colla, "nár dhéin an fear san riamh a leithéid de ghníomh".

"Chím", arsan Leagáid. "Níor dhein. Ní fhéadfadh sé é. Tá san soiléir go leór. Ach chuaigh manach éigin, nú duine éigin i riocht manaigh, suas go Luimneach ag triall ar an ngabha agus fuair sé macshamhail na heochrach uaidh. Chonaic Meargach iad go léir an lá ' thugas anuas anso é, agus ní fheacaigh sé orthu an manach a fuair an eochair uaidh. Is éagsamhlach an scéal é. Ní fheadar 'en tsaol cad is ceart dom a dhéanamh 'na thaobh mar scéal. Tá aon chúntúirt amháin os cionn an tsagairt óig seo agus is ceart é ' thabhairt as an gcúntúirt sin".

"Cad í an chúntúirt atá os a chionn, a Thiarna Easpaig?", arsa Colla. "Ar ndóin, tá ' fhios ag an saol ná féadfadh éinne an ghadaíocht san a chur 'na leith".

"Is fíor ná féadfá-sa ná mise í ' chur 'na leith", arsan Leagáid. "Ní gá dhúinn ach féachaint air. Ach féach conas mar a sheasaíonn an scéal. Bhí an chailís san *érdam* agus cúram an *érdaim* ar Art. Ní fheacaigh éinne an chailís ón lá a dh'imigh Art go dtí an lá a thánag-sa anso. Chuiris-se fios ar an mbosca iarainn an oíche sin. Bhí an bosca folamh. Raghaidh an scéal san amach luath nú mall. Pé áit 'na bhfuil Amhlaoibh tá ' fhios aige go raibh an bosca folamh an oíche sin. Neósfaidh Amhlaoibh an scéal san. Raghaidh an scéal ó bhéal go béal. Cad 'déarfar? Cad a bheidh le rá ach, 'Ní raibh éinne chun na cailíse ' thógaint ach fear an *érdaim*'".

"Tá an scéal go holc, a Thiarna Easpaig. Cad is dó' leat is ceart a dhéanamh?"

"Ní foláir a dhéanamh amach, ar dtúis, nách é Art a fuair an mhacshamhail don eochair ó Mheargach. Dá mbeadh an méid sin socair, bheadh Art ó bhaol. Dá bhféadfá-sa, gan aon ní do leogaint ort, a chur ' fhiachaibh ar Art culaith manaigh do chur uime agus dul ag déanamh gnótha an *érdaim*, d'fhéadfí* Meargach a thabhairt anuas, fé mar a thugas-sa anuas cheana é, agus leogaint do radharc ' fháil ar Art. Ansan do neósfadh sé dhúinn arbh é sin an manach a fuair an eochair nú nárbh é".

"Ach, a Thiarna Easpaig", arsa Colla, "ní gá dul chun na trioblóide sin in aon chor. Tá aithne mhaith ag Meargach ar Art le fada riamh. Dá mb'é Art a gheóbhadh an eochair, d'aithneódh Meargach é le línn na heocrach a thabhairt do".

"Ó, más mar sin é", arsan Leagáid, "ní gá dhúinn a thuilleadh de dhua an scéil a dh'fháil. Má deirtear aon fhocal choíche i gcoinnibh an tsagairt óig seo mar gheall ar an gcailís, glanfaidh Meargach é. Neósfaidh Meargach nách do a thug sé an eochair, agus beidh ' fhios ag gach éinne gurb é an fear a fuair an eochair a ghuid an chailís. Ní gá a thuilleadh de dhua an scéil a dh'fháil".

"Ní gá, a Thiarna Easpaig", arsa Colla, "dhúinn a thuilleadh de dhua an scéil a dh'fháil, chómh fada agus a théann aon amhras a bheith ar Art, ach ba mhaith liom, dá bhféadainn é, teacht suas leis an bhfear a fuair an eochair. Manach ab ea é de réir mar adeir Meargach. Bhí eólas na mainistreach go maith aige, agus eólas an *érdaim*. Bhí ' fhios aige an eochair a bheith agam-sa agus gan aon bhreith a bheith ag éinne ar í ' fháil as mo láimh. Bhí ' fhios aige gurbh é Meargach a dhein í. Cé hé an fear a dh'fhéadfadh an t-eólas san go léir a bheith aige agus nách duine de sna manachaibh é, agus a chuaigh suas ag triall ar Mheargach i riocht manaigh?"

"Ní fhéadfadh sé dul suas go Luimneach i riocht manaigh", arsan Leagáid, "gan culaith manaigh a bheith aige le cur uime".

"Ní féadfadh go díreach", arsa Colla, "agus cá raibh sí le fáil aige?"

"An dó' leat", arsan Leagáid, "a' bhféadfá a dhéanamh amach ó sna manaigh ar thug éinne acu culaith manaigh ar iasacht d'éinne le déanaí? Má cheistíonn tú iad air sin, seachain agus ná leog uait aon ní i dtaobh na cailíse. Dá mbeadh ' fhios ag an mbithiúnach go bhfuiltear ar a thóir, ní bheadh aon bhreith againn ar theacht suas leis".

"Níl agam ach an gnó ' dhéanamh chómh haicillí agus d'fhéadfad é", arsa Colla.

Ansan do tugadh aghaidh ar ghnóthaíbh eile agus do fágadh an scéal san ar an gcuma san.

Do chríochnaigh an Leagáid an gnó a bhí aige le déanamh in Éirinn. Ansan chuaigh sé go Ceann Cora agus d'fhág sé slán ag an Árdrí. D'fhág sé slán ag teaghlach an Árdrí. D'inis sé do Bhrian cad é an scéal áthais a bheadh aige don Phápa nuair a neósfadh sé dho na nithe móra a bhí déanta ag Brian don Chreideamh in Éirinn, agus na nithe ba mhó ná san a bhí i ndán do a dhéanamh anois nuair a bhí a chómhacht agus a ghradam agus a dhlithe i bhfeidhm ar Éirinn go léir. Duairt Brian leis go neósfadh sé an fhírinne don Phápa nuair a neósfadh sé na nithe sin do. Ansan do bhronn Brian seóide uaisle air, agus do scaradar.

D'fhág an Leagáid slán ag Murchadh, agus d'fhág sé slán ag Gormfhlaith.

Is é focal déanach aduairt sé le Colla agus é ag imeacht amach ar an loíng, ó Inis Cathaigh: "An cuímhin leat, a Cholla", ar seisean, "an focal úd aduart leat i dtaobh Bhriain agus an nímhe?"

"Is cuímhin, a Thiarna Easpaig", arsa Colla. "Do labhras leis an Rí-dhamhna. Tá gach ní socair díreach mar a chómhairlís".

"Labhair arís leis", ar seisean, "agus inis do go nduart leat labhairt arís leis".

"Déanfad, a Thiarna Easpaig", arsa Colla.

Chuaigh an Leagáid ar bórd na luinge agus do ghluais an long amach ó Inis Cathaigh, siar bhéal na Sionainne, thar Léim Chúchulainn, amach an fharraige mhór.

Do dhein na manaigh in Inis Cathaigh a ngnó de réir na rial. Bhí an scolaíocht insna scoileannaibh agus na húrnaithe insna heaglaisibh, an troscadh agus an tréanas agus gach gnó diaga eile ar siúl mar ba cheart, fé choimirce Sheanáin naofa. Bhí Colla go dícheallach agus go dúthrachtach ag féachaint i ndiaidh gach aon ní agus i ndiaidh gach aon duine. Bhí eochair an bhosca iarainn 'na sheilbh féin aige go haireach, agus ní fheidir éinne sa tigh ná go raibh an chailís dhaor úd istigh go daingean sa bhosca iarainn fén nglas. Ní raibh, áfach.

Leabhar a Dó

Caibideal 22: Cíos an Árdrí

*Chómh luath agus ' bhí Brian socair san Árdríocht, thosnaigh a chíos ar theacht chuige isteach ó gach aon pháirt d'Éirinn. Deirtear gur tugadh Brian Bórú air mar gheall ar an gcíos a dh'éilimh sé. Ní dó' liom go bhfuil fírinne san abairt sin. Ní hé Brian a cheap an cíos. Bhí cíos an Árdrí ceapaithe na céadta blian sara dtáinig Brian chun na hÁrdríochta. Nuair a tháinig Brian chun na hÁrdríochta do chuir gach rí cúige ag triall air an cíos a bhí ceangailte air, de réir dlí na hÉireann, do chur ag triall ar Árdrí Éireann. Deir cuid den tseanchas gurb é cúis 'nar tugadh Brian Bórú air ná so. Bóraimhe ab ainm don bhaile 'na raibh rí-theaghlach Bhriain, ag ceann na cora. Do tugadh, as san, "Ceann Cora" ar an rí-theaghlach agus do tugadh Brian Bóraimhe ar Bhrian féin toisc é ' bheith 'na chónaí ar an mBóraimhe. Measaim gur mó an chiall atá leis an gcainnt sin ná leis an gcainnt eile.

Lá Samhna an lá a bhí ceapaithe i gcónaí riamh chun cíosa an Árdrí do chur isteach, agus seo mar a bhí an cíos socair:

Caibideal 22: Cíos an Árdrí

Ó Chonnachtaibh ocht gcéad bó agus ocht gcéad muc.

Ó mhuíntir Chorca Mrua deich gcéad damh agus deich gcéad caíora* agus deich gcéad brat.

Ó Chorca Baoiscne deich gcéad damh agus deich gcéad molt agus deich gcéad muc agus deich gcéad brat.

Ó mhuíntir Chiarraí deich gcéad damh agus deich gcéad bó agus deich gcéad muc.

Ó mhuíntir Mhúscraí trí chéad bó ramhar agus trí chéad loilíoch agus trí chéad muc agus céad brat.

Ó Thír Chonaill chúig céad* bó agus chúig céad brat.

Ó Thír Eóin trí chéad muc agus trí chéad ualach iarainn.

Ó Chlann Rúraí trí caogaid bó agus trí caogaid muc.

Ó Oiriallaibh céad agus trí fichid bó.

Ó Chúige Laighean trí chéad bó ramhar agus trí chéad muc agus trí chéad ualach iarainn.

Mar sin dóibh mórthímpall na hÉireann go léir. Níl curtha síos anso agam ach fíor-bheagán de sna cíosannaibh, oiread díreach agus ' thispeánfaidh an tslí ar a ndíoltí an cíos, agus an fáltas cíosa a bhíodh ag titim ar na cineachaibh agus ar na dúthaibh fé leith.

Bhí a gcion den chíos ar na Lochlannaigh, leis, an chuid acu a bhí socair i mbailtibh móra na hÉireann. Bhí ar Lochlannaigh Bhaile Átha Cliath trí caogaid píopa fíona do thabhairt mar chíos d'Árdrí Éireann. Bhí ar Lochlannaigh Luimní trí chéad agus trí fichid píopa d'fhíon dearg a thabhairt mar chíos do.

Caibideal 22: Cíos an Árdrí

B'fhéidir go bhfiafródh duine conas ' fhéadfadh Lochlannaigh Luimní cíos a dhíol le hÁrdrí Éireann má bhíodar go léir díbeartha a Luimneach?

Bhí an chuid acu nár ghéill do Bhrian díbeartha, ach an chuid acu do ghéill do agus do gheall bheith dílis do, do fágadh ann iad. Fear eagnaí, tuisceanach, ab ea Brian. Daoine go raibh eólas mór acu ar gach gnó ceannaíochta ab ea na Lochlannaigh a bhí insna cathrachaibh cuan in Éirinn an uair sin. Do thuig Brian gurbh anathairbheach an rud do mhuíntir na hÉireann ceannaithe den tsórd san a bheith insna cathrachaibh a bhí ar na cuantaibh*. Go dtabharfaidís isteach ó dhúthaibh iasachta earraí nárbh fhéidir a dhéanamh in Éirinn agus go gceannóidís ó mhuíntir na hÉireann, le díol insna dúthaibh iasachta, na hearraí a déanfí in Éirinn agus nárbh fhéidir a dhíol in Éirinn. Mar gheall air sin is ea ' fhág sé na Lochlannaigh insna cathrachaibh a bhí ar na cuantaibh. D'fhág sé iad i mBaile Átha Cliath, i bPort Láirge, i gCorcaigh, agus i Luimneach, agus i mbailtibh beaga eile 'na bhféadfadh luingeas teacht isteach chúthu. Chuir sé fé chíos iad, áfach, agus ní raibh aon chur i gcoinnibh an chíosa acu. Ní raibh an cíos ró-throm agus an fhaid a dhíoladar an cíos bhíodar fé chosnamh Bhriain.

Thagadh an cíos isteach ó Éirinn go léir, gach aon Lá Samhna, go teaghlach Bhriain i gCeann Cora. Dob uathásach an saibhreas é. Ach do caití é go léir. Bhíodh suas le trí mhíle bó ann de bhuaibh ramhra, agus trí chéad déag muc, agus do hití an fheóil sin go léir, bhí an teaghlach chómh mór san, agus bhíodh oiread san daoine, uasal agus íseal, ag teacht agus ag imeacht ann coitianta. Bhíodh trí chéad agus chúig cínn fhichead* ann de phíopaí fíona, d'fhíon dearg, agus trí caogaid píopa de sna fíontaibh eile, agus d'óltí* an fíon go léir, mar bhí féile agus fairsinge i rí-theaghlach Bhriain, agus saibhreas agus uaisleacht, thar gach teaghlach Árdrí dá raibh in Éirinn ó aimsir Chormaic mhic Airt. Deirtí an uair sin go raibh Brian ar dhuine de sna trí hÁrdríthibh* ba ghlórmhaire dá raibh in Éirinn riamh. Conaire Mór mac Eidirsceóil* an chéad Árdrí dhíobh san, Cormac mac Airt an tarna hÁrdrí dhíobh, agus Brian Bóraimhe an tríú hÁrdrí dhíobh. Chimeád Brian an mhórgacht san agus an gradam san agus an chómhacht ríoga san 'na lán-neart agus 'na lán-tsoílse an fhaid a mhair a réim in Árdríocht na hÉireann.

Bhí sé ríoga 'na phearsain. Fear fionn árd dea-chúmtha dob ea é; fear géagach fuinniúil cuthaigh. Bhí a cheannatha solasmhar. Bhí éadan leathan árd bán air. Bhí srón fhada dhíreach air agus í beagáinín ró-théagartha, ba dhó' leat, don chuid eile dá cheannathaibh. Ní raibh puínn féasóige air agus féasóg dhonn ab ea an méid a bhí air sarar liath sí. An rud adéarfá leis an sróin, déarfá le gach ball eile dá cheannathaibh é nuair ' fhéachfá ar gach ball fé leith dhíobh, .i. go raibh an ball san beagáinín ró-mhór; ach nuair ' fhéachfá ar a aghaidh in éineacht, chífá go raibh na ceannatha go léir de réir a chéile cruínn. Is é rud is mó a thabharfá fé ndeara, áfach, ná go raibh, dar leat, an iomad báine 'na chúntanós. Ansan, nuair ' fhéachfá ar a phearsain ba dhó' leat, ar an gcéad amharc, go raibh na géaga pas beag ró-mhór, ró-théagartha, don chabhail, ach nuair a thómhaisfá an cliabh, chífá go raibh an cliabh san ní ba théagartha go mór ná cliabh aon fhir eile de sna fearaibh a bhí ar a theaghlach. Ansan ar ball, ní ró-mhór an iúnadh a bheadh ort nuair a chífá a chlaíomh aige á chasadh i dtreó gur dhó' leat ná beadh meáchaint slaite ann, agus nuair a bhéarfá id láimh féin ar an gclaíomh gcéanna go gcaithfá do dhá láimh a chur ar an ndornchar chun é ' chasadh in aon chor. Thuigfá i t'aigne ansan gurbh é téagar agus neart na ngéag fé ndeara don chabhail féachaint chómh caol.

Bhí an croí agus an aigne agus an mheabhair chínn, agus an tuiscint, agus an fhoighne, agus an fhaidearaí, agus an ghéire íntleachta, chómh maith ar gach aon tsaghas cuma le neart an chuirp agus na ngéag.

Nuair a bhíodh an fear san ag riar na sló agus dhá gcur in íonaibh catha agus nuair a labhradh sé leis na fearaibh, do hairítí an uile fhocal uaidh go hárd agus go glan, ó cheann ceann de pháirc an chamtha; agus i spéirling catha, dá labhradh sé árd, ag stiúrú na bhfear nú dhá ngríosadh chun an chómhraic, do mhothaíodh na fir a bhíodh in' aice píoparnach 'na gcluasaibh, bhí a leithéid sin d'uchtach aige agus a leithéid sin de neart 'na chliabh agus 'na cheann agus 'na ghuth. Nuair a labhradh an guth san i lár an chatha, do chritheadh an namhaid, agus is minic a bhaineadh fuaim an ghutha san a misneach díobh agus go n-iompaídís agus go dteithidís. Níorbh aon iúnadh an fear san do ghabháil trí shlóitibh namhad mar a ghoibh, agus é ' theacht chun Árdríocht na hÉireann mar a tháinig.

Bhí ana-dheallramh ag á mhac, Murchadh, leis. Bhí an téagar céanna ag Murchadh insna géagaibh, agus an fhéachaint chaol sa chabhail aige mar gheall ar théagar na ngéag. Bhí sé in aigne Dhúlainn Óig agus in aigne na bhfear eile 'na raibh aithne acu ar an mbeirt, gur thruime agus gur threise agus gurbh fheárr d'fhear Murchadh ná a athair an lá ab fheárr a bhí an t-athair.

Bhí an bheirt tréan go maith. Bhí fir thréana ar Dhál gCais, agus d'admhaíodar go léir ná raibh aon bhreith riamh ag aon fhear eile acu ar éinne den bheirt sin.

Caibideal 23: Mearathall Aigne

Nuair a bhí Brian socair san Árdríocht, do thosnaigh breis de sna huaislibh ar bheith ag teacht go Ceann Cora as gach áird i gcian agus i gcóngar. Níorbh fhada go mb'éigean tuilleadh slí ' dhéanamh sa rí-theaghlach. B'éigean an rí-theaghlach do chur i méid. B'éigean tithe nua do chur suas, in aice an tí mhóir, i dtreó, nuair a thiocfadh rí cúige nú priúnsa nú fear léinn, go bhféadfí é ' chur chun cónaithe ar a shuaimhneas, pé fada gairid ba mhaith leis fanúint.

Chuir an obair sin tuilleadh gnótha ar Mheargach agus ar na ceárdaithibh a bhí ag obair aige. Dá éaghmais sin, chómh luath agus ' bhí Brian in' Árdrí ar Éirinn bhí na ríthe eile, ríthe na gcúigí, ag cur fios go Ceann Cora ar gach aon tsaghas airm. Ní raibh aon mheas ar chlaíomh ná ar shleagh ná ar thuaigh mura bhféadfí a rá gur i gCeann Cora, i gceártain Mheargaigh, a deineadh iad. Do chuir san, leis, tuilleadh gnótha ar Mheargach. B'éigean do tuilleadh gaibhní agus tuilleadh de gach aon tsaghas ceárdaithe do chur ag obair. Bhí cúram mór air, ach bhí ní ar a aigne ba mheasa dho chuige ná an cúram, dá mhéid é. Bhí ' fhios aige go raibh an chailís dhaor úd guidithe as an mainistir agus gurbh é féin fé ndeár é. Bhí ' fhios aige gur dhein sé beart shímplí nuair a thug sé an mhacshamhail úd na heochrach isteach i láimh éinne le breith síos ag triall ar Cholla. Bhí ' fhios aige go raibh sé ceart aige féin dul síos agus í ' thabhairt isteach i láimh Cholla féin. Dá ndeineadh sé mar sin, thiocfadh an fhírinne amach láithreach, agus ní guidfí an chailís.

Bhí sé ag machnamh ar an méid sin ón lá a bhí an Leagáid ag cainnt leis agus dá mhéid machnamh a dhein sé ar an scéal is ea is mó a bhí an scéal ag breith ghreama ar a chroí. Bhí an scéal á chur amú ar a ghnó agus ag baint codladh na hoíche dhe. Níorbh fhéidir do labhairt le héinne 'na thaobh, ná cómhairle ' dh'iarraidh ar aon duine den mhuíntir a bhí 'na thímpall, ná ar aon duine de theaghlach Bhriain, le heagla gur tuilleadh díobhála a dhéanfadh sé. Fé dheireadh shocraigh sé ar dhul síos agus ar labhairt le Colla féin. Chuaigh sé síos agus do labhair sé le Colla.

"Féach, a Athair", ar seisean, "tá mo chroí briste ó bheith ag machnamh ar an gcuma úd 'nar deineadh amadán díom i dtaobh na heochrach agus i dtaobh na cailíse. Ní fhéadfainn fanúint a thuilleadh gan teacht chun cainnte le t'onóir. Ní foláir rud éigin a dhéanamh chun teacht suas leis an mbithiúnach, pé hé féin. Brisfidh mo shláinte nú imeód as mo mheabhair mura ndeintear rud éigin".

"Tá m'aigne féin chómh suaite le t'aigne-se mar gheall air, a dhuin' uasail", arsa Colla, "agus dá mbeinn ag machnamh go ceann bliana air, ní dó' liom go bhféadfainn cuímhneamh ar cad is ceart a dhéanamh. Dá dtagadh an tÁrdrí chúm anso agus go ndéarfadh sé gur mhaith leis an chailís a dh'fheiscint, cad a bheadh agam le rá leis?

Caibideal 23: Mearathall Aigne

B'fhéidir go ndéarfadh sé in' aigne féin go bhfuil an chailís sin ró-dhaor chun í ' fhágáilt anso. Níorbh aon iúnadh liom go ndéarfadh. B'fhéidir go dtuigfeadh sé in' aigne gur cheart cailís chómh luachmhar a thabhairt do phríomh-eaglais na hÉireann. Gur mhaith an tseóid í d'Árdrí Éireann le bronnadh ar phríomh-eaglais Éireann, ar eaglais Árd Mhacha*. Is ar eaglais Árd Mhacha ba cheart í ' bhronnadh. Sin é adéarfadh éinne a chífeadh í. Táim mar a bheinn in uisce bheirithe ó fuair Brian an Árdríocht agus ná feadar cad é an neómat a bheadh sé chúm isteach dhá rá gur mhaith leis an chailís sin a dh'fheiscint. Is trua chráite nár chimeád sé í an chéad lá agus gan í ' thabhairt in aon chor dúinn!"

"Cad 'déarfá, a Athair", arsa Meargach, "dá dtéinn agus an scéal a dh'ínsint do Mhurchadh ó thosach go deireadh?"

"Caithfar an scéal a dh'ínsint gan a thuilleadh ríghnis, do féin nú do Bhrian", arsa Colla. "D'ínseas féin an scéal don Leagáid, mar is eól duit. Dá n-iarrtí an chailís orm an fhaid a bhí an Leagáid anso, do neósfadh an Leagáid don Árdrí cad a bhí imithe uirthi. Bheadh an Leagáid idir me agus an tÁrdrí agam. Anois tá an Leagáid imithe agus tá scannradh orm le heagla go n-iarrfí an chailís orm. Má deir Brian, 'Cad 'na thaobh nár ínsis dúinn láithreach go raibh sí imithe?', cad a bheidh le rá agam? Déarfar gur breá a thugas uain don bhithiúnach ar imeacht slán agus an chailís a bhreith leis agus do chur ó aon fháil a bheith ar í ' thabhairt thar n-ais".

"B'fhéidir, a Athair", arsa Meargach, "go mbeadh sé chómh maith againn dul chun cainnte le Murchadh agus an scéal a dh'ínsint do ó thosach go deireadh. Mise fé ndeár an t-olc go léir. Ní raibh aon cheart agam gan teacht anso chun cainnte leat-sa sarar thugas uaim an eochair! Ní fheadar 'en tsaol cad d'imigh orm agus a leithéid de ghnó leanbaí ' dhéanamh. Nuair a chonac an aibíd agus an cochall, do baineadh dem chosaint me glan".

Caibideal 23: Mearathall Aigne

"Is uathásach an scéal é", arsa Colla. "Ní fheadar 'en tsaol cá dtáinig an aibíd. Thispeáin an Leagáid na manaigh go léir duit agus duairt sé go ndúraís nárbh éinne acu a bhí ann".

"Duart", arsa Meargach, "agus dob fhíor dhom é. Ní héinne acu a bhí ann".

"Ní miste dhom a dh'ínsint duit", arsa Colla, "go raibh sórd droch-amhrais ag an Leagáid ar an sagart óg so againn, ar an Athair Art mac Duibh, ach duart-sa leis dá mba dho san a thabharfá-sa macshamhail na heochrach go n-aithneófá é".

"D'aithneóinn, a Athair", arsa Meargach. "Tá a lán de sna manaigh atá anso agus d'aithneóinn iad, leis. An manach gur thugas an eochair do, ní fheaca roimis sin é ná ó shin".

"Ní baol go bhfeacaís ó shin é", arsa Colla, "agus ní dócha gur baol go bhfeicfir arís é má fhéadann sé cimeád as do radharc. Is dó' liom dá luathacht a bheidh an scéal go léir ínste do Mhurchadh againn gurb ea is feárr é".

D'imigh an bheirt suas go Luimneach agus as san go Ceann Cora. Fuaradar caoi ar chainnt a dhéanamh le Murchadh agus d'ínseadar do gach ní fé mar a thit amach, i dtaobh na cailíse. Cheistigh sé iad go dlúth, díreach mar a cheistigh an Leagáid Colla. Dá fheabhas a cheistigh sé iad, áfach, is ea ba mhó a chuaigh an scéal in aimhréidh air agus is ea ba dheocra dho aon tuairim a thabhairt do cérbh é an bithiúnach. Duairt sé leó gurbh fheárr gan an scéal do leogaint amach.

"Is é mo thuairim láidir", ar seisean, "pé hé an bithiúnach, ná fuil sé ró-fhada uainn an neómat so, agus go bhfuil sé ag faire go dlúth orainn, féachaint cad a dhéanfaimíd. Ní haon duine iasachta é. Thispeáin sé an iomad eólais. Bhí ' fhios aige cá raibh an chailís i gcimeád, agus bhí ' fhios aige cá raibh an eochair, agus bhí ' fhios aige cérbh é an gabha a dhein an eochair. Is iúntach an bob a bhuail sé ort, a Mheargaigh!", ar seisean, ag cur sceartadh gáire as. "Má airím-se aon fhocal ó m'athair", ar seisean, "dhá rá gur mhaith leis an chailís a dh'fheiscint, nú gur mhaith leis í ' chur go hÁrd Mhacha, cuirfidh mé dhe é. Ní mór dhúinn go léir bheith ag faire coitianta, féachaint an bhfaighimís aon phioc de radharc ná de bhalaithe an bhithiúnaigh".

Chuir an méid sin aigne na beirte chun suaimhnis mórán. Tháinig Meargach go Luimneach chun a ghnótha, agus tháinig Colla abhaile chun na mainistreach.

Nuair ' fhágadar Murchadh, do chrom seisean ar mhachnamh. Thuig sé áilleacht na cailíse agus a daoire. Bhí ' fhios aige, pérbh é an bithiúnach, go ndéanfadh an chailís sin fear saibhir de i gcaitheamh a shaeil, dá bhféadadh sé í ' dhíol, agus go ndéanfadh sí daoine saibhre dá shliocht ar feadh seacht nglún. Bhí ' fhios aige nárbh fhéidir í ' dhíol in Éirinn. Dá gceannaítí í in aon mhainistir ná in aon eaglais in Éirinn go n-aireófí teacht tháirsi go luath, ó bhéal go béal, i measc ríthe agus daoine, ar fuid na hÉireann go léir. Bhí ' fhios aige, dá bhrí sin, nárbh fhéidir í ' dhíol gan í ' chur amach a hÉirinn. Trí cheannaí éigin Lochlannach a caithfí san do dhéanamh. Bhí gach aon bhaol, dar leis, go raibh san déanta cheana. Bhí an iomad aimsire fálta ag an mbithiúnach, agus de réir an bhuib a bhuail sé ar Mheargach, níor bhithiúnach é do thabharfadh aon fhaillí san aimsir a tugadh do. Má bhí an chailís imithe thar farraige, ní raibh ann ach fiantas, dar leis, bheith ag cuímhneamh ar theacht suas léi go deó. "Ach níl agam le déanamh ach bheith ag faire chúm", ar seisean in' aigne féin.

"Ní chuirfinn thar mo leas-mháthair é!", ar seisean, a machnamh eile! "Is aici a bhí an chailís i gcimeád sarar cuireadh síos í go hInis Cathaigh. Agus is cuímhin liom go maith nách le haon dea-thoil a scar sí leis an seóid uasail. Ach cérbh é an manach? Agus cá bhfuair sé an aibíd agus an cochall má ba mhanach bréige é? Conas a fuair sé amach gurbh é Meargach a dhein an eochair? Ní dócha go gcuirfeadh sí féin aibíd agus cochall uímpi—ach cad é sin agam á rá! D'aithneódh an gabha í láithreach. Más í a dhein an gníomh, agus go deimhin, a ríogan, ní chuirfinn-se thort é, bhí duine éigin aici chun na hoibre ' dhéanamh di. Cérbh é an duine sin? Ní fheadar 'en tsaol. Níl agam ach bheith ag faire chúm. Ach caithfar féachaint id dhiaidh go géar, a ríogan, i nithibh eile leis. Ní gan chúis a thug an Leagáid an foláramh deirineach so dhom agus é ag imeacht, tar éis an fholáraimh chéanna a thabhairt dom tamall roimis sin. Ó, ambasa ní dhéanfaidh sé an gnó dhom aon mhíogarnach a theacht orm".

Caibideal 24: "Lady, Dost Thou Not Fear to Stray?"

*Cuid den chéad ghnó a dhein Brian, chómh luath agus ' bhí sé socair daingean san Árdríocht, ab ea na heaglaisí a bhí loitithe i ndiaidh na Lochlannach do dheisiú agus do shlánú agus do chur i dtreó arís. Chuir sé suas an eaglais mhór i gCíll Dálua; agus an eaglais in Inis Cathaigh; agus dhein sé athnóchaint ar an eaglais i dTuaim Gréine. Dhein sé bóithre móra ó thaobh taobh agus ó cheann ceann d'oileán na hÉireann, agus dhein sé droichid bhreátha leathana láidre insna háiteannaibh 'na dtéadh na bóithre sin treasna aibhní, i dtreó gur dhein sé tairbhe ana-mhór don phoiblíocht, mar gur chuir sé ar chumas daoine dul ar chuardaibh fada gan an iomad trioblóide. Bhí áthas mór ar an bpoiblíocht mar gheall ar na hoibreachaibh sin.

Dhein sé dúna agus daingeana láidre, leis, 'na lán áiteanna, agus chuir sé buíona maithe láidre fear isteach insna dúnaibh sin agus insna daingeanaibh sin, mar lucht cimeádta, i dtreó go mbeidís ann i gcónaí chun na tíre do chosaint agus chun smacht an Árdrí do chur i bhfeidhm ar aon duine, nú ar aon aicme daoine, do mheasfadh an smacht san do mhilleadh. Do neartaigh sé ar an gcuma san rí-theaghlach Chaisil, agus rí-theaghlach Cheann Fheabhrad, agus an rí-theaghlach in Inis Locha Cé, agus an rí-theaghlach in Inis Locha Guir, agus an rí-theaghlach i nDún gCrot, agus mórán eile de dhúnaibh agus de rí-theaghlachaibh ar fuid na hÉireann, agus chuir sé na buíona fear isteach iontu chun iad a chimeád agus do chosaint.

Caibideal 24: "Lady, Dost Thou Not Fear to Stray?"

Do neartaigh san a chómhacht féin go mór ar fuid na hÉireann go léir, i dteannta scáth agus eagla do chur ar a namhaid, amu' agus i mbaile.

Chuir sé lucht léinn agus eólais ag scrúdadh agus ag breithniú na seanndlithe agus dhá dtabhairt chun solais, an chuid acu a bhí imithe a cuímhne; agus fé mar a chonaic sé gá leó, chuir sé i bhfeidhm arís aon chuid acu a bhí imithe a feidhm le faillí nú de thoradh aimsire. Níor ró-dheocair do san a dhéanamh. Bhí a leithéid d'urraim i gcónaí riamh ag an nGael do dhlí na ríochta nár ghá a dhéanamh ach a chur in úil do go raibh an dlí ann chun a chur ' fhiachaibh air an dlí do chómhlíonadh. Bíonn iúnadh anois ar scoláirthíbh nuair a chíd siad ná raibh aicme áirithe, ceapaithe chun na dlí ' chur i bhfeidhm, in Éirinn fadó. Is dó' leó, agus is fíor dhóibh é, gurbh obair bhaoth dlí ' dhéanamh do sna daoine atá ar an saol anois, ná bheith ag brath air go ndéanfaidís an dlí sin do chómhlíonadh, mura gceapfí aicme láidir chun a chur ' fhiachaibh orthu an dlí ' chómhlíonadh. Ní thuigid siad conas a féadadh dlithe ' dhéanamh in Éirinn fadó agus ansan a dh'fhágáilt fé sna daoine féin na dlithe do chómhlíonadh. Do féadtí san do dhéanamh mar, chómh luath agus ' thuigeadh an phoiblíocht an dlí ' bheith ann, do chuireadh toil phoiblí na ndaoine ' fhiachaibh ar gach duine fé leith an dlí do chómhlíonadh. B'fheárr le gach duine fé leith go mór an dlí do chómhlíonadh ná fulag leis an ndroch-mheas phoiblí a bheadh air dá bhfeiceadh na daoine é ag tabhairt droch-mheas* nú tarcaisne don dlí. Tá solaoidí maithe againn ar fheidhm den tsórd san san aimsir seo féin. Má théann nós áirithe i bhfeidhm ar an bpoiblíocht anois féin, féach ca bhfuil an duine fé leith go mbeidh sé de mhisneach aige an nós san do bhriseadh! Aigne phoiblí na ndaoine is í ' chuireadh dlithe i bhfeidhm in Éirinn fadó, agus is feárr a chuireadh sí i bhfeidhm iad, agus is iomláine, ná mar a thagann le neart armála dlithe ' chur i bhfeidhm anois.

Ná measadh éinne, áfach, ná bristí dlithe in Éirinn fadó. Do bristí go deimhin. Ach nuair a thagadh an té ar a ndeintí an éagóir, os cómhair an bhreithimh, agus nuair a thugadh an breitheamh a bhreith, do glactí an bhreith ar gach taobh agus do deintí dá réir. Bhí sé daingean in aigne na ndaoine, éinne ná tispeánfadh an urraim sin don dlí ná beadh an rath air. Níor ró-dheocair dlithe fónta do chur i bhfeidhm i measc daoine den tsórd san.

Dhein Brian ní eile do chabhraigh go mór leis chun na ndlithe do chur i bhfeidhm. Ón lá a ghlac sé arm gaisce, agus gan é ach chúig bhliana déag, do thispeáin sé, 'na ghníomharthaibh agus 'na bhéasaibh agus ins gach aon tsaghas deighleála idir é féin agus daoine eile, go raibh beann thar bárr aige ar an gceart, ná déanfadh sé éagóir ar aon Chríostaí, peocu caraid* nú namhaid é, peocu íseal nú uasal é. Do tugadh an méid sin fé ndeara. Ansan, fé mar a leath cómhacht Bhriain agus fé mar a mhéadaigh a chreidiúint, do dhein daoine eile, uasal agus íseal, aithris air. Ar ball bhí acu go léir, nú dúradar go léir go raibh acu, beann thar bárr ar an gceart, fé mar a bhí ag Brian. Do glacadh an ceart 'na nós acu. Ansan bhí neart an nóis ag cur le neart an chirt. Bhí neart eile ag cur leis an dá neart san. B'é neart é sin ná neart an Chreidimh.

Ná bíodh aon iúnadh ar éinne gan aon ghá a bheith le neart armála chun dlithe ' chur i bhfeidhm nuair a bhí na trí nirt sin, neart cirt, agus neart nóis, agus neart Creidimh, ag oibriú as acfuinn a chéile chun dlithe ' chur i bhfeidhm.

Tugaimís fé ndeara cad a thit amach do Bhrian in aon phúnc amháin den cheart agus den bheann a bhí aige ar an gceart. Chonaic gach éinne go raibh aon bheart amháin éagóra ná ceadódh Brian ar aon tsaghas cleas ná réasún. B'í beart éagóra í sin ná masla ' thabhairt do mhnaoi. Chonaic na fir go léir, íseal agus uasal, go raibh gráin gan teóra ag Brian ar ghníomharthaibh den tsórd san. Mar gheall ar an urraim a bhí acu do Bhrian, do dhein na fir go léir, uasal agus íseal, aithris air sa ní sin, leis. Má b'uasal an rud do Bhrian an ghráin sin a bheith aige ar ghníomharthaibh den tsórd san, dob uasal an rud é, dar leó, d'aon fhear. As san duairt gach fear go raibh gráin aige féin ar ghníomharthaibh den tsórd san. As san do thug gach fear mar bhéas do féin bheith ag maíomh as nár thug sé riamh "masla ná tarcaisne do mhnaoi". Do lean an aithris ar Bhrian, agus do lean an chainnt, agus do lean an maíomh. As san do neartaigh an nós agus do tugadh fé ndeara, ar fuid na hÉireann, ná deineadh fir Bhriain gníomhartha den tsórd san. Fé mar a leath cómhacht Bhriain, do leath na nósa a bhí ag fearaibh Bhriain. Ar ball do tugadh fé ndeara ná deintí na gníomhartha gráinniúla úd in aon bhall in Éirinn.

Ansan, nuair a thagadh Niamh agus a hathair go Ceann Cora, agus nuair a chíodh na ríthe óga Niamh, do chuímhnídís ar an uaisleacht agus ar an nósmhaireacht a bhí tagaithe ar Ghaelaibh Éireann go léir agus deiridís eatarthu féin: "Níor mhiste dhi slat ríoga do thógaint 'na láimh, agus fáinne óir i mbarra na slaite, agus siúl 'na haonar ó Thonn Chlíona go Dún Sobhairce, agus ní baol go ndéanfadh aon fhear Gaelach, uasal ná íseal, oiread agus focal neamh-urramach do labhairt léi".

Dúradh an chainnt sin, nú cainnt den tsórd, chómh minic sin, agus do tuigeadh chómh maith san fírinne na cainnte, gur measadh, 'na dhiaidh san, nuair a bhí Brian agus Niamh agus an chuid eile acu san iúir, nár chainnt a bhí sa scéal ach gur dhein óig-bhean uasal éigin an siúl san, 'na haonar, ó Dhún Sobhairce go Tonn Chlíona, agus an tslat 'na láimh aici agus an fáinne óir ar an slait, agus ná fuair sí ar an slí ach an urraim agus an onóir ba mhó a dh'fhéadfí a thabhairt di. Do lean an scéal ar an gcuma san i seanchas na hÉireann go dtí go dtáinig an file Gallda, Ó Mórdha*, agus gur chúm sé an dán úd:

> "Lady, dost thou not fear to stray, &c".

Is fiú an scéal san machnamh a dhéanamh air. Is mó rí agus ímpire 'na bhfuil cúntas orthu i seanchas an domhain agus 'na bhfuil moladh mór ar a ngníomharthaibh agus ar a ngradam, ar an gcuma 'nar chuireadar tíortha fada fairseaga fé smacht a lámh, agus ar an gcuma 'nar chuireadar, má ba ríthe fónta iad, dlithe tairbheacha i bhfeidhm. Ní dó' liom, áfach, go bhfeaca riamh fós dá thabhairt, ar obair ná ar shaothar aon rí ná aon ímpire acu, moladh de shaghas an mholta so a thugann an scéal seanchais seo ar Bhrian. Ní nósmhaireacht, ná macántacht, ná gníomhartha onóracha, ná urraim do bhanntracht, is gnáth ag leanúint sló agus cogaidh agus armála agus cathanna fuilteacha. Neamh-shuím insna nithibh sin is ea is gnáth á leanúint riamh. Neamh-shuím i ngach dea-nós, neamh-shuím i gceart an fhir thall, neamh-shuím san urraim is dual do mhnáibh; an beithíoch allta dhá thispeáint féin sa duine; gabháil de chosaibh ins gach dualgas dá mbaineann le dlí, le dea-nós, le Creideamh; sin iad na nithe is gnáth ag leanúint cogaidh agus cómhraic agus cathanna fuilteacha.

Ní raibh Brian riamh, ó tháinig sé in aois a chúig mblian ndéag, ach sáite i gcogaíbh. Bhí a ghaolta go léir chómh sáite insna cogaíbh agus ' bhí sé féin. In ainneóin na gcogaí go léir, do thuíll Brian agus a shlóite an moladh atá sa scéal úd i dtaobh na mná óige agus i dtaobh na honóra a fuair sí ar feadh na slí go léir ó Dhún Sobhairce go Tonn Chlíona. Tá bua ag Brian sa méid sin ar chómhachtaibh agus ar ríthibh agus ar ímpiríbh an domhain riamh.

Táimíd anois ag dul sa deichiú céad blian ó fuair Brian agus a shlóite an bua san. Do chimeád ár sínsear cuímhne air. Thugadar dúinn-na an cuímhne sin le cimeád. Is ceart dúinn greim daingean a chimeád air. Caitear go minic insna súilibh orainn ná fuil aon ní ag baint lenár sínsear gur féidir dúinn aon mhaíomh ró-mhór a dhéanamh as. Tá againn, i scéal na mná óige sin, cúis mhaíte agus abhar creidiúna ná fuil a leithéid le fáil i seanchas aon tíre eile fé luí na gréine inniu. Tá ceangailte orainn, ní hamháin cuímhne ' chimeád ar an abhar creidiúna san, ach fós beart a dhéanamh dá réir.

Caibideal 25: Uisce-fé-Thalamh

Bhíodh Murchadh go minic i bhfad ó Cheann Cora ag féachaint i ndiaidh gnóthaí na hÁrdríochta fé chómhairle a athar. Nuair a bhíodh sé imithe ó Cheann Cora, bhíodh scannradh air le heagla go ndéanfí aon droch-ghníomh i ganfhios do. Bhí an fear friothála ceapaithe aige chun friothála ar an Árdrí, mar ba cheart agus mar ba ghnáth de réir nósa na haimsire sin. Ach ca bhfios do, dar leis, ná go nglacfadh an fear friothála breab dá ndeintí breab mhaith a thairiscint do. Thuig sé in' aigne gur i gcoinnibh mná a bhí ar an bhfear an cluiche ' dh'imirt, i gcoinnibh na mná ba bhreátha agus ba mheasa agus ba ghéire dá raibh in Éirinn an uair sin. Ca bhfios do, dar leis, cad iad na cleasa ' dh'imreódh sí ar an bhfear dá mba rud é go dtuigfeadh sí nárbh fhéidir é ' bhreabadh. Chonaic an Leagáid a diabhal coímhdeachta. Ca bhfios cad é an cúnamh a thabharfadh an diabhal coímhdeachta san di in aon droch-ghnó a bheartódh sí a dhéanamh.

"Ní haon mhaith", ar seisean in' aigne féin, "bheith ag brath air go bhféadfadh fear friothála bheith maith a dhóthain di féin agus dá diabhal coímhdeachta. Caithfidh mé bean a chur ag tabhairt aire dhi".

Ní fhéadfadh sé cuímhneamh ar aon mhnaoi chun na hoibre sin ach ar Niamh. Bhí ' fhios aige dá mbeadh Niamh in aice an Árdrí, agus ' fhios a bheith aici cad chuige go raibh sí ann, nár bhaol go bhféadfadh Gormfhlaith aon droch-ní ' dhéanamh i ganfhios di. D'imigh sé féin siar go hUíbh Máine. Do labhair sé le Niamh. D'inis sé dhi ó thosach go deireadh an scéal go léir.

"Ní fhéadfainn-se dul go Ceann Cora agus fanúint ann, a rí", arsa Niamh. "Ní fhéadfainn imeacht ó m'athair féin".

"Níl t'athair-se in aon chúntúirt, a ríogan", arsa Murchadh. "Ní mar sin do m'athair-se. Tá sé i gcúntúirt mhór. Dá bhféadainn féin fanúint sa bhaile, ní dó' liom go mbeadh aon bhaol air. Tá an iomad eagla aici rómham-sa. Nuair a bhím as baile, bíonn gach aon ní ar a toil aici, agus ní bhíonn aon eagla aici roim éinne. Níl aon phioc dá fhios age m'athair go bhfuil aon chúntúirt os a chionn. Dá neósfí dho é, ní fhéadfaimís é ' chosaint. Do leogfadh sé amach an scéal, mar ní chreidfeadh sé focal de. Tá ' fhios aige nách bean ró-mhaith í, ach ní chreidfeadh sé in aon chor go ndéanfadh sí aon iarracht ar é ' chur chun báis. Dá n-abradh éinne leis go ndéanfadh, is amhlaidh a thiocfadh fearg air. Déarfadh sé gur le corp droch-aigne adéarfadh éinne a leithéid. Thuigfeadh sé, dá mba ná beadh aon chúis eile aici le gan an gníomh san a dhéanamh, go seachnódh sí é ar mhaithe léi féin. Go gcuirfeadh bás an Árdrí í féin as an Árdríoganacht. Dá éaghmais sin, bean ró-ábalta is ea í. Tá curtha 'na luí aici ar aigne m'athar ná fuil aon ní is feárr léi ná é ' mhaireachtaint i bhfad, mar dá fhaid a mhairfidh sé gurb ea is sia a bhead-sa gan teacht san Árdríocht. Caithfar an t-aireachas a dhéanamh ar m'athair i ganfhios do, a Niamh".

"Ní fheadar, a rí", arsa Niamh, "an bhfuil aon bhaol go mbeadh dearúd ort-sa féin sa scéal?"

"Cad é an dearúd a dh'fhéadfadh a bheith orm, a ríogan?", ar seisean.

"Ba dhó' liom", ar sise, "go bhfuil gach aon deallramh ar an gcainnt sin adúraís i dtaobh an ruda atá curtha 'na luí aici, mar adeirir, ar aigne t'athar. Dá fhaid a mhairfidh t'athair is ea is sia a bheidh Gormfhlaith 'na hÁrdríogain agus is ea is sia a bheir-se gan teacht san Árdríocht. Má chuireann sí féin chun báis é, cuirfidh sí í féin as an Árdríoganacht láithreach, agus déanfaidh sí Árdrí dhíot-sa. Tá ' fhios aici go maith nách baol go nglacfaid fir Éireann éinne eile in' Árdrí. B'fheárr léi í féin do bhá ná thusa ' dh'fheiscint san Árdríocht. Sin dá dhíobháil mhóra aici á dhéanamh di féin leis an ngníomh. Ca bhfuil an tairbhe, a rí?"

"Tá sé chómh maith agam an scéal go léir a dh'ínsint duit, a Niamh", arsa Murchadh, "ach is fé rún atáim á ínsint duit. Tá níos mó go mór d'fhios a gnótha agam-sa ná mar is dó' léi. Tá, mar is eól duit, a mac 'na rí ar Lochlannaigh Bhaile Átha Cliath. Tá uisce-fé-thalamh aici á dhéanamh le fada riamh a d'iarraidh go bhfaigheadh na Lochlannaigh bua agus go mbeadh a mac féin in' Árdrí ar Éirinn. Éire ag Lochlannaigh agus Sitric in' Árdrí. Sin é atá uaithi. Ní fheadair éinne beó cad é an t-uisce-fé-thalamh a dhein sí chuige sin i gcaitheamh na haimsire roim chath Ghleanna Mháma. B'in é fé ndeár na

Lochlannaigh a bheith chómh líonmhar sa chath san agus an cath a bheith chómh dian, chómh fuilteach. Bhí sí deimhnitheach go mbeadh bua an chatha san ag Lochlannachaibh agus ná tiocfadh Brian ná éinne eile againn beó ón gcath. Tá an t-uisce-fé-thalamh céanna ar siúl anois arís aici. Is dó' léi ná fuil ' fhios agam-sa é*. Tá níos mó go mór d'fhios a gnótha agam ná mar is dó' léi. Tá rí Lochlann ag gléasadh armála agus ag déanamh luingeas agus á gcur ar uisce. Tá muíntir na hIorua dhá ngléasadh féin chun cogaidh, ach ní hínstear cad é an cogadh é ná cad chuige an gléasadh. Tá ollmhúchán ar siúl ar oileán Mhanann agus in oileánaibh Alban agus thuaidh in Ínsibh Orc. Ní deir éinne focal i dtaobh cad é an bun atá leis an obair go léir agus leis an ollmhúchán go léir. Tá ' fhios agam-sa go maith cad é an bun atá leis an ollmhúchán. Tá Gormfhlaith agus a mac, rí Lochlannach Átha Cliath, ag déanamh a ndíchill ar gach aon tsaghas cuma chun bheith ollamh ar chath uathásach eile do bhualadh ar son Árdríochta na hÉireann chómh luath agus ' gheóbhaid siad an chaoi cheart air. Dá bhfaigheadh m'athair bás díreach nuair a bheadh an t-ollmhúchán críochnaithe acu, do thiocfadh san agus a dtoil isteach lena chéile go hálainn".

"Tuigim thu, a rí", arsa Niamh. "Agus dá mba ná beadh aon fhonn ar t'athair bás d'fháil an uair ba mhaith leó é ' dh'fháil bháis*, is é do mheas go dtabharfadh Gormfhlaith cúnamh do chun báis a dh'fháil".

"Táim deimhnitheach de, a ríogan", arsa Murchadh. "Dá mbeadh a gcuid ollmhúcháin curtha chun cínn acu agus iad ollamh, agus ansan go bhfaigheadh m'athair bás obann, bheadh gnó na hÉireann 'na phraisigh, dar leó. Bheadh sé 'na chogadh dhearg idir mise agus M'leachlainn, féachaint cé ' bheadh in' Árdrí. B'fhéidir go mbeadh sé 'na chath trír, go ndéanfadh Ó Néill thuaidh iarracht ar an Árdríocht do shealbhú dho féin. Ansan dá bpreabadh neart maith láidir Lochlannach isteach chúinn, níor ró-dheocair dóibh Éire ' chur féna smacht agus Árdrí ' dhéanamh de Shitric".

Caibideal 25: Uisce-fé-Thalamh

"Ambasa, a rí", arsa Niamh, "is breá glan géar an fhéachaint atá aici á dhéanamh roímpi. Cad 'tá agaibh-se á dhéanamh! Ní dócha go bhfuiltí-se* 'núr suí díomhaoin agus iad súd dhá n-ollmhú féin chómh dícheallach".

"Ná bíodh eagal ort, a ríogan", arsa Murchadh. "Níl aon fhaillí againn á dhéanamh. Táimíd ag gléasadh sló ins gach aon chúinne den tír agus ag cur na n-arm is feárr 'na lámhaibh. Tá an t-ollmhúchán againn-na á dhéanamh chómh dian, chómh dícheallach agus atá acu san, nú b'fhéidir níos déine, ach táimíd dhá dhéanamh i ganfhios chómh maith agus ' fhéadaimíd é. Táid na mílte fear againn cheana féin insna dúnaibh agus insna daingeanaibh anso agus ansúd ar fuid na tíre. Níor dhó' le héinne ná beadh sáite 'nár n-obair go bhfuil oiread nirt againn agus atá".

"Ba dhó' liom-sa, a rí", arsa Niamh, "go bhfuil dearúd sa ní sin oraibh. B'fhéidir dá bhfeictí úr neart go n-éireófí as an ollmhúchán thall, mar go dtuigfí nárbh aon mhaith bheith a d'iarraidh bua ' fháil oraibh".

"Ní éireófí*, a ríogan", arsa Murchadh. "Is amhlaidh a déanfí tuilleadh díchill ar an ollmhúchán thall. Tá Gormfhlaith ró-cheapaithe ar an ndroch-obair atá curtha roímpi aici. Dá laige a mheasfaidh sí sinn-na ' bheith is ea is dóichí-de gan an iomad nirt a bheith cruinnithe aici 'nár gcómhair. Tá ' fhios aici go bhfuilimíd ag gléasadh sló ach níl ' fhios aici cad chuige go bhfuilimíd á ngléasadh. Níl ' fhios aici go bhfuil fios a hoibre féin againn mar atá. Is dó' léi gur chun na hÁrdríochta do chimeád ó Mh'leachlainn agus ó Ó Néill an gléasadh sló atá againn á dhéanamh. Dá mbeithá-sa* i gCeann Cora i bhfochair m'athar do thuigfeadh Gormfhlaith gur ag faire uirthi féin a bheithá ann. Ansan ní bheadh aon bhaol go ndéanfadh sí aon droch-ní air. Tá an iomad eagla aici rómhat-sa. Ní fheadar 'en domhan cad a dhéanfad mura bhféadair teacht go Ceann Cora agus fanúint ann".

"Ní fhéadfainn imeacht ó m'athair féin, a rí", arsa Niamh. "Ní haon mhaith dhuit bheith dhá iarraidh orm. Faigh duine éigin eile".

Caibideal 25: Uisce-fé-Thalamh

"Féach, a ríogan", arsa Murchadh, "cad é an bac atá ar t'athair teacht in éineacht leat! Ná déanfadh do dhriotháir aire ' thabhairt don ríocht so Uíbh Máine? Tá sé chómh ceangailte ar Thadhg Mhór Ó Chealla beart a dhéanamh i gcoinnibh namhad Éireann agus 'tá sé orm-sa, agus go deimhin, agus ní gá dhom san do rá le hinín Thaidhg, tá Tadhg Mór Ó Cealla chómh hollamh ar bheart a dhéanamh i gcoinnibh namhad Éireann agus 'tá aon fhear, uasal ná íseal, dá bhfuil beó in Éirinn inniu".

"An bhfuil ' fhios agat cad a dhéanfair, a rí", arsa Niamh. "Labhair le m'athair agus inis gach aon rud do, tríd síos, fé mar atá ínste agat dómh-sa. B'fhéidir ansan go dtuigfeadh sé gur ceart do dul go Ceann Cora agus fanúint ann, agus mise do bhreith leis agus do chimeád in' fhochair ann".

Do dhein Murchadh an ní sin. D'inis sé do Thadhg Mhór Ó Chealla an scéal go léir tríd síos, an t-ollmhúchán a bhí ar siúl thall i gcríochaibh Lochlann agus i gcríochaibh na hIorua agus insna hoileánaibh, agus an t-uisce-fé-thalamh a bhí ag an Árdríogan á dhéanamh chun na hÉireann a thabhairt fé smacht na Lochlannach agus Árdrí a dhéanamh dá mac féin, de Shitric. Thispeáin sé dho gach deimhne dá raibh aige ar an méid sin scéil. D'inis sé dho an dá fholáramh a thug an Leagáid do féin, trí bhéal Cholla. Nuair ' airigh Tadhg an scéal, is beag ná gurb amhlaidh a bhí sé ar buile toisc nár hínseadh fadó dho é. Shocraigh sé láithreach ar theacht go Ceann Cora agus Niamh a thabhairt leis. Do tugadh tigh breá glan uasal solasmhar dóibh, chun cónaithe ann, in aice thí mhóir Bhriain. Do fuaradh, mar ghnó súl le déanamh do Thadhg Mór bheith ag cabhrú leis an Árdrí i ngnóthaibh stáit. Níorbh aon iúnadh, ansan, Niamh do theacht ann. Do thuig gach éinne ná fanfadh sí sa bhaile i ndiaidh a hathar.

Caibideal 26: Púicíní

Cá bhfuair Murchadh an t-eólas a bhí aige ar an ollmhúchán a bhí ar siúl i gcríochaibh Lochlann, agus ar an mbun a bhí leis an ollmhúchán? Fuair sé an t-eólas ar an gcuma so. Bhí a ghiollaí turais féin aige agus bhí Caoilte aige mar cheann orthu. Dar leis an bpoiblíocht, is é gnó Bhriain a bhí orthu a dhéanamh, gnó na ríochta. Ach do thug Murchadh gnó eile, leis, le déanamh do chuid acu go raibh iúntaoibh aige astu. Bhí ' fhios aige go maith ná féadfadh Gormfhlaith a suaimhneas a cheapadh. Go gcaillfeadh sí an t-anam nú go mbeadh droch-obair éigin 'dir lámhaibh aici. Bhí ' fhios aige nárbh aon mhaith bheith a d'iarraidh cosc a chur léi. Dá gcurtí cosc léi in aon droch-obair amháin ná déanfadh sí ach aghaidh a thabhairt ar dhroch-obair eile agus é ' cheilt ní b'fheárr. Gurbh fheárr scaoileadh léi agus eólas cruínn a dh'fháil, i ganfhios di, ar gach aon tsaghas droch-oibre a bheadh ar siúl aici. Thug Murchadh an gnó san le déanamh do Chaoilte, d' "Fhear na gCos", a nduairt Conn. Níor mhiste an gnó ' thabhairt le déanamh do Chaoilte. Bhíodh sé ins gach aon chúinne d'oileán na hÉireann, agus ní sa riocht gcéanna a chítí é aon dá lá as a chéile. 'Na cheannaí Lochlannach a bhíodh sé uaireanta, istigh i gcathair Bhaile Átha Cliath, ag díol éadaí olla a deintí in Éirinn an uair sin ní b'fheárr ná mar a deintí iad in aon áit lasmu' d'Éirinn. 'Na ghrásaeir a bhíodh sé uaireanta eile agus stoc beag ba[*] seasca aige á dhíol le búistéiríbh Lochlannacha i gcathair Chorcaí. Nuair ' oireadh do eólas cruínn ' fháil agus gan bheith ag brath ar ráflaí, radharc a shúl féin a dh'fháil ar nithibh, théadh sé ar bórd luinge, 'na Lochlannach, mar dhea, agus théadh sé soir go Cathair na Beirbhe agus chíodh sé gach ní a bhíodh ar siúl ann. Chonaic sé lena shúilibh féin na slóite dá ngléasadh, agus d'airigh sé lena chluasaibh na daoine dhá ínsint dá chéile gur siar go hÉirinn a bhí na slóite sin go léir le dul chun cathanna crua do throid don Árdríogan uasal, do Ghormlóda. Gormlóda a thugaidís ar Ghormfhlaith. Bhí eólas ar chainnt na tíre sin ag Caoilte chómh maith agus dá mb'ann a tógfí é. Nuair a théadh sé i measc na ndaoine ann, ní bhíodh ' fhios ag éinne ná gur dhuine de mhuíntir na tíre é.

Fuair sé amach, ar a measc, ar dtúis gurbh í Gormfhlaith a bhí ag cur na hoibre go léir ar siúl, ach is fé rún a hínstí dho é. Fuair sé amach, leis, ar an gcuma gcéanna, go raibh Sitric, mac Ghormfhlaith, rí Lochlannach Átha Cliath, ag cabhrú le Gormfhlaith ar gach aon tsaghas cuma. Bhíodh sé coitianta anonn 's anall idir an dá chathair ag tabhairt gach aon tsaghas eólais do rí Lochlann ar ghnóthaibh na hÉireann, ar an gcuma 'na raibh Brian ag titim agus nárbh fhéidir do maireachtaint puínn eile aimsire. Nuair a gheóbhadh sé bás go dtitfeadh a chómhacht as a chéile. Ná beadh aon bhreith ag Murchadh ar fhearaibh Éireann a chimeád dlúite 'na chéile mar a bhíodar dlúite ag Brian. Go mbeadh ríthe na tíre, thuaidh agus theas, ag marú a chéile mar gheall ar an Árdríocht. Ná beadh aon bhac ar shlua Lochlannach preabadh chúthu isteach an uair sin agus gabháil de chosaibh iontu i ndiaidh ' chéile. Go mbeadh a leath ar thaobh na Lochlannach féin, i gcoinnibh an leath eile, chómh luath agus ' thiocfadh na Lochlannaigh. Gurbh é buac rí Lochlann an neart sló ba mhó ' fhéadfadh sé ' chruinniú ' bheith cruinnithe gléasta curtha le chéile aige i gcómhair bháis Bhriain, nú i gcómhair pé rud a thiocfadh. Do thuig rí Lochlann an ní sin go hálainn, agus bhí sé ag déanamh a dhíchill agus á dhéanamh go maith, agus má bhí ní raibh oiread agus cor aige á chur de, ná ag Sitric á chur de, ná raibh cúntas cruínn ag Caoilte á thabhairt do Mhurchadh air.

Théadh Caoilte go hoileán Mhanann, leis, agus chíodh sé cad a bhíodh ar siúl ann, agus chuireadh sé cúntas cruínn air ag triall ar Mhurchadh.

Thug sé cúpla cuaird ó thuaidh go hÍnsibh Orc agus chonaic sé cad a bhí ar siúl ann. Fuair sé go raibh ainm Ghormfhlaith i mbéalaibh na ndaoine ann, agus go raibh talamh saibhir geallta in Éirinn, saor ó chíos, d'aon fhear a thiocfadh ag cabhrú le Gormfhlaith agus le rí Lochlannach Bhaile Átha Cliath sa chogadh a bhí le teacht.

Caibideal 26: Púicíní

'Na chuardaibh go léir, nuair ' airíodh Caoilte an cómhrá ar siúl i dtaobh an chogaidh a bhí le teacht agus i dtaobh na dtalúintí saibhre saora a bhí le fáil de bhárr an chogaidh, thugadh sé fé ndeara, nuair adeireadh an fear, "Ní raghad-sa go hÉirinn. Is buan fear 'na dhúthaigh féin. Mharódh Murchadh me", go ndeireadh an bhean, "Is fear meata thu! Mura dtéir-se ann, raghad-sa ann! Nú má théann tú ann, raighimíd go léir ann in éineacht leat. Tá fir againn-na a bheidh maith a dhóthain do Mhurchadh, ní hea ach ró-mhaith dho. Is feárr dul go hÉirinn, pé crích a bhéarfaidh sinn, agus beatha bog sóil a bheith ag duine ar thalamh bhreá shaibhir, ná bheith a d'iarraidh beatha docht daor a bhaint as na riascaibh fiaine fuara so!"

Bhí aithne mhaith ar Mhurchadh an uair sin, ní hamháin i measc na Lochlannach a bhí 'na gcónaí in Éirinn, ach ar fuid tíre Lochlann go léir, agus ar fuid na hIorua, agus in Ínsíbh Orc, agus chómh fada ó thuaidh le hInis Tuile. Nuair ba mhaith le mnaoi eagla ' chur ar leanbh, ní deireadh sí ach, "Eist do bhéal nú glaofad ar Mhurchadh chút!" nú, "Chút Murchadh!"

Ní raibh Caoilte in' aonar san obair a bhí aige á déanamh. Bhí a theachtairí aige le cur uaidh go hÉirinn nuair a bhíodh eólas éigin ná fuiliceódh ríghneas aige le cur ag triall ar Mhurchadh. Chuireadh sé uaidh a theachtaire agus d'fhanadh sé féin thall ag faire chuige, ag lorg tuilleadh eólais.

Do thárla, lá dá raibh sé thall i gCathair na Beirbhe, gur ghluais ráfla ó bhéal go béal i measc na ndaoine.

"Ó", adéarfadh duine le duine, "ar airís an scéal nua?"

"Níor airíos airiú! Cad é an scéal nua é?", adéarfí á fhreagradh.

"Árdrí Éireann atá marbh!"

"Eist do bhéal!"

Caibideal 26: Púicíní

"Ó, go deimhin níl aon fhocal bréige ann. Lochlannach óg uasal ó Áth Cliath a thug an scéal nua anall anso ag triall ar an rí, agus dá chómhartha san féin is é Sitric, rí Lochlannach Átha Cliath, do chuir anall é. Tá Brian marbh agus beidh Sitric in' Árdrí anois".

Ansan déarfadh duine eile a thiocfadh suas:

"Tá an éagóir agat. Níor thugais an scéal sa cheart leat. Ní hé an tÁrdrí atá marbh. Níl éinne marbh. Is amhlaidh a chuir Sitric anall anso ó Áth Cliath an priúnsa óg, Amhlaoibh, dhá ínsint don rí go bhfuil Gormfhlaith go maith agus go bhfuil gach aon ní ag dul chun cínn aici ar a toil. Go bhfuair sí an saibhreas a bhí uaithi agus go bhfuil sí sásta".

"Cad é an saibhreas a bhí uaithi?", adéarfadh duine eile. "Nách í Árdríogan na hÉireann í? Tá an saibhreas san aici le fada anois. Nár bhuailtear* a thuilleadh úímpi! Cad a chuir i mbéal an amadáin seo Brian a bheith marbh?"

"Ní fheadar-sa san", adéarfadh an fear eile, "mura mar seo a dh'éirigh an focal. Duairt Gormfhlaith le hAmhlaoibh a dh'ínsint don rí go raibh Brian ag titim leis an aois go tiubh, agus ná féadfadh sé, agus a dhícheall a dhéanamh, seasamh puínn níos sia. Is dócha, nuair a leath an chainnt sin i measc na ndaoine gur chuireadar leis an gcainnt agus gur dheineadar a bhás as an gcainnt. Nuair a bhíonn ráfla ag gabháil tímpall, bíonn gach éinne ag cur leis".

Chuir an chainnt sin Caoilte ag machnamh. Cérbh é an tAmhlaoibh seo? Nú arbh fhéidir in aon chor gurbh é cara Thaidhg Óig Uí Chealla é?

"Ní foláir dom, má fhéadaim é, radharc ' fháil air", ar seisean in' aigne féin.

Caibideal 26: Púicíní

Chrom sé ar dhridim, ar feadh roinnt laethanta, i dtreó an rí-theaghlaigh le pé mangaireacht a bhí ar siúl aige. Bhíodh sé ag faire ar an huaislibh agus iad ag dul isteach 's amach. Theip air aon radharc ' fháil ar éinne de shaghas Amhlaoibh. Má theip bhí rud eile nár theip air. Níor theip air ceathrar lucht airm do theacht 'na thímpall de phreib agus príosúnach a dhéanamh de agus é ' chur isteach i gcarcair dhaingean, sara raibh ' fhios aige, ba dhó' leat, cad a bhí ag imeacht air. Níor labhradh oiread agus focal leis. Níor deineadh ach breith air agus a dhá láimh a cheangal laistiar de agus púicín a tharrac anuas ar a shúilibh agus é ' thógaint chun siúil. Nuair a bhí sé istigh sa phríosún, do cuireadh slabhra fan chuím air, agus bhí an ceann eile den tslabhra san daingean sa bhfalla. Do baineadh de an púicín agus do fágadh ansan é in' aonar. Tar éis roinnt aimsire do tugadh bia chuige agus do baineadh an ceangal dá lámhaibh an fhaid a bhí sé ag ithe an bhídh. Amáireach a bhí chúinn, tar éis cheithre huaire fichead a bheith caite aige in' aonar, do tugadh an bia chuige arís. Do tugadh an bia chuige mar sin gach aon lá. Gach aon uair a thagadh an bia, do labhradh Caoilte leis an dteachtaire, agus d'fhiafraíodh sé dhe cad é an chúis gur cuireadh isteach sa phríosún san é agus gan aon rud déanta as an slí aige. Ní thugadh an teachtaire aon fhreagra air ach fé mar a bheadh sé bodhar balbh. D'imigh lá agus oíche, agus d'imigh lá eile agus oíche eile, agus d'fhan Caoilte sa phríosún. D'imigh seachtain, agus ambasa bhí gach aon deallramh go bhfágfí sa phríosún san é, níorbh fhios cad é an fhaid. Bhí sé ag machnamh agus ag machnamh, agus ní fhéadfadh sé aon tuairim a thabhairt do cad fé ndeara príosúnach a dhéanamh de. Bhí ' fhios aige go maith go raibh sé ag cur eólais ag triall ar Mhurchadh go hÉirinn ar neart sló tíre Lochlann agus ar acfuinn na tíre agus ar gach aon tsaghas gnótha stáit dá raibh ar siúl san áit. Ach bhí ' fhios aige go maith, leis, ná raibh cogadh an uair sin idir an dá thír, idir Éire agus crích Lochlann, agus dá bhrí sin, pé eólas a chuirfeadh sé uaidh abhaile go hÉirinn, nárbh fhéidir spiaireacht do chur 'na leith. Má labhair sé cainnt na Lochlannach chómh maith agus do labhradar féin í, ní dhéanfadh san spiaire dhe nuair ná raibh aon chogadh ar siúl idir an dá thír.

Caibideal 26: Púicíní

Nuair a bhí breis agus seachtain caite sa phríosún aige, do labhair sé, lá, leis an dteachtaire, mar seo:

"A dhuine mhacánta", ar seisean, "níl aon lá a tháinís anso lem chuid bídh chúm nár fhiafraíos díot cad é an chúis gur deineadh príosúnach díom. Níor thugais aon fhreagra orm. Is maith liom anois an méid seo do rá leat, agus tá súil agam go raghaidh an focal ag triall ar rí Lochlann. Pé duine is bun le mise ' chur isteach sa phríosún so, gan aon droch-ghníomh do chur im leith, tá an dlí briste aige agus díolfaidh sé as. Má tugtar aon an-chor dom, díolfar as chómh daor agus a díoladh riamh a héagóir. Mura maith leat labhairt liom-sa, labhair le duine éigin eile agus inis an méid sin do. Labhair leis an té a dhein an gníomh so. Ní duine gan údarás a dhein an gníomh so".

D'imigh an teachtaire. Ní raibh sé i bhfad imithe nuair a tháinig an ceathrar céanna úd arís. Do rugadar ar Chaoilte. Bhaineadar an slabhra dá chúm. Shádar an púicín anuas ar a cheann agus ar a shúilibh. Do rugadar leó amach é agus síos agus chun an chuain, agus chuireadar ar bórd luinge é. Bhí an long ag dul go hÉirinn. Do cuireadh suas na seólta agus do ghluais an long. Nuair a bhí an long tamall amach ar uisce, do baineadh an púicín de Chaoilte agus do baineadh an ceangal dá lámhaibh. Ansan do shín an captaein leitir chuige. Sid é a bhí sa leitir:—

> "A 'Dhuínn', nú a 'Chaoilte', nú a 'Chosa Buí Árda', nú pé ainm 'nar maith leat freagairt do, tá t'anam á leogaint leat an turas so. Mar adeirir, níl cogadh idir rí Lochlann agus Árdrí Éireann. Ach má feictear sa tír seo arís tu, ní feicfar beó thu 'na dhiaidh san".

Do léigh sé an leitir agus chuir sé chuige í. Bhí an captaein agus é féin, agus an fhuireann, síbhialta go leór lena chéile go dtí gur sroiseadh cuan Chorcaí. Do cuireadh i dtír ag caladh an chuain sin é agus do fágadh ansan é. Bhí a dhóthain daoine muínteartha i gCorcaigh aige. Níorbh fhada an ríghneas a dhein sé eatarthu.

D'imigh sé ó thuaidh go Ceann Cora. Níorbh fhada go bhfeacaigh sé an rí-dhamhna, Murchadh. Thispeáin sé an leitir do, agus d'inis sé an scéal go léir do, tríd síos.

Caibideal 27: Dhá Amhlaoibh?

Nuair a hínseadh an scéal do Mhurchadh, ní miste a rá ná gur cuireadh ag machnamh é. Cérbh é an fear a scríbh an leitir sin a tugadh do Chaoilte? Cé ba bhun le breith ar Chaoilte agus é ' chur isteach i bpríosún? Sin cuid de sna ceisteannaibh a bhí ag Murchadh á fhiafraí dhe féin. D'inis Caoilte dho conas mar a dh'iarr Tadhg Óg Ó Cealla air bheith ag faire, 'na chuardaibh, féachaint an bhfaigheadh sé aon tuairisc ar an Amhlaoibh úd, an comrádaí a bhí ag Tadhg Óg i scoil Ínse Cathaigh. Nuair ' airigh sé na ráflaí, thall, i dtaobh an Amhlaoibh a tháinig ó Shitric, ó rí Lochlannach Átha Cliath, ag triall ar rí críche Lochlann, gur chuímhnigh sé ar an Amhlaoibh a bhí ar iarraidh agus gur bheartaigh sé in' aigne radharc ' fháil, dá mb'fhéidir é, ar theachtaire Shitric, le hionchas go mb'fhéidir gurbh é an tAmhlaoibh céanna é. Gur a d'iarraidh an radhairc sin a dh'fháil a bhí sé nuair a cuireadh an púicín air.

"Agus anois cad is dó' leat don scéal, a rí?", ar seisean le Murchadh.

"Tá roinnt nithe sa scéal, a Dhuínn", arsa Murchadh, atá soiléir go leór". (Bhí ' fhios ag Murchadh cérbh é Caoilte.) "An fear a dh'órdaigh an púicín do chur ort-sa, bhí ' fhios aige cad a bhí uait, gur theastaigh uait radharc ' fháil air féin. Bhí ' fhios aige go n-aithneófá é dá bhfaighfá radharc air. Fuair seisean radharc ort-sa sarar fhéadais-se radharc ' fháil air sin. Do rugadh 'na láthair thu nuair a bhí an púicín ort. D'fhéach sé go maith ort ansan. Is fear é go bhfuil cómhacht aige. Mura mbeadh go bhfuil, ní bheadh an lucht airm úmhal do. Tá ' fhios aige cé 'ra mac tu. Sin é cúis nár leog eagla dho aon an-chor a thabhairt duit. Tá an méid sin soiléir go leór. Cad 'na thaobh do a thabhairt le tuiscint duit, agus dúinn go léir, as an leitir seo, go bhfuil aithne mhaith aige ort? Inis an méid seo dhom, a Dhuínn. An raibh aithne ag an Amhlaoibh a bhí in Inis Cathaigh ort?"

"Ní raibh, a rí", arsa Caoilte.

"Is dó' liom, a Dhuínn, go dtuigim an scéal, ach b'fhéidir dearúd a bheith orm", arsa Murchadh. "Más éinne amháin an dá Amhlaoibh, do bhí aithne aige ort, ach cheap sé, agus dob fhíor dho é, go rabhais-se deimhnitheach ná raibh. Ansan do scríbh sé an leitir sin chun a chur 'na luí ort nárbh é féin an tAmhlaoibh go rabhais ar a lorg, mar go raibh aithne mhaith aige féin ort, agus go raibh ' fhios agat féin ná raibh aon aithne ag an Amhlaoibh eile ort. Is cuímhin liom an tAmhlaoibh a bhíodh ag teacht anso aníos ó Inis Cathaigh in éineacht le Tadhg Óg Ó Cealla. Mheasas gurbh ógánach dea-chroíoch macanta oscailte é, agus is dó' liom gurbh é sin meas gach éinne air. Is iúntach an scéal é má bhí doimhneas fíll ann laistigh den mhacántacht agus den oscailteacht go léir. B'fhéidir nárbh fhearra dhúinn rud a dhéanfaimís ná labhairt le Niamh agus an ní go léir do chur 'na cómhairle. Anso thall, féach, atá sí féin agus a hathair 'na gcónaí", agus thispeáin sé an tigh do Chaoilte.

"An bhfuil Niamh 'na cónaí anso, a rí?", arsa Caoilte, agus do las sé go bun na gcluas. Thug Murchadh fé ndeara an lasadh, ach d'iompaigh sé chómh hobann san, ag féachaint ar rud éigin eile, gur mheas Caoilte nár thug.

"Tá sí 'na cónaí anso le tamall maith anois. Tá sé chómh maith agam a dh'ínsint duit cad 'na thaobh".

Ansan d'inis sé do Chaoilte an dá fholáramh a thug an Leagáid uaidh, agus an scannradh a bhí air féin le heagla go ndéanfí aon iarracht ar nimh a thabhairt don Árdrí; conas nár fhéad sé a aigne ' chur chun suaimhnis go dtí gur chuir sé ' fhiachaibh ar Niamh teacht go Ceann Cora.

Caibideal 27: Dhá Amhlaoibh?

"Tá", ar seisean, "eagla ageam leas-mháthair roimena súil. An fhaid a bheidh sí anso, ní déanfar aon iarracht ar éagóir a dhéanamh ar an Árdrí. Tuigeann Niamh cad chuige go bhfuil sí anso, agus geallaim dhuit nách miste do Ghormfhlaith eagla ' bheith aici roimena súil. Ní thuigeann éinne eile sa teaghlach, ámh, ach Niamh agus a hathair, cad chuige go bhfuil sí anso. Tuigeann fear friothála an rí go bhfuil sé anso chun aire ' thabhairt do bhia an rí, díreach mar is gnáth aire ' thabhairt do bhia aon rí. Níl ' fhios aige go bhfuil aon chúntúirt fé leith ar m'athair. Tá sé chómh maith againn dul agus do scéal-sa a dh'ínsint do Niamh, féachaint a' ndéarfaidh sí go bhfuil dhá Amhlaoibh ann nú ná fuil".

Bhuaileadar araon anonn chun an tí 'na raibh Niamh agus a hathair 'na gcónaí ann. Chuir Niamh agus a hathair fáilte rómpu mar ba chóir.

D'inis Caoilte a scéal di, ó thosach go deireadh, agus thispeáin sé an leitir di.

"Cimeádfad an leitir seo, lenúr dtoil", ar sise, "agus tispeánfad do Thadhg í. Más é Amhlaoibh Thaidhg a scríbh í, aithneóidh Tadhg an scríbhinn".

"Ná beadh sé chómh maith agam-sa", arsa Caoilte, "preabadh siar go hUíbh Máine agus an leitir a thispeáint láithreach do?"

"Thar a bhfeacaís riamh", arsa Murchadh.

D'imigh Caoilte siar. Thispeáin sé an leitir do Thadhg Óg Ó Chealla.

"Cé 's dó' leat a scríbh an leitir sin, a Thaidhg", ar seisean.

D'fhéach Tadhg ar an leitir. Do léigh sé í. Do léigh sé arís í. D'fhéach sé ar Chaoilte.

Caibideal 27: Dhá Amhlaoibh?

"Cé is dó' leat a scríbh í?", arsa Caoilte leis.

"Airiú, ca bhfios dómh-sa cé ' scríbh í?", arsa Tadhg. "Níl aon phioc dá fhios agam cé ' scríbh í", ar seisean, "ná cad é an brí atá léi".

Do stad Caoilte. Chonaic sé nár aithin Tadhg an scríbhinn. Bhí sé i gcás 'dir dhá chómhairle ceocu ba cheart do an scéal go léir a dh'ínsint do nú nár cheart, gan cead ó Mhurchadh nú ó Niamh. Fé dheireadh thuig sé, ó thispeáin sé an leitir, gur cheart do a dh'ínsint cad 'na thaobh gur thispeáin sé í agus cad é an brí a bhí léi. D'inis sé an scéal go léir do, na ráflaí a dh'airigh sé thall i dtaobh bháis Bhriain agus i dtaobh an Amhlaoibh a chuaigh anonn ó Áth Cliath, ó Shitric, go rí Lochlann, agus i dtaobh na teachtaireachta a bhí ag an Amhlaoibh sin don rí thall, dhá rá leis go raibh Gormfhlaith go maith, agus an saibhreas a bhí uaithi, go raibh sé fálta aici. Ansan d'inis sé dho conas mar a chuaigh sé féin i gcóngar do rí-theaghlach rí Lochlann, féachaint a' bhféadfadh sé radharc ' fháil ar an Amhlaoibh úd, agus conas mar a cuireadh an púicín air, agus mar a cuireadh sa phríosún é, agus mar a cuireadh anall go Corcaigh é, agus conas mar a thug an captaein an leitir do.

D'éist Tadhg leis an ínsint go breá socair go dtí go raibh an focal deirineach ráite. Níor labhair sé ansan féin. D'fhan sé gan labhairt ar feadh tamaill mhaith. Nuair a bhí a mhachnamh déanta aige, do labhair sé.

"Cad é an saibhreas", ar seisean, "a bhí ó Ghormfhlaith agus a fuair sí?"

"Sin í díreach an cheist nách féidir le Niamh ná le Murchadh ná liom féin do réiteach", arsa Caoilte. (Níor mhaith leis trácht ar an gcailís gan cead ó Mhurchadh).

"Raghaidh mé leat soir go Ceann Cora", arsa Tadhg.

Caibideal 27: Dhá Amhlaoibh?

Do ghluais an bheirt soir. D'ínseadar nár aithin Tadhg an scríbhinn.

"Shamhlaíos féin gur mar sin a bheadh", arsa Niamh.

"Agus ar ndeóin", arsa Caoilte, "is tu aduairt an leitir a thispeáint do".

"Is me", ar sise. "Níorbh aon díobháil í ' thispeáint do. Ní hé an té do labhair an chainnt do scríbh an leitir. Fuair sé duine eile chun na scríbhinne ' dhéanamh".

Bhí Tadhg ana-ghruama. Ní raibh focal ag teacht as ach é ag machnamh. Bhí an triúr eile ag caitheamh tuairimí chómh maith agus d'fhéadadar é, agus bhí gach aon tuairim dár tugadh ag dúnadh isteach, i ndiaidh ar ndiaidh, dhá chur 'na luí air gurbh aon Amhlaoibh amháin an dá Amhlaoibh. An fhaid a bhí na tuairimí ar siúl, bhí a lán nithe beaga ag teacht chun cuímhne Thaidhg, nithe beaga nár chuir sé blúire suime iontu nuair a chonaic sé ar dtúis iad, ach gur chuir se mórán suime anois iontu, agus bhíodar dhá thispeáint do go raibh gach aon deallramh gurbh aon Amhlaoibh amháin an dá Amhlaoibh.

Thuig Murchadh gur cheart guid na cailíse d'ínsint do Thadhg. Do hínseadh do é. Níor bheag san.

"Ó", ar seisean, "nách me an t-amadán críochnaithe! Le feall is ea ' ghlac sé an Creideamh. Le feall is ea ' ghlac sé na mion-úird, chun go gcurfí isteach san *érdam* é. Ba cheart me ' chrochadh mar gheall ar leogaint do a leithéid d'amadán a dhéanamh díom! Feall ab ea an cion a bhí aige orm! Ó! Ní chuirfead náire an scéil díom an dá lá 's 'n fhaid a mhairfead! Dá mairinn céad, ní chuirfinn díom é. A Niamh, caithfir-se agus m'athair dul siar abhaile".

"Airiú, a Thaidhg, a lao", arsa Niamh, "cad é an gnó atá agat siar dínn? Ná fuil ' fhios agat cad chuige gur tugadh anso sinn? Cad 'tá chun tu féin a chosc ar aire ' thabhairt don áit thiar?"

Caibideal 27: Dhá Amhlaoibh?

"Nílim ag dul siar", ar seisean. "Leanfad an feallaire úd! Bainfead an geal-gháire dhe. Ó! An cladhaire! An bithiúnach fíll! Leanfad é agus tiocfad suas leis agus bainfead an ceann óna ghuaillibh de".

"Go réidh, a Thaidhg", arsa Murchadh. "Níl deimhne ceart in aon chor fós againn air gurb é an tAmhlaoibh a bhí in Inis Cathaigh do scríbh an leitir sin nú do labhair an chainnt atá inti. Dá mbeadh féin, ní healaí dhúinn gan féachaint rómhainn le heagla gurbh amhlaidh a chuirfimís ar a chumas tuilleadh díobhála ' dhéanamh dúinn. Más é a dhein an méid díobhála atá déanta, ní haon dóithín é. Ní foláir cuid dá ghastacht féin a dh'imirt 'na choinnibh. Éirigh-se siar abhaile agus fanadh Niamh agus t'athair anso. Ní gan fáth a cuireadh amach, thall i gcrích Lochlann, an ráfla úd i dtaobh bháis an Árdrí. Do cuireadh amach an ráfla i dtreó go mbeadh daoine ag dul i dtaithí an scéil agus nuair a thiocfadh an tásc ná déanfí iomad iúnadh dhe. Do cuireadh amach an ráfla le cúis eile, leis. Do cuireadh amach é mar chómhartha, dhá rá le rí Lochlann, 'Lean den ollmhúchán chómh dian agus ' fhéadfair é. Ní fheadraís cad é an neómat a gheóbhadh Brian bás. Bí ollamh'. 'Sé sin le rá, 'Cuirfimíd chun báis é chómh luath agus is féidir é, ach bídh-se ollamh!' Sin é brí atá leis na ráflaíbh".

"Gabhaim párdún agat, a rí", arsa Tadhg le Murchadh, "ach má tá daoine anso againn atá chómh ceapaithe sin ar an Árdrí do chur chun báis, cad 'na thaobh ná beirtear láithreach orthu agus a ndroch-bhearta do chur 'na leith agus iad do chur chun báis! Cad chuige bheith ag feitheamh go dtí go mbeidh an droch-bheart déanta acu? Cad é an leigheas ar an ndroch-bheart an cuirpeach do chur chun báis nuair a bheidh an droch-bheart déanta?"

"Is fíor dhuit, a Thaidhg", arsa Murchadh, "gur shuarach an leigheas ar dhroch-bheart an cuirpeach do chur chun báis nuair a bheadh an droch-bheart déanta. Ní hamhlaidh atáthar ag feitheamh go dtí go ndéanfaidh an cuirpeach an droch-bheart. Is amhlaidh atáimíd ag déanamh ár ndíchill chun an chuirpigh do chosc ar an ndroch-bheart a dhéanamh. Ní féidir cuirpeach do chur chun báis, pé droch-amhras a bheadh agat air, go dtí go mbeadh droch-ghníomh éigin agat le cur 'na leith. Mura mbeadh droch-ghníomh agat le cur 'na leith, cad a bheadh agat le déanamh ach tu féin a chosaint air? Sin é atá againn á dhéanamh, a Thaidhg. Táimíd dhár gcosaint féin ar an gcuirpeach. Éirigh-se siar abhaile, a Thaidhg, agus ná leog ort le héinne aon ní i dtaobh na cainnte seo atá déanta anso againn inniu. Ná bíodh aon eagal ort ná go dtabharfad-sa caoi dhuit, nuair a thiocfaidh an t-am chuige, ar t'aigne ' shásamh ar an bhfeallaire".

"Tá go maith, a rí", arsa Tadhg. "Tá t'fhocal agam chuige sin agus táim sásta. Tiocfaidh mo lá".

Agus d'imigh sé abhaile.

Caibideal 28: An tSí Gaoithe

Nuair a bhí Tadhg Óg Ó Cealla imithe, do labhair Murchadh le Caoilte.

"A Dhuínn", ar seisean, "pé hé an tAmhlaoibh do scríbh an leitir sin, nú do labhair an chainnt atá inti, tá botún mór déanta aige. Dá ghastacht é, tá dearúd déanta aige. Bainfead-sa geit as pé hé féin. Imigh ag triall ar Dhúlainn Óg agus abair leis buíon d'fhearaibh tofa do chur le chéile gan mhoíll agus tar chúm anso chómh luath agus ' bheid siad ollamh aige.

D'imigh Caoilte.

"Cad a mheasann tú a dhéanamh, a rí?", arsa Niamh.

"Raghad go hÁth Cliath, a Niamh", ar seisean, "agus labharfad le Sitric. Béarfad teachtaireacht ag triall air ón Árdrí. Táid Lochlannaigh Átha Cliath, agus Sitric leó, fé smacht an Árdrí. Tispeánfad an leitir sin do Shitric. Tá síocháin idir Éirinn agus tír Lochlann. Ó tá an tsíocháin sin ann, tá saor-chead chun gnóthaí ceannaíochta idir an dá thír, agus tá ' fhiachaibh ar gach tír acu cosnamh dlí a thabhairt do sna ceannaithibh a thagann ón dtír eile. Tá an cosnamh san againn-na á thabhairt do sna ceannaithibh Lochlannacha a thagann go hÉirinn. Tá geallúint againn ó rí Lochlann go dtabharfí an cosnamh céanna do cheannaithibh Gaelacha dá dtéidís anonn go Danmharg ag déanamh aon ghnótha ceannaíochta ann. Chuaigh ceannaí Gaelach anonn le déanaí. Bhí sé ag déanamh a ghnótha, gan aon chur isteach aige á dheanamh ar ghnó aon duine eile, agus gan briseadh ná milleadh ' dhéanamh ar aon dlí de dhlithibh na tíre sin. Tháinig ceathrar lucht airm, de lucht airm na tíre, agus do rugadar air, gan chúis gan abhar, agus chuireadar i bpríosún é, agus do cimeádadh sa phríosún é breis agus seachtain. Caithfar sásamh a dh'fháil ó rí Lochlann as an ngníomh san. Caithfar an ceart céanna a tugtar do cheannaithibh Lochlannacha in Éirinn do chur in áirithe do cheannaithibh Gaelacha thall i gcrích Lochlann. Ar scáth na hoibre sin, caithfar a dhéanamh amach más féidir é, an bhfuil an dá Amhlaoibh ann, nú an é an tAmhlaoibh a bhí anso againn atá anois 'na theachtaire idir Shitric agus an rí thall".

Lena línn sin, tháinig Caoilte thar n-ais.

"Tá Dúlainn agus na fir ollamh, a rí", ar seisean.

"Tá go maith, a Dhuínn", arsa Murchadh. "Tiocfair-se linn".

"Cathain a gheóbhaimíd aon scéala uaibh, a rí?", arsa Niamh.

"An túisce 'na mbeidh aon ní le hínsint gur fiú é é ' dh'ínsint curfar teachtaire thar n-ais chút, a Niamh", arsa Murchadh. "Ní gá dhom a rá leat aire mhaith a thabhairt dom leas-mháthair".

"Ná bíodh ceist ort, a rí", ar sise. "Tabharfad aire mhaith dhi. Ní chuirfidh sí cor di i ganfhios dom. Táimíd go hana-mhór lena chéile. Ach tá ' fhios aici, is dó' liom, cad é an gnó atá anso agam, agus tá sí ag déanamh a díchill chun a thispeáint dúinn go léir gur dearúd mór dúinn aon droch-amhras a bheith againn uirthi. Tá an dícheall san dhá cimeád ar fad ó aon ní a dhéanamh a chabhródh leis an ndroch-amhras. Beidh m'aigne féin ana-mhí-shásta, a rí", ar sise, "go dtí go mbeidh ' fhios agam cé hé an tAmhlaoibh seo, nú an aon Amhlaoibh amháin an dá Amhlaoibh".

"Curfar chút an t-eólas, a Niamh", arsa Murchadh, "chómh luath in Éirinn agus ' bheidh an t-eólas againn le cur chút".

D'imigh Murchadh agus Caoilte amach chun na háite 'na raibh Dúlainn agus na fir ag feitheamh leó. Ar marcaíocht a bhíodar le himeacht. Marcaigh mhaithe ab ea iad go léir. Marcach álainn ab ea Murchadh agus marcach álainn ab ea Dúlainn. Ach ní raibh aon bhreith ag éinne den bheirt, ná ag aon fhear in Éirinn an uair sin, agus M'leachlainn Mór féin do chur chuige, ar Chaoilte, chun capaill a mharcaíocht. An stail ba mhó agus ba threise agus ba thréine* dob fhéidir a dh'fháil, agus é ' bheith ag imeacht fiain, gan lámh duine do dhul ar a cheann go dtí go mbeadh sé in aois a sheacht mblian, do léimfeadh Caoilte ar a mhuin, gan srian gan iallait, agus dhéanfadh sé é ' mharcaíocht treasna na dútha go dtí go mbeadh an stail sin chómh mín le huan caeireach aige. Bhí Caoilte cúmtha chun na marcaíochta chómh maith díreach agus ' bhí sé cúmtha chun an reatha. Bhí an neart agus an fuinneamh go léir agus an bhreis bheag fhaid insna cosaibh aige. Aon chapall a geófí idir an dá chois sin, ní raibh aon bhreith aige, pé léimreach a dhéanfadh sé ná pé casadh a bhainfeadh sé as féin, ar dhul óna ngreim. Ní fhéadfadh sé an marcach a chur de ach le hé féin d'iomlasc ar an dtalamh. An túisce 'na gcuirfeadh an capall chun luite, bheadh an marcach 'na sheasamh in' aice, agus ansan, an túisce 'na mbeadh an capall ar a chosaibh arís, bheadh an marcach ar a mhuin arís. Níor bheag de radharc, uaireanta, bheith ag féachaint air féin agus ar chapall óg fhiain ag iomaidh le chéile go dtí go gcaitheadh an capall géilleadh dho sa deireadh.

Do ghluais an dírim marcach ó Cheann Cora agus thugadar aghaidh soir ó thuaidh ar Theamhair. Ba sheólta an ghluaiseacht acu é, fan an bhóthair álainn a bhí go breá leathan, leibhéalta, réidh, an bóthar a deineadh le hórdú Bhriain, ó Cheann Cora go Teamhair.

Tímpall deich míle soir ó thuaidh ó Cheann Cora bhí buachaill ag aeireacht bhó ar an dtaobh thuaidh den bhóthar. D'airigh sé, i bhfad siar ó dheas uaidh, mar a bheadh séideadh beag gaoithe trí chrannaibh. Do neartaigh ar an séideadh i dtreó gur mheas an buachaill gur stoirm a bhí ag teacht. Ansan do neartaigh ar an séideadh i dtreó gur mheas an buachaill nár shéideadh a bhí ann ach fuaim uisce ag gabháil le fánaidh gleanna. Ansan d'airigh sé mar a bheadh brú agus meilt agus fuadar cuisíochta, agus do ghluais an marc-shlua chuige amach ó scáth na coille a bhí ar thaobh an bhóthair agus a bhí dhá gclúdach uaidh go dtí san. Thánadar in' aice agus ghluaiseadar thairis, agus an fhaid a bhíodar ag gabháil thairis, shamhlaigh sé go raibh an talamh ag bogadh agus ag luascadh agus ag crith féna chosaibh le neart agus le brú agus le fuinneamh a ngluaiseachta agus iad ag imeacht mar ' imeódh an tsí gaoithe, agus an ceó bóthair ag éirí 'na ndiaidh, agus suip agus bileóga feóchta dá séideadh suas agus dá gcasadh agus dá scuabadh chun siúil, leis an ngaoith a tháinig ón ngluaiseacht. D'imíodar thairis agus chuaigh an ceó 'na shúilibh agus bhí an fothram 'na chluasaibh, agus nuair ' fhéad sé a shúile do ghlanadh agus féachaint arís orthu, bhíodar ag imeacht soir ó thuaidh as a radharc agus bhí an fothram ag maolú. Do mhaolaigh an fothram go dtí ná raibh ann ach mar a bheadh fuaim uisce. Do mhaolaigh sé ansan go dtí ná raibh ann ach mar a bheadh séideadh gaoithe trí chrannaibh. Ansan do mhaolaigh sé go dtí ná hairíodh an buachaill ach puth beag anois agus arís de. Ansan bhí sé imithe. Do cuireadh a leithéid de scárd i gcroí an bhuachalla gur fhan sé ar an áit sin gan corraí as ar feadh i bhfad.

Deich mbliana agus daichead 'na dhiaidh san, nuair a bhí an buachaill sin 'na sheanduine, bhíodh sé 'na sheasamh ar an áit gcéanna go minic agus d'airíodh sé an tsí gaoithe ag tosnú thiar theas, mar ar thosnaigh an séideadh gaoithe an uair sin, agus thagadh an tsí gaoithe chuige aniar aneas le fuinneamh, agus do scuabadh sí thairis soir ó thuaidh ag déanamh ceó bóthair agus ag scaipeadh na sop, agus bhíodh sé daingean in' aigne gurbh é Murchadh agus a mharc-shlua a bhíodh ann! Bhíodar go léir ar shlua na marbh an uair sin.

Ach tháinig Murchadh agus a mharc-shlua go Teamhair. Chuir sé teachtaire isteach ag triall ar Mh'leachlainn dhá rá leis gur mhaith leis roinnt cainnte ' dhéanamh leis. Tháinig M'leachlainn amach agus chuir sé míle fáilte roim Mhurchadh agus rómpu go léir. Do rug sé leis isteach iad agus dhein sé cúram mór díobh. Do cuireadh cóir bídh agus dí orthu. Ar ball d'inis Murchadh do Mh'leachlainn cad a thug é. Gur cuireadh duine de cheannaithibh na hÉireann i bpríosún, thall i bpríomh-chathair tíre Lochlann, gan chúis gan abhar. Ansan thispeáin sé an leitir.

"Táim ceapaithe, a rí", ar seisean, "ar dhul soir go hÁth Cliath agus ar labhairt le Sitric, ós é rí Lochlannach Átha Cliath é, agus ar a fhiafraí dhe an bhfuil aon eólas aige ar an té is bun leis an ngníomh éagórtha so do dhéanamh orainn. Dá leogaimís leó an gníomh so gan gearán a dhéanamh mar gheall air, níorbh fhada, b'fhéidir, go ndéanfí gníomh eile a bheadh ní ba mheasa ná é. Is lag an bheart dúinn-na a rá go mbeadh díon agus cosnamh againn á thabhairt do cheannaithibh Lochlannacha in Éirinn, agus ná cuirfimís díon ná cosnamh in áirithe do cheannaithibh Gaelacha thall i dtír Lochlann".

"Agus ca bhfuil an ceannaí Gaelach do cuireadh i bpríosún, a rí?", arsa M'leachlainn.

"Má séantar an gníomh, a rí", arsa Murchadh, "beidh an ceannaí le fáil".

"An amhlaidh ba mhaith leat mise ' dhul leat go hÁth Cliath, a rí?", arsa M'leachlainn.

"Dá mb'é do thoil teacht linn, a rí", arsa Murchadh, "ba dhian-mhaith an rud é. Thabharfadh sé le tuiscint do Shitric, agus trí Shitric do rí

Lochlann thall, agus do sna Lochlannaigh go léir, go bhfuilimíd ar aon aigne sa scéal. Do chuirfeadh san eagla ar an té ' dhein an gníomh pé hé féin".

"Tá go maith, a rí", arsa M'leachlainn. "Raghad-sa libh".

Bhí dhá bhuíon* acu ann ansan agus iad ag tabhairt aghaidh ar Áth Cliath. Ní raibh i mBaile Átha Cliath an uair sin ach cathair ana-bheag. Bhí an féar glas ag fás go saibhir ar fhormhór an tailimh atá fé thithibh móra agus fé shráideannaibh breátha fada leathana anois. Níor dheocair rí-theaghlach Shitric a dhéanamh amach. Thug an dá bhuíon aghaidh ar an rí-theaghlach. Do chonacthas ag teacht iad. Bhí Sitric agus Amhlaoibh thuas i bhfinneóig. Chonacadar an dá bhuíon ag teacht chun an rí-theaghlaigh. D'aithníodar Murchadh agus M'leachlainn. D'aithin Amhlaoibh Caoilte. Do rith Amhlaoibh agus chuaigh sé i bhfolach.

"Ná leog ort go bhfuil aon phioc eólais agat, a rí, ar ca bhfuilim-se ná an bhfuilim beó nú marbh", ar seisean le Sitric.

Chuaigh Sitric amach ag cur fáilte roim Mh'leachlainn agus roim Mhurchadh. Do tugadh isteach iad féin agus na huaisle a bhí in éineacht leó, agus do cuireadh gach aon chóir orthu. Ar ball d'inis Murchadh cad a thug é. Bhí ana-chathú ar Shitric nuair a hínseadh do an éagóir a deineadh ar an gceannaí Gaelach thall i gCathair na Beirbhe.

"Ó", ar seisean, "cuirfead-sa teachtaire anonn dhá ínsint don rí gur deineadh an éagóir sin, agus déanfar an uile shaghas deimhne agus urraíochta air nách baol go dtabharfar aon chaoi d'éinne ar a leitheid a dhéanamh arís".

"Tá san maith go leór, a rí", arsa Murchadh, "ach ní dhéanfaidh san an gnó anois. Tá órdú agam-sa ón Árdrí, má tá an fear a dhein an gníomh san in Éirinn anois, lucht cuardaigh do chur amach chun bertha air agus chun é ' thabhairt chun lámha. Ar mhaithe leis an dá thír, le hÉirinn agus le tír Lochlann, ní foláir an fear a dhein an gníomh san do chur chun báis. Is bíoba báis don rí é, mar do thóg sé chuige féin an t-údarás a bhaineann leis an rí. Is bíoba báis do mhuíntir na hÉireann é, mar do dhein sé gníomh i gcoinnibh anama fir Éireannaigh. Is bíoba báis é do Lochlannaigh, in Éirinn nú in aon tír eile, mar do dhein sé gníomh a chuirfidh ' fhiachaibh ar lucht gach tíre éirí 'na gcoinnibh, mura ndeintear an gníomh a dh'agairt, agus san go luath, ar an té a dhein an gníomh. Ar mhaithe linn go léir, a rí", arsa Murchadh, "ní foláir dómh-sa a bheith ar mo chumas a rá leis an Árdrí nuair a raghad abhaile, go bhfuil do bhriathar rí agam uait-se chuige go ndéanfair féin do dhícheall, agus go ndéanfaidh rí Lochlann a dhícheall, ar theacht suas leis an gcuirpeach a dhein an gníomh san agus é ' thabhairt chun lámha agus an bás atá tuíllte aige ' dh'imirt air".

"Is dó', b'fhéidir, a rí", arsa Sitric, "ná féadfadh ár ndícheall teacht suas leis".

"Ní duine suarach é, a rí", arsa Murchadh. "Ní fhéadfadh aon duine suarach an gníomh a dhein sé do dhéanamh. Ní bheadh lucht airm an rí úmhal do dhuine shuarach. An fear gur dhein lucht airm an rí rud air, mar a dheineadar air siúd, ní ró-fhuiriste dho dul i bhfolach ó ríogra na tíre".

"Ní fheadar 'en domhan, a rí", arsa Sitric. "Níl agam-sa le déanamh ach mo bhriathar rí a thabhairt duit go ndéanfad mo dhícheall ar é ' thabhairt chun lámha, agus go n-iarrfad ar rí Lochlann a dhícheall a dhéanamh, leis, chuige. Is é ár mbuac go léir, aon fhear a mhíllfidh ár smacht, é ' thabhairt chun lámha chómh luath agus is féidir é".

Nuair a bhí an méid sin cainnte déanta eatarthu, d'fhág Murchadh agus M'leachlainn slán ag Sitric agus thánadar uaidh. Bhí Amhlaoibh i bhfolach agus é ag éisteacht leis an gcainnt. Nuair a bhí an dá bhuíon imithe, tháinig sé amach, agus bhí a lán cainnte idir é féin agus Sitric, féachaint conas ' fhéadfaidís teacht as an gcrua-chás 'na rabhadar mar gheall ar an ngníomh a dhein Amhlaoibh.

Caibideal 29: Beirt Droch-bhuachaillí

"Déanfaidh an t-annscian san, Murchadh, díobháil dúinn, a rí", arsa Sitric. "Ní maith a dheinis é an fear do chur sa phríosún. B'fheárr scaoileadh leis agus faire do chimeád air".

"Sin é díreach a dhéanfainn mura mbeadh ' fhios a bheith agam go n-aithneódh sé me dá bhfaigheadh sé radharc orm", arsa Amhlaoibh. "Is dó' leó i gCeann Cora go bhfuilim marbh. Níl aon phioc dá fhios acu cérbh é Amhlaoibh ná an bhfuil sé beó. Dá bhfaigheadh an fear úd na gcos radharc orm, do neósfadh sé dhóibh cá bhfeacaigh sé me. Tá aithne aige orm, ach is dó' leis ná fuil aon aithne agam-sa air féin. Sin é ball 'na bhfuil an dearúd air. D'aithníos an peidléir thall chómh luath agus do leogas mo shúil air. Dá bhfeiceadh sé me sara bhfeaca-sa é, agus go n-imeódh sé gan me dhá fheiscint, d'imeódh sé abhaile láithreach agus do neósfadh sé dhóibh in Inis Cathaigh agus i gCeann Cora go bhfeacaigh sé me, agus cá bhfeacaigh sé me. Ansan do bheadh ' fhios acu go léir cé ' thóg an chailís. Chonaic Colla me i gCeann Cora an lá ' fhágas an áit. Do curfí so agus súd le chéile agus bheadh ' fhios acu go léir cad é an gnó a bhí agam i gCeann Cora an lá san. Thabharfaidís tuairim do ca bhfuil an chailís anois. Chaithfeadh do mháthair teitheadh lena hanam as an áit".

"Mo mháthair!", arsa Sitric.

"Ár máthair*, más ea", arsa Amhlaoibh. "Ní beag di a bhfuil le fulag aici eatarthu. Is feárr gan a thuilleadh eólais a thabhairt dóibh. Is dó' leó go bhfuil an chailís imithe thar farraige. Ní féidir dár máthair cor a chur di, de ló ná d'oíche, i ganfhios dóibh, tá an faire chómh géar san uirthi. Dá bhfaighinn-se mo thoil, ní raghadh fear na gcos thar n-ais ag triall orthu. Bhí eagal ar an rí, dá dtugtí aon an-chor do go dtiocfadh cogadh as, agus gan sinn ollamh fós, dar leis".

Caibideal 29: Beirt Droch-bhuachaillí

"Cad é an neart atá ollamh aige?"

"Tá ocht míle fear ollamh aige, in arm 's in éide. Dá nglaeití amáireach air, d'fhéadfadh sé dhá mhíle fear eile do chur leis an ocht míle sin. Ní dó' leis go bhfuilimíd leath láidir ár ndóthain. Tá scannradh Ghleanna Mháma fós air", arsa Amhlaoibh.

"Ní haon iúnadh go mbeadh", arsa Sitric. "Dhein Clann Chais obair uathásach an lá san".

"Bainfar móráil an lae sin díobh nuair a thiocfaidh an lá atá 'na gcómhair againn", arsa Amhlaoibh.

"Bainfar", arsa Sitric. "Ach is feárr féachaint rómhainn agus sinn féin d'ollmhú i gceart. Cad é an neart eile, nú na nirt eile, atá ollamh, nú ag ollmhú, in éaghmais nirt rí Lochlann agus ár neart féin in Éirinn anso?"

"Tá neart dá ollmhú ar oileán Mhanann", arsa Amhlaoibh, "agus ní neart suarach é. Tá chúig céad déag fear ann, ollamh aon lá a glaofar orthu. Níl oileán de sna hoileánaibh atá laistiar d'Albain gan míle nú cúpla míle fear ollamh ann. Is dó' liom go bhfuil trí mhíle fear ollamh ar oileán Scathaigh".

"Tá san maith go leór, a rí, ach an bhfuil aon eólas cruínn agat ar an ollmhúchán atá ag Brian á dhéanamh?", arsa Sitric.

"Imbriathar go bhfuil", arsa Amhlaoibh. "Níl aon mhíogarnach ar Bhrian. Tá sé dhá ollmhú féin chómh tréan agus d'fhéadfadh sé bheith dhá ollmhú féin dá mbeadh fios ár n-aigne aige chómh cruínn agus 'tá againn féin. Dá mbeadh sé deich mbliana níos óige ná mar atá sé, bheadh sé fuar againn bheith ag brath ar aon lámh uachtair a dh'fháil air. Ach tá sé an-aosta. Ní fios cad é an neómat a shínfidh sé a chosa. Ansan má bhímíd ollamh, beidh gach aon rud ar ár dtoil againn".

"Mheasas", arsa Sitric, "go raibh cúnamh aige le fáil chun iad a shíneadh".

"Is deocair an cúnamh a thabairt do, tá an faire chómh dlúth san", arsa Amhlaoibh. "Tá iníon Thaidhg Mhóir Uí Chealla san áit i gcónaí agus ní féidir aon ní a dhéanamh i ganfhios di".

"Airím a lán daoine ag teacht tháirsi sin dhá rá gur cailín ana-bhreá í. Cad é an saghas í?"

"Droch-shaghas", arsa Amhlaoibh. "Tá sí dathúil, deallraitheach, álainn go maith. Déarfainn gurb í an bhean is áille in Éirinn í, lasmu' den Árdríogain. Ach tá sí go holc".

"Ní hé sin adeirtear", arsa Sitric. "Is é rud atá i mbéalaibh daoine 'na taobh ná go bhfuil áilleacht a pearsan thar na beartaibh agus gur bhuaigh uaisleacht a haigne agus a méinne ar áilleacht a pearsan".

"Ná creid focal de", arsa Amhlaoibh. "Creid a mhalairt. An chéad uair riamh a chonac í, do chonac go raibh sí go holc. Droch-shaghas is ea í. Deirim leat é".

"Cad é an saghas a driotháir?", arsa Sitric. "Deir gach éinne go raibh ana-chion aige féin agus ag Amhlaoibh ar a chéile; an tAmhlaoibh úd a cailleadh nú d'imigh amú. Deirtear go raibh sé ag briseadh a chroí ag gol i ndiaidh Amhlaoibh".

"Ó, cúis gháire chúinn! An fear bocht. Níl ann ach leath-amadán", arsa Amhlaoibh. "Bhíodh ana-spórt agam air uaireanta. Ní leogainn m'aigne chuige, áfach. Bhíomair thuas i gCeann Cora lá agus bhí cleasaíocht ar siúl ann. Bhain sé an chos de mharcach bréige ann le buille ' thuaigh. Do leogas féin orm nár fhéadas an cleas a dhéanamh. 'Níor thugais a cheart féin don fhaobhar', ar seisean liom. Amadán is ea é, a rí. Ní miste fear láidir a thabhairt ar Mhurchadh, áfach. Ní dó' liom gur bhuail riamh fós umam fear chómh láidir le Murchadh.

Caibideal 29: Beirt Droch-bhuachaillí

Deirtear gur treise d'fhear é ná a athair an lá is feárr a bhí a athair. Is iúntach an fear é. Ní fhéadfá do shúile ' thógaint de dá bhfeicfá ag déanamh na lúth-chleas é. Níl aon teóra leis an neart atá suite ins gach ball dá bhallaibh".

"Tá súil agam ná buailfead uime sa chath so atá le teacht lá éigin", arsa Sitric. "Ach féach, a Amhlaoibh. Tá an scéal go holc agat-sa".

"Conas san, airiú?"

"Caithfar an ceann a bhaint díot".

"Ó, tuigim", arsa Amhlaoibh. "Agus tá do bhriathar rí tabhartha agat-sa do Mhurchadh agus do Bhrian go ndéanfair do dhícheall chun an chínn a bhaint díom. Nách símplí na daoine iad! Ach ar ndó', táim féin chómh símplí le héinne acu. Dá mb'áil liom-sa an ceann a bhaint d'fhear na gcos nuair a bhí greim agam air, ní bheadh an ceann le baint díom féin anois, agus ní bheadh do bhriathar rí tabhartha uait agat-sa chuige. Ach sin mar ' imíonn i gcónaí ar an nduine ná baineann an ceann dá namhaid nuair a gheibheann sé an lom air. Gheóbhaidh an namhaid sin lom air féin agus bainfidh sé an ceann de".

"An neósfair don rí gur tháinig M'leachlainn agus Murchadh anso?", arsa Sitric.

"Imeód soir láithreach agus neósfad an uile fhocal de dho, agus neósfad do go dtáinig fear na gcos anso in éineacht leó, agus ná tiocfadh dá mb'áil leis an rí leogaint dómh-sa an ceann a bhaint de in inead an phúicín a chur air", arsa Amhlaoibh. "Chuirfinn-se púicín air a chuirfeadh deireadh lena chuid spiaireachta. Ach ní haon mhaith bheith ag cainnt anois air mar scéal. An ceannaí! An peidléir! Is deas an obair bheith ag tabhairt ceart ceannaíochta dá leithéid sin! Ceart spiaireachta atá tugaithe dho!"

Caibideal 29: Beirt Droch-bhuachaillí

"Agus go mór mór ós duine tusa ná déanfadh spiaireacht in aon chor! Ba lag leat a leithéid a dhéanamh!", arsa Sitric.

"Cuir uait an magadh, a rí", arsa Amhlaoibh. "Ní cúrsaí magaidh é. Déanfaidh Donn mac Beathach díobháil fós dúinn, agus ní dhéanfadh dá ndeintí rud orm-sa nuair a bhí greim againn air. Ach é ' chur anall abhaile 'na shaol agus 'na shláinte! Ní féidir liom foighneamh leis mar scéal nuair a chuímhním air!"

Do scar an bheirt. D'imigh Amhlaoibh anonn go rí-theaghlach rí Lochlann agus d'inis sé dho gach ní i dtaobh teacht Mhurchadh agus Mh'leachlainn go hÁth Cliath, fé mar aduairt sé do neósfadh sé.

"Tá go maith", arsan rí. "Is feárr go mór an scéal a bheith mar atá sé ná é ' bheith mar a bheadh sé dá gcurtí an fear úd chun báis. Dá gcurtí chun báis é, ní bheadh Lochlannach beó in Éirinn um an dtaca so ach an méid acu do chuirfeadh iad féin go daingean fé smacht Bhriain. Ní fhéadfaimís-na cosc do chur lenár ndaoine féin anso. Do caithfí iad do ghléasadh agus do chur ar luingeas agus iad do bhreith go hÉirinn chun díoltais a dhéanamh ar Bhrian agus ar Ghaelaibh Éireann mar gheall ar mharú a gcine. Ní bheadh ach dithneas agus droch-ollmhú san obair. Ní raghadh ár neart go hÉirinn in éineacht. 'Na mbuínibh fé leith is ea do shroisfidís Éire. Ansan do mharódh Brian iad 'na mbuínibh fé leith. Is feárr go mór an scéal a bheith mar atá sé. Beidh uain againn ar thuilleadh nirt do chur le chéile. Agus féach, a Amhlaoibh, a mhic ó", ar seisean, "beidh uain ag Brian ar bhás a dh'fháil—má tá aon aidhm aige ar bhás a dh'fháil in aon chor!"

D'fhan an scéal mar sin agus do ghluais an t-ollmhúchán ar aghaidh, ins gach aon pháirt de chrích Lochlann agus ins gach aon pháirt d'oileán na hÉireann, go mór mór insna háiteannaibh a bhí dílis do Bhrian.

Caibideal 30: Marú le Soilbhreas

An fhaid a bhí an t-ollmhúchán ar siúl mórthímpall na hÉireann, bhí aghaidh na hÉireann ar Cheann Cora. Ní raibh lá gan priúnsa éigin, nú buíon éigin, d'uaislibh nú de mhaithibh móra, ó cheanntar éigin den tír, ag teacht go rí-theaghlach Bhriain, a d'iarraidh cómhairle, nú ag socrú cúise, nú dhá fhiafraí an mó fear a bheadh orthu do chur le chéile i gcómhair an chogaidh a thuig gach éinne a bhí ag teacht. Deiridís go léir, nuair a bhídís ag imeacht, ná raibh riamh in Éirinn rí chómh mór gradam le Brian; ná raibh riamh in Éirinn rí-theaghlach chómh greanta le rí-theaghlach Bhriain; ná raibh riamh in Éírinn, ná in aon tír eile, fir chómh huasal, chómh cróga, chómh tréan i gcath le Claínn Chais.

Ansan deiridís go léir, dá áilleacht agus dá nósmhaireacht agus dá uaisleacht ar gach aon tsaghas cuma, an rí-theaghlach agus a raibh ann, gur chuir an Bhannrín agus Niamh, ar an ngradam agus ar an uaisleacht agus ar an saibhreas agus ar an bhflúirse agus ar an rabairne, maise ná beadh orthu in aon chor mura mbeadh an bheirt sin a bheith san áit.

Gan amhras dob álainn an bheirt iad; agus ní aithneódh éinne do thiocfadh ann mar sin ar chuaird ná go raibh caradas idir an mbeirt. Is ar éigin ba dhó' le duine a thuigeadh Niamh féin uaireanta go raibh aon ní eatarthu ach caradas, bhíodh Gormfhlaith chómh caoin, chómh cneasta, chómh grámhar san léi. Bhíodh an tAifreann gach aon mhaidean, ag Maolshuathain, in eaglais an rí-theaghlaigh, agus bhíodh Gormfhlaith agus Niamh ag an Aifreann coitianta. Do chítí go minic i gcaitheamh an lae an bheirt i bhfochair a chéile, ag cainnt agus ag cómhrá go soilbhir agus go suairc agus go sultmhar, i dtreó ná bíodh aon phioc dá chuímhneamh ag éinne ná raibh fios bunús an scéil aige, go raibh aon ní idir an mbeirt ach caradas fírinneach. Ní raibh fios bunús an scéil ag Maolshuathain. Do tuigeadh gurbh fheárr an scéal a chimeád uaidh i dtreó ná tispeánfadh sé aon scáthúlacht 'na chainnt ná 'na chuideachtanas leis an Árdrí ná leis an Árdríogain. Ach bhíodh iúnadh mhór air nuair a thagadh Niamh chuige chómh minic roimis an Aifreann, ar maidin, agus nuair a dh'iarradh sí chómh dian, chómh dlúth air a guí do chur suas chun Dé sa Naomh Íbirt.

Bhí an aimsir ag gluaiseacht ar an gcuma san. Cómhacht Bhriain ag neartú ins gach aon bhall istigh in oileán na hÉireann, agus cómhacht Lochlann ag neartú ins gach aon bhall lasmu' d'oileán na hÉíreann. Na buíona insna daingeanaibh ag déanamh taithí de sna harmaibh agus ag leanúint ar an dtaithí chómh dícheallach agus ba cheart d'fhearaibh ná feidir cad é an neómat a chaithfidís na hairm sin do láimhseáil i gcoímheascar machaire chun iad féin a chosaint ar namhdaibh fíochmhara fuilteacha, mar a dhein cuid acu go minic cheana. Na ríthe agus na huaisle ar fuid na tíre ag cur a mbuíona féin le chéile, dhá múineadh agus dhá ngléasadh agus ag méadú a neart, ag toghadh na bhfear ab fheárr agus ag cur na n-iarmharán i leataoibh. An gabha, Meargach, ag obair go dian, na ceárdaithe dob fheárr le fáil aige, na tínte ar lasadh agus na builg ag séideadh aige, de ló agus d'oíche, agus gan ar a chumas na hairm a dhéanamh chómh tiubh agus ' bhí glaoch agus ceannach orthu, bhí a leithéid sin d'airc ar gach aon rud i bhfuirm fir chun arm a bheith 'na láimh aige. Bhí Tadhg Mór Ó Cealla i gCeann Cora, ach má bhí, bhí Tadhg Óg thiar sa bhaile, agus ní baol ná gur ghléas sé neart Uíbh Máine chómh maith díreach agus ' dhéanfadh Tadhg Mór féin dá mbeadh sé thiar.

Is amhlaidh a bhí faire agus formad agus iomarbháidh idir na ríthibh agus idir na cineachaibh, féachaint cé ab fheárr a dhéanfadh an t-ollmhúchán, agus cérbh iad an bhuíon dob fheárr a bheadh gléasta agus ba mhó do thispeánfadh neart nuair a thiocfadh an ghlao.

Bhí an feall a thuig sé a bhí déanta ag Amhlaoibh air ag déanamh ana-bhuartha do Thadhg Óg Ó Chealla. Nuair a chuímhníodh sé ar an bhfeall san, do chorraíodh a chuid fola agus thagadh allas te trína chroiceann amach le náire. Thuig sé in' aigne mura mbeadh an caradas a thispeáin sé féin don ropaire fíll, go mb'fhéidir ná beadh oiread iúntaoibh' ag Colla as agus do bhí. Thuig sé ansan go mb'fhéidir gur cheart do dul ó dheas chun na mainistreach agus an scéal go léir a dh'ínsint do Cholla, scéal Chaoilte a dh'ínsint do. Go mb'fhéidir go dtiocfadh droch-amhras ag Colla ar dhuine éigin eile, díreach fé mar a tháinig an droch-amhras ag an Leagáid ar an sagart óg, ar Art mac Duibh. Nuair a chuímnigh sé ar an méid sin, ba dhóbair do preabadh ó dheas láithreach. Ach ansan do chuímhnigh sé ar Niamh agus ar Mhurchadh, agus duairt sé leis féin gurbh fheárr dul soir ar dtúis go Ceann Cora agus labhairt le Niamh. Siúd soir é. Ní fhéadfadh sé fanúint socair. Ní fhéadfadh sé an oíche ' chodladh. Ní fhéadadh sé aon tsuaimhneas ' fháil ón' aigne ach an fhaid a bhíodh gnó éigin idir lámhaibh aige, gnó éigin a choiscfeadh é ar bheith ag machnamh. Nuair a bhíodh sé ag siúl, ní fhéadadh sé gan bheith ag géarú sa chuisíocht go dtí ná féadfadh éinne cimeád suas leis.

Tháinig sé go Ceann Cora. Nuair a bhí sé ag teacht i gcóngar an rí-theaghlaigh agus é ag siúl go géar, chonaic sé an bheirt bhan ag siúl roimis amach agus é ag teacht suas leó. Bhí sé ag siúl géar agus bhíodar san ag siúl go breá réidh. Bhí cainnt éigin ar siúl acu a bhí dhá gcur ag gáirí go hiúntach. Níor mhothaíodar ag teacht é go dtí go raibh sé nách mór buailte leó. D'iompaíodar agus thugadar aghaidh air. Do stad sé 'na choilg-sheasamh ar lár an bhóthair. Gormfhlaith agus Niamh is iad a bhí ann.

"Ó! Míle fáilte rómhat, a rí!", arsa Gormfhlaith go soilbhir. "Is fada ná feacamair thu", ar sise, agus shín sí a lámh chuige agus gáire 'na snua.

Do rug sé ar an láimh, ach dá bhfaigheadh sé Éire air, ní fhéadfadh sé focal do labhairt.

"Is dócha", ar sise, "ná fuairis aon tuairisc fós ar Amhlaoibh. Cuireann sé uaigneas orm, a Niamh", ar sise le Niamh, "Tadhg a dh'fheiscint agus gan Amhlaoibh a dh'fheiscint lena chois. Bhí ana-chion agam ar

Amhlaoibh. Ní fheadar 'en domhan cad d'imigh air. Ba mhór an trua aon droch-ní a dh'imeacht air".

Chomáin sí léi mar sin ag cainnt. Níor labhair Tadhg. Ní fhéadfadh sé labhairt. Bhí sé mar a sáfí le sciain é. Níor labhair Niamh ach chómh beag. Pé rud a bhí dhá cur ag gáirí sara dtáinig Tadhg suas, níor fhan aon chuímhne aici air agus níor fhan aon gháire aici.

"Is dó' liom", arsa Gormfhlaith, "go bhfuil rud éigin ag déanamh buartha dod dhriotháir, a Niamh, agus gur maith leis bheith ag cainnt leat i t'aonar. Fanaidh ansan ag siúl díbh féin go dtí go mbeidh úr gcainnt déanta agaibh, agus raghad-sa isteach. Ach ná cimeád i bhfad uaim í, a Thaidhg", ar sise. "Tá cleas ar obair shnáthaide aici á mhúineadh dhom agus ní bheidh mé sásta go dtí go mbeidh an cleas agam".

D'imigh sí uathu. Níor labhair éinne den bheirt go dtí go raibh sí as a radharc. Ansan do labhair Niamh.

"Airiú, a Thaidhg, a mhaíonach", ar sise, "cad 'tá ort?"

"Níl blúire ar domhan orm", ar seisean, "ach do bhain an bhean san a leithéid de phreib asam! Níor fhan léas meabhrach agam nuair a chonac an bheirt agaibh i bhfochair a chéile ar an gcuma san. Nách uathásach an earra í! Cad é mar ' fhéadann sí cainnt agus sult agus gáirí ' dhéanamh, gur dhó' le duine ná fuil cor ná lúb 'na croí ach oiread leis an leanbh! Do bhuaigh sí ar a bhfeaca riamh!"

"Ní fheadraís a leath, a Thaidhg. Ní fheadraís a leath", arsa Niamh. "Mura mbeadh m'athair a bheith anso i m'aice agam, chomáinfeadh sí as mo mheabhair me. Ní fheadar 'en tsaol cad a dhall Brian agus í ' thabhairt leis riamh! B'fheárr liom go mbeinn féin agus m'athair thiar sa bhaile agus go bhféadfaimís fanúint ann". Ansan do chrom sí ar ghol, agus bhí sí ag gol ar feadh tamaill mhaith.

Caibideal 30: Marú le Soilbhreas

Níor labhair Tadhg go dtí go raibh an greas san guil curtha dhi aici. Nuair a bhí sé curtha dhi aici: "'Sea!", ar sise, "is mór an t-éadromú ar mo chroí an méid sin".

"A Niamh, a lao", arsa Tadhg, "ní dhéanfaidh so an gnó go deó. Caithfar athrú ' dhéanamh ar an obair seo. Ní fágfar anso thusa níos sia. Tá cion agam ar Bhrian. Tá cion againn go léir air. Ach is measa liom-sa thusa ná é, agus ná a bhfuil beó dá mbaineann leis. Má thug sé leis í, agus má dhein sé dearúd nuair a thug sé leis í, ní healaí dhúinn tusa a bheith thíos leis an ndearúd san. Caithfidh Murchadh duine éigin eile do chur ag faire ar Ghormfhlaith. Bean éigin dá saghas féin ba cheart do chur ag faire uirthi. Is maith liom mar a thánag. Ní raibh aon choinne agam go rabhais 'na leithéid de chás aici. An bhfuil ' fhios agat cad 'tá ceapaithe aici? Tá sí ceapaithe ar do chroí a bhriseadh istigh id chliabh le corp soilbhris agus síbhialtachta! Is é a nádúr féin fuath fíochmhar a bheith aici laistigh den tsoilbhreas agus den gheal-gháire. Is amhlaidh a réitíonn san lena goile agus lena sláinte. Tá ' fhios aici go hálainn nách mar sin duit-se, ná réitíonn a leithéid led ghoile ná led shláinte. Tá ' fhios aici go gcuirfidh an obair sin sa chré thu ach leanúint air. Anois, ag féachaint dom ort, chím go bhfuilir ag dul as. Caithfar duine éigin a dh'fháil a bheith maith a dóthain di sa chleas so atá ar siúl aici".

"Is dó' liom, a Thaidhg", arsa Niamh, "go bhfuil an ceart agat, nú pé'n Éirinn é, go bhfuil cuid den cheart agat. Tá sí, is dó' liom, ceapaithe ar mo shláinte ' bhriseadh, nú murab é sin é, ar me ' dhíbirt as so. Is dó' liom gur cuma léi ach go mbeadh sí scartha liom, beó nú marbh. Má imím anois, beidh áthas uirthi agus déarfaidh sí léi féin go bhfuil éirithe go maith léi sa chluiche a shocraigh sí ar a dh'imirt. Ní maith liom an méid sin a thabhairt mar shásamh di agus gan cúrsaí an Árdrí do bhac in aon chor".

"Ní haon chúmparáid in aon chor tusa agus í féin, a Niamh. Ní haon chreidiúint duit-se an lámh uachtair a dh'fháil uirthi insna beartaibh atá curtha roímpi aici. Téanam agus labhraimís le m'athair. Agus féach airiú! Ba dhóbair dom an gnó a thug me do dhearúd. Táim dhá chuímhneamh, a Niamh, gur ceart dom dul síos go hInis Cathaigh agus a dh'ínsint do Cholla gurb é Amhlaoibh a ghuid an chailís".

"Agus ar ndeóin, a Thaidhg", arsa Niamh, ag cur smuta gáire aisti, "níl aon deimhne ceart fós agat air gurb é an tAmhlaoibh a bhí thíos in Inis Cathaigh do ghuid an chailís".

"Tá deimhne mo dhóthain agam air", ar seisean. "Nách tapaidh a tháinig an dúil sa Chreideamh aige! Bhí rud eigin dhá chur 'na luí orm i gcaitheamh na haimsire an fhaid a bhí sé dhá ollmhú féin chun an Chreidimh a ghlacadh ná raibh aon ghus san ollmhúchán. Bhí eagal orm dá ngéillinn don smaoineamh san go mbeinn ag déanamh éagóra ar an mbuachaill, bhí sé chómh símplí, chómh leanbaí sin, an ropaire! Ansan arís, nuair aduairt sé gur mhaith leis bheith 'na shagart, tháinig an smaoineamh céanna chúm. Cheapas nár mhothaíos an gus ceart 'na chainnt ná 'na mheón i dtaobh an ruda a bhí aige á chur roimis, dar liom. Thugas fé ndeara go minic folús éigin ná féadainn a thuiscint insna gnóthaíbh Creidimh a bhíodh ar siúl aige. An lá a bhí Brian agus na huaisle thíos, nuair a tháinig an Leagáid, d'airíos daoine ag cáineadh agus ag gearradh na Lochlannach os cómhair an Lochlannaigh óig. Bhí eagal orm go mbeadh fearg air. Níor chuir sé blúire suime 'na gcainnt, an ropaire fill! Is álainn a chimeád sé a aigne istigh, agus mise ag déanamh éagóra ar mo dhá shúil agus ar mo bhreithiúntas féin le heagla go ndéanfainn éagóir air sin. Níl aon phioc dá mhearathall orm, a Niamh. Is é ' ghuid an chailís, agus is chun í ' ghuid do leog sé air gur ghlac sé an Creideamh, agus is chuige do leog sé air gur mhaith leis bheith 'na shagart. Bhí ' fhios aige, chómh luath agus ' bheadh cuid de sna mion-órdaibh glacaithe aige, go gcuirfeadh Colla san *érdam* é. Ansan bhí gach aon chaoi aige ar an gcailís a ghuid. Bhíos chun dul síos agus an scéal go léir a dh'ínsint do Cholla, ach níor mhaith liom é ' dhéanamh gan é ' chur id chómhairle-se ar dtúis. Ca bhfios ná go mb'fhéidir go mbeadh sé ar dhuine éigin eile ag Colla. Téanam go bhfeicimíd m'athair, agus san am gcéanna, bí ag cuímhneamh i t'aigne ar cad is ceart dom a dhéanamh".

Chuadar isteach i dtigh Thaidhg Mhóir Uí Chealla, agus fuaradar Tadhg féin rómpu istigh.

Caibideal 31: Fuascailt

Bhí Tadhg Mór féin rómpu istigh agus níorbh aon iúnadh má gheal a chroí nuair a chonaic sé chuige isteach an bheirt. Ní raibh le feiscint in Éirinn an lá san ríogan óg a dh'fhéadfadh seasamh in aice na hiníne agus iomláine a háilleachta féin do chimeád. Pé áilleacht a chífí inti an fhaid a bheadh sí 'na haonar, do thiocfadh claíochló ar an áilleacht san nuair a curfí 'na seasamh in aice Niamh í. Bhí daoine ag tosnú ar a thabhairt fé ndeara ná bíodh iomláine blátha ar áilleacht Ghormfhlaith féin, le deiriní, nuair a chítí Niamh 'na haice. Níor chóir puínn iúnadh ' dhéanamh de sin, áfach, mar is ag teacht a bhí áilleacht Niamh agus bhí áilleacht Ghormfhlaith ag imeacht, nú ag tosnú ar imeacht. Agus i dtaobh an mhic. Bhí finne agus solasmhaire agus gileacht na hiníne ann, agus bhí folt óir na hiníne air; an t-ualach órga ar a cheann agus anuas ar a ghuaillibh agus ar a shlinneánaibh. Bhí an tsúil ríoga chéanna 'na cheann go glan agus go hoscailte agus go neamh-eaglach. 'Na theannta san, bhí sé groí cumasach láidir mar ba dhual athar do ' bheith. Ní raibh an chaoi fálta fós aige ar ghníomharthaibh gaile agus gaisce ' dhéanamh, mar a bhí fálta ag á athair, i gcathannaibh Bhriain in aghaidh na Lochlannach. Ach bhí an chaoi roimis, agus bhí gach aon deallramh go ndéanfadh sé na gníomhartha nuair a thiocfadh an chaoi, agus go mothódh na Lochlannaigh meáchaint a bhuille.

Níorbh aon iúnadh má gheal croí Thaidhg Mhóir Uí Chealla nuair a chonaic sé an bheirt chuige isteach.

"Dé bheatha-sa, a Thaidhg!", ar seisean. "Conas ' fhágais gach aon rud agus gach éinne id dhiaidh sa bhaile?"

Caibideal 31: Fuascailt

"Go mairir-se, a athair!", arsa Tadhg. "D'fhágas gach éinne agus gach aon rud im dhiaidh go maith, baochas le Dia! Bhí rud beag ag déanamh buartha dhom agus níor dheineas ach rith aniar chun go labharfainn le Niamh mar gheall air".

"An mó fear a bheidh agat i gcómhair an chogaidh, a Thaidhg?", arsa Tadhg Mór.

"Tá chúig céad déag fear againn cheana, a athair", arsa Tadhg Óg, "agus tá ' fhios agam go mbeidh chúig céad eile againn sara fada".

"Tá san ró-bheag, a mhic ó", arsa Tadhg Mór. "Ba cheart dúinn an trí mhíle* slán a bheith againn".

"Is mó an neart dhá mhíle ó Uíbh Máine, a athair, ná trí mhíle ó áiteannaibh eile. Tá a lán dár bhfearaibh agus tá muiríon óg orthu".

"Tá", arsa Tadhg Mór, "agus má gheibhid Lochlannaigh an lámh uachtair orainn cad a dhéanfaidh an muiríon óg? Beart lag, a Thaidhg, is ea d'aon fhear atá ábalta ar chlaíomh a chasadh fanúint siar anois. Nách dó' leat san, a Niamh?"

"Ní dó' liom, a athair", arsa Niamh, "go bhfanfaidh aon fhear siar in Uíbh Máine, aon fhear go bhfuil lúth a ghéag in aon chor aige".

"Ní dó' liom go bhfanfaidh, a 'níon ó", arsa Tadhg Mór. "Ach cad é seo oraibh, a Thaidhg?", ar seisean.

D'inis Tadhg do ansan conas a tháinig sé go hobann ar Ghormfhlaith agus ar Niamh agus cad a chonaic sé. Mhínigh sé dho conas mar, de réir a thuisceana féin, a bhí beartaithe ag Gormfhlaith sprid agus croí agus aigne Niamh do bhriseadh agus do mhilleadh le corp soilbhris agus le corp caradais, mar dhea.

Caibideal 31: Fuascailt

"Ní fhéadfaidh Niamh an rud san do sheasamh, a athair", ar seisean. "Tá sí ag dul as cheana féin. Ní fhágfaidh an bhean san goile ná sláinte aici. Ní feárr-de í aon uair a' chluig den aimsir a chaitheann sí i gcómhluadar na mná san. Crochaire mná is ea an bhean san! Má fágtar Niamh 'na fochair, cuirfidh sí Niamh san iúir, an rud atá beartaithe aici a dhéanamh".

D'fhéach Tadhg Mór ar Niamh.

"Imbriathar, a ghamhain", ar seisean, "gur dó' liom go bhfuil an ceart aige. Taíonn tú ag dul as. Nách olc uaim nár thug fé ndeara é!"

"Ó, a athair", arsa Niamh, "is trua chráite nár fhanamair thiar sa bhaile. Tagann tocht agus ualach ar mo chroí nuair a chím chúm í gach aon mhaidean agus í chómh séimh, chómh soilbhir, chómh geal-gháiriteach. Bím a d'iarraidh gáire ' dhéanamh léi i dtreó ná tabharfadh sí fé ndeara an tocht orm, ach is beag ná go mb'fheárr liom bás d'fháil ná fanúint a thuilleadh 'na fochair. Go maithidh Dia dhom é! Ní fhéadaim gan bheith dhá mheas go bhfuil droch-ní dhá leanúint".

"Ná bac í féin a thuilleadh, a 'níon ó", arsa Tadhg Mór. "Is trua nár labhrais níos túisce liom. Fanaidh araon ansan. Raghad anonn go teaghlach Bhriain. Beidh mé chúibh sara fada".

D'imigh sé amach agus anonn chun an teaghlaigh. Gormfhlaith an chéad duine a bhuail uime.

"Móra dhuit, a rí", ar sise leis. "Cad 'tá ag cimeád Niamh uaim? Is iúntach an t-eólas atá aici ar obair shnáthaide. Tá cleas ar an obair aici á mhúineadh dhom agus is é is fada liom* go mbeidh an cleas agam. An fada go dtiocfaidh sí, a rí?"

"Tá sí gan bheith ar fónamh, a Árdríogan", arsa Tadhg Mór. "Tá a driotháir ag cainnt léi. Is dó' liom gur inis sé rud éigin di a chuir trí chéile aigne uirthi. Bíodh foighne agat, a Árdríogan", ar seisean. "B'fhéidir nách fiú biorán is é. B'fhéidir go mbeadh sí chút gan puínn ríghnis. An bhfuil an tÁrdrí le feiscint, led thoil, a Árdríogan?"

"Anois díreach a chonac é féin agus an rí-dhamhna ag dul isteach", ar sise.

"Go ra' maith agat, a Árdríogan!", arsa Tadhg Mór, agus d'imigh sé isteach.

"'Sea!", arsa Gormfhlaith, 'na haigne féin, nuair a bhí sé imithe, "ní deirim ná go bhfuil teinneas croí curtha agam ar do pheata-sa. 'Tá sí gan bheith ar fónamh'. An cailín bocht! Dá mb'áil leó gan í ' chur im threó. Ní féidir aon ní a dhéanamh i ganfhios di. Ach is féidir rud a dhéanamh os a cómhair. Is féidir an croí do chrá inti os a cómhair".

Pé cainnt a bhí ag Murchadh á dhéanamh leis an Árdrí, níorbh fhada go raibh sí déanta. Ansan tháinig sé féin agus Tadhg Mór amach. D'inis Tadhg Mór a scéal do, agus ná féadfadh sé Niamh a dh'fhágáilt i gCeann Cora ní ba shia.

"Tá go maith, a Thaidhg, tá go hana-mhaith", arsa Murchadh. "Tagann san agus an rud ar a bhfuil socair isteach lena chéile go hálainn. Tá m'athair ag dul ar a chuaird rí. Fágfar an Árdríogan i gCeann Cora os cionn an rí-theaghlaigh. Ní féidir di aon droch-ní a dhéanamh an fhaid a bheidh an tÁrdrí ar a chuaird. Ní foláir duit-se dul leis, a Thaidhg, agus ní foláir duit Niamh a bhreith leat. Má tá sí ag dul as, tabharfaidh an chuaird thar n-ais 'na maise féin arís í, geallaim dhuit é".

Do tháinig Tadhg Mór thar n-ais chun a thí féin. D'inis sé don bheirt cad air go raibh socair. Bhí áthas mór orthu araon.

"Tá mo ghuí tabhartha dhom ag Dia, moladh go deó leis!", arsa Niamh. "Níl maidean le fada", ar sise, "nár iarras ar Mhaolshuathain mo ghuí do chur suas chun Dé sa Naomh Íbirt. Bhíos dhá iarraidh ar Dhia, trí ímpí Sheanáin, me ' dh'fhuascailt as an gcrua-chás 'na rabhas. Chuir Dia thusa chúm ar dtúis, a Thaidhg. Do labhrais-se le m'athair. Do labhair m'athair le Murchadh. Agus sin déanta an fhuascailt! Moladh go deó le Dia!"

"Is maith é sin", arsa Tadhg Óg. "Agus anois, ó tá do ghnó-sa déanta chun ár dtoile go léir, is mithid dómh-sa aghaidh a thabhairt ar mo ghnó féin. Tá mo chroí briste ó bheith ag cuímhneamh ar an ropaire fíll úd agus ar ghuid na cailíse agus ar an lámh a bhí agam féin sa ghadaíocht san".

"Airiú, a Thaidhg, an ar buile ataoi?", arsa Niamh. "An lámh a bhí agat féin sa ghadaíocht san! Cad é an lámh a dh'fhéadfá-sa ' bheith agat* sa ghadaíocht san?"

"Mura mbeadh an caradas a chonaic Colla, agus gach éinne eile, idir mise agus an ropaire úd, a Niamh", ar seisean, "ní bheadh oiread iúntaoibh' ag Colla as agus a bhí aige as. Mura mbeadh an iúntaoibh a bhí ag Colla as, ní curfí isteach san *érdam* é, agus ní bhfaigheadh sé an chaothúlacht a fuair sé ar an ngadaíocht a dhéanamh. Fuair sé caradas, a Niamh, ó m'athair agus óm mháthair, agus uaibh go léir, thiar in Uíbh Máine. Is trua chráite mar a chuir sé cos leis riamh san áit. Ní chuirfeadh sé cos leis san áit agus ní bhfaigheadh sé an caradas a fuair sé ann, a Niamh, mura mbeadh mise! Nuair a chuímhním air, bíonn náire orm ná féadfainn a dh'ínsint duit!"

Nuair ' airigh Niamh an méid sin cainnte, ní miste a rá ná go raibh náire a dóthain uirthi féin. Thuig sí go hálainn an uair sin, agus go minic roimis sin, cad é an saghas an grá a tugadh di gan labhairt. Thuig sí an uair sin, agus go minic roimis sin, ón lá a dh'inis Caoilte scéal an phúicín, cad é an saghas an glacadh Creidimh a dhein Amhlaoibh agus cad í an íntinn ar ar ghlac sé na hÚird. Bhí an dá mhachnamh úd tabhartha dá chéile aici cruínn go leór. Bhí náire a dóthain uirthi nuair ' airigh sí Tadhg á rá go raibh náire air. Ní duairt sí aon fhocal, áfach, amach as a béal i dtaobh an náire a bhí uirthi ná i dtaobh na cúise a bhí aici leis an náire; ní nár locht ar an gcailín!

"Ó, a Thaidhg", ar sise, "ná labhair ar an gcuma san. Bhí sé siúd chómh sleamhain, chómh geal-gháiriteach san go raibh báidh agus caradas ag gach éinne leis. Mheasamair go léir go raibh sé chómh símplí, chómh hoscailte leis an leanbh. Chuirfinn geall go n-admhódh Colla féin nách mar gheall ort-sa a thug sé aon iúntaoibh riamh a hAmhlaoibh, ach mar gheall ar Amhlaoibh féin. Ní healaí dhuit éagóir a dhéanamh ort féin, a Thaidhg. Níor dheinis ach an rud a dheineamair go léir. Níor bhuail sé ort-sa ach an bob a bhuail sé orainn go léir".

"Níor bhuail sé aon bhob ort-sa, a Niamh", arsa Tadhg, agus gan aon chuímhneamh aige ar an mbrí a bhí lena chainnt.

"Imbriathar gur bhuail", ar sise. "Do bhuail sé an bob orm a bhuail sé ar gach éinne. Ní raibh aon choinne agam ná gur bhuachaill shímplí oscailte dhea-chroíoch é*. Bhí áthas mór orm mar gheall ar charadas a bheith idir thusa agus a leithéid d'ógánach gheal-chroíoch uasal onóireach, dar liom".

Ba mhór go léir an suaimhneas aigne ar Thadhg an chainnt sin a dh'aireachtaint ó Niamh.

"Agus cad 'deirir liom", ar seisean, "i dtaobh dul síos agus an scéal go léir a dh'ínsint do Cholla?"

"Ní dó' liom", ar sise, "go bhfuil aon ghá leis. Ca bhfios duit ná go mb'fhéidir go bhfuil fios an scéil go léir ag Colla cheana chómh maith agus atá againn-na? Agus ca bhfios duit ná go mb'fhéidir gur mó an milleán atá ag Colla air féin ná mar atá aige ar éinne eile? Cad is gá dhuit-se dul agus tu féin a dhaoradh sa scéal? I dtaobh aon droch-amhrais a bheith ag Colla ar aon duine eile", ar sise, "ní baol go gcuirfidh Colla aon droch-amhras ar éinne gan labhairt le Murchadh.

Má labhrann sé le Murchadh, socróidh Murchadh an scéal do. Is í cómhairle ' thabharfainn-se dhuit, a Thaidhg", ar sise, "ná gan aon chur isteach ná amach a bheith agat ar an scéal a thuilleadh an fhaid ná déanfaidh éinne aon chur isteach ná amach ort mar gheall air. Do scaoilfinn thorm é dá mbeinn id chás".

"Is dó' liom, a Niamh", ar seisean, "go ndéanfaidh mé rud ort. Níl aon lorg in aon chor agam ar bheith ag dul ag cainnt le Colla mar gheall air. Is amhlaidh atá gráin agam air mar scéal, agus gráin agam orm féin mar gheall ar aon bhaint a bheith agam leis".

Níorbh fhada gur ghluais Brian ar a chuaird rí mórthímpall na hÉireann. Do ghluais Tadhg Mór Ó Cealla agus Niamh 'na chuallacht. Bhí saol breá ansan ag Niamh, agus níorbh fhada go raibh a croí agus a haigne féin arís aici.

Do fágadh Ceann Cora fé chúram na hÁrdríogana. Bhí ' fhios aici cad é an brí a bhí leis sin.

Caibideal 32: Cuaird Rí

Do ghluais Brian ar a chuaird rí. Bhí cuallacht uasal in éineacht leis. Bhí Murchadh in éineacht leis, agus Dúlainn Óg, agus Tadhg Mór Ó Cealla, agus Niamh. Bhí Tadhg Óg Ó Cealla imithe siar abhaile go hUíbh Máine chun aire ' thabhairt don ríocht san, in inead a athar, agus chun na bhfear do chur le chéile agus do ghléasadh agus d'ollmhú i gcómhair an chogaidh aduairt gach éinne a bhí ag teacht go luath. Ní raibh an cogadh fógartha. Bhí síocháin idir Árdrí Éireann agus rí Lochlann. Bhí síocháin idir é agus na ríthe eile go léir, lastoir agus lastuaidh. Ach bhí sé daingean in aigne na ndaoine, ar fuaid na hÉireann, go raibh an cogadh ag teacht agus nárbh fhada go mbeadh sé ann. Dá bhrí sin, bhí an t-ollmhúchán ar siúl ins gach aon bhall. Chun an ollmhúcháin sin do chur ar siúl ní ba ghéire dá mb'fhéidir é is ea ' chuaigh Brian ar an gcuaird rí sin. Theastaigh uaidh a dh'fheiscint lena shúilibh féin conas a bhí an gnó dá dhéanamh. Bhí cuid dá chlaínn mhac, agus uaisle eile a bhí tuisceanach i ngnóthaíbh cogaidh, imithe roimis mórthímpall chun na ndún agus chun na ndaingean a bhí curtha suas aige, chun a dh'ínsint go raibh sé ag teacht, agus chun na bhfear a bhí insna dúnaibh agus insna daingeanaibh sin do ghléasadh agus do chur i dtreó, ionas go mbeidís oiriúnach ar dhul féna shúil. Bhí scéala curtha, leis, ag triall ar na ríthibh, go raibh sé ag teacht, agus bhí gach rí acu ceapaithe ar pé neart fear a bhí aige do bheith chómh gléasta agus dob fhéidir iad a bheith, agus an méid ba mhó a dh'fhéadfadh sé dhíobh a bheith curtha le chéile aige i gcómhair an lae a thiocfadh Brian. Níorbh fhéidir aon bhob a bhualadh ar Bhrian i nithibh den tsórd san. Bhí an tsúil ró-ghéar aige. Do chífeadh sé ar an gcéad amharc an locht ba lú, insna fir nú insna hairm, nú sa ghléas. Chífeadh sé, leis, ar an gcéad amharc, an raibh cóir iompair agus cóir gluaiste agus sáith lóin, ag an rí sin do sna fearaibh sin, dá nglaeití chun bóthair orthu.

Ansan, bhí árdfhormad ag na ríthibh lena chéile, féachaint cé hé an rí a gheóbhadh moladh ó Bhrian nú cé hé a gheóbhadh cáineadh; nú, dá mba ná cáinfí éinne, cé ba mhó a gheóbhadh den mholadh. Bhí an formad san idir na fearaibh chómh mór díreach agus ' bhí sé idir na ríthibh, i dtreó nár ghá do sna ríthibh puínn de dhua na bhfear a dh'fháil chun iad a ghríosadh, mar go rabhadar féin ag gríosadh a chéile chómh dian agus dob fhéidir é. Ní raibh éinne do thuig an méid sin ní b'fheárr ná mar a thuig Brian é, agus ní raibh éinne dob fheárr a dh'fhéadfadh toradh ' bhaint as ná mar a dh'fhéad Brian toradh ' bhaint as.

Siar trí Chonnachtaibh a thug Brian aghaidh ar dtúis. Bhí ' fhios aige gur i gConnachtaibh ba lú a bhí gá le haimsir chun ollmhúcháin mar go raibh an t-ollmhúchán déanta cheana ann. Teaghlach Thaidhg Mhóir Uí Chealla an chéad theaghlach i gConnachtaibh ar ar thug sé aghaidh. Bhí Tadhg Óg imithe siar roimis agus bhí gach ní ollamh aige roimis.

Caibideal 32: Cuaird Rí

Nuair a thagadh Brian isteach mar sin ar chuaird, i dtiarnas rí, ar an eaglais a thugadh sé aghaidh ar dtúis. Dá mbeadh gá le haon ní a dhéanamh don eaglais, aon ní i bhfuirm saoirseachta, chun an tí ' chur i méid, nú chun slacht a chur air, thugadh Brian síntiús maith do rí na tíre sin chun na hoibre sin do dhéanamh. Ansan, dá mbeadh mainistir san áit, thabharfadh sé cuaird ar an mainistir agus dhéanfadh Maolshuathain féachaint i ndiaidh oibre na mainistreach, féachaint a' raibh gach aon rud 'na cheart, agus aon rud ba ghá a cheartú, dhéanfadh sé é ' cheartú.

Ba bheag eaglais ná mainistir ná *conbhint* ban rialta ná bíodh ní éigin tairbheach ag Brian le bronnadh orthu nuair a thagadh sé mar sin ar chuaird, agus do curtí gach eaglais agus gach mainistir agus gach *conbhint* ban rialta sa treó dob fheárr 'narbh fhéidir iad do chur nuair a bhíodh súil lena theacht.

Deireadh sé, i gcónaí, gur do sna gnóthaíbh a bhain le Creideamh ba cheart do ríthibh agus do dhaoine aireachas a thabhairt ar dtúis. Gur cheart gnó Dé a dhéanamh ar dtúis sara dtabharfí aghaidh ar ghnó an tsaeil seo. Gur dhóichí-de do dhuine an rath a bheith ar a ghnóthaíbh saolta nuair a dhéanfadh sé a dhícheall ar dhualgaisíbh an Chreidimh do chómhlíonadh. Ach, peocu ba thoil le Dia an rath do chur ar ghnóthaíbh saolta an duine nú gan a chur, go raibh ceangailte ar an nduine aitheanta Dé do chimeád.

Do mhúin Brian do sna ríthibh agus do sna daoine a bhí féna smacht an urraim is dual do bhanntracht, ach do mhúin sé dhóibh, 'na theannta san, an urraim is dual don cheart ar gach aon tsaghas cuma, agus chuir sé 'na luí ar a n-aigne go daingean gur i ndlí Dé atá brí agus bunús agus cúis agus fáth gach urrama dhíobh go léir. An té ná beidh eagla Dé air ná beann aige ar dhlí Dé, go bhfuil sé fuar ag éinne bheith ag brath air go staonfaidh an duine sin ó dhrúis ná ó chraos ná ó éagóir a dhéanamh ar a chómharsain má gheibheann sé an chaoi. Dá bhrí sin, gur ceart ar dtúis greim daingean a thabhairt don Chreideamh i gcroí agus in aigne an duine. Nuair a bheidh an greim sin ag an gCreideamh gurb ea is féidir an duine sin a dhéanamh úmhal do gach dlí agus do gach riail agus do gach dualgas bunaidh dá mbaineann leis an gCreideamh.

Na ríthe agus na rialtaisí atá sa tsaol anois, an chuid acu go bhfuil aon admháil in aon chor acu do Chreideamh, do cheadóidís an Creideamh le hionchas go ndéanfadh an Creideamh na daoine úmhal dóibh. Chómh maith agus gur chuige sin a cuireadh an Creideamh ar bun, chun daoine ' dhéanamh úmhal do ríthibh! Do thuig Brian nárbh ea. Gur chun daoine ' dhéanamh úmhal do Dhia a cuireadh an Creideamh ar bun. Ná fuil san úmhlaíocht a chuireann an Creidimh in áirithe do ríthibh ach cuid de thoradh an Chreidimh. Gur maith an rud do ríthibh an úmhlaíocht san a theacht mar thoradh as an gCreideamh ar an saol so, ach ná fuil sa méid sin de thoradh an Chreidimh ach neamhní seochas an toradh a fachtar as ar an saol eile. Go n-iompaítear nithe taobh síos suas nuair a curtar suím i dtoradh an Chreidimh ar an saol so agus neamh-shuím 'na thoradh ar an saol eile.

Do thuig Brian na nithe sin go léir agus dhein sé beart de réir a thuisceana. Bhí an Creideamh aige 'na chroí féin istigh agus do bhí an Creideamh san le feiscint go soiléir 'na ghníomharthaibh. Do mhúiscil an dea-shampla san Creideamh agus toradh an Chreidimh i gcroíthibh na ríthe agus na ndaoine a bhí féna smacht.

Thug sé tosach don Chreideamh insna háiteannaibh 'nar thug sé a chuarda. Nuair a bhíodh féachta aige ar na heaglaisíbh agus ar na mainistríbh agus ar chonbhintíbh na mban rialta, thugadh sé aghaidh ar na scoileannaibh, agus d'fhéachadh sé isteach go cruínn sa chuma 'na mbíodh an obair ag dul chun cínn. Agus thugadh sé aire mhaith, —ach níor ghá dho san mar do thugadh na manaigh féin aire mhaith dho—pé easnamh a bheadh ná ná* beadh, ar aon tsaghas eile ealaíon, ná caithfeadh aon easnamh a bheith, ná aon fhaillí a bheith, sa chuma 'na múintí an Creideamh do sna daoinibh óga. Bhí ' fhios ag Brian go maith, agus bhí ' fhios ag an uile dhuine de sna hoidíbh a bhí ag stiúrú na hoibre sin, ná fuil ach diabhal ó ifreann sa bhfear a gheóbhaidh scolaíocht gan Creideamh. Dá bhrí sin, níor ghá do Bhrian bheith ag féachaint 'na ndiaidh chun a chur ' fhiachaibh orthu an Creideamh do mhúineadh. Ach do bhíodh.

Nuair a bhíodh an obair sin go léir déanta ag Brian, san áit 'na mbíodh sé ar a chuaird, thugadh sé aghaidh ar an ollmhúchán armála a bhíodh ar siúl i gcómhair an chogaidh mhóir a bhí ag teacht, dar le gach éinne. Do tugtí na fir amach os a chómhair agus do curtí trína ngleacaíocht iad. Bhíodh oiread san eagla roimena shúil ag na fearaibh go léir, idir uasal agus íseal, go mbídís ag déanamh taithí den ghleacaíocht ar feadh mórán aimsire roim ré nuair a bhíodh súil lena theacht. Dheinidís a ndícheall chun ná faigheadh sé aon locht orthu. Agus bhíodh an formad ann, leis, idir na ríthibh, féachaint cé aige dob fheárr 'na mbeadh an t-ollmhúchán déanta, agus idir na buínibh, féachaint ceocu buíon ba mhó a thabharfadh sásamh do.

Thugadh sé tabharthaistí uaidh, do sna ríthibh agus do sna fearaibh, claíomh, nú sleagh, nú tua, nú brat álainn, nú capall breá, agus bhíodh an formad ann, féachaint cé ' gheóbhadh an tabharthas ba luachmhaire, mar, gan amhras, is don té ab fheárr a thabharfadh sásamh a tabharfí an tabharthas ab fheárr.

Bhí áthas an domhain ar Niamh nuair a fuair sí gur siar chun teaghlaigh a hathar a bhí Brian ag dul ar dtúis. Chuir Tadhg Mór teachtaire siar, chómh luath agus ' fuair sé an t-eólas, dhá ínsint do Thadhg Óg go raibh an tÁrdrí ag teacht. Ba mhaith le Brian féin dul siar chun na háite sin ar dtúis. Is ann a bhí a ghaolta ó thaobh a mháthar, agus is ann a bhí gaolta na clainne a bhí aige lena chéad mhnaoi. Drifiúr do Mhaolruanaidh na Paidre ab ea í[*]. Agus gan amhras bhí áthas an domhain ar an muíntir thiar go léir, leis, nuair a hínseadh dóibh go raibh sé ag teacht. Tháinig Maolruanaidh na Páidre, rí Ó bhFiachrach Áidhne, agus a lán eile d'uaislibh Connacht, tamall maith den tslí 'na choinnibh. Bhí Conn, mac Mhaoilruanaidh, i dteaghlach Bhriain cheana. Thugadar go léir aghaidh ar theaghlach

Thaidhg Mhóir Uí Chealla. Do cuireadh míle fáilte rómpu. Do cuireadh gach cóir orthu dár cheart go huasal agus go ríoga, agus duairt Niamh nár tógadh an ceó i gceart dá croí go dtí go bhfuair sí í féin arís i dteaghlach a hathar agus uaisle Connacht agus Cheann Cora 'na tímpall.

D'admhaigh an chuideachta gur shamhlaíodar an solas 'na tímpall, mar a bhíodh cheana, agus gurbh í an ga gréine céanna arís í ag teacht 'na measc.

Nuair a bhí an chuaird go hUíbh Máine tabhartha, chuadar go léir, le cois a chéile, go hUíbh Fhiachrach Áidhne agus chuir Maolruanaidh cóir uasal orthu.

Caibideal 33: Caradas ag Fás a Fuath

Nuair a bhí a chuaird agus a ghnó críochnaithe i gConnachtaibh ag Brian, thug sé aghaidh ó thuaidh ar Chúig' Uladh. Thug muíntir na cúige sin go léir an onóir do ba cheart a thabhairt don Árdrí, agus thug Brian dóibh na tabharthaistí ba cheart don Árdrí a thabhairt do ríthibh cúigí. D'fhéach sé ar na heagailsíbh agus ar na mainistreachaibh agus ar na scoileannaibh, fé mar a dheineadh sé ins gach aon bhall. Ghlaeigh sé chun na *gconbhintí* leis, agus ba mhór ag na mnáibh rialta an tÁrdrí do theacht dhá bhféachaint agus ag féachaint na scoileanna a bhí acu. Bhíodh mná óga acu 'na scoileannaibh agus iad ag múineadh gach aon tsaghas eólais do sna mnáibh óga san ar na nithibh a bhí riachtanach an uair sin do mhnaoi ' bheith ar eólas aici.

Ba mhór ag na mnáibh rialta an tÁrdrí a dh'fheiscint, agus Murchadh, agus Dúlainn Óg, agus gach fear eile de mhuíntir Bhriain 'na raibh a n-ainmneacha i mbéalaibh daoine ar fuid na hÉireann an uair sin. Ach ní raibh éinne beó ab fheárr leó a dh'fheiscint ná Niamh. Chuaigh a tuairisc roímpi eatarthu. Do hínseadh dóibh ná raibh ríogan óg eile ar thalamh na hÉireann an uair sin chómh breá ná chómh dathúil léi. Agus do hínseadh dóibh go raibh socair 'na haigne aici gan pósadh choíche. Go bhfanfadh sí ag tabhairt aire dá hathair an fhaid ab é toil Dé iad ' fhágáilt ar an saol so i bhfochair a chéile, agus ansan, dá mb'é a hathair ba thúisce a gheóbhadh bás, go bhfanfadh sí singil 'na dhiaidh ar an saol so go dtí go mbéarfadh Dia chuige féin í agus go mbeadh sí i bhfochair a hathar arís ar an saol eile.

Sara dtagadh sí chúthu, bhídís ag machnamh ar a háilleacht agus ag cuímhneamh ar na mnáibh óga dob álainne[*] agus ba bhreátha agus ba dhathúla dá bhfeacadar riamh, agus dhá shamhlú 'na n-aigne cad é an saghas í má bhí sí ní ba bhreátha le feiscint ná éinne acu súd. Ansan, nuair a thagadh sí agus do chídís í, do leathadh a súile orthu agus d'admhaíodís nár fhéad aon tsamhlú dár dheineadar teacht in aon ghiorracht don radharc a chonacadar nuair ' fhéachadar uirthi. Ansan, ní bhíodh aon iúnadh orthu nuair ' airídís i dtaobh an tsolais 'na tímpall agus i dtaobh an gha gréine. Do samhlaítí dhóibh féin, nuair a thagadh sí isteach sa *chonbhint* chúthu, go dtugaidís fé ndeara an solas 'na gnaoi agus 'na tímpall, agus gur chuma í nú ga gréine ag teacht isteach.

Is é céad rud a dheineadh na mná rialta, ins gach aon *chonbhint*, chómh luath agus ' bhíodh tamall de lá caite ann aici, ná cromadh ar thathant uirthi fanúint acu ar fad. Ghlacadh sise an tathant go breá réidh agus go breá séimh, ach ní baol go dtugadh sí aon chómharthaí uaithi ar ghéilleadh don tathant. Bhíodh áthas mór orthu an fhaid a bhíodh sí acu, agus bhíodh uaigneas mór orthu nuair a bhíodh cuaird na háite tabhartha, agus nuair a bhíodh Brian agus a chuallacht ag imeacht go háit eile.

Nuair a bhí Cúig' Uladh siúlta, do gabhadh tímpall trí Chúige Laighean. Do fanadh roinnt laethanta i gCúige na Mí, i dteaghlach Mh'leachlainn Mhóir. Níor chuaird in aistear cuaird chun an teaghlaigh sin. Do cuireadh cóir go fial agus go flaithiúil ar an Árdrí agus ar a chuallacht ann. Dá mbeadh i gcuallacht Bhriain an uair sin duine iasachta, duine ná beadh aon fhios aige ar cad a bhí titithe amach in Éirinn suím aimsire roimis sin, ní bheadh aon chuímhneamh in aon chor aige go raibh Brian tar éis Mh'leachlainn do chur as an Árdríocht. Shamhlódh sé gurbh é Brian an tÁrdrí i gcónaí agus go raibh M'leachlainn féna smacht i gcónaí. B'é an cleas céanna é ag an dá theaghlach. Níor leog teaghlach Mh'leachlainn orthu gurbh iad féin teaghlach an Árdrí riamh, agus níor thispeáin teaghlach Bhriain aon mhór-is-fiú ná aon éirí-in-áirde os cionn an teaghlaigh eile. Bhí an dá mhuíntir go séimh agus go soilbhir lena chéile, agus go hollamh chun gach urrama agus gach onóra ' thabhairt dá chéile.

Chuaigh an tÁrdrí agus a theaghlach ag triall ar Shitric, ar rí Lochlannach Bhaile Átha Cliath. Do cuireadh an chuaird sin chun cínn díreach mar a cuireadh i gcás Mh'leachlainn nú i gcás aon rí cúige eile in Éirinn. Do ghlaeigh Brian chun tithe na gceannaithe agus d'fhéach sé go cruínn ar an gcuma 'na ndeinidís a ngnó. D'fhéach sé ar na luingeas a bhí sa chuan. Do thuig sé in' aigne gur mhór go léir an tairbhe do mhuíntir na hÉireann dá mbeadh mórán de sna luingeas san sa chuan san, agus ins gach cuan eile de chuantaibh na hÉireann, agus mórán den obair cheannaíochta san acu dá chimeád ar siúl idir oileán na hÉireann agus dúthaíbh iasachta. An fhaid a bhí sé ag machnamh ar an gcuma san ar an dtairbhe a bhí ag cuan Bhaile Átha Cliath á dhéanamh, do chuímhnigh sé ar an gcothrom uathásach uisce atá ó chathair Luimní síos go hInis Cathaigh agus amach ar fad go Léim Chúchulainn, agus chuímhnigh sé ar an dtairbhe a dhéanfadh an cothrom uisce sin dá mbeadh sé clúdaithe le luingeas bhreátha mhóra do bhéarfadh earraí ceannaíochta amach ó Éirinn go cuantaibh an domhain, agus do thabharfadh earraí iasachta isteach go hÉirinn sa bhflúirse chéanna, ó chuantaibh an domhain.

Nuair ' fhág sé Baile Átha Cliath agus chuaigh sé ó dheas go teaghlach rí Laighean, teaghlach Mhaoilmhórdha, teaghlach driothár a chéile, bhí an machnamh céanna in' aigne i dtaobh uisce Béil

Sionainne. D'inis sé do rí Laighean cad a bhí in' aigne, agus duairt sé leis gurbh é a thuairim féin ná raibh le fáil in Éirinn, ná in aon áit eile, adhmad a dhéanfadh craínn seóil do lu

ingeas mhóra chómh maith agus do dhéanfadh an t-adhmad a bhí ag fás i gCúige Laighean.[*]

"Dá gcurfá chúm siar go Ceann Cora, a rí", ar seisean le Maolmhórdha, "trí cínn de sna crannaibh is feárr agat chun na hoibre, do chuirfinn trí luingeas dá ndéanamh gan a thuilleadh ríghnis".

"Cuirfead agus fáilte, a Árdrí", arsa rí Laighean.

D'fhan an scéal mar sin an uair sin.

Do ghluais Brian agus a chuallacht ó dheas isteach in Ur-Mhúmhain. Thug sé a chuaird chun teaghlaigh rí na nDéiseach. Mothla mac Faoláin ab ainm don rí sin. Bhí sé dílis do Bhrian, bíodh ná raibh i bhfad roimis sin ó bhris Brian cathanna fuilteacha ar a chine. Bhí sé in' aigne, fé mar a bhí in aigne gach éinne, go raibh tórmach cogaidh ar siúl, go raibh an spéir trom leis an dtórmach cogaidh sin, agus ná raibh aon fhear beó ach Brian a dh'fhéadfadh Éire ' thabhairt saor as an gcogadh san nuair a thiocfadh sé. Dá bhrí sin, bhí sé dílis do Bhrian.

Tháinig Brian agus a chuallacht go teaghlach athar Chaoilte. Fuair gach éinne amach ansan cérbh é Caoilte, gur mac rí é agus gur Donn ab ainm do, Donn mac Beathach. Nuair a fuair Conn, mac Mhaoilruanaidh na Paidre, gur mhac rí Caoilte, tháinig sé chuige agus do rug sé ar dhá láimh air.

"Ó, a Dhuínn", ar seisean, "cad 'na thaobh nár ínsis dom cérbh é thu! Bhí sé i m'aigne go mb'fhéidir go raibh braon éigin d'fhuil ríoga ionat, agus an bhfuil ' fhios agat cathain a chuímhníos air? Chuímhníos air nuair a thugas an tarcaisne dhuit agus nuair a chonac an chuma 'nar chimeádais srian le t'fheirg. 'Mura mac rí é', arsa mise i m'aigne féin, 'tá an fholaíocht ann pé ball 'na bhfuair sé í ' bheith ann'. Duart go deimhin. Nách mór an cleasaí Niamh! Chuir sí thusa ar theachtaireacht an lá úd. Do chuir más fíor bréag! Ní hea ach cheap sí sinn a chur ó chéile. Do rug sí mise i láthair Bhriain, agus geallaim dhuit gur cuireadh smacht orm. 'Bíodh ciall agat, a mhic ó', arsa Brian. Idir Bhrian agus an sagart agus Niamh, agus í imithe amach, níor fágadh léas meabhrach im cheann. Nuair a bhíos tagaithe amach agus roinnt machnaimh déanta agam is ea ' thuigeas i gceart cad a bhí imithe orm. 'Tá a haigne socair ag Niamh ar gan pósadh choíche', arsa Maolshuathain, agus, 'Bíodh ciall agat, a mhic ó', arsa Brian. Dheineadar amadán díom eatarthu".

"Agus nách maith nár dheinis aon dearúd den fhocal amháin úd, a rí", arsa Caoilte.

"Cad é an focal?", arsa Conn.

"An focal úd aduairt Maolshuathain, 'Tá a haigne socair ag Niamh ar gan pósadh choíche'".

"Ó, ambasa is fíor dhuit é", arsa Conn. "D'fhan an focal san 'na sheasamh i m'aigne ó shin. Tá sé 'na sheasamh i m'aigne anois chómh gléineach agus ' bhí sé nuair ' airíos ag teacht a béal Mhaoilshuathain amach é! 'Tá socair ag Niamh 'na haigne', ar seisean, 'gan pósadh choíche'. Dá mairinn míle blian, ní imeódh an méid sin cainnte as m'aigne".

"'Sé an scéal céanna agam-sa é", arsa Caoilte. "Duairt sí an chainnt sin díreach amach as a béal féin liom nuair a bhí sí 'om chur ar a' dteachtaireacht, mar dhea, agus tá an focal 'na sheasamh i m'aigne anois, agus beidh go deó".

"Féach, a Dhuínn", arsa Conn, "is maith a dhein sí é agus a haigne do shocrú ar an gcuma san. Dá bpósadh sí thusa, is dó' liom go mbainfinn an t-anam asat; agus dá bpósadh sí mise, is dócha go mbainfá-sa an t-anam asam-sa; agus dá bpósadh sí duine eile, is dócha go mbainfimís araon an t-anam as san. Ach nuair ná pósfaidh sí éinne choíche, ní bheidh éinne agam-sa ná agat-sa ná againn araon chun an anama ' bhaint as! Is dian-mhaith atá an scéal socair aici!"

"Is fíor dhuit sin, a Chuínn", arsa Caoilte. "Shocraigh sí é i dtreó go bhféadfaimíd bheith ag baint spóirt as, an rud atá agat-sa á dhéanamh anois, agus i dtreó go bhfuil ar ár gcumas bheith muínteartha caradach lena chéile. Tá gá againn anois le muíntearthas agus le caradas. Is dó' liom nách ró-fhada go mbeidh namhaid agus eascáirde ár ndóthain againn".

"Is fíor dhuit sin, a Dhuínn", arsa Conn. "Ná beadh sé chómh maith againn, agat-sa agus agam-sa adeirim, caradas daingean a bheith eadrainn, fé mar atá idir Mhurchadh agus Dúlainn, i dtreó nuair a bheimís i lár catha go bhféadfaimís a chéile ' chosaint. Tá ana-chion agam ort ón lá úd a bhuais orm sa rith".

"Ní mó an cion atá agat orm, a Chuínn", arsa Caoilte, "ná mar atá agam-sa ort-sa. Agus a' bhfhuil ' fhios agat cad é an chúis go bhfuil an cion san agam ort, a Chuínn?"

"An daighe ní fheadar, a Dhuínn", arsa Conn. "Ní heól dom gur dheineas aon ní riamh duit a thuíllfeadh cion dom uait".

"Neósfad-sa dhuit cad a chuir an cion im chroí ort. An grá a thispeánais a bheith agat do Niamh. Sin é a dhein é".

"Aililiú!", arsa Conn. "Ba dhó' liom gur éad, agus fuath dhom, agus gráin orm, a mhúiscleódh sé sin id chroí".

"Is ea, leis", arsa Caoilte, "go dtí go nduairt sí liom go raibh a haigne socair aici ar gan pósadh choíche. Nuair ' airíos an focal san uaithi bhí ' fhios agam gurbh fhíor an focal. Ansan nuair a chonac, agus nuair a thuigeas i m'aigne, an grá a bhí agat-sa dhi, tháinig trua agam duit. Ansan tháinig an cion agam ort. Sin mar a tháinig sé. Tá sé im chroí fós, chómh láidir díreach agus ' bhí sé an uair sin".

"Is iúntach an scéal é sin, a Dhuínn", arsa Conn. "Is é an scéal céanna óm thaobh-sa é ach nár thugas fé ndeara é chómh géar agus ' thugais-se fé ndeara é. Bhí ' fhios agam cad é an chúis 'na mbíodh Caoilte ag teacht fé dhéin teaghlaigh Thaidhg Mhóir Uí Chealla. Nuair a thánag amach ó Bhrian agus ó Mhaolshuathain, agus Maolshuathain tar éis an chínn a bhaint den scéal dom, dar leis, agus Brian tar éis cómhairle ' thabhairt dom ciall a bheith agam, chómh luath agus d'fhéadas mo mheabhair do chruinniú, agus níorbh fhuiriste é, 'Agus Caoilte bocht', arsa mise i m'aigne féin, 'cad a dhéanfaidh sé! Tá an scéal chómh holc aige agus 'tá sé agam-sa, nú b'fhéidir níosa mheasa'. Tá ana-bháidh agam leat ó shin. Agus féach, níor thugas fé ndeara an chúis go dtí anois nuair a dh'ínsis-se do thaobh féin den scéal dom".

Do shnadhmaigh an bheirt a gcaradas go daingean ansan, agus bhí móráil agus aiteas agus áthas croí orthu as san amach.

D'admhaíodar i gcónaí, as san amach, gur mhór an tabharthas ó Dhia dhóibh an caradas san a bheith eatarthu, agus gur ar Niamh a bhí a bhaochas acu Dia do thabhairt an tabharthais sin dóibh.

Caibideal 34: Ciúnas Roim Thóirthnigh

An fhaid a bhí Brian ar an gcuaird sin, mórthímpall na hÉireann, bhí sé ag táthú agus ag dlúthú agus ag méadú a nirt ar gach aon tsaghas cuma. Do bhíodh sé ag gríosadh na ndaoine a bhíodh neamh-shuimiúil. Bhí a lán neamh-shuimiúlachta insna daoine in áiteannaibh. Ní chreidfidís go raibh aon bhaol go dtiocfadh namhaid go dtí go bhfeicfidís ag teacht é. Ansan, nuair a maróífí a leath agus nuair a fágfí an leath eile dhíobh leath-mharbh, agus nuair a bheadh an namhaid imithe agus a gcuid 'en tsaol bertha chun siúil aige, ní chuirfeadh aon ní 'na luí orthu gur cheart dóibh iad féin d'ollmhú mar nár bhaol ná go dtiocfadh an namhaid sin arís. Nuair a thagadh Brian i measc daoine den tsórd san, ar a chuaird, bhíodh sé ag cainnt leó agus ag plé leó agus dhá ngríosadh agus ag spídiúchán orthu, go dtí go gcuireadh sé a bhfearg suas agus go socraídís ar na hairm a sholáthar agus ar thaithí ' dhéanamh díobh chómh maith le cách. Bhuaileadh duine uime uaireanta, áfach, agus ní fhéadadh a dhícheall aon spionnadh ' chur 'na mhisneach. Thug aon fhear amháin an freagra so air:

"Ná bí liom, a Árdrí", ar seisean. "Dá mbeadh sé in áirithe agam maireachtaint míle blian, b'fheárr liom gach aon lá den mhíle blian san do chaitheamh ar mhullach mo chínn sa lathaigh ag sclábhaíocht ná aon lá amháin do throid!"

B'éigean do Bhrian éirí as. Ní mór den tsaghas san, áfach, a bhuail uime ar a chuaird. Na fir a bhuail uime, pé neamh-shuimiúlacht a bhí orthu sarar labhair sé leó, do bhain a chainnt an neamh-shuimiúlacht díobh. Do tugadh dóibh na hairm agus do cuireadh ag déanamh na gleacaíochta iad agus stiúrthóirí 'na mbun, agus bhí gach aon deallramh nár ró-fhada go mbeidís ábalta ar aghaidh a thabhairt ar Lochlannach i gcath agus ar chleas a mhúineadh dho.

Um an am 'na raibh an chuaird dá críochnú, bhí measta in' aigne ag Brian go mbeadh suas le chúig mhíle fhichead fear ollamh aige i gcómhair na Lochlannach nuair a thiocfaidís. De réir a bhreithiúntais is go cuan Bhaile Átha Cliath a bhíodar le teacht. Bhí eólas maith tabhartha aige do Chlaínn Chais, agus do sna cineachaibh eile sa Mhúmhain, ar na bóithribh go Baile Átha Cliath. Ní raibh aon bhaol go mbeadh na slóite ag dul amú ná go mbeidís ag brú ar a chéile ná ag teacht crosta ar a chéile.

Bhí ' fhios aige, dá mbeadh fir Éireann go léir in éineacht aige, go mbeadh breis mhór agus daichead míle fear aige, agus bhí ' fhios aige, dá mbeadh san amhlaidh, ná tiocfadh aon chogadh, mar ná raibh aon chómhacht lasmu', in aon pháirt den domhan, a dh'fhéadfadh aghaidh a thabhairt ar chómhacht na hÉireann dá mbeadh fir Éireann go léir in éineacht. Ach bhí ' fhios aige go maith go mbeadh cuid d'fhearaibh Éireann ar thaobh na Lochlannach, agus go mbeadh cuid acu ná raghadh in aon chor sa chaismirt. Dhein sé a dhícheall, sa chuaird, ar an dá aicme sin do laígheadú an oiread agus dob fhéidir é. Chuir sé go soiléir os cómhair aigne na ndaoine, coitianta, agus ins gach áit 'nar labhair sé leis na daoine, dá bhfaigheadh na Lochlannaigh an lámh uachtair sa chogadh a bhí ag teacht, go ngeóbhaidís de chosaibh i nGaelaibh Éireann chómh tiubaisteach san gurbh fheárr go mór dá raibh de Chríostaithibh san oileán bás a dh'fháil sa chath a troidfí ná maireachtaint in Éirinn i ndiaidh an chatha san. Chuaigh an chainnt sin i bhfeidhm ar fhormhór na ndaoine. Thuigeadar go raibh an fhírinne sa chainnt. Shocraíodar a n-aigne ar an lámh uachtair a bheith acu féin nuair a thiocfadh an cath nú titim sa chath. Chuaigh an focal san amach i measc na ndaoine ins gach aon bhall. Ní har theacht ón gcath a bhíodh éinne ag trácht, ach ar thitim sa chath nú an namhaid do thitim. Chuaigh daoine i dtaithí an fhocail chómh mór san go raibh a n-aigne socair acu go breá réidh, gan aon chorrabhuais, ar dhul sa chath, nuair a thiocfadh an cath, agus ar gan teacht as. B'in é saol a gheárr gach fear amach do féin, go dtí go dtiocfadh an cath san.

Ní baol gur fhág Brian gan cur 'na luí orthu go léir, coitianta, an fear a thitfeadh sa chath gur bhás ar son an Chreidimh do é, agus bhí ' fhios acu féin, an té a dh'fhuiliceódh bás ar son an Chreidimh go raibh aoibhneas na bhFlaitheas in áirithe dho láithreach. Ní fhéadfadh bás i gcath scáth ná eagla do chur ar fhearaibh go raibh a n-aigne socair ar an gcuma san. Agus níor chuir, nuair a tháinig sé.

An fhaid a bhí an chuaird sin ar siúl, leis, bhí rud eile ar siúl. Bhí Caoilte ag imeacht coitianta ó áit go háit in Éirinn, agus bhíodh sé go minic imithe thar farraige i ganfhios d'éinne ach do Mhurchadh. Chuaigh sé soir go minic go crích Lochlann gan spleáchas don fholáramh úd a tugadh do sa leitir a fuair sé ó chaptaein na luinge a thug abhaile go Corcaigh é tar éis a thamall a thabhairt sa phríosún thall i gcathair rí Lochlann. Chuaigh sé anonn arís agus arís eile, agus thug sé leis anall, gach uair díobh, ag triall ar Mhurchadh, cúntas cruínn ar an neart fear a bhí thall ag rí Lochlann, agus ar an méid luingeas a bhí aige chun na bhfear a bhreith thar farraige, agus gur anall go hÉirinn a bhí na fir sin le tabhairt, chómh luath agus ' thiocfadh an t-am chuige.

Chuaigh sé ó thuaidh, agus níorbh aon uair amháin é, go hÍnsíbh Orc agus go hÍnsíbh Gall, agus chonaic sé lena shúilibh féin cad é an neart fear a bhí á dhéanamh suas insna hoileánaibh sin, agus cérbh é an rí a bheadh os cionn na bhfear san. Chuaigh sé, 'na chuardaibh, soir ó thuaidh go tír na hIorua, agus fuair sé ansan, leis, an t-eólas a bhí uaidh, agus eólas ná raibh coinne aige leis. Nuair a bhíodh roinnt eólais cruinnithe aige, thagadh sé abhaile agus thugadh sé an t-eólas do Mhurchadh, agus thugadh Murchadh do Bhrian é, 'sé sin, an méid ba mhaith a thabhairt do dhe. Bhí cuid den eólas agus níor tugadh do Bhrian é go dtí 'na dhiaidh san.

Do hínseadh do cad é an neart sló a bheadh ag teacht anall ó rí Lochlann agus cérbh iad na taoiseacha a bheadh 'na bhun. Do hínseadh do cad é an neart sló a bheadh ag teacht anall ó rí na hIorua agus cérbh iad na taoiseacha a bheadh 'na bhun. Do hínseadh do cad é an neart sló a bheadh ag teacht aduaidh ó Ínsíbh Orc agus ó Ínsibh Gall agus cérbh iad na taoiseacha a bheadh i mbun na sló san. Agus do hínseadh do nách namhaid ar fad a bheadh ag teacht; go mbeadh cúnamh fear agus nár chúnamh shuarach é, ag teacht anoir aduaidh ó Ghaelaibh Alban, chun buille ' bhualadh le Gaelaibh Éireann i gcoinnibh cómhacht Lochlann, agus go mbeadh an dá rí uasal*, an dá Mhaor Mhór*, i gceannas an chúnaimh sin. Fuair Caoilte amach, leis, go raibh slóite ag teacht anoir ón gceann tuaidh den Almáinn ag cabhrú le namhdaibh na nGael. Bhí, ba dhó' le duine, an Phágánacht go léir, thoir agus thuaidh, ag cruinniú agus ag éirí, mar a bheadh tonn mhór farraige, chun an oileáin seo na hÉireann do bhá agus do mhúchadh agus do thraochadh d'aon mhór-iarracht amháin.

Bhí an t-ollmhúchán ar siúl go huathásach ins gach aon bhall, ar fuid na hÉireann agus insna dúthaíbh thall, ach 'na thaobh san is uile ní raibh ach síocháin agus caradas ins gach aon bhall, in Éirinn agus thar lear. Ba chuma é nú an ciúnas roimis an dtóirthnigh. Bhí an tsíocháin ann. Dá bhrí sin, bhí neart do Chaoilte agus dá aicme féin ar bheith ins gach aon chúinne, ag faire agus ag fáil eólais, agus bhí, ar an gcuma gcéanna, neart don namhaid ar a lucht faire ' bheith acu ins gach aon chúinne d'oileán na hÉireann, ag féachaint agus ag iniúchadh agus ag fáil eólais, chómh maith agus dob fhéidir leó é.

Pé cúis a bhí leis, bíodh go ndeigh Caoilte anonn go minic go críochaibh Lochlann, agus anonn go Cathair na Beirbhe, níor deineadh aon iarracht ar aon chur isteach a dhéanamh air ná ar bhaint leis in aon tsaghas cuma. Thug sé féin aire mhaith gan aon dlí a bhriseadh.

Idir an dá aicme faire ba dheocair puínn eólais a bheith in Éirinn i ganfhios don namhaid, agus ba ró-dheocair don namhaid aon chor a chur díobh i ganfhios do Chaoilte. Ní raibh ag gach taobh le déanamh ach bheith dhá neartú féin chómh maith agus dob fhéidir leó é, agus bheith a d'iarraidh eólais a nirt do chimeád ón dtaobh eile chómh maith agus dob fhéidir leó é, go dtí go bpléascfadh an tóirthneach eatarthu.

Bhí dhá shaghas eólais ag gach taobh den dá thaobh á chruinniú. Bhí gach taobh a d'iarraidh eólais a dh'fháil ar na nithibh ab fheárr a dhéanfadh cur lena neart féin agus ar na nithibh ab fheárr a dhéanfadh baint ó neart an taoibh eile.

Caibideal 35: Cúnamh don Chúnamh

Ní raibh Brian i bhfad imithe ó Cheann Cora, ar a chuaird rí, agus Niamh agus a hathair imithe i gcuallacht Bhriain, nuair a tugadh fé ndeara daoine iasachta ag teacht ann. Níor cuireadh aon tsuím ró-mhór sa méid sin. Bhíodh daoine ag teacht ó gach aon pháirt d'Éirinn go ceártain Mheargaigh ag ceannach na n-arm. Bhí cúram teaghlaigh an Árdrí i gCeann Cora ar an Árdríogain, ní nárbh iúnadh, agus ba léir do gach éinne go raibh sí ábalta ar a smacht do chur i bhfeidhm agus ar mhuíntir an teaghlaigh do chimeád féna láimh, agus ar a gceann a chimeád fúthu, agus ar a chur ' fhiachaibh orthu a ngnó ' dhéanamh mar ba cheart. Dá bhrí sin, nuair a thagadh daoine iasachta ann, ní leogadh eagla d'éinne de mhuíntir an teaghlaigh aon rud a thabhairt fé ndeara ná aon chur isteach a dhéanamh ar nithibh nár bhain leó, dar leó féin.

In éaghmais na ndaoine iasachta eile dár tháinig ann, tháinig Amhlaoibh ann. San oíche is ea ' tháinig sé, agus bhí ' fhios ag Gormfhlaith roim ré go raibh sé ag teacht. Do shleamhnaigh sé isteach i ganfhios don teaghlach. Ní fheacaigh éinne é. B'éigean do teacht ar an gcuma san mar bhí an iomad aithne san áit air, agus dá bhfeictí ann é, do shroisfeadh an ráfla Inis Cathaigh agus Uíbh Máine. Ansan do shroisfeadh sé Murchadh agus Brian agus níorbh fhios cad a thiocfadh as. Tháinig sé ann san oíche, i ganfhios d'éinne. Nuair a bhí sé féin agus Gormfhlaith i bhfochair a chéile, i seómra a bhí i bhfad isteach, do chuir sí na mílte fáilte roimis. B'fhuiriste a dh'aithint ón gcuma 'nar ghlac sí é go raibh an gaol achomair go maith eatarthu. Ná féadfadh sé bheith ní b'achomaire.

"Ó! A mhic ó, a lao", ar sise, "nách fada gur fhéadais teacht! Shíleas ná tiocfá choíche. Conas 'tá an obair ag dul chun cínn? Cathain a buailfar an buille do shaorfaidh sinn ón annscian, ní hea ach ón slua annscian! Cathain a thiocfaidh an chabhair, a mhic?"

"Thiocfadh an chabhair amáireach, a mháthair", ar seisean, "dá mbeadh do thaobh-sa den obair déanta".

"Conas ' fhéadfainn mo thaobh den obair a dhéanamh anois agus gan Brian anso? An fhaid a bhí sé anso bhí an eascú san Thaidhg Mhóir ag faire orm ins gach aon chúinne gach aon ré sholais. Ní fhéadfainn cor a chur díom gan me féin a chur i gcúntúirt. Tá Murchadh ag faire orm. Tá Donn mac Beathach ag faire orm. 'Sé mo thuairim láidir gur dhein an t-easpag úd a bhí anso ón Róimh rud éigin, nú go nduairt sé rud éigin, do chuir iad go léir ar a gcosaint féin orm. Thugas fé ndeara é, cúpla uair, ag féachaint orm, agus níor thaithn an fhéachaint liom. Mheasas gur fhéach sé treasna thríom. Ní fheadar 'en domhan cad a chuir iad go léir ar a gcosaint féin mar atáid. Níor dheineas aon ní a dh'fhéadfadh aon rud do chur ar a súilibh dóibh. An fhaid a bhí Niamh anso ag faire orm, do leogas me féin féna súilibh chómh hoscailte agus dob fhéidir dom é. Dheineas gach aon rud, dar liom, chun a thispeáint di ná raibh brí ná bunús leis an bhfaireachán. Dheineas ní ba mhó ná san. Thugas me féin di chómh hiomlán san gur dó' liom dá bhfanadh sí i bhfad eile anso go mbeadh sí curtha fén gcré agam!"

"Airiú, cad a chuirfeadh fén gcré í, a mháthair? Ar ndóin, ní hamhlaidh a thabharfá dhi féin an rud 'na raibh sí ag faire ort sara dtabharfá do Bhrian é!", ar seisean.

"Ní hamhlaidh", ar sise. "Níor ghá dhom é. Cailín fíor-uasal 'na haigne is ea í. Do deineadh árdéagóir uirthi nuair a cuireadh anso í. Tá sí ana-ghéar-chúiseach, ach tá sé bun-os-cionn ar fad lena meón agus lena nádúr aon rud i bhfuirm faireacháin a thabhairt le déanamh di. Ní raibh fasc ag á hathair agus í ' thabhairt anso. Níor dheineas-sa ach í ' thachtadh agus do mhúchadh le séimhe agus le soilbhreas agus le geal-gháiriteacht. Go deimhin le fírinne dhuit, a Amhlaoibh, do bhíodh trua agam don chailín bhocht nuair a chínn í ag casadh le gáire ' dhéanamh agus gan aon gháire 'na croí. Mura mbeadh a luathacht a rugadar leó chun siúil í, bheadh sí ar an gclár acu".

"Bhí aithne agam uirthi", arsa Amhlaoibh. "Chonac í thiar sa bhaile cúpla uair. Níor mheasas gurbh aon rud fónta í".

"Aon rud fónta!", arsa Gormfhlaith. "Tabharfad a ceart féin di, a mhic, agus tuigim cad 'tá agam á rá. Is í cailín í is feárr agus is uaisle agus is gile agus is glaine croí agus aigne dár bhuail riamh fós umam-sa!

Déarfad an méid sin di dá ndeineadh sí oiread eile faireacháin orm. Níl fasc ag an muíntir a chuir anso í".

"Tá sí imithe anois, a mháthair, pé'r domhan é, agus tá an áit seo fút féin. Ba chóir go bhféadfá rud éigin a dhéanamh nuair a thiocfadh an tÁrdrí seo abhaile. Nár chóir go bhféadfá bheith ollamh i dtreó nár ghá dhuit tu féin a chur in aon chúntúirt nuair a bheadh sé sa bhaile? Tá sé an-aosta. Dá dtagadh an bás air díreach nuair a bheadh ár neart ag teacht isteach i gcuan Bhaile Átha Cliath, bheadh gach aon rud ar ár dtoil againn láithreach. Bheadh Éire againn gan a bheith orainn oiread agus aon fhear amháin do chailliúint. Do thitfeadh neart Bhriain as a chéile. D'éileódh M'leachlainn arís an Árdríocht a baineadh de chun í ' thabhairt do Bhrian. D'éileódh Murchadh an Árdríocht ós é an rí-dhamhna é. D'éireódh Ó Néill chun gan an Árdríocht d'fhágháilt ag éinne acu ach í ' bheith aige féin. Bheidís go léir ag marú a chéile láithreach bonn. Níor ghá dhúinn aon phioc dá ndua ' dh'fháil. Mharóidís féin a chéile dhúinn. Ní bheadh le déanamh againn ach scaoileadh leó agus bheith ag brú isteach orthu fé mar a bheidís ag lagú a chéile. Um an dtaca 'na mbeidís díscithe ag á chéile, bheimís-na i seilbh an oileáin. Dein rud éigin, a mháthair. Tabhair cúnamh éigin do Bhrian chun an tsaeil seo ' dh'fhágaint. Is mithid do imeacht".

"Déanfad mo dhícheall, a mhic ó", ar sise. "Ach caithfir aon ní amháin a gheallúint dom, a Amhlaoibh", ar sise.

"Geallfad aon rud is maith leat duit, a mháthair", ar seisean. "Cad é an rud é?"

"Geall dom", ar sise, "má éiríonn linn go bpósfair Niamh".

"Aililiú!", ar seisean, agus do leath a dhá shúil air. "Ag magadh athaíonn tú, a mháthair!", ar seisean.

Caibideal 35: Cúnamh don Chúnamh

"Ní hea, a mhic mo chroí!", ar sise. "Lom dáiríribh atáim. Níl cor 'na croí ná 'na haigne ná fuil ' fhios agam. Níor bhuail a leithéid eile riamh umam. Go dtí gur bhuail sí féin umam, níor mheasas go raibh a leithéid ar bith. Níor mheasas gurbh fhéidir a leithéid a bheith ar bith. An oíche úd a bhíúir go léir anso, nuair a chonac tu ag rínce léi, mheasas ná feaca riamh aon bheirt chómh hoiriúnach dá chéile. Ní mise amháin a mheas é. D'airíos an chogarnach: 'Ó! Nách álainn an lánú a dhéanfaidís!' An ngeallfair dom go bpósfair í má éiríonn linn?"

"Níl éirithe linn fós, a mháthair", ar seisean, "ach ní dó' liom gur miste dhom a gheallúint duit go bpósfad í—má phósann sí me. Tá sé i mbéal gach éinne go bhfuil socair aici 'na haigne gan pósadh choíche'.

"Ón aithne atá curtha agam uirthi, ní chuirfeadh san féin blúire iúnadh orm", arsa Gormfhlaith. "Tá meón ana-mhaith, ana-naofa, aici. B'fhéidir go n-athródh sí a haigne. Is cuímhin liom cogarnach eile ' dh'airíos an oíche chéanna id thaobh-sa. 'Ó', adeirthí, 'nách mór an trua sagart a dhéanamh de!' Cúis gháire chúinn! Ach pósfair í má phósann sí thu?"

"Tá go maith, a mháthair", ar seisean. "Ní dó' liom, áfach, go bpósfaidh sí me pé tathant a dhéanfair uirthi. Is éagsamhlach an bhean tu, a mháthair", ar seisean. "Mheasas go marófá me ní ba thúisce ná mar a leogfá dom í ' phósadh!"

"Dá dtuigthá a feabhas mar a thuigim-se é, ní mheasfá san", arsa Gormfhlaith.

Thugadar formhór na hoíche ag cainnt. Thug Amhlaoibh cúntas cruínn di ar an neart a bhí le teacht go hÉirinn chun seilbh na hÉireann do ghlacadh chómh luath agus ' gheóbhadh Brian bás. D'inis sé dhi cad é an neart fear a bhí ollamh ag rí Lochlann agus cad iad na luingeas a bhí ollamh ar uisce aige. D'inis sé dhi cad é an neart fear a bhí ollamh ag rí na hIorua, agus cad iad na luingeas a bhí ollamh ar uisce aige, agus conas mar a bhí beirt mhac an rí, an bheirt óig-fhear ba threise agus ba thréine i dtír na hIorua an uair sin, ag teacht 'na bhfearaibh cínn riain ar shlóitibh na hIorua.

D'inis sé dhi conas mar a bhí Sígurd mac Lódair, rí Ínsí hOrc, chun teacht agus mór-shlua aige d'fhearaibh luatha láidre crua ó Ínsíbh Orc agus ó Ínsíbh Gall, ó Scathaigh agus ó Cheann Tíre agus ó sna dúthaíbh sin go léir mórthímpall.

Thug sé gach aon chúntas mar sin di ar an gcuma 'na raibh neart Lochlann suite an uair sin agus ar an gcuma 'na raibh an neart ag méadú agus ag dul in acfuinní in aghaidh an lae. Agus chuir sé 'na luí ar a haigne ná raibh aon ní ag teastabháil feasta ach bás Bhriain.

D'fhan Amhlaoibh i gCeann Cora an chuid eile den oíche sin agus an lá a bhí chúinn. Níor thispeáin sé é féin d'éinne i gcaitheamh an lae. Chómh luath agus ' bhí am mhairbh na hoíche arís ann, d'imigh sé. Thug sé aghaidh ar Bhaile Átha Cliath. Chuaigh sé chun cainnte le Sitric, rí Lochlannach Bhaile Átha Cliath, agus d'inis sé dho an uile fhocal den chainnt a bhí idir é féin agus Gormfhlaith.

Bhí eagal ar an mbeirt ná déanfadh Gormfhlaith an bheart. Níor thaithn leó in aon chor an bháidh a thispeáin sí a bheith aici do Niamh. Thuigeadar 'na n-aigne má bhí cúnamh le tabhairt do Bhrian chun imeacht as an saol, agus má b'í Gormfhlaith a thabharfadh an cúnamh san do, nárbh fholáir cúnamh a thabhairt do Ghormfhlaith féin sa ghnó.

Conas a tabharfí an cúnamh san di, áfach, agus cad é an saghas an cúnamh a tabharfí dhi? B'in í an cheist acu agus níor cheist ró-bhog í.

Caibideal 36: Buille fé Thuairim; nú Fuadar ná Feadar

Bhí an bheirt istigh i seómra i rí-theaghlach Shitric i mBaile Átha Cliath agus iad ag cur 's ag cúiteamh i dtaobh an scéil.

"Ní dhéanfaidh sí an bheart", arsa Amhlaoibh. "Níl an scairt chómh láidir aici agus do mheasas. Sin é fé ndeár gan an gnó ' bheith déanta fadó. Do cuireadh Niamh ag faire uirthi. Is í Niamh a choisc í ar an obair a dhéanamh an fhaid a bhí Brian sa bhaile, ach ní leis an bhfaire do choisc sí í. Chuir Niamh Gormfhlaith ón ndroch-ghníomh i ganfhios do Ghormfhlaith féin. Deirim an méid seo leat, a rí. Dá bhfanadh Brian sa bhaile i gCeann Cora agus dá bhfanadh Niamh ann, agus í féin agus Gormfhlaith a bheith chómh mór i gcuideachtanas a chéile agus ' bhíodar, ní dhéanfadh Gormfhlaith an gníomh in aon chor. Bheadh sí ceapaithe ar an ngníomh a dhéanamh, ach an fhaid a bheadh Niamh ann agus í fé shúilibh Ghormfhlaith, agus a hanál ag dul fé Ghormfhlaith, agus a guth agus a gáire ag dul fé Ghormfhlaith, ní dhéanfadh Gormfhlaith an gníomh".

"Ach!", arsa Sitric. "Airiú, nách eólgaiseach an buachaill tu! Cá bhfuarais an fháidhiúlacht go léir? Ba dhó' le duine gur ag breithniú aigne an duine a chaithis do shaol".

"Abair do rogha rud, a rí", arsa Amhlaoibh, "i dtaobh conas a chaitheas mo shaol, ach bain-se an chluas anuas ón gceann díom mura bhfuil an ceart sa méid úd agam. Bheadh an rud atá uainn déanta fadó mura mbeadh Niamh a theacht go Ceann Cora. Chun na faire ' dhéanamh is ea do tugadh ann í. Dhein sí an fhaire, ach ní leis an bhfaire do choisc sí an gníomh, ach le hí féin a bheith ann".

"Ba dhó' liom gur conas a déanfar an gníomh an cheist anois agus nách conas a coisceadh é. Ó bhreithnís an cosc chómh maith, b'fhéidir go bhfuil breithniú éigin déanta agat ar conas a curfar an cosc as an slí", arsan Sitric.

Caibideal 36: Buille fé Thuairim; nú Fuadar ná Feadar

"Tá an breithniú san, leis, déanta agam, a rí", arsa Amhlaoibh.

"Is maith é sin. Scaoil chúinn toradh do mhachnaimh", arsa Sitric.

"An airís riamh", arsa Amhlaoibh, "conas a deineadh Árdrí de Dhiarmaid mac Céirbheóil?"

"Do maraíodh Tuathal Maolgharbh", arsa Sitric. "Ach ar airís-se cad d'imigh ar an bhfear a mhairbh Tuathal?"

"Do deineadh guin galáin de", arsa Amhlaoibh.

"Go díreach", arsa Sitric, "an rud a dh'imeódh láithreach bonn ar an té a mharódh Brian, ach so a bheith de dheifríocht idir an dá scéal. Do deineadh guin galáin den té ' mhairbh Tuathal, ach tar éis an ghnímh a deineadh de é. An fear a thabharfadh fé Bhrian a mharú, roimis an ngníomh a déanfí guin galáin de".

Bhí an bheirt ag cainnt ar an gcuma san. Tháinig seirbhíseach isteach.

"Tá duine sa phóirse agus ba mhaith leis labhairt leat, a rí", arsan seirbhíseach.

"Tabhair anso isteach é", arsa Sitric.

Do tugadh isteach é.

Sid é saghas duine a chonaic an bheirt nuair a tháinig sé isteach. Firín beag agus ceann mór air. Bhí folt odhar ar a cheann, folt trom agus é ag titim anuas ar a ghuaillibh agus siar síos ar a shlinneánaibh. Bhí mar ' bheadh raca beag óir ar gach taobh dá cheann, ag á uiseannaibh, ag cimeád a ghruaige siar dá éadan agus dá shúilibh. Bhí éadan leathan árd air agus fáibrí treasna ann, dhá thispeáint go raibh sé, an chuid ba lú dhe, trí fichid blian. Bhí srón fhada dhíreach air agus dhá shúil mhaithe mhóra sholasmhara aige, agus iad aibidh go maith. Bhí a cheannatha faid-leicneach agus bhí féasóg throm, liath-ghorm air agus í ag dul i bhfad síos ar a bhrollach. Bhí brat, nú clóca, den éadach saibhir ba cheart a bheith ar dhuin' uasal, aniar ar a shlinneánaibh.

"Cad é an gnó atá agat díom-sa, a dhuine mhacánta?", arsa Sitric leis.

"Liag is ea me, a rí", arsan duine iasachta. "Tá mórán de chríochaibh an domhain siúlta agam i gcaitheamh mo shaeil. Ón mBreatain anall a thánag le déanaí. Tá mórán taithí agam ar na galaraibh a thagann ar an nduine, agus ar na nithibh is feárr chun na ngalar san do leigheas. Thánag anso go dtí an chathair seo ag brath air go mb'fhéidir go bhféadfainn úsáid a dhéanamh ann den eólas atá agam agus roinnt tairbhe ' dhéanamh do dhaoine a bheadh 'na ghátar. Is léir duit féin, a rí", ar seisean, "gur ró-bheag an gnó a bheadh ageam leithéid ag teacht anso chun na hoibre sin a dhéanamh gan me féin do chur in úil ar dtúis don rí agus cead a dh'iarraidh air".

"Tá san fíor go leór", arsa Sitric, "ach ca bhfios dómh-sa nách díobháil a dhéanfá dom dhaoine dá dtugainn an cead san duit", agus chuir sé gáire as. "Ca bhfios dom", ar seisean, "ná gurb amhlaidh a thabharfá nimh dúinn go léir".

"Cúis gháire chút, a rí", arsan duine iasachta. "Ní gá dhom a dh'ínsint duit-se, a rí", ar seisean, "gurb é meón agus nádúr an liaig gur túisce leis go mór leigheas a dhéanamh ná aon díobháil sláinte ' dhéanamh d'aon duine. Tuigim go maith cad a bhaineann le nimh, agus cad a bhaineann le duine do leigheas ó nimh dá mbeadh sé tar éis an nímhe do thógaint, peocu le tionóisc nú le toil a bheadh an nimh tógtha aige. Ach ní gá dhom bheith dhá ínsint cad a dh'fhéadfainn a dhéanamh. Tá teistiméireachtaí anso agam ó ríthibh agus ó uaislibh agus ó choláistíbh móra, dhá thispeáint cad é an saghas me, agus cad é an saghas oibre a dheineas cheana insna háiteannaibh eile 'na rabhas sara dtánag anso".

Caibideal 36: Buille fé Thuairim; nú Fuadar ná Feadar

Tharraig sé amach beart pháipéar agus shín sé chun an rí iad. Thóg Sitric iad agus chrom sé ar iad do lé'. Thispeáin sé d'Amhlaoibh cuid acu. Do léigh Amhlaoibh iad.

"Chím astu so", arsa Sitric, "gur Lonán is ainm duit".

"Is ea, a rí", ar seisean. "Lonán m'ainm".

"Tá go maith", arsa Sitric. "Tá mo chead-sa agat chun aon tairbhe is féidir leat a dhéanamh do mhuíntir na cathrach so. Is dócha gur cuma leat ceocu Lochlannaigh nú Éireannaigh an mhuíntir 'na n-imreóir do chuid eólais orthu?"

"Is cuma, a rí", arsa Lonán. "Imreód mo chuid eólais ar an muíntir is mó a chífead 'na ghátar agus ar an muíntir is feárr a dhíolfaidh me".

"Ó, tuigim", arsa Sitric. "Ba dhó' liom féin, áfach", ar seisean, "go bhfaigheadh duine a shiúlaigh oiread agus ' shiúlaís-se ceannach ar a chuid eólais, agus díol as, níos feárr ná mar a gheóbhair-se sa chathair seo".

"Conas san, a rí, led thoil?", arsa Lonán.

"Ba dhó' liom gur mó rí, nú Árdrí, gur mhaith leis tusa ' bheith in' aice i gcónaí ag féachaint i ndiaidh a shláinte dho, agus go mb'fhéidir gurbh fheárr a dhíolfadh sé thu as do chuid eólais ná mar ' fhéadfadh daoine bochta na cathrach so thu ' dhíol", arsa Sitric.

Do gheal gnúis Lonáin.

"Tá go maith, a rí", ar seisean. "Níl aon rud ab fheárr a thaithnfeadh liom, más chuige atá t'onóir, ná an gnó san a dhéanamh do t'onóir-se. Thabharfainn aire mhaith don ghnó, agus is dó' liom, nuair a bheadh taithí agat ar m'eólas ar feadh tamaill, agus ar m'obair, nách go ró-bhog ba mhaith leat scarúint liom".

Caibideal 36: Buille fé Thuairim; nú Fuadar ná Feadar

"Ní horm féin a bhíos ag cuímhneamh nuair a labhras", arsa Sitric. "Is ar Árdrí Éireann, ar Bhrian, a bhíos ag cuímhneamh".

Do dhoirchigh gnúis Lonáin. Níor labhair sé. B'fhuiriste a dh'aithint go raibh rud éigin nárbh fhónta istigh aige i gcoinnibh an Árdrí. D'fhéach an bheirt eile ar a chéile. Ar ball do labhair Lonán.

"Gabhaim párdún agat, a rí", ar seisean, "agus agat-sa, a rí", ar seisean le hAmhlaoibh. "Tháinig ainm an fhir sin ró-obann orm. Tháinig ainm an Árdrí sin ró-obann orm", ar seisean. Do stad sé. "Mheasas gur ort féin a bhís ag trácht, a rí", ar seisean.

"Ní mheasaim", arsa Sitric, "go bhfuil aon ghrá ró-mhor agat don Árdrí".

Níor labhair Lonán, ach do dhoirchigh a ghnúis arís.

"Ach bíodh nách orm féin a bhíos ag cuímhneamh ar dtúis b'fhéidir nárbh fhearra dhom rud a dhéanfainn ná cuímhneamh orm féin anois. B'fhéidir nách i gcónaí a thiocfadh do leithéid-se crosta orm. Tar chúm anso amáireach agus b'fhéidir go bhféadfaimís socrú", arsa Sitric.

Do gheal gnúis Lonáin arís. Ba dhó' le duine air gur ríocht a bronnadh air, bhí sé chómh háthasach, chómh mórálach, chómh baoch.

D'imigh sé. D'fhéach an bheirt ar a chéile.

"Cad é an fuadar é seo fút anois?", arsa Amhlaoibh.

"Fágaim le huacht", arsa Sitric, "ná feadar cad é an fuadar é seo fúm!"

"Níl aon ghrá ag Lonán do Bhrian", arsa Amhlaoibh.

Caibideal 36: Buille fé Thuairim; nú Fuadar ná Feadar

"Tá an méid sin soiléir go leór", arsa Sitric. "Ní fheadar 'en domhan cad a dhein Brian air".

"Is mó duine nách é gur dhein Brian droch-bheart air", arsa Amhlaoibh.

"Bhí sé ar bharra mo theangan dhá uair a dh'fhiafraí dhe cad a dhein Brian air, ach bhí eagal orm go samhlódh sé go raibh cúis éigin agam leis an gceist a chur chuige", arsa Sitric.

"Tiocfaidh sé anso amáireach", arsa Amhlaoibh.

"Ní deirim ná go dtiocfaidh", arsa Sitric.

"Agus cad a dhéanfair leis?", arsa Amhlaoibh.

"B'fhéidir gur mó rud a féadfí a dhéanamh leis", arsa Sitric.

Do stad an bheirt agus iad ag machnamh. Bhí Sitric 'na shuí ar chathaoir agus bhí Amhlaoibh ag siúl síos is suas. Thug an bheirt tamall maith ar an gcuma san. Ar ball do labhair Amhlaoibh:

"Is fíor san", ar seisean. "Is mó rud, b'fhéidir, a féadfí a dhéanamh leis. Tiocfaidh sé anso amáireach. Ní gá dhom a rá leat aire mhaith a thabhairt. Faigh-se greim air más féidir é, ach ná leog do aon ghreim ' fháil ort".

"Ná bíodh eagal ort", arsa Sitric. "Mar aduart, níl aon phioc dá fhios agam fós cad a déanfar. Pé rud ar a socrófar is é Lonán féin a shocróidh air, uaidh féin".

"Sin í an chainnt", arsa Amhlaoibh. "Ansan, má scéann sé is air féin a scéifidh sé".

Do scar an bheirt i gcómhair na hoíche.

Caibideal 37: Cómhacht Luíbhneacha

Seachtain díreach tar éis na hoíche 'na raibh Sitric agus Amhlaoibh agus Lonán i bhfochair a chéile istigh i dteaghlach Shitric i mBaile Átha Cliath, bhí Gormfhlaith agus beirt dá mnáibh coímhdeachta ag siúl ar bruach glaise bige a bhí ag gabháil thar rí-theaghlach Bhriain i gCeann Cora. Chonacadar ag gabháil chúthu aníos ó threó Luimní capall agus carbad agus beirt sa charbad. Nuair a tháinig an carbad i gcóngar na háite 'na raibh na mná uaisle, do stad an carbad.

"Sin é rí-theaghlach an Árdrí agat anois", arsa duine den bheirt leis an nduine eile, "agus sin í an Árdríogan féin, Gormfhlaith, an bhean uasal is aoirde den triúr, an bhean 'na bhfuil an t-éadach corcra uirthi".

Tháinig an fear eile amach as an gcarbad.

"Ní dócha", ar seisean, leis an bhfear a dh'fhan istigh, "go mbeidh a thuilleadh gnótha agam díot-sa inniu. Tá sé chómh maith agat casadh thar n-ais".

Dhíol sé é agus chuir sé uaidh é, agus thug sé féin aghaidh ar an áit 'na raibh na mná uaisle ag siúl. Níor stadadar dá gcainnt, ná níor shamhlaigh sé gur chuireadar blúire suime ann go dtí go raibh sé ar a n-aghaidh amach. An uair sin féin, gheóbhaidís thairis gan féachaint air ná aon tsuím a chur ann mura mbeadh gur chaith sé é féin ar a dhá ghlúin ar aghaidh Ghormfhlaith amach agus gur shín sé leitir chúithi.

"Gabhaim párdún agat, a Árdríogan", ar seisean, "arbh é toil do Shoílse an leitir sin do lé'. Ó rí Lochlannach Átha Cliath is ea í".

"Déirc atá uaidh seo is dócha", ar sise leis na mnáibh coímhdeachta, agus do rug sí ar an leitir. D'aithin sí an scríbhinn a bhí ar an gcúmhdach. B'fhíor don duine é gur ó Shitric a fuair sé an leitir le tabhairt ag triall uirthi. D'oscail sí an leitir agus chrom sí ar í ' lé'. Ar ball d'fhéach sí ar an bhfear. D'fhéach sí go géar air. Firín beag ab ea é agus ceann mór air; an fear céanna a bhí istigh i dteaghlach rí Lochlannach Átha Cliath an oíche úd, seachtain roimis sin, ag cainnt le Sitric agus le hAmhlaoibh.

D'fhéach Gormfhlaith ar na mnáibh coímhdeachta.

"Téidh-se isteach, a chlann ó", ar sise. "Oireann dom labhairt leis an nduine seo in' aonar".

D'imigh an bheirt bhan.

"Chím", arsa Gormfhlaith leis an bhfear, "gur Lonán is ainm duit-se".

"Is ea, chun do thoile, a Árdríogan", ar seisean.

"Cad chuige gur cuireadh anso thu?", ar sise.

"Do réitigh an rí liom, a Shoílse", arsa Lonán, "chun go ndéanfainn, mar is gnáth a dhéanamh do rí, aireachas a thabhairt don bhia agus don digh a curfí os a chómhair le caitheamh, le heagla go ndéanfí éagóir air, le heagla go dtabharfí nimh do".

"Agus cad 'na thaobh nár chimeád sé thu?", arsa Gormfhlaith.

"Duairt sé liom, a Shoílse", arsa Lonán, "go mb'fhéidir gur mhó an gnó ' bheadh anso dhíom féin agus dem chuid eólais agus dem chuid foghlama ná mar a bhí aige féin díom. Is dócha gur inis sé sa leitir cad é an gnó ba dhó' leis a bheadh anso dhíom?"

"De réir mar a thuigim-se an chainnt atá sa leitir is mó gnó ' fhéadfadh ' bheith anso dhíot", arsa Gormfhlaith.

Caibideal 37: Cómhacht Luíbhneacha

"Ní mó na gnóthaí a dh'fhéadfadh ' bheith dhíom anso, a Shoílse", arsa Lonán, "ná na gnóthaí a dh'fhéadfainn-se a dhéanamh anso".

"Ach go ndíolfí thu astu, is dócha", arsa Gormfhlaith. "Agus is dócha", ar sise, "dá mhéid iad na gnóthaí gurbh ea ba mhó a bheadh le díol astu?"

"De réir dheallraimh, a Shoílse", arsa Lonán.

Do stad Gormfhlaith ar feadh tamaill mhaith. Bhog sí a béal chun labhartha cúpla uair agus níor labhair sí. Is amhlaidh a dhún sí a béal arís agus do lean sí dá machnamh. An fhaid a bhí sí ag machnamh bhí Lonán ag féachaint uaidh ar an sruthán agus gan aon chor aige á chur de. Do bhog sí a béal chun labhartha fé dheireadh agus do labhair sí.

"Tá sé chómh maith agam an ceann a bhaint den scéal duit", ar sise. "Tá oiread anso agus ' chrochfadh thu seacht n-uaire dá bhfaighfí amach ort é".

"Is fíor san, a Árdríogan", arsa Lonán.

"Nách breá bog a ghlacann tú é!", ar sise.

"Tá iúntaoibh agam asat, a Shoílse", ar seisean. "Duart leis an rí in Áth Cliath go raibh iúntaoibh agam asat".

"Do chruaigh a súil agus a gnúis agus thug sí droch-fhéachaint air.

"Ní fheicim", ar sise, "cad é an chúis go mbeadh an iúntaoibh sin agat asam-sa, a ghiolla. Níl crot na fírinne ar an gcainnt sin".

Thóg sí in áirde a lámh fé mar a bheadh cómhartha éigin aici á dhéanamh. Do rith chúithi anuas ón rí-theaghlach ceathrar d'fhearaibh luatha láidre agus a chlaíomh nocht i láimh gach fir acu.

Caibideal 37: Cómhacht Luíbhneacha

"Curtar sa charcair an fear san", ar sise go breá réidh. Ba dhó' le duine gur chun a dhínnéir a dh'órdaigh sí é ' bhreith, do labhair sí chómh cneasta san.

Do rugadh ar Lonán agus do cuireadh isteach sa charcair é. Do léigh Gormfhlaith an leitir arís, agus dhein sí a machnamh arís ar an gcainnt a bhí sa leitir. Sid í an chainnt a bhí sa leitir:

> "A mháthair,
>
> "Déanfaidh sé seo an gnó. Tá a chúis féin aige chun na hoibre ' dhéanamh. Ní miste, áfach, é ' dhíol go maith; ansan beidh dhá chúis aige chun na hoibre ' dhéanamh. Ní hobair thútach a dhéanfaidh sé. Tá an t-eólas thar bárr aige.
>
> "Tá ár neart go léir ollamh ar phreabadh isteach chúinn chómh luath agus d'aireóid siad an tásc.
>
> "Dá bhféadfí an gnó ' dhéanamh chómh luath agus ' bheadh an chuaird críochnaithe, b'in mar ab fheárr é. Bheadh fios na haimsire againn agus d'fhéadfaimís an aimsir d'fhriothálamh. Déanfaidh an fear so an gnó. Ná caill.
>
> "Is eól duit cé hé
>
> "Mise".

Nuair a bhí beagán aimsire caite agus uain fálta ag Lonán ar scannradh ' theacht i gceart air, do ghlaeigh sí arís ar an gceathrar.

"Tugtar chúm anso an fear úd", ar sise.

Do tugadh.

Caibideal 37: Cómhacht Luíbhneacha

Nuair a bhí an bheirt 'na n-aonar arís, do labhair sise. Bhí Lonán ag crith.

"Cad é an chúis a bhí agat-sa lena rá", ar sise, "go raibh iúntaoibh agat asam-sa?"

"Ní féidir do dhuine i gcónaí, a Shoílse", ar seisean, "a dh'ínsint cad é an chúis do iúntaoibh a bheith aige as duine eile. Ach is léir, a Árdríogan, mura mbeadh iúntaoibh a bheith agam-sa as do Shoílse-se ná tiocfainn anso in aon chor. Thánag chút anso, a Árdríogan, agus an téad ar mo mhineál. Ní dhéanfainn san mura mbeadh an iúntaoibh a bheith agam as do Shoílse".

"Ní dhéanfá", ar sise, "de réir dheallraimh. Ní dhéanfadh éinne é ach duine buile. Tá crot na fírinne air sin. Ach ní ínseann san cad é an chúis a bhí agat leis an iúntaoibh. Inis an chúis dom".

"Tá go maith, a Shoílse", ar seisean, "ach tabhair do bhriathar ríoga dhom ná tógfair orm é má ínsim an fhírinne dod Shoílse".

"A dhuine!", ar sise, agus bhuail sí speach dá cois sa talamh, "nách í an fhírinne atá uaim!"

"Tá scannradh orm rómhat, a Árdríogan!", ar seisean.

"Mo bhriathar ríoga dhuit", ar sise, "nách baol duit me. Inis dom an rud atá ar t'aigne".

"Tá sé i m'aigne, a Shoílse", ar seisean, "an gnó a thug mise anso agus an gnó ba thoil leat-sa a dhéanfainn anso gurb aon ghnó amháin iad. Dá bhrí sin, nuair a bhíos ag teacht anso chun an ghnótha san a dhéanamh, tháinig iúntaoibh agam asat-sa, a Árdríogan, agus mar gheall ar an iúntaoibh sin ' thánag anso, mar a chíonn tú, agus an téad ar mo mhineál. Ní raibh le déanamh ach me ' chur suas ar an gcroich!"

"Tá go maith", ar sise. "Táim sásta. An ndéanfair an gnó?"

"Déanfad, a Árdríogan", ar seisean.

"Gheóbhair do thuarastal go maith as an ngnó", ar sise.

"Thuigeas go bhfaighinn, a Shoílse", ar seisean.

Bhí an scéal socair eatarthu ansan. Níorbh fhada go bhfeictí iad coitianta ag imeacht tríd an ínse ar bhruach na glaise bige ag stathadh na luíbhneacha agus dhá mbreithniú. Do chítí sa gháirdín iad agus an gnó céanna ar siúl acu. Agus d'admhaíodh Lonán gurbh fheárr an t-eólas a bhí ag Gormfhlaith ar na luíbhneacha agus ar na cómhachtaibh a bhí iontu chun uilc nú chun maitheasa ná mar a bhí aige féin.

Níorbh fhada gur tugadh post gnótha sa teaghlach do Lonán. Do cuireadh 'na stíobhard os cionn an bhídh é, chun féachaint i ndiaidh an bhídh agus aireachas a thabhairt do gach aon tsaghas bídh a bheadh le húsáid sa teaghlach, i dtreó nár bhaol go dtabharfí chun búird ann aon bhia a bheadh mí-fholláin. Níor mhór stíobhard den tsórd san a bheith i dteaghlach a bhí chómh mór agus 'na mbíodh oiread san bídh dá ollmhú gach aon lá 'en tseachtain do dhaoinibh ann.

Ach is é gnó fé leith a bhí ceapaithe do Lonán ann ná féachaint chun an bhídh a hollmhófí* don Árdríogan, le heagla go gcurfí aon droch-ní ann.

Bhí Lonán ag déanamh na hoibre sin agus ag déanamh na hoibre go maith, agus bhí an aimsir ag gluaiseacht agus gach éinne ag cómhaireamh na laethanta agus ag breithniú na haimsire 'nar dhó' leó a bheadh an tÁrdrí agus a chuallacht ag teacht abhaile. Bhí uaigneas mór sa teaghlach i ndiaidh na ndaoine a bhí amu', agus b'é ab fhada le gach éinne go rabhadar ag teacht abhaile. Bhítí ag trácht go minic ar Niamh agus ar a hathair agus ar Chaoilte agus ar Chonn. Agus do cuímhnítí ar an rás agus ar an bhfeirg a bhí ar Chonn. Agus ar conas mar aduairt Brian leis ciall a bheith aige. Do cuímhnítí ar Mhurchadh agus ar Dhúlainn, agus ar an ngarsún óg, mac Mhurchadh[*], a dheineadh, adeirtí, gníomhartha nárbh é gach fear a dh'fhéadfadh iad a dhéanamh, agus go mbíodh daoine dhá rá, nuair a bheadh sé deich mbliana fichead go mbeadh sé chómh láidir le beirt de shaghas Mhurchadh an lá ab fheárr a bhí Murchadh riamh. Do cuímhnítí orthu go léir ar an gcuma san, agus b'é ab fhada le gach éinne go mbeidís ag teacht abhaile, mar, nuair a thiocfaidís, ní bheadh aon rud sa teaghlach, ar feadh i bhfad, ach spórt agus gleó agus pléisiúr agus caitheamh aimsire, rínce agus ceól agus ól agus imirt, agus an uile shaghas aoibhnis.

Ar an gcuma gcéanna is ea ' bhíodh an scéal ag an muíntir a bhí amu'. Bhídís ag féachaint rómpu amach chun an lae 'na mbeadh an chuaird críochnaithe agus iad go léir ag teacht abhaile go Ceann Cora in éineacht leis an Árdrí, agus a gcáirde sa bhaile ag cur na mílte fáilte rómpu agus ag cur an uile shaghas ceisteanna chúthu i dtaobh an chuma 'nar chaitheadar an aimsir an fhaid a bhíodar amu' agus i dtaobh na ndaoine a bhuail úmpu insna críochaibh iasachta, an rabhadar fial fáilteach, nú an rabhadar go do-thíosach. I gcaitheamh na cuairde bhídís a d'iarraidh cúntas cruínn a chimeád ar gach ní agus ar gach aicme daoine, agus go mór mór ar gach aon scéal sultmhar a bhuaileadh úmpu, i dtreó, nuair a thiocfaidís abhaile, go mbeadh a lán le hínsint acu, a lán a bhainfeadh gáirí agus sult amach, agus a lán a chuirfeadh daoine ag déanamh iúnadh de sna rudaí a neósfí dhóibh.

Thagadh teachtairí abhaile coitianta ón áit 'na mbíodh an tÁrdrí agus a chuallacht, agus d'ínseadh na teachtairí conas a bhíodh gach éinne agus gach aon rud. Ansan do bheireadh na teachtairí leó thar n-ais, ag triall ar an Árdrí agus ar a chuallacht, cúntas cruínn ar conas a bhíodh gach éinne agus gach aon rud sa bhaile.

Ní raibh Lonán i bhfad socair 'na phost i gCeann Cora nuair a bhí ' fhios go cruínn ag Murchadh agus ag Brian agus ag an gcuallacht go léir go raibh sé ann. Nuair a hínseadh an scéal i láthair Mhurchadh, níor labhair sé focal. Ní duairt sé olc ná maith leis an scéal. Nuair a hínseadh i láthair Bhriain é, níor dhó' le duine gur airigh sé in aon chor é, mar níor chuir sé suím ar bith ann. Ní hair, ná ar nithibh dá shórd, a bhí sé ag cuímhneamh. Bhí sé ag cuímhneamh ar na tuairiscíbh a bhí ag teacht chuige in aghaidh an lae, agus uaireanta go minic sa ló, tuairiscí ó chrích Lochlann anoir, agus ó chrích na hIorua, agus ó Ínsíbh Orc, agus ó áiteannaibh ná raibh chómh fada ó bhaile, agus gan insna tuairiscíbh go léir ach fuadar agus ollmhúchán, fuadar agus ollmhúchán, chun cogaidh, agus gan fios ró-chruínn ag éinne ar cá raibh an cogadh le bheith. Bhí ' fhios ag Brian agus ag Murchadh, agus ag an gcuid eile de lucht cómhairle Bhriain, cad é brí a bhí leis an ollmhúchán agus leis an bhfuadar. Bhí ' fhios acu go raibh gínte Lochlann go léir, agus a lucht cabhartha agus cúnta agus cómhluadair, dhá ngléasadh féin agus dhá gcórú féin agus ag cruinniú a neart chun aon iarracht amháin eile, bháis agus bheatha, do dhéanamh ar oileán na hÉireann do shealbhú dhóibh féin agus dá sliocht. Dá dhaingne a chuaigh an méid sin 'na luí ar aigne Bhriain agus ar aigne lucht cómhairle Bhriain is ea ba dhéine a dheineadar an uile shaghas díchill, i gcaitheamh na cuairde sin, ar neart na hÉireann do ghléasadh agus do chur i dtreó, ins gach aon bhall, insna daingeanaibh a bhí curtha suas ag Brian, agus i dteaghlachaibh na ríthe agus na n-uasal a bhí dílis do Bhrian, ionas, nuair a thiocfadh na gínte iasachta, go bhfaighidís an tseilbh—ach gur fén bhfód a gheóbhaidís an tseilbh.

Caibideal 38: Fód an Bháis do Sheasamh

Nuair ' airigh an chuid eile de chuallacht Bhriain Lonán a bheith i gCeann Cora agus an gnó a bhí aige á dhéanamh ann, bhí iúnadh orthu agus bhíodar ag cíoradh an scéil go tiubh. Bhídís á fhiafraí cérbh é; cá dtáinig sé; conas a fuair sé eólas ann; cé ba bhun leis an bpost san a thabhairt in aon chor do; agus ceisteanna den tsórd san.

Caibideal 38: Fód an Bháis do Sheasamh

Ansan do tháinig amach gurbh árdliag é, agus gur thug sé teistiméireachtaí móra leis ag triall ar an Árdríogan, agus gur thug an Árdríogan an post do i dtreó go mbeadh liag chómh mór san eólas agus chómh mór san tuiscint sa rí-theaghlach i gcónaí, chun féachaint i ndiaidh bídh an rí-theaghlaigh i dtreó go mbeadh an bia folláin i gcónaí, agus chun féachaint i ndiaidh sláinte na ndaoine sa rí-theaghlach, leis. I rí-theaghlach 'na raibh oiread san daoine ann nárbh fhios cad é an neómat, sa lá nú san oíche, do thiocfadh taom obann ar dhuine éigin de mhuíntir an rí-theaghlaigh, agus ansan dá mba ná beadh liag maith san áit go mb'fhéidir go bhfaigheadh an duine bás sara mbeadh dochtúir tagaithe ó áit eile, dá mbeadh ar an ndochtúir teacht i bhfad.

"Cad 'duairt Niamh, agus a hathair, agus Murchadh, leis an ngnó?", adéarfaidh duine éigin, b'fhéidir.

Pé rud adúradar leis an ngnó is eatarthu féin adúradar é. Níor leogadar aon fhocal de amach i measc na cod' eile den chuallacht. Bhíodar á chíoradh agus á bhreithniú eatarthu féin, áfach, chómh dian, ní hea ach ní ba dhéine go mór, ná mar a bhí an mhuíntir a labhair dhá chíoradh agus á bhreithniú. Chífar ar ball cad é an breithniú a bhí ag Niamh agus ag á hathair agus ag Murchadh á dhéanamh ar an scéal, agus cad é an chúis a bhí acu leis an scéal a bhreithniú go dlúth.

Pé breithniú a bhí ag Niamh ná ag á hathair ná ag Murchadh, ná ag éinne eile de chuallacht Bhriain á dhéanamh, i gcaitheamh na cuairde sin, ar an scéal san, ná ar aon scéal eile dá shórd a tháinig chúthu ó Cheann Cora, bhí aon bhreithniú amháin acu go léir á dhéanamh ar na scéalta a bhí ag teacht chúthu anoir agus aduaidh, agus anoir aduaidh, ón uile áird den domhan Lochlannach. Bhí na scéalta san ag teacht coitianta, agus fé mar a bhí an aimsir ag imeacht, bhíodar ag teacht ní ba thiúbha. Is é breithniú a bhí ag cuallacht Bhriain á dhéanamh ná so: nuair a thiocfadh na slóite a bhí chun teacht, nuair a thiocfadh toradh ar an dtórmach go léir, nuair a thiocfadh an cogadh a bhí geallta, nárbh fholáir do bheith 'na chogadh bháis do thaobh éigin, do Ghaelaibh Éireann nú do sna gíntibh a bhí ag teacht. Thuig gach éinne, agus duairt gach éinne lena chómharsain agus lena chomrádaí é, i gcaitheamh na cuairde sin, go raibh ceangailte ar gach aon fhear de shliocht Gael gan bheith beó i ndiaidh an chogaidh sin dá mb'ag na gíntibh a bheadh an bua sa chogadh. Duairt gach fear le gach fear eile, "Beidh bua ag Gaelaibh nú ní bhead-sa beó! Níl orm ach bás d'fháil aon uair amháin. Is feárr go mór bás d'fháil i lár an chatha ná bheith beó in Éirinn fé smacht na Lochlannach. Má bhíonn an bua acu, bíodh Éire acu ach ní bhead-sa acu! Ach geallaim an méid seo dhóibh. Más é mo bhás a bheidh acu, ní hin aisce a bheidh sé acu!"

Fé mar a thagadh na tuairiscí, bhíodh an saghas san cainnte le clos ní ba mhinicí, agus bhíodh an machnamh a bhíodh laistigh den chainnt ag dul i ngéire in aghaidh an lae go dtí, fé dheireadh, go raibh sé socair in aigne gach fir ná raibh aige le caitheamh ar an saol so ach go dtí lá an chatha mhóir sin a bhí le teacht, pé fada gairid go dtiocfadh sé, agus do thuig gach fear in' aigne ná raibh a thuilleadh saeil uaidh. Bás a dh'fháil an lá san, ar son Gael Éireann agus ar son Chreidimh Chríost, tar éis an éirligh ba mhó a dh'fhéadfadh sé do dhéanamh ar an namhaid iasachta, air sin is ea ' bhí aigne gach fir socair. Níor chuímhnigh éinne ar cad a dhéanfadh sé ná ar conas a mhairfeadh sé dá dtagadh sé saor ón gcath agus an bua ag Gaelaibh. Níor bheag, dar le gach duine, bheith ag cuímhneamh air sin nuair a bheadh san amhlaidh.

Bhí aigne na bhfear socair ar an gcuma san, ní hamháin i gcuallacht an Árdrí, ar an gcuaird, ach fós i dteaghlach gach rí cúige 'nar chaith an tÁrdrí roinnt laethanta ann, agus insna daingeanaibh a bhí curtha suas ag an Árdrí, agus ins gach aon bhall 'nar chuaigh cainnt na bhfear san agus a n-anál fén bpoiblíocht. Bhí aigne na mban chómh socair air sin agus ' bhí aigne na bhfear. Nuair a thiocfadh an lá, ní fhanfaidís sa bhaile i ndiaidh na bhfear. Do raighidís isteach sa chath agus do thabharfaidís gach cúnamh do sna fearaibh, agus dá mbeadh bua ag an namhaid iasachta, ní bheadh aon bhean acu beó in Éirinn i ndiaidh an chatha. Gheóbhaidís bás i dteannta na bhfear. Agus dá mbeadh aon fhear chómh meata san agus go dtarraiceódh sé siar ó fhód a bháis, do sheasódh bean ar an bhfód san agus thabharfadh sí aghaidh ar an namhaid agus do ghlacfadh sí an bás a sheachain seisean. Sin mar a labhraidís, pé rud a dhéanfaidís. Bhí cuid acu, agus níor chuid bheag é, do dhéanfadh an gníomh chómh dána díreach agus ' dhéanfadh aon duine de sna fearaibh é. Dhéanfadh Niamh é, bíodh ná duairt sí go ndéanfadh.

Dá mbeadh ' fhios ag an muíntir a bhí le teacht, agus a bhí ag socrú ar a mná agus a gclann a thabhairt leó chun cur fúthu in Éirinn, dá mbeadh ' fhios acu go raibh an saghas san aigne ag fás agus ag neartú agus ag aibiú in Éirinn 'na gcómhair, b'fhéidir go dtiocfaidís ar athrú aigne agus go bhfanfaidís thall. Ach ní raibh aon phioc dá fhios acu. Bhí daoine in Éirinn a bhí coitianta ag cur tuairiscí anonn ag triall orthu, ach níor ínseadar dóibh go raibh a leithéid siúd de dhásacht croí 'na gcómhair. B'fhéidir nár thuigeadar féin go raibh, agus b'fhéidir gur chuma leó ach bheith ag séideadh fén muíntir thall, i dtreó go dtiocfaidís, pé rud a thiocfadh as, thall ná abhus. Gormfhlaith agus Amhlaoibh macánta agus Sitric, rí Lochlannach Átha Cliath, a bhí dhá dhéanamh san. Bheadh Maolmhórdha, rí Laighean, driotháir Ghormfhlaith, dhá dhéanamh leó, ach, dar leis an dtriúr eile, leath-amadán ab ea é, agus níorbh aon iúntaoibh é chun aon ghnó chúntúrthach a thabhairt le déanamh do.

Do críochnaíodh an chuaird.

Tháinig Brian agus a chuallacht abhaile go Ceann Cora. Bhí lán a chroí d'áthas ar gach éinne; an mhuíntir a bhí sa bhaile ag cur gach aon tsaghas tuairiscí ar an muíntir a tháinig, agus an mhuíntir a tháinig ag cur gach aon tsaghas tuairiscí ar an muíntir a bhí sa bhaile. Nuair a bhí na ceisteanna go léir curtha, freagartha, ar gach taobh, agus na tuairiscí go léir tabhartha, thosnaigh ceist ar ghabháil tímpall i dtaobh an stíobhaird nua a bhí tagaithe ann chun bheith ag féachaint i ndiaidh an bhídh agus i ndiaidh na ndaoine a bheadh breóite, dá mba rud é go mbeadh a leithéidí ann.

"Cé hé sin?"

"Cad as é?"

"Cad a thug anso é?"

"Cé 'ra díobh é?"

Do freagradh na ceisteanna fé mar a féadadh teacht orthu agus fé mar a bhí eólas ag an muíntir 'nar cuireadh chúthu iad. Ansan do chuaigh gach éinne isteach in' áit féin, ag déanamh a ghnótha féin, agus chuaigh gach aon rud chun suaimhnis, gnó an rí-theaghlaigh dá dhéanamh go cruínn agus go slachtmhar mar ba ghnáth, na ríthe agus na huaisle, na sagairt agus na heaspaig, ag teacht gach aon lá chun cainnte ' dhéanamh leis an Árdrí, agus an t-uathás bídh agus dí, an t-uathás aráin agus ime agus fíona agus feóla, dá chaitheamh gach aon lá sa rí-theaghlach, mar ba ghnáth.

Cúpla lá tar éis Bhriain a theacht abhaile, do shocraigh Tadhg Mór Ó Cealla ar dhul siar abhaile go hUíbh Máine. Bhí Brian, i gcaitheamh na cuairde, tar éis a chur ar a súilibh do sna ríthibh go léir agus do thaoiseachaibh na sló, nárbh fhios cathain a thiocfadh an namhaid, agus nárbh fholáir do gach rí cúige agus do gach taoiseach airm agus do gach fear cínn riain, agus don uile dhuine a bhí in aon chor ábalta ar arm do láimhseáil, bheith ollamh, chómh luath agus ' gheóbhaidís an focal, chun aghaidh a thabhairt ar an namhaid pé áit 'na dtispeánfaidís iad féin. Níorbh fholáir do Thadhg Mhór Ó Chealla, ní nárbh iúnadh, dul siar go hUíbh Máine agus a mhuíntir féin do ghléasadh agus d'ollmhú, agus a chur ar a súilibh dóibh nár mhór dóibh bheith ollamh, chómh maith le các, chun aghaidh a thabhairt ar an namhaid chómh luath agus ' thiocfadh an ghlao.

Caibideal 38: Fód an Bháis do Sheasamh

Bhí Tadhg Óg Ó Cealla thiar cheana, ag déanamh na hoibre sin, agus ba mhaith chuige é, ach má bhí féin, agus má ba mhaith féin, do thuig an t-athair nárbh ealaí dho féin gan dul siar, leis, agus bheith ag féachaint i ndiaidh na hoibre. Bhí gach rí cúige in Éirinn, go mór mór na ríthe a bhí dílis do Bhrian, ag gléasadh a neart féin, féna súilibh féin, agus é daingean in aigne gach rí acu gurbh é fód an chatha, pé áit 'na raibh an fód san, fód a bháis. Bhí Tadhg Mór Ó Cealla chómh dílis do Bhrian le haon rí cúige acu, agus bhí an rud eile chómh daingean in aigne Thaidhg agus ' bhí sé in aigne éinne acu. Níorbh fhéidir do gan dul siar.

Agus níorbh fhéidir do Niamh gan dul siar in éineacht leis.

Is ar Thadhg Óg a bhí an t-áthas nuair a chonaic sé chuige iad.

"Ó! A Niamh", ar seisean, "is áláinn a dh'fhéachann tú! Dhein an chuaird sin ana-thairbhe dhuit. Tá do ghnaoi agus do dhá shúil féin arís agat".

Thug Niamh gach aon chúntas do ar an gcuaird, agus ar na tuairiscíbh agus ar na ráflaíbh a bhí ag gluaiseacht ins gach aon bhall i dtaobh na namhad iasachta a bhí ag teacht go hÉirinn chun clanna Gael do dhísciú agus seilbh na tíre do thógaint dóibh féin. D'inis sí dho go cruínn an obair a bhí déanta ag Brian chun neart na nGael do ghléasadh i gcómhair an chogaidh mhóir a bhí ag teacht, agus conas mar a bhí fir Éireann socair 'na n-aigne ar bhás a dh'fháil sa chogadh san nuair a thiocfadh sé, nú ar bhás a thabhairt don namhaid.

Thug sí dho go cruínn agus go mion tuairisc agus cúntas ar gach ní dár thit amach ins gach aon áit 'nar ghabhadar i gcaitheamh na cuairde. Agus d'inis sí dho go raibh Maolmhórdha, rí Laighean, ag teacht go Ceann Cora in achomaireacht, ag tabhairt na gcrann leis i gcómhair na luingeas a bhí le déanamh ar línn Luimní.

"Sin é anois agat, a Thaidhg", ar sise, "an scéal go léir, ón lá ' fhágamair an áit seo go dtí an lá a thánamair thar n-ais ann".

Caibideal 39: Scuab-bhuille ' Chlaíomh

An lá a chuaigh Niamh agus a hathair siar go hUíbh Máine, nú an lá 'na dhiaidh, tháinig Caoilte go Ceann Cora, agus níorbh fhios an mór den domhan a bhí siúlta aige. Chómh luath agus ' bhí bia caite aige, agus a thuirse curtha dhe aige, bhí sé féin agus Murchadh agus Brian i seómra fé leith agus é ag tabhairt eólais dóibh ar a chuardaibh agus ar cad a chonaic sé.

"Anonn go crích Lochlann a chuas ar dtúis", ar seisean, "a ríthe. Duart liom féin go dtabharfainn fúthu pé rud a dh'imeódh orm. Ní fheadar ceocu do haithníodh me nú nár aithníodh*. Má aithin éinne me níor leog sé air gur aithin sé me.

"Níor fhágas aon phioc dá neart gan féachaint, agus do bhreithníos a neart chómh cruínn agus d'fhéadas é ' bhreithniú. Táid na daoine go léir as a meabhair, ba dhó' le duine, le dúil teacht go hÉirinn agus seilbh a ghlacadh in oileán na hÉireann agus cur fúthu ann. Tá sé buailte isteach 'na n-aigne go bhfuil an t-oileán so chómh saibhir, agus an talamh chómh torthúil sin ann, nách gá do sna daoine gur leó é aon obair a dhéanamh ag saothrú an tailimh. Chím go soiléir go bhfuil daoine éigin anso in Éirinn atá ag séideadh fúthu agus ag cur nithe den tsórd san isteach 'na n-aigne. Pé cúis atá leis, níl aon mheas in aon chor acu ar a dtír féin, agus dá luathacht a bheid siad tagaithe anall anso in éineacht is ea is feárr é, dar leó. Táid na mná agus an chlann chómh mór buile chun teacht agus atáid na fir, nú níos mó. Tá oiread luingeas ollamh acu agus ' thabarfadh anoir fiche míle fear agus airm agus lón dóibh. Is dó' leó féin go mbeidh deich míle fear acu, agus go dtógfaid na mná agus an chlann suas oiread slí agus ' thógfadh deich míle eile fear.

Caibideal 39: Scuab-bhuille ' Chlaíomh

"Ní mheasaim féin, tar éis na cainnte go léir, go bhféadfaid siad deich míle fear do chur le chéile agus do thabhairt anso anoir. Ba mhaith an rud a bheadh déanta acu dá dtugaidís ocht míle fear leó i dteannta na mban agus na clainne.

"Chuas ó thuaidh go tír na hIorua. Tá an obair chéanna ar siúl ansan, agus an bhuile chéanna ar na daoine go léir chun imeacht as a dtír féin agus teacht go hÉirinn. Ní haon iúnadh an dithneas a bheith orthu san chun imithe* as a dtír féin. Níl sa bhaile acu ach beatha chruaidh, agus tuillid siad go cruaidh í. Talamh fuar fiain neamh-thorthúil atá acu. Tá obair chruaidh acu le déanamh coitianta, ag casadh leis an dtalamh a shaothrú, agus ansan, tar éis na sclábhaíochta go léir, ní bhíonn puínn de bhárr a saothair acu. Ní haon iúnadh dithneas a bheith orthu chun na tíre ' dh'fhágáilt agus teacht chun cónaithe i dtír a dhéanfaidh, dar leó, iad do chothú díomhaoin. Tá daoine éigin ó Éirinn ag séideadh fúthu san, leis, agus ag cur na smaointe sin isteach 'na n-aigne. Mura mbeadh go bhfuil, ní thiocfadh na smaointe chúthu".

"An mó míle fear is dó' leat, a Dhuínn, a dh'fhéadfaidh rí na hIorua do chur le chéile agus do thabhairt leis, má thagann sé?", arsa Brian.

"Déarfainn, a Árdrí", arsa Caoilte, "go gcuirfidh sé le chéile trí nú ceathair de mhíltibh fear. Tá beirt mhac aige, fir ana-chróga. Fén mbeirt sin is ea ' bheidh an tslua. Beidh, is dócha, trí nú ceathair de mhíltibh ban agus leanbh acu i dteannta na bhfear. Is mó an dithneas atá ar mhnáibh na hIorua chun teacht ná mar atá ar mhnáibh tíre Lochlann. Tá sé 'na n-aigne ná beidh acu le déanamh nuair a thiocfaid siad go hÉirinn ach bualadh isteach agus suí síos. Tá duine éigin, nú daoine éigin, dhá gcur amú, dhá gcur ar a n-aimhleas, ag cur an duibh 'na gheal ar na daoine bochta".

"Comáin leat, a Dhuínn", arsa Brian.

Caibideal 39: Scuab-bhuille ’ Chlaíomh

“Chuas ó thuaidh go hÍnsíbh Orc, a Árdrí”, arsa Caoilte. “Chuireas me féin i riocht file, agus thógas cláirseach liom agus thánag go rí-theaghlach an Iarla Sígurd, Iarla na n-Ínsí sin Orc. Bhí cuideachta le bheith ann. Bhí cuireadh tabhartha ag Sígurd don Iarla Gilli, fear atá pósta ag á dhrifiúr. Tháinig an tIarla Gilli, fear driféar Shíguird. Tháinig a lán eile uaisle ann. Bhí glaoch ar cheól agus thugas dóibh an ceól. Cé ’ bhuailfeadh chúinn isteach ach Sitric, rí Lochlannach Átha Cliath. Do cuireadh fáilte roimis féin agus roimena chuallacht. Bhí fear ann a tháinig aduaidh ó Inis Tuile. Bhí cúntas aige á thabhairt ar cad fé ndeara dho féin agus do roinnt eile de mhuíntir an oileáin sin imeacht ón mbaile. Dheineadar coir throm. D’éirigh idir iad agus duin’ uasal fónta a bhí ann, agus mheasadar an duin’ uasal do chur chun báis. Do theip orthu ar feadh i bhfad, mar bhí clann mhac ró-chróga aige agus do chosain an chlann mhac é. Fé dheireadh do fuaradar lom ar theaghlach an duin’ uasail do loscadh, agus do loisceadar ’na mbeathaidh é féin agus a bhean agus a chlann istigh ’na dtigh féin*. Niall ab ainm don duin’ uasal. B’éigean don mhuíntir a dhein an loscadh imeacht as an oileán. Thánadar, nú tháinig cuid acu, go teaghlach Shíguird in Inis Orc. Gunnar, nú Conchúr, ab ainm don fhear a bhí ag ínsint an scéil. An fhaid a bhí an scéal ar siúl tháinig fear chun an dorais, lasmu’, ach níor thispeáin sé é féin. Cairí ab ainm don fhear san, agus fear ana-chróga is ea é. Cliamhain is ea é don duin’ uasal a loisceadh, agus ba dhóbair go loisctí é féin mar bhí sé sa tigh an oíche do deineadh an loscadh. Bhí sé ar an dtaobh amu’ de dhoras rí-theaghlaigh Shíguird an uair sin, agus bhí sé ag éisteacht leis an scéal. Duine den mhuíntir a dhein an loscadh ab ea an fear a bhí ag ínsint an scéil. Bhí an dá Iarla ag an mbórd agus rí Lochlannach Átha Cliath eatarthu, agus iad ag éisteacht leis an scéal. Bhíos féin ag éisteacht leis an scéal agus mo chláirseach fé m’uillinn agam. Do labhair Sitric.

“‘Conas a dh’fhuilig Scraphádinn an tine, a Ghunnair?’, ar seisean.

“‘Maith go leór ar dtúis, a rí’, arsa Gunnar, ‘ach nuair a rug an teas i gceart air, do liúigh sé agus do ghoil sé mar a dhéanfadh seanabhean’.

Caibideal 39: Scuab-bhuille ' Chlaíomh

"Ar éigin a bhí an méid sin cainnte as a bhéal nuair a léim Cairí an doras isteach agus suas chun na háite 'na raibh Gunnar 'na shuí in aice an bhúird ar aghaidh an rí agus an dá Iarla amach. Sara raibh ' fhios ag éinne cad a bhí ar siúl aige, do tharraig Cairí a chlaíomh agus le haon* scuab-bhuille amháin do bhain sé an ceann den scéalaí. Chuir sé a leithéid sin d'fhuinneamh leis an mbuille gur léim an ceann isteach ar an mbórd, ar aghaidh Shitric agus an dá Iarla amach, agus go raibh an bórd lán d'fhuil, mórthímpall an chínn, sara raibh uain ag éinne ar a thuiscint cad a bhí titithe amach.* Níor dhein Cairí ach féachaint 'na thímpall agus ansan imeacht amach. Níor lean éinne é. Ar ball, nuair a bhí caoi agam air, do chromas ar dhuine a bhí i m'aice do cheistiú. Do labhras i gcainnt na hIorua.

"'Cé hé an rí sin, Sitric?', arsa mise.

"'Ó Éirinn aneas é sin', arsan duine liom. 'Is é rí Lochlannach Átha Cliath é'.

"'Agus cad a thug anso é?', arsa mise.

"'De réir mar a thuigim', ar seisean, 'is amhlaidh a tháinig sé dhá iarraidh ar an dá Iarla, ar Shígurd agus ar Ghilli, a neart do chur le chéile agus dul leis go hÉirinn ag cabhrú leis sa chogadh so atá le déanamh i gcoinnibh Bhriain'.

"'Agus cé hé Brian?', arsa mise go neamh-thuairimeach.

"'Ach!', ar seisean, 'an amhlaidh nách eól duit cé hé Brian!'

"'Agus cé hé féin, is dó'?', arsa mise.

"'Árdrí Éireann', ar seisean. 'Mheasas', ar seisean, 'ná raibh éinne beó gan aithne aige ar Bhrian'.

"'Is dócha', arsa mise, 'gur droch-rí é, treás go bhfuil an cogadh mór so dá bheartú 'na choinnibh'.

"'Ní droch-rí', ar seisean. 'Sin é iúnadh an scéil ar fad. Níl rí eile beó sa domhan atá chómh maith leis. Nuair a deintear feall air, maitheann sé an feall an chéad uair, agus má dheineann an duine sin feall air an tarna huair, maitheann sé an feall an tarna huair. Ansan, má dheineann an duine céanna feall air an tríú huair, tugann sé an cuirpeach suas don dlí. Sin rí fónta agat!', ar seisean.

"'Agus cad 'na thaobh an cogadh, más ea?', arsa mise.

"'Ní fheadar 'en tsaol', ar seisean, 'murab amhlaidh atá daoine éigin ag déanamh an fhíll an tríú huair air. Ní bheidís ag déanamh an fhíll an tríú huair air', ar seisean, 'dá mb'áil leis iad do chrochadh an chéad uair, nú, an chuid ba lú dhe, an tarna huair'.

"'An bhfuil Sígurd ag dul le Sitric?', arsa mise.

"'Deir gach éinne go bhfuil', ar seisean, 'agus Gilli, agus Ospac. Deir gach éinne', ar seisean, 'nách féidir do Bhrian agus do Ghaelaibh seasamh in aghaidh na slóite atá ag cruinniú as an uile áird 'na gcoinnibh. Go gcurfar clanna Gael go léir chun báis, agus ansan go mbeidh Éire gan chíos ag an muíntir a raghaidh ann anois ag déanamh an chogaidh'".

"An mór an neart is dó' leat a dh'fhéadfaidh Sígurd agus Gilli do thabhairt leó?", arsa Brian.

"Tá mórán luingeas acu, a Árdrí", arsa Caoilte "agus tá mórán luingeas ag Ospac. Tá taithí ag an uile shaghas lucht gadaíochta agus robála ar theacht ag triall ar Shígurd nuair a bhíonn sé ag dul ar chuaird thar farraige. Bíonn deimhne acu ar chuid mhaith den fhoghail a dh'fháil dóibh féin. Is deocair tuairim a thabhairt don méid nirt sló a dh'fhéadfaidh sé a thabhairt leis".

Caibideal 39: Scuab-bhuille ' Chlaíomh

"An bhfuil aon tuairim acu", arsa Murchadh, "don neart sló a bheidh 'na gcoinnibh in Éirinn?"

"Tá tuairim acu, a rí", arsa Caoilte, "nách in aisce a gheóbhaid siad seilbh na hÉireann, ach níl aon chuímhneamh acu go bhfuil aon bhaol ná go bhfaighid siad an tseilbh. Tá an méid sin curtha 'na luí ar a n-aigne go daingean, agus is ó Éirinn a cuireadh 'na luí ar a n-aigne é".

"Nách mór an iúnadh nár aithin Sitric thu, a Dhuínn", arsa Brian.

"Fágaim le huacht, a Árdrí", arsa Caoilte, "gur baineadh preab asam nuair a chonac ag teacht isteach é. Ach bhí an cheilt ró-mhaith orm. Thugas aire don chláirsigh, agus bhí a ghnó féin ag déanamh buartha dho san. Dá éaghmais sin, ní dó' liom go n-aithneódh sé me dá mba ná beadh aon cheilt orm. Ní ró-mhinic a chonaic sé riamh me, agus níor chuir sé puínn suime riamh ionam".

"Táimíd go léir fé chomaoine mhór agat, a Dhuínn", arsa Brian. "Níl aon teóra lena bhfuil d'eólas tabhartha agat chúinn, agus eólas tairbheach is ea é. Ní bheimís ollamh i gceart in aon chor mura mbeadh a bhfuil d'eólas tabhartha chúinn agat. Thiocfaidís i ganfhios orainn mura mbeadh tu!"

Um an dtaca 'na raibh deireadh an eólais tabhartha dhóibh ag Caoilte, do ghluais an focal tríd an rí-theaghlach go raibh Maolmhórdha, rí Laighean, ag teacht go Ceann Cora agus cuallacht lena chois agus na trí craínn mhóra acu á thabhairt leó, chun na gcrann seóil do sna luingeas a bhí le déanamh ar línn Luimní.

Caibideal 40: Cluiche Fichille, agus Poll i gCrann

*Nuair a bhí an t-eólas san go léir fálta ag Brian agus ag Murchadh, ó Chaoilte, do labhair Brian.

"Dúraís dhá uair nú trí, a Dhuínn", arsa Brian, gur daoine anso in Éirinn atá ag séideadh fé mhuíntir na ndúthaí iasachta so go léir agus á ngríosadh 'nár n-aghaidh. B'fhéidir go bhfuil obair den tsórd san ar siúl. Má tá, ní huathu féin atá na daoine sin, anso in Éirinn, ag déanamh na hoibre sin. Tá cómhachta atá níos treise ná cómhachta daonna, ag oibriú ag bun-phréimh na hoibre go léir. Cómhachta ifrinn is iad atá dhá n-oibriú féin 'nár gcoinnibh, i gcoinnibh an Chreidimh atá istigh 'nár gcroí. Táid cómhachta ifrinn ag spriocadh agus ag gríosadh na ndroch-dhaoine atá anso in Éirinn againn, chun na smaointe úd do chur isteach in aigne ár namhad, agus tá cómhachta ifrinn, ar an gcuma gcéanna, ag spriocadh agus ag gríosadh ár namhad, insna tíorthaibh sin go léir a shiúlaís, chun na smaointe sin do ghlacadh agus beart a dhéanamh dá réir. Tá cómhacht is treise ná cómhacht dhaonna 'nár gcoinnibh. Ní foláir dúinn-na, dá bhrí sin, cómhacht is treise ná cómhacht dhaonna do bheith ag cabhrú linn sa ghleic seo atá ag teacht orainn. Ba mhaith liom bheith ag cainnt le m'anamchara".

Do tugadh chuige Maolshuathain. Dheineadar an chainnt. Ansan duairt Brian le Maolshuathain teachtaireacht do chur mórthímpall ag triall ar chléir na hÉireann, dhá órdú guí na n-easpag agus guí na sagart agus guí na bpobal do bheith ag dul suas chun Dé coitianta, as san amach, dhá iarraidh ar Dhia, trí ímpí na Maighdine Muire agus na naomh go léir, agus trí ímpí Phádraig agus Bhríde agus Cholm Cille agus naomh Éireann go léir, an Creideamh agus sliocht Gael do thabhairt saor as an ngleic uathásach a bhí ag teacht orthu.

"Tá an ní san dá dhéanamh cheana, a Árdrí", arsa Maolshuathain. "Tá sé á dhéanamh ar fuid na hÉireann ins gach áit 'na bhfuil sagart agus pobal, agus Aifreann dá rá, agus tá sé á dhéanamh ins gach mainistir agus ins gach *conbhint* ban rialta. Ach cuirfead an teachtaireacht tímpall, mar sin féin. B'fhéidir gur déine-de a déanfar an guí an teachtaireacht do chur tímpall uait-se, a Árdrí. Ní fhéadfaidh an guí bheith ró-dhian".

"Ní fhéadfaidh", arsa Brian, "ná chómh dian agus ba mhaith é ' bheith. Ba mhaith liom, thar gach ní eile, go mbeadh Naomh Íbirt an Aifrinn dá dhéanamh coitianta ar an íntinn chéanna".

"Curfar san sa teachtaireacht, a Árdrí", arsa Maolshuathain.

Do cuireadh an teachtaireacht san mórthímpall na hÉireann.

An fhaid a bhí an chainnt sin ar siúl idir Bhrian agus Maolshuathain, bhí aos óg an bhaile imithe amach, gach bóthar agus gach cóngar, soir an treó 'na raibh rí Laighean agus a chuallacht ag teacht, chun go bhfeicfidís an rí, agus na huaisle iasachta, agus na craínn mhóra. Fé dheireadh do chonacadar an rí agus chonacadar na huaisle iasachta agus chonacadar na craínn. Bhí fiche fear, deichniúr ar gach taobh, fé gach crann acu. Bhíodar ag siúl go breá réidh. D'iompaigh an t-aos óg leó siar agus thánadar go Ceann Cora. Tháinig Brian amach agus chuir sé fáilte roim rí Laighean. Do leogadh na craínn anuas ar an bpáirc bhreá ghlas a bhí amach ón rí-theaghlach. Do rugadh na fir isteach agus do cuireach gach cóir orthu. Ansan d'imigh na fir abhaile agus d'fhan an rí i bhfochair Bhriain chun roinnt laethanta ' chaitheamh ag cainnt agus ag cómhluadar leis. Tháinig sé mar a raibh an Árdríogan, a dhrifiúr.

"Seo, a Ghormfhlaith", ar seisean, "do chailleas an cnaipe óir a bhí sa bhrat so agam. Féach a' bhféadfá cnaipe do chur ann dom".

"Conas a chaillis an cnaipe?", ar sise.

Caibideal 40: Cluiche Fichille, agus Poll i gCrann

"Nuair a bhíomair ag teacht leis na trí crannaibh", ar seisean, "bhí muíntir Uíbh Fáilge fé chrann acu agus muíntir Uíbh Faoláin fé chrann eile agus muíntir Mhuireadhaigh fén dtríú crann. Bhíomair ag teacht trí Shliabh an Bhogaidh. Níorbh fhéidir do sna trí buínibh gluaiseacht in éineacht. Níorbh fholáir dóibh gluaiseacht i ndiaidh ' chéile. D'éirigh eatarthu, féachaint ceocu buíon a bheadh ar tosach. Bhí fearg ag teacht orthu. Ní ghéillfeadh aon bhuíon acu do bhuíon* eile. Shíleas go mbeadh sé 'na bhruín chaorthainn eatarthu. Níor dheineas féin ach túirleacan dem chapall agus dul agus mo ghuala ' chur fén gcrann a bhí ag muíntir Uíbh Faoláin. Nuair a chonaic an dá bhuín eile an méid sin, tharraigeadar siar agus bhí an tsíocháin againn. Nuair a tháinig meáchaint an chraínn ar mo ghualainn, do sceinn an cnaipe as an mbrat agus do chailleas é".

Bhí Gormfhlaith ag éisteacht leis agus ag féachaint air an fhaid a bhí sé ag cainnt. Nuair a stad sé, níor dhein sí ach an brat do chaitheamh sa tine. Do las an brat agus do loisceadh 'na luaithrigh é os cómhair na beirte agus iad ag féachaint air. Brat ana-dhaor ab ea é. Níorbh fhada roimis sin ó thug Brian do rí Laighean é. Bhí iúnadh agus alltacht ar rí Laighean nuair a chonaic sé cad a bhí déanta ag Gormfhlaith. Ní fheidir sé 'en domhan cad a bhí ag éirí dhi. Níor fhág sí i bhfad gan eólas é. Do sheasaimh sí ar a aghaidh amach agus a gnúis álainn ar lasadh le buile feirge, agus a dhá súil, agus ba bhreá an dá shúil iad, ag taithneamh le solas éigin nárbh fhónta. Do chaolaigh na fabhraí anuas orthu agus do dhoirchigh a haghaidh, fé mar a thiocfadh scamall ar an ngréin, agus duairt sí, trína fiaclaibh, i gcogar nách mór:

"A rá gur rug sé im* beathaidh orm mo dhriotháir a bheith 'na bheithíoch iompair ag Brian!"

Nuair aduairt sí an focal san, d'iompaigh sí uaidh agus do ghluais sí ag rástáil síos agus suas an seómra. Do leath a dhá shúil air sin, agus ní fheidir sé cad ba mhaith dho a rá. D'iompaigh sí arís air sara raibh uain aige ar phuínn machnaimh a dhéanamh.

Caibideal 40: Cluiche Fichille, agus Poll i gCrann

"Ní ró-fhada", ar sise, "go mbeidh sé 'na bheithíoch iompair ag Murchadh, leis! Ansan is ea a bainfar obair as an mbeithíoch. Ansan is ea a curfar an t-ualach air, agus má chuireann sé stailc suas, ní bheidh ach an bata ' thabhairt do!"

"Tá an éagóir agat, a bhean!", ar seisean. "Ná tabhair a thuilleadh den chainnt sin dómh-sa, mar ní glacfar uait í. Níor dheineas aon rud ach an rud ba cheart do Chríostaí a dhéanamh chun daoine gan chiall do chimeád óna chéile ' mharú. 'Im beithíoch iompair ag Brian'! Is ró-mhaith an bhail ort nách fear thu! Dá mb'ea, ní déarfá an chainnt sin. Dá n-abarthá, ní déarfá an tarna huair í!"

Do stad sí arís ar a aghaidh amach agus do chaolaigh na súile i dtreó gur bheag ná go rabhadar dúnta.

"Ní déarfainn", ar sise. "Níor ghá dom é. Ní gá dhom an chainnt do rá anois. Déarfaidh daoine nách me í. Déarfaidh muíntir Uíbh Faoláin í, ag maíomh as an gcuma 'na bhfuaradar tosach ar an dá mhuíntir eile. Déarfaidh an dá mhuíntir eile í ag gearán ar an éagóir a deineadh orthu. Raghaidh an chainnt ó bhéal go béal ar fuid na hÉireann. Raghaidh an chainnt ó shliocht go sliocht an fhaid a bheidh sliocht Gael beó: 'Dhein rí Laighean beithíoch iompair de féin do Bhrian'. Conas a chuirfir-se ' fhiachaibh ar na daoine gan an focal do rá an tarna huair! Mairfidh an focal, a rí, an fhaid a mhairfir-se, an fhaid a mhairfidh éinne ded shliocht in Éirinn. Cad 'déarfaid Laighnigh feasta nuair a caithfar insna súilibh orthu go bhfuil an rí atá orthu 'na bheithíoch iompair ag Brian!"

An túisce 'na raibh an méid sin as a béal aici, bhí sí imithe amach doras a bhí in íochtar an tseómra agus an doras dúnta 'na diaidh aici agus an eochair casta sa ghlas aici.

D'fhág sí ansúd 'na sheasamh é agus a mheabhair bainte dhe nách mór. D'fhan sé ar feadh i bhfad gan aon chor a chur de. Fé dheireadh bhuail sé amach. Chuir sé an dínnéar agus an tráthnóna dhe gan puínn cainnte ' dhéanamh le héinne. Nuair a bhí an dínnéar caite agus an chuideachta scaipithe, bhuail sé isteach i seómra 'na raibh uaisle ag imirt fichille ann. Bhí Murchadh agus Conáing, beirt de mhacaibh Bhriain*, ag imirt chluiche, agus iad á imirt go dian. Bhí rí Laighean 'na sheasamh os a gcionn ag féachaint ar an gcluiche. Thug sé fé ndeara, dá n-aistríodh Conáing fear áirithe go mbuafadh sé an cluiche. Thug sé cómhartha éigin do Chonáing. Do dhein Conáing an t-aistriú agus do bhuaigh sé an cluiche.

Bhí ' fhios ag Murchadh gur thug rí Laighean an cómhartha uaidh.

"Is feárr an chómhairle a thugais do Chonáing anois, a rí", arsa Murchadh leis, "ná an chómhairle ' thugais do sna Lochlannaigh roim chath Ghleanna Mhάma. Do buadh orthu mar gheall ar an gcómhairle úd a thugais-se dhóibh".

"Tabharfad cómhairle a bheidh níos feárr ná an chómhairle sin dóibh lá eile", arsa rí Laighean.

"Más ea", arsa Murchadh, "ná dein aon dearúd de chrann a bheidh folamh 'na lár a bheith in aice na háite agat chun dul i bhfolach ann, fé mar a chuais sa chrann i nGleann Mhάma*. Agus bíodh an poll mór a dhóthain i dtreó go bhféadfair do chosa ' tharrac isteach. Mura mbeadh do chosa ' bheith lasmu' den pholl a bhí sa chrann úd i nGleann Mhάma, ní fheicfinn tu ann in aon chor".

D'iompaigh rí Laighean agus do rith sé an doras amach.

"Ó, a Mhurchadh", arsa Conáing, "tá cathú orm nár leogas orm nár thuigeas an cómhartha! Tá fearg air. Beidh an tÁrdrí ar buile chúinn mar gheall air".

"Ná féadfadh sé é féin d'iompar!", arsa Murchadh.

"Is trua mar a thráchtais in aon chor ar an gcrann!", arsa Conáing.

Caibideal 40: Cluiche Fichille, agus Poll i gCrann

"Dá mba ná beadh agat ach aon gháire amháin, a Chonáing", arsa Murchadh, "dhéanfá an gháire sin dá bhfeicfá é nuair a rugas ar dhá chois air agus tharraigeas amach a poll an chraínn é. Ní raibh aon choinne in aon chor agam gurbh é a bhí agam go dtí go raibh sé tarraicthe amach agam. Tá sé riamh ag gabháil páirt na Lochlannach i ganfhios. Gabhadh sé a bpáirt os cómhair an tsaeil, agus ní déarfad focal leis! Ach dhá leogaint air go bhfuil sé dílis dúinn agus ansan ag déanamh an fhíll orainn!"

Ní fheacadar rí Laighean an chuid eile den oíche. D'imigh sé roim lá agus thug sé aghaidh soir abhaile. Nuair a tháinig an mhaidean, do fuaradh go raibh sé imithe. Do hínseadh do Bhrian an rud a thit amach i dtaobh an chluiche. Chomáin Brian teachtaire i ndiaidh rí Laighean dhá iarraidh air casadh agus go ndéanfí leórghníomh san easonóir a tugadh do. Go raibh tabharthaisí ag Brian le bronnadh air mar gheall ar na craínn a thabhairt chuige.

Tháinig an teachtaire suas leis. Thug sé a theachtaireacht do. Bhí bata 'na láimh ag rí Laighean. Níor dhein sé ach cúpla buille den bhata ' thabhairt sa cheann do theachtaire an Árdrí, agus comáint leis soir. Ar ghuaillibh fear a tugadh abhaile an teachtaire*. Nuair a chonaic muíntir rí-theaghlaigh Bhriain an cor a bhí ar an dteachtaire, d'iarradar ar Bhrian leogaint dóibh rí Laighean do leanúint agus é ' thabhairt thar n-ais 'na phríosúnach. Ní thoileódh Brian chuige sin.

"Is do rí Laighean a tugadh an easonóir ar dtúis", arsa Brian. "Leogtar do imeacht slán abhaile. Ansan raighimíd soir agus bainfimíd sásamh de ag doras a thí féin".

Chómh luath agus a fuair Gormfhlaith go raibh rí Laighean imithe i bhfeirg agus go raibh an easonóir tabhartha aige do theachtaire Bhriain, bhí ' fhios aici go raibh sé 'na chogadh dhearg eatarthu. Sin a raibh uaithi. Chomáin sí teachtaire go Baile Átha Cliath ag triall ar Shitric agus ar Amhlaoibh dhá ínsint dóibh cad a bhí titithe amach.

"Anois an t-am agaibh!", ar sise. "Tagadh úr neart go léir chómh tapaidh agus is féidir é. Beidh an gnó eile déanta agam-sa agus ag Lonán sara mbeidh úr neart cruinnithe tagaithe".

Caibideal 41: Rí Laighean

Duine ab ea rí Laighean nár chuir éinne puínn suime in aon rud a dhéanfadh sé ná in aon ní adéarfadh sé. Fear baoth ab ea é. Mheas sé féin ná raibh duine ar bith dob fheárr ciall agus tuiscint ná é, ach níorbh é sin meas daoine eile air. Bhí sé ollamh i gcónaí chun daoine eile do chómhairliú. Do leogadh daoine orthu go nglacfaidís an chómhairle, ach ní ghlacaidís. Thugadh sé a aigne do gach éinne agus ní thugadh éinne a aigne dho san. Dá dtugaidís, ní chimeádfadh sé rún. Bhí sé ar thaobh na Lochlannach i gcath Ghleanna Mháma agus bhí sé amu' air gur mar gheall ar chómhairle éigin a thug sé dhóibh a chuaigh an lá 'na gcoinnibh. Tar éis an chatha, bhí Murchadh agus Dúlainn Óg ag gabháil tímpall ag féachaint i ndiaidh na bhfear ngunta. Chonacadar crann agus poll dreóite ann agus a lár folamh. Bhí dhá chois duine amach as an bpoll. Do rug Murchadh ar an dá chois agus tharraig sé an duine amach a poll an chraínn. Cé ' bheadh aige ach Maolmhórdha! Dhein Murchadh agus Dúlainn gáirí a ndóthain nuair a chonacadar cé ' bhí acu. Do deineadh rí ar Laighnibh 'na dhiaidh san de trí chómhairle Ghormfhlaith agus Shitric.

Níor thug Gormfhlaith ná Sitric ná Amhlaoibh fios ná eólas do ar an uisce-fé-thalamh a bhí ar siúl acu i gcoinnibh Bhriain agus Mhurchadh. Ní fhéadfaidís é. Do scoilfeadh air nú do leogfadh sé amach é. Do leogadar do go dtí go raibh gach aon ní ollamh acu i gcómhair an chogaidh. Theastaigh uathu ansan é féin agus slóite Laighean a bheith ar a dtaobh féin, i gcoinnibh Bhriain, sa chogadh. Chuige sin is ea ' chuir Gormfhlaith an fhearg air nuair a chuaigh sé go Ceann Cora leis na crannaibh. Dhein sí an gnó go feilmeanta. Tháinig sé go Ceann Cora an uair sin agus gan idir é agus Brian ach an caradas ba threise agus ba dhílse. D'fhág sé Ceann Cora agus gan 'na chroí do Bhrian ach fuath agus fíoch agus fearg, agus a chroí dá loscadh ag an bhfocal úd a chuir Gormfhlaith isteach 'na chluais, é ' bheith 'na "bheithíoch iompair ag Brian!" Bhí sé lán-cheapaithe ar dhul, gan stad gan ríghneas, ag triall ar Shitric agus ar a dh'ínsint do cad é an tarcaisne a tugadh do i gCeann Cora, agus ar a iarraidh air cabhrú leis chun an tarcaisne do dhíogailt ar Bhrian agus ar Mhurchadh agus orthu go léir.

Nuair a bhí san mar sin, bhí a haidhm féin curtha chun cínn go hálainn ag Gormfhlaith. Bhí rí Laighean gofa isteach go daingean aici ar a taobh féin, sa chogadh a bhí ag teacht, agus ní raibh aon phioc dá fhios ag rí Laighean ná gurbh é a ghnó féin a bhí aige dá dhéanamh; ná gurbh é a fhuath féin agus a mhioscais féin a bhí aige dá shásamh i gcoinnibh Bhriain. Bhí gnó Ghormfhlaith aige dá dhéanamh chun a toile go hiomlán agus ní raibh aon bhaol go leogfadh sé amach aon rún, mar níor tugadh do aon rún.

Sara raibh uain ag Maolmhórdha ar bheith sa bhaile ó Cheann Cora bhí teachtaire Ghormfhlaith i mBaile Átha Cliath dhá ínsint do Shitric cad a bhí déanta. Chómh luath agus do shrois Maolmhórdha an baile siúd, isteach go Baile Átha Cliath é dhá ínsint do Shitric cad d'imigh air i gCeann Cora agus dhá iarraidh air a pháirt do ghabháil i gcoinnibh Bhriain.

"Geóbhad*, a rí", arsa Sitric, "do pháirt i gcoinnibh Bhriain, agus ní mise amháin a gheóbhaidh do pháirt 'na choinnibh. Geóbhaidh rí Lochlann do pháirt 'na choinnibh. Agus geóbhaidh rí na hIorua do pháirt 'na choinnibh. Agus geóbhaid ríthe nách iad do pháirt 'na choinnibh. Comáinfead teachtairí láithreach ag triall orthu dhá iarraidh orthu teacht anso go cuan Bhaile Átha Cliath chómh luath in Éirinn agus is féidir é, chun do pháirt-se ' ghabháil, agus díoltais a dhéanamh ar Bhrian agus ar a chlaínn mar gheall ar a bhfuil d'olc déanta acu ar chlannaibh Lochlann le fada ' bhliantaibh. Imigh-se abhaile, a rí", ar seisean, "agus cruinnigh do neart agus cuir thu féin i dtreó, agus bí anso led shlóitibh nuair a thiocfaidh an neart iasachta".

D'imigh rí Laighean abhaile agus dhírigh sé ar a shlóite do chruinniú agus do ghléasadh. D'inis sé do gach éinne cad é an tarcaisne a tugadh do i gCeann Cora, conas mar a caitheadh Gleann Mháma insna súilibh air féin agus ar Laighneachaibh, agus conas mar aduairt Murchadh, mac Bhriain, leis féin agus leis na Laighneachaibh gan aon dá chuid a dhéanamh dá ndícheall.

Do chealg an chainnt sin na Laighneacha, agus dúradar go mbeadh lá eile acu féin agus go ndíolfadh Brian agus Murchadh, agus Clann Chais go léir, a Gleann Mháma. Bhíodar ag déanamh na hoibre a bhí geárrtha amach dóibh ag Gormfhlaith, agus ní raibh aon phioc dá fhios acu gurbh í sin obair a bhí acu á dhéanamh. Ba dhoimhinn agus ba ghasta agus ba dhroch-aigeanta an bhean Gormfhlaith, agus dob ábalta an bhean í. Ach bhí cluiche bháis is bheatha aici dá imirt le daoinibh a bhí beagán ró-dhoimhinn di, agus ró-ghasta dhi, agus ró-ábalta dhi. Do thuigeadar an cluiche a bhí aici dá imirt agus do scaoileadar léi. Bhí bob aici dá bhualadh ar rí Laighean agus ar na Laighneachaibh, agus ní raibh aon phioc dá fhios aici go raibh a chómhthrom, agus breis, de bhob dá bhualadh, i láthair na huaire céanna, uirthi féin.

Leabhar a Trí

Caibideal 42: Cor in Aghaidh an Chaím

Roinnt laethanta tar éis rí Laighean a dh'imeacht i bhfeirg ó Cheann Cora, bhí Brian agus Murchadh agus Dúlainn Óg i bhfochair a chéile i gcómhairle. Bhí a lán nithe acu á bhreithniú. Bhíodar ag áireamh na mílte fear a féadfí ' thabhairt as gach triúch nuair a thiocfadh an ghlao. Thuigeadar gur isteach i gcuan Bhaile Átha Cliath a thiocfadh an namhaid iasachta. Bhíodar ag breithniú na mbóithre a bhí ó Cheann Cora go Baile Átha Cliath; agus ó Uíbh Máine go Baile Átha Cliath; agus ó Chaiseal go Baile Átha Cliath; agus ó thír na nDéise go Baile Átha Cliath; agus ó Chiarraí go Baile Átha Cliath; agus mar sin, ó gach aon áit 'na raibh cuid de neart sló Bhriain go dtí an áit in aice Bhaile Átha Cliath 'na gcaithfeadh a shlóite go léir teacht agus cruinniú i gcoinnibh na sló namhad iasachta a bhí ag teacht go hÉirinn ón uile pháirt den domhan Lochlannach. Ansan is ea do tuigeadh go hálainn tairbhe na hoibre a bhí ag Brian á dhéanamh ar feadh i bhfad roimis sin, nuair a bhí na bóithre breátha leathana aige á dhéanamh ins gach aon bhall agus nuair a bhí na drochaid bhreátha láidre aige á chur ar na haibhníbh. Do tuigeadh, leis, an uair sin gur deineadh maitheas mór nuair a rugadh slóite Bhriain go minic roimis sin go Cíll Mhaighneann in aice Bhaile Átha Cliath, an áit 'nar ghnáth le Brian dul agus longphort a dhéanamh agus roinnt aimsire ' chaitheamh, nuair a bhíodh gnó aige le déanamh, aighneas a shocrú idir ríthibh, nú a smacht féin do chur i bhfeidhm. Bhí aithne mhaith ag Dál gCais ar na bóithribh ó Cheann Cora go Cíll Mhaighneann.

Nuair a bhí cuid mhaith aimsire caite sa chómhairle, agus cainnt agus breithniú déanta ar a lán nithe, tháinig an t-am chun dul agus bia ' chaitheamh. Tháinig teachtaire dhá rá go raibh an bia ollamh. D'éirigh an triúr agus thánadar go seómra an bhídh. Shuíodar chun an bhúird. Tháinig Gormfhlaith agus shuigh sí in aice an Árdrí. Bhí sí go séimh agus go soilbhir agus go geal-gháiriteach leó, agus go mór mór leis an Árdrí. Bhí sí ag déanamh grínn agus suilt den chuma 'nar chuir rí Laighean fearg ar Mhurchadh nuair a dhein sé an bhagairt ar Chonáing sa chluiche.

"Níor dheineas aon iúnadh dem dhriotháir", ar sise. "Fear is ea é, is dó' liom, nár theip an tuathal riamh air. Ach go deimhin agus go dearfa, níor mheasas go ndéanfadh Murchadh an rud a dhein sé".

"Cad a dheineas, a Árdríogan?", arsa Murchadh.

"Nuair a thagann fearg ort, a rí", ar sise, "ní haon dóithín tu. Ach ní gnáth leat fearg a theacht ort gan puínn cúise".

Caibideal 42: Cor in Aghaidh an Chaím

"Is fíor dhuit, a Árdíogan", ar seisean. "Ní raibh aon cheart agam a dhéanamh den scéal ach neamhní, mar ní raibh ann ach neamhní. Is trua ná táinig* sé thar n-ais nuair a tháinig an teachtaire suas leis. Dá dtagadh, d'adhmóinn láithreach go raibh an éagóir agam agus d'iarrfainn air mo leathscéal do ghabháil".

Níor chuir Brian ná Dúlainn aon fhocal isteach sa chómhrá san. Níor mhaith leó trácht in aon chor ar an easonóir a tugadh do theachtaire an Árdrí. Dar leó, d'fhéadfadh rí Laighean diúltú do chasadh agus gan an teactaire do bhualadh. Cuid ab ea é sin den tuathal nár theip riamh ar rí Laighean.

Ba ghnáth, i ndeireadh gach dínnéir, sólaist éigin, nú mísleán éigin, do thabhairt isteach agus do chur ar an mbórd. Bhí gaidhrín na hÁrdríogana ar a ghlúin ag Murchadh agus é ag cimilt a bhaise dhá dhrom, ag feitheamh leis na mísleáin. Lonán a bhí ag friothálamh. Do tógadh chun siúil na miasa móra. Tháinig Lonán isteach agus trí miasa beaga aige agus sórd éigin bídh orthu, agus aon mhias bheag amháin agus dhá úll uirthi. Chuir sé an mhias ar a raibh na húlla os cómhair na hÁrdríogana, agus na trí miasa eile os cómhair an trír fear. D'fhéach sé ar Mhurchadh. Chuir Murchadh a lámh anonn láithreach agus tharraig sé chuige an mhéisín a cuireadh os cómhair Bhriain agus an mhéisín a cuireadh os cómhair Dhúlainn. Dhein sé an méid sin go tapaidh, i dtreó ná raibh uain ag éinne acu ar aon phioc den bhia ' chur 'na bhéal. Ansan do thóg sé blúire den bhia agus chuir sé i mbéal an ghaidhrín é agus do scaoil sé an gaidhrín uaidh ar an dtalamh. Shiúlaigh an maidrín beagán ar an úrlár. Ansan do thit sé. D'iompaigh sé na cheithre cosa in áirde. Do chroith na cosa ar feadh tamaill bhig agus bhí an gaidhrín marbh.

D'fhéach Murchadh ar Ghormfhlaith.

"Dheinis láidir ár ndóthain dúinn é!", ar seisean.

Caibideal 42: Cor in Aghaidh an Chaím

Thug sé fé ndeara a lámh aici á chur isteach 'na brollach. Do phreab sé anonn agus do rug sé ar an láimh.

"Ná dein é sin, a Árdríogan!", ar seisean. Is amhlaidh a bhí scian 'na brollach aici agus mheas sí Lonán do shá leis an sciain.

Nuair a bhí greim ag Murchadh ar a láimh, d'fhéach sí ar Lonán, agus ba dhó' leat go sáfadh sí é lena súilibh. An mhuíntir a bhí láithreach an uair sin agus do chonaic a haghaidh agus í ag féachaint ar Lonán, ní miste a rá ná go bhfeacadar a diabhal coímhdeachta má chonaic éinne riamh é.

"Do dhíolais me!", ar sise le Lonán.

"Cad é an brí atá leis an obair seo?", arsa Brian, agus d'fhéach sé ó dhuine go duine dá raibh láithreach.

"Tá, a Árdrí", arsa Murchadh, "go bhfuil oiread nímhe sa méid bídh atá ar na trí miasaibh beaga san agus ' mharódh trí naonúir, ní áirím triúr".

D'fhéach Brian ar Lonán.

"Cad chuige dhuit a leithéid de ghníomh a dhéanamh?", ar seisean.

"Níor dhein sé ach an rud adúradh leis a dhéanamh", arsa Murchadh.

"Ní shaorfadh san in aon chor é!", arsa Brian.

"Oscail do bhéal agus inis an fhírinne don Árdrí", arsa Murchadh le Gormfhlaith.

"Oscail-se féin do bhéal", arsa Gormfhlaith, "agus inis an scéal go léir do. Is dó' liom gur tu is feárr eólas air".

Caibideal 42: Cor in Aghaidh an Chaím

"Cad é an ainm atá ort-sa?", arsa Murchadh le Lonán.

"Lonán mac Beathach, a rí", arsa Lonán.

"Airiú, an driotháir do Dhonn tu?", arsa Brian.

"Ó! Ó! Ó!", arsa Gormfhlaith.

"Is ea, a Árdrí", arsa Lonán.

"Tar i dtosach an scéil, a Lonáin", arsa Murchadh, "agus inis don Árdrí é, tríd síos".

"Déanfad scéal gairid de dhuit, a Árdrí", arsa Lonán. "Thánag abhaile anso go hÉirinn tar éis scoileanna agus coláistí an domhain do shiúl, ag cruinniú eólais ar ghearántaibh agus ar thaomaibh an duine, agus ar na leighseannaibh is feárr orthu. Ní rabhas i bhfad sa bhaile nuair a chuir mo dhriotháir, Donn, ní im chómhairle.

"'Táthar ar tí an tÁrdrí do chur chun báis le nimh', ar seisean. 'Tá aireachas maith á thabhairt do', ar seisean, 'ach tá scannradh orainn go léir le heagla go bhfaighfí caoi ar an ngníomh a dhéanamh in ainneóin ár n-aireachais. D'fhéadfá-sa beart a dhéanamh', ar seisean, 'a chuirfeadh an tÁrdrí ó bhaol'.

"'Cé atá ar a thí?', arsa mise.

"'Tá Gormfhlaith', ar seisean, 'agus a mac, rí Lochlannach Átha Cliath'.

"'Cad é an tairbhe a dhéanfaidh a bhás dóibh?', arsa mise.

"'Ní sa tairbhe a dhéanfaidh a bhás dóibh atá an cheist', ar seisean, 'ach sa tairbhe is dó' leó a dhéanfaidh a bhás dóibh. Tá Gormfhlaith', ar seisean, 'agus Sitric ag obair, fé thalamh agus os cionn tailimh, chun gínte críche Lochlann agus críche na hIorua do chruinniú agus do thabhairt anso go hÉirinn chun na nGael do dhísciú agus Éire ' bheith acu féin, agus Sitric a bheith in' Árdrí ar Éirinn. Dá bhfaigheadh Brian bás le línn an chruinnithe ' bheith déanta, do thitfeadh, dar leó, cómhacht Bhriain as a chéile. Bheadh ríthe Éireann go léir ag marú a chéile chun teacht ar an Árdríocht, agus ba ró-fhuiriste do chómhacht Lochlannach bualadh isteach agus an Árdríocht do sciobadh uathu go léir. Chuige sin', ar seisean, 'tá Gormfhlaith ag faire, féachaint an bhfaigheadh sí caoi ar nimh a thabhairt do Bhrian, agus táimíd-na ag faire uirthi chun gan an chaoi a thabairt di. Thugamair Niamh, iníon Thaidhg Mhóir Uí Chealla, go Ceann Cora, chun na faire ' dhéanamh, ach tá Gormfhlaith ró-ghlic do Niamh. Dá éaghmais sin, ní réitíonn faireachán den tsórd san le meón ná le haigne Niamh. Thugamair fé ndeara go raibh a sláinte ag imeacht uaithi san obair. Tá an aigne ró-uasal ag Niamh. Do mharódh faireachán den tsórd san í. Díreach nuair a bhíomair i gcás ná raibh ' fhios againn cad ba mhaith dhúinn a dhéanamh, shocraigh Brian ar dhul ar a chuaird rí. An fhaid a bheidh sé ar an gcuaird agus Gormfhlaith i gCeann Cora, níl baol air. Ach nuair a bheidh an chuaird tabhartha ní fheadar 'en tsaol cad a dhéanfaimíd'.

"'Inis an scéal go léir do Bhrian féin', arsa mise.

"'Ní bheadh aon mhaith ann', ar seisean. 'Ní chreidfeadh sé go ndéanfadh sí é, agus ansan is amhlaidh a bheadh an chúntúirt ní ba mhó'.

"'Agus cad 'tá agam-sa le déanamh?', arsa mise.

"'Éist go cruínn liom', ar seisean, 'agus neósfad duit cad 'tá agat le déanamh. Níl Sitric sásta nuair ná fuil an gnó dá dhéanamh chómh tapaidh agus ba mhaith leis é. Dá bhfaigheadh sé duine a dhéanfadh an gnó níos tapúla, do thabharfadh sé tuarastal maith dho as an obair a dhéanamh. Imigh-se go Baile Átha Cliath, id dhochtúir, mar dhea. Leog do Shitric tu ' dh'fháil amach. Tuigeadh sé uait, i ndiaidh ar ndiaidh, ná fuil aon ghrá agat do Bhrian. Nuair a thuigfidh sé an méid sin, measfaidh sé go ndéanfair-se an gnó. Curfar siar go Ceann Cora thu. Beidh tú ann nuair a thiocfaidh Brian abhaile. Ceapfar tu chun na hoibre ' dhéanamh agus geallfar tuarastal maith dhuit. An fhaid a bheidh an gnó ar do láimh-se, ní baol go gcurfar ar aon láimh eile an gnó. Luigh isteach chun ha hoibre chómh maith agus dá mbeithá dáiríribh. Dein gach aon rud díreach mar adéarfar leat é ' dhéanamh. Tabhair a toil féin do Ghormfhlaith. Dein rud uirthi ins gach aon ní a chuirfidh sí os do chómhair. Ansan, nuair a thiocfaidh an t-am ceart chuige, féadfair scéith uirthi'.

"Chuas go Baile Átha Cliath. Thit gach ní amach díreach mar a mheas Donn a thitfeadh. Is uathásach an bhean í!", ar seisean, agus d'fhéach sé anonn ar Ghormfhlaith, mar ' fhéachfadh duine ar éan éigin neamh-choitianta, nú ar bheithíoch neamh-choitianta.

D'fhéach sise air, idir an dá shúil.

"Ní foláir a dh'admháil", ar sise, "gur dheinis do ghnó go maith. Bhuailis bob ar Shitric, agus bhuailis bob ar fhear atá níos géire go mór ná Sitric. Bhuailis bob ar Amhlaoibh. Mura mbeadh san, ní bhuailfá an bob orm-sa mar a bhuailis. Is ábalta an buachaill tu", ar sise. "Tháinig amhras i m'aigne cúpla uair go mb'fhéidir go rabhais 'om mhealladh, ach chuiris m'aigne chun suaimhnis gach uair acu led shímplíocht. Ó, is sleamhain an bioránach tu! Is trua nách ag triall orm féin a tháinís ar dtúis! Ach nuair a tháinís chúm ón mbeirt sin, cad ' fhéadfainn a rá! Cad é an díobháil dom ach Amhlaoibh!"

"Cé hé Amhlaoibh?", arsa Brian.

Chrom gach éinne a cheann.

"Nách é sin an t-ógánach úd a thagadh anso aníos ó Inis Cathaigh in éineacht le mac Thaidhg Mhóir Uí Chealla?", arsa Brian.

Caibideal 42: Cor in Aghaidh an Chaím

Níor labhair éinne, ach do las gnúis Mhurchadh.

"Ná neósfaidh éinne dhom cé hé an t-ógánach úd?", arsa Brian.

"Níl ach éinne amháin anso a dh'fhéadfadh an cheist sin do fhreagairt duit, a athair", arsa Murchadh, agus do labhair sé go han-íseal.

D'éirigh Brian ón mbórd agus d'imigh sé amach gan féachaint ar Ghormfhlaith.

"Cimeádtar 'na príosúnach í", arsa Murchadh le Dúlainn, agus d'imigh sé amach i ndiaidh an Árdrí.

"Tá carbad na hÁrdríogana féin ollamh amu' chun bóthair", arsa Lonán. "Bhíomair chun imeacht ar cos in áirde go Baile Átha Cliath", ar seisean, "chómh luath agus ' bheadh an gníomh déanta", agus chuir sé gáire as.

"Imigh amach agus inis an méid sin do Mhurchadh", arsa Dúlainn. "Tabharfad-sa aire dhi seo".

D'imigh Lonán amach. Bhí Brian agus Murchadh amu' agus iad ag siúl síos agus suas agus Brian ag cainnt. D'airigh sé an t-aon fhocal amháin ó Bhrian.

"Ní mac d'Amhlaoibh é. Tuigim an scéal go léir anois".

Chonaic sé Lonán ag teacht 'na dtreó.

"A Lonáin, a mhic ó", ar seisean, "tá comaoine mhór curtha agat orm! Chuiris t'anam féin i gcúntúirt ar mo shon".

"Is suarach le rá m'anam-sa seochas t'anam-sa anois, a Árdrí", arsa Lonán. "Ach a leithéid seo, a rí", ar seisean le Murchadh. "Tá carbad na hÁrdríogana ollamh chun bóthair. Bhí socair aici ar dhul láithreach go hÁth Cliath agus ar mise ' bhreith léi. Do crochfí me chómh luath agus ' bheinn thíos dá mbeadh an scéal aici mar a mheas sí a bheadh sé. Sin é tuarastal a gheóbhainn uathu", agus chuir sé gáire as.

"Tá san go maith! Tá san go hana-mhaith!", arsa Brian. "Níl aon phioc dá fhios ag éinne cad 'tá titithe amach. Cuir isteach sa charbad í, a Mhurchadh, agus cuir buíon fear léi síos go Baile Átha Cliath, agus fágtar thíos í".

D'imigh Brian isteach 'na sheómra féin, agus d'imigh Murchadh agus Lonán chun an ruda a dh'órdaigh sé do dhéanamh. Thánadar isteach mar a raibh Dúlainn agus Gormfhlaith, agus an gaidhrín marbh.

"Tuigim go bhfuilir ag dul go hÁth Cliath, a Árdríogan", arsa Murchadh. "Tá do charbad féin ollamh duit".

D'éirigh sí, gan labhairt, agus bhuail sí amach in éineacht leis. Tháinig Lonán in éineacht leis an mbeirt. Thug sé cogar do Mhurchadh. Thánadar mar a raibh an carbad gofa ollamh chun bóthair.

"Tá an Árdríogan ag dul go hÁth Cliath, a ghiolla", arsa Murchadh leis an ngiolla. "Tabhair aire mhaith do sna capaillibh".

D'fhéach Murchadh isteach sa charbad. Chonaic sé bosca beag deas istigh ann. Thóg sé amach an bosca.

D'fhéach Gormfhlaith air. D'fhéach seisean uirthi. Níor labhair éinne acu.

Do ghluais an carbad.

Caibideal 43: Breall ar an bhFeall

Nuair a bhí an carbad ag gluaiseacht bhí beirt bhan uasal sa charbad in éineacht le Gormfhlaith, beirt dá mnáibh coímhdeachta, beirt a tháinig léi go Ceann Cora nuair a phós Brian í. Bhí Dúlainn agus dírim marcach aige chun dul, mar ghárda, in éineacht leis an gcarbad. Le Gormfhlaith féin ab ea cúigear de sna marcachaibh. Thánadar léi go Ceann Cora nuair a bhí sí ag teacht ann. Ní raibh aon phioc dá fhios ag éinne acu, ná ag éinne de sna mnáibh coímhdeachta, cad a bhí titithe amach. Chimeád Gormfhlaith an gnó go léir idir í féin agus Lonán. Bhí socair aici ar imeacht láithreach nuair a bheadh an gníomh déanta. Dá mbeadh Brian agus Murchadh agus Dúlainn chómh marbh leis an ngaidhrín, bheadh sí féin agus Lonán, agus an méid dá muíntir féin a bhí i gCeann Cora, bheidís leath na slí go hÁth Cliath sara mbeadh teaghlach Chínn Cora tagaithe as an sceón, dar léi. Bheidís socair, ó bhaol, in Áth Cliath sara mbeadh teaghlach Chínn Cora ábalta ar aon tsaghas gnímh a dhéanamh, bheadh a leithéid sin de mheascán mearaí ar an áit agus ar na daoine, dar léi. Ansan d'fhéadfí Lonán a chrochadh agus ní bheadh ' fhios ag éinne beó cé ' dhein an gníomh. Chimeád sí féin agus Lonán an rún chómh maith san ná raibh aon phioc dá fhios ag éinne ach acu féin go dtí gur scéigh Lonán, ach amháin ag Murchadh, agus ag Caoilte, driotháir Lonáin. An mhuíntir a bhí ag gluaiseacht in éineacht leis an gcarbad an uair sin, lasmu' de Dhúlainn, ní raibh aon choinne acu ná go mbeidis ag teacht thar n-ais arís in éineacht leis an gcarbad gcéanna, agus an Árdríogan istigh ann acu, i gceann beagán aimsire, nuair a bheadh a cuaird go hÁth Cliath tabhartha aici.

Nuair a drideadh soir ó Cheann Cora, chuir Dúlainn beirt de sna marcachaibh, beirt de mhuíntir Ghormfhlaith, uaidh, ní ba ghéire ná mar a bhí an chuid eile ag gluaiseacht, agus leitir acu do rí Lochlannach Átha Cliath, dhá rá leis dírim marcach a thabhairt leis agus teacht 'na gcoinnibh chun na hÁrdríogana do thógaint uathu agus í ' thiúnlacan an chuid eile den tslí. Ansan do ghluais Dúlainn go réidh i dtreó go mbeadh Sitric tamall maith ar an slí 'na gcoinnibh.

Caibideal 43: Breall ar an bhFeall

An uair a scar Murchadh leó, do thóg sé leis an bosca agus chuaigh sé go seómra Bhriain. D'oscail sé an bosca i láthair Bhriain, agus thóg sé rud amach as agus chuir sé ar an mbórd é.

"Cad chuige gur tugadh an chailís sin aníos ón mainistir, a Mhurchadh?", arsa Brian.

D'inis Murchadh cúrsaí na cailíse dho ó thosach go deireadh. Níor labhair Brian aon fhocal amach as a bhéal an fhaid a bhí Murchadh ag ínsint an scéil do.

"Bhí ' fhios againn", arsa Murchadh, ag críochnú an scéil, "gur anso ' bhí an chailís agus cérbh é an bithiúnach. D'inis Caoilte do Lonán an scéal. Ní raibh Lonán i bhfad anso nuair a fuair sé amach gur sa bhosca san a bhí an chailís. Bhí socair aici, nuair a bheimís go léir sínte chómh marbh leis an ngaidhrín, an bosca ' bhreith léi. Bhí sé aici anois sa charbad. Chonaic Lonán é agus thug sé an cogar dom. Thógas an bosca os cómhair a súl. Níor dhein sí ach féachaint orm. Níor labhair sí focal. Labharfaidh an coileán úd léi nuair a raghaidh sí síos ag triall air féin agus ar an gcoileán eile".

"Is feárr", arsa Brian, "an chailís do chur síos arís go mainistir Ínse Cathaigh, mar a raibh sí cheana. In onóir do Sheanán is ea ' thugas don mhainistir í. Cuir síos ann arís í, a Mhurchadh. Agus féach. Is ceart a dh'ínsint do Mheargach gur fuaradh í. Beidh áthas air. Ní deirim ná go bhféachfaidh sé roimis sara ndéanfaidh sé macshamhail eochrach arís, an fear bocht! Is dó' liom, leis, go dtabharfaidh Colla aireachas níos feárr di féin agus do gach aon chailís eile dá bhfuil aige".

Do cuireadh síos an chailís go dtí an mhainistir. Ní miste a rá ná go raibh áthas ar Cholla. Do hínseadh an scéal do Mheargach. Bhí áthas air. Bhí seirithean, leis, air, chuige féin. Níorbh fhuiriste a bhreithniú, áfach, ceocu ag an áthas nú ag an seirithean a bhí an lámh uachtair in' aigne.

Caibideal 43: Breall ar an bhFeall

Do hoscladh an cóthra láidir san *érdam* agus do tógadh amach as an bosca iarainn a bhí folamh. Do cuireadh an chailís dhaor isteach sa bhosca bheag iarainn sin, mar a raibh sí cheana, sara dtáinig an t-ógánach Lochlannach úd, an t-ógánach breá dathúil úd, a bhí chómh naofa, chómh séimh, chómh grianach, chómh geal-gháiriteach, chómh hoscailte 'na mheón, gur dhó' le duine ná raibh 'na chroí ar fad ach fírinne agus dílse. Dhein Meargach glas eile agus eochair eile don bhosca agus ní baol gur dhein sé macshamhail den eochair sin.

Ní bhfuair Art mac Duibh amach riamh go raibh sé ar feadh tamaill 'na leithéid de chúntúirt. Ní bhfuair na manaigh amach, ón lá a cuireadh an chailís sa bhosca san ar dtúis go dtí an lá a cuireadh iad féin as an oileán, go raibh an bosca folamh ar feadh tamaill agus an chailís dhaor imithe.

Tháinig an Leagáid céanna arís, tar éis suím blianta. B'í céad cheist a chuir sé ar Cholla, chómh luath agus d'fhéad sé labhairt i ganfhios leis, ná "An bhfuaradh an chailís?"

Do tispeánadh do í. Bhí áthas mór air. Do hínseadh an scéal go léir do; conas a ghuid Amhlaoibh an chailís; conas a cuireadh Niamh ag faire ar Ghormfhlaith le heagla go dtabharfadh sí nimh do Bhrian; conas ab éigean Niamh a thógaint as an obair sin mar go raibh Gormfhlaith dhá cur chun báis le neart soilbhris agus cuideachtanais agus geal-gháirí. Ansan do hínseadh do conas a himreadh an cleas ar Ghormfhlaith; conas a cuireadh Lonán chúithi ag cabhrú léi, mar dhea, chun an ghnímh a dhéanamh, agus conas mar a bhí Brian ó bhaol ar fad an fhaid a bhí an cabhrú san ar siúl, agus cad é an deireadh a bhí ar an gcabhrú. Do gháireadh an Leagáid arís agus arís eile nuair a chuímhníodh sé ar an gcuma na mbíodh an bheirt, Gormfhlaith agus Lonán, ag déanamh a ngnótha chómh discréideach, agus an discréid go léir ag Lonán á thabhairt do Mhurchadh i gcaitheamh na haimsire.

“Ó”, adeireadh sé, “do tugadh a srian féin di ar áilleacht an domhain! An bhean bhocht!”

Do shrois an bheirt mharcach an chathair. Thánadar go doras rí-theaghlaigh an rí. Do rugadh an leitir isteach. Do léigh Sitric í. Bhí Amhlaoibh ann. Bhí an bheirt ag faire agus ag feitheamh. Bhíodar ag brath in aghaidh gach neómait, ar scéal uathásach a dh’aireachtaint ó Cheann Cora. Nuair a tháinig an leitir, bhí an bheirt deimhnitheach go raibh an scéal a bhí uathu sa leitir. Ní raibh aon ní iúntach sa leitir. Leitir ó Dhúlainn ab ea í dhá ínsint go raibh an Árdríogan ag teacht agus dhá iarraidh ar an rí, ar Shitric, dul ’na coinnibh chun í ’ thiúnlacan go hÁth Cliath. Tháinig an bheirt amach mar a raibh an dá mharcach. D’fhéachadar orthu, agus d’fhéachadar ar a chéile.

“Cad é an scéal ó Cheann Cora agaibh é, a fheara?”, arsa Sitric.

“Mar ba ghnáth, a rí. Níor thugamair aon nuacht linn”, arsa duine den bheirt.

“Conas ’tá an tÁrdrí?”, arsa Sitric.

“Go hana-mhaith, a rí”, arsan fear a labhair.

“Agus an Rí-dhamhna, conas ’tá sé?”, arsa Sitric.

“Go hálainn, a rí”, arsan fear.

“Agus Dúlainn, conas ’tá sé?”, arsa Sitric.

“Tá sé go maith, a rí”, arsan fear. “Is féna láimh atá na fir atá ag tiúnlacan na hÁrdríogana”, ar seisean.

Caibideal 43: Breall ar an bhFeall

"Tá go maith", arsa Sitric. "Téidh-se isteach go gcurfar cóir oraibh. Ní iarrfar* oraibh dul chun bóthair arís inniu".

"Go ra' maith ag úr Soílse!", arsan fear, agus d'imigh an bheirt.

"Cad 'deirir leis an scéal?", arsa Sitric le hAmhlaoibh.

"Ní féidir liom tón ná ceann a dh'fháil air!", arsa Amhlaoibh.

D'imigh Sitric agus chuir sé dírim marcach ar bóthar, agus ghluais sé chun siúil. Níor fhéad sé gan gluaiseacht ana-ghéar. Chonaic an dírím eile chúthu é i bhfad sarar mheasadar a chífidís é. D'úmhlaíodar dá chéile mar ba chóir. Thug Dúlainn an Árdríogan suas dá mac, agus d'iompaigh sé féin agus a chuallacht abhaile. Níorbh fhada go raibh an chuallacht eile sa chathair. Focal amach as a béal níor labhair Gormfhlaith go dtí go raibh an triúr i bhfochair a chéile istigh agus gan éinne ann ach iad. Ansan do labhair sí agus níor mhaith leat bheith ag éisteacht léi.

"'Sea!", ar sise, "dheiniúir go deas é! Ní miste gnó ' thabhairt do bheirt agaibh le déanamh!"

"Cad a dheineamair, a mháthair?", arsa Sitric.

"Inis an méid seo dhom", ar sise. "Cá bhfuarais Lonán? Nú, an bhfuil ' fhios agat cé hé?"

"Liag tuisceanach is ea é", arsa Sitric. "Tá an t-eólas a dh'oir duit aige. Do shiúlaigh sé chuige. Cad é sin dúinn-na cé hé, ach, mar aduart leat, é ' chrochadh chómh luath agus ' bheadh an obair déanta".

Bhí sí ag féachaint ó dhuine go duine acu an fhaid a bhí sé ag cainnt.

"Ó", ar sise, "is deocair do dhuine foighneamh lenúr leithéidí de bheirt amadán! Driotháir do Chaoilte is ea é". (Do léim an bheirt 'na seasamh.) "Tháinig sé anso chúibh-se dhá leogaint air go raibh fuath aige do Bhrian. Chuiriúir-se ag triall orm-sa é, an rud a bhí uaidh. Bhí iúntaoibh agam-sa as mar gheall ar é ' theacht chúm uaibh-se. D'oibríomair araon a láimh a chéile. Níor chuireamair cor dínn nár inis sé do Mhurchadh chómh luath agus ' chuireamair dínn é. Díreach nuair a bhí an obair nách mór déanta, do scéigh sé. Chuir sé na trí miasa nímhe os cómhair an trír. Tharraig Murchadh chuige na trí miasa sara raibh uain ar éinne den bheirt eile ar an mbia do bhlaiseadh. Thug Murchadh blúire den bhia dom ghaidhrín. Thit an gaidhrín marbh os cómhair ár súl go léir. Ansan d'inis Lonán dóibh cérbh é agus cad é an bob a bhí buailte aige orm-sa. Ní féidir liom gan urraim a bheith agam do. Chosain sé Brian orm chómh hálainn agus do cosnadh éinne riamh. Conas ' fhéadfainn-se aon bheart eile ' tharrac chúm an fhaid a bhí an iúntaoibh agam a Lonán agus sinn ag oibriú a láimh a chéile! Níorbh fhéidir an gníomh a dhéanamh gan sinn araon á dhéanamh. Níor bhaol do Bhrian an fhaid a bhí lámh Lonáin sa ghníomh, ní nách iúnadh. Ní bheadh a lámh sa ghníomh mura mbeadh é ' theacht chúm uaibh-se. Ó, táid siad go léir ag cur a n-anama amach ag gáirí umainn agus ag magadh fúinn! Agus gan amhras, tá a chúis acu".

Chomáin sí léi ag cainnt. Níor labhair éinne den bheirt eile go ceann i bhfad. Ar ball do labhair Amhlaoibh.

"Ar thugais leat an chailís?", ar seisean.

"Níor thugas!", ar sise. "Bhí sí agam sa charbad agus me ag fágaint na háite. Chonac Lonán, an ropaire!, ag cogarnaigh le Murchadh. Tháinig Murchadh chúm anall agus thóg sé leis an bosca 'na raibh an chailís. Ó, dheiniúir an gnó go hálainn ar fad nuair a chuiriúir Lonán chúm! Dá mb'áil leis teacht ar aon chuma eile chúm ach uaibh-se! Is gasta a dhein sé é. Go deimhin, ní féidir liom gan urraim a bheith agam do".

D'iompaigh dath dubh ar ghnúis Amhlaoibh nuair a fuair sé go raibh an chailís imithe.

"Dá mb'áil liom-sa", ar seisean, "a mhalairt de chúram a chur ar Fhear na gCos nuair a bhí an chaoi agam air!"

"Eist, a Amhlaoibh", arsa Sitric. "Ní fiú biorán is an gnó go léir. Tá ár máthair anso againn beó. Is iúntach an scéal iad dhá leogaint uathu chómh bog. Beidh caoi arís agat ar shocrú le Fear na gCos uair éigin. Tá ár neart ollamh ins gach aon bhall. Ba mhór go léir an tairbhe dhúinn neart Gael a bheith gan cheann, dá n-éiríodh linn. Ach tá sé an-aosta. Is cuma nú bheith gan cheann dóibh an ceann a bheith chómh haosta. Ná habraimís a thuilleadh mar gheall ar Lonán ná ar a ghnó. Ní dó' liom go bhfuil puínn dá fhios ag éinne go raibh an gnó ar siúl. Tugaimís aghaidh ar an obair atá rómhainn. Comáinimís teachtairí mórthímpall dhá rá lenár neart cruinniú, gan a thuilleadh ríghnis, sa chuan so amu'; go bhfuil gach aon rud ollamh. Tá Maolmhórdha ar dearg-bhuile, a mháthair. Dheinis an méid sin go maith. Tá néal chun cogaidh i Lochlannachaibh na hÉireann, agus is ag triall ar rí Laighean atáid siad ag teacht. Buafaimíd fós ar Bhrian agus ar Chlaínn Chais!"

Caibideal 44: An Dá Lonán

Chómh luath agus ' bhí an cogar tabhartha ag Lonán do Mhurchadh agus an bosca tógtha ag Murchadh as an gcarbad, d'imigh Lonán isteach chun an tseómra a bhí aige sa rí-theaghlach ó tháinig sé ann 'na dhochtúir, agus 'na stíobhard ar gach córú bídh dá mbeadh le déanamh ann. Ní fheacaigh éinne riamh ó shin an Lonán céanna ag teacht amach as an seómra san. Tháinig fear amach as an seómra, ach níorbh é an Lonán céanna é, dar le héinne a chonaic an Lonán a chuaigh isteach, agus ansan, an Lonán a tháinig amach. Bhí folt odhar, ag titim siar síos ar a shlinneánaibh, ar an Lonán a chuaigh isteach. Bhí folt breá fionna-rua, ag titim siar síos ar a shlinneánaibh, ar an Lonán a tháinig amach. Bhí féasóg fhada liath-ghorm ar an

Caibideal 44: An Dá Lonán

Lonán a chuaigh isteach. Bhí féasóg rua ná raibh ró-fhada, ar an Lonán a tháinig amach. Firín beag agus ceann mór air ab ea an Lonán a chuaigh isteach. Níorbh fhear ró-mhór an Lonán a tháinig amach, ach bhí an ceann tar éis dul i laíghead, agus ansan níor fhéach an fear chómh beag agus d'fhéach sé fén gceann mór. Bhí na fáibrí imithe as an éadan, ach bhí an t-éadan leathan go maith agus árd go maith ag an Lonán a tháinig amach, díreach mar a bhí ag an Lonán a chuaigh isteach. Bhí an Lonán a chuaigh isteach trí fichid, mura raibh sé os a chionn. Ní raibh an Lonán a tháinig amach aon lá os cionn seacht mbliana fichead. Dá bhfeiceadh Amhlaoibh, nú Sitric, nú Gormfhlaith, an Lonán a tháinig amach, thabharfaidís an leabhar ná feacadar riamh é. Dá bhrí sin, níor ghá don Lonán a tháinig amach puínn eagla ' bheith aige roimis an gcainnt a bhí ar siúl idir an dtriúr, istigh i rí-theaghlach Shitric in Áth Cliath, nuair a bhíodar dhá mhaíomh agus dhá dhearbhú go ndéanfaidís so 's súd leis an Lonán a bhuail an bob orthu, chómh luath agus ' gheóbhaidís greim air.

Is iad a bhí go loiscithe scólta 'na gcroí agus 'na n-aigne, ag cuímhneamh ar an gcuma 'nar bhuail sé an bob san orthu, díreach nuair a mheasadar gurbh iad féin a bhí á bhualadh air sin go hálainn. Bhí Caoilte i gCeann Cora an uair chéanna agus is mó gáire mhaith a bhí aige féin agus ag Lonán agus ag Murchadh agus Lonán ag seanchas don bheirt eile ar an gcuma 'na mbíodh sé féin agus Gormfhlaith ag toghadh na luíbhneacha agus ag áireamh na gcómhacht a bhí iontu.

"Tá an méid seo agam le rá, áfach", arsa Lonán leis an mbeirt. "Tríd an obair go léir ní mise do chúm ná do cheap ná do bheartaigh ná do thosnaigh aon droch-ní. Í féin a thosnaíodh gach aon rud. Níor thugas di aon bhlúire droch-eólais ná raibh aici cheana. Nuair a bhí an bia againn dá ollmhú chun an ghnímh a dhéanamh, níor dheineas ach gach aon rud do shocrú agus do chórú díreach mar a dh'órdaigh sí dhom é ' dhéanamh".

Caibideal 44: An Dá Lonán

"Tá ' fhios agam-sa aon rud amháin a dheinis, a bhithiúnaigh, agus níor órdaigh sí dhuit é ' dhéanamh", arsa Murchadh.

"Cad é an rud é sin, a rí?", arsa Lonán agus iúnadh ag teacht air.

"Níor órdaigh sí dhuit an bhagairt úd a dhéanamh orm-sa", arsa Murchadh.

"Ó!", arsa Lonán. "Is fíor dhuit, a rí", agus gháireadar, mar do baineadh iarracht de gheit a Lonán.

"Tá aon ní amháin sa scéal agus ní ró-mhaith a thaithneann sé liom", arsa Caoilte.

"Cad é an rud é?", arsa Murchadh.

"Tá Gormfhlaith in Áth Cliath", ar seisean, "agus tá cead a cos aici, agus cead a cínn, agus cead a béil. Is trua nár cimeádadh anso í. Déanfaidh an bhean san díobháil dúinn. Tá sí ar dearg-bhuile mar gheall ar an gcuma 'na bhfuil stáicín áiféis' déanta dhi os cómhair an domhain. Ní chuirfeadh sé blúire iúnadh orm dá dtéadh sí féin, de shiúl a cos dá mb'fhéidir é, soir chun cainnte le rí Lochlann, agus as san ó thuaidh chun cainnte le rí na hIorua, agus mórthímpall chun gach rí agus chun gach tíre 'nar dhó' léi go bhfaigheadh sí a bheag nú a mhór d'aon rud i bhfuirm nirt sló le tabhairt léi chun díoltais a dhéanamh ar Árdrí Éireann agus orainn go léir. Daoine ná cuímhneódh in aon chor ar theacht, meallfaidh sí léi iad agus tiocfaid siad. Is mór an trua nár cimeádadh anso í!"

"Tá an ceart agat sa méid sin, a Chaoilte", arsa Murchadh. "Duart féin leis an Árdrí gur í ' chimeád anso ba cheart. Ní dhéanfadh. Ba lag leis é. Níl againn ach aon ghnó amháin a dhéanamh de pé neart a thiocfaidh. Dá mhéid a thiocfaidh díobh, má thugaimíd Gleann Mháma an tarna huair dóibh, rud a thabharfaimíd, is ea is lú is baol iad do theacht go deó arís chúinn. Táid siad fada a ndóthain ag teacht.

Caibideal 44: An Dá Lonán

Is mithid deireadh ' chur lena gcuardaibh. Ní raibh fir Éireann riamh chómh ceapaithe ar dheireadh ' chur le cómhacht Lochlann agus atáid siad anois. Ach ní hag cainnt is ceart dúinn a bheith. Téanaídh. Tá cainnt ag an Árdrí le déanamh liom-sa agus le beirt agaibh-se".

Chuadar i láthair an Árdrí. Bhí a lán eile de sna giollaíbh turais cruinnithe rómpu ann. Bhí Maolshuathain ann agus leitreacha aige á scrí' chómh tiubh agus d'fhéadadh sé an cleite ' chomáint. Fé mar a bhíodh gach leitir scríofa aige, chuireadh Brian a ainm thíos léi, agus do tugtí do dhuine de sna giollaíbh turais í agus chuireadh sé sin an talamh de.

Ag triall ar na ríthibh agus ar na taoiseachaibh a bhí cuid de sna leitreachaibh ag dul. Sid é bunús na cainnte a bhí iontu san:

"A rí onóraigh,

"Tá an lá buailte linn. Ní fios cad é an neómat a thiocfaidh scéala chúinn dhá ínsint dúinn luingeas rí Lochlann agus luingeas rí an hIorua agus luingeas Shíguird, rí Ínsí hOrc, a bheith i gcuan Átha Cliath. Ní healaí dhúinn gan bheith ollamh dóibh. Cruinnigh do neart, a rí, agus tabhair aghaidh ar Chíll Mhaighneann. Ní bheidh aon uaigneas ort ar an slí. Beid fir Éireann 'na míltibh ag bualadh umat. Tá socair againn go léir 'nár n-aigne gan teacht abhaile beó nú teacht abhaile le bua. Abair le gach fear dá bhfuil agat gur feárr go mór bás d'fháil i gcath ná luí fé smacht Lochlannach anois.

"Mise Brian".

Bhí cuid de sna leitreachaibh ag dul ag triall ar easpagaibh agus ar shagartaibh agus ar mhainistreachaibh. Seo bunús na cainnte a bhí iontu san:

"A Thiarna Easpaig,

Caibideal 44: An Dá Lonán

"Cuir do ghuí suas chun Dé ar ár son chómh dian, chómh dícheallach agus ' chuiris guí suas chun Dé riamh. Tá an lá cruaidh buailte linn fé dheireadh. Tá ár namhaid ag cruinniú chúinn as an uile áird. Má bheireann an namhaid seo bua anois orainn, tá deireadh linn; tá deireadh le sliocht Gael in Éirinn agus tá deireadh leis an gCreideamh a thug Pádraig chúinn trí ghrásta Dé. Cuir féin do ghuí suas chun Dé dhá iarraidh ar Dhia gan an bua ' thabhairt don namhaid. Iarr ar na poblaibh go léir a nguí ' chur suas chun Dé ar an íntinn gcéanna. 'Éisteann Dia le guí na ndaoine'.

"Brian".

Chómh luath agus ' fuair gach rí agus gach taoiseach a leitir, do thosnaíodar ar na fir do chruinniú. Do thuig na daoine go léir an focal úd, "gur feárr go mór bás d'fháil i gcath ná luí fé smacht Lochlannach anois". Thuig gach éinne gurbh fheárr an fharraige do theacht isteach ar Éirinn agus gan aon Chríostaí ' dh'fhanúint beó ar an oileán ná sliocht Gael do luí fé smacht na Lochlannach an uair sin. Dá bhrí sin, na mná agus na seandaoine a bhí ag fanúint sa bhaile, níor dheineadar buairt ná gol ná olagón. Má bhí an bhuairt orthu, agus is dócha go raibh, níor thispeánadar puínn de.

Na mná a bhí pósta agus go raibh cúram clainne orthu, d'fhanadar sa bhaile, ach má fhanadar níor airigh éinne osna ó éinne acu, ná ní fheacaigh éinne deóir lena súil. Is dócha gur shileadar a ndóthain díobh nuair ná raibh éinne ag féachaint orthu. Níor fhan na cailíní óga sa bhaile. Chuadar in éineacht lena ndriothárachaibh chun bídh a dh'ollmhú dhóibh ar an slí agus chun éadaigh a ní dhóibh nuair ba ghá é, agus chun banaltranais a dhéanamh orthu tar éis an chatha dá mbeadh gá acu leis. Bhí mná na nGael go léir, óg agus críonna, ana-thuisceanach san obair sin.

Chómh luath agus ' fuair na heaspaig agus na sagairt agus na habanna insna mainistreachaibh na leitreacha, do cuireadh an guí ar siúl ins gach aon bhall láithreach. Bhí na hAifrinní insna heaglaisibh gach maidean ar an íntinn sin Bhriain agus na pobail ag guí ar an íntinn gcéanna, agus na manaigh ag guí insna mainistreachaibh, ní hamháin sa lá ach i gcaitheamh na hoíche leis. Chaithidís an oíche i láthair na hAltórach dhá iarraidh ar an Slánaitheóir, trí ímpí na Maighdine Muire agus trí ímpí Phádraig agus Bhríde agus Cholm Cille, gan an bua ' thabhairt do sna Lochlannaigh sa chath uathásach a bhí ag teacht. Ní miste a rá ná gur dheineadar a nguí go dúthrachtach, mar bhí ' fhios acu go dian-mhaith cad a bhí le himeacht orthu féin agus ar na mainistreachaibh dá mbeireadh na Lochlannaigh bua. Bhíodar go léir ollamh, gan amhras, ar bhás a dh'fhulag ar son an Chreidimh, ach bhí ' fhios acu, dá mbeireadh na Lochlannaigh bua an chatha san a bhí ag teacht an uair sin, go gcuirfidís an Creideamh féin ar neamhní i dteannta na ndaoine do chur chun báis. Dá bhrí sin, do leanadar ag guí go cruaidh, de ló agus d'oíche, agus ag déanamh troscaidh go dian, an fhaid a lean an chúntúirt.

Níorbh fhada go bhfeacathas ag gluaiseacht na bóithre soir ó thuaidh, ó gach aon pháirt den Mhúmhain, mar a bheadh sochraidí móra fada, na fir chróga, fir bhreátha óga láidre, fir go raibh socair 'na n-aigne acu gan teacht thar n-ais beó ón gcogadh dá mbeadh bua ag Lochlannaigh. Ag machnamh ar an ní sin dóibh, shocraíodar 'na n-aigne ná tiocfaidís thar n-ais beó pé taobh a bhuafadh. Shocraíodar 'na n-aigne dá laíghead eagla ' bheadh acu roimis an mbás gurbh ea ab fheárr a dhéanfaidís an troid agus gurbh ea ba mhó an t-éirleach a dhéanfaidís ar na Lochlannaigh, agus, as san, gurbh ea ba dhóichí-de an bua ' bheith ag Gaelaibh agus an cath do bhriseadh ar na Lochlannaigh. Chuaigh an socrú san 'na luí chómh daingean san ar a n-aigne gur ghnáth eatarthu, 'na gcómhrá, agus gan acu á dhéanamh de ach cúis gháire, an focal, "Pé duine ' thiocfaidh thar n-ais ná ná tiocfaidh, ní thiocfad-sa thar n-ais".

"Sin í an chainnt! Ní chun teacht thar n-ais atáimíd ag dul sa chath so!", adéarfadh duine eile.

"Caithfead bás a dh'fháil uair éigin. Ní thiocfaidh uair choíche a bheidh níos feárr ar gach aon tsaghas cuma chun báis a dh'fháil ná an uair a chífead na bithiúnaigh ar m'aghaidh amach agus an t-arm im láimh!", adéarfadh an tríú duine.

"Agus dá éaghmais sin", adéarfadh an ceathrú duine, "is bás ar son an Chreidimh é, agus an té a dh'fhuiliceóidh bás ar son an Chreidimh, raghaidh a anam suas láithreach go haoibhneas na bhFlaitheas! Dá dtagainn thar n-ais agus maireachtaint fiche bliain eile, b'fhéidir nár ró-mhór an deimhne a bheadh agam air sin. Déanfaid na Lochlannaigh a ngnó go holc nú ní thiocfaidh aon chos díom-sa thar n-ais".

Sin é saghas cainnte a bhíodh ar siúl acu agus iad ag gluaiseacht na bóithre soir ó thuaidh 'na sochraidíbh móra fada. Bhíodh na seandaoine ar na cnucánaibh ag féachaint orthu ag gluaiseacht, agus do lasadh a gcuid fola le dásacht, agus, "Ó!", adeiridís, "Nách trua gan me óg arís!" Chídís na fir agus na gathanna breátha fada 'na lámhaibh acu agus reanna glasa crua géara na ngathanna san ag taithneamh agus ag spréacharnaigh sa ghréin, agus na tuanna ar ghuaillibh na bhfear, agus na bratacha ar a gcrannaibh i dtosach gach buíne, ag luascadh sa ghaoith; agus gach buíon ag gluaiseacht go breá réidh stuama, cos le cois, guala le gualainn, agus an bhuíon ag casadh fé mar a chasadh an bóthar agus ag díriú nuair a dhíríodh an bóthar. Chíodh na seandaoine ar na cnucánaibh an obair go léir, agus do ghluaiseadh an tsean-fhuil trí sna sean-fhéitheachaibh, 'na caisíbh tine, agus thagadh luas croí ar na seandaoinibh, agus, "Ó!", adeiridís, "Nách trua chráite gan me óg arís!"

Caibideal 45: Ospac in Inis Cathaigh

Ag triall ar na ríthibh ba shia ó dheas is ea do cuireadh an chéad chuid de sna leitreachaibh, ó b'iad ba shia ó áit an choinne. Ansan do cuireadh iad ag triall ar ríthibh Connacht; ag triall ar na dúnaibh; ag triall ar rí na nDéise, agus mar sin. Chuaigh Lonán ó dheas go Ciarraí

Luachra, ag triall ar a athair, Mac Beathach. Chuaigh Caoilte siar go hUíbh Máine agus leitir aige do Thadhg Mhór Ó Chealla. Ní raibh puínn gá le leitir a chur ag triall ar Thadhg. Bhí an méid nirt a bhí acu gléasta, ollamh chun bóthair aige féin agus ag á mhac. Bhí ráflaí ar siúl ann ar conas mar ba dhóbair go gcurtí Brian agus Murchadh chun báis le nimh, agus gurbh í an Árdríogan a mheas an gníomh a dhéanamh ach gur chaill an fear tís uirthi nuair a bhí gach aon rud ollamh aici. Ansan gur mhairbh sí an fear tís agus gur imigh sí síos go hÁth Cliath ag triall ar a mac, Sitric.

Thug Caoilte an scéal 'na cheart dóibh. Nuair a tugadh dóibh an scéal 'na cheart, dúradar go léir an focal céanna aduairt Caoilte féin, gur mhór an trua nár cimeádadh an Árdríogan 'na príosúnach.

Nuair ' airigh Niamh an scéal 'na cheart, "Ó!", ar sise, "níl aon teóra libh! Níl aon teóra leat, a Chaoilte", ar sise, "agus cuímhneamh ar a leithéid de chleas".

"Mura mbeadh Lonán a bheith agam, ní chuímhneóinn air, a ríogan", arsa Caoilte. "Dheineamair dochtúir iasachta de Lonán i dtreó nár aithin a athair féin é, ná a mháthair, nuair a bhí sé socair againn. Ní raibh aon bhaol go dteipfeadh an t-eólas air mar is ag foghlaim chun bheith 'na dhochtúir atá a shaol go dtí so caite aige. Dhein sé a ghnó go hálainn. Dá mba ná beadh agat ach aon gháire amháin, dhéanfá an gháire sin dá mbeithá ag éisteacht leis dhá ínsint conas a chaith sé féin agus Gormfhlaith an aimsir, ag piocadh luíbhneacha agus dhá mbreithniú".

I lár a gcod' cainnte dhóibh, siúd chúthu isteach teachtaire aníos ó Inis Cathaigh.

"Ó! A ríthe", ar seisean, "tá an fharraige go léir, ó Inis Cathaigh amach go Léim Chúchulainn, lán de luingeas iasachta. Is dócha go bhfuil an mhainistir trí thine um an dtaca so agus na manaigh go léir marbh!", agus chas sé an dá olagón déag* agus é ag greadadh a dhá bhas.

Siúd gach éinne dhá cheistiú:

"Cathain a thánadar?"

"Cad iad na luingeas iad?"

"Ar labhair éinne leó?"

"An bhfeacaís féin iad?"

"Ca bhfios duit an luingeas namhad iad?"

Ní raibh uain aige ar aon fhreagra ' thabhairt ar na ceisteannaibh nuair siúd isteach teachtaire eile.

"Eist do bhéal, a amadáin!", arsan tarna teachtaire. "Is tu ' dhein an fothram gan ghá gan riachtanas! Táid na luingeas ann, a ríthe", ar seisean, "ach ní luingeas namhad iad. Is luingeas carad iad. Ospac is ainm don rí atá orthu. Tháinig sé isteach chun na mainistreach i mbád, agus do labhair sé le Colla agus d'inis sé dho cad a thug é agus gach aon rud. Tá an chabhlach luingeas ansúd mórthímpall an oileáin agus tá Ospac agus Colla imithe soir go Ceanna Cora chun labhartha leis an Árdrí. Deir na fir atá ar na luingeas go bhfuil cabhlach eile ag Bruadar. Bhí an dá rí (beirt driothár is ea iad) muínteartha go maith lena chéile ar feadh tamaill, go dtí gur thoiligh Bruadar chun an chogaidh seo atá dhá dhéanamh i gcoinnibh Bhriain.* Do thuig Ospac in' aigne gurbh éagóir an cogadh agus dhiúltaigh sé d'aon lámh a bheith aige ann. Bhí luingeas Ospaic agus luingeas Bhruadair istigh in aon chuan amháin lastuaidh in áit éigin. Do leath Bruadar a luingeas féin ar bhéal an chuain chun gan luingeas Ospaic do leogaint amach. Cheangail sé a luingeas féin dá chéile le téadaibh móra láidre agus cheangail sé long acu den talamh tirim ar gach taobh. Níor leog

Ospac air gur thug sé fé ndeara an gníomh san. Nuair a tháinig an oíche agus bhí Bruadar agus a mháirnéalaigh 'na gcodladh, chuir Ospac a luingeas go léir i ndiaidh ' chéile in aon líne amháin agus d'órdaigh sé gan aon tsolas do lasadh ar aon loíng acu. Ansan do bhog sé chun gluaiste iad i ndiaidh ' chéile, i dtreó na háite 'na raibh long na lámha deise de luingeas Bhruadair ceangailte den talamh tirim. Chuaigh fuireann i mbád agus do ghearradar an téad gan aon fhothram a dhéanamh. Ansan do shleamhnaigh na luingeas go léir amach. Nuair a tháinig solas na maidine, chonaic Bruadar an cuan laistigh de folamh, agus luingeas Ospaic i bhfad amach ar an bhfarraige agus iad ag imeacht siar ó dheas fé lán a seól. Thánadar anso go dtí an línn seo Luimní chun a dh'ínsint do Bhrian cad a bhí chuige, agus chun pé cabhair a bheadh ar a gcumas do thabhairt do. Dá mb'áil leat-sa", ar seisean leis an gcéad teachtaire, "beagáinín foighne ' bheith agat níor ghá dhuit an rith a dheinis do dhéanamh anso aníos, agus níor ghá dhómh-sa bheith ag briseadh mo chos agus ag cur saothair orm féin ag rith aníos id dhiaidh chun gan leogaint duit an dúthaigh a chur as a meabhair".

"'Sea!", arsa Tadhg Mór Ó Cealla, "is mithid dúinn go léir bheith ag gluaiseacht. Cad 'duairt Ospac a bhí Bruadar ar aigne ' dhéanamh?", ar seisean leis an dteachtaire.

"Duairt sé le Colla, a rí", arsan teachtaire, "gurbh é a thuairim go mbeadh Bruadar 'na cheann ar luingeas rí Lochlann agus go mbeadh Sígurd agus pé luingeas a bheadh aige fé smacht Bhruadair. Agus duairt sé gurbh é a thuairim go bhfuilid siad go léir istigh i gcuan Átha Cliath um an dtaca so, nú geall leis".

"Ó! Foth, foth!", arsa Tadhg Mór. "Ní bheimíd in am in aon chor!"

Lena línn sin, cé ' bhuailfeadh chúthu isteach ach Tadhg Óg Ó Cealla agus Conn agus athair Chuínn, Maolruanaidh na Paidre, rí Ó bhFiachrach Áidhne. Do cuireadh fáilte roimis an rí agus roim Chonn.

Caibideal 45: Ospac in Inis Cathaigh

"Bhíomair díreach ollamh ar imeacht", arsa Maolruanaidh, "ach ní bheadh Conn sásta gan teacht féachaint an rabhúir-se ollamh. Deir sé, agus is dócha gur fíor dho é, gur fearra dhúinn cimeád in aice ' chéile ar an slí, agus ansan cimeád in aice ' chéile sa chath, leis, má fhéadaimíd é".

"Tá an ceart aige, a rí", arsa Caoilte. "Is mó cuma 'na ndéanfaimíd áise dá chéile má chimeádaimíd in aice ' chéile, 'sé sin, ach gan bheith ró-achomair dá chéile. An mó fear a bheidh agaibh, a Chuínn?", ar seisean.

"Beidh breis agus fiche céad fear, is dó' liom", arsa Conn. "An bhfuil Niamh ag teacht?", ar seisean.

"Tá, Niamh ag teacht", arsa Niamh féin; "ná bíodh aon phioc dá mhearathall ort-sa ná ar éinne eile", ar sise.

"Ní fhanfaidh Niamh in aon bhall i ndiaidh a hathar", arsa Tadhg Mór Ó Cealla.

"Is maith an iníon a thug Dia dhuit, a rí", arsa Maolruanaidh, "nuair a thug sé Niamh duit. Tá súil agam go gcuímhníonn tú go minic air sin, agus go dtugann tú baochas do Dhia mar gheall air".

Rí ana-dhiaga ab ea Maolruanaidh na Paidre. Bhíodh sé coitianta ag machnamh i láthair an Athar Síoraí, agus, as an machnamh, bhíodh sé coitianta ag labhairt leis an Athair Síoraí. Thuigeadh sé in' aigne ná raibh aon tsaghas cainnte ba chirte chun labhartha leis an Athair Síoraí ná an chainnt a chuir ár Slánaitheóir i mbéalaibh na gCríostaithe chun labhartha leis an Athair Síoraí. Dá bhrí sin, nuair a labhradh sé leis an Athair Síoraí is, "Ár nAthair atá ar neamh, &c". adeireadh sé. Bhíodh sé ag rá na Paidre sin coitianta, agus do tugadh an ainm, "Maolruanaidh na Paidre", air mar gheall air sin. Fear ana-láidir, ana-chróga, ab ea é, agus mura raibh eagla ag na Lochlannaigh roimena Phaidir, ní baol ná go raibh eagla acu roimena thuaigh.

Caibideal 45: Ospac in Inis Cathaigh

Níorbh fhada go rabhadar go léir ollamh chun bóthair. Bhí carbad álainn ag Niamh, agus bhí beirt dá mnáibh coímhdeachta sa charbad in éineact léi, ach thugadh sí a lán dá haimsir i measc na mban óg eile a bhí ag dul ón mbaile, in éineacht leis na fearaibh, agus í dhá stiúrú agus dhá thispeáint dóibh conas na héadaí lín a theastódh uathu ar ball do chur chúthu agus do chimeád in eagar.

D'fhan an dá bhuíon san, buíon Thaidhg Mhóir Uí Chealla agus buíon Mhaoilruanaidh na Paidre, in aice ' chéile ar an slí, agus bhíodh Conn agus Caoilte i gcómhluadar a chéile go mór. B'éigean do Chaoilte an scéal go léir ó thosach go deireadh a dh'ínsint do Chonn, conas a chuir Sitric agus Amhlaoibh an fear ó Áth Cliath chun Briain do chur chun báis le nimh, agus gurbh é fear a chuireadar uathu chun na hoibre sin a dhéanamh ná Lonán, driotháir Chaoilte, an fear, thar a raibh d'fhearaibh in Éirinn, dob fheárr a dhéanfadh Brian do chosaint ar an mnaoi a bhí ceapaithe ar an nimh a thabhairt do.

Do ghluais na buíona eile ó gach aon pháirt de Chúige Connacht, na bóithre soir, i dtreó na háite 'nar ghnáth le Brian longphort a dhéanamh, in aice Átha Cliath. Tháinig an dá bhuíon, buíon Ó Máine agus buíon Ó bhFiachrach Áidhne, go Ceann Cora, chun bheith in éineacht le buín an Árdrí. Ansan do ghluaiseadar féin agus buíon an Árdrí an bóthar soir ó thuaidh.

Díreach sarar fhágadar Ceann Cora, tháinig teachtaire ó rí Laighean ag triall ar an Árdrí agus thug sé leitir don Árdrí, agus sid iad na focail a bhí sa leitir sin.

> "A Árdrí Éireann,
>
> "Do tugadh easonóir dómh-sa id rí-theaghlach-sa i gCeann Cora. Tar anois agus cosain thu féin orm, mar táim ceapaithe ar an easonóir sin do dhíogailt ort-sa agus ar do chlaínn, agus ar Dhál gCais.

Caibideal 45: Ospac in Inis Cathaigh

"Mise Maolmhórdha

"Rí Laighean".

Do léigh Brian an leitir. Ansan do scríbh sé ar dhrom na leitre na focail:

"Táim ag teacht, a dhriotháir. Féach chút féin.

"Mise Brian".

"Seo, a ghiolla", ar seisean leis an dteachtaire. "Beir thar n-ais í".

Thóg an teachtaire an leitir agus do rug sé leis thar n-ais í.

Ní raibh um an dtaca san bóthar aneas ná bóthar aniar ná bóthar ó thuaidh trí Chúige Laighean ná raibh clúdaithe leis na buínibh fear agus iad ag gluaiseacht 'na míltibh, féna ríthibh agus féna dtaoiseachaibh, agus a n-airm ar a nguaillibh, agus a mbratacha breátha síoda in áirde ar a gcrannaibh ag lúbadh agus ag luascadh sa ghaoith, agus a n-aghaidh go léir ar an áit 'nar ghnáth le Brian a longphort a dhéanamh, in aice Átha Cliath. Agus ní raibh insna buínibh sin go léir oiread agus aon fhear amháin ná raibh socair go daingean in' aigne aige gan teacht thar n-ais beó.

"Más ag Lochlannaigh a bheidh bua", adeiridís, "is feárr gan teacht thar n-ais beó. Más ag Gaelaibh a bheidh bua, bíodh a thoradh ag an muíntir atá sa bhaile 'nár ndiaidh. Pé taobh ar a mbeidh bua, díolfaid na Lochlannaigh as".

Caibideal 46: Mícheál Rua

Bhí Brian agus a ghnáth-theaghlach tamall soir ó Cheann Cora, ar bhóthar Átha Cliath, agus iad ag gluaiseacht go hálainn agus go stuama agus go mileata. Bhí buíon Thaidhg Mhóir Uí Chealla agus buíon Mhaoilruanaidh na Paidre ag teacht 'na ndiaidh. Bhí Niamh 'na carbad i dtosach buíne Thaidhg. Tháinig bean agus clóca uirthi, agus cochall an chlóca amach ar a ceann aici, i gcóngar don charbad. Bhagair sí ar Niamh. Do stad an carbad. Do shín an bhean leitir isteach chun Niamh agus d'imigh sí. Do léigh Niamh an leitir. D'fhéach sí 'na tímpall. Ní raibh Caoilte i bhfad ón áit. Duairt sí le duine de sna fearaibh glaoch air. Tháinig sé. Thug sí dho an leitir. Do léigh sé í.

"Cad is feárr a dhéanamh, a ríogan?", arsa Caoilte.

"Measaim gur feárr an leitir sin a thabhairt do Mhurchadh", ar sise.

"Is fíor", arsa Caoilte.

D'imigh sé amach i ndiaidh ghnáth-theaghlaigh an Árdrí, agus thug sé an leitir do Mhurchadh. Bhí iúnadh ar Mhurchadh nuair a léigh sé an leitir.

"Tá go maith, a Chaoilte", ar seisean.

Tháinig Caoilte thar n-ais.

Lar-na-mháireach an lae sin tháinig giolla turais ag triall ar Chaoilte, duine dá ghiollaíbh turais féin, agus shín sé leitir chuige. Do léigh Caoilte í. Siúd ag triall ar Niamh é agus shín sé chúithi an leitir. Do léigh sí í.

"Ó!", ar sise. "Imigh láithreach, a Chaoilte", ar sise, "agus tabhair í seo leis do Mhurchadh". Do dhein.

I dtreó go dtuigfar brí agus bunús an dá leitir* sin, ní foláir dul siar beagán agus a dh'ínsint conas a dh'imigh le Gormfhlaith ó fhág sí Ceann Cora agus ó tháinig sí go teaghlach rí Lochlannach Átha Cliath.

Caibideal 46: Mícheál Rua

Do hínseadh i dtosach an scéil seo conas mar a thug Brian a iníon le pósadh do Shitric, le hionchas go ndéanfadh an cleamhnas san a chómacht féin do neartú leis an gcaradas, dar leis, a thiocfadh as idir Lochlannaigh Átha Cliath agus Clann Chais. Béibheann ab ainm don iníon* san Bhriain, ainm a mháthar féin*. Ríogan ana-chiallmhar, ana-thuisceanach ab ea í. Do cimeádadh uaithi an t-uisce-fé-thalamh a bhí á dhéanamh i gcoinnibh a hathar an fhaid a bhí Niamh ag déanamh na faire, agus ansan, an fhaid a bí Lonán dhá leogaint air go raibh sé ag cabhrú le Gormfhlaith sa droch-obair a bhí ar siúl aici. Chimeád a muíntir féin an scéal ó Bhéibheann i gcaitheamh na haimsire sin chun gan bheith ag cur buartha uirthi gan ghátar, agus i dtreó gur shuaimhneasaí a bheadh an saol aici nuair a chífeadh Sitric go soiléir ná raibh aon phioc d'fhios na droch-oibre aici. Chimeád Sitric an t-eólas uaithi díreach mar a dhein sé a dhícheall ar é ' chimeád ó gach éinne ba dhó' leis a dhéanfadh aon iarracht ar an ndroch-obair do chosc.

Ach nuair a tháinig Amhlaoibh thar n-ais ó Inis Cathaigh chómh hobann, agus nuair nár hínseadh d'éinne cad é an chúis, agus ansan, nuair a thug sí fé ndeara an discréid agus an chogarnach ag Amhlaoibh agus ag Sitric, agus an bheirt ag stad de pé cainnt a bhíodh eatarthu nuair a thagadh sí 'na láthair, thuig sí 'na haigne go raibh rud éigin nárbh fhónta dá bheartú acu. Dá shoiléire a thuig sí an ní sin is ea ba lú a leog sí uirthi gur thuig sí é féin ná aon ní dhá shórd, agus is ea ba lú a bhí aon chuímhneamh acu san gur thuig sí é féin ná aon ní dhá shórd. Bhí sí ag faire orthu go géar agus ní raibh aon choinne acu go raibh. Dá fheabhas faire a dhein sí, áfach, níor fhéad sí teacht suas le haon ní áirithe do thabharfadh eólas cruínn di ar cad a bhí ar siúl acu, ná ar cé 'na choinnibh go raibh an t-uisce-fé-thalamh á dhéanamh.

Do lean an scéal mar sin go dtí go dtáinig Gormfhlaith go hÁth Cliath. Ansan do thuig Béibheann go raibh donas éigin thar na beartaibh déanta. Níorbh fhada gur tugadh le tuiscint di ná raibh Gormfhlaith ag dul thar n-ais ag triall ar Bhrian. Ansan do stadadh de bheith ag déanamh aon chimeád ar cad 'na thaobh gur tháinig sí uaidh ná ar cad 'na thaobh ná raibh sí ag dul thar n-ais. Do thárla go raibh an ceathrar i bhfochair a chéile agus gur éirigh fearg Ghormfhlaith. Do léim sí agus do spriúch sí. Do chaith sí insna súilibh ar Shitric agus ar Amhlaoibh an bob a bhuail Lonán orthu, agus ansan, an bob a bhuail sé uirthi féin nuair a chuaigh sé siar ag triall uirthi agus teistiméireacht aige uathu san. Ansan do thuig Béibheann cad é an brí a bhí leis an ndiscréid agus leis an gcogarnach* agus leis an stad cainnte nuair a thagadh sí féin. Níor labhair sí aon fhocal amach as a béal mar gheall ar an ngníomh a measadh a dhéanamh ar a hathair. Duairt sí, 'na haigne féin: "Do theip an méid sin oraibh. Ní stadfaidh sibh anois. Déanfaidh sibh iarracht eile. Ní mór dhom faire níos feárr a dhéanamh, le heagla go mb'fhéidir ná teipfeadh an tarna hiarracht oraibh".

Níor dhein sí aon cheilt ar an ndroch-mheas a bhí aici orthu, ná ar an bhfeirg a bhí uirthi mar gheall ar an rud a cheapadar a dhéanamh. Ach níor dhein sí trácht ar imeacht as an áit mar gheall air. Níorbh fhada gur thit rud amach a thispeáin di gur mhaith a dhein sí é agus fanúint.

Tháinig rí Laighean ann.

"'Sea!", arsa Gormfhlaith leis, "measaim gur dheineas éagóir ort nuair aduart gur bheithíoch iompair ag Brian tu. Measaim gurbh fhearra dho go scaoilfeadh sé thairis an beithíoch. Airím go bhfuil do neart agat dá chruinniú go cuthaigh. Fíorfair an focal úd adúraís le Murchadh: 'Má cailleadh Gleann Mháma tríom chómhairle', arsa tusa, 'buafar Gleann Mháma eile tríom chómhairle'. An t-annscian! Mura mbeadh an bheirt seo ' bheith chómh símplí", ar sise, "bheadh sé féin agus a athair agus Dúlainn fén bhfód go tréith anois".

"Ní gá dhuit é ' chur ar an mbeirt seo, a mháthair", arsa Amhlaoibh. "Bhí aimsir do dhóthain agat chun an ghnímh a dhéanamh sara ndeigh Lonán ag triall ort, agus níor dheinis é. Níor dheinis, agus ní dhéanfá ó shin é, pé caoi a bheadh agat air, an fhaid a bheadh iníon Thaidhg Mhóir Uí Chealla i t'aice! Is dó' liom", ar seisean, "dá mbeadh sí i bhfad i t'aice go ndéanfadh sí míorúilt ort, a mháthair", agus chuir sé dranna-gháire as. Níor dheas an dranna-gháire é, bhí sé chómh diablaí agus an ghnúis chómh hálainn, chómh hóg. An té a chífeadh an ghnúis sin an uair sin agus an dranna-gháire, déarfadh sé go raibh duine in éaghmais Ghormfhlaith gurbh fhéidir a dhiabhal coímhdeachta a dh'fheiscint uaireanta. Chonaic Béibheann diabhal coímhdeachta Amhlaoibh an uair sin, agus chimeád sí cuímhne air.

"Cad é sin agat dhá rá, a choileáin?", arsa Gormfhlaith. "Cad í an mhíorúilt a dhéanfadh sí orm?"

"Dhéanfadh sí naomh díot, a mháthair", ar seisean, "agus ba mhór an mhíorúilt é", agus do leathnaigh an dranna-gháire.

Do stad sí agus í ag féachaint air.

"Ní dhéanfadh míorúilt féin naomh díot-sa!", ar sise.

"Foth, foth!", arsa Maolmhórdha, "níl aon tairbhe le teacht as an saghas san cainnte. Cuiridh uaibh í. Ní deirim ná go bhfuil rud déanta agam-sa do chuirfidh chun cínn an bheart so do theip ar thriúr agaibh-se".

Do léim Sitric agus chuir sé bas ar bhéal rí Laighean, agus shín sé a mhéar i dtreó na háite 'na raibh Béibheann 'na seasamh i lúib na finneóige. Dhrid sí isteach sa lúib sin nuair a thosnaigh an chainnt ar dhul in olcas idir Ghormhflaith agus Amhlaoibh. D'airigh sí an focal, áfach, a béal rí Laighean, ach níor leog sí uirthi gur airigh. Do rith cailín isteach, duine de mhnáibh coímhdeachta Bhéibheann.

"Ó!", ar sise, "tá an cuan lán de luingeas!"

Do rith gach éinne amach ach Béibheann.

Caibideal 46: Mícheál Rua

"Tar i leith, a lao", ar sise leis an gcailín. "Tháinís anso in éineacht liom-sa", ar sise. "Tá ' fhios agam nách miste dhom rún a thabhairt duit. Tá, mar is eól duit, mar is eól do gach éinne, Lochlannaigh an domhain ag cruinniú a neart in aghaidh na hÉireann agus in aghaidh Árdrí Éireann. Tá an tÁrdrí ag cruinniú neart na nGael chun na hÉireann do chosaint. Tuigid ríthe Lochlannach dá mbeadh Árdrí Éireann as an slí go dtitfeadh cómhacht na nGael as a chéile agus nár dheocair an lámh uachtair a dh'fháil orthu. Tá, dá bhrí sin, iarracht mhallaithe dá déanamh le fada ar an Árdrí do chur chun báis le nimh. Tá teipithe glan ar an iarracht san. Sin é fé ndeara Gormfhlaith a bheith anso anois. Tá iarracht eile dá dhéanamh anois. Tá feall éigin eile dá dhéanamh anois ar m'athair. D'airíos an focal ó chiainibh ó rí Laighean. 'Tá rud déanta agam-sa', ar seisean, 'do chuirfidh chun cínn an bheart so do theip ar thriúr agaibh-se'. Ní duairt sé a thuilleadh mar do chuir Sitric lámh ar a bhéal. Ní dó' leó gur airíos-sa an focal. Ní mór scéala ' chur láithreach ag triall ar an Árdrí. Inniu an lá chun an fhíona do chur siar go Sórd Cholm Cille. Imigh, a lao, agus cuir an fíon sa bhosca mar is gnáth leat a dhéanamh, fíon Aifrinn, agus tar chúm anso nuair a bheidh san déanta agat".

D'imigh an cailín agus chuir sí an fíon sa bhosca. Ba ghnáth le Béibheann an fíon san do chur chun na mainistreach san, agus dá bhrí sin níor chuir éinne aon tsuím sa rud a bhí ag an gcailín á dhéanamh. Nuair a bhí an bosca i dtreó aici, tháinig sí ag triall ar an mBannrín mar adúradh léi.

"Seo anois", arsan Bhannrín léi, "cuir chút an dá leitir seo. Tabhair an dá leitir don Airchinneach, do Ghiolla Phádraig, agus dein an rud adéarfaidh sé leat".

D'imigh an cailín agus do rug sí léi an bosca, agus an capall agus an carbad aici, mar ba ghnáth. Chonaic Sitric agus Amhlaoibh agus Gormfhlaith ag imeacht í. Chonacadar an bosca fíona. Níor chuímhníodar ar aon ní eile ' bheith aici, agus níor chuireadar blúire suime inti.

Caibideal 46: Mícheál Rua

Tháinig sí go Sórd Cholm Cille. Thug sí an dá leitir don Airchinneach. D'oscail sé leitir acu, mar do féin ab ea í. Do léigh sé í. Thug an cailín fé ndeara gur iompaigh a líth ann.

"An bhfuil ' fhios agat cad 'tá sa leitir seo atá léite agam?", ar seisean leis an gcailín.

"Tá tuairim agam do, a Athair", ar sise.

"An mbéarfá-sa an leitir eile seo ag triall ar inín Thaidhg Mhóir Uí Chealla?", ar seisean. "Deir Béibheann ná fuil éinne is feárr a dhéanfaidh an gnó ná mar a dhéanfair-se é".

"Agus ca bhfuil iníon Thaidhg Mhóir Uí Chealla le fáil?", arsan cailín.

"Tá sí le fáil", arsan tAirchinneach, "i mbuíon* a hathar, sa mhór-shlua atá ag teacht aniar ó Cheann Cora. Cuirfead carbad agus giolla leat. Thabharfainn an leitir don ghiolla le breith siar ach deir an Bhannrín gan an leitir a thabhairt d'éinne ach duit-se. Agus deir sí go gcaithfir do cheann a chimeád folaithe go maith, le heagla go n-aithneófí thu. Caithfidh Niamh an leitir a dh'fháil i ganfhios d'éinne, agus caithfidh sí an leitir a dh'fháil gan ' fhios a bheith aici cé uaidh go bhfaighidh sí í".

"Tá go maith", arsan cailín. "Duairt Béibheann liom go neósfá-sa dhom cad a bheadh le déanamh agam".

"Nuair a bheidh an leitir tabhartha do Niamh agat, féadfair an carbad agus an giolla do bhreith leat siar abhaile ag triall ar do mháthair. Cuirfidh Béibheann fios ort arís i ndiaidh an chatha. Ní fios cé ' bheidh beó an uair sin, áfach".

Do gabhadh capall agus carbad, agus do cuireadh an cailín sa charbad agus do cuireadh an tsrian i láimh an ghiolla.

Caibideal 46: Mícheál Rua

"Dein an dithneas is mó a dh'fhéadfair", arsan tAirchinneach leis an ngiolla, "ach gan súile na ndaoine ' tharrac ort ach chómh beag is is féidir é".

Do ghluais an carbad. Níor fhéad an giolla oiread dithnis a dhéanamh agus a measadh a dhéanfadh sé, mar bhí na bóithre go léir lán de dhaoine. Ach thánadar fé dheireadh chun buíne Thaidhg Mhóir agus, mar adúradh cheana, do tugadh an leitir do Niamh agus chuir Niamh chun Murchadh í. Chómh luath agus do léigh Murchadh an leitir, d'imigh sé chun na háite 'na raibh Brian agus d'athraigh sé na fir a bhí in aice le pearsain an Árdrí.

Nuala ab ainm don chailín a thug an leitir sin do Niamh. Chómh luath agus ' bhí an leitir tabhartha uaithi aici, d'imigh sí amach chun na háite 'nar fhág sí an giolla agus an carbad. Bhailíodar leó amach a brú na sló, agus thugadar aghaidh siar go Cúige Connacht, chun na háite 'na raibh máthair an chailín 'na cónaí.

Is é cúis go ndúradh le Nuala a ceann do chimeád folaithe ná so. Do thuig Béibheann go raibh Maolmhórdha tar éis breibe ' gheallúint d'fhear éigin ach dul in aice an Árdrí sa ghluaiseacht agus sleagh do shá ann, nú é ' chur chun báis ar chuma éigin mar sin. Bhí eagal uirthi, dá mb'ar an gcuma san a bheadh an scéal, go mb'fhéidir go n-aithneódh an fealltóir Nuala agus ansan go bhfaigheadh Sitric amach an scéal go léir, agus go maródh sé í féin. Níor fhág sí ar a chumas Nuala do mharú, pé rud a thitfeadh amach, mar duairt sí léi dul siar abhaile. Chimeád Nuala a ceann folaithe agus níor aithin éinne í. Níor aithin Niamh féin í, bíodh go raibh aithne mhaith thiar sa bhaile aici uirthi féin agus ar a máthair.

Um thráthnóna an lae a dh'imigh Nuala ó rí-theaghlach Shitric agus an capall agus an carbad agus an bosca fíona aici, do thárla gur airigh duine eile de mhnáibh coímhdeachta Bhéibheann cainnt idir an dá rí, idir Shitric agus Maolmhórdha.

Caibideal 46: Mícheál Rua

"Ná bíodh ceist ort, a rí", arsa Maolmhórdha. "Déanfaidh Mícheál Rua an bheart. Tá sé i ngnáth-theaghlach an Árdrí anois le cheithre bliana, agus tá árdiúntaoibh ag Brian as. Tá iúntaoibh acu go léir as. Is dó' le Murchadh ná fuil fear eile sa rí-theaghlach chómh dílis leis. Gormfhlaith a thug aithne dhom air. Is cuma leis ceocu ' curfar chun báis é nú ná curfar nuair a bheidh an gníomh déanta, mar tá geallta againn do go mbeidh fearann saor go deó ag á mhnaoi agus ag á shliocht má chuireann sé Brian as an slí uainn. Dá mbeadh Brian as an slí, bheadh gach aon rud ar ár dtoil againn".

D'imigh an bhean choímhdeachta agus d'inis sí do Bhéibheann an chainnt a dh'airigh sí. D'imigh Béibheann agus chomáin sí ar siúl giolla turais i lár na hoíche agus leitir eile aige le tabhairt do Niamh. D'aimsigh sé capall maith. Bhí aithne ar an bóithribh agus ar na cóngair aige. Do shrois sé an áit 'na raibh buíon Thaidhg Mhóir Uí Chealla. Thug sé an leitir do Chaoilte, mar adúradh, agus thug Caoilte do Niamh í, agus chuir Niamh ag triall ar Mhurchadh í. Do léigh Murchadh í. D'fhéach sé 'na thímpall. D'fhéach sé ar an ngárda a chuir sé, inné roimis sin, ó bheith in aice Bhriain. Bhí aithne mhaith aige ar Mhícheál Rua. Ní raibh Mícheál Rua le feiscint in aon bhall. Nuair a deineadh an t-athrú inné roimis sin, do thuig Mícheál in' aigne go raibh scéite ag duine éigin air. D'éalaigh sé san oíche as an áit. Chómh luath agus ' fuair Murchadh imithe é, do scaoil sé an focal i measc na bhfear, breith air agus é ' thabhairt thar n-ais. Níorbh fhada gur tugadh thar n-ais é. Bhí an iomad aithne air. Do tugadh i láthair Mhurchadh é.

"Pé duine ' thabharfadh cúl le cath", arsa Murchadh leis, "níor mheasas gur tusa ' dhéanfadh é! Seasaimh ansan i t'inead, agus ná fág an áit arís".

Cheap Mícheál nuair a tugadh thar n-ais é go gcrochfí é. Bhí ' fhios aige go raibh an chroch tuíllte aige. Nuair nár deineadh ach a rá leis dul agus seasamh in' inead féin, bhí iúnadh air. Níor thug sé fé ndeara an bhagairt a dhein Murchadh ar na fearaibh eile.

Dá gcrochtí é, b'fhéidir go raghadh an scéal ó bhéal go béal agus go sroisfeadh sé rí Lochlannach Átha Cliath, agus nárbh fheárr-de Béibheann san. Dá bhféadadh sé imeacht slán go hÁth Cliath nuair a dh'éalaigh sé, thiocfadh an díobháil chéanna as, b'fhéidir.

Sheasaimh sé in' inead féin i measc na bhfear an lá san—ach ní feacathas 'na dhiaidh san é beó ná marbh.

Caibideal 47: Éigean ar Ríocht na bhFlaitheas

Nuair a bhíodh Caoilte in Albain ag breithniú an nirt a bhí ag Lochlannaigh in Ínsibh Orc agus insna hoileánaibh eile ann, is i dteaghlach Dhónaill mhic Éimhin, i Mágh Geirrghinn, a chaitheadh sé an chuid ba mhó den aimsir. Thugadh sé, sa chainnt a bhíodh eatarthu, tuairisc cruínn do Dhónall ar an gcuma 'na raibh gach aon rud ag dul chun cínn in Éirinn. Bhíodh Dónall coitianta dhá cheistiú i dtaobh Bhriain agus i dtaobh Mhurchadh agus i dtaobh Dhál gCais go léir.

Thugadh Caoilte cuid dá aimsir, leis, i bhfochair Mhuireadhaigh, Mór-mhaor Leamhna, agus chaitheadh sé na tuairiscí céanna ' thabhairt do san ar an gcuma 'nar sheasaimh cómhacht Bhriain, agus ar gach dóchas a bhí go bhféadfadh sé seasamh in aghaidh na mór-chómhacht a bhí ag cruinniú as gach áird 'na choinnibh.

Bhí ana-bháidh ag an mbeirt sin le Brian agus le Gaelaibh. Níorbh iúnadh báidh a bheith ag Dónall le Brian, mar ó Oilioll Olum do shíolraigh an bheirt. Ó Ghaelaibh a shíolraigh Muireadhach leis. Dá éaghmais sin, níorbh aon iúnadh dúil mhór a bheith ag an mbeirt go mbuafadh Brian sa mhór-chath a bhí ag teacht, mar dá mb'ag na gíntibh a bheadh an bua, do chuirfidís deireadh leis an gCreideamh a mhúin Colm Cille do Ghaelaibh agus do Chruithneachaibh Alban, agus níor mhiste deimhin a dhéanamh de go ndéanfaidís Gaeil Alban do dhísciú.

Caibideal 47: Éigean ar Ríocht na bhFlaitheas

Bhíodh Caoilte dhá ínsint don bheirt cad é an saghas fir Brian, agus cad é an saghas fir Murchadh, agus cad é an saghas fir Dúlainn, agus Maolruanaidh na Paidre, agus Tadhg Mór Ó Cealla.

"Agus", arsa Dónall, "cad é an saghas an cailín seo, iníon Thaidhg Mhóir Uí Chealla, go bhfuilimíd bodhar ag gach éinne ag moladh a háilleachta?"

Nuair a cuireadh an cheist sin chuige, do las Caoilte go bun na gcluas. Ansan do bhánaigh sé chómh bán le cailc.

D'fhéach Dónall air agus thuig sé an scéal go léir láithreach, dar leis féin.

"Is dócha", ar seisean, "gur fíor an chainnt adeirtear, go bhfuil sí níos áille ná Gormfhlaith féin".

"Is fíor, a rí", arsa Caoilte. "Tá sí níos áille ná mar a bhí Gormfhlaith riamh. Ní hé an saghas céanna áilleachta atá iontu. Tá sé chómh maith agam an scéal go léir a dh'ínsint duit, a rí", ar seisean le Dónall.

Ansan tháinig sé i dtosach an scéil agus d'inis sé do Dhónall, ó thosach go deireadh, gach aon rud a bhí aige le hínsint i dtaobh Niamh; conas a bhain a háilleacht a mheabhair shaolta dhe an céad uair a chonaic sé í; conas mar a bhí éad ar Chonn chuige mar gheall uirthi; conas mar aduairt sí leis féin, agus leis an gcuid eile de sna ríthibh óga, go raibh socair aici 'na haigne gan pósadh in aon chor, ach fanúint i bhfochair a hathar an fhaid a mhairfeadh a hathair, agus ansan maireachtaint singil ar an saol so go dtí go leanfadh sí é.

Fear breá dathúil uasal cumasach ab ea Dónall. D'éist sé le Caoilte an fhaid a bhí Caoilte ag cainnt. Thuig se in' aigne nárbh fholáir nú gurbh uathásach an áilleacht a bhí sa ríogan óg san. Duairt sé leis féin gur dhócha gurbh é cúis go nduairt sí go raibh a haigne socair ar gan pósadh mar nár thaithn éinne de sna fearaibh óga san léi. Go mb'fhéidir dá bhfeiceadh sí an fear a thaithnfeadh léi go n-athródh sí an socrú san. Níor leog sé air le Caoilte go raibh aon mhachnamh den tsórd san in' aigne. Bhí sé i mbéalaibh na ndaoine go léir go raibh Sitric chun a mháthar féin, Gormfhlaith, a thabhairt le pósadh d'Iarla Ínsí hOrc. Bhí tuairim ag daoine go raibh sí geallta aige dho ní ba mhó ná an tIarla san. Gan amhras bhí Gormfhlaith ag dul amach insna bliantaibh. Ach má bhí féin, bhí na geallúna úd ann. Is dócha gur thuig Sitric go mb'fhéidir go socródh an cath, nuair a thiocfadh sé, a lán den tsaghas san geallúna.

Thuig Dónall in' aigne dá bhféadadh sé féin Niamh a dh'fháil go mbeadh bean aige a bheadh ní b'áille, agus ní b'fheárr ar gach aon tsaghas cuma, ná an bhean so a bhí á geallúint do gach éinne ach teacht ag cabhrú le Sitric.

Pé'r domhan é, bhí Dónall socair ar theacht go hÉirinn ag cabhrú le Brian i gcoinnibh na Lochlannach, ach nuair ' airigh sé an moladh a dhein Caoilte ar inín Thaidhg Mhóir Uí Chealla, bhí sé socair ní ba dhaingne, naoi n-uaire ní ba dhaingne, ar theacht, agus ar an uile fhear a dh'fhéadfadh sé do thabhairt leis. Do labhair sé leis an Mór-mhaor eile, Mór-mhaor Leamhna a tugtar air sa tseanchas, agus chuir sé suas é chun a nirt go léir do chruinniú ar an gcuma gcéanna agus teacht go hÉirinn ag cabhrú le Brian.

"Má buaitear ar Bhrian", ar seisean, "sa chath so atá ag teacht, tá sé chómh maith ag Gaelaibh imeacht a hAlbain. Dísceófar sinn go léir. Is fearra dhúinn titim i gcath ag cabhrú le Brian ná na Lochlannaigh a theacht agus sinn a mharú anso sa bhaile má buaitear ar Bhrian".

Do chruinnigh an bheirt a neart go léir. Tháinig chúthu an uile shaghas fir a dh'fhéadfadh aon ní i bhfuirm airm do láimhseáil. Níor fhan sa bhaile ach seandaoine agus mná agus leanaí.

Is ró-bheag dá chuímhneamh a bhí ag Niamh gurbh í fé ndeár an méid sin den chúnamh a tháinig ag triall ar Bhrian a bheith chómh láidir agus ' bhí sé. Díreach mar a bhí sí gan aon phioc dá chuímhneamh aici, nuair a bhí sí ag faire ar Ghormfhlaith chun gan leogaint di nimh a thabhairt do Bhrian, nách leis an bhfaire do chosain sí Brian ach leis an gcosc a chuir a cómhluadar fónta, agus a cuideachtanas fónta, agus a hanál fhónta, le droch-íntinn Ghormfhlaith, i ganfhios di féin agus i ganfhios do Ghormfhlaith.

An fhaid a bhí na slóite ar an slí, bhí mórán tairbhe ag Niamh á dhéanamh, i ganfhios di féin, ar an gcuma san. Bhí dúil ag na fearaibh go léir gach gnó ' dhéanamh ar an gcuma ba dhó' leó dob fheárr a thaithnfeadh léi; agus i mbuínibh na mban ní raibh aon ní ba mhó ag na mnáibh ná focal molta ' dh'fháil uaithi nuair a bhíodh sí ag gabháil eatarthu ag féachaint ar an gcuma 'na mbíodh a ngnó acu á dhéanamh. Dheinidís go léir a ngnó ní b'fheárr go mór, ar gach aon tsaghas cuma, ná mar a dhéanfaidís é dá mba ná beadh sí ann.

Ach dhein sí, leis, mórán tairbhe agus ní hi ganfhios di a dhein sí é, ach le hiomláine feasa agus machnaimh.

Do hínseadh cheana cad é an chúis gur tugadh "Maolruanaidh na Paidre" ar rí Ó bhFiachrach Áidhne. Gur thuig sé in' aigne a bheith ceangailte ar an gCríostaí bheith coitianta ag guí chun an Athar Síoraí, agus ná fuil aon chainnt is oiriúnaí chun labhartha leis an Athair Síoraí, moladh is glóire leis, ná an chainnt a mhúin ár Slánaitheóir dúinn.

Do labhair Niamh anois is arís le cuid de sna fearaibh. Do thrácht sí leó ar an gcuma 'na rabhadar go léir lán-cheapaithe ar gan teacht thar n-ais ón gcath. Chuir sí i gcuímhne dhóibh gur ar son an Chreidimh, chómh maith le har son na hÉireann, a bhí an ceapadh san déanta acu go léir. Bhí focal aici le rá, ó am go ham, ar rí Ó bhFiachrach Áidhne agus ar an gcuma 'na mbíodh an Phaidir ar siúl aige i gcónaí. Chuir sí 'na luí orthu go raibh gach duine acu chómh ceapaithe ar bhás a dh'fháil sa chath a bhí rómpu agus ' bhí Maolruanaidh. Dá bhrí sin, go raibh gach duine acu chómh mór i ngá leis an bPaidir agus ' bhí Maolruanaidh.

"Is dócha", ar sise, "go bhfuil oiread gá agam féin leis agus atá ag éinne", agus thosnaigh sí ar an bPaidir do rá coitianta.

"Má tá gá ag Niamh leis an bPaidir", arsa duine de sna fearaibh, "is deocair a rá ná go bhfuil gá agam-sa leis!", agus thosnaigh sé ar an bPaidir do rá coitianta. Níorbh fhada go raibh an Phaidir ar siúl ag gach duine dá raibh ar an mór-shlua.

Bhí a lán sagart ar an mór-shlua. Ní raibh gnáth-theaghlach rí ann gan sagairt fé leith, nú b'fhéidir beirt shagart dá mbeadh a lán daoine sa ghnáth-theaghlach. Do chabhraigh na sagairt go mór leis an bPaidir do chur ar siúl i measc na bhfear, agus ansan, i measc na ndaoine go léir a bhí ag leanúint na sló. Ní baol ná go ndúradh an Phaidir sin ó chroí go dúthrachtach. Thuig gach éinne dá mba ná beadh lámh Dé go láidir le Gaelaibh Éireann sa chath a bhí ag teacht ná beadh an bua acu. Dá mhéid a tuigeadh an ní sin is ea is dúthrachtaí adúradh an Phaidir agus is ea is aoirde do glaodh ar Dhia, le gach saghas úrnaithe, dhá iarraidh air cabhrú le Gaelaibh agus leis an gCreideamh. Do glaodh ar an Slánaitheóir ó b'é do mhúin an Phaidir do sna Críostaithibh. Do glaodh ar an Maighdin Muire, ó b'í Máthair an tSlánaitheóra í. Do glaodh ar Mhícheál Naofa an tÁrdaingeal, ar Naomh Eóin Baiste, ar Pheadair agus ar Phól, ar Phádraig agus ar Bhríd agus ar Cholm Cille, agus ar na naoimh go léir, dhá iarraidh orthu a nguí ' chur suas chun an tSlánaitheóra agus chun an Athar Síoraí ar son na nGael agus ar son an Chreidimh, ionas go dtabharfadh Dia an bua do Ghaelaibh sa mhór-chath a bhí rómpu.

Do thuig Brian cad a bhí ar siúl agus do ghoibh sé a bhaochas go dúthrachtach le Dia, agus do neartaigh a ghuí féin chun Dé ar son na sló a bhí dhá leanúint chun an chatha mhóir, slóite ná fíllfeadh aon duine acu ón gcath san dá mbeadh bua ag an namhaid, slóite ná fíllfeadh duine as an gcéad acu pé taobh ar a mbeadh bua.

Caibideal 47: Éigean ar Ríocht na bhFlaitheas

Ní sa mhór-shlua amháin a bhí éigean dá dhéanamh ar Ríocht na bhFlaitheas ar an gcuma san le guí daoine. In sna mainistribh agus insna heagailsibh, ar fuid na hÉireann, bhí sagairt agus manaigh agus mná rialta, de ló agus d'oíche, gan bhia gan deoch gan chodladh gan suan, ag briseadh a gcroí ag glaoch go hárd ar Dhia, trí ímpí na Maighdine Muire agus na naomh go léir, gan bua an chatha a bhí ag teacht do leogaint leis an namhaid.

Ar an gcuma gcéanna, ins gach aon pháirt d'Éirinn, go mór mór i ngach lín tí go raibh duine de mhór-shlua Bhriain tagaithe as, bhí an t-éigean céanna á dhéanamh, ar Ríocht na bhFlaitheas, an t-athair agus an mháthair agus an chuid eile den chlaínn dhá iarraidh ar Dhia an té a bhí amu' uathu do thabhairt saor ón gcath agus é ' thabhairt chúthu thar n-ais slán. Bhí na paidreacha agus na húrnaithe ba ghnáth ar siúl ins gach tigh, agus in éaghmais na n-úrnaithe ba ghnáth, bhíodh na húrnaithe móra ar siúl, Mairineamh Phádraig, agus Amhra Cholm Cille, agus Lúireach Phádraig, agus mórán úrnaithe den tsórd san in onóir do naoimh fé leith, dhá iarraidh orthu a nguí ' chur chun Dé ar son duine éigin fé leith a bhí sa mhór-shlua agus an duine ' thabhairt saor.

Bhí gach fear de sna fearaibh a bhí sa mhór-shlua ceapaithe ar gan filleadh ón gcath, ach bhí a mhalairt sin d'aigne ag an muíntir a bhí sa bhaile 'na ndiaidh. Bhí an mhuíntir a bhí sa bhaile ag déanamh a gcroí díchill dhá iarraidh ar Dhia iad do thabhairt abhaile slán.

Ba bheag aon treabhchas fé leith gan naomh de naoimh Éireann fé leith acu. Bhí Seanán ag muíntir gnáth-theaghlaigh Bhriain. Bhí Breandán ag muíntir Chiarraí. Bhí Íta ag muíntir Uíbh Chonaill Ghabhra. Bhí Déaglán ag muíntir na nDéise. Bhí Barra ag muíntir Chorcaí. Mar sin dóibh. Agus bhí na húrnaithe ag dul suas coitianta chun gach naoimh acu san, ón muíntir a bhí féna choimirce, a d'iarraidh a n-ímpí* chun Dé, an uair sin thar gach uair dár tháinig riamh roimis sin.

Caibideal 47: Éigean ar Ríocht na bhFlaitheas

Idir mhór-shlua ag gluaiseacht chun an chatha agus gaolta 'na ndiaidh sa bhaile, ní raibh ach aon ghuth úrnaithe ag dul suas chun Dé ó Ghaelaibh Éireann go léir.

Caibideal 48: Connla

Bhí mac ag Murchadh agus Toiréalach ab ainm do. Ní raibh sé ach trí bliana dh'aois nú mar sin nuair a tháinig Tadhg Óg Ó Cealla agus Amhlaoibh go hInis Cathaigh chun na scolaíochta ' dh'fháil. Tímpall na haimsire céanna san, do rugadh an leanbh siar go rí-theaghlach Mhaoilruanaidh na Paidre, toisc an gaol a bheith ann. Ní fada a bhí sé thiar sa rí-theaghlach san nuair a tháinig Niamh ann ar chuaird, ó rí-theaghlach a hathar in Uíbh Máine. Do chuir an leanbh aithne ar Niamh. Má chuir, do cheangail sé suas di. Nuair a bhí sí ag dul abhaile, bhí an leanbh ag briseadh a chroí ag gol. B'éigean dóibh leogaint do imeacht in éineacht léi go hUíbh Máine. As san amach is mó dá aimsir a chaith sé in Uíbh Máine ná in aon áit eile. Bhíodh sé ann nuair a thagadh Tadhg Óg Ó Cealla agus Amhlaoibh ar a gcuardaibh ó Inis Cathaigh aníos ann. Tháinig árdchion aige ar Amhlaoibh an chéad uair a chonaic sé é. Bhí cion aige ar Thadhg Óg, agus bhí cion aige ar Thadhg Mhór, agus ar gach éinne sa teaghlach. Ach do fuair Amhlaoibh inead 'na chroí ná fuair aon duine eile an uair sin, lasmu' de Niamh féin.

Chonaic Niamh an ní sin. Chonaic gach éinne é, ach níor chuir éinne eile puínn suime ann. Ní raibh ann, dar leó, ach mian linbh. Chonaic Tadhg Óg é, agus bhí áthas air, mar, dar leis, tháinig mian an linbh agus an caradas a bhí idir é féin agus an Lochlannach óg isteach lena chéile. Chuir Niamh suím ana-mhór i mian an linbh an uair sin, ach níor leog sí uirthi gur chuir. Do chuir sí an suím ann, mar, dar léi, do thispeáin an cion san a tháinig ag an leanbh san ar Amhlaoibh an uair sin nách gan abhar a tháinig an ní eile úd 'na haigne agus 'na croí féin an uair chéanna i dtaobh an Amhlaoibh chéanna.

Caibideal 48: Connla

Bhí san mar sin. Bhíodh Niamh agus an leanbh i bhfochair a chéile coitianta. Ní raibh aon teóra leis an leanbh san chun ceistiúcháin, agus Niamh a chaitheadh na ceisteanna go léir a fhreagairt do. Bhíodh ceisteanna aige le cur chúithi i dtaobh an uile shaghas ní; an spéir; an talamh; na cnuic; na haibhní; an ghrian; an ghealach; an duine; an bás; an saol eile; gach aon rud ar a bhféadadh sé cuímhneamh. Bhí an chiall agus an breithiúntas go hálainn aici sin agus, gan a leogaint uirthi go raibh sí dhá dhéanamh, chuir sí isteach in aigne an linbh sin eólas ar an gCreideamh chómh cruínn agus chómh hiomlán agus chómh fórlíonta agus a dh'fhéadfadh Colla féin a dhéanamh. Ní déarfainn ná gur dhein sí an gnó ní b'fheárr ná mar ' fhéadfadh Colla é ' dhéanamh. Mar gheall ar an gcion a bhí ag an leanbh uirthi, agus aici air, do tugadh an t-eólas agus do glacadh an t-eólas ar chuma nárbh fhéidir é ' thabhairt ná é ' ghlacadh dá mb'é Colla, nú duine mar é, a bheadh in inead Niamh.

Nuair a bhíodh na ceisteanna a bhaineadh leis na nithibh a thagadh féna shúilibh réitithe do, d'iompaíodh an leanbh ar na ceisteannaibh a thagadh os cómhair a aigne, agus ansan ar na ceisteannaibh a bhain le hÉirinn agus le ríthibh Éireann, agus le naoimh na hÉireann, le teacht an Chreidimh go hÉirinn agus le dílse na nGael don Chreideamh. Ansan, do cheistíodh sé í ar theacht na Lochlannach agus ar an léirscrios tine agus fola a dheinidís i gcónaí nuair a thagaidís, agus d'ínseadh sí dho gach aon rud fé mar a bhíodh le hínsint. Ní baol ná gur mhínigh sí dho go soiléir na gníomhartha móra a dhein a sheanathair ar na Lochlannaigh i gcaitheamh a shaeil, agus na gníomhartha a dhein a athair féin, Murchadh, orthu, agus driotháracha a athar.

Leanbh mór ab ea é dá aois. Nuair a bhí sé chúig bhliana dh'aois bhí sé chómh mór le leanbh a bheadh seacht nú hocht de bhlianaibh. Bhí an dúchas garbh ann agus thug sé leis an dúchas. Níorbh fhada go raibh sé ag breith suas ar bheith chómh hárd, geall leis, le Niamh féin. Chíodh na daoine in éineacht iad ag gluaiseacht ar fuid na mbánta agus an ceistiúchán ar siúl.

Caibideal 48: Connla

Nuair a chíodh na daoine mar sin iad, do chuímhnídís ar "Eachtra Thaidhg mhic Céin", agus ar "Chonnla Rua", mac Chuínn Chéad-chathaigh, agus ar an mnaoi do rug léi Connla.* Bhí ' fhios ag gach éinne gurbh óig-bhean ana-naofa ana-dhiaga Niamh, agus bhí ' fhios acu go raibh Toiréalach óg lán de naofacht agus de Chreideamh agus de gach aon tsaghas eile dea-thréithe aigne, mar gheall ar an oiliúint aigne a bhí aige dá fháil ó Niamh.

Níorbh fhada gur thug na daoine "Connla" mar ainm cheana air. Níor thugadar "Connla Rua" air, mar ní rua a bhí sé ach donn. Nuair a bhí "Connla" ag gach éinne air is "Connla" a bhíodh ag Niamh air.

Nuair a tháinig an scéal áthais go hUíbh Máine go raibh Amhlaoibh ag glacadh an Chreidimh, bhí áthas ana-mhór ar Chonnla. Bhí oiread áthais air agus ' bhí ar Niamh.

"A Niamh", ar seisean léi, "an bhfuil ' fhios agat cad a dhéanfainn-se dá mbeinn i m' Árdrí?"

"Ní fheadar, a Chonnla", ar sise. "Is dócha gur rud éigin fónta a dhéanfá".

"Chuirfinn ' fhéachaint ar na Lochlannaigh go léir", ar seisean, "an Creideamh do ghlacadh".

"Ach, a Chonnla", ar sise, "ní bheadh aon tairbhe sa ghníomh san".

"Cad 'na thaobh, a Niamh?", ar seisean.

"Ní féidir Creideamh a ghlacadh", ar sise, "ach le saor-thoil. Ní Creideamh in aon chor é mura nglactar é le saor-thoil".

"Tuigim", ar seisean. "D'fhéadfadh duine a rá 'Creidim' 'na chainnt, agus gur 'Ní chreidim' a bheadh istigh 'na chroí".

Caibideal 48: Connla

“Go díreach”, arsa Niamh.

“Más ea”, arsa Connla, “chuirfinn an Creideamh dá mhúineadh dhóibh, agus ansan, nuair a bheadh an t-eólas acu, do ghlacfaidís an Creideamh le saor-thoil”.

“Ní dhéanfadh an t-eólas féin an gnó, a Chonnla”, arsa Niamh, “gan rud eile i dteannta an eólais”.

“Cad é an rud eile ’ bheadh uathu, a Niamh?”, arsa Connla. “Ar ndóin, nuair a bheadh eólas ar an bhfírinne ag duine, ní fhéadfadh sé gan an fhírinne ’ chreidiúint”.

“D’fhéadfadh duine cur i gcoinnibh an Chreidimh, a Chonnla”, arsa Niamh, “pé eólas a múinfí dho ar na fírinníbh, mura bhfaigheadh sé cúnamh agus solas ó ghrásta Dé”.

“Ó, tuigim”, arsa Connla, “agus tugann Dia a ghrásta don té a dheineann a dhícheall óna thaobh féin”.

“Tugann”, arsa Niamh, “agus tugann sé a ghrásta don duine sin chun an díchill sin a dhéanamh”.

“Moladh go deó le Dia!”, arsa Connla.

Tháinig an tuairisc go raibh Amhlaoibh chun bheith ’na shagart. Ansan is ea ’ bhí an obair ag Niamh chun gan a leogaint uirthi le Connla go raibh an dá mhachnamh úd os cómhair a haigne agus é ag teip uirthi iad do thabhairt dá chéile. Dhein sí an bheirt, áfach, maith go leór. Bhí Connla ró-óg. Ach dá óige a bhí sé, do chuaigh ’na luí ar a aigne nár thaithn an scéal ró-mhaith le Niamh. Níor fhéad sé dul a thuilleadh.

Nuair a tháinig an scéal uathásach ná raibh aon tuairisc ar Amhlaoibh, bhí iúnadh agus alltacht i gceart ar Chonnla. Chonaic sé an bhuairt go léir ar Thadhg Óg Ó Chealla. Bhí uaigneas agus buairt a dhóthain air féin. Chonaic sé go raibh buairt ar Niamh, ach níor mheas sé gurbh í an bhuairt cheart í. Do lean sé ar feadh tamaill ag cur ceisteanna chúithi 'na thaobh, dhá fhiafraí a' raibh aon tuairisc air; cad ba dhó' léi a bhí imithe air; a' raibh aon tsúil go dtiocfadh sé thar n-ais; cérbh iad a mhuíntir; agus a lán ceisteanna den tsórd san. Ní raibh aon eólas aici le tabhairt do go dtí go bhfuair Caoilte gach aon rud amach i dtaobh Amhlaoibh. Ansan féin do cimeádadh an scéal ó Chonnla go dtí go raibh an Árdríogan, Gormfhlaith, imithe agus na slóite ar na bóithribh ag dul go háit an choinne chun an chatha mhóir do throid i gcoinnibh na Lochlannach.

Nuair a bhí an t-ollmhú chun gluaiste dá dhéanamh i rí-theaghlach Bhriain i gCeann Cora, do measadh Connla ' dh'fhágáilt thíos in Inis Cathaigh fé láimh Cholla. Ní fhanfadh sé ann.

"Táim chúig bhliana déag", ar seisean. "Ní raibh m'athair ach chúig bhliana déag nuair a mhairbh sé Maolmhuaidh i mBealach Leachta. Ní raibh mo sheanathair ach chúig bhliana déag nuair a thóg se claíomh i gcoinnibh na Lochlannach. Tá sé chómh ceart agam-sa claíomh a thógaint agus me in aois mo chúig mblian ndéag agus ' bhí sé ageam athair agus ageam sheanathair".

B'éigean a shlí féin a thabhairt do, agus do tugadh. Bhí áthas ar Bhrian agus ar Mhurchadh nuair a fuaradar é chómh ceapaithe ar dhul sa chath. Bhí rud eile, leis, sa scéal. Bíodh ná raibh Connla ach na chúig bhliana déag, ba bheag ná go raibh sé chómh hárd len' athair agus bhí an ghairíocht agus an neart insna géagaibh aige mar a bhí ag á athair. An Lochlannach a thiocfadh 'na choinnibh sa chath, níorbh fholáir do bheith láidir go maith nú bheadh Connla maith a dhóthain do.

Nuair a bhí an méid sin socair agus an mhór-shlua ar an slí, do labhair Connla le Niamh.

Caibideal 48: Connla

"A Niamh", ar seisean, "tá ceist agam le cur chút, agus caithfidh tú labhairt agus an cheist do fhreagairt dom".

"Déanfad gan amhras, a Chonnla", ar sise, "má fhéadaim é".

"Féadfair", ar seisean. "An t-eólas atá uaim tá sé agat-sa. Tá an t-eólas céanna ag Tadhg Óg. Ar feadh tamaill tar éis Amhlaoibh a dh'imeacht, bhí ana-bhuairt ar Thadhg, díreach mar a bhí orm féin, agus mar is dó' liom a bhí ort-sa. Le déanaí, má thráchtann éinne ar Amhlaoibh i láthair Thaidhg, dúbhann gnúis Thaidhg. Tá fuath fíochmhar aige d'Amhlaoibh. Sin í mo cheist, a Niamh. Ca bhfuil Amhlaoibh? An bhfuil sé beó? Peocu beó nú marbh do, inis dom cad a dhein sé ar Thadhg?"

B'éigean di teacht i dtosach an scéil agus é go léir a dh'ínsint do, ó thosach go deireadh.

D'éist Connla le Niamh an fhaid a bhí sí ag ínsint an scéil agus é 'na shuí lena hais sa charbad, agus iad féin agus an tslua ag gluaiseacht go réidh. D'inis sí dho i dtaobh na cailíse; i dtaobh na heochrach; i dtaobh an phúicín a cuireadh ar Chaoilte thall i gCathair na Beirbhe; i dtaobh na leitre a tugadh do nuair a bhí sé ar an loíng ag teacht anall go Corcaigh; agus i dtaobh conas mar a dheineadar amach gurbh aon Amhlaoibh amháin an dá Amhlaoibh agus gur chun caoi a dh'fháil ar an gcailís a ghuid do leog sé air an Creideamh a ghlacadh agus na mion-úird do ghlacadh. D'éist Connla leis an scéal go léir gan focal do labhairt. Bhí iúnadh ar Niamh a rá go raibh sé chómh ciúin. Bhí a chúis féin aige leis.

Nuair a chonaic sé Amhlaoibh ag teacht ar dtúis go Ceann Cora agus go hUíbh Máine agus nuair a bhíodh an rínce ar siúl, ba chuímhin leis gur airigh sé an focal: "Nách álainn an lánú a dhéanfaidís!" Níor thaithn an focal an uair sin leis, dá óige a bí sé. Ba leis féin Niamh, dar leis, agus níor theastaigh uaidh aon éileamh a bheith ag Amhlaoibh ná ag éinne eile uirthi. Bhí cion an uair sin aige ar

Amhlaoibh, mar a bhí ag gach éinne, ach má bhí féin, níor thaithn an focal úd leis.

An fhaid a bhí sí ag ínsint an scéil do, bhí sé ag cuímhneamh ar an bhfocal úd agus bhí uabhar agus bochtaineacht agus fearg agus diomá agus buile seirithin 'na chroí, a rá gur labhradh an chainnt sin riamh agus gur cuireadh in aice ' chéile sa chainnt Niamh agus a leithéid de ropaire fíll agus éithigh agus dí-chreidimh.

Nuair a bhí cúrsaí na cailíse ínste aici dho, d'inis sí dho gnóthaí Ghormfhlaith agus conas mar a bhí sí féin i gCeann Cora chómh fada agus í ag faire le heagla go dtabharfadh Gormfhlaith nimh don Árdrí.

Níor bhain sí aon fhocal cainnte as go dtí gur inis sí obair Lonáin do. Ansan do gháir sé a dhóthain, agus nuair a bhí an scéal go léir ínste dho, do sceartadh sé ar gháirí, as a mhachnamh, nuair a chuímhníodh sé ar an gcleas a dhein Lonán.

Ach do lasadh an fhearg arís, ar buile, gach aon uair a chuímhníodh sé ar an bhfocal úd, "Nách álainn an lánú a dhéanfaidís!", Agus ' fhios aige ná raibh ag Amhlaoibh á dhéanamh i gcaitheamh na haimsire go léir ach feall!

Bhí an doimhneas ann, óna sheanathair, agus níor thug Niamh fé ndeara in aon chor go raibh a leithéid d'fhearg air. Ach bhí.

Caibideal 49: Geallta do Bheirt

An uair úd do rith an cailín isteach mar a raibh Sitric agus Maolmhórdha agus Amhlaoibh agus Gormfhlaith ag cainnt, agus aduairt sí go raibh an cuan lán de luingeas, do rith, mar adúradh, an ceathrar amach go bhfeicidís na luingeas. Chonacadar iad ach ní raibh oiread acu ann agus ' mheasadar ba cheart a bheith ann. Ní raibh ann ach luingeas Shíguird ó Ínsibh Orc. D'aithin Sitric iad.

Caibideal 49: Geallta do Bheirt

"Is ceart dúinn dul amach chun cainnte leis an Iarla", arsa Gormfhlaith.

"Is fíor san, a mháthair", arsa Sitric, "ach ní mór dhom ní áirithe a dh'ínsint duit-se ar dtúis".

"Cad é an ní é?", ar sise.

"Ní a bhainfidh gáire asat", ar seisean, agus do stad sé.

"Scaoil chúinn é!", ar sise. "Má bhaineann sé gáire asainn, ní miste dhuit é ' scaoileadh chúinn. Cad é an greim atá agat air?"

"Gheallas ní don Iarla so. Ní thiocfadh sé liom go dtí gur thugas an gheallúint do". Do stad sé arís. (Bhí Maolmhórdha láithreach.)

"Ochón!", ar sise, "is agat atá an greim air. Cad a gheallais do?"

D'iompaigh sé uirthi agus d'fhéach sé uirthi.

"Gheallas tusa dho!", ar seisean.

"Is maith a dheinis é", ar sise, "rud a gheallúint do ná raibh ar do chumas a thabhairt do. Ní dó' liom, áfach, gur maith a dhein seisean é agus an gheallúint sin do ghlacadh uait".

"Do ghlac sé an gheallúint agus do tháinig sé. Mura mbeadh gur thugas an gheallúint do, ní thiocfadh sé. Dar leis, agus dar leó go léir, níl bean eile sa domhan chómh breá leat-sa".

"Agus conas a bheidh an scéal agat ar ball má dhiúltaím-se don gheallúint do chómhlíonadh?"

"Bhí san sa mhargadh. Gheallas go bhfaigheadh sé thu lem lán-toil-se. Bhí ' fhios aige go maith ná féadfadh sé thu ' dh'fháil i gcoinnibh do thoile féin. Mar adeirir, is ceart dul amach agus labhairt leis, agus fáilte ' chur roimis agus roimena mhuíntir, roimis na daoine a tháinig in éineacht leis. Ná leog ort leis, a mháthair, go bhfuil ' fhios agat gur gheallas do go bhfaigheadh sé thu, ach bí chómh séimh, chómh cneasta leis agus a dh'fhéadfair a bheith. Fear láidir tréan cuthaigh is ea é, agus má gheibheann sé thusa séimh geal-gháiriteach leis is truime-de a bheidh a bhuille ar fhearaibh Éireann nuair a thiocfaidh an cath".

"Tá go maith, a mhic ó", ar sise. "Téanam agus feicimís é, agus feiceadh sé sinn".

Do ghluais an ceathrar síos chun an chaladh. Ag gabháil síos an uair sin dóibh is ea ' chonacadar an cailín agus an bosca fíona aici agus í ag dul siar go Sórd. Níor chuireadar aon tsuím inti. Chuirfidís suím inti dá mbeadh ' fhios acu go raibh an dá leitir úd istigh 'na brollach aici. Ní raibh aon phioc dá fhios acu, agus chomáineadar leó gan aon tsuím a chur inti.

Chuadar isteach sa bhád, bád an rí. Bhí fir an rí ann i gcónaí agus iad ollamh ar an mbád do ghléasadh, fé sheóltaibh dá mbeadh gaoth ann, nú fé bhataíbh rámha dá mba ná beadh gaoth ann. Bád breá mór órnáideach ab ea é, agus bhí gach aon chóir dá uaisleacht agus dá dhaoire ar bórd air*, mar ba cheart a bheith ar bhád an rí. Pé áit 'na bhfeictí ar an gcuan é, do haithnítí é mar gheall ar ghlaine agus ar uaisleacht a dhathanna.

Bhí gaoth ann an lá san agus do cuireadh suas na seólta. Do ghluais an bád an cuan amach, i dtreó na háite 'na raibh na luingeas iasachta. D'aithin Sitric long an Iarla. Do tugadh aghaidh ar an loíng sin. Do tagadh* 'na haice. Chómh luath agus ' bhíodar in aice na luinge, d'aithin an tIarla Sitric. Do cuireadh an dréimire síos láithreach idir an long agus an bád agus chuaigh an ceathrar ar bórd na luinge. Chuir an tIarla na mílte fáilte roimis an rí, rí Lochlannach Átha Cliath, agus roim Ghormfhlaith. Ní raibh aithne roimis sin aige ar

Mhaolmhórdha ach do cuireadh aithne acu ar a chéile. Bhí sean-aithne aige ar Amhlaoibh. Théadh Amhlaoibh ó thuaidh go minic go hÍnsibh Orc ag breith teachtaireachtaí ag triall ar an Iarla ó Shitric, agus ag tabhairt eólais do ar an gcuma 'na mbíodh gach ní ag dul chun cínn in Éirinn. Bhí Amhlaoibh tar éis a dh'ínsint don Iarla, ar na cuardaibh sin, conas mar a bhí Brian an-aosta agus conas mar a bhí gnó ar siúl a chuirfeadh Brian as an slí, díreach um an dtaca 'na mbeadh cómhacht Lochlann ollamh ar theacht go hÉirinn chun an ghnímh a dhéanamh. Ní baol, áfach, gur thug Amhlaoibh aon eólas don Iarla ar cé a bhí chun an ghnótha ' dhéanamh do Bhrian nuair a thiocfadh an t-am. Dá bhrí sin, ba bheag ná gurbh í céad cheist a chuir an tIarla chúthu ná conas a bhí Brian.

"Tá sé chómh maith, a rí", arsa Maolmhórdha, "agus is féidir d'fhear a bheith san aois atá aige, ach ní fheadramair cad é an neómat a gheóbhaimís tásc a bháis".

"An amhlaidh atá aon bhreóiteacht air, a rí?", arsan tIarla.

"Ní hamhlaidh, a rí", arsa Maolmhórdha. "Is amhlaidh atá duine curtha agam-sa ag tabhairt aireachais do, duine dá mhuíntir féin, duine den bhuín a bhíonn 'na seasamh in' aice coitianta, duine dá bhuín chosanta. Curfar sleagh 'na chroí nuair is lú a bheidh coinne aige leis. Ansan ní bheidh 'na mhór-shlua ach mór-shlua gan cheann. Titfidh a chómhacht as a chéile. Beidh Éire againn féin, agus beidh Sitric in' Árdrí ar Éirinn".

D'fhéach an tIarla ar Shitric, chómh maith lena rá, "An é sin a gheallais-se dhómh-sa?" Do labhair sé:

"De réir mar a thuigim-se an scéal", ar seisean, "dá n-imíodh aon ní ar Bhrian anois, bheadh Éire ag an Árdríogain, agus ag an bhfear a phósfadh í".

Do phreab aigne Ghormfhlaith nuair ' airigh sí an focal san.

"Ó", ar sise, 'na haigne. "Ní mise a bheadh uait ach an Árdríocht! 'Mo ghrá thu agus rud agat'".

Ní raibh focal a héinne ar feadh tamaill. Do labhair Amhlaoibh agus é ag gáirí.

"Gan dabht!", ar seisean. "Dá n-imíodh aon rud ar Árdrí Éireann is ag an Árdríogain a bheadh an Árdríocht, agus ag an té go dtabharfadh sí dho an Árdríocht. Maraímís Brian ar dtúis agus ansan beidh ' fhios againn cad a dhéanfaidh an Árdríogan".

"Is fíor", arsan tIarla. "Maraímís Brian ar dtúis. Níl brí ná éifeacht le cainnt go dtí go mbeidh san déanta ar dtúis. An fear san a chuiris-se ag tabhairt aire do Bhrian", ar seisean le Maolmhórdha, "má dheineann sé a ghnó go maith, agus go luath, beidh caoi ag an Árdríogan* ar a taobh féin den ghnó ' dhéanamh. Ansan is ea ' bheidh éifeacht le cainnt. Go dtí san, ná deintear a thuilleadh cainnte".

"Dar so 's súd!", arsa Gormfhlaith 'na haigne féin, "ach má bhíonn Árdríocht agam-sa le tabhairt d'éinne, ní baol gur duit-se ' thabharfad í, a bheithígh allta! Ó! Is mór idir thu agus Brian, dá olcas é! Agus is mór idir thu agus Bruadar!"

"Barra na teangan go mbaintear amach as do bhéal, a bhrealláin!", arsa Sitric, in' aigne féin, le Maolmhórdha.

"Ba mhaith linn na fir a thugais leat a dh'fheiscint, a rí", arsa Amhlaoibh leis an Iarla.

Do rug an tIarla leis iad ó loíng go loíng agus thispeáin sé a shlua dhóibh. Ní ró-shuaimhneasach an aigne a bhí ag éinne den cheathrar tar éis an méid úd cainnte, agus ní suaimhneas ar fad a chuir an radharc a tispeánadh dóibh orthu. Chonacadar fir mhóra láidre agus airm mhaithe ghéara 'na lámhaibh acu, agus a dheallramh orthu go rabhadar ábalta ar úsáid a dhéanamh go neamh-eaglach agus go cróga de sna hairm. Chuir san sásamh aigne ar an gceathrar. Ach do chonacadar, in éaghmais na bhfear, sloigisc ban agus leanbh agus gan iontu, nách mór, ach daoine fiaine. Is ceart a dh'admháil go dtáinig uabhar agus bochtaineacht ar an uile dhuine den cheathrar nuair a thuigeadar 'na n-aigne cad é an cor a bheadh ar Éirinn agus ar Ghaelaibh Éireann nuair a leogfí an tsloigisc sin isteach orthu agus an bua acu. Ach má bhí uabhar agus bochtaineacht orthu, do bhrúdar fúthu é. Chimeádadar istigh é. Níor dheineadar oiread agus a dh'admháil dá chéile 'na gcainnt gur mhothaíodar istigh é. Sin mar a bhíonn i gcónaí ag an té a dheineann an droch-ghníomh. Chun sásamh aigne ' thabhairt do féin is ea ' dheineann sé an droch-ghníomh, agus ar ball is é rud a thagann as do ná mí-shásamh aigne, agus seirithean aigne, agus buaireamh aigne, agus canncar agus trí chéile aigne. Ansan bíonn an trí chéile aigne laistigh aige agus an geal-gháire lasmu' aige, agus is mór an trua é.

Tháinig an ceathrar abhaile go rí-theaghlach Shitric agus dheineadar an ceann ab fheárr den ghnó, chómh maith agus d'fhéadadar é, 'na gcainnt. Mholadar an tIarla mar gheall ar a mhéid agus ar a neart. Dar leó, ní raibh aon fhear ar theaghlach Bhriain a dh'fhéadfadh seasamh 'na láthair agus é ' throid. Mholadar na fir a bhí aige, agus na hairm a bhí acu. Ní dúradar puínn i dtaobh na mban agus na leanbh. Níor mhaith le Gormfhlaith cuímhneamh orthu in aon chor, bhíodar chómh meánna, chómh salach, chómh fiain.

D'imigh Maolmhórdha. Bhí a shlóite féin ag teacht isteach ó árdaibh Cúige Laighean. Níor mhór do dul agus féachaint chúthu.

Nuair a bhí sé imithe do labhair Sitric.

"Greadadh chuige", ar seisean, "ba dhóbair do an donas a dhéanamh orainn! Mura mbeadh Amhlaoibh, bhí an donas déanta aige. Nách uathásach an scéal ná féadfadh sé a bhéal a dh'oscailt gan toirmeasc éigin a dhéanamh! Mura mbéadh a thapúlacht a labhair Amhlaoibh, do dhéanfadh sé an donas".

Caibideal 49: Geallta do Bheirt

"Tá ' fhios ag an dtalamh", arsa Amhlaoibh, "gur mheasas go mbeadh an scéal go léir scaoilte amach aige sara mbeadh uain agam ar labhairt!"

"Ní fheicim cad é an díobháil a bheadh déanta dá dtigeadh* leis an scéal go léir do scaoileadh amach", arsa Gormfhlaith.

"Ní bheifá mar sin, a mháthair", arsa Sitric, "dá mbeadh fios an scéil go léir agat. Dá mbeadh an chuid eile den scéal agat, chífá go hálainn cad é an díobháil a dhéanfadh sé agus cad é an díobháil ba dhóbair do a dhéanamh".

"Aililiú!", ar sise. "Inis-se dhom an chuid eile den scéal, a Amhlaoibh, nuair ná neósfadh sé seo dhom é".

"Níl puínn deifríochta", arsa Amhlaoibh, "idir an dtaobh atá agat agus an taobh eile. Gheall Sitric go dtabharfadh sé thusa don Iarla. Ansan, nuair a bhí sé ag cainnt le Bruadar, gheall sé dho go dtabharfadh sé thusa dho! Taíonn tú geallta dhóibh araon, a mháthair. Má gheibhid siad araon amach é, beidh spórt againn!"*

Chaith sí í féin i gcathaoir agus ba dhó' leat go dtitfeadh an t-anam aisti le neart gáirí. Do gháir sí, agus do gháir sí arís.

"Ó!", ar sise fé dheireadh, "féach air sin! An mó duine eile gur gheallais me dhóibh?" (Bhí ' fhios aici go raibh sí geallta do Bhruadar.)

"Níor gheallas tu ach don bheirt sin, a mháthair", arsa Sitric.

"Ach!", ar sise, "is olc a dheinis é! Bhíos ag brath air go mb'fhéidir gur gheallais me do bheirt mhac rí na hIorua. Ar gheallais-se d'éinne me?", ar sise le hAmhlaoibh.

"Níor gheallas, a mháthair", ar seisean, "ach is dócha go mbeidh Bruadar, agus luingeas rí Lochlann aige, ag teacht isteach sa chuan so ar maidin amáireach. Chuamair amach chun cainnte leis an Iarla, leis an bhfear mór mileata meirgeach. Ní foláir dul amach chun cainnte le Bruadar nuair a thiocfaidh sé. Dá n-airíodh sé gur chuais-se amach chun cainnte leis an bhfear meirgeach agus gan tu ' dhul amach chun cainnte leis féin, b'fhéidir go dtiocfadh éad air".

"Tá go maith", ar sise. "Raighimíd amach chun cainnte leis". Agus chuir sí sceartadh gáire eile aisti.

"Seachain, a mháthair", arsa Sitric, "agus ná tuigeadh sé uait go bhfuilir geallta don Iarla".

"Ní baol duit", ar sise. "Is amhlaidh a bheidh sé a d'iarraidh a thuiscint go bhfuilim deimhnithe dho féin".

Caibideal 50: Cad a Thiocfaidh As?

Nuair a tháinig an mhaidean, d'fhéachadar amach ar an gcuan. Bhí cabhlach luingeas a bhí dhá uair chómh mór le cabhlach an Iarla tar éis teacht isteach sa chuan agus tar éis inead do ghlacadh laistigh de chabhlach an Iarla, fan na trá, ar an dtaobh thuaidh den chuan. Bhí a lán de sna fir, a cabhlach an Iarla, tar éis imeacht as na luingeas agus dul i dtír, lastuaidh den chuan, agus cábáin a chur suas dóibh féin, agus tínte do lasadh chun bídh a dh'ollmhú agus leapacha ' dhéanamh dóibh féin agus tuirse na farraige ' chur díobh. Bhí na daoine a bhí sa chabhlach mhór a tháinig i gcaitheamh na hoíche ag tosnú ar an rud céanna ' dhéanamh. Bhí na báid, agus iad lán de dhaoine agus d'abhar na gcábán, ag fágáilt na luingeas agus ag imeacht amach trí chúr na trá, chun an tailimh thirim.

Níor bheag d'uathás a raibh de luingeas sa dá chabhlach. Nuair a bhí na hanncaireacha curtha amach acu agus iad 'na stad, agus iad in aon líne amháin, fan na trá, do shrois an líne ó Bhínn Éadair go hÁth Cliath nách mór.

Do ghluais bád Shitric amach arís ón gcaladh in aice an rí-theaghlaigh, agus do ghluais sé i dtreó na luinge ar a raibh Bruadar. Chuaigh Gormfhlaith agus Sitric agus Amhlaoibh ar bórd na luinge sin. Chuir Bruadar na mílte fáilte rómpu.

"Ó", ar seisean le Gormfhlaith, "nách óg a dh'fhéachann tú, a Árdríogan!"

"Ní haon iúnadh é sin, a rí", ar sise. "Ní haon iúnadh me ' bheith ag féachaint óg an fhaid atáim óg. Ní rabhas ach seacht mbliana déag nuair a rugadh é seo", ar sise, (b'é sin Sitric) "agus níl sé seo puínn thar fiche bliain fós.* Ní ceart seanabhean a thabhairt orm go dtí go mbeidh mé a daichead an chuid is lú dhe".

"Ní tabharfar seanabhean ort choíche, a Árdríogan", ar seisean. "Taíonn tú ag féachaint chómh hóg an neómat so agus ' bhís an lá a phósais Amhlaoibh. Mheasas ná raibh agat ach aon mhac amháin le hAmhlaoibh agus go bhfuair Amhlaoibh bás sarar rugadh an mac san".

"Is iúntach an fear chun plámáis tu, a rí", arsa Amhlaoibh. "Dheinis tuathal ar dtúis nuair a dheinis an iúnadh d'í ' bheith ag féachaint chómh hóg, ach do leighsis an tuathal nuair adúraís go mbeadh sí ag féachaint óg go deó".

"Tá dearúd ort sa méid úd, a rí", arsa Gormfhlaith. "Sid é an mac a rugadh tar éis bháis Amhlaoibh".*

"Ó, tuigim", arsa Bruadar. "Sid é an tAmhlaoibh Óg. Cad 'na thaobh nár ínsis riamh dom cérbh é t'athair, a bhithiúnaigh?", ar seisean le hAmhlaoibh.

Caibideal 50: Cad a Thiocfaidh As?

"Le heagla go ndéanfainn bréag, a rí", arsa Amhlaoibh. "Nách in í an Árdríogan tar éis a rá leat ná feaca-sa m'athair riamh. Conas ' fhéadfainn a dh'ínsint duit cérbh é agus ná feaca riamh é?"

"Is fíor", arsa Bruadar. "Ach is cuma dhuit ceocu.[*] Tá géar-chúis do mháthar agat, agus tá a croiceann agus a bláth ort".

Níor thug Gormfhlaith uain do ar a thuilleadh plámáis a dhéanamh. Níor bheag léi a raibh ráite aige. Bhí sé ag taighde ar nithibh nár oir di é féin ná éinne eile ' bheith ag taighde orthu.

"Thánamair chun go bhfeicfimís do neart sló, a rí", ar sise.

"Tá go maith, tá go maith, a Árdríogan", ar seisean.

Do rugadh ó loíng go loíng iad, agus do tispeánadh gach aon rud dóibh. Chonacadar na slóite fear armtha, agus ba bhreá an radharc iad. Fir mhóra láidre chumasacha, agus na hairm ar áilleacht acu. Do tispeánadh dóibh an deich gcéad fear 'na raibh na héidí mitil orthu. Duairt Bruadar leis na fearaibh na héidí do chur úmpu go bhfeicfeadh an Árdríogan iad. Do chuireadar.

"Ó!", arsa Gormfhlaith. "Geóbhaid siad san trí shlóitibh Bhriain mar a gheóbhadh buanaithe trí pháirc cruithneachtan a bheadh aibidh!"[*]

Do rugadh iad chun na luinge ar a raibh beirt mhac rí na hIorua, Caroll Cnút agus Anrud.[*]

Ní fheacaigh an bheirt sin Gormfhlaith riamh go dtí san, ach d'airíodar teacht tháirsi. D'airíodar daoine a chonaic í ag trácht ar a háilleacht. Bhí ' fhios acu gur bhean álainn thar bárr í. Ach nuair a chonacadar í, ba dhóbair dóibh a mbéasa agus a stuaim do chailliúint, chuir a háilleacht a leithéid sin d'iúnadh orthu. Ní fhéadaidís gan bheith ag féachaint uirthi, agus ansan nuair ' fhéachaidís uirthi, ní fhéadaidís a súile ' bhogadh dhi.

Caibideal 50: Cad a Thiocfaidh As?

Bhí an tslua ar an gcuma gcéanna. An fhaid a bhíodh sí ag gabháil thórsu, ní fhéadaidís aon rud a dhéanamh ach bheith ag féachaint uirthi. Dá mb'iad na mná féin iad, bhí an scéal ar an gcuma gcéanna acu. Nuair a ghabhadh sí thórsu, do rithidís tímpall chun teacht roímpi agus radharc eile ' dh'fháil uirthi.

Thugadar a lán den lá ag gabháil tímpall ó loíng go loíng. Nuair a bhí an fhéachaint déanta acu, thánadar abhaile go rí-theaghlach Shitric.

"'Sea!", arsa Gormfhlaith, nuair a bhíodar 'na suí ar a suaimhneas in aice na tine, "tá m'aigne sásta. Níl aon bhreith ag Brian ar bhuachtaint sa chath so atá le troid anois aige. Bhí an t-eagla i gcónaí orm roim Mhurchadh agus roim Dhál gCais, ach an deich gcéad úd insna héidíbh práis, cuirfid siad san deireadh, glan, le Dál gCais. Nuair a bheidh deireadh le Dál gCais, beidh deireadh le cómhacht Bhriain. Má dheineann Mícheál Rua an bheart atá geallta aige a dhéanamh is amhlaidh is feárr é, ach peocu ' dhéanfaidh nú ná déanfaidh, níl baol orainn anois".

"Is maith liom mar a thaithneann an mhór-shlua leat, a mháthair", arsa Sitric. "Do fuaradh a lán dá dua. Níorbh aon ghnó ró-shuarach an dá chabhlach luingeas san, agus na mílte fear san, do thabhairt ansan amu' ar uisce an chuain sin chút! Tá obair mhór déanta ag rí Lochlann agus ag rí na hIorua agus ag an Iarla, dá mhéid de bheithíoch é. Tá obair mhór déanta acu go léir. Ní deintear obair mhór den tsórd san gan súil le díol as".

"Cad í an ghruaim seo anois ort?", arsa Gormfhlaith.

"Tá eagal air", arsa Amhlaoibh, "má bhuaid na ríthe seo ar Bhrian go gcimeádfaid siad toradh an bhua dhóibh féin".

"Bhuailis do mhéar air, a Amhlaoibh", arsa Sitric. "Ní sheasaíonn sé le cóir ná le ceart ná le réasún go dtiocfadh na fir seo anso agus go dtroidfidís cath fuilteach dúinn-na i gcoinnibh Bhriain, agus ansan, nuair a bheadh Brian marbh, agus Murchadh, agus M'leachlainn Mór, agus Dál gCais go léir, go n-árdóidís a seólta agus go n-imeóidís soir abhaile, agus ó thuaidh abhaile, arís agus go bhfágfaidís Éire againn-na".

"Cad é sin agat dá rá mar sin?", arsa Gormfhlaith. "Ná fuil slí dhóibh go léir, agus dúinn-na 'na dteannta, in Éirinn?"

"Sin é díreach atá orm, a mháthair", arsa Sitric. "Tá eagal orm ná fuil, 'slí dhóibh go léir agus dúinn-na 'na dteannta, in Éirinn'. An focal úd aduairt an tIarla, an 'beithíoch', a ndúraís féin, an focal úd aduairt sé le rí Laighean, tá sé daingean im chroí ó shin mar a bheadh dealg. 'Beidh an Árdríocht ag Gormfhlaith', ar seisean, 'agus ag an bhfear a phósfaidh í'. Is dócha go bhfuil an rud céanna istigh in' aigne féin ag Bruadar. Agus tá ' fhios ag an saol nách chun na hÁrdríocht* do chur in áirithe dhómh-sa, ná d'éinne den bheirt sin, a tháinig beirt mhac rí na hIorua anso go hÉirinn agus luingeas a n-athar acu, agus slóite a n-athar, agus a dtír féin curtha fé chostas mhór throm acu. Tá eagal orm go bhfuil aimhleas, agus nách aimhleas beag é, déanta againn, agus nách fios conas a thiocfaimíd uaidh. B'fheárr liom bheith fé Árdríocht Bhriain, a mháthair, ná fé Árdríocht éinne den cheathrar".

"Ní mac duit-se an fear san in aon chor, a mháthair!", arsa Amhlaoibh. "Mac d'Amhlaoibh is ea é. Deir a lán daoine liom nách mac d'Amhlaoibh mise. Measaim go bhfuil an ceart acu. Mac duit-se is ea me. Cad is gá dhuit-se, a Shitric, bheith fé smacht éinne den cheathrar! Cuir i gcás go ndéanfaid na buanaithe an obair ar an gcruithneacht* aibidh, agus go mbeidh Brian agus Dál gCais 'ar slí na fírinne', mar adéarfadh Colla, cad a thitfidh amach? Iompóidh Bruadar agus an 'Beithíoch' ar a chéile agus troidfid siad cath fuilteach, féachaint cé aige go mbeidh Gormfhlaith agus an Árdríocht. Iompóid* beirt mhac rí na hIorua orthu araon, nú ar an té a bheidh beó dhíobh, dhá chur in úil nách ag éinne acu is ceart an Árdríocht so do bheith ach ag duine acu féin, mar gurb iad is sia ó bhaile do tháinig dhá hiarraidh. Measaim, nuair a bheidh a gcuid coímheascair déanta ag an gceathrar, ná beidh puínn éilteóirí ag teacht idir thusa agus an Árdríocht, a mhic t'athar! Inis an fhírinne, a mháthair; nách é an coímheascar san idir an gceathrar an rud a chuir tusa ag cur an anama amach ag gáirí aréir nuair a hínseadh duit go rabhais geallta do bheirt acu?"

"Fágaim le huacht, a Amhlaoibh", arsa Gormfhlaith, "gur bhuailis do mhéar go cruínn ar an rud a chuir ag gáirí me. Ní rabhas, áfach, ag cuímhneamh ach ar an mbeirt, ar Bhruadar agus ar an Iarla. Do chonac go soiléir conas a féadfí an bheirt sin do chur ag dísciú a chéile agus gur me féin a dh'fhéadfadh an bheart san a dhéanamh. Ach chím anois go bhféadfar an ceathrar do chur ag dísciú a chéile go feilmeanta. Féadfar é ' dhéanamh agus déanfar é. Ná bíodh ceist ná eagal ort, a Shitric. Dísceóid siad cómhacht Bhriain duit ar dtúis. Ansan dísceóid siad a chéile dhuit. Ansan beidh Árdríocht na hÉireann agat 'na ndiaidh go léir!"

"Níl aon teóra libh!", arsa Sitric. "Ach deinidh féachaint bheag a thabhairt ar an dtaobh so den scéal. Cuir i gcás go bhfuil a ngnó déanta ag an meitheal buanaithe seo atá cruinnithe againn, agus go bhfuil an gort cruithneachtan ar lár. Chím an ceathrar i gcómhairle.

"'Is liom-sa an Árdríocht agus an Árdríogan', adeir an tIarla.

"'Cad a bhéarfadh gur leat-sa iad?", adeir Bruadar.

"'Mar do gheall Sitric féin dom iad, agus mura mbeadh gur gheall, ní thiocfainn anso', adeir an tIarla.

"'Ní dhuit-se a gheall Sitric iad', adeir Bruadar. 'Is dómh-sa a gheall sé iad.'

"'B'fhéidir', adeir duine de mhacaibh rí na hIorua, 'gur gheall sé do bheirt agaibh iad', agus cuireann sé gáire as. Gheibhtear amach gur thugas an ghealláint don bheirt. Éiríd siad ar buile.

"'Téanaídh', adeirid siad. 'Cuirimís ár neart le chéile agus tugaimís do Shitric an rud atá tuíllte aige!' B'fhéidir go neósfadh Amhlaoibh agus a mháthair do mhac Amhlaoibh cé air go ndéanfar dísciú ansan".

"Stad go fóill, a mhic Amhlaoibh", arsa Amhlaoibh. "Ca bhfios duit an mó duine den cheathrar a thiocfaidh saor ón gcath?"

"Ní fheadar; ná an mó duine againn féin a thiocfaidh saor ón gcath", arsa Sitric.

"Agus ar ndóin, an té ná tiocfaidh saor ón gcath", arsa Amhlaoibh, "cad é sin do san cad a dhéanfaidh an Árdríocht?"

"Ná an Árdríogan, an ea?", arsa Sitric.

"Is dó' liom, a bhuachaillí", arsa Gormfhlaith, "nách feárr rud a dhéanfaidh beirt agaibh anois ná dul a chodladh".

Chuadar a chodladh.

Caibideal 51: Oscailt Súl do Shitric

Níor chodail Sitric aon néal an oíche sin. Chómh luath agus ' tháinig solas an lae, bhí sé thuas ar bharra an rí-theaghlaigh agus é ag féachaint soir ó thuaidh ar an líne fada luingeas a bhí sínte ar an uisce ó Bhínn Éadair go hÁth Cliath, agus ar an líne cábán a bhí sínte fan chiúmhais na trá, amu' ar an dtalamh tirim, agus é chómh fada le líne na luingeas. Bhí an machaire, lasmu' de sna cábánaibh, clúdaithe le slóitibh dúbha daoine agus iad ag cur nithe i dtreó dhóibh féin i gcómhair bhéile na maidine. Bhí Sitric ag féachaint ar na luingeas agus ar na cábáin agus ar na slóite daoine, agus bhí a aigne anathrína-chéile.

"Is eagal liom", ar seisean in' aigne féin, "nách é mo leas a dheineas nuair a thugas ansan sibh. Dá mbeadh sibh go léir sa bhaile arís, gach duine agaibh 'na dhúthaigh féin, bheadh sibh ann tamall sara dtabharfainn-se as sibh. Tá sé déanach agam anois bheith ag cuímhneamh air sin".

Níor mhothaigh sé an Bhannrín, Béibheann, ag teacht in' aice. Chuir sí a lámh ar a chuislinn agus bhí méar na lámha eile ar a béal féin aici, mar chómhartha do gan fothram a dhéanamh. D'fhéach sé uirthi.

"Ná labhair, a rí!", ar sise leis i gcogar. "Tá ní agam le hínsint duit. Tar chun mo sheómra".

An fhaid a bhí an méid sin cainnte aici dá rá bhí a méar sínte aici i dtreó na háite 'na raibh na luingeas agus na slóite, mar dhea gur orthu a bhí sí ag féachaint agus ag trácht. Níor mhór di an gliocas. Ní raibh ach an cogar críochnaithe aici nuair a bhí Gormfhlaith laistiar di. Do lean sí ag cainnt go réidh, mar dhea nár mhothaigh sí Gormfhlaith ag teacht:

"Nách seóigh a' bhfuil ann díobh!", ar sise. "Féach", ar sise, "is dócha gurb í an long mhór san i lár baíll long an Iarla".

"Ní hí, a ríogan", arsa Sitric. "Sin í long Bhruadair. An bhfeiceann tú an long mhór eile úd thoir ar fad? An long go bhfuil an buthaire mór deataigh ag éirí aisti?"

"Chím í", arsa Béibheann.

"Sin í long an Iarla", arsa Sitric.

"Is moch ar maidin atáthaoi* araon dhá n-iniúchadh, a chlann ó", arsa Gormfhlaith laistiar den bheirt.

Do baineadh geit dáiríribh a Sitric mar níor mhothaigh sé ag teacht í. Do leog Béibheann uirthi gur baineadh geit aisti féin, leis, agus dhein sí an leogaint uirthi chómh maith san gur shamhlaigh an Árdríogan gur baineadh.

Thug an triúr tamall san áit ag breithniú na luingeas agus na sló. Ansan duairt Béibheann go raibh an mhaidean glas, agus d'imigh sí. Níorbh fhada go nduairt Gormfhlaith gurbh fhíor do Bhéibheann é, go raibh an mhaidean glas, agus d'imigh sí. Chómh luath agus a thuig Sitric ná raibh éinne dhá thabhairt fé ndeara, tháinig sé go seómra Bhéibheann.

"Cad é seo ort, a Bhéibheann?", ar seisean.

"Tá sé buailte isteach i m'aigne, a rí", ar sise, "go bhfuil éagóir á dhéanamh ort, éagóir throm".

"Cad a bhuail an ní sin isteach i t'aigne?", ar seisean.

"Inis dom ar dtúis", ar sise, "agus bí chómh cruínn agus d'fhéadfair ar na foclaibh, cad í an chainnt adúradh idir an gceathrar agaibh inné, idir thusa agus Bruadar agus Amhlaoibh agus do mháthair".

D'inis sé dhi an chainnt chómh maith agus d'fhéad sé é. D'éist sí leis go dtí go raibh an chainnt ráite aige.

"'Sea!", ar sise, "thugais leat an chainnt cruínn go leór".

Ní fheidir sé 'en domhan cad a bhí ag teacht.

"Bhíos ag éisteacht libh aréir", ar sise, "i ganfhios díbh. Admhaím é agus níl aon náire 'na thaobh orm. D'airíos do mháthair dhá rá libh dul a chodladh. Chuaúir a chodladh. Ní fheadar ar chuais-se a chodladh, ach tá ' fhios agam ná deigh Amhlaoibh a chodladh. D'fhíll sé thar n-ais agus thug sé féin agus do mháthair tamall maith den oíche ag cainnt. Do tarraigeadh anuas an uile fhocal den chainnt a bhí eadraibh ar bórd na luinge. Dheineadar ana-shult den chuma 'nar dhein sí amach ná rabhais-se ach fiche bliain d'aois agus gurbh é Amhlaoibh an mac léi a rugadh tar éis bháis a athar, 'sé sin tar éis bháis Amhlaoibh, agus gur mar gheall air sin a tugadh Amhlaoibh óg air. Ba dhó' leat go gcuirfidís araon an t-anam amach ag gáirí, féna n-anál*, an fhaid a bhí an méid sin ar siúl acu. Ach níorbh aon rud an méid sin suilt seochas an sult a bhí acu nuair a tharraigeadar chúthu conas mar a chuir do mháthair cosc leis an gcainnt ar eagla go leogfadh Bruadar amach scéal áirithe éigin, ní éigin a theastaigh ón dtriúr a chimeád uait-se.

"Sid iad anois agat, a rí, na ceisteanna atá os cómhair m'aigne agus atá ag déanamh buartha dhom. Cad é an ní é seo atá acu dá chimeád uait-se? Cad é an t-eólas é seo atá ag Bruadar agus ná fuil agat-sa, agus nárbh fholáir an chainnt do chosc ar eagla go leogfadh Bruadar amach, id láthair, aon bhalaithe dhe? Cad é an brí a bhí ag Amhlaoibh leis an sult a dhein sé, id láthair féin, amu' ar an loíng, den rud gur dhó' le héinne go n-éistfeadh sé a bhéal 'na thaobh? 'Cad 'na thaobh, a bhithiúnaigh', arsa Bruadar, 'nár ínsis dom ná feacaís t'athair riamh?' 'Le heagla', arsa Amhlaoibh, 'go ndéanfainn bréag', agus 'nách in í mo mháthair dhá ínsint duit ná feaca m'athair riamh?' Tá sé daingean i m'aigne, a rí, go bhfuil níos mó idir an dtriúr ná mar a thuigeann éinne ach iad féin. Tá uisce-fé-thalamh dá dhéanamh id choinnibh, a rí, agus neósfad duit cad é an t-uisce-fé-thalamh é. Má thiteann m'athair-se, táthar chun Árdrí ' dhéanamh de Bhruadar".

"Eist! eist! a ríogan", arsa Sitric. "Taíonn tú as do mheabhair".

"Féach isteach sa scéal", arsa Béibheann, agus breithnigh é, agus meáigh é, agus cuirfead geall go ndéarfair go bhfuil an ceart agam. Cad 'tá acu dá chimeád uait? Sin í an cheist. Cad 'tá acu le cimeád uait? Níor chimeádais-se aon ní uathu san riamh. Cad é an scéal é seo atá idir iad féin agus Bruadar agus nách maith leó aon ghaoth dhe do leogaint chút-sa?"

Caibideal 51: Oscailt Súl do Shitric

Do léim Sitric 'na sheasamh. Shiúlaigh sé an seómra síos agus suas ar feadh tamaill, díreach mar a dhéanfadh a mháthair. Nuair a bhí greas rástála déanta aige, do stad sé ar aghaidh na Bannríne amach:

"Dar so 's súd, a Bhéibheann", ar seisean, "ach tá an ceart agat! Chím anois é go soiléir. Cad a dhall me? Nách é é 'na steille-bheathaidh! Agus ó, nách athairiúil an mac é! Ó, cad a dhall me! Cad a dhall me! Déanfaidh sí Árdrí dhe! Ansan déanfar Árdrí d'Amhlaoibh 'na dhiaidh. Táim-se sa tslí. Cad a chómhairleófá dhom a dhéanamh, a Bhéibheann?"

"Ná leog ort go bhfuil aon bhlúire droch-amhrais agat orthu", ar sise. "Scaoil leó. Tá slua mhaith láidir agat-sa féin i gcómhair an chatha so. Leog iad súd i dtreó Dhál gCais sa chath. Socróid Clann Chais a lán de sna ceisteannaibh seo".

"Is maith í do chómhairle, a Bhéibheann", ar seisean. "Is trua chráite nách í do chómhairle a ghlacas ó thosach in inead cómhairle Ghormfhlaith. Ó, nách baileach a chimeád sí uainn an méid úd!"

"Nuair a bhí Amhlaoibh i gCeann Cora agus in Inis Cathaigh is ea ' thug sí an t-eólas do", arsa Béibheann.

"Is uathásach an bhean í!", arsa Sitric, "agus tá Amhlaoibh maith a dóthain di. Tá sé athairiúil, máithriúil".

"Tá", arsa Béibheann, "ach ní hé an taobh fónta den dúchas a thug sé leis ó athair ná ó mháthair".

"Ní puínn fóntachta a dh'fhéadfadh sé a thabhairt ó aon taobh acu", arsa Sitric.

Bhí an t-am ann chun dul fé dhéin béile na maidine. Chuadar isteach i seómra an bhídh. Bhí Gormfhlaith istigh rómpu.

Caibideal 51: Oscailt Súl do Shitric

"Móra dhíbh, a chlann ó!", ar sise. "Ní hiúnadh liom a lán cainnte ' bheith agaibh le déanamh inniu. Ní dócha go mbeidh puínn eile caoi ar chainnt agaibh go dtí go mbeidh bua an mhór-chatha so ar thaobh éigin. Ansan beidh gach aon ní ar úr dtoil agaibh má bhíonn an bua ar an dtaobh gceart".

"Agus má bhíonn an bua ar an dtaobh eile, a mháthair, cad a dhéanfaimíd?", arsa Sitric.

"Má bhíonn an bua ar an dtaobh eile", arsa Gormfhlaith, "ní bheidh aon ghá le cainnt againn. Deineadh gach fear a ghníomh féin sa chath agus ní baol ná go mbeidh an bua ar ár dtaobh féin".

"Cad 'tá ag cimeád Amhlaoibh?", arsa Béibheann.

"Ní fheaca inniu é", arsa Gormfhlaith. "Is dócha go mb'fhéidir go bhfuil tuirse air tar éis an lae 'nné".

Chríochnaíodar an bhéile. Níor tháinig Amhlaoibh.

"Is feárr glaoch air", arsa Sitric. "Raghad agus glaofad air".

D'imigh sé. Níorbh fhada gur fhíll sé.

"Níl sé 'na sheómra", ar seisean.

"Is mór an iúnadh", arsa Gormfhlaith, "é ' dh'éirí chómh moch. Más ag féachaint ar ár mór-shlua a bhí sé, nách mór an iúnadh ná feacamair é".

"Níor luigh sé ar a leabaidh in aon chor aréir, a mháthair", arsa Sitric.

Tháinig iúnadh uirthi, díreach mar a thiocfadh dá mb'i ganfhios a thiocfadh an scéal uirthi. Níorbh eadh. Bhí ' fhios aici go maith nár chodail sé sa rí-theaghlach an oíche roim ré. Dhein sí an iúnadh chómh maith san gur mheas an bheirt eile go raibh an iúnadh uirthi dáiríribh.

Bhí Amhlaoibh imithe amach go loíng Bhruadair agus teachtaireacht aige do Bhruadar ó Ghormfhlaith.

Do ghluais Gormfhlaith ar fuid an rí-theaghlaigh ag ceistiúchán ar na seirbhísigh, féachaint cé ba dhéanaí a chonaic an tiarna óg, Amhlaoibh, agus canad a chonacthas é. Ní bhfuair sí aon tuairisc air, ní nárbh iúnadh. Ní fheacaigh éinne acu é ó chonacadar go léir é féin agus an rí agus an Árdríogan ag teacht isteach ar an mbád um thráthnóna inné roimis sin.

Dhein Gormfhlaith dearúd. Dhein sí an iomad ceistiúcháin. Nuair a chonaic Béibheann an ceistiúchán, thuig sí ná raibh ann ach púicín. Thug sí cogar don rí.

"Níl sa cheistiúchán san ach púicín, a rí", ar sise. "Tá ' fhios ag Gormfhlaith ca bhfuil Amhlaoibh imithe. Pé ball 'na bhfuil sé imithe, a rí", ar sise, "ní har* mhaithe le rí Lochlannach Átha Cliath atá a thriall".

"Is fíor", arsa Sitric. "Ní foláir féachaint go cruínn chun an méid sin scéil", ar seisean.

Ansan do labhair sé leis an mbeirt, le Béibheann agus le Gormfhlaith.

"Féachaídh, a ríogana", ar seisean. "Inniu an Mháirt. Ní dó' liom gur ró-fhada uainn an cath. Tá slóite an Árdrí nách mór cruinnithe i gCíll Mhaighneann. Ní mór dómh-sa imeacht agus neart sló Lochlannach na hÉireann do chur san inead atá ceapaithe dhóibh ar thalamh an chatha. Beid siad féin agus slóite rí Laighean in aice ' chéile. Is dó' liom go bhfuil na Laighnigh ollamh cheana féin. Fágfar anso oiread nirt agus ' chosnóidh an rí-theaghlach so pé cuma 'na ngeóbhaidh an cath. Fanaidh-se araon anso istigh go dtí go mbeidh an bua ar thaobh éigin. Má bhíonn an bua ag Brian, ní baol go ndéanfaidh sé aon an-chor a thabhairt d'éinne agaibh-se. Má bhíonn an bua againn féin, beidh gach aon rud go maith".

D'imigh sé agus d'fhág sé ansan an bheirt.

B'in iad an bheirt ná raibh aon ghrá ró-mhór acu dá chéile. Ach an té a chífeadh iad i bhfochair a chéile, ní hé sin ba dhó' leis.

Caibideal 52: Fuadar agus Flosc agus Giodam

Um an dtaca 'na raibh slóite na Lochlannach agus a lucht cúnta socair 'na gcábánaibh ar an machaire, fan na trá, ar an dtaobh thuaidh de chuan Átha Cliath, bhí slóite Bhriain ag teacht go tiubh isteach ar mhachaire Cille Maighneann, mar ar ghnáth le Brian longphort a dhéanamh i gcónaí nuair a thagadh sé féin agus a shlóite aneas ón Múmhain, ag cur smachta ar Lochlannachaibh Átha Cliath, nú ag cur eagla a chómhachta ar na Gaelaibh a ghabhadh a bpáirt. Chuaigh gach rí de sna ríthibh a tháinig aneas an uair sin chun na háite 'nar ghnáth leis dul, é féin agus a bhuíon, agus chuireadar suas a gcábáin ann, fé mar ba ghnáth leó a dhéanamh. Bhí gach rí agus a bhuíon féin ag cur a gcábán suas fé mar a shroisidís an áit, agus ní raibh aon bhuíon ag teacht sa tslí ar bhuín eile, ná ní raibh aighneas ná díospóireacht ná abhcóidíocht ar siúl.

Bhí cábán Thaidhg Mhóir Uí Chealla san áit 'na mbíodh sé i gcónaí, in aice le cábán an Árdrí, agus bhí cábán Mhaoilruanaidh na Paidre in aice le cábán Thaidhg Mhóir. D'fhág san caoi ag Conn agus ag Tadhg Óg Ó Cealla ar bheith go minic i bhfochair a chéile, agus bhíodh Caoilte agus Lonán i bhfochair na beirte sin chómh minic agus d'fhéadaidís é. Minic go maith ab ea san, mar ní raibh cábán a n-athar ró-fhada ón áit. D'fhág san, leis, caoi ag Niamh ar bheith go minic 'na bhfochair go léir, agus ar a lán eólais a dh'fháil ó Chaoilte ar an gcuma 'na raibh an tslua go léir suite, agus ar cad é an saghas an namhaid agus cad a bhí acu dá dhéanamh. B'é gnó an ghiolla turais gach eólas den tsórd san do sholáthar agus do bheith aige, agus ní baol ná go raibh Caoilte tugtha go maith chun an ghnótha san do dhéanamh, agus chun gach aon bhlúire eólais, fé mar a thagadh sé suas leis, do thabhairt ag triall ar Niamh. Do thugadh sé ag triall ar Niamh é chómh luath agus ' thugadh sé ag triall ar Bhrian é.

Bhí cuid mhaith de sna Lochlannaigh a bhí 'na gcónaí in Éirinn an uair sin, ar mhór-shlua Bhriain, i gCíll Mhaighneann, ag cabhrú leis sa chath san, agus bhí ceart Éireannach, de réir dlithe na hÉireann, curtha i bhfeidhm aige dhóibh féin agus dá sliocht, mar gheall ar an gcabhrú san.

Bhí Ospac ann agus an méid nirt sló a tháinig aduaidh leis ó sna hoileánaibh nuair a dh'éalaigh sé ó Bhruadar. Do ghlac sé féin agus a dhaoine an Creideamh*, agus do bhaist Colla iad in Inis Cathaigh, agus chuireadar fé choimirce Sheanáin iad féin. Ansan do thánadar, in éineacht le mór-shlua Bhriain, chun an mhór-chatha. Do thuigeadar go raibh an cath le troid ar son an Chreidimh, agus bhí ' fhios acu go raibh neamh le fáil ag an té do thitfeadh i gcath a troidfí ar son an Chreidimh.

Bhí M'leachlainn Mór ann, rí na Mí, agus deich gcéad fear aige.

Tháinig a lán d'fhearaibh Uladh ann agus do luíodar isteach insna buínibh, fé mar a bhí aithne acu ar na fearaibh nú ar na ríthibh. Fir ab ea iad ná leogfadh a gcroí ná a n-aigne dhóibh fanúint sa bhaile nuair a bhí a leithéid de chath le bualadh, agus Éire go léir 'na leithéid de chúntúirt, agus an Creideamh 'na leithéid de chúntúirt.

Bhí an dá rí ó Albain ann agus neart maith láidir de Ghaelaibh Alban in éineacht leó.

De réir gach seanchais, bhí suas le fiche míle fear ag Brian i gCíll Mhaighneann an uair sin nuair a bhíodar go léir cruinnithe. De réir na gcúntaisí gcéanna bhí aon mhíle fhichead ag an namhaid. Ach bhí an deich gcéad fear insna héidíbh práis ar thaobh na Lochlannach, agus do measadh gur mhó le rá an deich gcéad san, i bhfrithghuin catha, ná deich míle de sna fearaibh ná raibh orthu ach na "léinteacha sróil".

Bhí Caoilte agus na giollaí eile ag teacht isteach coitianta ó bheith ag féachaint ar an namhaid agus dhá mbreithniú.

As na tuairiscibh a thugadar leó, do mheas Brian ná tiocfadh an namhaid amach chun catha go ceann seachtaine eile pé'r domhan é. Bhí Luan na Failme an uair sin ann. Bhí a neart go léir cruinnithe in aice Átha Cliath ag rí Laighean i gcómhair an chatha. Bhí Cúige Laighean gan chosaint. Dob ana-mhaith an rud, an fhaid a bheifí ag feitheamh leis an gcath, an Chúige sin do scrios agus bia don mhór-shlua do thabhairt aisti; a chur ' fhéachaint ar ríocht Mhaoilmhórdha an mhór-shlua do chothú.

Chuir Brian amach a mhac, Donncha, chun Cúige Laighean do scrios. Do ghluais Donncha i dtosach na hoíche, i dtreó ná feicfí ag imeacht é agus go mbeadh na creacha istigh aige sara mothódh an namhaid go raibh an gnó á dhéanamh in aon chor. Níor rug Donncha leis ar an gcuaird sin puínn thar cúig nú sé ' chéadaibh fear. Ní raibh aon ghnó aige dá thuilleadh.

An oíche do ghluais Donncha ó Chíll Mhaighneann, chun na hoibre sin a dhéanamh, b'in í díreach an oíche do chuir Gormfhlaith Amhlaoibh leis an dteachtaireacht, ó rí-theaghlach Shitric, ag triall ar Bhruadar, i ganfhios do Shitric agus i ganfhios do Bhéibheann. Bhí Amhlaoibh ábalta ar cheilt a chur air féin 'na lán de riochtaibh, agus ar é ' dhéanamh go maith. Nuair a bhí sé ag imeacht ón rí-theaghlach, do chuímhnigh sé in' aigne gur mhaith an rud do gabháil trí Chíll Mhaighneann, féachaint an bhféadfadh sé teacht suas le haon bhlúire eólais a bheadh tairbheach do Bhruadar. D'aimsigh sé mála agus chuir sé ar a mhuin é, mar dhea ná raibh ann ach duine de lucht leanúna an tslóigh agus go raibh sé ag díol nithe beaga a bheadh áiseach d'fhearaibh an tslóigh. Cá dtabharfadh sé aghaidh ach i dtreó an bhaíll 'na raibh Donncha agus a bhuíon ag tosnú ar ghluaiseacht ó dheas. Bhí iúnadh air. Do luigh sé ar chainnt le cuid den lucht leanúna a thárla in' aice. Níorbh fhada gur bhailigh sé uathu an toisc ar a raibh an bhuíon ag imeacht ó dheas, agus cé ' bhí 'na cheann orthu. Do bhailigh sé é féin amach ón lucht leanúna chómh tapaidh agus d'fhéad sé é gan aon droch-amhras a tharrac air féin. Chómh luath agus ' bhí sé bailithe uathu, thug sé aghaidh soir ó thuaidh, agus níorbh fhada go raibh sé ag cainnt le Bruadar. Ní baol gur ag triall ar Mhaolmhórdha a chuaigh sé chun a ínsint do go raibh buíon fear imithe ó dheas chun a thíre do scrios. Dá ndeineadh, b'fhéidir go ngluaiseódh Maolmhórdha ó dheas chun a thíre do chosaint, agus do lagódh san mór-shlua na Lochlannach i gcómhair an chatha. Ag triall ar Bhruadar a thug sé aghaidh.

"Is maith a dheinis é, a mhic ó!", arsa Bruadar leis. "Tá súil agam ná faighidh rí Laighean amach go bhfuil san ar siúl 'na thír. D'imeódh sé uainn láithreach agus ní oirfeadh dúinn scarúint le hoiread agus aon fhear amháin. Tá an scéal céanna díreach anso sa leitir seo agam ód mháthair, pé cuma 'na bhfuair sí amach é. Deir sí gur ceart dúinn an cath do throid láithreach sara mbeidh uain ag Donncha ar theacht thar n-ais".

"Is é mo thuairim-se, a rí", arsa Amhlaoibh, "go mbeidh easnamh níos mó ná easnamh Dhonncha agus a bhuíne ar an Árdrí nuair a thiocfaidh an cath".

"Cad é an t-easnamh eile a dh'fhéadfadh a bheith air?", arsa Bruadar.

"Tá rí cúige éigin ag déanamh a dhíchill chun a chur ' fhéachaint ar chuid de sna ríthibh eile tarrac siar ó Bhrian agus ó Dhál gCais nuair a thosnóidh an cath", arsa Amhlaoibh.

Caibideal 52: Fuadar agus Flosc agus Giodam

"Dar so 's súd ach má deintear san, beidh an cath ar ár dtoil féin againn!", arsa Bruadar. "An dó' leat", ar seisean, "an bhfuil ag éirí leis an rí cúige sin?"

"De réir mar ' airíos an chainnt", arsa Amhlaoibh, "do bheartaíos go raibh ag éirí leis maith go leór".

"Ó, is maith é sin!", arsa Bruadar. "Imigh, a lao", ar seisean, "agus cuir chúm an draoi".

Fear ab ea Bruadar a dhein, i dtosach a bheatha, an rud céanna díreach a dhein Amhlaoibh nuair a bhí sé in Inis Cathaigh. Do ghlac sé an Creideamh, agus ansan do ghlac sé na hÚird i dtreó gur deineadh *deacon* de.* Dhá *dheacon* ab ea é féin agus Amhlaoibh. Ansan níor lean Bruadar den Chreideamh. Do shéan sé é agus chaith sé uaidh é, díreach mar a dhein Amhlaoibh. Nuair a chaith sé uaidh an Creideamh, d'iompaigh sé ar dhiablaíocht agus ar dhraíocht agus ar dheamhnaibh agus ar phiseógaibh, agus ar an uile shaghas deismireachta den tsórd san, i dtreó go ndeirtí go raibh ar a chumas a lán nithe iúntacha do dhéanamh le cómhacht deamhan.

Tháinig an draoi. D'inis Bruadar do conas mar a bhí cuid de shlua Bhriain imithe amach ag creachadh Cúige Laighean, agus conas mar a bhí cuid de sna ríthibh ag iompáil i gcoinnibh Bhriain.

"Agus anois", ar seisean leis an ndraoi, "cad í do chómhairle dhom? Is mise, mar is eól duit, is fear cínn riain ar an mór-shlua so. Is agam atá lá an chatha do cheapadh. Dá dtugainn an t-órdú anois", ar seisean, "bheimís ollamh chun an chatha do thosnú go moch ar maidin Dé hAoine. Cad 'deirir liom?"

Do stad an draoi ar feadh tamaill. Tar éis machnaimh do labhair sé.

"Má troidtear an cath so Dé hAoine", ar seisean, "titfidh Brian. Má troidtear an cath aon lá eile, titfidh sibh-se go léir".

Caibideal 52: Fuadar agus Flosc agus Giodam

Nuair a bhí an méid sin ráite aige, d'iompaigh sé ar a sháil agus d'imigh sé chun a chábáin féin.

Do stad an bheirt, Bruadar agus Amhlaoibh, ag féachaint 'na dhiaidh. Nuair a bhí sé imithe as a radharc, do labhair Bruadar.

"Tuigim é", ar seisean. "Má throidimíd Dé hAoine, beidh Donncha gan filleadh agus beidh an rí cúige seo adeirir-se in earraid le Brian. Má fantar níos sia gan an cath do throid, beidh Maolmhórdha imithe chun a chúige do chosaint, beidh Donncha tagaithe thar n-ais agus na creacha aige. Chífidh an rí cúige seo adeirir-se an dá ní sin, Maolmhórdha imithe agus Donncha tagaithe agus na creacha aige, agus luífidh sé isteach in' inead féin sa chath. Ansan beidh Brian ró-láidir dúinn go léir. Sin é brí na cainnte sin aduairt an draoi. Ní foláir an focal do chur amach anois i measc na sló so go léir go bhfuil an cath le tosnú ar maidin Dé hAoine".

Do cuireadh amach an focal. Do hínseadh, leis, don mhór-shlua go léir, an focal aduairt draoi Bhruadair, dá dtroidtí an cath Dé hAoine go dtitfeadh Brian, ach dá bhfágtí gan troid é ní ba shia ná go hAoine go dtitfeadh na Lochlannaigh agus a lucht cúnta go léir. Do thuig an mhór-shlua as san dá dtroidtí an cath Dé hAoine a bhí chúinn go mbeadh an bua ag na Lochlannaigh.

Dá bhrí sin, chómh luath agus ' fuaradar an focal, thosnaíodar go léir ar iad féin d'ollmhú i gcómhair an chatha. Ní raibh puínn thar ocht n-uaire is daichead acu an uair sin chun an ollmhúcháin a dhéanamh. Níor bheag leó an méid sin aimsire. Dá luathacht a troidfí an cath dob ea ab fheárr é, dar leó. Bhíodar deimhnitheach go mbuafaidís. Bhíothas tar éis a chur 'na luí orthu go daingean ná raibh ag Brian de mhór-shlua ach sloigisc a bhí ní ba thugtha go mór chun iompáil ar a chéile ná mar a bhíodar chun troda ' dhéanamh le namhaid. Go raibh cuid de sna ríthibh cúige agus ná rabhadar ach ag feitheamh leis an gcath do thosnú chun druím lámha ' thabhairt le Brian agus é féin agus Clann Chais do thréigean. Go raibh cúis a ndóthain ag á lán acu chuige sin, mar go raibh lámh Bhriain ana-dhian orthu, agus dá dhéine a bhí lámh Bhriain orthu gur thuigeadar go mbeadh lámh Mhurchadh ní ba sheacht ndéine orthu nuair a thiocfaidís fúithi. Nuair a thosnódh an cath gurbh ea do chífí an neamh-ghus a bhí i gcómhacht Bhriain, dá mhéid leatha a bhí faoi* agus dá aoirde cáil a bhí air. Ach pé breith a bheadh aige ar bhuachtaint sa chath dá mbeadh an dá shlua mar a chéile i dtaobh arm, ná raibh aon bhreith in aon chor aige ar bhuachtaint nuair a bhí an deich gcéad fear insna héidíbh práis ag na Lochlannaigh. Go siúlódh an deich gcéad fear san rómpu trí mhór-shlua Bhriain agus go ngeóbhaidís de chosaibh iontu. Dá luathacht, dá bhrí sin, a troidfí an cath dob ea ab fheárr é, dar leó, mar b'in mar ba thúisce a dh'fhéadfaidís iad féin do leathadh isteach ar mhachairibh breátha míne na hÉireann agus seilbh a ghlacadh iontu. Bhí fonn agus flosc agus giodam agus meanmna agus mór-chroí, dá bhrí sin, orthu féin agus ar a mnáibh, agus fuadar an domhain fúthu, nuair a rith an focal mórthímpall eatarthu go dtroidfí an cath ar maidin Dé hAoine a bhí chúinn. Níor chodail éinne acu an chuid eile den oíche sin, bhí a leithéid sin d'fhothram agus de ghleó ar siúl ó cheann ceann den longphort.

Níorbh fhada go bhfuaradh amach i longphort Bhriain cad a bhí ar siúl, agus cad fé ndeár an gleó agus an fothram. Bhí Caoilte agus a ghiollaí turais anso agus ansúd, fé cheilt, i measc na Lochlannach. Thugadar leó ag triall ar mhór-shlua Bhriain tuairisc cruínn ar an ollmhúchán. Thosnaigh na Gaeil ar iad féin d'ollmhú láithreach. Bhí an t-ollmhúchán ar siúl go tréan sa dá longphort i ndeireadh na hoíche sin agus i gcaitheamh an lae amáirigh, agus i gcaitheamh na cod' eile den aimsir as san go hAoine.

Caibideal 53: Daoine Ciallmhara ag Féachaint Rómpu Amach

Dá mhéid a bhí deimhne ag Bruadar agus ag Amhlaoibh, agus ag an gcuid eile acu, ar bhuachtaint sa mhór-chath a bhí ag teacht, is ea ba mhó a bhíodar ag féachaint rómpu amach agus ag cuímhneamh ar na nithibh a dhéanfaidís tar éis an chatha.

Do labhair Amhlaoibh le Bruadar.

"A leithéid seo, a rí", ar seisean. "Is tusa a bheidh in Árdríocht na hÉireann tar éis an chatha so".

"B'fhéidir é", arsa Bruadar, "ach ca bhfios duit-se sin?"

"Táim deimhnitheach de", arsa Amhlaoibh. "Do gheall Sitric duit go dtabharfadh sé mo mháthair duit. Ní foláir do an ghealluint sin do sheasamh. Ansan, an té go mbeidh an Árdríogan aige, beidh an Árdríocht aige".

"Mheasas", arsa Bruadar, "gur chun na hÁrdríochta ' thabhairt do Shitric a tosnaíodh an obair seo ar dtúis".

"Mheasas-sa, leis, é", arsa Amhlaoibh, "ach measaim rud eile anois. Chím athrú ar aigne mo mháthar ó thosnaigh na slóite móra so ar chruinniú féna súil. Ní déarfainn ná go bhfuil ' fhios agat féin, a rí, gur duit a tabharfar an Árdríocht, agus nách inniu ná inné do thosnaís ar ' fhios a bheith agat".

"Nár gealladh Árdríogan agus Árdríocht don Iarla?", arsa Bruadar.

"Ní ceist ag lorg eólais í sin, a rí", arsa Amhlaoibh. "Tá freagra na ceiste sin agat féin cheana agus ní gá dhómh-sa í ' fhreagairt duit".

"Is fíor, a mhic ó", arsa Bruadar, "ach cad 'tá uait? Tá ' fhios agam go dteastaíonn uait ní éigin a dh'iarraidh orm nuair a bhead i m' Árdrí, agus gur maith leat an ní sin do chur in áirithe dhuit féin roim ré".

"Sin é díreach a theastaíonn uaim, a rí", arsa Amhlaoibh.

Caibideal 53: Daoine Ciallmhara ag Féachaint Rómpu Amach

"Tá go maith. Comáin leat. Ach ba dhó' liom, ó tá ' fhios agat anois cé hé thu, go dtuigfá i t'aigne ná fuil aon ghá leis an gcur in áirithe roim ré. Ach comáin leat", arsa Bruadar.

"Nuair a bhíos-sa in Inis Cathaigh", arsa Amhlaoibh, "chuireas aithne ann ar mhac do Thadhg Mhór Ó Chealla. Tá aithne agat ar Thadhg Mhór Ó Chealla".

"Tá. An fear so adeirtear atá níos treise agus níos cróga ná Murchadh féin", arsa Bruadar.

"Sin é é", arsa Amhlaoibh. "Chuireas aithne ar a mhac. Buachaill bocht símplí is ea é. Ach do chuamair ar chuaird ó thuaidh go hUíbh Máine, go rí-theaghlach Thaidhg Mhóir. Chonac ríogan óg ansan, iníon do Thadhg Mhór. Niamh a tugtí uirthi. Ní fheacaigh mo dhá shúil riamh roimis sin, ná ó shin, aon ní i riocht duine chómh hálainn léi. Mheasas gur bhain a háilleacht mo radharc díom. Ach san am gcéanna, ar an gcéad amharc, do buaileadh isteach i m'aigne go raibh sí go holc. Ní hí a bhí go holc ach mise. Tháinig sí go Ceann Cora 'na dhiaidh san chun bheith ag faire ar mo mháthair le heagla go dtabharfadh sí nimh do Bhrian. Chuir mo mháthair aithne uirthi. Bhíos ag cainnt lem mháthair uair, i gcaitheamh na haimsire 'na raibh Brian ar a chuaird rí. Duairt sí liom go raibh dearúd mór déanta agam i dtaobh Niamh. Thuigeas gurbh fhíor di é. Do chaitheas a gheallúint di dá n-éiríodh ár n-obair linn go bpósfainn Niamh".

"An nduairt sí leat", arsa Bruadar, " go bpósfadh Niamh thu?"

"Táim féin deimhnitheach, ón gcéad amharc úd, go bpósfaidh. Is é rud atá agam le hiarraidh ort, nuair a bheir-se in Árdríocht na hÉireann, go dtabharfair ríghe Connacht dómh-sa agus do Niamh".

"Ambasa, a mhic ó", arsa Bruadar, "tabharfad agus fáilte. Tabharfad ríghe Connacht duit peocu ' thógfaidh sí thu nú ná tógfaidh".

Caibideal 53: Daoine Ciallmhara ag Féachaint Rómpu Amach

In áit eile, sa mhór-shlua chéanna, bhí beirt eile agus iad ag féachaint rómpu ar an gcuma gcéanna agus iad ag socrú nithe go hálainn, dar leó. B'iad beirt iad san ná Maolmhórdha agus Sitric. Níor ró-fhuiriste do Shitric nithe do shocrú i gcómhairle le Maolmhórdha, mar fear ró-bhaoth, ró-bhéal-scaoilte, ab ea Maolmhórdha, agus ní féadfí aon eólas a thabhairt do ach eólas nár mhiste a leogaint amach.

"Is dócha, a rí", arsa Sitric le Maolmhórdha, "ná fuil aon teip ná go mbuafaimíd sa chath so atá le troid Dé hAoine".

"Níl, a mhic ó", arsa Maolmhórdha. "Ní fhéadfadh a bheith. Chuirfeadh an deich gcéad fear so insna héidíbh práis in áirithe dhúinn é dá mba ná beadh aon ní eile chun é ' chur in áirithe dhúinn. Ach tá a lán nithe chun é ' chur in áirithe dhúinn. Airím-se go bhfuil socair ag M'leachlainn Mór ar tharrac siar ón gcath chómh luath agus ' thosnóidh an cath. Ní haon iúnadh in aon chor go mbeadh socair aige ar a leithéid".

"Agus cad 'na thaobh nár fhan sé thiar sa bhaile agus gan teacht in aon chor, fé mar a dh'fhan tuilleadh acu?", arsa Sitric.

"D'fhanfadh, leis, ach go bhfuil socair aige ar níos mó díobhála ' dhéanamh do Bhrian ná mar a dhéanfadh sé dho dá bhfanadh sé thiar sa bhaile", arsa Maolmhórdha.

"Agus cad é an díobháil eile atá beartaithe aige a dhéanamh?", arsa Sitric.

"Tá sé ag brath air go mbéarfaidh sé leis as an gcath beirt nú triúr eile de sna ríthibh atá dílis fós do Bhrian. Ní fhéadfadh rí na nDéiseach aon ghrá ró-mhór a bheith aige do Bhrian; ná rí Ó nEachach Múmhan; ná tuilleadh acu", arsa Maolmhórdha.

"Agus cogar, a rí", arsa Sitric, "cad is dó' leat a dhéanfaidh mo mháthair tar éis an chatha?"

Caibideal 53: Daoine Ciallmhara ag Féachaint Rómpu Amach

"Cad a dhéanfadh sí", arsa Maolmhórdha, "ach an rud atá geallta aici ó thosach, thusa ' chur san Árdríocht?"

"Mura dtiocfadh aon lucht droch-chómhairle chúithi a chuirfeadh suas í chun a haigne d'athrú", arsa Sitric.

"Cé hé an droch-chómhairleóir a dh'fhéadfadh í ' chur suas chun a haigne ' dh'athrú'?", arsa Maolmhórdha.

"Ní fheadar 'en domhan, a rí", arsa Sitric, "ach tá roinnt nithe agam á thabhairt fé ndeara le déanaí agus ba ró-mhaith liom do chómhairle-se ' dh'fháil 'na dtaobh. B'fhéidir go bhfuil an éagóir agam. Má tá, sin mar is feárr é. Ach ní dhéanfaidh do chómhairle-se aon díobháil dom peocu 'tá an éagóir agam nú ná fuil".

"Cad 'tá agat dá thabhairt fé ndeara?", arsa Maolmhórdha.

"Tá so agam á thabhairt fé ndeara", arsa Sitric. "I dtosach na hoibre seo is dómh-sa a thugadh sí an chuid ba mhó dá haigne. Im chómhairle-se a chuireadh sí gach aon rud, go mór mór na nithe ba mhó a dheineadh buairt di. Ansan, fé mar a ghluais an aimsir, bhíodh an triúr againn in éineacht ins gach cómhairle, mise agus Amhlaoibh agus í féin. Táim á thabhairt fé ndeara le déanaí gur d'Amhlaoibh a thugann sí a haigne ar fad. Nuair a chuir sí ó thuaidh me chun a dh'iarraidh ar Bhruadar teacht agus a neart sló ' thabhairt leis, duairt sí liom a gheallúint do, dá mba rud é ná cuirfeadh aon rud eile ' fhéachaint air teacht, a gheallúint do go dtabharfainn í féin do agus Árdríocht na hÉireann, dá mbeirimís bua. Mheasas an uair sin ná raibh insna geallúnaibh ach neamhní. Is eagal liom anois nách neamhní in aon chor iad. Agus is eagal liom go bhfuil ' fhios ag Amhlaoibh nách neamhní iad".

"Ó 'sea!", arsa Maolmhórdha, "agus go bhfuil Amhlaoibh ag cabhrú le Bruadar san obair!"

Caibideal 53: Daoine Ciallmhara ag Féachaint Rómpu Amach

"Bhuailis do mhéar air, a rí", arsa Sitric.

"Tá go maith, a mhic ó", arsa Maolmhórdha. "Is maith a dheinis an méid sin a dh'ínsint dom. Ná leog aon ní ort leó. Nuair a bheidh an ruagairt curtha againn ar shlóitibh Bhriain, iompóimíd araon, tusa agus mise, ar shlua Bhruadair, agus dísceóimíd iad. Ansan ní bheidh éinne chun teacht idir thusa agus an Árdríocht".

Shocraíodar an méid sin chun a dtoile go hálainn. Nuair a bhí an socrú déanta acu, áfach, bhí socrú nárbh é in' aigne féin ag gach duine acu.

"Is agam-sa féin a bheidh an Árdríocht i ndeireadh bára, agus ní hagat-sa ná ag Bruadar!", arsa Maolmhórdha, in' aigne féin.

"Ní haon iúntaoibh tu, a dhriotháir mo mháthar", arsa Sitric, in' aigne féin. "Níl agam", ar seisean, "ach an úsáid is feárr a dh'fhéadfad a dhéanamh díot, agus ansan—me féin do sheachaint ort chómh maith agus d'fhéadfad é!

Bhí beirt eile in áit eile, sa mhór-shlua, agus bhí cainnt eatarthu, leis. B'iad beirt iad san ná Cnút agus Anrud, beirt mhac rí na hIorua.

"Ar airís, a dhriotháir", arsa Cnút, "cé 'tá le bheith in' Árdrí ar Éirinn i ndiaidh an chatha so a troidfar Dé hAoine?"

"D'airíos a lán ráflaí", arsa Anrud, "ach ní fheadar an ceart puínn suime ' chur iontu. D'airíos ar dtúis gur do Bhruadar a tabharfí an Árdríocht agus an Árdríogan. D'airíos ansan gur do Shitric, rí Lochlannach Átha Cliath, a tabharfí an Árdríocht. Ach tá muíntir an Iarla deimhnitheach gurb é an tIarla a bheidh in' Árdrí; gur gheall Sitric an Árdríocht agus an Árdríogan in éineacht do".

"Tá an scéal go léir cruínn agat", arsa Cnút. "is léir, as na ráflaíbh sin ná fuiltear socair i gceart ar cé aige go mbeidh an Árdríocht".

"Is fíor san, a dhriotháir", arsa Anrud, "ach cad é sin dúinn-na ceocu atáthar socair air nú ná fuiltear?"

"Is mórán nithe dhúinn é", arsa Cnút. "Ar thánamair-na anso, sinn féin agus ár mór-shlua, tar éis mórán costais do chur ar ár dtír féin, treasna farraigí fuara, chun ár n-anama ' dh'imirt i bhfrithghuin catha, i gcoinnibh Bhriain agus Dál gCais, i dtreó go bhfaigheadh Bruadar Árdríocht agus Árdríogan?"

"Ní mheasaim gur chuige sin a thánamair", arsa Anrud.

"Ar thánamair i dtreó go bhfaigheadh an tIarla iad?", arsa Cnút.

"Ní mheasaim gur thánamair", arsa Anrud.

"Ar thánamair chun Árdrí ' dhéanamh de Shitric?", arsa Cnút.

"Ní mheasaim é", arsa Anrud. "Ní cneasta an fhéachaint a thabharfadh ár n-athair orainn nuair a raighimís abhaile dá mba ná beadh de bhárr ár gcuarda againn ach Árdrí ' dhéanamh de Shitric", ar seisean. "Ach cad 'tá beartaithe agat?"

"Neósfad-sa san duit", arsa Cnút. "Tá sé daingean i m'aigne, chómh luath agus ' bheidh buaite againn ar mhór-shlua Bhriain go n-éireóid na ríthe seo go léir chun a chéile agus go mbeidh sé 'na chogadh dhearg eatarthu. Leogaimís dóibh a chéile do dhísciú, agus ansan bíodh Éire againn féin!"

"Is maith an chómhairle í", arsa Anrud. "Nuair a bheidh Éire againn féin, tiocfaidh m'athair anall agus déanfaimíd Árdrí dhe".

"Thar a bhfeacaís riamh!", arsa Cnút.

Níor chodail an bheirt sin puínn an oíche sin ach ag socrú an scéil sin, agus shocraíodar é chun a dtoile go hálainn.

Caibideal 54: Rosc Catha Bhriain

Ar éirí lae ar maidin Dé hAoine, ar maidin Aoine an Chéasta, bhí Béibheann agus Gormfhlaith thuas i mbarra rí-theaghlaigh Shitric in Áth Cliath, agus iad ag féachaint anonn treasna an chuain ar na línte fada cábán. Chonacadar na slóite go léir ag gluaiseacht amach agus dhá gcur féin in eagar. Níorbh fhada go bhfeacadar na híona fada dhá riaradh féin, fan na trá, lasmu' de sna cábánaibh.

Chonacadar lasmu' arís, i bhfad amach, ar aghaidh na Lochlannach anonn, íona eile dhá gcur féin in eagar, agus do thuig an bheirt ríogan go raibh na híona amu' chómh fada, chómh líonmhar, chómh láidir ar gach aon tsaghas cuma le híonaibh na Lochlannach.

"Ní mheasaim go bhfuil puínn sa mbreis ag aon taobh acu ar a chéile i dtaobh nirt sló", arsa Béibheann.

"Ní líonmhaire a dheineann neart i gcónaí", arsa Gormfhlaith, "ná ní hé a bheireann bua".

"Is fíor", arsa Béibheann. "Dá bhfeicinn-se m'athair agus Murchadh agus Dál gCais i láthair catha agus a dtrí n-oiread nirt sló 'na gcoinnibh, ní bheadh aon eagal orm ná go mbeadh an bua acu".

"Fan leat go fóill", arsa Gormfhlaith, "go bhfeicir lucht na n-éidí práis úd thall ag tabhairt aghaidh orthu. Ansan is ea ' chífir cad a dhéanfaidh Murchadh agus Clann Chais".

"Is fíor!", arsa Béibheann.

Bhí na híona catha, ó gach taobh, ag teacht fé dhéin a chéile. Bhí na Lochlannaigh ag gluaiseacht go hana-réidh. D'órdaigh na ríthe agus na taoiseacha dhóibh siúl go réidh i dtreó ná beadh saothar orthu nuair a thiocfaidís lámh le láimh agus ucht le hucht leis an namhaid. Bhí íona na nGael, leis, ag teacht go réidh agus go stuama.

Caibideal 54: Rosc Catha Bhriain

Do hórdaíodh do sna Gaelaibh stad. Do stadadar.

Nuair a bhíodar 'na stad tháinig an tÁrdrí amach os a gcómhair agus é ar muin capaill agus beirt fhear ag ceann an chapaill agus greim acu ar an sriain. Bhí a chlaíomh nocht in áirde ag an Árdrí, 'na láimh dheis, an claíomh a bhí tar éis rian a bhéil do chur ar Lochlannachaibh ins gach aon pháirt den Mhúmhain agus ins gach aon pháirt d'Éirinn. D'aithin an tslua go léir an claíomh san, agus nuair a chonacadar in áirde é, thugadar trí gártha molta do féin agus don Árdrí. Le línn na ngártha san a thabhairt dóibh, d'árdaigh gach fear a chlaíomh féin. Bhí an ghrian díreach ag éirí. Do thaithn solas na gréine ar na claimhtibh go léir agus iad in áirde, i dtreó gur mheas Béibheann agus Gormfhlaith go raibh slóite Bhriain trí thine.

Do thóg Brian in áirde, 'na láimh chlé, an Chrois Chéasta agus íomhá an tSlánaitheóra uirthi. Ansan do cuireadh an capall ag siúl go réidh, fan na n-íona, ar aghaidh na sló amach, agus do labhair an tÁrdrí mar seo:

"A Chlanna Gael, a ríogra Éireann, táimíd go léir le tamall maith dhár n-ollmhú féin i gcómhair an lae seo. Tá aon ní amháin socair againn agus measaim gur feárr d'ollmhú é ná aon ollmhú eile atá déanta againn. Tá socair ag gach fear againn gurb é an lá inniu lá a bháis féin pé taobh ar a mbeidh bua. Más ag ár namhaid a bheidh bua, ní bheidh a smacht orainn-na, mar ní bheimíd beó acu chuige. Más againn-na a bheidh bua an lae seo, bíodh a thoradh ag an muíntir atá 'nár ndiaidh sa bhaile.

"An té go bhfuil socair in' aigne aige ar bhás d'fháil sa chath so atá le troid againn ní baol go n-iompóidh sé ón gcath. Dá mba ná beadh aon ní eile chun bua do chur in áirithe dhúinn, cuirfidh san in áirithe dhúinn é. Dá mbeadh ' fhios ag an namhaid go bhfuil ár n-aigne socair mar sin againn-na, ní ró-mhór an misneach a bheadh anois orthu. Gheóbhaid siad amach ar ball é".

Caibideal 54: Rosc Catha Bhriain

Do labhair sé focal fé leith le gach rí agus le gach *cinel* fé mar a tháinig sé ar a n-aghaidh amach, focal éigin a chuir a n-uaisleacht féin agus a gcrógacht i gcuímhne dhóibh, agus conas mar a bhí Dia agus daoine ag faire ar an gcuma 'na ndéanfaidís gníomh an lae a bhí rómpu. Nuair a tháinig sé ar aghaidh Dál gCais, duairt sé:

*"A Chlann Chais, a shliocht ríoga! A mhuíntir na n-arm ngéar agus na gcrua-lámh, nár staon agus nár stríoc do namhaid fós riamh, i gcath dá thruime, in éigin dá ghéire, i spéirling dá dhéine, mo sheasamh inniu oraibh!"

Ansan d'árdaigh sé a ghlór agus do sheinn a ghuth mar a sheinnfeadh fuaim adhairce, i dtreó gur hairíodh agus gur tuigeadh an uile fhocal uaidh ó cheann ceann den mhór-shlua:

"Féach* ansúd iad!", ar seisean, ag síneadh a chlaímh i dtreó na Lochlannach, "cruinnithe cnósta os úr gcómhair. Tá rian úr lámh go daingean cheana orthu. Ní thugann san ciall dóibh. Is minic le fiche bliain a chuiriúir-se anaithe agus teitheadh agus ár agus dearg-ruathar orthu, ar fuid réithe agus gleannta agus machairí Éireann. Is mór dá gcuid fola agus feóla atá ag cur geamhair agus féir ghlais ag fás in Éirinn inniu. Go dtí so, ba chuma iad nú corrmhíola; dá mhéid a maraítí dhíobh, ní samhlaítí easnamh ná laíghead orthu. Is fada sinn cráite acu, iad ag faire ar ár gcuantaibh agus ar ár mbailtibh puirt, ag preabadh chúinn isteach nuair ná bíodh coinne leó, ag bradaíol agus ag sciobadh agus ag coscar. Is minic a leogadh as iad agus croch tuíllte acu. B'é a mbaochas teacht arís agus feall ní ba mheasa do dhéanamh. An fada a curfar suas leis an obair sin? Is dócha gur dó' leó go leogfar as inniu iad mar a leogadh chómh minic cheana. Bíodh san de dhearúd orthu, a chlann ó! Ná téadh fear ínste scéil abhaile dhíobh! Níor cuireadh fios orthu. Do thánadar uathu féin. Is minic adúradh leó go dtiocfaidís agus ná himeóidís. Deintear deimhin inniu de dhóibh. An amhlaidh a cheapadar ná raibh éinne 'na chónaí ar an oileán so? Má dheineadar dearúd, bíodh orthu féin anois.

"Tá aon mhaith amháin sa dearúd atá déanta acu. Do thánadar go léir. Féachaidh, a chlann ó, féach an tsloigisc sin. Tá 'an chráin 's a hál go léir' ansan agaibh. Tá a bhfuil beó de chlannaibh Lochlann ansan agaibh. Táid siad bailithe ansan agaibh ó Bhreatain agus ó Shasana, ó Albain agus aduaidh ó sna hoileánaibh, anall ó Mhanainn agus anoir ó chríochaibh Danmharg agus ó riascaibh na hIorua. Níl a thuilleadh 'na ndiaidh sa bhaile gur fiú iad d'áireamh. Múchaidh an saithe san inniu, agus tá deireadh le réim Lochlannach go brách na breithe!"

Lena línn sin, do chonacadar go léir M'leachlainn agus a dheich gcéad fear ag imeacht as a n-inead. Duairt Brian:

"Chím cuid agaibh ag amharc anonn treasna na páirce sin. Ní maith an radharc atá le feiscint ann. Is mairg do Mh'leachlainn, díreach mar is mairg do Mhac Giolla Phádraig agus dá Laighnibh, caismirt an lae inniu do sheachnadh. Déanfar gníomh an lae inniu gan a gcabhair. Béarfar bua an lae inniu os cómhair a súl agus gan iad páirteach ann. Beidh san de mhasla agus de ghuith ar a gclú agus ar a gcáil an dá lá 's an fhaid a bheidh grian ar spéir agus daoine ar talamh.

"Tá cuid dár muíntir féin amu' uainn. Ná bac san. Tá oiread againn anso agus ' shocróidh cúntas leis an sloigisc sin thall. Is cúntas fada é. Is mithid é ' shocrú. Anois an t-am chun é ' shocrú. Is iad ár namhaid iad. Is iad namhaid ár gCreidimh iad. Tá rian na tine ar eaglaisíbh agus ar mhainistríbh Éireann 'na ndiaidh. Beidh lámh Dé linn dhá dhíogailt san inniu orthu.

"Cad é an lá é seo inniu againn? Inniu an Aoine. Is í Aoine an Chéasta féin í", agus d'árdaigh sé an Chrois Chéasta i radharc an tslóigh go léir. "I gcuímhneamh an lae inniu", ar seisean, "is ea d'fhuilig ár Slánaitheóir Íosa Críost bás ar chrann na Croise chun an Chreidimh do chur ar bun. Táimíd-na anso inniu ag tabhairt aghaidh ar an mbás chun an Chreidimh do chosnamh. An dó' leat ná go mbeidh lámh chómhachtach an tSlánaitheóra linn sa ghleó? An dó' leat ná go mbeidh meanmna ó Dhia inniu i gcroí gach fir a thabharfaidh aghaidh ar an namhaid sin? Beidh; agus más anso atá fód ár mbáis, beidh bás an tSlánaitheóra féin mar urrús againn air go raghaidh ár n-anam saor ón bhfód so go Flaitheas na ngrást".

Ansan d'éirigh a ghlór ní b'aoirde agus ní ba bhinne:

"Gabhaidh chúthu, a chlann ó, in ainm Dé agus Mhuire. Tugaidh an faobhar dóibh! Gabhaidh de chosaibh iontu! Ní hé an chéad uair agaibh é. Ná téadh aon mhac máthar acu beó uaibh. Ná cuiridh suím 'na gcótaibh iarainn. Cótaí troma is ea iad. Tá aon mhaith amháin iontu: cimeádfaid siad na fir díbh-se chun na gceann a bhaint díobh. Do thánadar chun fanúint. Fanaidís, in ainm Dé. Tá slí fén bhfód anso dhóibh. Tugtar dóibh é go fial!"

Ansan do labhair sé le Dál gCais:

"A chlann ó, a óga mo chroí, a chine uasal! Is maith is eól dómh-sa úr ngníomh. Feiceam an gníomh san inniu uaibh, agus geallfad díbh go mairfidh a thoradh agus a chlú an fhaid a bheidh uisce ag rith agus féar ag fás in Éirinn!"

Um an dtaca 'na raibh an méid sin cainnte déanta ag Brian, bhí an namhaid ag teacht i gcóngar. Tháinig Tadhg Mór Ó Cealla agus Murchadh agus tuilleadh de sna ríthibh, agus chuireadar ' fhiachaibh ar Bhrian dul agus fanúint 'na chábán, mar go raibh sé ró-aosta chun dul sa chath, agus dá dtitfeadh sé sa chath go gcuirfeadh san misneach ar an namhaid. Dhein sé rud orthu, agus do cuireadh lucht cosanta tímpall ar an gcábán.

Caibideal 55: An Cath

Um an dtaca 'na raibh Brian socair 'na chábán agus an lucht cosanta 'na thímpall, bhí an dá shlua i ngiorracht cúpla péirse dá chéile. Do léim fear mór amach a slua na Lochlannach agus do labhair sé.

Caibideal 55: An Cath

"An bhfuil Dónall mac Éimhin anso?", ar seisean.

"Tá sé anso", arsa Dónall, ag teacht amach a slua na nGael.

Thug an bheirt aghaidh ar a chéile. Do bhuail gach fear díobh aon bhuille amháin ar an bhfear eile agus do thit an bheirt marbh ar an bhfód.

Ansan do séideadh na hadharca ar gach taobh, do rith an dá shlua chun a chéile agus do thosnaigh an t-éirleach. Bhí solas na gréine ag neartú agus ní raibh an solas insna súilibh ar aon tslua acu, mar bhí an ghrian ag taithneamh anoir díreach, ar láimh dheis na Lochlannach agus ar láimh chlé na nGael. I dtosach an chómhraic, ní raibh puínn de sna fearaibh ag titim ar aon taobh, mar bhí an chosaint chómh maith leis an mbualadh. Aon áit sa tímpall 'na raibh cnucán ná árdán, bhí mná agus daoine óga in áirde ar na hárdánaibh ag faire ar an gcómhrac. Níor mhar a chéile cómhrac an uair sin agus cómhrac anois. Ní fhéadfadh éinne dul in aon ghaobhar do chómhrac anois mar gheall ar an arm tine. An uair sin, d'fhéadfadh mná agus mion-daoine teacht achomair go maith don chómhrac. Bhí mná na Lochlannach cruinnithe ins gach sórd áite 'nar fhéadadar aon radharc a dh'fháil ar an gcómhrac. Do chonacadar na claimhte dá gcasadh agus iad ag taithneamh sa ghréin. Chonacadar gach buille dá chosaint, le faobhar nú le sciath, chómh tiubh agus do thagadh sé. D'airíodar fuaim na mbuillí ar na sciathaibh agus screadach na bhfaobhar i gcoinnibh a chéile, agus guthanna árda na dtaoiseach ag labhairt leis na fearaibh, agus dranntán na namhad chun a chéile le línn na mbuillí do bhualadh dhóibh, agus do mheasc na fuaimeanna san ar a chéile ó dhaichead míle namhad, i dtreó dá ndúnadh duine a shúile agus éisteacht leis an ngleic, gur dhó' leis gur choíll mhór a bhí trí thine, agus an lasair ag búirthigh agus an t-adhmad ag cnagarnaigh le neart na tine.

Do lean an cómhrac ar an gcuma san ar feadh i bhfad agus an ghrian ag dridim suas ar an spéir, agus is go hana-mhall a bhí sí ag dridim suas. Ansan, do thosnaigh na fir ar thitim. Bhí saothar agus tuirse ag teacht ar chuid acu agus bhí an chosaint ag teip.

Maolmhórdha agus a Laighneacha is iad a bhí aghaidh ar aghaidh le Dál gCais agus bhí slua mhór de sna Lochlannaigh ag cabhru leó.

Nuair a bhíodh tuirse ag teacht ar a namhaid is ea ba ghnáth le Dál gCais breis nirt agus breis fuinnimh do theacht iontu. Bhí san ag teacht iontu an uair sin. Bhí idir Laighneacha agus Lochlannaigh ag titim féna mbuillibh, agus bhí an chuid nár thit díobh ag dul i ndiaidh a gcúil go ríghin. Ba dheocair iad do chur i ndiaidh a gcúil. Bhí greim maith acu ar an bhfód.

Ach bhí Clann Chais ábalta ar a ngreim a bhogadh ón bhfód. Bhí Murchadh ann agus a dhá chlaíomh aige, mar ba ghnáth, agus nuair a thugadh sé aghaidh ar fhear, do thiteadh an fear san gan a thuilleadh cáirde. Bhí Dúlainn ann agus é chómh tapaidh, chómh maraitheach leis an león. "Fear na mbuillí dtroma" a thugadh na Lochlannaigh air. Bhí mac Mhurchadh ann agus an dá chlaíomh aige, mar a bhíodh ag á athair. Dar leis na Lochlannaigh, bhí sé chómh holc len' athair. Ní haithneófí ó chéile iad ach gan an fhéasóg a bheith ar an mac.

B'é focal deirineach aduairt Niamh ar maidin le Dúlainn ná "A Dhúlainn, ná tabhair do cheann leat ón gcath so má leogann tú buille i gceann Chonnla!"

Ní rabhadar i bhfad sa chath nuair a chonaic Dúlainn nár ghá d'éinne ceann Chonnla do chosaint; go raibh a lámh dheas féin ábalta ar a cheann do chosaint go feilmeanta. Agus ar nós Clainne Chais go léir, is ag dul i bhfuinniúlacht a bhí a chroí agus a ghéaga fé mar a bhí an cath ag dul i ndéine. Bhí an namhaid ag dul i ndiaidh a gcúil, agus iad ag titim, agus Dál gCais ag brú orthu agus dhá leagadh; agus bhí an ghrian ag dridim suas ar an spéir go mall. Bhí an ghaoth anoir agus í go maith láidir ionnuar anamúil, agus ba mhór an tairbhe an méid sin do sna fearaibh, ar gach taobh, mar bhí allas ag teacht orthu agus teas an chómhraic ag cur orthu, go mór mór ar an gcuid acu ná raibh taithí ró-mhaith acu ar an saghas san oibre. Níor ghoíll teas an chómhraic puínn ar Dhál gCais. Do cruadh iad go maith leis an ngleacaíocht a bhíodh ar siúl coitianta i gCeann Cora. Nuair a bhíodar sa mhór-chath, is amhlaidh a bhíodar ar nós an chapaill ráis 'na mbíonn an fholaíocht ann. Nuair ba dhó' le duine gur cheart tuirse ' bheith ag teacht air, is amhlaidh a bhíonn buile nirt agus misnigh agus fuinnimh ag teacht ann.

Bhí cuid de sna Lochlannaigh a bhí ar an gcuma gcéanna, agus ba ró-dheocair iad do chur i ndiaidh a gcúil. Ach bhíodar ag dridim siar agus bhí Dál gCais ag brú orthu go dian. Bhí Maolmhórdha ag déanamh a dhíchill chun iad do chimeád gan dul siar, ach ní fhéadadh sé é. Thugadh sé aire mhaith, áfach, gan teacht aghaidh ar aghaidh le Murchadh ná le Dúlainn. Mheasadh sé go bhfeiceadh sé dhá Mhurchadh ann, an Murchadh go raibh an fhéasóg air agus an Murchadh ná raibh, agus go raibh an Murchadh ná raibh an fhéasóg air chómh cúntúrthach de theangmhálaí leis an Murchadh go raibh.

An fhaid a bhí san mar sin sa cheann san den chath, bhí nithe ar a mhalairt de chuma sa cheann eile. Bhí Lochlannaigh Átha Cliath agus an deich gcéad fear ón Ioruaidh go raibh na héidí práis orthu i gcoinnibh na Muímhneach eile (lasmu' de Dhál gCais), agus bhí lucht na n-éidí práis ag brú na nGael rómpu agus dhá marú go tiubh. Ba mhó go mór an t-éirleach a bhí ag lucht na n-éidí práis á dhéanamh ar Ghaelaibh an chínn sin den chath ná mar a bhí ag Dál gCais á dhéanamh ar Lochlannaigh an chínn eile. Bhí Bruadar ar tosach ar lucht na n-éidí, agus bhí na Muímhnigh ag titim 'na sraitheannaibh ins gach treó 'na dtugadh sé aghaidh.

Bhí Béibheann agus Gormfhlaith thuas ar barra rí-theaghlaigh Shitric agus iad ag féachaint ar an éirleach a bhí ag lucht na n-éidí á dhéanamh ar na Muímhneachaibh.

Caibideal 55: An Cath

"Is maith na bunaithe iad san, a Bhéibheann!", arsa Gormfhlaith. "Táid siad ag leagadh an arbhair go tiubh. Beidh uathás oibre déanta acu i gcómhair na hoíche".

"Tá an lá óg fós, a Árdríogan", arsa Béibheann. "Is mó cor a dh'fhéadfadh an saol a chur de 'dir seo agus an oíche".

Chonaic Murchadh conas a bhí lucht na n-éidí ag marú na Muímhneach rómpu. D'fhéach sé 'na thímpall. Ní raibh Caoilte i bhfad uaidh.

"Téanam, a Chaoilte", ar seisean. "Ní mór cosc do chur leó súd thiar. Beir ar do thuaigh agus lean me. Dein-se an rud céanna", ar seisean le Dúlainn. "Agus tusa, a mhic", ar seisean le Connla. "Seasaíodh an chuid eile an fód anso".

D'imigh an ceathrar siar as an gcath agus siúd siar ó dheas iad chun na háite 'na raibh lucht na n-éidí agus iad ag marú rómpu.

"An tua! An tua! An tua, a fheara!", arsa Murchadh.

Lena línn sin, do léim sé chun Lochlannaigh mhóir a bhí ag déanamh éirligh agus ná téadh aon bhuille ' chlaíomh i bhfeidhm air. Dhein Murchadh dhá leath dá cheann, idir phrás agus cloigeann, le buille ' thuaigh. Bhí na tuanna go léir in áirde láithreach. Ansan is ea do chonacthas an obair.

"Tugtar sleagh dhom!", arsa Murchadh.

Do tugadh. Thug sé sá d'fhear mhór eile de lucht na n-éidí. Do rith an tsleagh tríd an éide mar a rithfeadh snáthad trí bhréid, agus do thit an fear. Ansan is ea do fíoradh an focal aduairt Brian ar maidin. "Ná cuiridh suím 'na gcótaíbh iarainn", ar seisean. "Cótaí tróma is ea iad". Chuímhnigh gach éinne ar an bhfocal. Do sheasaimh na Muímhnigh an fód. D'oibríodar an tua agus an tsleagh. Níorbh fhada go raibh lucht na n-éidí ag titim go tiubh. Níor chuadar i ndiaidh a gcúil mar ní ró-mhaith a dh'fhéadfaidís é. Bhí tuirse agus allas orthu, agus bhí an éide ró-throm. Níor dheineadar ach seasamh agus iad féin a chosaint chómh maith agus dob fhéidir leó é. Níor ró-mhaith a dh'fhéadadar iad féin a chosaint, mar bhí an bhuile agus an fhearg ar na Muímhneachaibh nuair a fuaradar go raibh ar a gcumas na héidí uathásacha san do ghearadh le tuaigh nú do shá le sleagh chómh saoráideach. Níor thit puínn eile de sna Muímhneachaibh an uair sin, agus do chosain lucht na n-éidí iad féin maith go leór. Do coireadh iad, áfach, agus fé mar a coirtí iad, ní fhéadaidís aon chosaint a dhéanamh orthu féin, agus ansan do maraítí iad.

Do lean an cómhrac, gan stad gan staonadh, ó cheann ceann de pháirc an chatha. Na hÉireannaigh lán-cheapaithe, fé mar a bhí socair go daingean acu i bhfad roim ré, ar bhás a dh'fháil sa chath san, pé taobh ar a mbeadh bua an chatha. Iúnadh agus alltacht ar na Lochlannaigh go léir, idir ríthe agus daoine, a rá go raibh a leithéid de sheasamh ag na Gaeil á dhéanamh. "Má seasaítear 'nár gcoinnibh puínn eile aimsire ar an gcuma so, buafar orainn!", adeiridís lena chéile, agus iúnadh a gcroí orthu. Ghéaraíodar sa chómhrac, mar dhea go scuabfaidís na Gaeil rómpu. Do chaitheadar iad féin i gcoinnibh na nGael díreach mar a chaitheann an fharraige í féin i gcoinnibh na carraige lá gaoithe. Ní raibh aon mhaith dhóibh ann. Do sheasaimh Clanna Gael 'na gcoinnibh díreach mar a sheasaíonn an charraig i gcoinnibh uisce na farraige.

Thug na Lochlannaigh ní eile fé ndeara. Thugadar fé ndeara ná raibh blúire eagla roimis an mbás ag na hÉireannaigh, ná aon doicheall acu roimis an mbás. I ndiaidh ar ndiaidh, do chuaigh 'na luí ar aigne na Lochlannach ná raibh aon tsúil go n-iompódh na hÉireannaigh ón gcath. Go seasóidís an fód an fhaid a bheidís beó, agus gur le háthas a ghlacfaidís bás.

Níorbh fhéidir leis na Lochlannaigh an ní sin do thuiscint. Do thuigfidís é, b'fhéidir, dá mbeadh ' fhios acu cad é an socrú aigne a bhí déanta ag na Gaelaibh i bhfad sara dtáinig lá an chatha san; do thuigfidís é dá mbéadh ' fhios acu go raibh Naomh Íbirt an Aifrinn dá dhéanamh chun Dé, ó tháinig an chéad léas de sholas an lae an mhaidean san, ins gach eaglais agus ins gach mainistir in Éirinn. Do thuigfidís é dá dtuigidís conas mar a bhí sagairt agus manaigh agus mná rialta ar fuid na hÉireann, i gcaitheamh na maidine sin agus i gcaitheamh na hoíche roim ré, ag briseadh a gcroí dhá iarraidh ar Dhia na glóire, trí ímpí na Maighdine Muire, agus trí ímpí Phádraig agus Bhríde agus Cholm Cille, gan bua an chatha san do leogaint leis na Lochlannaigh. Do thuigfidís é dá mbeadh ' fhios acu conas mar a bhí an tÁrdrí aosta, an fear a thispeáin an Chrois Chéasta don tslua an mhaidean san, an fear a bhí ceapaithe ag Dia an uair sin chun cómhacht na Lochlannach do bhriseadh agus do chloí in Éirinn, conas mar ' bhí sé ar a dhá ghlúin, istigh 'na chábán, dhá iarraidh go cruaidh ar an Slánaitheóir Gléigeal gan an bua do leogaint le namhaid an Chreidimh. Ní raibh aon phioc d'fhios an méid sin go léir ag na Lochlannaigh, agus dá bhrí sin níor thuigeadar cad fé ndeara do sna Gaelaibh a leithéid de sheasamh a dhéanamh sa chath agus bás do ghlacadh lena leithéid d'áthas.

Do lean an cómhrac gan sos gan staonadh gan lagú, agus bhí an ghrian ag dridim go ríghin chun a háite ar an spéir i meán lae. Bhí an bualadh agus an t-éirleach cómh-dhian, ba dhó' le duine, ó cheann ceann den mhachaire. Bhí na mná agus na mion-daoine ar na hárdánaibh ag faire. Bhí buairt agus eagla ag tosnú ar theacht ar na mnáibh a tháinig ar na luingeas. Ní raibh aon choinne acu go leanfadh an cath chómh fada, ná go seasódh na Gaeil an fód chómh daingean. Bhí a lán dá bhfearaibh féin, agus dá macaibh, sínte marbh ar an bpáirc. Bhí ag dul 'na luí ar a n-aigne gur bhaol ná raibh seilbh i dtalamh na hÉireann le fáil acu chómh saoráideach agus do mheasadar. Ach do ghluais an cómhrac agus shamhlaíodar gur ag dul i ngéire agus i ndéine agus i dtruime a bhí an chaismirt, agus gan aon chló lagachair ná aon deallramh géilleadh* ar shlóitibh na nGael. Dá ndúnadh bean acu a súile an uair sin agus éisteacht leis an ngleó, d'aireódh sí an choíll mhór trí thine agus an lasair ag búirthigh agus an t-adhmad ag cnagarnaigh, agus d'aireódh sí mar a bheadh daichead míle fear agus daichead míle tua acu agus iad ag gearradh na gcrann agus dhá leagadh!

Bhí na craínn ag titim, na craínn bheaga ar dtúis agus ansan na craínn mhóra, agus ní raibh aon taobh ag déanamh aon ghéilleadh don taobh eile, nú má géilltí beagán ar thaobh anois agus arís, do buaití an beagán san thar n-ais gan puínn ríghnis; agus bhí an ghrian ag dridim siar. Bhí ceó éigin odhar ag éirí ón machaire, agus bhí an ghaoth ag séideadh an cheóigh sin os cionn na bhfear a bhí ag troid, agus isteach fén dtír. Ceó fola ab ea an ceó san. D'éirigh, leis, ar an machaire, fuar-bhalaithe gránna trom, balaithe na fola. Bhí an balaithe chómh láidir, chómh trom san go mb'éigean do chuid de sna mnáibh a bhí ar na hárdánaibh imeacht. Nuair a chuaigh an balaithe sin fúthu, d'iompaigh a ngoile, bhí an balaithe chómh trom san. Ach níor chuir faobhar ná fuil, ceó ná balaithe, ' fhéachaint ar lucht an chómhraic staonadh ón gcath ar aon taobh. Chomáineadar leó ag bualadh agus ag leagadh agus ag titim, an dua agus an saothar agus an cruatan dhá dtnáitheadh agus an tart dhá loscadh, agus an ghrian ag dridim siar go ríghin.

Tá tobar breá fíor-uisce sa mhachaire ar a raibh an cómhrac ar siúl. Deirtear go dtéadh na taoisigh Ghaelacha chun an tobair sin, ó am go ham, chun a lámh a dh'fhuaradh sa n-uisce agus chun dí ' dh'ól, agus ansan go bhfillidís chun an chómhraic agus a lán-neart acu. Thug na Lochlannaigh fé ndeara an ní sin. Bhí buíon chosanta ag na Gaelaibh ar an dtobar. Tháinig buíon Lochlannach chun an tobair a bhaint díobh. Do throid an dá bhuíon go fíochmhar. Do loiteadh an tobar. Nuair a tháinig taoiseach Gaelach chuige ar ball, bhí sé lán d'fhuil agus de chré, agus na cuirp 'na gcruachaibh air.

Ní fheadar féin conas ' fhéad na fir Ghaelacha imeacht ón gcath chun dí ' dh'ól as an dtobar murab amhlaidh a dheinidís uanaíocht ar a chéile. Pé rud a dheinidís do lean an t-éirleach gan sos gan staonadh, agus bhí an ghrian ag dridim siar go mall.

Caibideal 55: An Cath

Is é Sígurd, Iarla Ínsí hOrc, agus a shlua, a bhí i ngleic leis na Connachtachaibh. I dteannta na gConnachtach a bhí ceapaithe do Mh'leachlainn Mhór seasamh. Nuair a dh'imigh M'leachlainn agus a dheich gcéad as an gcath, d'fhág sé easnamh mór agus leath-lámh mhór ar na Connachtachaibh. Ach do sheasaimh na Connachtaigh an cómhrac, gan dul órlach i ndiaidh a gcúil, i gcaitheamh an lae go léir. Thug an dá shlua fé ndeara na gníomhartha uathásacha a dhein Tadhg Mór Ó Cealla i gcaitheamh an lae. Thug a lán de sna fearaibh láidre a bhí ar na Lochlannaigh aghaidh air, i gcaitheamh an lae, ach do thit gach fear díobh lena láimh. Fé dheireadh do thug Bruadar féin aghaidh air. Bhí éide ana-chruaidh ar Bhruadar. Bhí a shleagh i láimh Thaidhg Mhóir. Thug sé sá den tsleagh do Bhruadar. Níor chuaigh an tsleagh tríd an éide ach do caitheadh Bruadar siar ar fleasc a dhroma, bhí a leithéid sin de neart leis an sá a tugadh do. D'éirigh sé agus thug sé fogha eile fé Thadhg. Do leagadh arís é ar an gcuma gcéanna. Thug sé an tríú fogha. Do baineadh an tríú leagadh as. D'éirigh sé agus do rith sé isteach i gcoíll a bhí in aice na háite. Lena línn sin, tháinig Sígurd i ngar do Thadhg, agus sara raibh uain ag Tadhg ar a shleagh do bheartú arís, do bhuail Sígurd sa cheann é le tuaigh. Do thit Tadhg marbh. Is ar éigin a bhí sé ar lár nuair a bhí Sígurd ar lár, chómh marbh leis, agus a cheann agus a chabhail, síos go caol a dhroma, scoilte glan le buille ' thuaigh ó Mhurchadh.* Chonaic an dá shlua an buille sin. Do bhrúigh slua Shíguird isteach chun báis a rí do dhíogailt. Bhí Dúlainn agus Caoilte agus Connla in aice Mhurchadh. Do dhrid na Connachtaigh amach 'na dteannta. Bhí slua Shíguird ag titim láithreach chómh tiubh agus do féadtí na buillí do tharrac orthu. Chonaic beirt mhac rí na hIorua an t-éirleach san. Do ritheadar araon fé dhéin na háite. Lena línn sin, tháinig Tadhg Óg Ó Cealla chun na háite 'na raibh a athair sínte. Bhí bean ar a glúinibh ag ceann an athar agus a cheann idir a dhá láimh aici.

Bhí Murchadh ag rith fé dhéin na beirte a bhí ag teacht 'na choinnibh. Bhí na Connachtaigh ag déanamh an éirligh ar mhuíntir Shíguird. Caroll Cnút an chéad duine den bheirt a tháinig i gcoinnibh Mhurchadh. Do thit Caroll láithreach fé thuaigh Mhurchadh. Pé rud a bhí imithe ar láimh dheis Mhurchadh, chaith sé uaidh an tua. Tháinig Anrud chuige agus é ar buile mar gheall ar mharú a dhriothár. Do chosain Murchadh é féin air leis an gclaíomh a bhí 'na láimh chlé aige. Thug sé únthairt éigin do i dtreó gur leag sé é. Ansan do chuir sé an claíomh i gcoinnibh a uchta féin agus a bharra ar ucht Anruid agus do luigh sé len' ucht ar an gclaíomh agus chuir trí éide agus trí chliabh Anruid é. Nuair a chrom Murchadh chuige sin, do thug Anrud snap ar an sciain a bhí i gcrios Mhurchadh. Do tharraig sé an scian as a' truaill agus sháigh sé suas in ucht Mhurchadh í, agus do thit Murchadh anuas air.

An fhaid a bhí an méid sin ar siúl, bhí Tadhg Óg Ó Cealla ag déanamh an éirligh, i dteannta na gConnachtach, ar shlua Shíguird, ag díogailt bháis a athar orthu. Bhí a athair sínte laistiar de agus an bhean ar a glúinibh ag á cheann. Cé ' léimfeadh chuige amach a lár an namhad ach Amhlaoibh agus a thua 'na láimh aige.

"Tabharfad a cheart féin don fhaobhar anois, a Thaidhg!", arsa Amhlaoibh, agus sara raibh uain ag Tadhg ar an iúnadh a tháinig air do chur de ná ar aon chosaint a dhéanamh air féin, do bhuail Amhlaoibh sa cheann é leis an dtuaigh. Do thit Tadhg. Chómh luath agus do thit Tadhg cé ' chífeadh Amhlaoibh 'na seasamh ar a aghaidh amach ach Niamh!

D'fhéach an bheirt ar a chéile. Níorbh ionann an fhéachaint sin agus an chéad fhéachaint úd a thug an bheirt chéanna ar a chéile. Pé rud a chonaic Amhlaoibh sa chéad fhéachaint, chonaic sé sa tarna féachaint rud éigin uathásach, rud éigin a bhain a mheabhair de glan. Do thit an t-arm as a láimh. Do leath a bhéal agus a dhá shúil. D'iompaigh sé ar a sháil agus do rith sé as an áit. Do rith sé in am agus ní raibh ann ach san. Bhí Connla díreach ag teacht agus a thua 'na láimh aige, tua a bhí chómh dian ar na Lochlannaigh an lá san le tuaigh Mhurchadh féin. Nuair a rith Amhlaoibh, do rith Connla 'na dhiaidh.

Caibideal 55: An Cath

Bhí Amhlaoibh chómh cosmhail sin le Bruadar gur measadh go minic i gcaitheamh an lae gurbh é Bruadar Amhlaoibh agus gurbh é Amhlaoibh Bruadar. Do deineadh an dearúd céanna go minic i gcaitheamh an lae i dtaobh Mhurchadh agus Chonnla, go mór mór nuair ' drideadh amach sa lá agus nuair a bhí na fir go léir clúdaithe le fuil agus le salachar i dtreó nárbh fhéidir a dh'fheiscint ceocu a bhí féasóg ar dhuine nú ná raibh.

Nuair a chonaic an dá shlua an bheirt ag rith, do buaileadh isteach láithreach in aigne gach éinne gurbh é Bruadar a bhí ag teitheadh agus gurbh é Murchadh a bhí ar a thóir. Nuair a chonaic na Lochlannaigh, dar leó, Bruadar ag teitheadh agus Murchadh ar a thóir, d'iompaíodar go léir agus do theitheadar. D'éirigh an liú fhiaigh ó sna Gaelaibh mórthímpall i dtreó gur chrith an machaire fé chosaibh na bhfear. Nuair ' airigh an deich gcéad a bhí ag M'leachlainn an liú uathásach san, níor fhéadadar fanúint socair a thuilleadh. Bhí páirc threafa idir iad agus an cath. Siúd amach iad, treasna na páirce agus siúd ar thóir na Lochlannach iad. Dheineadar obair mhaith, dá dhéanaí a thánadar. Mura mbeadh iad, ní curfí ar na Lochlannaigh an t-ár uathásach a cuireadh orthu. Bhí na fir a bhí sa chómhrac fan lae ró-bhuailte amach le tuirse, an méid díobh ná raibh cneathacha go tiubh orthu agus mórán fola caillte acu.

Do ghluais an teitheadh agus an tóir agus an marú. Thug na mná aghaidh ar na bádaibh chun dul ar bórd na luingeas. Chuaigh an iomad acu isteach ins gach bád. Chómh luath agus ' dhrid na báid amach, do chuadar fé uisce agus do bádh na daoine a bhí orthu. Thug formhór na bhfear a bhí ag teitheadh aghaidh ar rí-theaghlach Shitric in Áth Cliath. Bhí an Tulchainn ar an slí rómpu, agus bhí sé ana-dhoimhinn, mar bhí an taoide lán um an dtaca san. Do bádh na céadta dhíobh san abhainn sin.

Bhí Gormfhlaith agus Béibheann thuas ar bharra an rí-theaghlaigh. Chonacadar an teitheadh agus an tóir.

"Measaim", arsa Béibheann, "gur feárr na buanaithe atá ag obair anois ná iad súd a bhí ag obair i dtosach an lae".

Níor dhein Gormfhlaith ach buille ' dhorn a thabhairt sa bhéal di, agus cúpla fiacal a bhaint aisti.*

Caibideal 56: An tÁr-mhá

Nuair a rith Amhlaoibh, do rith Connla 'na dhiaidh, agus ansan do rith an méid a bhí gan marú de mhuíntir Shíguird. Do ghluais ar a dtóir an méid a bhí ábalta ar rith de sna Connachtachaibh. Do ghluais Caoilte sa tóir in éineacht leó. Níor chuaigh Caoilte i bhfad. Bhí ' fhios aige go raibh Niamh san áit 'na raibh a hathair sínte marbh. Do chas sé thar n-ais le heagla go gcasfí buíon Lochlannach sa treó agus go mb'fhéidir go mbeadh Niamh gan chosaint.

Nuair a tháinig sé, is amhlaidh a fuair sé a lán de mhuíntir Uíbh Máine ann roimis, agus de mhuíntir Mhaoilruanaidh na Paidre. Bhíodar ró-chréachtnaithe chun leanúint ar an dtóir, ach bhíodar ábalta ar Niamh a chosaint go maith. Bhí sise ar a glúinibh ag ceann cuirp a hathar. Bhí sagart ann, leis, agus manach. Ag tabhairt aire do Thadhg Óg Ó Chealla is ea ' bhí an sagart. Ní raibh Tadhg Óg marbh, bíodh go raibh sé gortaithe go maith. Níor thug Amhlaoibh "a cheart féin don fhaobhar". Bhí clogad maith láidir ar cheann Thaidhg. Do chuir an tua stangadh doimhinn sa chlogad agus do gortaíodh an ceann, ach níor gearradh an clogad ná an ceann. Bhí Lonán ann agus níorbh fhada go raibh Tadhg tagaithe chuige féin fé láimh Lonáin.

Bhí ceann Thaidhg Mhóir, áfach, 'na dhá leath, ach níor chorraigh Niamh uaidh.

Bhí Conn ann agus é tar éis teacht ón áit 'na raibh a athair féin, Maolruanaidh na Paidre, sínte marbh. Do mhair Maolruanaidh tamall maith tar éis a ghunta, agus bhí sagart in' aice ó fuair sé an ghuin go dtí go bhfuair sé bás.

Caibideal 56: An tÁr-mhá

Nuair a chonaic Niamh Caoilte agus Conn, do labhair sí leó.

“Ca bhfuil Connla?”, ar sise.

“D’imigh sé ar thóir na Lochlannach, a ríogan”, arsa Caoilte.

“Is trua san!”, ar sise. “Má imíonn aon ní air, tá Éire creachta glan”.

Bhí tuilleadh de sna Connachtaigh ag teacht ón dtóir. Chuir sí tuairisc Chonnla orthu. Ní fheacaigh éinne Connla ach do chonaic gach éinne Murchadh agus é ar thóir Bhruadair agus Bruadar ag teitheadh uaidh.

“Ní fhéadfadh Murchadh ’ bheith ar thóir Bhruadair”, arsa duine a tháinig, “mar tá Murchadh ansúd thall sínte agus beirt shagart in’ fhochair. Do thit Murchadh díreach nuair a bhí an teitheadh agus an tóir ag tosnú”.

“An é radharc mo shúl a mheasfá a bhaint díom?”, arsan chéad duine. “Ná feacaigh mo dhá shúil Bruadar ag teitheadh agus Murchadh ar a thóir?”

“Ní fheacaís Bruadar ag teitheadh”, arsa Niamh, “mar do leag m’athair é trí huaire as a chéile, agus ansan do rith sé isteach sa choíll bheag san thuas”.

Lena línn sin, d’fhéachadar suas agus cad a chífidís ach Bruadar féin ag rith ’na dtreó ón áit ’na raibh puball an Árdrí, agus é ag liúirigh:

“Scaoiltear an focal ó bhéal go béal!”, ar seisean, “gur mhairbh Bruadar Brian!”*

Siúd chuige an bhuíon chosanta do fágadh ar phuball Bhriain. Do ritheadar ar thóir na Lochlannach agus d’fhágadar an puball gan chosnamh. Tháinig Bruadar amach as an gcoíll, mar a raibh sé i bhfolach. Fuair sé an tÁrdrí gan chosnamh, agus chuaigh sé isteach agus mhairbh sé an tÁrdrí. Do rug an bhuíon chosanta ar Bhruadar agus chuireadar chun báis é. Ba shuarach an leigheas é sin ar an ndíobháil a bhí déanta. Dá dtugaidís aire don ghnó a cuireadh 'na chúram orthu, tá gach aon deallramh go mbeadh a mhalairt de scéal againn go léir, riamh ó shin agus inniu, seochas mar atá.

Deir cuid den tseanchas gur chosain Brian é féin go cróga. Ní fheadar ceocu a dhein nú nár dhein, agus is cuma liom. B'fheárr liom go mór a bheith ar chumas an tseanchais a rá gur chosain na fir é 'nar cuireadh mar chúram orthu é ' chosaint. Is trua gan a n-ainmneacha againn! Chuireadar pionós ar Bhruadar. Ba mhór go léir an leigheas é sin ar an bhfaillí a dheineadar féin, nárbh ea!

Ag teacht thar n-ais ó thóir na Lochlannach a bhíodar nuair a bhuail Bruadar úmpu agus an gníomh déanta aige. Dheineadar go hainnis a ngnó!

Nuair a fuair Niamh go raibh Brian marbh, d'éirigh sí 'na seasamh:

"Téanam!", ar sise le Caoilte agus le Conn. "Caithfimíd Connla ' dh'fháil. Tá Brian marbh, agus is dócha go bhfuil Murchadh marbh. Tá Árdrí againn fós, áfach, má tá Connla beó".

Siúd chun siúil iad. Do leanadar an treó do lean na Connachtaigh sa tóir. Bhí cuid de sna Connachtaigh ag teacht thar n-ais. D'iompaíodar in éineacht leis an dtriúr nuair a fuaradar cad a bhí uathu. Dheineadar gach aon tsaghas cuardaigh agus chuireadar gach aon tsaghas tuairisce, ach ní bhfuaradar aon bhlúire eólais. D'inis fiche duine dhóibh go bhfeacathas Bruadar ag teitheadh agus Murchadh ar a thóir, ach ní fheacaigh éinne Connla.

Bhí an oíche ag titim. Bhí an machaire go léir lán de chorpaibh, agus bhí a lán de sna Lochlannaigh a leagadh sa tóir agus ná rabhadar marbh ar fad, agus go raibh fonn orthu sleagh nú tua nú scian do chaitheamh le haon Éireannach a chífidís. Do tuigeadh go raibh sé ró-chúntúrthach leogaint do Niamh dul ní ba shia sa chuardach. Do socraíodh ar dhul thar n-ais. Go mb'fhéidir go raibh Connla tagaithe ann um an dtaca san. Mura raibh, go bhféadfadh na fir teacht arís ag cuardach agus Niamh a dh'fhágáilt ar a suaimhneas in áit a bheadh gan bhaol.

Thánadar thar n-ais. Ní raibh aon tuairisc ar Chonnla. Bhí an oíche dhubh ann um an dtaca san, agus chun na hoíche ' dhéanamh ní ba dhuíbhe do leath ceó isteach ón bhfarraige i dtreó ná feicfeadh duine a lámh dá síneadh sé í.

Ní raibh aon rud le déanamh ach dul fé dhéin an longphuirt i gCíll Mhaighneann. Dhein muíntir Thaidhg Mhóir agus muíntir Mhaoilruanaidh dhá chróchar agus do rugadar leó an dá chorp chun an longphuirt. Bhí na sagairt agus na manaigh ann, agus bhíodar ag cantainn úrnaithe na marbh ar an slí. Nuair a thánadar go Cíll Mhaighneann, fuaradar go raibh a lán sochraidí beaga eile tagaithe ann rómpu, agus ag teacht ann 'na ndiaidh, agus an obair chéanna ar siúl acu. Bhí na sagairt agus na manaigh go léir ann, ó Shórd Cholm Cille, agus an uile shaghas córacha tabhartha leó acu, mar atá líon geal chun cneathach do dhúnadh agus fuil do chosc, agus deocha chun nirt, agus banndaí lín-éadaigh, agus cliathacha chun cnámh do chur, agus mar sin. Bhí flúirse de sna nithibh sin tabhartha leó ón mbaile ag na mnáibh a tháinig, ach níor mhiste an tuilleadh.

Bhí na buíona beaga ag teacht i gcaitheamh na hoíche agus a nduine marbh féin ag gach buín díobh. Tháinig cuid de theaghlach Mhurchadh agus Murchadh ar chróchar acu, ach ní raibh sé marbh. Mhair sé go dtí amáireach a bhí chúinn. Bhí na sagairt in' aice san áit 'nar thit sé, anuas ar mhac rí na hIorua. D'fhan sagart in' fhochair go dtí gur tharraig sé an anál.

Ní raibh aon bhuíon a tháinig mar sin i gcaitheamh na hoíche ná raibh Niamh a' faire orthu, féachaint cathain a chífeadh sí buíon ag teacht agus Connla acu, nú féachaint cathain a chífeadh sí Connla féin ag teacht ar bhuín acu agus duine aige á thabhairt leis. Níor tháinig sé mar seo ná mar siúd.

Tháinig solas an lae. Do ghlan an ceó.

"Téanam", arsa Niamh le Caoilte agus le Conn, "go gcuardaímíd an machaire, féachaint a' bhfaighimís Connla beó nú marbh".

Ghluaiseadar amach. Thánadar ar áit an chatha. Ba ghránna an radharc an uair sin é mar mhachaire. Bhí an talamh go léir, ó Bhínn Éadair go hÁth Cliath agus ó chiúmhais na trá i bhfad amach sa tír, clúdaithe le corpaibh daoine. Bhí, anso agus ansúd ar fuaid an mhachaire, rudaí beó ag gluaiseacht i measc na gcorp. Daoine ab ea cuid de sna rudaíbh beó san, daoine a bhí ag lorg corp a gcarad féin. Bithiúnaigh ab ea cuid de sna rudaíbh beó; bithiúnaigh a bhí ag guid an tsaibhris agus na n-órnáidí a bhí ar chorpaibh na Lochlannach uasal agus na nÉireannach uasal. Gadhair ab ea cuid de sna rudaíbh beó, leis; gadhair ghránna mhóra chúntúrthacha a tháinig isteach ón dtír nuair a rug an ghaoth balaithe na fola amach ag triall orthu.

Shiúlaigh Niamh agus a cuallacht an machaire, soir agus siar agus anonn agus anall, ach ní bhfuaradar aon radharc ar aon chorp go raibh aon chosúlacht aige le Connla. Do chíodh Niamh uaithi go minic corp a bhíodh, dar léi, cosmhail le Connla. Ansan nuair a thagaidís in' aice, chíodh sí nárbh é é, agus bhíodh áthas uirthi.

Bhí an mhaidean ag gluaiseacht agus an ghrian ag dridim suas ar an spéir, agus fir ag teacht go tiubh, as gach aon treó baíll, le hórdú na sagart, agus rámhainní agus sluaiste acu, chun na gcorp do chur fé thalamh. Do leath na fir sin iad féin ins gach aon bhall ar fuaid an mhachaire agus do chrom gach aon triúr nú ceathrar acu ar thrínse ' dh'oscailt. Ba ghéarr go raibh oiread san acu ann go mb'éigean do sna gadhair agus do sna bithiúnaigh glanadh as an áit. Má bhí saibhreas le fáil ar chorpaibh na marbh, do thuig na fir a bhí ag déanamh na hoibre gurbh iad féin dob fheárr ceart chun an tsaibhris sin. Bhí an obair ar siúl ins gach aon pháirt den mhachaire, agus insna háiteannaibh 'na raibh na cuirp 'na gcruachaibh in áirde ar a chéile, b'éigean trínsí móra leathana doimhne ' dhéanamh, agus na cuirp a chur 'na gcruachaibh fé thalamh, díreach mar a bhíodar 'na gcruachaibh os cionn tailimh. Bhí an taoide lán arís agus bhí cuirp na mban agus na leanbh aici á chaitheamh isteach ar an dtráigh. Fé mar a dhrid an taoide amach, bhí sí ag fágaint na gcorp ar an dtráigh 'na diaidh. B'éigean trínsí móra leathana doimhne ' dhéanamh dóibh sin, leis, agus iad do chur 'na gcruachaibh fé thalamh. Nuair a bhí na trínsí sin lán de sna corpaibh agus an chré curtha suas orthu is amhlaidh a bhí árdán mór árd san áit 'nar deineadh gach trínse. Táid na hárdáin sin le feiscint san áit fós, nú cuid acu.

Chonaic Niamh, agus an mhuíntir a bhí lena cois sa chuardach, a lán daoine cruinnithe tímpall na háite 'na dtéann an Tulchainn isteach sa bhfarraige. Thánadar chun na háite. Bhí an Tulchainn lán de chorpaibh na Lochlannach i dtreó go rabhadar ag cimeád uisce na habhann siar ón dtaoide do leanúint. Bhí na fir ag tógaint na gcorp as an abhainn agus dhá síneadh ar an bport in aice ' chéile. Nuair a tháinig Niamh, chonaic sí dhá chorp sínte ar an bport in aice ' chéile. D'aithin sí láithreach iad. Amhlaoibh agus Connla is iad a bhí ann. D'aithin gach éinne Connla. Mheas cuid den lucht oibre gurbh é Bruadar an fear eile. D'ínseadar do Niamh, agus don mhuíntir a bhí lena cois, gurbh amhlaidh a fuaradh an bheirt agus cruach mhór de chorpaibh Lochlannach anuas orthu, agus dhá láimh Chonnla daingean i bhfolt Amhlaoibh, agus a chorp anuas ar chorp Amhlaoibh.*

D'fhéach Niamh ar an mbeirt agus iad sínte in aice ' chéile go breá socair. Bhí dhá shúil Amhlaoibh ar dian-leathadh, agus bhí 'na sheasamh iontu, agus 'na ghnúis ar fad, an sceón míllteach a chonaic sí iontu díreach nuair a thit an tua as a láimh agus do theith sé. Bhí gnúis Chonnla chómh sámh, chómh socair, chómh suaimhneasach agus dá mba 'na chodladh ' bheadh sé. Chómh luath agus do chonaic sí iad do bhánaigh a haghaidh i dtreó go dtáinig Caoilte agus Conn 'na haice, duine acu ar gach taobh di. Mheasadar go raibh sí i riocht titim. Ní raibh. Do gháir sí nuair a chonaic sí an t-eagal orthu. Tháinig sí ar a glúinibh in aice Chonnla agus chrom sí ar phaidir a rá len' anam. Tháinig an bheirt eile ar a nglúinibh agus dúradar an phaidir in éineacht léi.

"Go maithidh Dia do pheacaí dhuit, a Amhlaoibh!", ar sise, "agus dúinn go léir".

D'éiríodar. Dheineadar cróchar agus chuireadar corp Chonnla air, agus do rugadar leó é chun an longphuirt.

"Dob uathásach an cath é!", arsa Conn agus iad ag teacht, "agus is fada a bheidh cuímhne in Éirinn air".

"Is fada", arsa Caoilte, "agus an bhfuil ' fhios agat cad a chuirfidh iúnadh ar an saol go deó?"

"Cad a chuirfidh?", arsa Conn.

"An deich gcéad úd go raibh na héidí mitil orthu, tá an uile dhuine acu marbh!", arsa Caoilte.

"An uile dhuine acu?", arsa Conn.

"An uile dhuine riamh acu", arsa Caoilte.

Caibideal 57: I nDiaidh an Chatha

Nuair a tháinig Niamh agus an mhuíntir a bhí lena cois go dtí an longphort, agus corp Chonnla acu, bhí Donncha, mac Bhriain, tagaithe thar n-ais ó Chúige Laighean agus mórán creach aige. Bhí iúnadh ar Dhonncha nuair a fuair sé go rabhthas tar éis an mhór-chatha do throid. Bhí iúnadh, leis, air féin agus ar gach fear de sna fearaibh a bhí in éineacht leis, mar gheall ar dhéine an chatha agus ar mhéid an áir ar gach taobh. D'fhiafraigh sé conas a thárla gur deineadh a leithéid de dhísciú ar Dhál gCais agus ar na Connachtaigh agus ar na Muímhneachaibh, agus M'leachlainn Mór agus a shlua bheag do dhul as chómh maith.

Do hínseadh do conas mar a tharraig M'leachlainn agus a dheich gcéad siar ón gcath i dtosach an lae agus conas mar a chuireadar an pháirc threafa idir iad agus an cath. Ach do hínseadh do conas mar a dheineadar rud maith um thráthnóna, gur ghluaiseadar ar thóir na Lochlannach, agus mura mbeadh iad, go mb'fhéidir ná brisfí an cath ar na Lochlannaigh chómh hiomlán agus a deineadh. Pé'r domhan é, ná curfí ar na Lochlannaigh an t-ár a cuireadh orthu mura mbeadh M'leachlainn agus a dheich gcéad.

"Ar ghluais sé ar thóir na Lochlannach", arsa Donncha, "sara raibh ' fhios aige go raibh m'athair marbh?"

Níor fhéad éinne an cheist sin do fhreagairt do.

Bhí sé in aigne gach éinne, áfach, lasmu' den méid a bhí beó de Dhál gCais, gurbh é M'leachlainn Mór a bheadh in' Árdrí ar Éirinn i ndiaidh Bhriain.

D'oibrigh M'leachlainn agus Donncha, agus na huaisle eile, a láimh a chéile, go dtí go raibh gach aon rud déanta chun na marbh a dh'adhlacadh mar ba chóir, agus go dtí go raibh corp Bhriain tabhartha suas don chléir le breith ó thuaidh go hÁrd Mhacha.

Nuair a bhí corp Bhriain tabhartha don chléir, do labhair Caoilte.

"Bhí Murchadh le hais Bhriain", ar seisean, "ins gach cath dár throid sé riamh ó chath Bhealaigh Leachta go cath Ghleanna Mháma. Is le láimh Mhurchadh do thit laochra agus uaisle Lochlann agus Laighean i gcath an lae inné. Ní ceart Murchadh agus Brian do dheighilt ó chéile anois!"

Caibideal 57: I nDiaidh an Chatha

Do tugadh corp Mhurchadh don chléir le breith ó thuaidh go hÁrd Mhacha in éineacht le corp Bhriain.

Ansan do labhair Niamh.

"Tá sé chómh ceart", ar sise, "gan a mhac do chimeád ó Mhurchadh agus atá sé gan a mhac do chimeád ó Bhrian".

Níor ghá dhi a thuilleadh cainnte ' dhéanamh. Do tugadh Connla don chléir agus do rugadh ó thuaidh é go hÁrd Mhacha, in éineacht le Murchadh agus le Brian, agus do hadhlacadh thuaidh an triúr.

Ansan do chruinnigh Donncha an méid a bhí beó de Chlaínn Chais, agus thug sé féin agus iad féin aghaidh siar ó dheas fé dhéin Chínn Cora.

Éinne gur maith leis ' fhios a bheith aige conas a dh'éirigh leó ar an slí, níl aige ach leabhar an tseanchais do sholáthar agus do lé'. Chífidh sé roinnt nithe ná cuirfidh puínn áthais air sa tseanchas san. Chífidh sé gníomh gránna ó Mhac Giolla Phádraig úd 'nar thrácht Brian ar a ainm nuair a bhí sé ag labhairt leis an slua maidean lae an chatha. Chuir sé in aice ' chéile Mac Giolla Phádraig agus M'leachlainn Mór. Is é cúis gur chuir sé in aice ' chéile iad mar bhí an gníomh céanna déanta acu araon. Do dhiúltaigh Mac Giolla Phádraig don chath nuair a chuaigh giollaí turais Bhriain ag triall air dhá rá leis teacht. Do sheachain M'leachlainn an cath os cómhair súl fear Éireann go léir, maidean lae an chatha. Chuir Brian an bheirt in aice ' chéile 'na chainnt dhá thispeáint go raibh gníomh Mh'leachlainn ar aon dul le gníomh Mhac Giolla Phádraig chómh fada agus a chuaigh náire agus aithis agus spriúnlaitheacht.

Nuair a fuair Mac Giolla Phádraig go raibh Clann Chais lag, d'éirigh sé chúthu agus cheap sé smacht a chur orthu. Níor éirigh leis, áfach, mar a chífir sa tseanchas má léann tú é.*

Caibideal 57: I nDiaidh an Chatha

Ní le Claínn Chais ná le Mac Giolla Phádraig a bhaineann an scéal so, áfach, ach le Niamh, agus le Caoilte, agus le Conn. Bhí Tadhg Mór Ó Cealla marbh, agus bhí Niamh gan a hathair. Bhí uirthi déanamh gan a hathair fé dheireadh. Ba chruaidh an cás é. Ach ní raibh leigheas air. Bhí Maolruanaidh na Paidre marbh, leis. D'fhág san Conn gan athair chómh maith le Niamh. Agus bhí athair Chaoilte marbh. D'fhág san Caoilte agus Lonán gan athair.

Níorbh fholáir do Chaoilte agus do Lonán dul agus buíon a n-athar, an méid a bhí beó acu, do chruinniú agus do chur i dtreó chun dul ó dheas abhaile. Níorbh fholáir do Chonn dul agus an rud céanna ' dhéanamh do bhuín Ó bhFiachrach Áidhne, don méid a bhí beó dhíobh, agus níor mhór é. Bhí a neart agus a mhisneach ag casadh ar Thadhg Óg Ó Chealla i dtreó go raibh sé ábalta, maith go leór, é féin agus Niamh, ar mhuíntir Uíbh Máine do ghléasadh agus do chur i dtreó chun dul abhaile.

Ach níor mhaith le Conn ná le Caoilte scarúint le Niamh go dtí go bhfeicfidís thiar sa bhaile i rí-theaghlach a hathar í.

"Socraímís an scéal ar an gcuma so", arsa Tadhg Óg Ó Cealla. "Deinimís aon bhuíon amháin de sna trí buínibh agus gabhaimís aon bhóthar amháin go dtí go mbeimíd i gCeann Cora".

"Déanfaidh san an gnó go hálainn", arsa Caoilte, "agus ní chuirfidh sé aistear ar aon bhuín againn, mar tá aghaidh na mbóithre is feárr agus is dírí ar Cheann Cora ón áit seo; agus ansan, is ó Cheann Cora atá na bóithre is feárr agus is dírí ag gach buín dínn chun dul abhaile".

Bhí aithne ag Caoilte ar na bóithribh. Do socraíodh an scéal ar an gcuma san. Do tugadh na trí buíona chun a chéile. Níor ghluaiseadar chun bóthair ró-thapaidh. Ghlacadar a suaimhneas go dtí go mbeadh na fir ghunta a bhí orthu láidir a ndóthain chun gluaiste. Ba mhór an mhaith do sna trí buínibh iad do thabhairt chun a chéile ar an gcuma san agus aon bhuíon amháin a dhéanamh díobh. Bhí cuideachtanas a chéile acu, agus cúnamh a chéile nuair ba ghá é. Bhí na Connachtaigh bertha go mór leis an socrú, mar bhí an dochtúir acu. Dá n-imíodh na Muímhnigh leó féin, ní bheadh Lonán ag na Connachtaigh. Chaithfeadh sé imeacht lena mhuíntir féin. Nuair a bhí na trí buíona i dteannta ' chéile, bhí Lonán acu go léir. Ba mhaith an bhail orthu san. Bhí a lán acu, idir Chonnachtaigh agus Muímhnigh, gunta go dian, agus gheóbhaidís bás in ainneóin gach aon rud mura mbeadh Lonán a bheith ag féachaint chúthu agus an t-eólas thar na beartaibh a bheith aige ar a ghnó. Fuair cuid acu bás in ainneóin a dhíchill.

Bhí eólas maith ag Niamh, leis, agus tuiscint mhaith, agus bhíodh sí coitianta i measc na n-othar, ag tabhairt aire dhóibh, agus ag cur misnigh orthu, agus ag friothálamh orthu, agus mheasaidís ná bíodh éinne ba thúisce ' thuigeadh cad a bhíodh in easnamh orthu ná mar a thuigeadh Niamh é. An t-áthas croí a thagadh orthu nuair a thagadh sí ag friothálamh orthu, shamhlaídís go gcuireadh sé feabhas sláinte orthu. Bhí aithne aici ar gach duine fé leith de mhuíntir Uíbh Máine agus Uíbh Fiachrach, agus níorbh fhada go raibh aithne aici, leis, ar gach duine fé leith de sna Muímhneachaibh.

Bhí Lochlannaigh ann. De mhuíntir Ospaic ab ea cuid acu. Do maraíodh Ospac féin sa chath. Driotháir do Bhruadar ab ea é. Tar éis an chatha, chuaigh cuid dá mhuíntir i mbuín Dhonncha, mhic Bhriain, agus tháinig cuid acu i mbuín Thaidhg Óig Uí Chealla. Bhíodh Caoilte mar fhear teangan idir iad agus na Gaeil. Bhí cuid acu gunta go dian, agus do tugadh aireachas dóibh chómh maith díreach agus a tugadh do sna Gaelaibh féin.

Cáirde ab ea muíntir Ospaic, ach bhí cuid de mhuíntir a dhriothár ann, leis, agus do tugadh an t-aireachas céanna dhóibh, bíodh gurbh é an driotháir sin a dhein an gníomh ba mheasa ar na Gaelaibh dár deineadh sa chath, .i. marú Bhriain.

Bhí aon fhear amháin ann agus níor féadadh a dhéanamh amach ar feadh i bhfad cérbh é ná cárbh as é. Bhí sé ar éadromacht. Bhain éirleach an lae sin a mheabhair shaolta dhe. Bhí focal éigin aige dá rá coitianta, ach níor thuig éinne é go dtí gur tháinig Caoilte chuige. Fuair Caoilte amach uaidh gur aduaidh ar fad ó Inis Tuile a tháinig sé. Is é focal a bhíodh 'na bhéal aige, agus nár tuigeadh, ná: "A Pheadair Naofa, tabhair saor ón lá so me agus raghaidh mé trí huaire go dtí an Róimh ag triall ort im mhaidrín!"

Do tugadh saor ón gcath é. Tháinig a mheabhair do i ndiaidh ' chéile nuair a fuair sé an caradas agus an t-aireachas. Ansan ní shásódh aon rud é ach go gcaithfeadh Niamh an Creideamh a mhúineadh dho. B'éigean do Chaoilte bheith sa mhúineadh, leis, go dtí go raibh an fear bocht ábalta ar an nGaelainn a thuiscint.

Do ghlac na Lochlannaigh eile a bhí ann an Creideamh, leis, chómh luath agus do féadadh é ' mhúineadh dhóibh. Is amhlaidh adeiridís, an Creideamh a bhí ag Niamh go raibh sé maith a dhóthain d'éinne sa domhan; ná féadfadh sé gan bheith 'na Chreideamh fhónta agus é ' bheith ag Niamh. Ansan, nuair a múintí dhóibh é, do thuigidís a mhaitheas agus a thairbhe ann féin.

Fé dheireadh thiar thall, bhí na daoine gunta, an méid ná fuair bás díobh, ag dul i bhfeabhas. Bhí an aimsir, leis, ag dul i bhfeabhas agus na laethanta ag dul i bhfaid, agus bhí an focal i mbéal gach éinne gur mhithid bheith ag cuímhneamh ar an mbaile. Do gabhadh na capaill agus do cuireadh na hualaí orthu. Do cuireadh na daoine leicthe ar charraíbh agus leapacha fúthu. Bhí oiread san capall agus carraí acu nár ghá d'éinne bheith 'na chuis. Bhí mórán lóin acu, agus mórán earraí, agus mórán stuic. Bhí ba agus caoire a ndóthain acu, loilíocha chun bainne, agus ba seasca chun mairteóla. Chuireadar gach aon rud i dtreó chun gluaiste agus ghluaiseadar an bóthar siar ó dheas fé dhéin Chínn Cora.

Sarar fhágadar an chómharsanacht, chuaigh Niamh go Sórd chun go bhfeicfeadh sí uaigh Dhúlainn agus uaghanna na n-uasal eile a bhí curtha ann. Chuaigh Tadhg Óg agus Caoilte agus Conn agus Lonán in éineacht léi. Ghoileadar a ndóthain ar uaigh Dhúlainn agus ar na huaghannaibh eile. Bhí uaigh Thaidhg Mhóir agus uaigh Mhaoilruanaidh in aice ' chéile. D'fhan Niamh i bhfad os cionn uagha a hathar. Ba mhaith léi, dá mb'é toil an Tiarna é, uaigh eile ' bheith le hais na huagha san agus í féin a bheith sínte ann, agus a hanam a bheith i bhfochair anama a hathar. Ach do thuig sí nárbh é toil Dé é, agus go raibh gnó eile curtha 'na chúram ag Dia uirthi, agus d'fhág sí an áit.

Chomáin na trí buíona leó, agus iad in aon bhuín amháin, an bóthar siar ó dheas go breá réidh socair. Ní fhéadfaidís gluaiseacht ró-mhear, dá mba ná beadh aon ní chun ríghnis a chur orthu ach na slóite daoine a bhíodh ag teacht rómpu ar an slí ag fáiltiú rómpu, agus dhá moladh agus ag cur gach aon tsaghas beannacht orthu. Bhí tuairisc an chatha tar éis leathadh ar fuid na hÉireann um an dtaca san, agus bhí ualach tógtha de chroí na ndaoine. Bhí na daoine ag imeacht as a meabhair le neart áthais agus le neart baochais ar Dhia agus ar na fearaibh do throid an cath agus do bhuaigh an cath. Bhí ' fhios acu go maith cad a bhí 'na gcómhair go léir dá mba ag na Lochlannaigh a bheadh an bua sa chath san. Bhí ' fhios acu, leis, ag an uile dhuine acu, gur ag na Lochlannaigh a bheadh an bua mura mbeadh a thréine do throid na Gaeil. Agus bhí ' fhios acu ná raibh fir sa chath ba thréine do throid ná na trí buíona san a bhí an uair sin ag gluaiseacht an bóthar san siar ó dheas, in aon bhuín amháin. Dá bhrí sin, is amhlaidh a bhídís 'na gcéadtaibh agus iad ar a nglúinibh, ar dhá thaobh an bhóthair, agus iad ag liúirigh agus ag gol agus ag gáirí, ag breith a mbaochais le Dia mar gheall ar an bhfuascailt a tugadh ar Éirinn, agus dhá iarraidh ar Dhia na glóire a bheannacht do chur go deó, sa tsaol so agus ar an saol eile, ar na fearaibh a dhein an troid uathásach agus do bhuaigh an cath uathásach.

Thar gach éinne eile dá raibh ann, bhíodh na daoine a d'iarraidh radharc ' fháil ar Niamh. Bhí a hainm i mbéalaibh daoine ins gach aon bhall. Bhí sé in aigne na ndaoine, pé cuma 'nar cuireadh isteach 'na n-aigne é, gur mhó a cúnamh chun slóite Bhriain do ghléasadh agus do dhlúthú lena chéile, agus chun na hárdaigne a bhí acu do dhúiseacht iontu i gcómhair an chatha, ná cúnamh aon duine eile lasmu' de Bhrian féin. Dá bhrí sin, pé duine eile a chídís, ní bhídís sásta go dtí go bhfeicidís Niamh. Bhíodh na fir agus na mná ar na hárdánaibh agus ar na clathachaibh agus iad ag iniúchadh agus ag cuardach lena súilibh go dtí go bhfeicidís Niamh. Ansan bhídís ag árdú na leanbh suas 'na lámhaibh i dtreó go bhfeicfidís Niamh.

Níor ghá don chuallacht aon eagla ' bheith orthu go mbeadh aon rud in easnamh orthu ar an slí. Bhí an t-ím agus an bainne agus na huíbhe, agus an uile shaghas toradh talún, ag teacht chúthu isteach ó gach taobh den bhóthar. Ní raibh aon ghá acu leis. Bhí breis agus a ndóthain de gach aon tsaghas bídh acu féin. Thugadar san le tuiscint do sna daoine. Ní raibh aon mhaith ann. Tháinig an bia. Duairt Niamh é ' chur i gcimeád agus go bhféadfí é ' thabhairt do dhaoine bochta ar ball.

Caibideal 58: "Na Mílte Olagón"

Nuair a tháinig Niamh agus a cuallacht go Ceann Cora, bhí dúbhadh na gcnuc agus na gcoíllte den uile shaghas daoine cruinnithe roímpi ann. Do hairíodh in Uíbh Máine go raibh na trí buíona, in aon bhuín amháin, ag dul in éineacht go Ceann Cora, agus do ghluais an uile dhuine sa dúthaigh sin 'na raibh ann siúl in aon chor, soir ó dheas go Ceann Cora. Do hairíodh an scéal céanna in Uíbh Fhiachrach Áidhne agus do deineadh an ghluaiseacht chéanna. Tháinig, in éineacht leis an dá chine sin, gach aon treabhchas go raibh cuid dá ndaoine sa chath, féachaint an mór acu a bhí ag teacht abhaile slán, nú beó féin.

An rud a hairíodh thiar in Uíbh Máine agus in Uíbh Fhiachrach Áidhne, do hairíodh é theas i gCiarraí Luachra agus insna tíorthaibh mórthímpall, agus do ghluais na daoine as na tíorthaibh sin, díreach mar a ghluais na daoine as na tíorthaibh thuaidh, fé dhéin Chínn Cora.

Caibideal 58: “Na Mílte Olagón”

Nuair a tháinig na trí buíona do cuireadh trí gártha móra fáilte rómpu. Do tógadh na gártha arís agus arís eile, bhí a leithéid sin d’áthas ar na daoine a bhí ag feitheamh nuair a chonacadar tagaithe an mhuíntir a bhí uathu. Bhí áthas an domhain ar an muíntir aneas nuair a chonacadar Caoilte agus Lonán. Bhí áthas ba mhó ná an t-áthas san féin ar mhuíntir Uíbh Máine nuair a chonacadar Niamh agus a driotháir, agus bhí áthas chómh mór leis an áthas san ar mhuíntir Uíbh Fhiachrach Áidhne nuair a chonacadar Conn. Ní har a mhuíntir féin amháin a bhí áthas mór i dtaobh Chuínn do theacht slán, ach ar an uile dhuine dá raibh tagaithe san áit. Ógánach dea-chroíoch, uasal, fónta, diaga, ab ea é, mar ba dhual athar do ’ bheith, agus bhí cion ag gach éinne, thuaidh agus theas, air.

Tar éis na bhfáiltí, do tháinig an fhiafraí. Fuair muíntir Uíbh Máine amach gur fágadh Tadhg Mór agus formhór na bhfear a bhí lena chois sínte thíos i gCluain Tairbh. Fuair muíntir Uíbh Fhiachrach amach gurbh é an scéal céanna acu féin é. Fuair muíntir Chiarraí amach gur fágadh a rí féin agus na fir a bhí aige san áit chéanna. Ar ball do fuair gach éinne amach gur fágadh duine leis féin thíos, nú b’fhéidir beirt, nú b’fhéidir triúr. Ansan is ea ’ dh’éirigh na gártha, agus níor ghártha áthais iad ach gártha guil. Ansan is ea ’ dh’éirigh “na mílte olagón”! Na mná do thosnaigh é. Bhíodar ag sileadh ar dtúis ar feadh tamaill. Ansan do chas bean olagón. Ansan do ghluais an t-éirleach lógóireachta óna raibh de mhnáibh san áit. Ní raibh bean ann gan a fear nú a mac nú b’fhéidir an bheirt in éineacht in easnamh uirthi.

Ansan duairt duine éigin, “Ó! Ca bhfuil Brian?”

Duairt duine eile, “Ca bhfuil Murchadh? Agus ca bhfuil Dúlainn? Agus ca bhfuil Connla?”

Ansan do chas na fir “na mílte olagón”, agus bhuaileadar a mbasa. Fir láidre chrua. Fir go raibh taithí acu ar bhás agus ar chogadh agus ar ár, agus gur ró-dheocair osna ' bhaint ón gcroí acu ná deór a bhaint óna súilibh.

Is mó duine a dh'fhéadfadh éisteacht le gol agus le holagón ó mhnáibh agus ná bainfí aon chorraí ar a chuid fola. Ach nuair a bhaineann buairt uathásach fáscadh a croí fir i dtreó go gcaitheann sé an t-olagón do scaoileadh amach 'na lán-neart nú go bpléascfadh a chroí istigh 'na chliabh, is deocair d'éinne éisteacht le gol an fhir sin gan tocht agus fáscadh do theacht ar a chroí féin ná scarfaidh a chuímhne leis an chuid eile dá shaol.

Nuair a ghluais an gol, bhí Niamh ag sileadh. Níor ' airigh éinne a guth an fhaid ná raibh ag gol ach na mná. Ach nuair ' éirigh gol na bhfear, agus nuair ' airigh sí ainm Bhriain agus ainm Mhurchadh agus ainm Chonnla agus ainm a hathair, do ghluais an t-olagón uaithi chómh hárd agus do ghluais sé ó éinne eile dá raibh ann.

Bhí Colla ann, agus cuid de sna sagairt agus de sna manaigh, aníos ó Inis Cathaigh. Do scaoil sé leis an ngol ar feadh tamaill. Ansan tháinig sé in áirde ar árdán agus chrom sé ar chainnt. Do stad an gol in aice na háite 'na raibh sé ag cainnt. I ndiaidh ar ndiaidh, do stad an gol ins gach aon bhall, agus bhí na daoine go léir ag éisteacht leis. Seo mar a labhair sé:

"A dhaoine", ar seisean, "ní haon iúnadh dhúinn go léir buairt ár ndóthain a bheith orainn". (Bhí a dhá shúil féin fliuch go maith.) "Tá cúis ghuil againn má bhí sé ag aon daoine riamh. Ach seo rud nách ceart dúinn a dhearúd i lár ár mbuartha. Tá abhar áthais againn inniu má bhí abhar áthais ag aon daoine riamh. Do buaileadh, thíos i gCluain Tairbh, an lá fé dheireadh, cath nár buaileadh a leithéid in Éirinn ní fios cad é an fhaid ó shin. Do buaileadh an cath san idir Ghaelaibh Éireann agus Lochlannaigh an domhain. Dá bhfaigheadh na Lochlannaigh an lámh uachtair sa chath san is ag na Lochlannaigh a bheadh an t-oileán so na hÉireann inniu. Ní fágfí oiread agus fód de thalamh na hÉireann againn! Thug na Lochlannaigh leó a mná agus a gclann, bhíodar chómh ceapaithe sin ar thalamh na hÉireann do ghlacadh chúthu féin agus ar shliocht Gael do dhísciú, do chur chun báis, do ghlanadh as an oileán gan oiread agus duine acu ' dh'fhágáilt beó ann. Thug Dia dhúinn (moladh agus glóire agus baochas leis!) gur bhuaigh Brian agus a mhór-shlua orthu. Do thit Brian agus a lán dá mhór-shlua sa chath. Dá dtugadh Dia, mar gheall ar ár bpeacaíbh-na, an bua do sna Lochlannaigh, do thitfeadh Brian agus a mhór-shlua go léir, agus ansan do thitfimís-na go léir, ins gach aon pháirt d'Éirinn. Dá mbeadh an bua ag na Lochlannaigh, ní fhágfaidís Brian ná éinne dá mhór-shlua beó, agus bheidís ag gluaiseacht anois ar fuid na hÉireann ag marú na bhfear aosta agus na mban agus na leanbh agus ní bheadh Brian ná éinne dá mhór-shlua ann chun iad do chosaint.

"Má fhéachaim im thímpall anois anso agus má fhéadaim a dh'fháil amach cé hí an bhean is mó atá creachta leis an gcath so, deirim léi, agus is fíor dhom é, gur mó go mór an t-abhar áthais atá tabhartha ag an gcath dhi ná an t-abhar buartha atá tabhartha aige di. Is mó atá sí buaite leis an gcath ná mar atá sí caillte leis. Pé méid dá muíntir atá titithe sa chath, bheidís titithe ann dá ngabhadh an cath 'nár gcoinnibh, agus bheadh sí féin agus an chuid eile acu marbh um an dtaca so ag an slua Lochlannach a bheadh leata anois ar fuid na hÉireann agus iad ar buile ag déanamh díoltais orainn mar gheall ar dhéine an chatha.

"Cuirimís uainn an gol, dá bhrí sin, agus an bhuairt, agus in inead bheith ag gol agus ag déanamh buartha, tugaimís ár mbaochas ó chroí do Dhia na glóire mar gheall ar an gcuma 'nar thug sé saor sinn óna leithéid de chúntúirt. Nuair a dh'éireóidh an bhuairt 'nár gcroí, cuirimís chúinn féin an cheist seo. Conas a bheadh an scéal againn anois dá mb'ag na Lochlannaigh a bheadh an bua?

"Tá ' fhios agaibh-se chómh maith agus atá ' fhios agam-sa conas mar a bhí socair go daingean in' aigne ag an uile dhuine de sna fearaibh a dh'fhág an baile chun dul sa chath so, ar gan teacht beó ón gcath pé taobh ar a mbeadh bua. Tá sé buailte isteach i m'aigne mura mbeadh an socrú san a bheith déanta roim ré acu, ná déanfaidís an troid chómh dian agus ' dheineadar é. An beagán acu do tháinig ón gcath, bhí a n-aigne socair ar gan teacht chómh daingean agus ' bhí ag an muíntir a thit sa chath. Ach do tháinig as an socrú go raibh an troid chómh dian san gur briseadh an cath ar na Lochlannaigh sarar thit a thuilleadh dár ndaoine. Áthas, dá bhrí sin, is ceart dúinn a bheith orainn inniu agus ní buairt.

"Tá abhar eile áthais againn, a dhaoine. Na fir a thit sa chath so is ar son Creidimh Chríost do thiteadar. Tá ' fhios againn go léir, an té a dh'fhuiligeann bás ar son an Chreidimh, go dtugtar aoibhneas na bhFlaitheas do láithreach. Ní ceart dúinn bheith ag déanamh buartha nuair a thuigimíd 'nár n-aigne go bhfuil aoibhneas na bhFlaitheas anois, le cúnamh Dé, ag an muíntir a baineadh dínn sa chath so".

Dhein sé a lán cainnte leó ar an gcuma san, níos feárr go mór ná mar a thagann liom-sa an chainnt a chur síos anso. Chuir sé a n-aigne chun suaimhnis. Thuigeadar gur cheart bheith sásta le toil Dé.

Lena línn sin, cé ' chífidís ag teacht chúthu, an bóthar anoir, ach Donncha, mac Bhriain, agus an méid a bhí beó den bhuín a tháinig leis ón longphort i gCíll Mhaighneann. Bhí cuid mhaith acu ar chrócharaibh, mar ní rabhadar ábalta ar siúl, agus bhí an chuid eile dhá n-iompar.

Chuir Colla an cogar tímpall i measc na ndaoine a bhí ann dhá rá leó gan a thuilleadh guil a dhéanamh. Níor bheag san. In inead aon ghuil a dhéanamh is amhlaidh a cuireadh suas go bríomhar gáir mholta agus fáilte.

D'inis na fir a tháinig conas mar a chuir Mac Giolla Phádraig an ríghneas orthu ar an slí, agus conas mar a mheas sé cath do chur orthu. Bhí fearg mhór ar gach éinne mar gheall air sin. Do féachadh chun na bhfear ngunta agus do cuireadh gach aon chóir orthu.

Ní raibh Donncha agus a chuallacht i bhfad tagaithe nuair a labhair Colla arís.

"A ríthe agus a uaisle agus a dhaoine", ar seisean, "do thit Brian i gcath Chluain Tairbh. Do thit Murchadh sa chath, leis. Tá Árdrí againn in inead an Árdrí do thit. Is é Donncha mac Briain Árdrí Éireann anois!"

Ansan is ea do cuireadh suas an liú mholta i gceart. Do tógadh an liú arís agus arís eile.

Ansan do tháinig a raibh de dhaoine ann chun na háite 'na raibh Bile Mór Mágha Adhair agus do hóirneadh Donncha mac Briain in' Árdrí ar Éirinn. Dhein Colla an obair i láthair na ndaoine, agus bhí áthas agus móráil ar gach éinne.

Níor ghlac fir Éireann, 'na dhiaidh san, áfach, Donncha in' Árdrí ar Éirinn, ach do glacadh é 'na rí ar an Múmhain.

Nuair a bhí an méid sin déanta, bhí gach éinne sásta. Do scar na daoine agus d'imigh gach treabhchas abhaile chun a ndútha féin. Chuaigh Caoilte agus Lonán abhaile go dúthaigh a n-athar. Chuaigh Conn ó thuaidh go hUíbh Fhiachrach Áidhne. Chuaigh Niamh agus Tadhg Óg Ó Cealla ó thuaidh go hUíbh Máine. Bhí Conn agus iad féin in éineacht, áfach, an tslí go léir nách mór.

Caibideal 59: An Ga Gréine Céanna

Do ghluais an dá bhuín, muíntir Uíbh Máine agus muíntir Uíbh Fhiachrach Áidhne, siar ó thuaidh i dtreó a dhá ndúthaigh féin. Bhí in éineacht leis an méid acu a tháinig ó Chíll Mhaighneann an méid a tháinig 'na gcoinnibh go Ceann Cora, i gcás ná raibh aon uaigneas orthu. Nuair a thánadar i gcóngar don bhaile, do scaradar ó chéile. Ba bheag ná gur éirigh an gol agus "na mílte olagón" arís nuair a shroiseadar an t-aos óg agus na seandaoine nár fhéad dul go Ceann

Cora. Ach do cuireadh cosc leis an mbuairt. Do hínseadh cad 'duairt Colla nuair a bhí sé ag cainnt leis an bpobal mór thíos ag Ceann Cora. Do cuireadh na seandaoine chun suaimhnis.

Chómh luath agus ' bhí a dtuirse curtha dhíobh ag an muíntir a tháinig abhaile ón gcath, thosnaíodar ar bhualadh um á chéile agus ar bheith ag cainnt agus ag cuímhneamh ar cad a déanfí feasta. Bhí an saol ana-chiúin, ana-shuaimhneasach acu, agus an aimsir ag dul i mbreáthacht. An phráinn agus an bhruid agus an fáscadh aigne a bhí ar na daoine i gcaitheamh na haimsire an fhaid a bhí an t-ollmhúchán ar siúl i gcómhair an chogaidh, agus an fhaid a bhí na slóite ag imeacht ó bhaile agus ag cruinniú chun an chatha, agus an fhaid do lean an scannradh i dtaobh conas a gheóbhadh an cath, bhíodar go léir imithe. Bhí gach aon rud ciúin suaimhneasach socair.

Do hóirneadh Conn 'na rí ar Uíbh Fhiachrach Áidhne, agus do hóirneadh Tadhg Óg Ó Cealla 'na rí ar Uíbh Máine. Bhí roinnt gnótha le déanamh acu araon ar feadh tamaill ag socrú nithe idir chlaínn na bhfear a fágadh i gCluain Tairbh. Do deineadh a lán cleamhnaisí sa tsocrú. Dhein Niamh dhá chleamhnas, cleamhnas do Thadhg Óg le drifiúr do Chonn, agus cleamhnas do Chonn le drifiúr di féin.

Nuair a bhí an méid sin déanta, thug Niamh agus a driotháir cuaird ó dheas go hInis Cathaigh. Bhí áthas mór ar Cholla nuair a chonaic sé iad. Cé ' bheadh ann rómpu, ar chuaird, ach Caoilte! Ba bheag ná gur baineadh radharc a shúl arís de Chaoilte nuair a chonaic sé iad, díreach mar a baineadh an chéad lá úd a chonaic sé Niamh. Bhí sé 'na rí an uair sin ar Chiarraí Luachra in inead a athar. D'ínseadar do conas a bhí gach aon rud socair lastuaidh in Uíbh Máine agus in Uíbh Fhiachrach Áidhne, agus d'inis seisean dóibh gach aon ní a bhí aige le hínsint i dtaobh a dhútha féin.

"Ba mhaith liom an chailís úd a dh'fheiscint, a Athair, más é do thoil é. Ní fheaca riamh fós í", arsa Niamh.

Caibideal 59: An Ga Gréine Céanna

Do rug sé isteach san *érdam* iad agus thispeáin sé an chailís dóibh.

Ba bhreá an radharc le feiscint í. D'fhéadfadh duine fanúint ar feadh leath an lae ag féachaint uirthi agus ní bheadh a shúile ná a aigne cortha dhi. Dá fhaid a bheadh sé ag féachaint uirthi is amhlaidh ba mhaith leis tamall eile ' thabhairt ag féachaint uirthi. Chimeádfadh saibhreas an óir greim ar a shúilibh. Chimeádfadh uaisleacht agus ealaíontacht a hórnáide greim ar a shúilibh, agus é dhá fhiafraí dhe féin conas a dh'fhéad lámh duine riamh a leithéid d'obair a dhéanamh. Chimeádfadh an crios, na clocha lómhara, greim ar a shúilibh, agus iad ag taithneamh agus ag spréacharnaigh, agus eisean dhá fhiafraí dhe féin cá bhfuaradar an solas! Dá éaghmais sin go léir, bhí sa riocht 'na raibh an chailís sin cúmtha rud éigin a chimeádadh greim ar shúilibh an té a chíodh í, agus do chuireadh áthas isteach in' aigne trína shúilibh.

D'fhéach Niamh uirthi, go dlúth agus go daingean, ach níor labhair sí aon fhocal amach as a béal. D'fhéach an bheirt eile uirthi go dlúth agus go daingean, leis, agus níor stadadar ach dhá moladh.

"Ba mhaith liom labhairt leat-sa, a Athair", arsa Niamh le Colla.

D'imíodar i leataoibh.

"A leithéid seo, a Athair", ar sise. "Tá m'aigne socair agam le mórán aimsire ar me féin a thabhairt suas don tSlánaitheóir i dtigh ban rialta. Ba mhaith liom do chómhairle ' dh'fháil, a Athair, i dtaobh an teaghlaigh ban rialta 'nar ceart dom dul, de réir do bhreithiúntais".

"Ar mhiste dhom a dh'fhiafraí, a 'níon ó", ar seisean, "cad é an fhaid aimsire ó shocraís an ní sin i t'aigne ar dtúis?"

"Bhí sé i m'aigne, a Athair, ar feadh i bhfad", ar sise, "sarar dhaingnigh sé ann. Ní dó' liom go bhféadfainn a dh'ínsint duit cruínn, a Athair, cad é an fhaid atá sé daingean, ach tá sé daingean le tamall maith".

Caibideal 59: An Ga Gréine Céanna

Do stad sé ar feadh tamaill.

"An dó' leat, a 'níon ó", ar seisean, an bhféadfá a dh'ínsint dom cad a chuir an ní sin isteach i t'aigne ar dtúis?"

"Féadfad", ar sise. "Nuair a thosnaigh an t-ollmhúchán i gcómhair an chogaidh mhóir seo atá curtha dhínn againn, thugas fé ndeara conas mar a bhí na fir go léir dhá cheapadh agus dhá shocrú 'na aigne go ndéanfaidís íbirt anama ar son na hÉireann agus ar son an Chreidimh. Ní raibh éinne ba ghéire dhá gcur go léir suas chun na híbirte sin a dhéanamh ná mise. Ansan do thuigeas i m'aigne, nuair ná raibh ar mo chumas an íbirt a dhéanamh ar an gcuma 'na rabhadar san dhá déanamh, gurbh é ba lú ba ghann dom í ' dhéanamh ar an gcuma 'na raibh ar mo chumas í ' dhéanamh. Dheineas ar an gcuma san í. Ghabhas orm féin i láthair Dé ceangal gan céile eile do ghlacadh choíche ach an Slánaitheóir, moladh go deó leis! Sin é mo chuid-se den íbirt, a Athair. Tá an ceangal san orm. Ní fhéadfainn imeacht ó m'athair an fhaid a bhí sé beó. Níl aon rud anois chun me ' chosc ar dhul isteach i dteaghlach ban rialta agus an íbirt do chur i ngníomh".

"I dtreó ná beadh aon bhaol go ndéanfí aon dearúd, a 'níon ó", arsa Colla, "ba mhaith liom aon cheist amháin eile do chur".

"Cuir aon cheist is maith leat chúm, a Athair", arsa Niamh, "agus neósfad an fhírinne dhuit".

"Nuair a dheinis an íbirt sin, nuair a thugais tu féin suas mar sin don tSlánaitheóir, an dó' leat a' raibh aon éileamh ag éinne eile ort?"

"Ní raibh, a Athair", ar sise, "aon éileamh ag éinne eile, ná níl anois". Do stad sí. "Ach is dócha", ar sise, "gur ceart dom an méid seo a dh'ínsint duit. Is cuímhin leat an t-ógánach Lochlannach úd a tháinig anso fadó, nuair a bhí mo dhriotháir Tadhg anso?"

"Is cuímhin liom é go maith", arsa Colla.

Caibideal 59: An Ga Gréine Céanna

"Chuaigh sé suas go hUíbh Máine in éineacht le Tadhg. An chéad uair a chonac é, tháinig ana-chion agam air. Tháinig grá agam do. Sin í an fhírinne. Thuigeas i m'aigne go dtáinig an grá céanna aige sin dómh-sa. Níor labhramair. Ach do tuigeadh an scéal eadrainn. Nuair a tháinig an scéal go raibh sé ag glacadh an Chreidimh, bhí áthas mór orm. Ansan, nuair a tháinig an scéal go raibh sé chun bheith 'na shagart, níorbh fhéidir liom an scéal a thuiscint in aon chor. B'é deireadh mo mhachnaimh ar an ngnó gur thuigeas i m'aigne go raibh ceangailte orm é ' chur as mo chroí ar fad. Do dheineas san. Ní raibh aon bhaint in aon chor, a Athair, ag an méid sin scéil leis an gceangal so adeirim leat do ghlacas orm féin i dtaobh an tSlánaitheóra".

"Tá go maith, a 'níon ó", arsa Colla. "Déanfad-sa an ní seo atá agat dá iarraidh orm. Ní mór dhom, áfach, beagán aimsire chuige. Cuirfead scéala chút ó thuaidh chómh luath agus ' bheidh an áit ceapaithe agam agus gach aon rud socair agam".

Do scaradar. Bhí Tadhg agus Caoilte imithe ar fuid na mainistreach, Tadhg ag tispeáint na mainistreach do Chaoilte, agus Caoilte ag cur aithne ar na manachaibh, go mór mór ar an muíntir go raibh sean-aithne ag Tadhg orthu.

Seachtain díreach i ndiaidh an lae sin, tháinig Colla féin go hUíbh Máine. D'imigh Tadhg agus Niamh agus é féin soir go Cíll Dara, go teaghlach Bhríde. Bhí áthas nárbh fhéidir a dh'ínsint ar Chómharba Bhríde agus ar an uile dhuine de sna mnáibh rialta nuair a fuaradar go raibh Niamh le fanúint acu. D'fhan sí acu, agus má ba gha gréine í fadó, ag teacht i gcuideachtain, i dteaghlach a hathar, b'í an ga gréine céanna í ag gluaiseacht i measc na maighdean naofa, i dteaghlach Bhríde, go dtí gur lean sí a hathair.

CRÍOCH

Timeline

(some dates are necessarily approximate; events not covered in Niamh *are also included to give a fuller picture of the historical record)*

AD 967: The battle of Solchaid: Mathúin mac Cinéide, king of the Dál gCais in Co. Clare, inflicts a defeat on the Norse.

AD 976: Mathúin is killed by Maolmhuaidh, king of Deas-Mhúmhain, of the Eóghanacht Raithlinn dynasty. Maolmhuaidh becomes king of the whole of Munster. Mathúin is succeeded as king of the Dál gCais by his brother, Brian Bórú.

AD 977: Brian Bórú's capture of Inis Cathaigh.

AD 978: The battle of Bealach Leachta: Brian Bórú defeats the Eóghanacht Raithlinn. Maolmhuaidh is killed, and Brian Bórú becomes king of Munster.

AD 980: M'leachlainn Mór inflicts a great defeat on the Norse of Dublin.

AD 982: Brian's attack on Ossory leads to conflict with M'leachlainn, who invades and cuts down the sacred tree of the Dalcassians.

AD 983: Brian attacks Ossory again, capturing the king and taking hostages.

AD 984: Brian forms an alliance with the Norse of Waterford to attack Leinster and Dublin. He subjugates Ossory and ravages M'leachlainn's own lands in Meath.

AD 985: The Decies revolt against Brian's rule in Munster, leading to an invasion and the devastation of the Decies territories.

AD 988: Brian attacks Connacht and Meath. The invasion of Connacht is successfully defeated.

AD 989: M'leachlainn invades Munster.

AD 991: Brian invades Leinster again.

AD 992: M'leachlainn leads an expedition against Connacht. The two sides (Brian and the Connachtmen, and the forces of Leinster) retire without battle in Westmeath.

AD 993: Brian wages war against Connacht again, and devastates Breifne in the north.

AD 996: Brian seizes hostages in Leinster. He is now dominant in the whole of Southern Ireland.

AD 997: Brian and M'leachlainn agree to divide Ireland. M'leachlainn will rule the North and Brian the South.

AD 999: The Leinstermen ally with the Norse and revolt against Brian. Brian defeats them at Gleann Mháma, and attacks Dublin.

AD 1000: Sitric, the king of Dublin, is expelled, but then submits to Brian and is restored to his kingdom.

AD 1002: M'leachlainn is forced to submit to Brian when the Northern Uí Néill fail to come to his assistance. The northern kingdoms still resist Brian, but Brian retires from a battle against them without a fight.

AD 1005: Brian marches to Armagh, and gives twenty ounces of gold to the cathedral there. He receives hostages from most of the northern kingdoms.

Timeline

AD 1006: Brian makes a fresh circuit of the north, and receives hostages from some kingdoms.

AD 1008: Flaithbheartach Ó Néill of Cineál Eóghain in the North submits to Brian, but Cineál Chonaill still hold out against him.

AD 1011: Brian attacks Cineál Chonaill, capturing the king and bringing him back to Ceann Cora, where he finally submits to Brian. Brian is now recognised as an overking by the whole of Ireland. Njáll Þorgeirsson and his family are killed in an infamous burning in Iceland.

AD 1012: Brian falls out with Maolmhórdha, king of Leinster, attributed by later annals to the scheming of Queen Gormfhlaith. Maolmhórdha encourages the northern kings to revolt. Cineál Eóghain attack Cineál Chonaill, while the Norse of Dublin attack Leinster.

AD 1013: Brian sends his son Murchadh to attack Leinster. Brian's army arrives to join in a blockade of Dublin from September until Christmas. Brian's forces then return home. Gunnar Lambason is slain by Kári Sölmundarson in the court of Jarl Sigurd in the Orkneys.

AD 1014: Knowing that Brian will return, Sitric visits the Orkneys and the Isle of Man to appeal to the Norse there to aid him in preparing his defence against Brian. The Northern kings refuse to join in the coming struggle, and most of the Connacht kingdoms refuse to rally to Brian's side. M'leachlainn withdraws his Meath troops from Brian's forces after a quarrel, leaving Brian with the support of Munster and south Connacht alone to attack the forces of Leinster and Dublin on Good Friday. The sides are evenly matched, but Brian's army eventually prevails, although retreating Norsemen kill Brian. Murchadh, Maolmhórdha, Sigurd of the Orkneys and Bróðir of the Isle of Man are killed. Sitric remains in the city and avoids the battle (or in some accounts is put to flight in the battle but survives it). Brian's body is buried in Armagh. M'leachlainn becomes high king of Ireland again until his death in AD 1022.

Notes

Caibideal 1

35 Some of the events in this chapter—Brian Bórú's burning of Limerick, his pursuit of the Norse to Scattery Island and the capture of Íomhar, Amhlaoibh and Duíbhgeann there—are mentioned in FFÉ Book 2 Chapter 23. Historically speaking, Brian Bórú's capture of Scattery Island took place in AD 977.

35 *Lámh le farraige agus lámh le tír*: *láimh le* means "close by, hard by, alongside". See PUL's *Na Cheithre Soisgéil* (pp202-203), where we read *nuair a bhí sé ag teacht i ngar do Bhetphagé i mBetánia, láimh leis an sliabh ar a dtugtar Olibhet*. The dative was not given in the original text of *Niamh* in this phrase. The fact that two *lámh*'s are mentioned may play a role here, but evidence that would resolve the issue one way or the other is lacking in Muskerry literature.

Notes

36 *I gcoinnibh namhad an Chreidimh*: in GCh there is a "rule" against concatenation of genitives. Gerald O'Nolan, in his *Studies in Modern Irish, Part I,* offers an alternative presentation of Irish grammar that dovetails better with PUL's usage (see pp158-160 therein). Rather than prohibiting successive genitives, O'Nolan's exposition holds that noun phrases standing where the oblique cases would be expected can be given in the nominative absolute in what he calls the Bracketed Construction, where the noun phrase as a whole is bracketed off and undeclined. However, the Unbracketed Construction, where all nouns are given in their logical cases, is also correct, and the choice of usage depends on whether the author wished to view the noun phrase as a unit, or as a succession of nouns. In other words, *ar son mhuíntir na hÉireann* and *ar son muíntire na hÉireann* are both equally grammatically correct. The Unbracketed Construction is often found in PUL's works after prepositions or prepositional phrases that take the genitive, including *tar éis, chun* and *i gcoinnibh. Ag déanamh gach aon tsaghas friothála* in chapter 8 here is an example of the Bracketed Construction: nouns phrases with *saghas* regularly stand in the nominative absolute.

37 *Ins gach cloch díobh*: the dative *cloich* is not given here, but *gach cloch díobh* may be seen as a noun phrase in the Bracketed Construction.

37 *Scolaibh*: this is a variant dative plural derived from an older nominative plural, *scola.* PUL normally uses *scoileannaibh* in the dative (see, for instance, chapter 2 here).

Caibideal 2

39 *Mac do Thadhg Mhór Ó Chealla*: note the historically correct lenition of the surname in the dative.

41 *Ón ngalar gcéanna*: eclipsis of the adjective in the dative singular is sometimes found in WM Irish. Eclipsis is more likely to be employed when the noun itself is also eclipsed. Certain phrases, such as *san am gcéanna* and *ar an gcuma gcéanna* are consistently found with the adjective eclipsed. Compare *leis an láimh dheis* later in chapter 2 here with *leis an láimh ndeis* in chapter 10.

41 *Buille ' thuaigh*: "an axe-blow". This is a truncation of *buille dhe thuaigh.*

42 *Sin ar chuir*: "that is all it managed to do". *Ar* here is the comprehensive relative particle ("all that") combined with the perfective particle.

Caibideal 3

44 *Ríthibh Éireann*: the use of *Éireann* in the genitive without the article denotes something fundamentally, concretely or essentially Irish, such as *fir Éireann,* "the men of Ireland", rather than a part or a temporary or incidental attribute of Ireland, as in *cómhacht na hÉireann,* "the power of Ireland", and *ar fuid na hÉireann,* "throughout Ireland". The distinction is to some extent idiomatic, as *muíntir na hÉireann* has the article.

44 *Fiann Éireann*: a warrior band led by Fionn mac Cúmhaill in defence of Ireland in the Fenian cycle of myths.

Notes

45 *Mar a ghléas Fionn é*: note that PUL doesn't appear to realise that the events recounted in the Fenian cycle of myths are not historically attested events.

Caibideal 4

45 The battles of Bealach Leachta and Gleann Mh//áma are mentioned in FFÉ Book 2 Chapter 23.

46 *Ag dul i neartmhaire*: "getting stronger". This construction (*ag dul i bhfuaire, i laíghead, i neartmhaire*, etc) is used in WM Irish in preference to *ag éirí* (*ag éirí fuar, beag, neartmhar*, etc). See "Seachain!" in *An Músgraigheach*, Uimhir 1, Meitheamh 1943, p29.

46 *Chúig bhliana déag*: note that *cúig* is normally lenited in WM Irish, save in counting, when it appears as *a cúig*. *Chúig* usually lenites even a plural noun governed by it.

46 The battle of Fán Chonradh is briefly mentioned in FFÉ Book 2 Chapter 23, where Dónall mac Faoláin is wrongly referred to as Dónall Ó Faoláin, which usage is therefore also found in *Niamh* here. PUL's account confuses two campaigns—the battle of Fán Chonradh in AD 979, and a campaign in AD 995 that led to Dónall mac Faoláin's death.

47 *An fear ag titim agus fear eile in' inead láithreach*: "a man falling and another man immediately in his place". See PUL's comments in NIWU (p5) where he explains that in *chonaic sé an duine agá chosaibh* "this use of the definite article is peculiar to Irish speech. Its effect here is to intensify the idea of the presence of a person in the place. It makes for vividness of description, as if to express that the person, at that moment, was a very 'definite' thing for him".

48 *Cé 'ra*: this form is used in WM Irish before the indirect relative of the copula, and corresponds simply to *cér* in GCh. *Cé 'ra díobh é* here means "what family he was from, where he originated from". PUL spelt this *cé 'ra* and as *cé 'ro* in his novel *Séadna*. The authorised *Foclóir do Shéadna* indicates that *cé 'ra* is an abbreviation of *cé gurab*.

48 PUL's comments regarding the great joy of the chieftains at being subject to Brian Bórú may be cited as an example of the mistaken understanding of the social realities of early Ireland this book is criticised for.

49 Sitric married a daughter of Brian Bórú in AD 1012 who is incorrectly identified as Béibheann later in this work. Note that the chronology of the historical events is rather different to that presented in this fictional work.

49 Drowning is a typical mode of suicide frequently mentioned in traditional Irish literature.

Caibideal 5

50 *Ag cogarnaigh*: "whispering". This would be *ag cogarnach* in GCh, but as a feminine verbal noun in *-ach* the dative is calcified in *-igh* in such phrases in traditional WM Irish. *Cogarnach* is part of a class of similar verbal nouns, often referring to noises of people or animals (*ag amhastraigh*, "barking"; *ag géimrigh*, "lowing", of cattle; *ag siosraigh*, "neighing"). All such verbal nouns tend to take

the dative only when used as verbal nouns with *ag* (compare, for example, *leis an gcogarnach* in chapter 46 here).

Caibideal 6

54 *Ní raibh duine ba mhó áthas ná Niamh*: "there was no-one filled with greater joy than Niamh". All such constructions have the comparative followed by a noun in the *bun-fhuirm*, which covers both nominative and accusative case usages following the disappearance of a morphologically distinct accusative form in Modern Irish. Gerald O'Nolan explained this case usage as being the Accusative of Specification ("there was no-one who was greater in terms of joy than Niamh"). See *Studies in Modern Irish, Part I*, p213.

54 *Lena chara*: note that the dative *charaid*, used elsewhere in this work, is not used here.

55 *Gach aon tsaghas urrama agus onóra acu á thabhairt*: despite the plural antecedent, we have *á dhéanamh* and not *á ndéanamh*, reflecting a rule in WM Irish that where the agent (*acu*) precedes the verbal noun, the pronoun object of the verbal noun does not agree with the antecedent. This rule was explained in a letter written by PUL to O'Nolan on November 23rd 1914, later published in O'Nolan's autobiography, *Beatha Dhuine a Thoil* (pp133-135).

56 *Cad chuige gur thispeáin sé an grá úd di an chéad lá má bhí aon chuímhneamh aige ar bheith 'na shagart?*: This passage reflects PUL's lack of knowledge of church history. Clerical celibacy began to be imposed in AD 1074 in the Gregorian reforms, but the Irish church was not under the control of Rome at the time, and only came gradually under Roman influence after a series of synods in the 12th century following the Anglo-Norman conquest. Priests and bishops frequently raised families in early Ireland (hence the Gaelic surnames Mac an tSagairt and Mac an Easpaig), and clerical celibacy only became strictly enforced in Ireland from the AD 1383 Synod of Armagh.

56 *Deacon*: note that PUL's religious vocabulary is generally English, probably reflecting the dominance of the English language in the nineteenth-century Roman Catholic Church in Ireland. *Deagánach* is the form used in GCh.

56 *Érdam*: this word occurs in modern dictionaries, despite PUL's claim the word did not exist in modern Irish, as *eardhamh*. Note that PUL's use of *sacraistí* is a further example of his preference for Anglophone vocabulary in ecclesiastical matters.

Caibideal 7

56 This entire chapter is remarkable for its sense that Brian Bórú's wars were being conducted with noble aims, to defend Ireland, the church and wider Christendom. The papal legate appears to be encouraging Brian in his wars—and even encouraging him to slaughter the Norse-Gaels *en masse*. This seems to be another instance of PUL's limited understanding of early Ireland or the way in which he reads Irish history backwards from an early twentieth-century perspective—Brian was one warlord among many engaged in a struggle for

power, not for the defence of Irish or wider European culture. The Celtic Church in Ireland was not under Roman control, and there was no Papal legate to Ireland.

57 *Ceann an Teampaill, Fear Inid Íosa Críost*: "the head of the church, the vicar of Christ", i.e. Roman Catholic terms for the Pope.

57 *I gcoinnibh na slua págánach*: *págánach* is either an adjective in the genitive plural or a noun in the genitive plural: "the pagan hosts" or "the hosts of pagans".

58 *Do bheadh an greim a bhí uathu acu ar oileán na hÉireann um an dtaca so, fé mar atá acu ar Shasana*: once again, the chronology appears inexact, as the time period under discussion here corresponds to the earlier part of the Anglo-Saxon reign of Æthelred the Unready. The Danish king, Sweyn Forkbeard, did not take the English throne until AD 1013, the year before the Battle of Clontarf in Ireland.

58 *Rí Ó nEachach*: "the king of Iveagh". The nominative of this placename is Uíbh Eachach (see under Uíbh Eachach in the *Index of Placenames*), reflecting fossilisation of a locative dative. If the Bracketed Construction had been used here, we could have had *rí Uíbh Eachach.* PUL used the Unbracketed Construction here, declining *ó* in the genitive plural. See also further explanation of such placenames under Uí Fighinti in the *Index of Placenames.*

Caibideal 8

63 *Agus tháinig*: adjusted from *agus táinig*. There was an occasional tendency in WM Irish for a *t* to be delenited after an *s*. Cf. *shíos agus tsuas* (i.e. *thíos agus thuas*) in PUL's *Séadna* (p12).

64 *A lán-ndóthain bídh agus dí acu*: "complete sufficiency of food and drink". It is worth noting the transference of eclipsis following the possessive particle to the second element of the compound word *lán-dóthain.*

64 The recounting to the Papal legate of the battle of Sulcoit of AD 967/968 shows that PUL is mixing up the dates of many battles—this battle occurred decades before the time period covered in *Niamh.* The battle of Sulcoit is briefly mentioned in FFÉ Book 2 Chapter 23. See also the account in CGG §LII.

64 *Maghnas mac Arailt*: PUL has Maghnas mac Arailt dying on Scattery Island in the campaign in AD 977 or 978 that led to the death of King Íomhar of Limerick, but in fact there is no historical record of his death, which is assumed to have been in the late 980s, when references to him cease in the annals. It is clear that PUL is confusing many different events.

65 *I ngach*: PUL normally uses the WM form *ins gach*, but occasionally uses the form found in GCh, *i ngach.*

Caibideal 9

67 *Tabhair chúinn anso an bosca iarainn úd 'na raibh an chailís óir ann*: it is interesting that the preposition *i* appears to be used twice in this phrase in that *'na* is etymologically derived from *i.* Grammatically speaking, *'na raibh an*

chailís óir would have been sufficient, or it could have been phrased *go raibh an chailís óir ann.* Where *'na* and *'nar* are used in PUL's works to create indirect relative clauses, they have lost their connection with the preposition *i*, just as the original derivation of *go* and *gur*, used to create indirect relative clauses, from the preposition *ag* has become obscured. It is for this reason, as well as to reflect the pronunciation, that such forms cannot be edited as *ina.* The lack of any remaining link between *i* and *'na* is also why *'na*, when used as a helping preposition to create indirect relative clauses, is generally found as *n-a*, with no apostrophe, in PUL's works, as in the original text here, which had *tabhair chúghainn anso an bosca iarainn úd n-a raibh an chailís óir ann.*

67 *Mise aduairt gur cheart í ' chur anso*: it is worth nothing that in such relative clauses *mise* is followed by a third-person verb *duairt.* This contrasts with hypercorrect English usage ("it is I who am...", "it is you who are..."), although the Irish here is similar to the pattern found in colloquial English ("it is you who is...", etc). *Mise aduairt* may be seen as elliptical for *mise an té aduairt.* Contrast PUL's statement in a letter to Risteárd Pléimeann dated February 27th 1918, part of the G1,277 (1) collection of manuscripts held in the National Library of Ireland, where he states that *ní duine mise gur mhaith liom* is the correct Irish for "I am not a person who would wish", and not *ní duine mise gur mhaith leis.*

69 *Sa ríogan óg*: note that the dative *ríogain* is not given here.

71 *'Na leithéid seo ' chuma*: a truncation of *'na leithéid seo dhe chuma.* Lenition of *de* often allows the preposition to drop out in speech (and, as shown here, in writing too).

71 *Ceann So-fheicse an Chreidimh*: "the Visible Head of the Faith", a phrase used by PUL to refer to the Pope.

Caibideal 10

73 *Mura mbeadh Murchadh, bhí Gleann Mháma ag na Lochlannaigh*: the use of the preterite *bhí* rather than the conditional *bheadh* here is emphatic in tone.

75 *I t'Árdríogain ar Éirinn go léir ó Dhonncha Dí go Tigh Mháire!*: a set phrase, meaning from the easternmost point to the westernmost point of Ireland. For further discussion, see *Donncha Dí* and *Tigh Mháire* in the *Index of Placenames.*

Caibideal 11

79 *Déarfaidís an rud úd aduairt Cathal leis an gcleasaí. "Airiú, a mhic léinn", arsa Cathal, "cad fé ndeara dhuit bheith as do mheabhair!"*: PUL is here referring to the story he updated into modern Irish in *An Craos-Deamhan* (p60). The words quoted were addressed by Cathal (king of Cashel and Munster) to Mac Conglinne when the latter ground his teeth loudly against a stone to attract Cathal's attention in a bid to rescue Cathal from the demon of gluttony.

Caibideal 12

81 I have been unable to discover a reference to an Irish saint promising woe to whoever would look in a woman's face.

Notes

82 *Ag Éire*: note that the dative *Éirinn* is not given here.

87 *"Cad iad na gnóthaí iad, a Athair?" "Tá, maithe móra a bheith tagaithe ann"*: this introductory *tá* was explained by PUL in NIWU (p116) as an introductory particle asserting the truth of the subsequent answer. The example given there is *cad é an sgéal é? Tá, sgéal ait* (quoted from *Séadna*, p53).

87 *Glacfaid cáirde Mh'leachlainn arm*: note the use of the plural verb with the plural subject in this and the subsequent sentence. PUL regularly uses this syntax in the present and future tenses, and there are occasional examples in the other tenses (cf. *nuair a chuadar na fir abhaile* in *Séadna*, p54).

Caibideal 13

89 *Mura héagóir dá dhaoine féin*: the use of h-prefixation here is worth noting. This appears to be unique in the published corpus of Muskerry Irish. *Maran* is found in AÓL's Irish where *mura/mara* is followed by the (deleted) present-tense copula and a predicate, although no examples with a predicate starting with a vowel are available.

91 *Ar ar thrácht an Leagáid*: this construction is equivalent to *gur thrácht an Leagáid air. A* (and in the past tense *ar*) as an indirect relative particle is used directly after a preposition, whereas *go/gur* is used where the preposition is shifted, as is more usual, to the end. The first *ar* here is therefore the preposition and the second *ar* is the relative particle. These are not pronounced identically: the pronunciation is /er′ ər/, as indicated by PUL in NIWU (p118), where he states that *ar ar* in such constructions is "pron. *air ur*".

Caibideal 14

94 *Bertha*: the verbal adjective of the verb *beirim, breith* is generally spelt *beirthe*, but the pronunciation is /b′erhə/, with a broad *r*. The spelling *beirthe* is also somewhat suboptimal in terms of indicating the WM pronunciation, as an epenthetic vowel is sometimes produced between an *r* and a *th*. *Beirthe* might therefore imply a pronunciation of /b′er′ihi/, which is in fact the pronunciation of *beirithe*, the verbal adjective of the verb *beirím, beiriú*, "boiled". Consequently, it seems clearer, both in terms of differentiation from *beirithe* and in terms of showing the pronunciation, to edit *beirthe* as *bertha*.

95 *Míle ' shlí*: a truncation of *míle dhe shlí*, "a mile's distance".

98 *Níor mhiste "gasra nár dhó'" a thabhairt ar an mór-shlua san, mar a tugtar sa tsean-amhrán*: I haven't been able to identify this song.

Caibideal 15

98 This chapter appears to be partly based on the account in FFÉ Book 2 Chapter 24, which relates how M'leachlainn was forced out of the high kingship by the kings of Ireland because Brian Bórú was doing more to rid the country of the Viking incursions. However, M'leachlainn did oppose the Vikings, and his defeat of the Vikings in the AD 980 Battle of Tara is seen by modern historians as of greater consequence than the AD 1014 Battle of Clontarf in weakening the Kingdom of

Dublin. Professor Ó Corráin explains "the battle at Clontarf was not a struggle between the Irish and the Norse for the sovereignty of Ireland; neither was it a great national victory which broke the power of the Norse forever (long before Clontarf the Norse had become a minor political force in Irish affairs). In fact, Clontarf was part of the internal struggle for sovereignty and was essentially the revolt of the Leinstermen against the dominance of Brian, a revolt in which their Norse allies played an important but secondary role" (*Ireland before the Normans*, p130). Seathrún Céitinn relates how M'leachlainn was given a month by Brian Bórú to prepare his forces to defend the high kingship (see also CGG §LXXII), how Aodh Ó Néill refused to come to M'leachlainn's help, and how Brian Bórú gave M'leachlainn an additional year to prepare to defend his position (see CGG §LXXV).

98 *Seacht cathanna*: note that eclipsis is often omitted in PUL's works after *seacht*, *ocht* and *deich*, as the /t/ or /h/ at the end of these numerals would tend to devoice the first consonant of the following noun. Further examples are found in *Niamh*. Gerald O'Nolan explained in his *New Era Grammar of Modern Irish*, "*deich cinn, deich pearsana, deich toibreacha*—10 heads, person, wells—are heard. The reason is that the final *h* sound of *deich* unvoices the consonant resulting from eclipsis, and thus restores the original one. Then *seacht cinn*, etc., follow these analogically" (§97).

101 While Brian Bórú forced M'leachlainn to step down in AD 1002 after his Northern Uí Néill kinsmen refused to come to his aid, and so the high kingship was surrendered peacefully, Brian was a military warlord who had subjugated all the tribes of southern Ireland in battle and was not averse to bloodshed. PUL seems to be developing the point made in FFÉ Book 2 Chapter 25 about how Brian Bórú could have had M'leachlainn killed, but chose not to do so.

101 *Géill*: *géill* means "hostages (human pledges)". Patrick S. Dinneen's translation of FFÉ Book 2 Chapter 24 says "sureties and hostages".

101 This section contains a long digression comparing Brian Bórú's supposedly generous way of taking the high kingship to the seizure of the English throne in AD 1399 from Richard II by Henry IV, known as Bolingbroke. Richard II was murdered after his deposition.

102 A reference to the apparent murder of "the princes in the tower", Edward V and Prince Richard, imputed to the Duke of Gloucester in AD 1483, thus enabling the latter to ascend the throne of England as Richard III.

102 A reference to the Norman Conquest of England in AD 1066 by William, Duke of Normandy, later William I of England.

102 Richard II made an expedition to Ireland in May-July 1399, just as Bolingbroke was gathering his forces. Soon after his return to England, in late September 1399, he was forced to abdicate in favour of Bolingbroke.

103 In fact, Brian Bórú's elevation to the high kingship was followed by military campaigns in Ulster and Leinster in the following decade to subdue the regional kings, and it was not until AD 1011 that Brian had forced all the regional kings to submit to him. The high kingship had been a very loose form of suzerainty

until then, but Brian's subjugation of the regional kings is the basis for the assertion of historians that he was the first real king of the whole of Ireland.

103 The story of Conchúr mac Neasa and Feargas mac Róigh is taken from the Ulster cycle of myths. These are not attested historical events. Further details are given under these names in the *Index of Personal Names*.

104 *Firu Éireann*: *firu*, "men", was the vocative and accusative plural of *fer* (whence *fear*) in Old Irish. PUL had little knowledge of Old or Middle Irish, and so appears to think that *firu* was the Old Irish nominative plural, which was in fact *fir*.

Caibideal 16

107 *I reachtaibh an anama ' bhaint as a chéile*: the use of the genitive where the whole noun-verbal noun phrase is governed by an antecedent that takes the genitive is not found in GCh, but is a feature of traditional forms of WM Irish.

107 *Tá an scéal go háiféiseach*: it is worth noting that use of *go* with predicative adjectives is much more widespread in PUL's works than in GCh, which limits this to a handful of adjectives. PUL explained that the use of *go* with a predicate adjective is an intensifier and that "what the grammars say about turning an adjective into an adverb by prefixing *go* gives very little genuine information" (NIWU, p135). *Go háiféiseach* here means "absurd and no mistake".

108 *Ag magadh faoi*: this is a rare example in PUL's works of *faoi*, which is the form accepted in GCh, instead of the usual WM form *fé*.

Caibideal 17

110 *Trí ' fhoclaibh*: a truncation of *trí dhe fhoclaibh*.

112 *Drifiúr do Mhaolruanaidh na Paidre*: the first wife of Brian Bórú, Mór, is recorded as being the daughter of one of the kings of Uíbh Fhiachrach Áidhne, although it is not clear which king it was. In particular, PUL's view that she was the sister of Maolruanaidh na Paidre is problematic, as Maolruanaidh was the first of the Ó hEidhin kings of Uíbh Fhiachrach Áidhne. Mór was the mother of Murchadh and some of Brian Bórú's other children.

116 *An droch-obair a bhíodh tagaithe, is minic a bhíodh sé curtha ar neamhní aici*: this sentence is a good illustration of the fact that a feminine antecedent (*droch-obair*) can be referred to by *sé*. The focus is not fully on the noun and its grammatical gender as such, but rather on the thing that the noun represents.

Caibideal 18

118 *Ar Chúige na Mí is ea ' dh'fhág Brian 'na rí é*: PUL makes it sound as if Brian Bórú "appointed" M'leachlainn king of Meath after he surrendered the high kingship. However, M'leachlainn was historically king of Meath AD ca. 975 to 1022, as well as high king of Ireland from AD 980 to 1002, when he surrendered the high kingship to Brian Bórú, who was high king until he died in the Battle of Clontarf, whereupon M'leachlainn resumed the high kingship, 1014-1022.

Notes

Caibideal 19

119 *Duais shaibhir*: given as *duais saibhir* in the original text of *Niamh*, probably reflecting an obscuring of the /h/ of *shaibhir* after the /ʃ/ of *duais*.

122 *Buille ' chasúr*: "hammer blow", a truncation of *buille dhe chasúr*.

124 *Gurb in é gnó a bhí agam díot-sa inniu, chun na híomhá san a bhreith síos ag triall air*: in *Papers on Irish Idiom* (p53) PUL explains that the definite article may be omitted before a noun in copula sentences defined by a subsequent relative clause. The example given there is *do b'é céad* (or *an chéad*) *duine a tháinig é. Gnó* here is similarly defined by a relative clause, and so the definite article can be dropped.

124 *Ataoi-se*: note the use of *ataoi*, an older second-person singular combined with the relative particle, corresponding to *atá tú* in GCh, or to *atánn tú* and *ataíonn tú* in more recent forms of Munster Irish.

Caibideal 21

131 *D'fhéadfí*: PUL does not normally lenite the autonomous form of the verb in any tense, but *d'fhéadfí* seems to be something of an exception to this rule; *do féadfí* is rarely found in PUL's works. By contrast, the autonomous forms of the preterite and past habitual are *do féadadh* and *do féadtí*.

Caibideal 22

134 The list of taxes paid to Brian Bórú while he was high king appears to be based on FFÉ Book 2 Chapter 25.

135 *Deich gcéad damh agus deich gcéad caíora*: *céad* takes the nominative singular (e.g. *céad bean*, as stated by PUL in *Irish numerals and how to use them*, p11). Such usage historically reflects the fact that the genitive plural and nominative singular of first- and second-declension nouns are often identical, yet *céad bean* shows it is now the nominative singular and not the genitive plural that should be used. Nevertheless, PUL's works regularly have *céad blian*, and not *céad bliain*, either as a calcified form or as a general exception that applies where the genitive plural of a noun is identical to the nominative singular save for its having a broadened ending. (It is difficult to find attestation, but *céad súl* and *céad glún* may work in the same way.)

135 *Chúig céad bó*: non-lenition of *céad* in the phrase *chúig céad* is the norm in WM Irish due to the coincidence of homorganic consonants across the word boundary.

136 This passage implies that Brian allowed the Norse to inhabit the port cities of Ireland through some kind of calculation of the economic benefit that their trading skills would bring to Ireland. In fact, an Ireland divided into small kingdoms was in no position to expel the Norse—and Dublin, Waterford and Cork were all founded as Viking settlements.

136 *Chúig cínn fhichead*: *fichead* is lenited after plural nouns ending in a slender consonant (as well as after singular nouns whether they end in broad/slender consonants or vowels).

136 *D'óltí*: "would be drunk". This is the past habitual autonomous form, and notable for the failure to use h-prefixation (cf. *do hití* earlier in the paragraph). The few attested examples of this phrase in WM Irish are all of *d'óltí.*

136 *De sna trí hÁrdríthibh*: h-prefixation after *trí* was not given in the original.

136 PUL doesn't seem to realise the reigns of Conaire Mór mac Eidirsceóil and Cormac mac Airt are not historically attested. The list of the three most glorious high kings of Ireland may have been taken from FFÉ Book 2 Chapter 25.

Caibideal 23

140 *Eaglais Árd Mhacha*: Professor Ó Corráin notes that Armagh's status as the primatial see was advanced by Brian Bórú's recognition of its primacy in AD 1005 (see *Ireland before the Normans*, p127). FFÉ Book 2 Chapter 25 tells how Brian presented 20 ounces of gold to the church in Armagh.

Caibideal 24

143 This chapter, mentioning Brian Bórú's renovation of churches, support for learning and the building of roads mirrors the discussion in FFÉ Book 2 Chapter 25. The placenames mentioned in this chapter and the story of how a lady travelled in Ireland without being violated or robbed as a result of the peace of Brian's reign are also taken from FFÉ and CGG §LXXX. Professor Ó Corráin indicates that Brian Bórú made an attempt to bring the church under his control, with important churches and monasteries staffed by Dalcassian loyalists or even members of the Dalcassian dynasty, but also notes that the claim that Brian exhibited a reforming spirit greater than that of previous kings, founding churches and schools and serving as a patron of learning, lacks historical foundation and is simply twelfth-century propaganda, projecting the values of a later century back into the Ireland of Brian's time (*Ireland before the Normans*, pp127-128).

144 *Ag tabhairt droch-mheas*: *meas* and *droch-mheas* are often undeclined in the genitive, reflecting the fact this noun is often followed by *ag* or *ar*, which in any case begin with a vowel that could be confused with the vowel appended to *meas* in the genitive.

145 *Peocu caraid nú namhaid é*: this is an unusual example in PUL's works of *caraid*, the dative, being used as a nominative, possibly influenced by the symmetry with *namhaid*, which is also historically a dative form, but which has replaced the erstwhile nominative *namha* both in WM and elsewhere.

146 *Ó Mórdha*: what follows is a poem by Thomas Moore (1779-1852), written in 1808. Moore was born in Dublin; his father was from an Irish-speaking area of Co. Kerry and his mother from Co. Wexford. Yet PUL describes him as *gallda*. While there are Moores in Ireland of both English and Norman origin, the spelling Ó Mórdha is also attested as a surname of Irish Gaelic origin.

Notes

Caibideal 25

150 *Is dó' léi ná fuil ' fhios agam-sa é*: PUL explained in NIWU (pp144-145), that the final *é* in such sentences is not redundant and cannot be omitted, because it stands for a whole clause.

150 *É ' dh'fháil bháis*: this phrase stood in the original as *é ' dh'fháil báis*. Lenition is added here in line with the majority usage of PUL's works.

151 *Go bhfuiltí-se*: an older second-person plural form corresponding to *go bhfuil sibhse.*

151 *Ní éireófí*: note the failure to prefix *h* to the autonomous form here. Compare *ní haithneófí* in chapter 55.

151 *Bheithá*: both *bheithá* and *bheifá* are found in WM Irish in both the conditional and past subjunctive.

Caibideal 26

153 *Stoc beag ba seasca*: note the lack of the traditional genitive plural, *bó,* which can be explained by use with an adjective here (qualified use can allow the Bracketed Construction).

156 *Nár bhuailtear*: PUL generally uses the autonomous form of regular verbs unlenited (*ní buailtear, níor buaileadh, ní buailfar, ní buailfí, ní buailtí*), but the present subjunctive autonomous after *nár* is an exception to that rule. See also *nár chúitighthear a saothar léi* in PUL's *Séadna* (p75).

Caibideal 28

167 *Ba threise agus ba thréine*: note how PUL uses both the irregular and the regular comparative, *treise* and *tréine,* together in the same passage, for emphasis or enhanced description.

170 *Dhá bhuíon*: note that the correct dual *dhá bhuín* is not given here, indicating that the dual number had become haphazard in usage by the early twentieth century. *Dhá bhuíon* is also found elsewhere throughout *Niamh.*

Caibideal 29

172 Amhlaoibh is apparently an entirely fictional character; there is no historical evidence that Gormfhlaith had a son called Amhlaoibh.

Caibideal 31

184 *An trí mhíle*: numerals above one are correctly used with the singular definite article, particularly when the amount is seen as a unified whole.

185 *Is é is fada liom go mbeidh an cleas agam*: "I can't wait until I've mastered that trick". The doubling of the copula in forms like *is é is fada* and *b'é ab fhada* is emphatic. See the discussion in Gerald O'Nolan's *Studies in Modern Irish Part I,* pp16-17.

187 *Cad é an lámh a dh'fhéadfá-sa ' bheith agat sa ghadaíocht san?*: "what hand could you have had in that theft?" This is an interesting construction because of

the way in which *an lámh a bheith agat* has *lámh* governing *bheith* as its subject, and yet we don't have **cad é an lámh a dh'fhéadfadh bheith agat?*, and, at first glance, it might seem that *lámh* has been reinterpreted as the object of a verb "to have", with the *rud do bheith agat* construction brought fully into line syntactically with the English verb "to have". The explanation is rather that in Irish the final *é* in *d'fhéadfá-sa é* is required, and that *lámh a bheith agat* replaces this *é* in such sentences.

188 *Gur bhuachaill shímplí oscailte dhea-chroíoch é*: this passage is noteworthy for its use of lenition on the adjective as well as the noun following *gur*. This might appear to be a typographical error, but for the fact that PUL wrote in a letter to Risteárd Pléimeann (dated December 3rd 1919 and held in the G1,277 manuscript collection in the National Library of Ireland), "I have often heard the *gur* covering the two words. E.g. *bíodh gur dhuine mhacánta é*".

Caibideal 32

192 *Pé easnamh a bheadh ná ná beadh*: PUL explained in NIWU (pp128-129) the difference beween *ná ná* and *nú ná*. *Nú ná* is a disjunctive negative, used where there are two distinct contingencies, as in *ní osgalóchad an doras pé'cu thiocfidh sé nú ná tiocfidh sé* ("I will not open the door whether he comes or does not come"), where there are two distinct circumstances mentioned. By contrast, *ná ná* is a total negative, as in *ní osgalóchad an doras pé duine a thiocfidh ná ná tiocfidh* ("I will not open the door no matter who comes or does not come").

193 Brian Bórú's first wife, Mór, the mother of Murchadh, was the daughter of one of the kings of Uíbh Fhiachrach Áidhne. See the notes to chapter 17 above.

Caibideal 33

195 *Dob álainne*: "most beautiful". Both *álainne* and *áille*, found elsewhere in *Niamh*, are found in WM Irish as comparatives of *álainn*.

197 FFÉ Book 2 Chapter 25 relates how Brian Bórú asked Maolmhórdha, the king of Leinster, to send him some trees to serve as ship masts.

Caibideal 34

203 *An dá rí uasal*: note the lack of a plural adjective; historically the dual took a plural adjective (*uaisle*). This sentence is analogous to the one found in the manuscript of PUL's *Don Cíochóté* (with *an dá ríogain uasal*) that Osborn Bergin raised with PUL (see "Comhfhreagras idir an Athair Peadair agus an tAimhirgíneach", by Seán Ua Súilleabháin, in *Celtica*, Vol 24, 2003, p283), only to be told that PUL's native Irish sense would not permit the plural adjective there. Such phrases may have occurred only rarely in speech, and it seems PUL was unsure of his ground here, later writing to Shán Ó Cuív, "Feuch. Nílim ró-dheimhnightheach cé cu 'dhá ríogain uasal' an ceart nu 'dhá ríogain uaisle', ach tá fhios agam gur 'don dá ríogain uasail' an ceart" (see an undated note to Shán Ó Cuív, part of the G1,276 collection of manuscripts held in the National Library

of Ireland). This implies that in that phrase, where the dual phrase is in the dative, PUL preferred the dative singular feminine adjective.

203 *An dá Mhaor Mhór*: once again, *an dá Mhaor Mhór* fails to use the plural adjective after a noun in the dual.

Caibideal 37

221 *Chun an bhídh a hollmhófí don Árdríogan*: as PUL does not lenite the autonomous form (in any tense other than the present subjunctive), it follows that the relative particle *a* causes no change to a consonant, but prefixes *h* to an autonomous verb form starting with a vowel.

222 *Mac Mhurchadh*: this seems to be a reference to Murchadh's son, Toiréalach, who is introduced later in this work.

Caibideal 39

229 *Nár aithníodh*: note the lack of h-prefixation before the autonomous here.

230 *Chun imithe*: *imithe* is the genitive of the verbal noun, but the genitive of the verbal noun was not consistently used in PUL's works, as seen in *chun imeacht* in the preceding clause. Cf. *chun labhairt* in *Mo Sgéal Féin*, p56, and *chun labhartha* in *Séadna*, p51. The genitive of the verbal noun is used consistently with a possessive particle (cf. *chun a dhéanta* in both *Mo Sgéal Féin*, p138, and *Séadna*, p172).

231 This event is related in the Icelandic *Njáls saga*, which PUL appears to draw on for some background material.

232 *Le haon scuab-bhuille*: the expected h-prefixation before *aon* was not given in the original and is supplied here.

232 The story of how Cairí slew the killers of Niall in Sígurd's court in front of Sitric is told in the Icelandic *Njáls saga* (ch. 154).

Caibideal 40

235 The story of how trees were transported from Leinster to serve as tree masts, and how Maolmhórdha helped the Uí Faoláin carry the tree after a dispute arose between the three teams of carriers, is found in FFÉ Book 2 Chapter 25 and CGG §LXXXI. However, in FFÉ it is a silver clasp (or a silver button in CGG), and not a gold button, that Maolmhórdha lost on that occasion. Gormfhlaith's casting of the cloak into the fire and her scolding of Maolmhórdha for serving as Brian's beast of burden are also recounted in FFÉ and CGG, as was the story of the chess-game that led to Maolmhórdha's falling out with Murchadh.

237 *Do bhuíon eile*: note that the dative, *bhuín*, is not used here.

237 *Im beathaidh*: note delenition of *bheathaidh* across the labial boundary.

239 Conáing was historically the nephew, rather than the son, of Brian Bórú, being the son of Brian Bórú's elder brother, Donn Cuan mac Cinéide, as is clear from the account in FFÉ.

239 Irish annals relate how Murchadh found Maolmhórdha hiding in a yew tree after the Battle of Gleann Mháma in AD 999. See CGG §LXXI.

Notes

240 The beating of the messenger, Cogarán, to the extent that the bones of his skull were broken, is related in FFÉ (see also CGG §LXXXIII, where the messenger is called Cocarán).

Caibideal 41

242 *Geóbhad*: *geóbhad* is the first-person future of *gabháil*, corresponding to *gabhfaidh mé* in GCh. The forms of *gabháil* and *fáil* are therefore partly aligned in WM Irish. The first-person future of *fáil* is *gheóbhad*, with lenition in PUL's Irish, but can also be found as *geóbhad* in WM Irish.

Caibideal 42

245 *Ná táinig*: this form is retained here, as the verb *tagaim* was often used without the *ro* particle. In other words, forms such as *go dtáinig* and *ná táinig* are found alongside forms such as *gur tháinig* and *nár tháinig* in PUL's works.

Caibideal 43

256 *Ní iarrfar*: note the failure here to prefix *h* to *iarrfar* (compare *an fhaid a bhéad-sa beó ní h-iarfar airís ar chléireach dul ar aon tslógadh liom* in *An Craos-Deamhan*, p64). As PUL does not lenite the autonomous form any tense (save the present subjunctive and with the additional exception of some irregular verbs), autonomous forms of the verb are, or can be, subject to h-prefixation in the same circumstances where an autonomous verb form beginning with a consonant would resist lenition.

Caibideal 45

266 *An dá olagón déag*: I haven't been able to find out more on the 12 lamentations, but these are also mentioned in "Filí agus Filíocht Mhúsgraighe" in *An Músgraigheach*, Uimhir 2, Fóghmhar 1943, p10, where we read, *sheasaimh sé os cionn na huagha agus do chas sé an dá olagón déag*.

266 The dispute between Bruadar and Ospac and how Ospac's fleet escaped from Bruadar are recounted in the Icelandic *Njáls saga* (ch. 154-155).

Caibideal 46

271 *Brí agus bunús an dá leitir sin*: the genitive dual is an interesting point of grammar. Theoretically, the genitive dual is formed like the genitive plural, but it doesn't seem to be used with any of the weak declensional plurals, which are a relatively recent innovation in the modern Irish. Here we have the older genitive plural, *leitir*, rather than the weak declensional form *leitreacha*. It is worth noting that this applies to the weak plural endings *-acha*, *-anna* and *-(a)í* (e.g. *ag marú an dá mhadra*, where the weak plural *madraí* would not be used in the genitive dual).

272 *Don iníon*: the dative *inín* is not given here.

272 Historically speaking, the daughter who married Sitric was probably called Sláine; Béibheann married Flaithbheartach Ó Néill, king of the Northern Uí Néill.

273 *Leis an gcogarnach*: the dative *cogarnaigh* is not given here and is only used in PUL's works when part of a verbal noun construction (*ag cogarnaigh*).
276 *I mbuíon*: the dative *buín* is not given here.

Caibideal 47

284 *Bhí na húrnaithe ag dul suas coitianta chun gach naoimh acu san, ón muíntir a bhí féna choimirce, a d'iarraidh a n-ímpí chun Dé*: *gach naoimh* here is genitive singular and referred to by the masculine singular possessive particle in *féna choimirce* despite the fact that *gach naomh acu* is essentially plural in meaning. Yet later in the sentence, the plural possessive particle in *a n-ímpí* refers back to a grammatically singular antecedent (*muíntir*). Irish exhibits the same laxity with regard to the agreement of persons as is found in colloquial English, where "they" may refer to a singular antecedent.

Caibideal 48

287 The story of the adventure of Tadhg mac Céin to Paradise, given in the *Book of Lismore*, relates how one of Adam's immortal daughters lured a beautiful youth, Connla, to Paradise. In other versions of the story, it is a fairy maiden who lures Connla away from Ireland to the fairy world.

Caibideal 49

293 PUL may have known little or nothing about boats of the period under discussion, which were unlikely to have been extremely luxurious.
293 *Do tagadh*: a past-tense autonomous form, normally found in PUL's works as *do tánathas* and as *do thánathas* in works by other writers of WM Irish.
295 *Ag an Árdríogan*: the expected dative form, *Árdríogain*, is not given here.
297 *Dá dtigeadh leis*: *tigim* is the classical form of *tagaim* and is occasionally used by PUL. *Dá dtigeadh leis* therefore corresponds to *dá dtagadh leis*, "if he had been able to".
297 The story of how Gormfhlaith's hand and the high kingship of Ireland were offered by Sitric to both Jarl Sígurd and Bruadar is recounted in the Icelandic *Njáls saga* (ch. 154).

Caibideal 50

299 Gormfhlaith is believed to have been born around AD 960, with Sitric's birth around AD 970. These dates are clearly inexact, and Gormfhlaith could have been in her late teens when Sitric was born, but by 1014, at the time of the Battle of Clontarf, Gormfhlaith was around 50, and Sitric around 40. Gormfhlaith, by claiming Sitric was not much past 20 and that she gave birth to him when she was 18, is trying to make out she is younger than she really is in this passage.
299 Amhlaoibh Cuarán, the first husband of Gormfhlaith, died in AD 981, which would put the birth of this fictional posthumous son, Amhlaoibh, around AD 981 too.

Notes

300 This passage possibly indicates that this fictional Amhlaoibh may not have been the posthumous son of Amhlaoibh Cuarán. PUL does not spell out his intention here, but after Amhlaoibh Cuarán's death, Gormfhlaith was married to M'leachlainn before her eventual marriage to Brian Bórú. There is also a slight hint in this and the subsequent chapter that Bruadar may have been his real father.

300 *Geóbhaid siad san trí shlóitibh Bhriain mar a gheóbhadh buanaithe trí pháirc cruithneachtan a bheadh aibidh!*: PUL has Gormfhlaith making this statement while watching the Battle of Clontarf; in CGG §CVIII it is Sitric who says this.

300 *Caroll Cnút agus Anrud*: FFÉ Book 2 Chapter 25 relates how Maolmhórdha asked the Norwegian king to send forces to take part in the Battle of Clontarf, and states that the forces that were sent were commanded by Norwegian princes named Carolus Cnutus and Andreas.

302 *Chun na hÁrdríocht*: note the failure here to decline *Árdríocht* in the genitive. PUL normally gives the historically correct genitive of such nouns, but AÓL's regular failure to decline feminine nouns ending in *-cht* in the genitive was noted by Donncha Ó Cróinín in *Béaloideas*, Vol 35/36, *Scéalaíocht Amhlaoibh Í Luínse* (1967/1968), p327.

302 *Ar an gcruithneacht*: note that the dative *cruithneachtain* is not used here.

302 *Iompóid beirt mhac*: note how the noun *beirt*, while grammatically singular, takes a plural verb, in line with its plural meaning, much the same as words like "majority" often take a plural verb in English.

Caibideal 51

305 *Atáthaoi*: *atáthaoi* is an older second-person plural form of the present tense of the verb *táim*, combined with the relative particle. *Atánn sibh* (or *atá sibh*) would mean the same thing. PUL seems only to use these archaic second-person plural forms with the verbs *táim* and *deirim* (see *deirthí* in *Na Cheithre Soisgéil*, p44, where *deirthí* is not the autonomous form of the verb in the past habitual, but a second-person plural present-tense form).

307 *Féna n-anál*: note the lack of the dative *anáil* here.

310 *Ní har mhaithe le rí Lochlannach Átha Cliath*: h-prefixation of the vowel after the negative copula *ní* was not given in the original text. For a further example of the failure to insert an *h*, see *an méid beag oideachais atá agam ní ar an sgoil a fuaras é* in *Cómhairle Ár Leasa* (p41).

Caibideal 52

315 Ospac's conversion to Christianity and his baptism and that of his men before joining forces with Brian Bórú is related in the Icelandic *Njáls saga* (ch. 155).

312 The Icelandic *Njáls saga* relates how Bruadar had accepted Christianity and become a deacon, only to revert to paganism (see ch. 154). The saga also recounts Bruadar's reputation for sorcery and how druids told him that Brian Bórú would win the Battle of Clontarf if it were held on Good Friday, but would

fall in battle himself; whereas, if battle were joined before Good Friday, all of Brian's opponents would fall in battle (ch. 156).

317 *Faoi*: note the use of *faoi* instead of the more usual *fé*.

Caibideal 54

326 *A Chlann Chais, a shliocht ríoga!*: from this point onwards, the text of Brian's war cry follows, with only minor textual changes, the text of the war cry written by PUL as "Rosg Catha Bhriain i gCluain Tairbh" and published by Connradh na Gaedhilge in *An tAithriseóir* in 1900 (p4ff). The text was also published in *Staraidheacht: Pieces for Recitation in Irish*, published by Muinntir na Leabhar Gaedhilge in 1905 (pp53-55). Similar texts were carried in *The Cork Weekly Examiner* in June 1898 and *Fáinne an Lae* in September 1898—in Fr. Shán Ó Cuív's bibliography of PUL's works the latter version is listed as a "redaction prepared for [the] Mount Melleray Speech Day" (*Materials for a Bibliography*, p12), which suggests a speech on this subject may have been delivered at the Mount Melleray Seminary in Cappoquin, Co. Waterford, in 1898. These prior versions of the war cry evince PUL's longstanding interest in the patriotic quality that could be ascribed to a war cry by Brian Bórú at the Battle of Clontarf.

326 *Féach ansúd iad!*: it's worth noting that PUL does not use the plural imperative here, although Brian Bórú is addressing large numbers of people. The implication is that each member of Brian's troops is being addressed individually by the high king. Later on in Brian's battle address, we read *féachaidh, a chlann ó!*, where the plural imperative is required because of its proximity to the collective noun in the vocative.

Caibideal 55

334 *Aon deallramh géilleadh*: "any sign of yielding". Theoretically, the genitive of *géilleadh* should be *géillte*, but verbal nouns used as real nouns often eschew the genitive, particular where the genitive in question would be identical to the verbal adjective, possibly because the genitive could be misconstrued as an adjective qualifying the preceding noun. A similar example is *an mhuinntir ba mhó cáil droch iompair agus droch mhúine ins gach aon bhall* in PUL's *Catilína* (p34), where the genitive *droch-mhúinte* is not used.

336 The death of Sígurd is recounted in the Icelandic *Njáls saga*, although it is not recorded in that saga who killed him (ch. 156).

339 Béibheann's comment on the Dalcassians' victory at Clontarf is recounted in CGG §CX, where it is Sitric, and not Gormfhlaith, who strikes her for it, with some readings of CGG adding that a tooth was knocked out of her head by the blow.

Caibideal 56

340 The Icelandic *Njáls saga* tells how Bruadar killed Brian Bórú, but was captured and subsequently disembowelled by Brian's men (ch. 156). CGG §CXIV has a

probably fictionalised account, where Brian Bórú managed to cut off one of Bruadar's legs at the knee and the other at the foot, before being slain by him.

344 The death of Toiréalach is recounted in CGG §CX, where it is stated that he pursued the foreign troops into the sea and was drowned by a tidal wave, while managing to pin a foreign soldier under him, another one in his right hand and another in his left hand, so killing three as he drowned himself.

Caibideal 57

347 FFÉ Book 2 Chapter 26 relates how Mac Giolla Phádraig, the king of Ossory, harassed the retreating troops of Brian's army, which was then under the leadership of Brian's son, Donncha. The account states that 150 men died during the skirmishes with the men of Ossory, leaving only 850 men, the remnants of Brian's original army, to return home. CGG §CXXI has Mac Giolla Phádraig declining battle with the Dalcassians, being intimidated by the bravery of the wounded soldiers, 150 of whom then expired once the excitement was over.

Index of Personal Names

(the correct Middle Irish or Old Norse names are briefly indicated where they are known; otherwise the forms used by PUL in this work are used throughout)

Amhlaoibh: 1) Amlaíb or Olaf in Middle Irish and Norse. The son of Íomhar of Limerick who was killed AD 977 or 978 on Scattery Island. 2) Amlaíb mac Sitric, also known as Amlaíb Cuarán, or Óláfr Sigtryggson in Old Norse. He was Norse king of Northumbria and Dublin and the first husband of Gormfhlaith before his death in AD 981. 3) The main character called Amhlaoibh in this work is a fictional Amhlaoibh, supposed to be a son of Gormfhlaith (the subtext of chapters 50 and 51 may be read as implying that this fictional son born after Amhlaíb Cuarán's death was actually Bruadar's son; at any rate, Amhlaoibh is not confident enough to state that Amhlaíb Cuarán was his father). Amhlaoibh is pronounced /au'li:v'/. The association of the name Amhlaoibh with the name Humphrey is entirely spurious.

Anrud: possibly the Norwegian prince called Andreas in FFÉ. According to some accounts, he was slain at Clontarf by Murchadh, son of Brian Bórú, but managed to slay Murchadh in turn with his dying blow. He may have been son of Eiríkr Hákonarson, or Eric of Norway, Norwegian regent AD 1000-12 (note that this Eric was no longer king or regent of Norway by the time of the Battle of Clontarf, contrary to what is stated in the text of *Niamh* here).

Aodh Ó Néill: Áed mac Dómnaill ua Néill, king of Aileach AD 989-1004. The high kingship of Ireland rotated for centuries before Brian Bórú's accession between septs of the Uí Néill dynasty, who claimed descent from Niall Noígíallach, legendary high king of Ireland around AD 400. The kings of Aileach belonged to the northern branch of the Uí Néill; the kings of Mide (Meath), of whom M'leachlainn was one, belonged to the southern branch of the Uí Néill.

Index of Personal Names

Art mac Duibh: a monk from Muskerry.

Barra: St. Finbarr, the patron saint of Cork, who lived on a hermitage in the scenic spot of Gougane Barra. Died AD 623. Also called *Fionnbhárr.*

Béibheann: daughter of Brian Bórú; Bé Binn was the Middle Irish spelling and Béibionn was the spelling used in the original text of *Niamh*, showing no lenition of the medial *b*. She is recorded as having married Flaithbertach ua Néill, the king of the Northern Uí Néill dynasty. PUL seems to confuse her with a third daughter, possibly called Sláine, who married Sitric, the Hiberno-Norse king of Dublin in AD 1012. According to FFÉ, Brian Bórú's mother was also called Béibheann, as is mentioned here in chapter 46.

Bolingbroke: the nickname of Henry IV of England, who was born in Bolingbroke Castle in Lincolnshire.

Breandán: St. Brendan, born in Ciarraí Luachra in Co. Kerry. St. Brendan, one of the Twelve Apostles of Ireland, died around AD 577. Pronounced /br΄aun'dɑ:n/.

Brian Bórú: Brian Bóruma, high king of Ireland, son of Cennétig mac Lorcáin of the Dál gCais dynasty, who was killed AD 1014 during the Battle of Clontarf, at the age of 88 if the account in FFÉ is accurate. However, the Annals of Ulster have Brian as 73 years of age at Clontarf, a figure thought more likely to be correct (see the note in ARÉ, Vol 2, p772). Brian Bórú is the ancestor of the O'Briens. Brian is an old Celtic given name, thought to mean "high" or "noble". Bórú has a number of interpretations, but there is a word *bórumha*, "cattle tribute", and so it may refer to his capacity to levy tribute. An alternative explanation is advanced by PUL in chapter 22, that the name is connected with the placename Béal Bóraimhe in Co. Clare.

Bríd: St. Brigid/Bridget. Reputedly born in Co. Louth, St. Brigid founded monastic institutions for both men and women in Kildare before her death in AD 525.

Bruadar: Bróðir, a Viking based in the Isle of Man, and the brother of Ospac. Unlike his brother, he fought against Brian Bórú at the battle of Clontarf. The Icelandic *Njáls saga* credits him with killing Brian Bórú in that battle, although accounts differ. Bruadar also died in the battle.

Cairí: Kári Sölmundarson, the Icelander who, according to *Njáls saga*, escaped being burnt with Njál (see under *Niall* here) and his family, and pursued the arsonists, killing Gunnar Lambason in the court of Jarl Sígurd of Orkney. Cairí was Niall's son-in-law.

Caoilte: a nickname in this work for Donn mac Beathach. The nickname is probably a reference to Caílte mac Rónáin, the Fenian warrior and nephew of Fionn mac Cúmhaill in the Ulster cycle of myths, said to have been able to run very fast.

Caroll Cnút: a Norwegian prince called Carolus Cnutus in FFÉ. According to some accounts, he was the son of Eiríkr Hákonarson, or Eric of Norway, Norwegian regent AD 1000-12; note that this Eric was no longer king or regent of Norway by the time of the Battle of Clontarf. Killed at Clontarf according to FFÉ. Both *Carrol Cnút* and *Caroll Cnút* are found in the original; Caroll is standardised on here. He is also referred to here simply as Cnút.

Index of Personal Names

Cathal: an Irish masculine name, originally meaning "valour", and spuriously associated with the English name Charles. The Cathal mac Finguine referred to here was king of Cashel and Munster before his death in AD 742. He was portrayed in the Middle Irish *Aislinge Meic Con Glinne* as possessed by a demon of gluttony, which story was updated by PUL into modern Irish in his *An Craos-Deamhan.*

Cian mac Maolmhuaidh: Cian mac Máelmuaid. He was son of Maolmhuaidh mac Briain, king of Munster, who married Sadhbh, daughter of Brian Bórú.

Clíona: Clídna, queen of the Tuatha Dé Danaan in Irish mythology. *Tonn Chlíona,* "Clíona's wave", was one of the three famous waves in Irish waters, said to be in Glandore Bay, Co. Cork. This was spelt *Tonn Clíona* in the original, without lenition on the *c,* possibly in imitation of a older Irish original form, being adjusted in this edition to *Tonn Chlíona.*

Cnút: see under *Caroll Cnút.*

Colla: the name of the abbot of Inis Cathaigh mentioned in Irish annals as dying in AD 995. PUL's novel is based very loosely on the history of the period and so later in the book he finds no problem showing Colla alive well after the period of his real recorded death.

Colm Cille: St. Columba. One of the Twelve Apostles of Ireland, St. Columba was born in Donegal and preached the Gospel among the Picts of Scotland before his death in AD 597. Pronounced /koləm k'il'i/.

Conáing: son of Brian Bórú in this work. This appears to be a mistake: FFÉ shows Conáing was the son of Donn Cuan mac Cinéide, the elder brother of Brian Bórú, and so was Brian Bórú's nephew. According to FFÉ, Conáing was killed at the Battle of Clontarf.

Conaire Mór mac Eidirsceóil: Conaire Mór mac Eterscél, a legendary high king of Ireland whose reign is dated to the early BC period.

Conchúr: Conchobar mac Nessa or Conchúr mac Neasa, king of Ulster in the Ulster cycle of myths. Pronounced /kro'xu:r/.

Conn: son of Maolruanaidh na Paidre in this work. Pronounced /ku:n/. PUL has Conn succeeding his father as king of Uíbh Fhiachrach Áidhne in 1014, but historically Maolruanaidh na Paidre was succeeded by an unnamed grandson of an early king, Comhaltan Ó Cléirigh.

Conn Céad-chathach: known as Conn Cétchathach ("Conn of the Hundred Battles") in early forms of Irish, Conn Céad-chathach is a legendary high king of Ireland who took the northern half of Ireland, Leath Chuínn, in a legendary second-century carve-up of the island with his foe, Mogh Nuat (Mug Nuadat).

Connla: in Irish legends Connla was a son of Conn Céad-chathach who fell in love with a fairy queen and went with her to the fairy world; in one version of the story, it is one of Adam's immortal daughters who lures him to Paradise on account of his beauty. Also known as Connla Rua on account of his reddish hair. Used here as a nickname for Toiréalach, grandson of Brian Bórú.

Cormac mac Airt: a legendary high king of Ireland, whose reign is variously dated to the second or fourth centuries AD. *Cormac* is pronounced /korəmək/.

Index of Personal Names

Cúchulainn: an Irish hero from the Ulster cycle of myths and nephew of Conchúr mac Neasa.

Déaglán: St. Declan, who played a role in the conversion of the Decies to Christianity in the fifth century AD.

Diarmaid mac Céirbheóil: Diarmait mac Cerbaill, the last pagan high king of Ireland, who is thought to have died around AD 565.

Dónall mac Duibh: Dómnall mac Duib-dá-Bairenn (son of Dub-dá-Bairenn mac Dómnaill, king of Munster AD 957-959). Dónall mac Duibh was killed in battle in AD 1015 by Donncha, king of Munster and son of Brian Bórú and Gormfhlaith.

Dónall mac Éimhin: Dómnall mac Éimen in older forms of Irish. Mentioned in FFÉ as the mormaer of Mar in Scotland who died in the battle of Clontarf in AD 1014. PUL has him as a member of an Eóghanacht clan governing an area of eastern Scotland.

Dónall Ó Faoláin: Dómnall mac Faeláin, king of the Decies, who died in battle in AD 995. PUL's use of *ó* instead of *mac* possibly reflects a copying of historical detail from FFÉ Book 2, Chapter 23 of which uses the same incorrect appellation.

Donn mac Beathach: a prince in this work who works as a messenger for Brian Bórú. Son of Mac Beathach, king of Ciarraí Luachra. Donn mac Beathach goes under the nicknames of Caoilte, Caoilte Cosach, Fear na gCos and Cosa Buí Árda in this work.

Donnabhán: Donnubán mac Cathail, king of the Uí Fighinti, who died in AD 980. He allied with his father-in-law, Íomhar, the last Viking king of Limerick, and with Maolmhuaidh mac Briain, king of Deas-Mhúmhain, against the Dál gCais.

Donncha mac Briain: Donnchad mac Briain, son of Brian Bórú and Gormfhlaith. After the battle of Clontarf, he became king of Munster. Upon his deposition in 1063, he went on a pilgrimage to Rome and died there in 1064. Note that *Donncha, mac Bhriain* is found in the original here, with lenition on the *b* where the phrase *mac Bhriain* is parenthetical, whereas *Donncha mac Briain*, with no comma, is found as this man's name or proper appellation.

Duíbhgeann: given as *Duíbhghean* in the original, this name is the equivalent of the tenth-century form Dubcenn. Duíbhgeann was one of the sons of Íomhar of Limerick, who was killed AD 977 or 978 on Scattery Island. Such names do not necessarily have a normative pronunciation in WM Irish, but a pronunciation /di:g′ən/ could be suggested here, in line with the /g/ pronunciation of *díogras* and *díogailt* (from historical *díoghras* and *díoghailt*).

Dúlainn Óg: one of Murchadh's key lieutenants in this work. Possibly based on the young warrior, Dunlang O'Hartugan, mentioned in CGG §XCVIII.

Eóin Baiste: St. John the Baptist.

Feargas mac Róigh: also known as Fergus mac Róich or Fergus mac Rossa, where Róech was his mother's name, representing the remnant of an ancient matrilineal system in the Ulster cycle of myths. Feargas was a mythological king of Ulster tricked out of the kingship by Conchúr mac Neasa. When Feargas fell in love with Neasa, she agreed to marry him on condition the kingship was briefly transferred to her seven-year-old son, Conchúr, who then proceeded to rule wisely with his mother's help in such a way that Feargas was unable to regain the throne. Pronounced /farəgəs/. The modern equivalent of the name, Fearghas, would be pronounced /fa'ri:s/.

Fionn mac Cúmhaill: also known as Finn McCool, a warrior in the Fenian cycle of myths.

Gilli: Norse-Gael earl or *jarl* of an area in the Southern Hebrides in Scotland, mentioned in the Icelandic *Njáls saga*, which PUL seems to have drawn on for some historical background. The name Gilli appears to be of Gaelic origin, possibly being a truncation of a Gaelic compound name consisting of *giolla* and another name. Gilli was the brother-in-law of Jarl Sígurd the Stout of Orkney.

Giolla Phádraig: the herenach of Sórd Cholm Cille. Spelt *Giolla Pádraig* with no lenition on the *p* in the original, possibly in imitation of the form found in early Irish works.

Gormfhlaith: Gormflaith ingen Murchada, daughter of Murchadh mac Finn, king of Leinster, and mother of Sitric II Silkbeard, king of Dublin. Born around AD 960, she died in AD 1030. As the widow of Amhlaoibh Cuarán, Norse-Gael king of Dublin, who died in AD 981, she married in succession M'leachlainn and then Brian Bórú in AD 999. Following her divorce from Brian Bórú, she played a key role in organising opposition to him in the run-up to the Battle of Clontarf in AD 1014. The name Gormfhlaith has previously been anglicised as Gormley and appeared in the Icelandic *Njáls saga* as Kormloð, gaelicised as *Gormlóda* in one passage here. The Irish name means "blue/illustrious princess". Pronounced /gorəmlə/.

Gunnar: Gunnar Lambason, an Icelander who was killed in Jarl Sígurd's court AD 1013 as he related the story of the burning of Njál (see under *Niall*). This event is recorded in the Icelandic *Njáls saga*. PUL sees a connection between the Old Norse name Gunnar and the Gaelic Conchúr.

Hamhrí IV: or Henry IV, king of England, who took the throne after deposing Richard II in 1399. Also known by the soubriquet Bolingbroke. PUL's spelling would suggest a pronunciation of /hau'r'i:/ or /hau'ri:/.

Íomhar: Ímar or Ivar, the last Norse king of Limerick, who was killed AD 977 or 978 on Scattery Island.

Íosa Críost: Jesus Christ. In his *New Era Grammar of Modern Irish*, Gerald O'Nolan indicates that the final vowel of this name is commonly unvoiced or murmured (p3).

Íta: St. Ita, native of Co. Waterford, was head of a community of nuns in Co. Limerick before her death in AD 570.

Lódair: Hlodvir Thorfinnsson, father of Sígurd the Stout, earl or *jarl* of Orkney (mentioned in *Njáls saga*, ch. 84).

Loíngseach mac Dúlainn: Loingsech mac Dubhlaing, a king of the Uí Chonaill Ghabra in this work. While there were a number of Irish kings called Loíngseach, it is not clear where PUL got this name from. There does not appear to have been a king of the Uí Chonaill Ghabra with this name.

Lonán mac Beathach: a fictional character who is one of the sons of the king of Kerry, Mac Beathach, in this work. Lonán disguised himself as a doctor and was employed by Sitric and Gormfhlaith to attempt to poison Brian Bórú.

M'leachlainn: pronounced /ml′axəliŋ′~mr′axəliŋ′~br′axəliŋ′/, this is the modern form of the name Máel Sechnaill, meaning "disciple of St. Seachnaill". The king here being referred to was known in Middle Irish as Máel Sechnaill mac Dómnaill, king of Meath and high king of Ireland, also known as Máel Sechnaill Mór. M'leachlainn opposed the Vikings, and fought the battle of Tara in AD 980 against Amlaoibh Cuarán; the Vikings were defeated in that battle, leading to Dublin's occupation by M'leachlainn. M'leachlainn was deposed by Brian Bórú in AD 1002. Until then the high kingship had remained for centuries in the hands of the Uí Néill dynasty, to the Clann Cholmáin sept of which M'leachlainn belonged. Brian Bórú became high king of Ireland in AD 1002 until his death at the battle of Clontarf in AD 1014. The Vikings were defeated at Clontarf owing to M'leachlainn's decision to intervene with his army towards the end of the battle, whereupon M'leachlainn resumed the high kingship until his death in AD 1022, being succeeded by Brian Bórú's grandson Toiréalach. The title of high king was somewhat nominal between 1014 and the 1050s owing to turmoil in Ireland.

Mac Beathach: Mac Bethad, son of Muiredach Claen, king of Ciarraí Luchra (a kingdom in North Kerry, in the Sliabh Luachra area) in AD 1004-1014, shown in FFÉ as dying in the battle of Clontarf in AD 1014.

Mac Giolla Phádraig: Donnchad mac Gilla Pátraic, king of Ossory, a kingdom in Leinster, AD 1003-39. He is excoriated in this work for refusing to join in the battle of Clontarf. Spelt *Mac Giolla Pádraig* with no lenition on the *p* in the original, possibly in imitation of an early work.

Maghnas mac Arailt: Maccus Haraldsson, a Scandinavian or Norse-Gael king thought to have been king of the Isle of Man and to have taken part in raids on both shores of the Irish Sea before his death between AD 984 and 987. His attack on Scattery Island in AD 974 is recorded in the Annals of Innisfallen. PUL has Maghnas mac Arailt dying on Scattery Island in a campaign in AD 977 or 978, but in fact there is no historical record of his death, which is assumed to have been in the late 980s, when references to him cease in the annals. IWM §349 shows *Maghnas* is pronounced /meːnəs/ in WM Irish, but PUL's choice of spelling may point to a pronunciation /məinəs/.

Maolmhórdha: Máel Mórda mac Murchada (sometimes Anglicised as Mailmora), brother of Gormfhlaith and king of Leinster, killed in the battle of Clontarf, AD 1014. This is not a modern name, but a pronunciation /meːl-'(v)oːrə/ could be suggested. There is no lenition of the medial *m* in the nominative of this name in the original text, possibly reflecting the influence of older source materials or to give an archaising flavour to the text. The genitive is given here as *Maoilmhórdha.*

Maolmhuaidh: Máel Muaid mac Briain, or Molloy, king of Munster AD 959/963 to AD 970, king of Desmond AD 970 to AD 976, and then king of the whole of

Munster again AD 976 to AD 978 until his death in the battle of Bealach Leachta. The English version of the name, Molloy, implies that the medial *m* is lenited and then passed over in pronunciation: a pronunciation /me:l 'uəg'/ or /mə 'luəg'/ could be suggested. It is worth noting that, unlike other names in *Maol-* used in this work, PUL does not give a genitive in *Maoil-* (the genitive here was spelt *Maolmuaidh* in the original, identical to the nominative), possibly influenced by the sources he used or because the name is truncated in any case in the manner I have suggested. There is no lenition of the medial *m* in the original text, once again possibly reflecting the influence of older source materials or to give an archaising flavour to the text.

Maolruanaidh na Paidre: Máelruanaid na Paidre ua hEidhin, or Mulroney of the Prayer O'Heyne, king of Uíbh Fhiachrach Áidhne in Co. Galway, who died in AD 1014 at the Battle of Clontarf. PUL explains that this king was noted for his talismanic devotion to the Lord's Prayer and thus its constant repetition. The genitive here is *Maoilruanaidh.*

Maolshuathain: a priest in this work. A poet called *Maolsuthain*, probably Maolsuthain ua Cearbhaill, is mentioned in Seathrún Céitinn's FFÉ, and this may be where PUL got the name from. The genitive here is *Maoilshuathain.*

Mathúin mac Cinéide: Mathgamain mac Cennétig, king of Munster from about AD 970 till his death in AD 976. The genitive of this name is *Mathúna.* The spelling of *Cinéide* with a single *n* appears to reflect an eschewing of /ŋ'/ following an earlier *c* or a *g* and a short vowel in WM Irish (cf. *cinniúint* and *glinniúint*, etc, pronounced *ciniúint* and *gliniúint*), and consequently the pronunciation is /k'i'n'e:d'i/.

Meargach: the blacksmith in this work; the name refers to a "crusty" appearance. Pronounced /m'arəgəx/.

Mícheál Naofa: St. Michael the Archangel.

Mícheál Rua: a guard in Brian Bórú's household troops who is encouraged by King Sitric of Dublin to attempt to kill the high king.

Mórling: the daughter of Tadhg Mór Ó Cealla in this work, usually referred to by the nickname *Niamh.* There appears to be no historical attestation of this figure.

Mothla mac Faoláin: apparently a mistake in the original, referring to Mothla mac Dómnaill, also called Mothla ua Faeláin, king of the Decies AD 996-1014, who was killed in the Battle of Clontarf. He was the son of Dónall mac Faoláin.

Muire (an Mhaighdean Mhuire): the Virgin Mary. It is notable that *Muire* is lenited in the phrase a*n Mhaighdean Mhuire*, as if of adjectival force. (The dative is *ar an Maighdin Muire*, with no such lenition.)

Muireadhach: given here as the name of a mormaer of Lennox in Scotland. Pronounced /mi'r'i:x/.

Murchadh: Murchad in older forms of Irish, sometimes Anglicised as Murrough, the son of Brian Bórú. Murchadh was killed in the battle of Clontarf AD 1014, according to some accounts by the Norwegian prince Anrud. FFÉ relates that Murchadh, depicted here as physically strong, was 63 years old at the age of his death; this figure is unlikely to be correct, as there are questions over the age of

Brian Bórú himself in 1014. Murchadh's mother was Mór, possibly the sister of Maolruanaidh na Paidre. Pronounced /murəxə/.

Neasa: or Ness, princess of the royal house of Ulster in the Ulster cycle of myths. Neasa was the mother of Conchúr mac Neasa.

Niall: Njáll Þorgeirsson, an Icelandic man the burning of whom (with his wife and children) is related in the Icelandic *Njáls saga* (ch. 128).

Niamh: Mórling in this work went by the nickname Niamh, a reference to Niamh Chínn Óir, Niamh of the golden hair, the name of a mythological figure who lured Oisín away from Ireland in the Fenian cycle of myths. As a noun, *niamh* means "brightness, lustre, sheen", and was pronounced by AÓL at least /n′iav/ (and not /n′i:v/ or /n′iəv/), as stated in CFBB (p167).

Nuala: one of Béibheann's ladies-in-waiting.

Ó Cealla: the surname Ó Ceallaigh, pronounced /o: k′alə/, in line with dialectal rules on the pronunciation of *-igh* in surnames and given simply as *Cealla* in the original text of *Niamh.*

Ó Mórdha: pronounced /o: mo:rə/, this name, anglicised as Moore, is a true Gaelic name, or is sometimes so. O Mórdha refers here to the Irish poet Thomas Moore (1779-1852). Thomas Moore is described here as *gallda,* despite his Irish descent. This might be because, while he supported the 1829 Roman Catholic Relief Act that repealed penal laws against Irish Catholics, he regarded this step as sufficient and opposed what he saw as the 'demogoguery' of Daniel O'Connell. Although his father came from a Gaeltacht area of Co Kerry, Stephen Gwynn's biography of Moore states, "he had not a word of Gaelic, and (like O'Connell) desired to see it die out" (*Thomas Moore,* p177).

Oilioll Olum: Ailill Aulom in early forms of Irish, the son of Mogh Nuat (or Mug Nuadat), legendary king of Leath Mogha in second-century Ireland. Oilioll Olum, who became king of Southern Ireland, was reputedly the ancestor of the Eóghanacht dynasty through his son Eóghan, and possibly the ancestor of the mormaers of Mar in Scotland.

Ospac: or Óspak, a Viking based in the Isle of Man mentioned in the Icelandic *Njáls saga.* Ospac fought on Brian Bórú's side in the AD 1014 Battle of Clontarf, whereas his brother Bruadar fought against Brian Bórú.

Pádraig: St. Patrick; pronounced /pɑ:d(ə)rig′/.

Peadair: St. Peter. The spelling given in the original text here shows the slender *r* in the WM pronunciation, /p′adir′/.

Pól: St. Paul.

Risteárd II: or Richard II, king of England, whose expedition to Ireland in May-July 1399 took place just as Bolingbroke (who became Henry IV) was gathering his forces. Soon after his return to England, in late September 1399, Richard II was forced to abdicate in favour of Bolingbroke. He was murdered in 1400.

Risteárd III: or Richard III, king of England, said to have murdered "the princes in the tower", Edward V and Prince Richard, in AD 1483, thus enabling him to take the throne.

Scraphádinn: Skarphéðin, an Icelander and the son of Njál (Niall), who was burned along with him in an event related in the Icelandic *Njáls saga* (ch. 128, 154).

Seanán Naofa: St. Senán, one of the twelve apostles of Ireland, who was born in Co. Clare AD 488.

Sígurd: Sigurd Hlodvisson, or Sigurd the Stout, earl or *jarl* of Orkney, AD ca. 960-1014. Son of someone called Hlodvir Thorfinnsson. Sígurd fought against Brian Bórú at the Battle of Clontarf and was killed in the battle.

Sitric: Sigtrygg II Silkbeard Olafsson, Norse-Gael king of Dublin AD 989-994; 995-1000; and from 1000 till his abdication in 1036. He died in AD 1042. Sitric was the son of Amhlaoibh Cuarán and Gormfhlaith and married a daughter of Brian Bórú, who PUL names as Béibheann, but who other accounts indicate was possibly called Sláine, in 1012. Pronounced /ʃit′ir′ik′/.

Tadhg: an ancient Celtic name, probably derived from a Celtic root meaning "badger". Pronounced /təig/. In this work we find: 1) Tadhg Mór Ó Cealla, or Tadg Mór ua Cellaigh, a historical figure who was the 36th king of Uí Maine and the first chief of the Ó Ceallaigh name. Allied with Brian Bórú, he died in AD 1014 in the battle of Clontarf. The Ó Ceallaigh surname originated with this Tadhg, as he was the grandson of someone called Cellach mac Finnachta. 2) Tadhg Óg Ó Cealla, the son of the former. Tadhg Óg seems to be a fictional character in this work. PUL has Tadhg Óg succeeding his father as king of Uí Maine in 1014, but historically it was a son called Conchúr (Concobar mac Tadg ua Cellaigh) who succeeded Tadhg Mór. 3) Tadhg mac Céin, grandson of the legendary king Oilioll Olum. Legends (told in the *Book of Lismore*) have him wandering to Paradise and meeting one of the immortal daughters of Adam. His father, Cian, was the son of Oilioll Olum and Sadb, daughter of Conn Cétchathach.

Toiréalach: the son of Murchadh and grandson of Brian Bórú, killed in PUL's novel at the age of 15 during the Battle of Clontarf. FFÉ also has a son of Murchadh called Toiréalach who died in the battle; he is stated as being not more than 15 years old in CGG §CX. The spelling *Toirdhealbhach* is used in the original text here, corresponding to Toirdelbach in Middle Irish. However, the pronunciation is /tre:ləx/. Toiréalach is frequently referred to here by the nickname Connla.

Tuathal Maolgharbh: Túathal Máelgarb ("bald and rough") or Túathal mac Cormaic, high king of Ireland, who died in the 540s. Some late glosses in the Irish annals, thought to have come from a much later date, hold that Tuathal was killed by Diarmaid mac Céirbheóil's half-brother or adoptive kinsman, who was then killed on the spot. PUL used the spelling *Maolgarbh* in the original, with no medial lenition (*maolgarbh*), possibly in imitation of a Middle Irish original.

Uilliam I: William I, the Duke of Normandy who conquered England in AD 1066.

Uisneach: or Uisnech. In the Ulster Cycle of myths, Conchúr mac Neasa's killing of the sons of Uisneach was the proximate cause for the renunciation of Feargas' loyalty to him and his going over to the court of Connacht instead.

Index of Placenames and Population Groups

Alba: Scotland. With *na hAlban* in the genitive and *Albain* in the dative. Pronounced /ɑləbə/.

Almáinn (an Almáinn): Germany, generally *an Ghearmáin* in GCh, pronounced /ɑlə'mɑ:ŋ′/. Compare *Almaine* and *Almany*, obsolete English terms for Germany.

Árd Mhacha: Armagh, the metropolitical seat of the Irish church, where *Macha* is a personal name.

Áth Cliath: the name of a ford over the river Liffey that Dublin (Baile Átha Cliath) is named after. Hence, Dublin itself.

Baile Átha Cliath: Dublin. Pronounced /bl′a: 'kl′iəh/. See *Áth Cliath.*

Béal Bóraimhe: a fort in Co. Clare north of Killaloe that may be the origin of the appellation Bórú.

Bealach Leachta: a place near Macroom, known in Middle Irish as Belach Lechta, which saw a battle in AD 978, where Brian Bórú emerged as the king of Munster.

Beann Éadair: Howth, Co. Dublin, or the Ben of Howth hill nearby. This is given here in a dative context, *ó Bhínn Éadair,* spelt *ó Bheinn Éadair* in the original. *Éadar* in this placename is believed to be a personal name.

Breatain (an Bhreatain): Wales.

Caiseal: Cashel, Co. Tipperary, a placename meaning "stone ringfort".

Cathair Chonstantín: Constantinople. PUL generally does not attempt to impose Irish orthographical rules on foreign names; consequently, this is not *Cathair Chonstaintín.*

Cathair na Beirbhe: the placenames index in an early edition of *Niamh* asserts that this placename is Copenhagen in Denmark, and a number of passages in this work imply that the city is in Denmark. However, the city properly referred to as Cathair na Beirbhe is Bergen in Norway. The original text shows no lenition of the second *b* (*Cathair na Beirbe*), possibly in imitation of a Middle Irish original. *Beirbhe,* or at least the modern version of the word with a lenited *b,* would be pronounced /b′e'r′i:/.

Ceann Cora: Kincora, the O'Brien stronghold near Killaloe, Co. Clare, built by Brian Bórú in AD 1002.

Ceann Fheabhrad: a location near the border between counties Cork and Limerick, identified by some as Seefin in Co. Limerick. See the entries under *Ceann Abhrad* and *Ceann Feabhrad* in the index of placenames in PSD's edition of FFÉ.

Ceann Tíre: Kintyre, Scotland.

Ciarraí Luachra: or Ciarraige Luachra, a kingdom in North Kerry, in the Sliabh Luachra area.

Ciarraí: Kerry.

Cíll Chaoi: Kilkee, a resort in Co. Clare ("the Church of St. Caoi").

Cíll Dálua: Killaloe, Co. Clare, the village where Brian Bórú's palace, Kincora, stood.

Index of Placenames and Population Groups

Cíll Dara: Kildare, where St. Brigid founded the first convent in Ireland.

Cíll Mhaighneann: Kilmainham, Co. Dublin ("the Church of St. Maighnenn"). Pronounced /k′i:l′ vəin′ən/.

Clann Chais: an alternative term for the Dál gCais or Dalcassians.

Clann Rúraí: a reference to the Ulaid people who occupied Ulster in ancient times, said to be descendants of a legendary high king of Ireland, Rudraige mac Sitric. Spelt in the original text with a slender medial *r* (*Clann Rudhríghe*), but adjusted here in line with the form used in PUL's other works.

Cluain Tairbh: Clontarf, Co. Dublin, the scene of a major battle in AD 1014 that saw the death of Brian Bórú and many Irish leaders. The placename is usually found as *Cluain Tarbh*. The form used in this book is pronounced /kluən′ tɑr′iv′/. The use of *Cluain Tairbh* by native speakers of Muskerry Irish may reflect the influence of local placenames, including Drom Tairbh, Dromtariff, a ridge not far from PUL's home in the Muskerry Gaeltacht.

Connachta: Connacht, the western province of Ireland. Note that, as a plural noun, the genitive is *Connacht* and the dative given here is *Connachtaibh*. CFBB (p110) shows that later speakers of WM Irish, including AÓL, had *i gConnacht* in the dative. PUL consistently uses the historically correct dative plural in his works.

Connachtach: a native of the province of Connacht.

Corca Baoiscne: the Corca Baiscinn or Corcu Baiscind, a group who held an early kingdom in Co. Clare later absorbed into the territory of the Dalcassians.

Corca Mrua: Corcomroe in Co. Clare. Given as Corca Modhruadh in the original.

Corcaigh: Cork. This placename is derived from *corcach*, "marsh", but, in common with many placenames, the erstwhile dative has come to be the standard form of the placename.

Crích Lochlann: Scandinavia. Note that PUL's usage in this work (e.g. in chapter 39) shows he viewed this term as meaning "Denmark", possibly in line with his mistaken conception that *Cathair na Beirbhe* (properly Bergen in Norway) referred to Copenhagen, so Caoilte is shown in chapter 39 as first going to Crích Lochlann and then to Norway, when in fact Norway may properly be considered part of Crích Lochlann.

Cruithneach: Pict, a member of an ancient ethnic group in Scotland. Pronounced /krin′'hɑx/.

Dál gCais: the Dalcassians, a powerful dynasty who held a kingdom in Thomond, or North Munster, in the 10th century. *Dál* means "people, sept, tribe". The Dál gCais claimed descent from Cormac Cas, a legendary king of Munster killed by the invading Déisi Muman (or the Decies kingdom) near Limerick in AD 713. The eclipsis of *Cais* reflects calcification of the name, according as it does with the grammar of an earlier form of Irish. The Dál gCais were the descendants of a Decies group (the Déisi Tuisceart; see *Déiseach*) who settled in Co. Clare in the early eighth century (see *Ireland before the Normans*, p114), and later claimed a genealogical connection, deemed by modern scholars to be spurious, with the Eóghanacht dynasty that held sway in Southern Ireland from the seventh to the tenth century.

Index of Placenames and Population Groups

Danar: Dane; or less specifically, "barbarian, foreigner". PUL sometimes uses this term in reference to the Vikings in general.

Danmharg: Denmark, or *Danmhairg* in GCh. This is found once as *Danmharg* and once as *Danmarg* in the original, with the latter being adjusted in this edition to *Danmharg.*

Deas-Mhúmhain: Desmond or South Munster, an area later divided into Cork and Kerry. This placename was spelt *Deas-Múmhain* in the original, with no lenition on the first *m*, possibly in imitation of a Middle Irish original. Pronounced /d′as-'u:n′/.

Déiseach: an inhabitant of the territory held by the Déisi Muman (Déise Múmhan), who held the Decies kingdom in Co. Waterford and Co. Tipperary. *Déis* meant "vassal, subject", and so the kingdom may have emerged from a population group linked via social status in ancient Ireland. *Rí na nDéiseach*, "king of the Decies"; also given here as *rí na nDéise*, using the genitive plural of *déis.* Other Decies groups existed elsewhere in Ireland, including the Déisi Tuisceart from whom the Dál gCais dynasty emerged, but modern scholars believe the various Decies groups were not related to each other.

Donncha Dí: this appears to be an incorrect rendering of the Co. Down placename, Donaghadee, which is the easternmost point of the Irish mainland. The correct Irish form is *Domhnach Daoi*, "Daoi's church". The phrase "from Donaghadee to Tigh Mhóire" refers to the eastern and western extremities of Ireland. See also *Tigh Mháire.*

Dún gCrot: a fort in the Galtee mountains in Co. Tipperary.

Dún Sobhairce: Dunseverick, a rock three miles to the east of the Giant's Causeway, Co. Antrim, with ruins of an ancient castle.

Éire: Ireland, with *Éireann* in the genitive (*na hÉireann*) and *Éirinn* in the dative.

Fán Chonradh: This placename was mentioned in the Dublin copy of the *Annals of Innisfallen* as being the location of a battle that took place in AD 979. Seathrún Céitinn's FFÉ refers to it as *Fan mic Connrach*, which PSD's edition stated as being in Co. Waterford. This placename was found as both *Fán Chonradh* and *Fán Conradh* in the original, and the former form is standardised on in this edition.

Frainnc (an Fhrainnc): France. The traditional double *n* is needed here to show the diphthong: /fraiŋk′/.

Gleann Mháma: a place in Co. Wicklow, known as *Glenn Máma* in Middle Irish, that saw a battle in AD 999, in which Brian Bórú crushed the Leinster revolt against his rule.

Inis Cathaigh: Iniscathy or Scattery Island, Co. Clare.

Inis Locha Cé: an island in Loch Cé, or Lough Key, Co. Roscommon; or identified by some as a dry lake near Knockaney, Co. Limerick.

Inis Locha Guir: the island of Lough Gur, Co. Limerick.

Inis Tuile: Iceland. The mythological island of Thule in Northern Europe has had a number of interpretations (Greenland and Iceland among others), but the term is used here to refer to Iceland.

Index of Placenames and Population Groups

Ínsí Gall: the Hebrides.

Ínsí hOrc: the Orkney islands, or *Inse Orc* in GCh. The *h-* reflects the grammatical norms of earlier forms of Irish. PUL also uses *Inis Orc* in one passage here. The king of the Orkneys submitted to the Romans at Colchester in AD 43. However, there is no historical evidence of a conquest of the Orkneys by the Romans that PUL alludes to here.

Iodáil (an Iodáil): Italy. Pronounced /i'dɑ:l'/.

Ioruaidh (an Ioruaidh): Norway, pronounced /i'ruəg'/, with the genitive *na hIorua.*

Iúróip (an Iúróip): "Europe", or *Eoraip* in GCh. The original spelling here was *Euróip.* PUL told Osborn Bergin the pronunciation was /u:'ro:p'/ (see "Comhfhreagras idir an Athair Peadair agus an tAimhirgíneach", by Seán Ua Súilleabháin, in *Celtica,* Vol 24, 2003, p281).

Laighin: Leinster, the eastern province of Ireland. A fifth-declension masculine plural noun with genitive *Laighean* and dative *Laighnibh.* Pronounced /lain', lain, lain'iv'/.

Laighneach: Leinsterman. Both *Laighneacha* and *Laighnigh* (which is accepted in GCh) are found in the nominative plural here. Pronounced /lain'əx/.

Leamhain (an Leamhain): the river Laney, Co. Cork.

Leamhain: Lennox in Scotland, with the genitive *Leamhna.*

Leath Chuínn: or Leth Cuinn, Conn's Half of Ireland, referring to Connacht, Ulster and Meath in a legendary second-century carve-up of the island following the battle of Maynooth said to have taken place in AD 123 between Mug Nuadat (or Mogh Nuat) king of Munster and the high king of Ireland Conn Cétchathach.

Leath Mhogha: or Leth Moga, Mogh's Half of Ireland, referring to Leinster and Munster in a legendary second-century carve-up of the island following the battle of Maynooth said to have taken place in AD 123 between Mug Nuadat (or Mogh Nuat) king of Munster and high king of Ireland Conn Cétchathach. Also referred to as *Leath Mhogha Nuat.*

Léim Chúchulainn: Cúchulainn's Leap, Loop Head, Co. Clare.

Loch Guir: Lough Gur, near Bruff, Co. Limerick.

Luimneach: Limerick. Often *Luimne,* /lim'in'i/, in WM Irish (see *go Luimne,* CFBB, p16). See also GCD (§222), where Diarmuid Ó Sé states that *Luimneach* becomes *Luimne* in the dative in Chorca Dhuíbhne Irish. PUL has *Luimneach* in both the nominative and dative (see *a Luimneach* in chapter 4 here) and *Luimní* in the genitive.

Mágh Adhair: Myra Park, Co. Clare, the location of a sacred tree (*Bile Mór Mágha Adhair*) where the Dalcassian kings were inaugurated. Irish annals relate that the tree was cut down in AD 982 during an invasion of Dál gCais territory by M'leachlainn Mór.

Magh Chromtha: Macroom, Co. Cork. While this placename appears to mean "crooked plain" in modern Irish, it is thought that it refers rather to the Celtic god Cromm Crúaich, or Crom Cruach, whose worship included human sacrifice. Worship of Crom Cruach is said to have been put a stop to by St. Patrick. PUL stated that the initial *m* of *Magh Chromtha* is never lenited, by way of an exception (see NIWU, p75). This placename was given as *Mághchromtha* in the original (a single word, with a long *a*), but IWM §148 shows the pronunciation to be /mə 'xroumhə/. The use of a short vowel in *magh* appears to be the case only with *Magh Chromtha*; other placenames with *mágh* have a long vowel. See under *mágh* in the *Glossary*.

Mágh Geirrghinn: the plain of Circenn, thought to be the Angus and the Mearns area of eastern Scotland, ruled by a dynasty said to be a branch of the Eóghanacht dynasty prominent in Ireland.

Mí: the province of Meath or Mide. Ireland originally had five provinces, and Meath was the province in the middle of the country and the location of Teamhair na Rí.

Móin Mhóir (an Mhóin Mhóir): this is the name of numerous villages in several counties of Ireland, and it is not clear which of these PUL is claiming saw a battle at which the Vikings were put to flight. Possibly Moanmore in Co. Tipperary.

Muímhneach: Munsterman, native of the province of Munster. Pronounced /mi:n′əx/.

Múmhain (an Mhúmhain): Munster, the southern province of Ireland. This is one of many words where the historical dative has replaced the erstwhile nominative (*an Mhumha*) in Cork Irish. The genitive is *na Múmhan*, the article of which is sometimes not given (as in *rí Múmhan*, *uaislibh Múmhan* and *Gaelaibh Múmhan* found here), in the same way that the genitive of *Éire* is sometimes *Éireann* and sometimes *na hÉireann*. Pronounced /ə(n) vu:n′, (nə) mu:n/.

Múscraí: Muskerry, the district in Co. Cork of which PUL was a native. Pronounced /mu:z'gri:/, this is one of the few words in WM Irish with a *z* in the pronunciation. Often written *Músgraí*.

Oileán Mhanann: the Isle of Man. The original text had *Manain* in both the genitive and dative (*Oileán Mhanain, ó Mhanain*). The usual form of this placename is *Oileán Mhanann*, with *Manann* in the genitive and *Manainn* in the dative. *I Manainn* is used in the dative in PUL's *An Cleasaidhe* (p3).

Oileán Scathaigh: the Isle of Skye. PUL's name for this island is rather unusual, as the accepted term is *Oiléan Scitheanach*. PUL may have subscribed to the theory that the island's name was connected with Scáthach, a Scottish warrior maiden mentioned in the Ulster Cycle of myths.

Oirialla: Oriel, an ancient Irish kingdom based in Counties Louth and Monaghan. As a plural noun the dative is *Oiriallaibh*. Pronounced /ir′iələ/.

Port Láirge: Waterford. One theory holds that *Port Láirge* means "Lárag's port". Waterford is derived from the Norse name for the city, Veðrafjörður. Waterford is Ireland's oldest city, founded by the Vikings in AD 914.

Róimh (an Róimh): Rome; *na Rómha* in the genitive. Pronounced /ro:v′/, with /ro:/ in the genitive.

Sasana: England.

Sionainn (an tSionainn): the River Shannon.

Index of Placenames and Population Groups

Sliabh an Bhogaidh: explained as a minor placename of no importance in the index of placenames in early editions of *Niamh.* The placename seems to have been garnered by PUL from FFÉ; PSD's edition of that work locates *Sliabh an Bhogaidh* somewhere between the river Feegile on the Offaly/Kildare border and Kincora. *Bogadh* means "soft, boggy land".

Solán (an Solán): the river Sullane in Co. Cork (in the Muskerry Gaeltacht).

Solchaid: Solohead in Co. Tipperary, the location of a battle in AD 967 or 968, fought between King Íomhar of Limerick and Mathúin mac Cinéide, then king of Thomond, later king of Munster, and elder brother of Brian Bórú. The battle is referred to in older Irish as the battle of Sulcoit.

Sórd Cholm Cille: Swords in Co. Dublin. This is derived by PSD from the word *sórd,* "sward, an area of ground covered by grass", although other theories contend the placename means "the well of St. Columba". In this work, Swords is the place where the tribute or tax for the high king was received. Brian Bórú's body is believed to have been brought to Swords Abbey to rest for a day or two after his death during the Battle of Clontarf. Also abbreviated as *Sórd.*

Teamhair (Teamhair na Rí): Tara in Co. Meath, the seat of the high kings of Ireland. Pronounced /t′aur′/. The genitive is *na Teamhrach,* pronounced /nə t′aurəx/. *Teamhair* means "elevated place, assembly hill".

Tigh Mháire: this appears to be PUL's incorrect rendering of *Tigh Mhóire,* a place on Dunmore Head, Co. Kerry. The phrase "from Donaghadee to Tigh Mhóire" refers to the eastern and western extremities of Ireland. See also *Donncha Dí.*

Tír Chonaill: Tyrconnell, an ancient kingdom including parts of Co. Donegal and other counties.

Tír Eóin: Co. Tyrone; also the name of an ancient kingdom in that area of Ireland.

Tuaim Gréine: Tomgraney, Co. Clare, once the location of an abbey. *Tuaim* means "funeral mound".

Tulchainn (an Tulchainn): the River Tolka in Dublin, referred to as *An Tulcha* in GCh. PUL uses a dative form for the nominative here. PUL had an unlenited *c* in the original, possibly influenced by the English form of the river name or by a Middle Irish version of the name. Pronounced /tuləxiŋ′/.

Uí Fighinti: the Uí Fidgenti, anglicised as the Hy Fidgenti, a dynasty that held a kingdom in Co. Limerick between the fifth and twelfth centuries. Historically speaking, the dynasties that ruled ancient kingdoms generally have the word *Uí* in their names in the nominative (and *Ó* in the genitive and *Uíbh* in the dative), with the territories they ruled being referred to in the same way. However, there was a later tendency for the dative form *Uíbh* to creep into nominative and genitive usage of placenames. *Uí* lenites in modern Irish, whereas *Uíbh* requires no lenition, but consonant mutation in placenames became confused at an early date, as shown by PUL's confused usage of names of dynasties and places beginning with *Uí* and *Uíbh,* which are maintained in this edition as given in the original.

Uí Mhuireadhaigh: the dynastic name of the Ó Tuathail family in Co. Kildare. Pronounced /i: vi′r′i:g′/.

Uíbh Chonaill Ghabra: a territory in Co. Limerick ruled by a sept of the Uí Fighinti.

Uíbh Eachach (Múmhan): Iveagh in south-west Cork, ruled by a branch of the Eóghanacht dynasty known in Middle Irish as the Eoganacht Raithlind, referring to their seat or fort at Raithleann. Both *rígh ua Neathach* and *rígh ua n-Eachach* in the original text have been edited as *rí Ó nEachach* here. Pronounced /i:v′ ɑx, ri: o: n′ɑx/.

Uíbh Fáilge: *Uí Fhailí* in modern Irish, or Offaly, an ancient kingdom and modern county in the centre of Ireland. The dynasty holding the kingdom traced its descent from a sixth-century king, Fáilge Berraide.

Uíbh Faoláin: a territory in Co. Kildare held by the Uí Bhriain (O'Byrnes of Leinster) dynasty.

Uíbh Fhiachrach Áidhne: the Hy Fiachrach, a kingdom in Co. Galway held by a dynasty claiming descent from Fiachrae, a fourth-century prince. This becomes *Ó bhFhiachrach Áidhne* in the genitive plural.

Uíbh Máine: usually found as *Uíbh Maine*, with a short *a*, and occasionally anglicised as Hy Many, an ancient kingdom in Co. Galway and Co. Roscommon ruled by the Ó Ceallaigh family.

Ulaidh: Ulster, the northern province of Ireland. As a plural noun, the genitive is *Uladh* and the dative *Ultaibh*. Pronounced /olə, oulhiv′/.

Ultach: Ulsterman, native of the province of Ulster, pronounced /oulhəx/.

Ur-Mhúmhain: Ormond or East Munster. This placename is spelt *Urmúmhain* in the original, possibly in imitation of a Middle Irish original. Pronounced /ur-'u:n′/.

Glossary

(the GCh equivalents are given where appropriate)

-na: an emphatic suffix appended to first-person plural prepositional pronouns. Usually written as one word with the pronoun, as in *againne* and *dúinne* in the original text, the pronunciation is with a separate syllable with a broad *n*, /ə'guŋ′nə/ and /du:ŋ′nə/, and often written as *againn-na* and *dúinn-na* in PUL's works (see, for example, *Sgéalaidheachta as an mBíobla Naomhtha*, Vol 4, pp415, 462). The latter spelling is adopted in this edition. Similarly, *sinne* is pronounced /ʃiŋ′nə/, and so is *sinn-na*. Also appended to verbs: *táimídne*, pronounced /tɑ:m′i:d′nə/ and edited here as *táimíd-na*.

'na, 'nar, 'narbh: PUL frequently uses *i* as the helping preposition to form indirect relative clauses, producing forms such as *'na*, *'nar* and *'narbh* where *go*, *gur* and *gurbh* (etymologically derived from the use of *ag* as the helping preposition) would be more common today. However, just as *go* has lost its connection with *ag*, the etymological connection of *'na* with *i* has been lost, and consequently these should not be edited as *ina, inar, inarbh*. PUL generally draws the distinction, writing *'n-a* where *'na* still functions as a preposition (*i n-aice na* *h-áite 'n-a raibh sé ag caint* in the original spelling in chapter 58 here) and *n-a*, with no apostrophe, where *'na* functions purely as a relative particle (*duine ana naomhtha n-ar bh'ainim dó Colla* in the original spelling in chapter 1 here).

a dhe: "really, indeed". The notes to PUL's *An Cleasaidhe* (p76) state that *a dhe* may be derived from *a Dhé!*, although the etymology is unclear. Pronounced /ə 'je/.

a: "from", or *as* in GCh, pronounced /ɑ/. The preposition *as* historically appeared with an *s* only before the singular and plural articles (*as an, as na*), the relative pronoun (*as a*), possessive adjectives (*as mo*), and before *gach*. *A* prefixes an *h* to a vowel, as in *a hÉirinn* (=*as Éirinn*).

ab: "abbot". PUL uses *abanna* in the plural, where GCh has the classical form *abaí* (originally spelt *abadha*).

abha: "river". The genitive is *abhann* and the dative *abhainn*, but the dative has replaced the nominative in GCh. Pronounced /au, aun, auŋ′/. The plural here is *aibhni*, corresponding to *aibhneacha* in GCh, pronounced /əi'ŋ′i:/.

abhaile: "home", pronounced /ə'vɑl′i/.

abhar: "material", or *ábhar* in GCh. WM Irish distinguishes between *abhar* (originally spelt *adhbhar*, now pronounced /aur/), "material", and *ábhar* (sometimes written *ádhbhar*, pronounced /ɑ:vər/), "amount". This word is found in *Niamh* only in the sense of "material". *Abhar cainnte*, "topic for discussion". *Abhar na gcábán*, "material for making the tents". *Abhar machnaimh*, "food for thought". *Abhar an tsagairt*, "the makings of a priest, a trainee priest". *Abhar tine*, "fuel".

abhcóidíocht: "debating, discussing", or *abhcóideacht* in GCh, pronounced /au'ko:d′i:xt/.

abhus: "on this side", pronounced /ə'vus/.

acfuinn: "capacity, means", or *acmhainn* in GCh. Pronounced /ɑkfiŋ′/ in WM Irish. *Acfuinn aigne*, "mental capacity". *As acfuinn a chéile*, "working in a united fashion, with their powers put together".

acfuinneach: "capable, substantial", or *acmhainneach* in GCh.

acfuinní: "capacity, power, resources", or *acmhainní* in GCh. *Ag dul in acfuinní*, "becoming more substantial". This word is not listed as a noun in dictionaries, but *acfuinní* is an abstract noun formed from the comparative of the adjective *acfuinneach*.

ach: "but". *Do rith sé in am agus ní raibh ann ach san*, "he ran away in time, but only just".

acrach: "handy, convenient", pronounced /ɑkərəx/.

adharc: "horn", with *adhairce* in the genitive. Pronounced /əirk, əirk′i/.

adhlacaim, adhlacadh: "to bury", pronounced /əiləkim′, əiləkə/.

adhmad: "wood", pronounced /əiməd/.

adhsáideach: "convenient, easy", or *aosáideach* in GCh, pronounced /əi'sɑ:d′əx/.

admhaím, admháil: "to admit", pronounced /ɑdə'vi:m′, adə'vɑ:l′/.

aduaidh: "from the north", pronounced /ə'duəg′/. *Ó thuaidh*, "northwards".

áfach: "however". PUL has the standard form of this word, which is found in other speakers of the WM dialect as *áfaigh*.

Glossary

ag: "at". *Ag mo* and *ag do* appear here as *ageam* and *agead/ageat*, pronounced /ig′əm, ig′əd~ig′ət/. The combination *ag á*, corresponding to *ag a* in GCh, is pronounced /i'g′ɑ:/. *Ag* combines with the plural of the definite article once here as *age sna*, pronounced /i'g′e snə/, reflecting the influence of the *s* found in *insna*. See under *dá, dhá, dhár* for discussion of the combination of *ag* with pronoun objects of the verbal noun (*'om, 'od, á*, etc).

aghaidh: "face", pronounced /əig′/. The phrase *in aghaidh*, "against; for (each)", often loses its final consonant, as in *in aghaidh an lae*, "by the day, daily", pronounced /nəin 'le:/. *Ag tabhairt aghaidh orthu* in chapter 54 shows the genitive is *aghaidh* and not the *aghaidhe* given in FGB. (*Aghaidhe* is extremely rare, but is found in PUL's manuscript translation of Genesis 3:19.)

agraim, agairt: "to avenge", or *agraím, agairt* in GCh, pronounced /ɑgərim′, ɑgirt′/.

aibíd: "habit, religious dress".

aibidh: "ripe, mature, keen", or *aibí* in GCh. Pronounced /ab′ig′/.

aibím, aibiú: "to ripen, mature".

aicillí: "agile, supple; adroit", or *aclaí* in GCh. Pronounced /ak′i'l′i:/.

aidhm: "desire, inclination", pronounced /əim′/.

aifliain: "the new year, the following year", or *athbhliain* in GCh, which regularly writes *ath-* regardless of the quality of the vowel in the prefix. Pronounced /af′l′iən′/.

aifreann: "Mass", pronounced /af′ir′ən/. PUL uses the plural *Aifrinni*, /af′ir′iŋ′i:/, whereas GCh has *Aifrinn*. *Aifreanntai* and *Aifreannai* are also found in WM Irish, *Aifreannai* being the form used by AÓL, according to CFBB (p4). Note *ag an Aifreann* in chapter 30 here: FGB shows that both *ag* and *ar* are found, but PUL consistently uses *ag* in his works.

aighneas: "contention, argument", pronounced /əin′əs/.

aigne: "mind", pronounced /ag′in′i/. *Fírinne aigne gan nochtadh aigne*, "honesty without indiscretion".

áilteóir: "practical joker, trickster", pronounced /'ɑ:l′ho:r′/ according to IWM §233, with unexpected stress on the first syllable.

aimhleas: "disadvantage, mischief", pronounced /ail′əs/.

aimhréidh: "entanglement", pronounced /əi'r′e:g′/. *Dul in aimhréidh*, "to get tangled, confused".

aimsím, aimsiú: "to find, get", pronounced /aim'ʃi:m′, aim'ʃu:/.

ainm: "name", pronounced /an′im′/. This noun is feminine in PUL's works, but masculine in GCh.

ainmním, ainmniú: "to name, specify", pronounced /an′im'n′i:m′, an′im'n′u:/.

ainneóin: "unwillingness". *In ainneóin*, "in spite of". *Dá lom deiridh ainneóna*, "in spite of his utmost efforts to the contrary", where *lom* is a noun meaning "a rank or pure state" (cf. *lom an donais*, "rank bad luck") and *deiridh* is an adjective meaning "uttermost". Pronounced /i'ŋ′o:n′/.

ainnis: "wretched". *Go hainnis*, "in a sorry way". Pronounced /aŋ′iʃ/.

airc: "greed".

Glossary

airchinneach: "hereditary steward of a church; herenach; prior". Pronounced /ar′hiŋ′əx/.
áird: "direction, quarter of a compass". *As gach áird,* "from all directions". *Ó árdaibh Cúige Laighean,* "from all over Leinster".
aireachas: "care, attention", pronounced /i'r′ɑxəs/.
airgead: "silver", pronounced /ar′ig′əd/. The genitive, *airgid,* has adjectival force.
airím, aireachtaint: "to hear", or *airím, aireachtáil* in GCh. Pronounced /a'r′i:m′, i'r′ɑxtint′/. This verb is more common in WM Irish than *cloisim, clos.*
áirím, áireamh: "to reckon, count". The past tense would be *d'áirigh* in GCh, but WM Irish normally has a slender -*v* in the pronunciation in the preterite singular and imperative where a *v* sound occurs in the verbal noun (*áireamh*). The past tense is therefore *d'áirimh,* /dɑ:r′iv′/. *Ní áirím,* "let alone, never mind".
áirithe: "certainty; lot". *Rud do chur in áirithe dhuit,* "to secure something for yourself".
airiú!: "why! really! indeed!", or *arú!* in GCh. Pronounced /i'r′u:~e'r′u:/.
áirseóir: "adversary", or *áibhirseoir* in GCh. *An tÁirseóir,* "the Devil". Note this word has initial stress in Munster Irish; see "Contributions to the Study of Word Stress in Irish", by Diarmuid Ó Sé, in *Ériu,* Vol. 40 (1989), p171. This stress pattern reflects the original trisyllabic spelling.
ais: "verge, side". Found in the phrase *le hais,* "besides", pronounced /l′ahiʃ/.
áise: "convenience", or *áis* in GCh. *Áise dhéanamh do dhuine,* "to do someone a favour".
aistear: "journey; roundabout way". *Aistear a chur ar dhuine,* "to take someone out of his way". *Cuaird in aistear,* "a wasted journey".
aistrím, aistriú: "to move around", pronounced /aʃt′i'r′i:m′, aʃt′i'r′u:/.
aiteas: "delight". This word is given in FGB as "pleasantness, fun", but PUL states in NIWU (p4) that this word means "intense delight", a stronger word than *áthas.*
aithis: "disgrace".
aithne: "acquaintance", pronounced /ahin′i/.
aithním, aithint: "to recognise, discern", pronounced /an′'hi:m′, ɑhint′/.
aithris: "imitation; an act of imitating or mimicking". Pronounced /ahir′iʃ/.
áitím, áiteamh: "to argue, establish, persuade, prove". *Ní áiteódh an saol air (go),* "nothing could have convinced him (that)".
ál: "litter, brood".
álainn: "beautiful". The comparatives *áille* and *álainne* are found here.
allta: "wild, fierce", pronounced /aulhə/. *Beithíoch allta,* "wild beast".
allúrach: "foreigner; pirate".
altaím, altú: "to give thanks, say grace", pronounced /ɑl'hi:m′~ɑl'hu:/. PUL uses the spelling *athlughadh* in the original text.
altóir: "altar", with *altórach* in the genitive singular where GCh has *altóra.*
amach: "out", pronounced /ə'mɑx/.
amáireach: "tomorrow", or *amárach* in GCh. Pronounced /ə'mɑ:r′əx/. This word is declinable, as in *i gcaitheamh an lae amáirigh* here. *Amáireach a bhí chúinn,* "the next day".

Glossary

ambasa: "indeed", or *ambaiste* in GCh. This appears to mean, literally, "by my hands", but the alternative form *ambaiste* indicates a more likely derivation from an oath meaning "upon my baptism". Pronounced /əm'bɑsə/.

amháin: "one; only", pronounced /ə'vɑ:n′/.

amharc: "sight", pronounced /ɑvərk/.

amhlaidh: "thus, so", pronounced /aulig′/, but often reduced to /aulə/.

amhra: "poem, eulogy, lamentation". Pronounced /aurə/. This word is especially used in reference to *Amra Cholm Cille,* a eulogy to St. Columba that may have been written in the seventh century. *Amhra Colm Cille* in the original text did not give lenition of *Colm Cille,* probably with archaising intent. The Dublin Institute of Advanced Studies published a version of this work under the title *Amrae Coluimb Chille: a critical edition* in 2019.

amhrán: "song", pronounced /ɑvə'rɑ:n/.

amu': "outside", or *amuigh* in GCh. PUL here used the spelling *amuich,* probably to forestall a pronunciation in /g′/, as the pronunciation is /ə'mu/.

an-, ana-: "very". *Ana-* is frequently found before a vowel in the original (*ana aosta, ana íseal,* etc), possibly reflecting PUL's view that *ana* was a separate word and not a prefix (see NIWU, p3). These have been edited as *an-aosta,* etc, here.

an-chor: "ill-treatment", pronounced /'ɑn'xor/.

anaithe: "storm; terror", or *anfa* in GCh. Pronounced /ɑnihi/. The spelling *anaithe* was given in the original text.

anál: "breath", or *anáil* in GCh. *Anáil* is found in the dative in many of PUL's works, but *anál* is used even in dative contexts in *Niamh. Féna n-aná(i)l,* "under their breath". *An anál do tharrac,* "to draw one's last breath; expire". *T'anál ag dul fé dhuine,* "to influence someone".

anall: "over here, from that side"; pronounced /ə'naul/.

anamchara: "confessor, chaplain". Pronounced /'ɑnəmˌxɑrə/.

aneas: "from the south", pronounced /i'n′as/. *Ó dheas,* "southwards", pronounced /o: 'jas/.

angar: "want; hunger", or *angar* in GCh, pronounced /auŋgər/. *Ní raibh aon angar sa tseómra mhór,* "the large room was stocked with everything; it lacked nothing". Spelt *amhgar* in the original.

aniar: "from the west", pronounced /i'n′iər/. *Aniar aneas,* "from the southwest".

aníos: "up (from below)", pronounced /i'n′i:s/.

anncaire: "anchor", or *ancaire* in GCh. A double *n* is inserted in this edition to show the diphthong: /auŋkir′i/; the spelling *anncaire* is found in PUL's *Lúcián* (p26 and elsewhere). Note the plural here is *anncaireacha,* in contradistinction to *ancairí* in GCh. The plural *ancairí* is also found in PUL's works (*Guaire,* Vol 2, pp194-195, and *Gníomhartha na n-Aspol,* p367).

annscian: "terror, fury, wildness; a wild or violent person", or *ainscian* in GCh. Pronounced /aunʃk′iən/. This word is feminine in FGB, but found as *an t-annscian* here, in reference to Murchadh.

anoir: "from the east", pronounced /ə'nir′/. *Anoir aduaidh,* "from the northeast".

Glossary

anois: "now". A broad *n* is shown in IWM (§142), but Brian Ó Cuív uses the spelling *anis* in CFBB (e.g. p11), and the various LS editions of PUL's works prepared by Shán Ó Cuív and Osborn Bergin use *inìsh*. A slender *n* is preferable in this word, /i'n′iʃ/.

anonn: "over there, to that side", pronounced /ə'nu:n/. *Curtha anonn*, "sent off". *Anonn* is used in preference to *sall* in WM Irish.

ansan: "then; there", or *ansin* in GCh; pronounced /ən'son/.

anso: "here", or *anseo* in GCh, pronounced /ən'so/.

ansúd: "there" (more distant), or *ansiúd* in GCh, pronounced /ən'su:d/.

anuas: "down (from above)", pronounced /ə'nuəs/.

aoibhneas: "bliss, delight", pronounced /i:v′in′əs/.

Aoine: "Friday". *Dé hAoine*, "on Friday". This word originally meant "fasting, abstinence", referring to Christian observances on Fridays.

aoirde: "height", or *airde* in GCh.

aol: "limestone".

aon bhall: "anywhere", pronounced /e:(n) vəl/.

aon chuma: "anyway", pronounced /e:(n) xumə/.

aon rud: "anything", pronounced /e:(n) rəd/.

aoraim: "to herd", with the verbal noun *aeireacht*, pronounced /e:rim′~e:r′əxt/. Traditionally spelt *aodharaim* and *aodhaireacht*.

aos: "age". In this meaning, this word would be *aois* in GCh. Pronounced /e:s/.

ar fuaid, ar fuid: "throughout", pronounced /er fuəd′, er fid′/, "throughout", or *ar fud* in GCh. PUL wrote that *ar fuaid* should be used for broad areas (*ar fuaid na paróiste*) and *ar fuid* for small areas (*ar fuid an tí*) (NIWU, p54), but it is clear from *Niamh* that this distinction is not always adhered to (cf. *ar fuid na hÉireann* here). The distinction seem historical or forced, as Brian Ó Cuív wrote that he had never heard *ar fuid* (CFBB, p273).

ar ndeóin: see under *ar ndó'*.

ar ndó': a variant of *dar ndó'* (*dar ndóigh* in GCh), "of course, no doubt". The variant forms *ar ndóin* and *ar ndeóin* are also found here (spelt *ar nóin* and *ar neóin* in the original). *Dóin* is explained in PSD as a corruption of *dóigh*. See also under *dó'*.

ar ndóin: see under *ar ndó'*.

ár-mhá: "battlefield". Note this word is masculine here, but feminine in GCh. This is noteworthy, because, in theory, the second element of a compound word should give the gender. Compare *an mágh so na h-Éamhna* in *Eisirt* (p65).

ar: "on", pronounced /er′/, reflecting a general tendency for prepositions to become aligned with the third-singular prepositional pronoun, *air*. Note *orm*, "on me", with an epenthetic vowel: /orəm/. *Ar* does not lenite definite placenames, and so we find *ar Gleann Mháma* and similar phrases here. This principle only applies when the meaning is "in/at a place"; such phrases as *thugadar aghaidh ar Cheann Cora* and *thugadar aghaidh ar Bhaile Átha Cliath* show correct lenition of the placename. *Ca bhfios ná go mb'fhéidir go mbeadh sé ar dhuine éigin eile ag Colla*, "who knows if maybe Colla would blame someone else?"

Glossary

ár: "slaughter, massacre".
araon: "both", pronounced /ə're:n/.
arbhar: "corn", pronounced /ɑ'ru:r/.
árd-dhearúd: "a great mistake".
árd: "high". Note the genitive used in *i gcómhair an Aifrinn Aoird*, "for the High Mass", here, where *an Aifrinn Aird* would stand in GCh. Similarly, the comparative here is *aoirde*, where GCh has *airde*.
árdaigne: "high spirits". *Árdaigne do dhúiseacht iontu i gcómhair an chatha*, "to arouse their enthusiasm for the battle". Pronounced /'ɑ:rdag′in′i/.
árdfhearg: "great anger", pronounced /'ɑ:rdɑrəg/.
árdríogan: "high queen". It is not clear that such a title existed in ancient Ireland, but PUL uses this word here to refer to the wife of the high king. If this word existed in GCh it would be *ardríon*. This becomes *árdríogana* in the genitive and *árdríogain* in the dative. The genitive was spelt *árdríghna* in the original, but PUL's *Eisirt* has *ríogna* for the genitive of *ríogan* (see p50 therein), and it seems likely /'ɑ:rd'ri:gənə/ would be the desired pronunciation of the genitive singular.
árdríoganacht: "high queenship", the office of the wife of the high king. If this word, apparently concocted *ad hoc*, existed in GCh, it would be *ardríonacht*.
aréir: "last night", pronounced /ə're:r′/, with a broad *r* in the middle of the word.
argain: "destruction, plunder", pronounced /ɑrəgin′/.
argóint: "argument", pronounced /ɑrə'go:nt′/.
arís: "again". PUL used the spelling *airís*, indicating a slender *r*, /i'r′i:ʃ/. This word is shown with a broad *r* in IWM (§274, line 85), but PUL's spelling and transcription of this word as *irìsh* in the LS editions of PUL's works show the slender pronunciation.
arm: "army" or "weapon". This word can be used as a collective singular to refer to weapons. Pronounced /ɑrəm/. *An lucht airm*, "the soldiers, the armed men".
armáil: "army", pronounced /ɑrə'mɑ:l′/.
armtha: "armed", or *armáilte* in GCh. Pronounced /ɑrəmhə/.
athairiúil: "like one's father", or *aithriúil* in GCh. While this word was spelt *aithreamhail* in the original text of *Niamh*, CFBB (p18) indicates this word is pronounced /ahi'r′u:l′/, and this is supported by the spelling used in PUL's *Sgéalaidheachta as an mBíobla Naomhtha*, where we read *deiridís gur bh'é mac ab athaireamhla é d'á bhfeacadar riamh* (Vol V, p568).
athnóim, athnóchaint: "to renew, renovate", or *athnuaim, athnuachan* in GCh. Pronounced /ɑn'ho:m′, ɑn'ho:xint′/.
athraím, athrú: "to change", pronounced /ɑhə'ri:m′, ɑhə'ru:/.
bacaim, bac: "to hinder, prevent", or *bacaim, bacadh* in GCh.
bacán: "hook, peg".
bagairt: "an act of nodding or winking". *Bagairt a dhéanamh ar dhuine*, "to give someone the nod".
baic: "twist, crook", found in the phrase *baic miníl*, "the nape of the neck".

Glossary

báidh: /bɑ:g′/, "sympathy, liking". This word is *bá* in GCh, but the final *-idh* in the historical spelling is audible in the nominative/dative singular in WM Irish. The genitive was originally spelt *báidhe* or *bádha*, but is edited as *bá* here.

bail: "success, prosperity". *Measaim gur maith an bhail ort gan M'leachlainn a bheith ag éisteacht leat*, "I think you're lucky M'leachlainn is not listening to you".

baileach: "exact; totally, completely", pronounced /bi'l′ɑx/.

bailím, bailiú: "to collect". *Bailiú leat (amach)*, "to slip away, be off".

báim, bá: "to drown". Pronounced /bɑ:m′, bɑ:(h)/.

bainim, baint: "to cut". *Baint de*, "to remove or take from". *Baint le*, "to touch; to concern or be connected with something". Pronounced /bin′im′, bint′/.

bainntreach: "widow", or *baintreach* in GCh. The double *n* here shows the diphthong: /baint′(i)r′əx/.

balaithe: "smell", or *boladh* in GCh. This is corrected from *balaith* in the original text. *Balaithe a dhul fút*, "to smell something, perceive a smell".

balbh: "dumb, mute", pronounced /bɑləv/.

ball: "place, spot". *In aon bhall*, "anywhere", pronounced /ə'ne:vəl/.

banaltranas: "nursing; to nurse", pronounced /bɑnərhlənəs/.

bannda: "band of cloth, bandage", or *banda* in GCh. The traditional *nn* is retained here, as it showed the diphthong: /baundə/.

bannrín: "queen", or *banríon* in GCh. Pronounced /bau'ri:n′/ in WM Irish. The genitive is *bannríne*. The *r* is broad: a spelling *bannraín* would show the pronunciation better, but the connection with *rí* and *ríogan* would be obscured.

banntracht: "womankind, womenfolk", or *bantracht* in GCh. Pronounced /bauntrəxt/.

baoch: "grateful", or *buíoch* in GCh, pronounced /be:x/ in WM Irish. *Buidheach* stood in the original.

baochas: "thanks", pronounced /be:xəs/; *buíochas* in GCh. *Buidhchas* stood in the original.

baol: "danger". *Ní baol ná go*, "there is no fear but that, it is certain that, it is highly likely that".

bára: found in the phrase *i ndeireadh bára*, "when all is said and done, after all". *Bára* is derived from *báire*, "a game; a hurling match", but the pronunciation is /bɑ:rə/ in this phrase. *I ndeireadh báire* is found in GCh.

bárr, barra: "top", or *barr* in GCh. Pronounced /bɑ:r, bɑrə/. Both forms are found in WM Irish, with *barra* typically found in the dative (according to *Foclóir do Shéadna*, p15), although this use is not limited to the dative. *Dá bhárr*, "as a result of it". *Mar bharra ar*, "in addition to". *Barra na teangan*, "the tip of the tongue". *Thar bárr*, "excellent, to an exceeding degree". *Bárr a leogaint le duine*, "to let someone get ahead/take the lead". Note *ar bárr/barra*, "on top (of), atop", with *ar bhárr/bharra* meaning "on the top of, at the tip of" something. This distinction is poorly evidenced in PUL's published works: in *Niamh* we read *ar barra rí-theaghlaigh Shitric* in one passage and *ar bharra an rí-theaghlaigh* in another. Essentially, *ar barra* is a discrete adverbial phrase, and *ar barra rí-theaghlaigh Shitric* can be parsed as *{ar barra} {rí-theaghlaigh Shitric}*, i.e. as an adverbial phrase followed by a noun phrase, whereas *ar bharra mo theangan* found here contains a preposition and a noun phrase thus: *ar {bharra mo theangan}*. The grouping of words is made in the mind and so lenition and non-lenition are both correct in such phrases. See PUL's comments in NIWU (p144): "*Ar bruach na faraige*, on the sea-shore. *Ar bhruach na faraige*, on the shore of the sea". See under *bruach* for further discussion of generic adverbial phrases such as *ar barra*.

barra: "bar". *Barra ciomalta*, "file". See under *cimlim, cimilt*.

bas: "palm of the hand", with *baise* in the genitive. The GCh form is *bos*. See *cimlim, cimilt*.

bata: "stick". *Capall bata*, "a wooden horse".

beacht: "precise, exact, perfect".

beag: "small, little", pronounced /b′og/. The spelling has not been altered in the editing process here, as this is a common word. Compare *ní beag dóibh é*, "it is enough for them", with *ní beag leó é*, "they think it sufficient". *Níor bheag san*, "that was enough".

beagán: "a little bit", pronounced /b′ə'gɑ:n/.

béal-scaoilte: "indiscreet".

béal: "mouth", but also "blade" of a sword.

bean: "woman", with *mná* in the genitive singular and *mnaoi* in the dative singular (*mnaoi* is now rare in WM Irish).

beárna: "gap, breach", with *beárnain* here in the dative. CFBB (p27) shows that *beárnainn* was also found in the dative singular. Pronounced /b′a:rnə, b′a:rnin′~b′a:rniŋ′/.

beart: "bundle", feminine here, but masculine in GCh. *Beart pháipéar*, "a bundle of papers".

beart: "deed, action, move", feminine here, but masculine in GCh. *Thar na beartaibh*, "beyond expectation", i.e. "exceedingly".

beartaím, beartú: "to wield or brandish a weapon", as well as "to decide, think, estimate".

béile: "meal". *Béile*, which is masculine in GCh, is normally feminine in PUL's works, but *an béile* was found in chapter 51 here. This may have been a typographical error in the original text: *an bhéile* has been used in this edition. *Béile na maidine*, "breakfast".

beirim, breith: "to bear, take, carry", and numerous other meanings. Note that the *r* of the preterite *rug* is pronounced slender in lenitable circumstances, e.g. *do rug*, /də r′ug/. Compare the autonomous form *nuair a rugadh mise* in *Mo Sgéal Féin* (p20), transcribed in the LS version, *Mo shgiàl fén* (p9), as *nuer a rugag mishi*, showing a broad *r* in the autonomous form, which resists lenition. Yet AÓL had *riugag* in the autonomous (*Seanachas Amhlaoibh*, p217). *Beirthe*, the past participle of *beirim*, is pronounced /b′erhə/, with a broad *r*, and is accordingly edited as *bertha* here. This falls in line with the point made by PUL in a letter to Risteárd Pléimeann dated March 10th 1918 and held in the G1,277 (1) collection of manuscripts in the National Library of Ireland: "Take the Irish word for 'born'. It consists of two syllables *ber* and *tha*. Put them together and you have the word *bertha*. But the pedant, using his eye, not his ear, insists on writing it *beirthe*, a word which no Irish speaker has ever spoken! It is very near the sound of the Irish word for 'boiled', i.e. *beirithe*". *Cad a bhéarfadh gur leat-sa iad?*, "how come they are yours?" *Breith ar*, "to seize": *beir ar do thuaigh*, "grab your axe". *Bertha le rud*, "advantaged by something, the better off on account of something". *Níorbh fhada go raibh sé ag breith suas ar bheith chómh hárd, geall leis, le Niamh féin*, "it wasn't long before he was catching up, almost, with Niamh herself in terms of height".

beirithe: "boiled". *In uisce bheirithe*, "in boiling water", i.e. in a panic or fix of some kind.

bia: "food". *Bídh*, the genitive singular, is pronounced /b′i:g′/ in WM Irish. The genitive is *bia* in GCh.

bile: "sacred tree", such as the *Bile Mór Mágha Adhair* in Co. Clare.

bíoba: "enemy, wrongdoer", or *bíobha* in GCh. *Bíoba báis*, "an inveterate enemy". This word is consistently given as *bíodhba*, and not *bíodhbha*, in the original text. See IWM (§368) for discussion of similar words (*Banba, diablai*, etc) that see a delenition of a classical *bh* in WM Irish.

biorán: "pin", pronounced /br′ɑ:n/. *Ní fiú biorán is é*, "it is worthless".

bioránach: "lad, fellow".

bithiúnach: this is glossed in FGB as "scoundrel", but generally means, more specifically, "thief".

bithiúntas: "thievery". See under *bithiúnach*.

bob: "trick".

bochtaineacht: "humiliation".

bodhar: "deaf", pronounced /bour/.

bogha: "bow", pronounced /bou/.

bolg: "stomach", with the plural *builg* meaning "bellows". Pronounced /boləg, bil′ig′/.

bonn: "ground, foundation", pronounced /boun/. *Láithreach bonn*, "on the spot, instantly".

bórd: "table", with *búird* in the genitive singular and nominative plural *búird*. Compare *bord* and *boird* in GCh. *Ar bórd luinge*, "on board ship". See under *bruach* for discussion of generic adverbial phrases such as *ar bórd*.

bóthar: "road", with *bóithre* in the plural. Pronounced /bo:hər, bo:r′hi/.

brách: "judgement, doomsday". *Go brách na breithe*, "till doomsday".

bradaíol: "pilfering", or *bradaíl* in GCh. It is generally the case that verbal nouns in *-aíl* (*-ghail* in the older spelling) have a broad *l* in WM Irish (see *camastaíol* and many others in CFBB, p48 and elsewhere).

braighdineas: "captivity", or *braighdeanas* in GCh. IWM §95 shows AÓL had a broad *n* in this word, but PUL consistently spelt it slender.

bratach: "flag, standard", pronounced /brə'tɑx/.

breall: "defect". *Breall ar an bhfeall*, possibly "the evil is thwarted, comes to nothing".

breis: "addition, increment". This word is usually found with eclipsis after *sa*: *sa mbreis*, "in addition".

breithiúntas: "judgement", or *breithiúnas* in GCh.

breithním, breithniú: "to consider, examine", or *breathnaím, breathnú* in GCh. Pronounced /br′en′ˈhi:m′, br′en′ˈhu:/. However, IWM §321 has *breathnaigh*, showing both forms existed.

breóite: "sick". Note that the traditional distinction between *breóite*, "sick", and *teinn*, "sore", is maintained in WM Irish. GCh only has the latter, spelt as *tinn*.

breóiteacht: "sickness".

brí: "meaning". This word is masculine here, but feminine in GCh.

bríomhar: "vigorous, forceful", or "stirring" of a song, used in reference to cheering in chapter 58 here.

brollach: "breast, bosom". Pronounced /bərˈlɑx/ according to IWM §420, and spelt *borlach* in PUL's *Cath Ruis na Rí for Bóinn* (p2).

bronntanas: "gift, present", pronounced /brountənəs/.

bruach: "bank, shore". *Ar bruach na farraige*, "on the seashore", with no lenition of the *b* in generic reference. This principle was set out by PUL in NIWU (p144), where he draws a distinction between *ar bruach na faraige* (so spelt), "on the sea-shore", and *ar bhruach na faraige*, "on the shore of the sea". PUL's comments in a letter to Risteárd Pléimeann (dated February 6th 1918 and held in the G1,277 manuscript collection in the National Library of Ireland) on *ar muin a bheithíg féin* are quoted in full in the Preface here, and show the distinction lies in the generic nature of the adverbial expression: *ar muin* just means "riding", and not "on the upper back of" anything as such (there is no clear focus on "back" as a specific noun). We have an adverbial phrase (*ar muin*) followed by a noun phrase (*a bheithígh féin*), producing the correct parsing *{ar muin} {a bheithíg féin}*. Other apposite examples include *ar bórd luinge* and *ar bórd na luinge* found here ("on board a ship" or "on board the ship"), parsed as *{ar bórd} {na luinge}*, and *bhíos i gCeann Tuirc ar Caibidiol, mé féin agus na sagairt eile a bhain leis an áit* in PUL's *Mo Sgéal Féin* (p120), where *ar caibidiol* (*ar caibideal*) is a generic adverbial phrase meaning "at chapter", as of a priest convening with other clergymen.

Consequently, in theory *ar bruach* just means "by, along", and not literally "on the bank of". However, it is difficult to infer this distinction in each case in PUL's published Irish. In addition to *ar bhruach an tSoláin* here, we also have *ar bruach na Sionainne*, and it would seem a little forced to have the one meaning "on the (actual) bank of the Sullane" and the other just as "along the Shannon". Gerald O'Nolan argues (in his *New Era Grammar*, p113) that 'dynamic lenition' is used to create additional "psychological distinctions", generally where the nuance is of reference to a particular person or thing rather than generic. If so, such usage seems haphazard, if PUL's published works are held to correctly give the lenition or non-lenition in such phrases. The large number of glaring typographical errors in PUL's works further complicates the issue, as it is difficult to be certain that his published works correctly represent his Irish.

bruid: "hurry, pressure of work", or *broid* in GCh.

bruidiúil: "busy", or *broidiúil* in GCh. The spelling with *ui* is retained here as clarifying the pronunciation.

bruíon chaorthainn: *'na mbruín chaorthainn,* "in uproar". This phrase is a reference to the tale *Cath Bruíon Chaorthainn* in the Fenian cycle of myths, which relates how the *Fianna* were tricked into an enchanted house of rowan trees (*bruíon chaorthainn*), where they were held by a spell until their captors were killed and the spell broken.

buac: "pinnacle; one's best interests", or *buaic* in GCh.

buaim, buachtaint: "to win, gain a victory", or *buaim, buachan* in GCh.

buile: "rage". *Buile misnigh,* "a frenzy of courage".

buille: "blow". *Buille fé thuairim,* "a random, haphazard blow".

buíon: "troop, company or band of soldiers", with *buín* in the dative. The plural here is *buíona,* but would be *buíonta* in GCh. *Buíon chosanta,* "bodyguard".

búirtheach: "an act of bellowing, roaring", or *búireach* in GCh. The *th* is preserved, as the pronunciation is /bu:r′həx/ in traditional WM Irish. Note that as this verbal noun is feminine, it becomes *ag búirthigh* /ə bu:r′hig′/ in the dative, a distinction not observed in GCh, which has *ag búireach.*

bun-áit: "base, military base, headquarters".

bun-os-cionn le: "at variance with". Pronounced /bin′iʃ 'k′u:n/ according to IWM §202, although a slender *n* is not shown in PUL's works. LASID has /bunəs 'k′u:n/.

bun-phréamh: "taproot; root, cause, origin", or *bunfhréamh* in GCh. The dative is *bun-phréimh. Ag bun-phréimh na hoibre go léir,* "behind the whole business".

bunaidh: "essential, basic", an adjective derived from the genitive singular of *bunadh,* "origin"; pronounced /bunig′/. *Áit bhunaidh,* "headquarters".

buthaire: "cloud/column of smoke", or *puthaire* in GCh. Often found as *buthaire deataigh.*

cá/ca: "where?" The vowel is generally short in *ca bhfios?,* "who knows?", which is pronounced /kɑvəs/ according to IWM (§257). Some of PUL's works, including *Lúcián* (e.g. p16), use the spelling *ca bh'fhios.* Similarly, *ca bhfuil?* is used in this edition. There is an annotation added to *ca bhfuilid siad?* in PUL's manuscript translation of Deuteronomy 32:26 held in Maynooth, which may be in Risteárd Pléimeann's handwriting, saying "(not *cá*)". Compare *Scéalaíocht Amhlaoibh Í Luínse* (p20), which has *ca bhfuil?* GCD indicates that *cá* is pronounced short in Corca Dhuíbhne Irish when combined with the present tense of the verb *bheith* (see §533, where *cá bhfuil* can be /kavəl′/, /kal′/ or /koul′/). PUL's *Lúcián* (e.g. p22) has *ca bhfuil.*

cábán: "cabin, tent, booth".

cabhail: "torso", pronounced /koul′/.

cabhlach: "fleet, navy". Note: this noun is feminine here, but masculine in GCh. Pronounced /kouləx/.

cabhraím, cabhrú: "to help". Note that the verbal adjective here is *cabhartha,* pronounced /kourhə/, where *cabhraithe* stands in GCh.

Glossary

cad 'na thaobh?: "why?", or *cén fáth?* in GCh. Pronounced /kɑnə 'he:v/. *Cén fáth?* is not found in PUL's works, but *cad fáth?, cad chuige?, cad é an chúís?, cad fé ndeár é?, cad ar a shon?, cad uime?* and *cad* on its own (e.g. *cad ba ghá?*) are all attested.

cad é mar: "how", but generally confined to exclamations or rhetorical utterances. *Cad é mar 'fhéadann sí cainnt agus sult agus gáirí ' dhéanamh,* "how she can talk and have fun and laugh!"

caibideal: "chapter", *or caibidil* in GCh. PUL consistently uses the spelling *caibidiol* in his works, and so seems to have pronounced this word with a broad *l*, /kab′id′əl/, although a slender *l* is more common in other writers, and a slender *l* is shown in all of the LS editions of PUL's works (e.g. *Eshirt,* p1).

cailís: "chalice".

caillim, cailliúint: "to lose", or *caillim, cailleadh* in GCh. *Ná caill,* "don't fail; don't let me down".

cáinim, cáineadh: "to condemn".

cainnt: "talk, talking", or *caint* in GCh. The traditional double *n* is shown here to indicate the diphthong, /kaint′/. The original text of *Niamh* does not give a double *n,* but the traditional spelling can be found in PUL's other works.

caíora: "sheep", or *caora* in GCh, with the plural here *caoire,* corresponding to *caoirigh* in GCh. The genitive singular and plural is *caorach/caeireach.* Pronounced /ki:rə/ and /ki:r′i/, with the genitive /ke:rəx~ke:r′ex/.

cáirde: "respite, delay". *Gan a thuilleadh cáirde,* "with no more ado".

caise: "stream, flood". *Caise deór,* "a flood of tears".

caismirt: "conflict, contention". *Dul sa chaismirt,* "to enter the fray". Pronounced /kɑʃm′irt′/.

caladh: "landing-place, jetty". *Caladh cuain,* "wharf, jetty". This word was spelt *calaith* in the original, possibly to prevent the *-idh* of the genitive (*calaidh* in GCh) from being pronounced as /g′/. As in both the nominative and the genitive this word is pronounced /kɑlə/, the genitive here is undeclined, as *caladh.*

cam: "bend, twist". *Cor in aghaidh an chaím,* "tit for tat, giving as good as you get". PUL states in NIWU (p26) that the genitive of this word is pronounced *caím.* The whole phrase is /kor (ə) nəin xi:m′/.

camtha: "camp", or *campa* in GCh. Pronounced /kaumhə/.

canad: "where?", or *cá háit?* in GCh.

canaim, cantainn: "to chant", equivalent to *canaim, canadh* in GCh. *Cantain* is a noun meaning "chanting, singing" in GCh. *Canadh* is also found as the verbal noun in PUL's works, for example, in *Críost Mac Dé,* Vol 1, p28 (*tá an chantic sin d'á labairt, agus d'á canadh leis na míltibh saighseana ceóil, i dteangthachaibh an domhain ins gach páirt de'n domhan*). The LS version of *Aithris ar Chríost* transcribes *cantainne* (found on p58 of that work) as *cantuingi* (p142 of the LS edition) showing the pronunciation of the verbal noun to be /kɑntiŋ′/, with no diphthong in the first syllable, because *cantainn* is related to the English word chanting and/or the Latin *cantare.*

canncar: "canker, anger, spleen", or *cancar* in GCh. The traditional double *n* is given here to show the diphthong, /kauŋkər/, although the original spelling used here was *cancar*.
caogad: "fifty", or *caoga* in GCh. The plural *caogaid* is found here (*trí caogaid*, "one hundred and fifty" in chapter 22), for some reason universally spelt *caoghaid* in the original text of *Niamh*. CFBB (p49) shows *caogaid* to be the general form of this numeral in WM Irish, but *caogad* in the singular is found in PUL's works.
caoi: "opportunity", pronounced /ke:/.
caoin: "gentle, refined".
caol-dromach: "narrow-ridged", of a nose here.
caol: "the slender part of something". *Caol droma*, "the small of the back".
caothúil: "convenient, suitably situated", or *caoithiúil* in GCh. Pronounced /ke:'hu:l'/.
caothúlacht: "convenience", or *caoithiúlacht* in GCh, pronounced /ke:'hu:ləxt/.
capall: "horse". Note that the dative plural has a slender *l* in WM Irish: *capaillibh*.
captaein: "captain", or *captaen* in GCh.
cara: "friend", with the genitive (singular and plural) *carad*, the dative *caraid* and the plural *cáirde*. Note that this was until recently a rare word in native Irish speech, as "friends", whether relatives or not, were generally *daoine muínteartha* (see PUL's comments in NIWU, p81). However, in the specific context of the allies of various kings (*cáirde Bhriain, cáirde Mh'leachlainn*), the word makes more sense than *daoine muínteartha*, explaining its use here. Since PUL's day, the word *cara* has been adopted by modern speakers of Irish as a one-for-one equivalent of the English word "friend".
caradach: "friendly", or *cairdiúil* in GCh.
caradas: "friendship", or *cairdeas* in GCh.
carbad: "chariot". This is spelt *cárbad* (once, in chapter 20) and *cárbat* (34 times, including *chárbat*) in the original. The spelling *carbad*, accepted in FGB and PSD, was not found in the original edition of *Niamh*, but is used elsewhere in PUL's works (for example, *Lúcián*, p8, and *Táin Bó Cuailnge*, p3). *Carbad* is a literary word that may not have been in frequent use among the Irish-speaking community PUL grew up in, and it seems he may at one point have thought it should be pronounced /kɑ:rbət/. However, *cárbait* in the genitive in PUL's *Eisirt* (p58) is transcribed in the LS edition, *Eshirt* (p59), as *carabuid*, indicating a pronunciation (in the nominative) of /kɑrəbəd/, one likely to be more generally accepted as the 'correct' pronunciation of this word in Munster Irish.
carcair: "prison, jail".
carra: "wagon", with *carrai* in the plural. The GCh forms are *carr* and *carranna.*
casaim, casadh: "to turn". *Casadh giorraithe*, "turning of hares (in hare coursing)". *Casadh le*, "to endeavour to (do something)". *A neart ag casadh air,* "his strength returning to him".
casúr: "hammer".
cath: "battle", with *cathanna* in the plural.
cathain: "when?", pronounced /kə'hin'/.

Glossary

cathair: "city", with *cathrach* in the genitive. Pronounced /kahir′, kahərəx/.

céad: "first". This numeral would ordinarily not lenite a *t* or a *d*, but we find *an gcéad thigh* in the original text of chapter 14 here, as well as *an gcéad teachtaire* elsewhere. *Thigh* may be a typographical error in the original, particularly as there is only a slight difference indicated in pronunciation between *gcéad thigh* and *gcéad tigh*, and so the spelling has been adjusted to *an gcéad tigh* here. *An chéad cuid* in chapter 45 has also been adjusted to *an chéad chuid*, in line with the general usage in PUL's works. The general plural of *céad* is *céadta*, found here, for example, in *[thagaidís] 'na gcéadtaibh agus 'na míltibh*, "they came in their hundreds and thousands, in great numbers". Where the meaning is more specifically numeric, PUL uses *céadaibh* in the dative plural, as in chapter 52 here: *cúig nú sé ' chéadaibh fear*, "five or six detachments of men", where each detachment presumably comprised 100 men. Compare also the Feeding of the Five Thousand in PUL's *Na Cheithre Soisgéil* (p104): *do shuidheadar 'n-a mbuidhnibh, 'n-a gcéadaibh agus 'n-a gcaogadaibh*, "they sat in groups, in groups of a hundred and in groups of fifty". In *Séadna* we read *ní 'n-a sgillingibh ná 'n-a phúntaibh atá an t-airgead ag imtheacht uaidh, ach i n-a fhichidibh agus 'n-a chéadaibh púnt* (p127). *Deich gcéad*, "a thousand".

cealgaim, cealgadh: "to beguile, deceive", pronounced /k′aləgim′, k′aləgə/.

ceangal: "bond, obligation". *Ceangal a ghabháil ort féin*, "to enter into an obligation, take on an obligation".

ceanglaim, ceangal: "to bind, tie", or *ceanglaím, ceangal* in GCh. Pronounced /k′aŋəlim′, k′aŋəl/.

ceann-ísleacht: "submissiveness".

ceann: "head; end". *Fear cínn riain*, "leader, captain". *Dheineadar an ceann ab fheárr den ghnó*, "they made the best of it". *Ó cheann ceann den longphort*, "from one end of the camp to another". The use of *de* after *ó cheann ceann* was commented on by PUL in NIWU (p19), where he explained the phrase *ó cheann ceann den tír*, and said, "*ó cheann ceann na tíre* would not be correct. The full expression is, *ó cheann de'n tír go dtí an ceann eile de'n tír*. In *ceann na tíre* there is question of only one end, whereas in the text there is question, not of the country's end, but of two ends of the country. The genitive in this case is a partitive genitive". Yet FGB gives only *ó cheann (go) ceann na tíre* with *ceann* followed by the genitive case (see under *ceann*) and other speakers of WM Irish seem to accept the genitive here. See, for instance, *ó cheann ceann na bliana* in *Seanachas Amhlaoibh Í Luínse* (p99) and *ó cheann ceann na bliadhna* in Diarmuid Ua Laoghaire's *An Bhruinneall Bháin* (p123).

ceannach: "demand" for something, used with *ar*. Pronounced /k′ə'nax/.

ceannatha: "facial features", or *ceannaithe* in GCh. This was spelt *ceannacha* in the original text, but this word is pronounced /k′ə'nahə/, as stated by PUL in NIWU (p60).

ceanntar: "district", or *ceantar* in GCh, pronounced /k′auntər/.

ceárd: "trade". The dative singular *ceird* (i.e. *céird* here) is used as the nominative in GCh. *Lucht ceárd*, "craftsmen".

ceárdaí: "artisan, craftsman".
ceárdúil: "well-wrought, the product of good craftsmanship".
ceart: "right". *I gceart*, "in the right way; properly, really; out and out, good and proper". *Sa cheart*, "in the proper manner, correctly".
ceárta: "forge", with the genitive *ceártan* and dative *ceártain*.
céasadh: "torment; crucifixion". *Aoine an Chéasta*, "Good Friday". *An Chrois Chéasta*, "the crucifix". See also under *crois* for further discussion.
ceataí: "inconvenience, awkwardness, a problem". This appears in GCh as *ciotaí*, but *ceataighe* is the traditional spelling, and the pronunciation in WM Irish is /k′a'ti:/. Note the spelling of the cognate word *ciotach*, "awkward". The divergence in spelling seems to reflect the fact that unstressed vowels are usually reduced in the pretonic position in WM Irish, except where /i:/ or /u:/ occurs in the stressed syllable.
ceathrar: "four people", pronounced /k′ahərər/.
ceathrú: "quarter; thigh", with *ceathrúin* in the dative. Pronounced /k′ar'hu:/. GCD §475 shows this word is not end-stressed when it means "fourth", as in *an ceathrú Hamhrí* here.
ceirtlín: "a ball of thread; a round ball", pronounced /k′ar'hl′i:n′/.
ceocu: "which? which of them?" From *cé acu* or *cé'cu*. Pronounced /k′ukə/. Often followed by a relative clause. See further discussion under *peocu*.
cheana: "already", pronounced /hɑnə/.
cheithre: "four", or *ceithre* in GCh. Pronounced /x′er′hi/.
chím, feiscint: "to see", or *feicim, feiceáil* in GCh. The past particle is given here as *feicithe* (cf. *feicthe* in GCh). These forms are pronounced /x′i:m′, f′iʃk′int′, f′ik′ihi/. Note the past-tense forms *chonac, chonaic sé, chonacadar*, and the autonomous *chonacthas*, PUL's spellings of which do not all correspond well to the pronunciations /xnuk, xnik′ ʃe:, xnik′ədər, xnik′əhəs/ used by AÓL (i.e. *chonaiceadar, chonaictheas*, etc, would be possible spellings of these words in WM Irish). It seems likely PUL used /xnukədər, xnukəhəs/. Also note the dependent autonomous form in the past tense, *feacathas*.
chúig: "five", generally found lenited in WM Irish, other than in counting. *Chúig* often lenites a plural noun in PUL's Irish: both *chúig bliana* and *chúig bhliana* were found in the original text, with *chúig bhliana* being standardised on in this edition.
chun: "towards". The combined forms of this preposition are distinctive in WM Irish: *chúm, chút, chuige, chúithi, chúinn, chúibh, chúthu*. GCh has *chugam, chugat, chuige, chuici, chugainn, chugaibh, chucu*.
ciardhubh: "jet-black; raven (of hair colour)", pronounced /k′iəruv/.
cimeádaim, cimeád: "to keep", or *coimeádaim, coimeád* in GCh. PUL used the classical spelling with a broad *c* in the original here, but manuscripts of his private correspondence held in the National Library of Ireland show that he did write *cimeád*, and *cimeád* was used in the published texts of some of PUL's other works, including *Aithris ar Chríost*. Also note that the distinction given in FGB

between *coimeád*, "keep", and *coimhéad*, "watch over", does not obtain in WM Irish. *Cimeád suas*, "support, upkeep". *Lucht cimeádta*, "keepers, guards".

cimlim, cimilt: "to rub", or *cuimlím, cuimilt* in GCh. Pronounced /k′im′il′im′, k′im′ihl′/. *Barra ciomalta*, "a file, an iron file", would be *barra cuimilte* in GCh. Pronounced /bɑrə k′iməlhə/. *Cimilt do bhaise (de rud)*, "to stroke something with your palm".

cine: "race". Note the plural used here is *cineacha*, /k′i'n′ɑxə/ (or /k′in′əxə/, to avoid confusion with *ceannatha*, /k′ə'nɑhə/, "features, face"), where *ciníocha* is used in GCh.

***cinel*:** "kind, sort; kindred, tribe". This word is *cineál* in modern Irish (historically *cinéal*). *Do labhair sé focal fé leith le gach rí agus le gach* cinel *fé mar a tháinig sé ar a n-aghaidh amach*, a sentence in which an incorrect form *cineil* stood in the original, may use *cinel* to give an archaising flavour to the text, mimicking phrases found in old texts referring to kindred groups such as *Cinel Conaill* or *Cenél Conaill*.

cíoraim, cíoradh: "to comb; examine minutely, thresh out in discussion".

ciúmhais: "edge, margin", pronounced /k′u:ʃ/.

ciúnas: "quietness", or *ciúineas* in GCh.

cladhaire: "rogue, trickster", pronounced /kləir′i/.

claí: "fence". Note the plural here is *clathacha*, whereas *claíocha* is found in GCh. The plural found here—which was also given in *Seanachas Amhlaoibh Í Luínse* (p4) as AÓL's form of this word—would appear to be pronounced /klə'hɑxə/—but *cladhacha* was found in PUL's novel *Séadna* (p240), with the transcription in LS being *clycha* (see *Shiàna*, p97). GCD has /klahəxə/ in the plural in Corca Dhuíbhne (§277), but IWM (§236) states that AÓL regularly shifted the stress in such words. The definition of *claí* is wider than the English word "fence": PUL glossed this in his NIWU (p21) as "any sort of rampart of earth or of stones or of both".

claíochlaím, claíochló: "to deteriorate, change for the worse". This verb would be *claochlaím, claochlú* in GCh, and is generally found with *ao* in PUL's works (*claochlaím, claochló*), but *claoídhchlódh* was given in the original text of chapter 31 here. *Do chlaoidhchlóidh a gcumas* is also found in PUL's *Táin Bó Cuailgne*, p233. Consequently, it seems there may have been variation in the vowel, and that this word was pronounced /kle:'xli:m′~kli:'xli:m′, kle:'xlo:~kli:'xlo:/.

claíomh: "sword", with *claimhte* in the plural. *Scéalaíocht Amhlaoibh Uí Luínse* (p16) and the LS version of PUL's *Séadna* (see *cluitiv* in *Shiàna*, p85, for *claidhmhtibh* in *Séadna*, p210) both show the vowel to be short in the plural: /kli:v, klit′i/.

cláirseach: "harp".

clann: "children" (not "family"), with *clainne* in the genitive and *claínn* in the dative. Pronounced /klaun, kliŋ′i, kli:ŋ′/.

Clanna Gael: the Gaels, the Gaelic race.

clár: "board, table". *Bheith ar an gclár*, "to be laid out (dead)".

cleamhnas: "marriage, match". The GCh plural is *cleamhnais*, but PUL uses *cleamhnaisi* here. *Cleamhnaisí* and *cleamhnaisti* are both found in PUL's novel *Séadna*, and the latter is the more frequent form in WM Irish.

cleas: "game, trick". *Ní ... ar aon tsaghas cleas*, "not on any account". *Ní ... ar aon tsaghas cleas ná réasún*, "not on any account or for any reason".

cléir: "clergy".

cleite: "feather; quill".

cliamhain: "son-in-law". Pronounced /kl′iən′/, as PUL indicated in NIWU (p22).

cliathach: "lattice frame; splint (to set bones with)", with *cliathacha* in the plural. Pronounced /kl′i'hɑx, kl′i'hɑxə/.

cliste: "clever". This word can be pronounced /gl′iʃt′i/ in WM Irish.

cló: "form, appearance". *Cló duine*, "the form or appearance of a person", as in a picture or image. *Cló lagachair*, "an appearance of weakness".

cloch araige: "a casting stone for throwing in contests". This is listed as *cloch airgthe* in PSD, where it is interpreted as derived from a corruption of *airligthe*, "tossed", but the derivation is uncertain.

clogad: "helmet".

cloigeann: "skull, head", pronounced /klog′ən/.

cloím, cloí: "to subdue".

cloisim, clos: "to hear", or *cloisim, cloisteáil* in GCh. *Airím, aireachtaint* is used by preference in WM, but PUL occasionally uses this verb too.

cluas: "ear". *Bain-se an chluas anuas ón gceann díom (má/mura)*, literally "cut my ear off (if/unless)", used to emphasise a statement, in a manner similar to the English "I'll eat my hat (if/unless); you can be sure that..."

cluiche: "game". This word is masculine in PUL's works, but note the lenition of *bháis is bheatha* here in *cluiche bháis is bheatha*, "a game of life and death", in chapter 41 here. *Báis agus beatha* is usually lenited in phrases: see also ag *cruinniú a neart chun aon iarracht amháin eile, bháis agus bheatha, do dhéanamh ar oileán na hÉireann do shealbhú dhóibh féin agus dá sliocht* in chapter 37 here; *bhí cumas bháis agus bheatha ag an máighistir ar na daoíne* (*Sgothbhualadh*, p55); and *i n-aimhdeóin a dhíchil bháis agus bheatha* (*Mo Sgéal Féin*, p191).

cluigín: "little bell", or *cloigín* in GCh. The spelling with *ui* is retained here as clarifying the pronunciation.

cnagarnach: "cracking, crunching". Note that as a feminine verbal noun, this becomes *ag cnagarnaigh*, /ə knɑgərnig′/, in the dative.

cnaipe: "button".

cneadh: "wound", or *cneá* in GCh. Along with a number of other words where the older spelling is in *-adh* or *-agh* (see *sleagh* here), *cneadh* has a short vowel, /kn′a(h)/. The nominative plural is given as *cneadhacha* in the original text here, with *cneádhthach* in the genitive plural. These appear to indicate pronunciations of /kn′i'hɑxə/ and /kn′a:həx/ respectively, although it is unclear how reliable the long *a* in *cneádhthach* is, and the genitive plural may be /kn′i'hɑx/. These forms have been edited here as *cneathacha* and *cneathach*. The nominative and genitive plurals are given as *cneadha* and *cneadh* (see *Táin Bó*

Cuailnge, p188 and p183 respectively) in PUL's other works, indicating pronunciations of /kn′a:/ and /kn′ah/.

cnósaím, cnósach: "to collect, gather", or *cnuasaím* and *cnuasach* in GCh. While the original spelling here was *cnuasta* (the past participle), it seems likely that PUL had /o:/ in this word, as is generally the case in WM Irish, as the spelling *cnósach* is found in his *Táin Bó Cuailnge* (pp120, 123), *Cómhairle Ár Leasa* (p54) and *Sgothbualadh* (p167). *Cnósta,* "gathered, grouped", is found as *cnuasaithe* in GCh.

cnuc: "hill", or *cnoc* in GCh, with *cnuic* in the plural. Pronounced /knuk, knik′/. Similarly, *cnucán,* "hillock", is found here for *cnocán.*

cochall: "hood".

cogadh: "war". *Cogadh dearg,* "a bloody war; a right to-do".

cogarnach: "whispering", a feminine verbal noun that becomes *ag cogarnaigh* when used as a verbal noun in the dative; this distinction is not observed in GCh. Other than in the verbal noun construction *ag cognarnaigh,* the dative is *cogarnach* in PUL's works, as in *sa chogarnach dóibh* in chapter 9 here.

coileán: "cub, whelp; trickster".

coilg-sheasamh: found in the phrase *'na choilg-sheasamh,* "bolt upright", or *ina cholgsheasamh* in GCh. Pronounced /nə xil′ik′ 'hɑsəv/.

coímhdeacht: "accompaniment". *Diabhal coímhdeachta,* "an evil genius". *Bean choímhdeachta,* "lady-in-waiting". Pronounced /ki:nl′əxt/ according to IWM (see the note to §409); this pronunciation is not shown in PUL's works, and PUL may have had a *d* here.

coímheascar: "struggle, mêlée", pronounced /ki:skər/. *I gcoímheascar machaire,* "in the heat of battle".

coimirce: "protection, patronage". PUL used the older spelling *comairce* in the original, but this has been adjusted to *coimirce,* the form accepted in GCh, as IWM shows the pronunciation to be /kim′irk′~kim′irk′i/ (see the note to §351). *Fé choimirce,* "under the patronage of".

coinníoll: "condition", pronounced /ki'n′i:l/ as if written with a single *n,* reflecting a tendency in WM Irish not to use a tense slender *n* (/ŋ′/) where *c* or *g* occur earlier in the preceding syllable. The dative of this word is consistently *coinghíoll* in the original text of *Niamh,* whereas PUL's novel *Séadna* had *coinghíll* in the dative. The authorised *Foclóir do Shéadna* (p31) shows this word is masculine, but is declined in the singular as if in the second declension (i.e. with *coinnílle* in the genitive and *coinníll* in the dative).

coir: "crime", pronounced /kir′/.

cóir: "equipment, means; proper provision", with *córacha* in the plural. *Cóir iompair,* "transport, means of transport". *Cóir gluaiste,* "provisions or equipment required to move out". *Cóir bídh agus dí ' chur ar dhuine,* "to provide someone with food and drink".

coirim, cor: "to tire, exhaust", pronounced /kor′im′, kor/. The verbal adjective, given here, is *cortha (de rud),* "tired (of something)". It is worth noting that, in PUL's published works, *cortha dhe,* with a lenited *dhe,* is only found at the end of a sentence, as in *tá eagal orm go bhfuil na daoine cortha dhe* in *Cómhairle Ár Leasa* (p94). Where a noun or a whole clause follows, the *de* stands unlenited, as in *cortha de Mh'leachlainn* here and *cortha de bheith ag feuchaint ortha* in *Séadna* (p256). The choice of *de* or *dhe* is partly a matter of euphony, but also reflects the mental division of the sentence: compare *go bhfuil na daoine (cortha dhe)* and *cortha (de Mh'leachlainn).*

coisricim, coisreacan: "to consecrate". Pronounced /koʃir'ik'im', koʃir'əkən/.

coitianta: "regular, habitual". Pronounced /ko't'iəntə/.

coláiste: "college", pronounced /klɑ:ʃt'i/.

comáinim, comáint: "to drive", or *tiomáinim, tiomáint* in GCh. *Comáinim liom*, "I proceed". *Teachtaire ' chomáint*, "to send out a messenger". Both *comáinim* and *tomáinim* (with a broad *t*) are found in WM Irish.

Comaoine: "Holy Communion", or *Comaoin* in GCh. This word also means "a favour": *comaoine ' chur ar dhuine*, "to do someone a favour".

cómh-dhian: "equally severe, just as hard".

cómhacht: "power, authority; property (of a herb)", or *cumhacht* in GCh, pronounced with a long *o* in WM Irish: /ko:xt/. The plural is *cómhachta*, as opposed to the *cumhachtaí* of GCh.

cómhachtach: "powerful, commanding", *cumhachtach* in GCh, but pronounced /ko:xtəx/ in WM Irish.

cómhairím, cómhaireamh: "to count", or *comhairim, comhaireamh* in GCh, pronounced /ko:'r'i:m', ko:r'əv/.

cómhalta: "foster-brother; fellow student at school", pronounced /ko:lhə/.

cómharba: "the successor to the founder of a monastery or church". *Cómharba Bhríde*, the Abbess of Kildare. Pronounced /ko:rbə/.

cómharsa: "neighbour", with the plural here *cómharsain* where GCh has *comharsana*. The dative singular here is also *cómharsain*. Pronounced /ko:rsə/.

cómharsanacht: "vicinity".

cómhartha: "sign", pronounced /ko:rhə/.

cómhluadar: "company, society". The use as a verbal noun, as in *ag cómhluadar leis*, "spending time with him, in his company", in chapter 40 here, is not indicated in FGB.

cómhnaois: "person of the same age", or *comhaois* in GCh; pronounced /ko:'ni:ʃ/.

cómhrac: "fight, fray", pronounced /ko:rək/.

cómhthrom: "an equal weight of something; an equivalent amount of something". CFBB (pp66, 69) shows this is pronounced /ko:rhəm/ in this meaning (a *chómhthrom óir*), and /korhəm/ where it means "a supply, a sufficiency". A long vowel is used in this edition in this sentence: *a chómhthrom, agus breis, de bhob dá bhualadh uirthi féin*, "a trick equally great, and in fact greater, being played on her". The original text had *a chothrom*, but "equal weight, equivalent amount" is the meaning here. See *a chómhthrom de cheangal ar an dTromdháimh* (*Guaire*, Vol 1, p48) and *deir lucht ealadhan nách foláir do gach neart a chómhthrom de thoradh a thabhairt* (*Sgothbhualadh*, p122).

comrádaí: "comrade". Pronounced /kumə'rɑ:di:/.

***conbhint*:** "convent", or *clochar* in GCh. PUL argued that *conbhint* was the correct Irish word, as it was used by the Four Masters (NIWU, p25). However, it is also likely that ecclesiastical terminology was generally Anglophone in the nineteenth-century Irish Roman Catholic church. This is also reflected in PUL's use of *deacon* rather than *deagánach* and *sacraisti* instead of *eardhamh.*

cóngar: "a shortcut".

cóngarach: "near to", or "terse, curt, glib", as of advice in chapter 18 here.

cóngas: "closeness, relationship, affinity", a broader relationship than *gaol,* "consanguinity", as it includes relationships by marriage, adoption and the spiritual link with godparents.

cor: "throw, cast; condition, situation". *In aon chor,* "at all", pronounced /ə'ne:xər/. *Cor do chur díot,* "to budge, move".

cora: "weir, dam".

córach: "shapely, comely, well-proportioned".

córaím, córú: "to arrange, dress", e.g. for battle or referring to the dressing of food; *cóirím, cóiriú* in GCh. CFBB (p68) shows that both *córú* and *cóiriú* are found in WM Irish.

corcra: "purple", pronounced /korkərə/.

corp: "body", but used in the phrase *le corp* to refer to the emotion or motivation with which something is done: *le corp droch-aigne,* "out of malice, with evil intention".

corrabhuais: "uneasiness, consternation".

corrmhíol: "midge". Note the plural used here is *corrmhíola,* in contradistinction to *corrmhíolta* in GCh. Pronounced /korə'v′i:l/.

cos: "leg, foot". Note that the dative/dual, *cois,* is normally pronounced /koʃ/, but the phrase *'na chuis,* "on foot", is pronounced /nə xuʃ/ (cf. CFBB, p286). Compare *lena cois,* "along with him", /l′ənə xoʃ/. *Do chosa ' shíneadh,* "to die, kick the bucket". *Ar cos in áirde,* "at a gallop".

cosach: "with long legs". Pronounced /kə'sɑx/.

coscar: "mangling; slaughter". This is used as a verbal noun here, corresponding to *coscairt* in GCh. The finite verb is *coscraím* in GCh and probably *coscraim* in traditional WM Irish, but usage in PUL's works of any form other than *coscar* itself is not attested.

cosmhail: "like, resembling". *Cosmhail le duine,* "resembling someone". IWM §361 shows the pronunciation /kosvil′/. *Cosúil,* /ko'su:l′/, is also found in Munster Irish, but as each instance of this word was spelt *cosmhail* in the original text, and not *cosamhail,* this word has not been edited with *ú* here. See also under *cosúlacht.*

cosnaim, cosnamh/cosaint: "to defend", or *cosnaím, cosaint* in GCh. Both verbal nouns are found in this work, and PUL stated in NIWU (p29) that there is a difference in meaning: *cosnamh* means "protecting, shielding" and *cosaint* "defending". An epenthetic vowel was sometimes written out in forms of this verb (e.g. *cosanadh* in the original text of chapter 43 here and *chosanóchaidh* in chapter 51). The hand of editors may have played a role in the final spelling of

PUL's works, but it seems most likely that PUL had an epenthetic vowel here, whereas CFBB (p68) shows that AÓL, who had *cosnaím* in the second conjugation, did not. This reflects a wider issue with *sn*, with *thosnaigh* having no additional vowel according to IWM and CFBB, but often transcribed with one in LS versions of PUL's works (e.g. *hosanuig* in *Eshirt*, p4). Consequently, it is likely that some speakers did use an additional vowel in the *sn* combination. Given that more is known about AÓL's pronunciation of Irish, for the purposes of learners of WM Irish the pronunciation of this word can be given as /kosnim′~kos'ni:m′, kosnəv~kosint′/.

cosnamh: "protecting, guarding". *Gan c.* is listed in the glossary to the early edition of *Niamh* as meaning "undisputed", a rare, literary use, and this appears to relate to the following passages: *do chuir Leath Mhogha, gan chosnamh, fé láimh Bhriain* and *tabharfad an Árdríocht duit gan chosnamh* in chapter 15. This is more frequently found as *gan cosnamh* (e.g. in *Bricriu*, p165), but may be accepted with lenition if the meaning is "without any dispute". The two instances of *gan chosnamh* in chapter 56 are more straightforward, meaning "unguarded". Once again, *gan cosnamh* could be expected, but the meaning here seems to be "without any defence".

cosúlacht: "likeness, resemblance". The spelling in the original (*cosamhlacht*) suggests the pronunciation /ko'su:ləxt/, which is adopted in GCh too. *Cosmhalacht*, pronounced /kosvələxt/, is also found in WM Irish, as a *v* sound is generally retained and not vocalised after an *s* (see IWM §361).

cóta: "coat". *Cóta iarainn*, "iron armour, chain-mail".

cóthra:"coffer, chest", or *cófra* in GCh, pronounced /ko:rhə/.

cothrom: "a sufficiency of something". AÓL pronounced this /korhəm/. Donncha Ó Céileachair (*Nótaí do 'Scéal mo bheatha'*, p55) stated that his father, Dónall Bán Ó Céileachair, had /kohərəm/. *An cothrom uathásach uisce*, "the terrific expanse of water". See also *cómhthrom*.

craidhreac: "blood-red, scarlet", or c*ródhearg/craorag* in GCh. Pronounced /krəir′ək/. PSD states under *craorach* that this word derives from *cróidhearg*, "scarlet, crimson, blood-red", or *caordhearg*, "berry-red, bright red". FGB has an entry for *croidhreac*, cross-referenced to *craorag*.

cráin: "sow", or other female animal. In chapter 54 *'an chráin 's a hál go léir'* is a set phrase or saying, meaning "we have the whole brood (in our grasp)".

crann seóil: "mast of a ship", normally found as *seolchrann*.

crann: "tree", but also "pole". *Bratacha ar chrannaibh*, "flags or standards on poles".

creach: "spoil, plunder". In the plural, *na creacha* means "the spoils", as in "spoils of war".

creachaim, creachadh: "to plunder, despoil". The past participle is *creachta*.

créachtnaím, créachtnú: "to wound", or *créachtaím, créachtú* in GCh. IWM (§99) states that the word *créacht* is pronounced /kr′e:xt/, influenced by verse pronunciation. Consequently, *créachtnaím, créachtnú* should be /kr′e:xt'ni:m′, kr′e:xt'nu:/.

crích: "end, fate; territory, region", or *críoch* in GCh. The historical dative has replaced the nominative in WM Irish, although *críoch* is used here to denote the end of the book (and is also found in PUL's Irish in the genitive plural *na gcríoch*). *Crích a bhreith duine*, "to end up in a certain way, to suffer a certain fate". *Fé crích a bhéarfaidh sinn*, "whatever happens to us".

críochnaithe: "finished". *Amadán críochnaithe*, "a total fool".

crios: "flint", with *creasa* in the genitive. *Tine chreasa*, "sparks, frictional sparks".

Críostaíocht (an Chríostaíocht): "Christendom".

croch: "the gallows", with *croich* in the dative. Pronounced /krox, kroh/.

cróchar: "stretcher".

croí díchill: "utmost", or *croídhícheall* in GCh. PUL consistently uses this phrase as two words, with no lenition on the *ḋ*. We read in the original in chapter 47 *ag déanamh a gcroí dícheall dhá iarraidh ar Dhia iad do thabhairt abhaile slán*, "doing their utmost asking God to bring them back safe", which failed to give the correct genitive, *a gcroí díchill*. This has been corrected in this edition in line with the form found in PUL's other works, including *Sgothbhualadh*, pp 70, 113).

croí: "heart". *Briseadh do chroí (ag déanamh ruda)*, "to break your heart (doing something)/to put great emotional effort into doing it".

croiceann: "skin", or *craiceann* in GCh. Pronounced /krek′ən/ or /krok′ən/ in traditional WM Irish.

croiméal: "moustache", pronounced /kro'm′ial/.

crois: "cross", or *cros* in GCh. The historical dative often replaces the nominative in PUL's Irish, especially in the phrase *crois chéasta*, "crucifix" (compare *daoine gur fonn leó Cros Íosa d'iomchar* in *Aithris ar Chríost*, p84; *cros mhór sholasmhar* in the section on the cross of Constantine in PUL's *Lúcián*, p155; and *d'iompair an Slánuightheóir an chruis chéasta go barr an chnuic sin* in *Sgéalaidheachta as an mBíobla Naomhtha*, Vol 1, p35). The genitive and dative *croise* and *crois* (often spelt *cruise* and *cruis* in PUL's other works) are pronounced /kriʃi, kriʃ/ according to PUL's *An Choróinn Mhuire* (pp18-19, where the ordinary spelling and LS are given on opposing pages), which pronunciation is also shown in IWM (§142, 304). The LS edition of PUL's *An Teagasg Críostaidhe* shows the pronunciations /kroʃi, kroʃ/ (see *An Teagasc Crísdy*, p23).

croithim, crothadh: "to shake", or *croithim, croitheadh* in GCh. The spelling *do chroth* was used in the original, being adjusted to *do chroith* here.

cromán: "hip", pronounced /krə'mɑ:n/.

crosta: "cross-wise, across". *Rud a theacht crosta ort*, "for something to befall you/happen to you".

crot: "appearance". This word is distinguished from *cruth*, "form, shape", although the difference is not made in GCh. *Níl crot na fírinne ar an gcainnt sin*, "what you said does not have the ring of truth".

crua-lámh: this word, found in chapter 54 here, is not a standard word listed in any dictionary, and so is an *ad hoc* form, meaning "strong, hard hands" (in the genitive plural here).

cruach: "heap, stack". *'Na gcruachaibh*, "in heaps".

cruadas: "hardness", or *cruas* in GCh. The original spelling was *cruadhas*, but PUL stated that a clear *d* was pronounced in this word: /kruədəs/ (NIWU, p30).

cruaidh: "hard, severe", or *crua* in GCh. Pronounced /kruəgʹ/ in WM Irish. The plural, traditionally spelt *cruadha*, is edited as *crua* here.

cruaim, cruachtaint: "to harden", or *cruaim, cruachan* in GCh. The verbal noun is not found here, but is attested in PUL's other works (see *Lúcián*, p7).

cruithneacht: "wheat", with *cruithneachtan* in the genitive where GCh has *cruithneachta*. The dative is given here as *cruithneacht*, in place of the expected *cruithneachtain*. Pronounced /kriŋʹ'hɑxt/.

cruth: "appearance, state, condition". This word is masculine, but is often feminine in the dative, *cruith*. By contrast, a masculine dative *cruth* can also be found in PUL's works.

cuaird: "visit", or *cuairt* in GCh. Note the genitive here, *cuairde*. *Cuarda* is also found in the genitive singular in PUL's works (for example, *Mo Sgéal Féin*, p93); GCh has *cuairte*. The plural here is *cuarda*, where GCh has *cuairteanna*.

cuallacht: "company; the group of people attending someone".

cuid: "part, share". The final syllable of the genitive, *coda*, is elided here in *i gcaitheamh na cod' eile den aimsir*.

cuideachta: "company, the people present", with *cuideachtan* in the genitive and *cuideachtain* in the dative. PUL's spelling indicates a pronunciation of /ki'dʹaxtə/, but /ki'lʹaxtə/ is also found (see IWM §409); that the pronunciation with /l/ is more common in Munster Irish today is indicated in GCD §253 (the Corca Dhuíbhne pronunciation is /klʹaxtə/). Bhí *dóthain na cuideachtan de rí i mBrian*, "Brian was an adequate king for the company present".

cuideachtanas: "company", and as a verbal noun, "keeping company", pronounced /ki'dʹaxtənəs~ki'lʹaxtənəs/. CFBB (p75) shows that, whereas some Muskerry speakers used an *l* in this word, more careful speakers such as AÓL kept a *d* here. PUL explained the difference in nuance between this word and *cómhluadar* in a letter to Risteárd Pléimeann dated February 27th 1918, catalogued under G1,277 (1) in the Shán Ó Cuív papers held in the National Library of Ireland: *i gcómhluadar a chéile* means "in each other's company", whereas *i gcuideachtanas a chéile* places more stress on the *enjoyment* of each other's companionship.

cúige: "province". This is feminine here, but masculine in GCh. This word often appears in PUL's works with an elided final vowel (*cúig'*), particularly before a following vowel.

cuireadh: "an invitation", pronounced /kirʹi/.

cuirim, cur: "to put; to bury". The verbal noun is retained as given in the original, although *cur* is often pronounced with slender *r*, i.e. /kur~kirʹ/. See Brian Ó Cuív's spelling in CFBB, pix: *chun Gaeulainge na sean-daoine chuir ó bhaol bháis*. (GCD §564 indicates that this is a wider phenomenon in Munster Irish, where, it is stated, *cur* has a broad *r* only in the meaning of "planting, burying" and at the end of a sentence.) *Rud do chur ar dhuine*, "to blame someone for something". *Teas do chur ort*, "to be affected by the heat". *Cuirim chúm*, "I appropriate, put away on my person", as in *cuir chút an dá leitir seo*, "put these two letters in your pocket". Also found in chapter 45 in this work: *éadaí lín do chur chúthu*, "to gather up linen cloths". *Cur chuige*, "to try your hand at it": *ní raibh aon bhreith ag éinne, agus M'leachlainn Mór féin do chur chuige, ar Chaoilte, chun capaill a mharcaíocht*, "no one, not even M'leachlainn Mór, could compete with Caoilte as far as riding horses was concerned". A related meaning is "to set about doing something": *an túisce 'na gcuirfeadh an capall chun luite*, "as soon as the horse lay down". *Cur de*, "to get through" in various senses: *chuireamair cruach dínn*, "we got through a heap/we accomplished the killing of a heap of them"; *aimsir a chur díot*, "for time to pass"; *tuirse na farraige ' chur díot*, "to recover from the weariness of a sea journey". *Cnámh a chur*, "to set a bone". Note the present and future autonomous forms, *curtar* and *curfar*, where *cuirtar* and *cuirfar* would be more usual in other works in WM Irish. The conditional and imperfect autonomous forms are *curfí* and *curtí*, as the *f* and *t* are slender in WM Irish *(cuirfí* and *cuirtí* are the more usual forms). PUL wrote in a letter to Risteárd Pléimeann dated December 21st 1917, catalogued under G1,277 (1) in the Shán Ó Cuív papers held in the National Library of Ireland, "I say *curfí* with *r* broad and *f* slender, or *cuirfí*, with *r* and *f* slender. I could never say *curfaí*. I must have the *f* always slender". Similarly, the second-person singular conditional form *churfá* is found in most of PUL's works, in preference to *chuirfá* in other works in WM Irish. The original text used a variety of spellings of these forms (*curtar* 3 times, *cuirtear* once; *curfar* 13 times, *cuirfear* once; *curtí* 7 times; *curfaí* 11 times; and *dá gcurfá* once), but the forms *curtar, curfar, curfí, curtí* and *curfá* are so frequently found in PUL's works, that they seem likely to have been the forms he used and have therefore been standardised on here.

cuirpeach: "malefactor, villain", or *coirpeach* in GCh. Pronounced /kir′ip′əx/.

cuisí: "foot-traveller, a person on foot", or *coisí* in GCh. The *-ui-* of the original text is accepted here.

cuisíocht: "pace, gait, steps", or *coisíocht* in GCh.

cuisle: "vein; forearm", with *cuislinn* in the dative.

cúitím, cúiteamh: "to compensate, requite". *Ag cur 's ag cúiteamh*, "to argue, weigh the pros and cons".

cúl dín: "refuge".

cúl: "back of the head". *I ndiaidh a chúil/gcúil*, "backwards". *Cúl a thabhairt le rud*, "to abandon, forsake, turn aside from something".

culaith: "suit of clothes", pronounced /klih/. *Culaith manaigh*, "a monk's vestments". The lack of lenition after a feminine noun is noteworthy: Gerald O'Nolan advanced the view in his *New Era Grammar* that *culaith shagairt* would mean vestments for a *particular* priest according to the principle of 'dynamic lenition' (see p113). O'Nolan's explanation contrasts with the entry under *culaith* in FGB showing that *culaith mairnéalaigh* means "a sailor's uniform", whereas *culaith mhairnéalaigh* means "a sailor uniform". PUL's *An Craos-Deamhan* (p44) has *culaith chléirigh*, and so it seems lenition gives the following noun an adjectival flavour ("a police uniform"/"clerical vestments" rather than "a policeman's uniform"/"vestments of a cleric"), although the difference in nuance is slight.

cúm: "waist", or *coim* in GCh. The genitive is *cuím.*

cumaim, cumadh: "to form, shape". Declined forms of this verb that are either monosyllabic or where the *m* precedes a consonant have a long *u* in WM Irish: *do chúm, cúmfad, cúmtha,* /də xu:m, ku:mhəd, ku:mhə/.

cumas: "ability, control". *Níor fhág sí ar a chumas Nuala do mharú,* "she didn't leave him any opportunity to kill Nuala".

cúmparáid: "comparison", or *comparáid* in GCh. Pronounced /ku:mpərɑ:d′/.

cúnamh: "help". *Cúnamh fear,* "auxiliary force", and hence, "a body of men".

cúntanós: "countenance", or *cuntanós* in GCh, pronounced /ku:ntəno:s/.

cúntas: "account", or *cuntas* in GCh. Pronounced /ku:ntəs/. The plural here is *cúntaisí,* where GCh has *cuntais.*

cúntúirt: "danger", or *contúirt* in GCh.

cúntúrthach: "dangerous, risky", or *contúirteach* in GCh.

cúpla: "couple", pronounced /ku:pələ/, used with the nominative singular.

cúr: "froth, foam".

curadh: "warrior", with the plural *curaí* where GCh has *curaidh.* Pronounced /kurə, ku'ri:/. *Curaí na Craoibh-rua,* the Knights of the Red Branch. In Irish mythology, Conchobar mac Nessa, king of Ulster, ruled from Eamhain Macha, or Navan Fort, in Co. Armagh, and one of his palaces was called Cróeb Ruad, thought to be on the site of the townland of Creeveroe in Co. Armagh. Modern retellings of the Ulster cycle of myths turn this into an order of knights, the Knights of the Red Branch.

cuthach: "rage, fury". The genitive of this word, *cuthaigh,* is used as an adjective meaning "furious, fierce". Pronounced /kə'hɑx, kuhig′/.

dá, dhá, dhár: *dá* and *dhá* are found where a verbal noun governs a third-person pronoun object. PUL used *dá* in passive senses (*dá dhéanamh,* "being done") and *dhá* (*'ghá* in the original) with a pronoun object (*dhá dhéanamh,* "doing it"). Where the latter is given in the original as *'á,* this has been edited here as *á.* Both uses would be likely to be written *á* and pronounced /ɑ:/ by later speakers of the WM dialect, and *á* is also the usage of the GCh in both meanings.

PUL used *a'm/am'* and *ad'* in the original text where the verbal noun takes a first- or second-person singular pronoun object (corresponding to *do mo* and *do do* in GCh). These are edited here as *'om* and *'od.* With a first-person plural pronoun object, the original text has *'ghár,* being edited here as *dhár* (*táimíd dhár gcosaint féin,* "we are defending ourselves"). This latter form is found as *dár* in GCh. The pronunciation of this form would be likely to be /ɑ:r/.

daighe: found in *an daighe,* "the Dagda" (a powerful god in Irish mythology) and, by extension, "really, indeed!" Pronounced /ən dəi/. *An daighe* is given as *don daighe* in FGB, but the etymology is unclear and the first syllable may just be the definite article.

daingean: "firm", with *daingne* in the comparative. Pronounced /dɑŋ′ən, dɑŋ′in′i/.

Glossary

daingean: "fortress, garrison", with the plural here *daingeana*, where GCh has *daingin*.
daingním, daingniú: "to make fast or secure (e.g., of a door); to become secure". Pronounced /dɑŋ'i'n'i:m', dɑŋ'i'n'u:/.
dáiríribh: "actually, really", or *dáiríre* in GCh. *Lom dáiríribh*, "actually, in dead earnest". PUL stated in NIWU (p35) that "in earnest" is *dáiríribh*, not *i ndáiríríbh*, although the latter form is given in PSD as a variant. Yet at least one instance of *i ndáiríribh* is found in PUL's works, *iad 'á labhairt i sult agus i bhfeirg, i magadh agus i ndáiríríbh, i n-aighneas agus i síothcháin* in *Sgothbhualadh* (p21), where the context is slightly different, and the phrase means not "in earnest, actually, seriously", but rather "in circumstances where you are in earnest/serious".
damh: "ox, stag".
dán: "calling, profession". *De réir a ndán*, "by rank".
dán: "lot, fate". *I ndán do*, "in store for, predestined for, fated for".
daor-aicme: "an unfree class of people", an inferior group of people of some kind.
daor: "hard, severe".
Dar fia!: "by Jove!" *Fia* means "Lord, God", but the word was frequently confused with the word *fia*, meaning "deer"—the former was *fiadha* and the latter *fiadh* in the old script—producing the Hiberno-Irish form, "by the deer!"
dar ndó': see under *ar ndó'*.
dar so 's súd: "I swear; as God be my witness, etc"; literally, "by this and that".
dásacht: "daring, audacity".
de: "of, from". The simple preposition is pronounced in the same way as *do* in WM Irish, /də/. Usage in the original work was inconsistent, with *gabháil de chosaibh* on one page and *gabháil do chosaibh* on another, but it has been thought better to edit these with the historically correct prepositions, as they would stand in GCh. Note that PUL was particularly insistent on writing *do réir*, which he held was either pronounced /də re:r'/ or /d'r'e:r'/—in other words, the slender *d* only appeared when run together as a single word—but this has been edited as *de réir* here. Similarly, *do ghnáth* and *do phreib* are edited here as *de ghnáth* and *de phreib*. PUL's usage with *macshamail* (*macshamhail don eochair*) was also consistent; this has been edited here as *macshamhail den eochair*. The alignment of *do* and *de* in pronunciation only applies to the simple preposition; the prepositional pronoun *de* (written *dé* in the original) is pronounced /d'ə~d'i/. With the plural article, *de sna* is found here, the *s* of which developed by analogy with *insna*. See also *do*.
dé: an obscure word used in salutations. *Dé bheatha-sa*, "welcome". *Dé* doesn't appear to have anything to do with the word *Dia*, "God". The phrase rather appears a corruption of the Old Irish *rotbia de bethu*, "may you have much life", literally, "there will be life to you", where *t* is an infixed pronoun that has survived in the *d* of *Dé*. The phrase appears to have been inaccurately reanalysed as some sort of copula sentence, with *dé (do) bheatha-sa* then seeming to mean "God is your life".

Glossary

dea-chúmtha: "well-built, attractive", or *dea-chumtha* in GCh. See under *cumaim, cumadh.*

dea-mhéinn: "goodwill", or *dea-mhéin* in GCh. Pronounced /d′əi'v′e:ŋ′/.

dea-nós: "good custom, good habit". Pronounced /d′əi'no:s/. PUL comments as follows in NIWU (p36): "*Deagh-nós,* civilisation. The prefix *deagh-* is often pronounced *deigh-*, apart from the rule *caol le caol*; e.g. *deighmhac,* a good, dutiful son".

dea-shampla: "good example"; /d′a'haump(ə)lə/.

***deacon*:** PUL uses an Anglophone word here, where GCh has *deagánach.*

déaga: *ná déaga,* "the teenage years".

dealg: "thorn", pronounced /d′aləg/.

deallraitheach: "resplendent; handsome". Pronounced /d′aurihəx/. Spelt *dealraitheach* in GCh.

deallramh: "appearance", or *dealramh* in GCh. Pronounced /d′aurəv/. *De réir dheallraimh,* "very probably, according to every indication". *Agus a dheallramh orthu (go),* "and it looked like they...".

deamhan: "demon", pronounced /d′aun/.

dearbhaím, dearbhú: "to affirm, swear, attest". Pronounced /d′arə'vi:m′, d′arə'vu:/.

dearfa: "sure, certain", pronounced /d′arəfə/.

dearg-bhuile: "rage, fury", pronounced /'d′arəg'vil′i/. *Ar dearg-bhuile,* "raging mad, furious".

dearg-ruathar: "a fierce onslaught, a precipitate rout", literally "a red charge", pronounced /'d′arəg'ruəhər/.

dearg: "red", pronounced /d′arəg/.

dearúd: "mistake", or *dearmad* in GCh. *Dearúd a dhéanamh,* "to make a mistake". *Dearúd a bheith ort,* "to be mistaken".

dearúdaim, dearúd: "to forget", or *dearmadaim, dearmad* in GCh.

deatach: "smoke", pronounced /də'tɑx~d′ə'tɑx/. This word is written with a slender *d* here, as well as in PUL's other works; yet CFBB shows AÓL had a broad *d* in this word (p272).

deichniúr: "ten people", pronounced /d′en′'hu:r/.

deifríocht: "difference", or *difríocht* in GCh. The pronunciation shown in CFBB (p85) is /d′ef′ə'ri:xt/, but the original spelling here was *deifrígheacht,* and it seems possible that PUL had a slender *r* in this word, where AÓL had a broad *r.*

deighleáil: "dealing, transaction", or *déileáil* in GCh. Pronounced /d′əi'l′a:l′/.

deighlim, deighilt: "to separate", pronounced /d′əil′im′, d′əihl′/.

deimhin: "certain, sure", pronounced /d′əin′/.

deimhne: "certainty", pronounced /d′əin′i/. This word occurs twice here as *deimhne ceart,* showing it to be masculine in the text here, but feminine in GCh. This may reflect a wider uncertainty among native speakers of the gender of some rarer abstract nouns. See also *an lán deimhne céadna* in PUL's *Sgéalaidheacht na Macabéach,* Vol 2, p233.

deimhním, deimhniú: "to affirm, assure, etc", pronounced /d′əi'n′i:m′, d′əi'n′u:/. *Deimhnithe dho féin,* "assured to him" in chapter 49 here.

deimhnitheach: "certain", or *deimhneach* in GCh. Pronounced /d′əin′ihəx/.

déine-de: "all the harder". This is a 'second comparative' form, similar to *feárr-de, usa-de, miste,* meaning "all the more X for it".

deinim, déanamh: "to do", or *déanaim, déanamh* in GCh, where use of the historical dependent form is generalised. *Deinim* derives from a corruption of the historical absolute form, *do-ghním.* Pronounced /d′in′im′, d′ianəv/. *Cad é sin do san cad a dhéanfaidh an Árdríocht?,* "what difference does it make to him what happens to the high kingship?" *Déanamh amach (go),* "to make out, claim". *Déanamh gan a hathair,* "to make do without her father".

deirim, rá: "to say". Note that in the combinations *á rá, a rá,* and *do rá* the *r* can be slenderised, /ɑ: r′a:, ə r′a:, də r′a:/, and such usage was shown in the LS versions of PUL's works. PUL generally eschews the historically correct dependent form of the verb, *abraim,* using forms in *abr-* only in the subjunctive: *dá n-abradh duine leó,* "if someone were to say to them", where *abradh* is pronounced /ɑbərəx/. The past-tense forms are given here as *duart, duaraís, duairt sé, dúradar, dúradh.* Lenition of the *t* is retained in the past habitual autonomous form *adeirthí* where it was given in the original.

deirineach: "final", or *deireanach* in GCh. Note that PUL generally wrote a slender *r* and a slender *n* in this word (although counterexamples exist), suggesting /d′er′in′əx/; AÓL had a a slender *r* and a broad *n*; LASID has /d′erənəx/. PUL explained in NIWU (p38) that *deirineach* means "final", whereas *déanach* means "late". See also under *deirini.*

deiriní: "lateness", or *deireanaí* in GCh. Pronounced /d′er′i'n′i:/ (or /d′er′ə'ni:/). *Le deiriní,* "recently". This phrase is equivalent in meaning to *le déanaí,* calling into question PUL's claimed distinction between *deirineach* and *déanach.* It seems these words are often interchanged.

deismireacht: "incantation, spell". Pronounced /d′eʃm′ir′əxt/.

deocair: "difficult", or *deacair* in GCh. Pronounced /d′okir′/, with the comparative *deocra, deacra* in GCh, pronounced /d′okərə/. *Is deocair a rá ná go,* "it is hard to imagine anything other than (that)".

deoch: "drink", with *di* in the genitive, *digh* in the dative and *deocha* in the plural (where GCh has *deochanna*).

deóir: "tear", with the plural here generally *deóracha,* where *deora* stands in GCh. *Deóra* is also found as the plural in PUL's works (cf. *Na Cheithre Soisgéil,* p112). In chapter 58 *agus gur ró-dheocair osna ' bhaint ón gcroí acu ná deór a bhaint óna súilibh* the older nominative singular *deór* is given: *osna* and *deór* are often found in collocation together.

dí-chreideamh: "unbelief". PUL used the spelling *díthchreidimh* in the original of *Niamh,* apparently confusing the (etymologically related) use of *dí-* as a prefix and the use of *díth* governing a following noun in the genitive (as in *díth céille*).

diabhal: "devil", pronounced /d′iəl/. See under *coímhdeacht.*

diablaí: "diabolical", or *diabhlaí* in GCh. This word was spelt both *diablaídhe* and *díoblaidhe* in the original, but IWM shows it is pronounced /diə'bli:/ (§368).

diablaíocht: "devilry, wizardry", or *diabhlaíocht* in GCh. Pronounced /d′iə'bli:xt/.

diaidh: "wake, rear", pronounced /d′iəg′/. The *-dh-* ending is not always pronounced: *'na dhiaidh san*, /nə jiə son/; *i ndiaidh na hoibre*, /(i) n′iə nə heb′ir′i/; *i ndiaidh an lae*, /(i) n′iən le:/ (cf. the transcription of similar phrases in the LS edition of PUL's work *Séadna*); and *i ndiaidh ' chéile*, "one after the other", pronounced /(i) n′iə x′e:l′i/.

dian-leathadh: found in the phrase *ar dian-leathadh*, "wide open".

díbrim, díbirt: "to banish, drive out", with *as*. *Díbrím, díbirt* in GCh. Pronounced /d′i:b′ir′im′, d′i:b′irt′/.

dílis: "faithful, loyal". Brian Ó Cuív wrote in IWM that the comparative *dílse* could be pronounced either /d′i:l′ʃi/ or /d′i:l′iʃi/ (see §415).

dínnéar: "dinner". *Dinnéar* in GCh. Pronounced /d′i:′ŋ′e:r/.

díobháil: "harm". *Cad é an díobháil dom ach Amhlaoibh!*, "I wouldn't have minded/it wouldn't have been so bad if it hadn't been Amhlaoibh!"

díogailt: "to avenge, punish", or *díoghail* in GCh. The verbal noun is spelt both *díoghalt* and *díoghailt* in the original (and edited here as *díogailt*), but PUL's replies to a letter from Risteárd Pléimeann dated January 4th 1918, catalogued under G1,277 (1) in the Shán Ó Cuív papers held in the National Library of Ireland indicate that there is a *g* in the pronunciation of this rare, literary word, but not in the related word *díoltas* (traditionally spelt *díoghaltas*). Use of a finite verb *díoglaim* is not attested in PUL's works; although FGB does have an entry for the finite verb, it seems likely the verbal noun is the only viable member of this paradigm.

díolaim, díol: "to sell", but also "to betray".

díoltas: "vengence, revenge".

diomá: "disappointment", or *díomá* in GCh.

díospóireacht: "disputing, debating, argument". The vowel in the first syllable is generally written short in PUL's works, but this appears to reflect the regular reduction of long vowels in pretonic position in the dialect. AÓL had *díospóireacht*.

dírim: "band, posse, squadron", or *díorma* in GCh.

díscím, disciú: "to destroy, exterminate".

discréid: "discretion; a secret".

discréideach: "discreet, secret".

dithneas: "haste, urgency". Pronounced /d′ihinəs~d′ehin′əs/ (transcriptions given in IWM and LASID respectively).

dlí: "law". The plural used here is *dlithe*; this would be *dlíthe* in GCh, but the WM pronunciation is /dl′ihi/. This word is feminine here, but masculine in GCh.

do-thíosach: "inhospitable, churlish".

do: "to, for". Note that the classical spelling of the preposition pronoun *dó* is adopted in GCh, but this is pronounced /do/ in the WM dialect and so edited as *do* here. *Daoibh*, "for you (plural)", is pronounced /d′i:v′/, and therefore edited as *díbh* here. The emphatic form *dómh-sa* has a long vowel, /do:sə/. With the plural article, *de sna* is found here, the *s* of which developed by analogy with *insna. Dúr* is the combination of *do* and *úr* (*bhur*), "to/for your (pl)". See also under *de.*

dó': "hope, expectation; source of expectation", or *dóigh* in GCh. This occurred as *dó'* and *dóich* in the original, but is uniformly edited as *dó'* here, in line with the pronunciation. *Gasra nár dhó'*, "a warrior band not to be trifled with". *Is dó'*, "however, indeed, well". *Cé hé féin, is dó'?*, "who is he, though?" See also under *ar ndó'*. *Cad is dó' leat don scéal?*, "what do you think of the matter?": this usage might appear to give *do* for *de*, but *cad is dóich leat dóibh anois, a rígh?* in PUL's *Eisirt* (p60) shows the idiom correctly uses *do*.

dóbair: "it nearly happened", originally the preterite of the rare verb *fóbraim* ("to attack; attempt"). *Ba dhóbair do preabadh ó dheas láithreach*, "he nearly started off to the south immediately".

docht: "hard, tough".

doicheall: "reluctance; inhospitality", used with *roim*. Pronounced /dohəl/.

dóichí-de: "all the more likely". This is a 'second comparative' form, similar to *feárr-de, usa-de, miste*, meaning "all the more X for it".

doilíos: "sorrow, melancholy". Pronounced /do'l'i:s/.

doimhinn: "deep", or *domhain* in GCh, pronounced /dəiŋ'/. The plural, *doimhne*, is pronounced /deŋ'i~doŋ'i/.

doimhneacht: "depth", pronounced /deŋ'əxt~doŋ'əxt/.

doimhneas: "depth", pronounced /deŋ'əs~doŋ'əs/.

doircheacht: "darkness", pronounced /dor'ihəxt/, or *dorchacht* in GCh.

doirchím, dorchú: "to darken". Pronounced /dor'i'hi:m', dorə'xu:/. These forms are interesting, because PUL has *dorchú* for the verbal noun, but conjugated forms of the verb are usually derived from *doirchím*, with a slender *rch*, as with *do dhoirchigh* here, pronounced /ɣor'ihig'/. GCh has *dorchaím, dorchú.*

dóirseóir: "doorkeeper, porter".

dóithín: "source of expectation". *Ní haon dóithín é*, "he is not to be trifled with". See also under *dó'* for a related expression.

dorn: "fist", pronounced /dorən/.

dornchar: "hilt of a sword", or *dornchla* in GCh. Pronounced /dorənxər/.

draíocht: "magic".

dranna-gháire: "a mocking smile", or *drannghháire* in GCh.

dranntán: "act of growling, snarling", pronounced /draun'tɑ:n/. The double *n* shows the diphthong; GCh has *drantán.*

draoi: "druid, wizard".

dridim, dridim: "to get close to, approach, move near", but often more generally simply "to move"; *druidim, druidim* in GCh. *Dridim suas*, "to move up". *Dridim isteach*, "to move in(to)". The original spelling here was *druidim*, but some of PUL's works use *dridim* (see *Aithris ar Chríost*, p14), which is the pronunciation shown in IWM (§407).

drifiúr: "sister", or *deirfiúr* in GCh. The genitive here is *driféar* and the plural *driféaracha*. IWM (see the note to §287) shows that both *drifíur* and *driofúr* were found in WM Irish, but a slender *f* was used in the original spelling here. PUL's *Séadna* is unusual among PUL's published works in using a broad *f* (e.g. p18). Pronounced /dr'i'f'u:r~dr'i'fu:r, dr'i'f'e:r, dr'i'f'e:rəxə/.

driotháir: "brother", or *deartháir* in GCh.
driuch: "facial appearance", or *dreach* in GCh.
droch-bheart: "an evil deed", pronounced /'drov′art/.
droch-fhéachaint: "a nasty look", pronounced /dro'hiaxint′/.
droch-ghnóthach: "up to no good". See under *Proverbs.* Pronounced /dro'ɣno:həx/.
droch-ní: "something wrong, something bad", pronounced /dro'n′i:/.
droch-obair: "mischief", pronounced /'drohobir′/.
droch-ollmhú: "poor preparation, lack of proper preparation", pronounced /ˌdroho'lu:/.
droch-sheasamh: "a bad stand, a poor show of resistance". See under *Proverbs.* pronounced /'drohɑsəv/.
drom: "back", or *droim* in GCh. In his works, PUL uses *drom* (in the nominative and dative) for the actual back of a person or a thing (cf. *ar dhrom na leitre* in chapter 45), but *druím* for more metaphorical usages (*druím lámha*, "back of a hand", and thus "forsaking, abandonment", etc). Pronounced /droum/.
druím: "back". See the note under *drom. Druím lámha ' thabhairt le Brian*, "to abandon Brian". Pronounced /dri:m′/.
drúis: "lust".
dua: "trouble, pain". *Dua (ruda) a dh'fháil*, "to go to some trouble, to put yourself out in connection with a matter".
duais: "prize, reward".
dual: "natural, to be expected of someone". *Is dual athar do é*, "he takes after his father in that respect".
dualgas: "duty". The plural here is *dualgaisí*, where *dualgais* stands in GCh.
dubh: "black", with *dúbha* in the plural and *duíbhe* in the comparative. Pronounced /duv, du:, di:/.
dúbhaim, dúbhadh: "to darken", or *dubhaím, dúchan* in GCh; pronounced /du:m′, du:/. *Dúbhann*, /du:n/, is found in the present tense here, whereas *dhúbhaigh*, /ɣu:g′/, in the second conjugation, is found in the past tense in PUL's *Séadna* (p73). *Dúbhadh* is the verbal noun given here, but *dúchtaint* is the verbal noun used in PUL's *Mo Sgéal Féin* (p90). *Dúbhadh na gcnuc agus na gcoíllte den uile shaghas daoine*, "so many people of all types gathered there sufficient to darken the hills and the woods".
dúchas: "nature, heritage". In chapter 48, *bhí an dúchas garbh ann agus thug sé leis an dúchas* means "there was a tendency towards ruggedness/physical sturdiness in his family, and he had inherited the tendency".
dul: "condition, state". *Ar aon dul le*, "in line with, of a piece with". *Ar an ndul 'na raibh sé cheana*, "in the state it was in before".
dún: "fort", with the plural here *dúna*, where GCh has *dúnta*.
dúthaigh: "land, region, district", with the genitive singular *dútha* and the plural *dúthaí*. This is *dúiche*, with the plural *dúichí*, in GCh.
dúthrachtach: "fervent, earnest, devoted", pronounced /du:rhəxtəx/.
eachtra: "adventure; tale, story", pronounced /ɑxtərə/.

éadromacht: "lightness". *Ar éadromacht*, "out of your senses, out of your mind". GCh has *éadroime.*

éadromú: "lightening", of a burden.

eagal: "fear". This form of *eagla* tends to be used before prepositional pronouns using *le* and *ar*: *is eagal liom, tá eagal orm.*

éaganta: "giddy, silly, senseless".

éaghmais: "absence, lack", or *éagmais* in GCh, pronounced /iamiʃ/. *Dá éaghmais sin*, "in spite of that". *In éaghmais*, "besides, other than".

eagla: "fear", masculine here, but feminine in GCh. Pronounced /ɑgələ/.

eaglais: "church". The genitive is given consistently as *eagailse* here (compare *eaglaise* in GCh) and the dative plural variously as *eaglaisíbh* (3 times), *eaglaisibh* (3 times), *eagailsíbh* (once) and *eagailsibh* (once), all of which forms are retained here. An article on PUL's translation of the Rosary in *An Músgraigheach* pointed out that although *eaglaise* is found in some of PUL's works, *eagailse* is the correct form: "*eaglaise* atá sa leabhar anso, ach is dócha gur dearmhad é. Sgríobhadh an tAth. P. *eagailse* do ghnáth agus siné an ceart" (see "An Choróinn Mhuire", in *An Músgraigheach*, 6, Fóghmhar 1944, p15). *An eaglais* is pronounced /ən 'ɑgəliʃ/, with a broad *n* (see CFBB, p270). The genitive singular and dative plural are pronounced /ɑgil′ʃi/ and /ɑgil′'ʃi:v′/.

eagnaí: "wise", pronounced /ɑgə'ni:/.

éagóir: "injustice". The plural here is *éagórtha*, where *éagóracha* stands in GCh.

éagórtha: "unjust", or *éagórach* in GCh.

éagsamhlach: "extraordinary, uncommon", or *éagsúlach* in GCh. Pronounced /iag'sauləx/. PUL commented on this word, "prefixes do not alter the pronunciation of the main word" (NIWU, p43), and consequently the word is not *éagsúlach.*

ealaí: "art, skill", with *ealaíon* in the genitive (*lucht ealaíon*, "skilled artisans"). *Ní healaí dhómh-sa é*, "it is not fitting for me, it does not behove me". *Ealaí* is found in GCh as *ealaín*, the historical dative.

ealaíonta: "artistic, skilful".

earra: "a good", as in "goods, wares". Note this is feminine here, but masculine in GCh. *Nách uathásach an earra í!*, "isn't she a terrible piece of work!" The original spelling here in this context was *ara*, probably indicating that in *an earra*, the *n* is broad. Where the meaning is "goods, wares", PUL's spelling here was *earaí.*

earraid: "contention, strife", pronounced /ɑrid′/. Usually found in the phrase *in earraid le*, "at variance with, at odds with".

eascara: "foe", with *eascáirde* in the plural. Pronounced /'ɑsˌkɑrə, ɑs'kɑ:rd′i/.

eascú: "eel, snake; wily person", or *eascann* in GCh.

easnamh: "want, shortage". Pronounced /ɑsnəv/.

easpag: "bishop", pronounced /ɑspəg/.

éide: "vestments, uniform, armour". *Gléasta in arm 's in éide*, "equipped with arms and accoutrements". *Éide Aifrinn*, "Mass vestments". *Éidí mitil*, "metal armour".

éigean: "violence, force". *Éigean ar ríocht na bhflaitheas le guí daoine*, "assaulting the kingdom of heaven with prayers". This word is masculine (becoming *éigin* in the genitive), but seems to be feminine in the dative, producing forms such as *ar éigin* ("barely, hardly") and *in éigin dá ghéire* ("in violent clashes/dire straits, no matter how severe"). The variant *éigint* (in *ar éigint*), found frequently in AÓL's Irish, is not found in PUL's published works.

eile: "all, every", or *uile* in GCh. Both /il'i/ and /el'i/ are found, and *eile* was the spelling of *'na theannta san is eile* in chapter 13 here (compare *'na thaobh san is uile* in chapter 34).

éilím, éileamh: "to claim, demand". As with many verbs with *-mh* in the verbal noun, the preterite here also has *mh*, *d'éilimh*, where GCh has *d'éiligh*.

éineacht: found in the phrase *in éineacht*, "together", and *in éineacht le*, "together with". This is adjusted from *aonfheacht* in the original text. However, AÓL had *aonacht* in *Scéalaíocht Amhlaoibh* (e.g. p2). Pronunciations of /in′ e:n′əxt/, /in′ e:nəxt/ and /ən e:nəxt/ are found.

éinne: "anyone", or *aon duine* in GCh, spelt *aoinne* in the original text of *Niamh*.

éirím, éirí: "to rise". This word is pronounced /əi'r′i:m′, əi'r′i:/ in WM Irish. *Éirí in áirde*, "airs, uppishness". *Cad a bhí ag éirí dhi*, "what was coming over her" (in chapter 40 here).

éirleach: "slaughter, havoc". *Éirleach cainnte*, "a tremendous amount of conversation".

eisean: "he", the disjunctive form of the emphatic pronoun. Pronounced /iʃən/.

éistim, éisteacht: "to listen" or "to keep silent". Note that *éist* is normally /e:ʃt′/, but a by-form *eist*, pronounced /eʃt′/, is also found. This is generally found in the phrase *eist do bhéal*, "hold your tongue", or as an imperative meaning "hush".

eochair: "key", with *eochracha* in the plural and *eochrach* in both the genitive singular and genitive plural. Pronounced /oxir′, oxərəxə, oxərəx/.

eólas: "knowledge". *An t-eólas* is pronounced /ən to:ləs/, with a broad *t* (see CFBB, p270). *Eólas a dh'fháil go háit*, "to find your way somewhere, to get there".

eólgaiseach: "knowledgeable", or *eolach* in GCh.

***érdam*:** "sacristy". PUL uses this word here, while stating it was an obsolete Irish word that had no equivalent in modern Irish. PUL used the Anglophone word *sacraistí*. *Eardhamh* is listed in FGB, and could be pronounced /ɑ'ru:v/, although it is unlikely to be in use in any Gaeltacht community.

fágaim, fágáilt/fágaint: "to leave", or *fágaim, fágáil* in GCh. Both *fágáilt* and *fágaint* are found as the verbal noun in the text of *Niamh*.

fáibre: "notch, groove; wrinkle", or *fáirbre* in GCh. Pronounced /fɑ:b′ir′i/.

faid-leicneach: "with long cheeks", or *fadleicneach* in GCh. Pronounced /fɑd′-l′ek′in′əx/.

faid: "length", or *fad* in GCh. *An fhaid*, "while", equivalent to *fad* or *a fhad* in GCh. *Dhá shlait ar faid*, "two yards in length". *Faid saeil*, "long life". *Dá fhaid*, "however long", and by extension "the longer" (in sentences such as *dá fhaid a mhairfidh t'athair is ea is sia a bheidh Gormfhlaith 'na hÁrdríogain*, "the longer your father lives, the longer Gormfhlaith will be high queen"). *Ag dul i bhfaid*, "getting longer".

Glossary

faidearaí: "long-suffering", or *fadarai* in GCh. PUL's spelling here (*faidearaídhe*) implies a slender *d*, /fɑd′a'ri:/, but /fɑdɑ'ri:/ is also found; see for example *fadaraighe* in PUL's *Aithris ar Chríost* (p21).

fáidhiúlacht: "prophetic powers", pronounced /fɑ:'g′u:ləxt/.

faillí: "neglect, negligence".

failm: "palm branch or tree", or *pailm* in GCh. Pronounced /fɑl′im′/. This is one of a number of words where WM Irish has *f* for *p* (cf. *féire* for *péire*); see the discussion in IWM §409. *Luan na Failme*, "the Monday after Palm Sunday".

faire: "to watch, keep a lookout". *Faire chút*, "to keep an eye out, be watchful or cautious" (this common phrasal verb isn't mentioned in FGB). Note that both *an faire* and *an fhaire* are found in the nominative here, whereas the genitive is consistently *na faire*. The word is feminine in GCh.

fairseag: "wide, extensive", or *fairsing* in GCh. Pronounced /fɑrʃəg/. *Fairsing* was given in the original text of *Niamh*, but see *fairseag* in PUL's *Cómhairle Ár Leasa* (p201) for evidence that he did have a broad *g* here. The plural is edited here as *fairseaga*; CFBB (p60) shows the comparative of the adjective and the cognate abstract noun retain *ng*.

fairsinge: "lavishness".

fáiscim, fáscadh: "to squeeze, press, tighten, bind". *Fáscadh chun reatha*, "to set off on a run".

falla: "wall", or *balla* in GCh.

fáltas: "a little supply of something", and by extension "a fair amount of something", pronounced /fɑ:lhəs/.

fan: "along", a contraction of *feadh an*. *Fan chuím air*, "around his waist".

fánaidh: "slope", or *fána* in GCh. *Fánaidh*, pronounced /fɑ:nig′/, is found in the dative here, although usage in PUL's *Críost Mac Dé* (Vol 1, p116) shows that he had *fánaidh* in the nominative of this word too: *tá tuitim an tailimh, nú an fhánaidh, síos ó chnoc Carmeil, agus ó Nasaret, go Caphárnum.*

fanaim, fanúint: "to wait, stay", or *fanaim, fanacht* in GCh.

faobhar: "sharp edge". Pronounced /fe:r/.

faoi: see under *fé.*

faoistin: "confession".

fasc: "an iota of sense".

fáscadh: "squeezing". *Fáscadh ' bhaint a croí fir* (or *fáscadh do theacht ar a chroí*), "for something to wring a man's heart with grief". *Fáscadh aigne (ar dhuine)*, "mental pressure".

fé dhéin: "towards, to meet, in aid of". In chapter 17, we find *féna ndéin*, "towards them", a form that AÓL pronounced as /f′e:nə ŋ′e:n′/ (see *Scéalaíocht Amhlaoibh*, p8). Direct evidence of PUL's own pronunciation of this phrase is not available, but PUL did state that he pronounced *ageam mhac* as *ageam bac*, (see NIWU, p1), and so this sort of delenition was a feature of his Irish and consequently it is likely he would also have delenited *déin* to *géin*, but without necessarily showing it in the spelling.

fé mar: "just as, according as". The *fé* here is derived from *féibh*, "precisely, just as", and not from *fá*, although the GCh form is *faoi mar*, as if this were derived from *fá*. *Fé mar* takes a direct relative clause.

fé ndeár, fé ndeara: *thug sé fé ndeara*, "he noticed". This would be *thug sé faoi deara* in GCh. Pronounced /f′e: n′a:r~f′e: n′arə/. *Fé ndeár* also has an additional meaning, "cause, reason". Gerald O'Nolan points out in his *A Key to the Exercises in Studies in Modern Irish (Part I)* (pp3-4) that in Munster Irish it is usual to say *tabhairt fé ndeara* for "to notice", but *fé ndeár* for "cause".

fé: "under", or *faoi* in GCh. *Fé* can also denote "having or possessing" in various sense: *fé bhórdaibh fada*, "with long tables". *Faoi* is also found twice in the original and so retained here where found. *Fé* can also mean "over" with a sense of motion, as in *isteach fén dtír* here, "over the land".

féachaim, féachaint: "to look (at)". *Féachaint chun ruda*, "to attend to something". *Féachaint rómhat (amach)*, "to be careful, think twice (before adopting a course of action), look ahead with foresight". *Féach isteach sa scéal*, "consider the matter". The plural imperative is found as both *féachaidh* and *féachaídh* here: the former seems preferable in WM Irish, but GCD (§511, 512) states that end-stressed plural imperatives in the first declension are found elsewhere in Munster Irish.

féachaint: *cur ' fhéachaint ar*, "to force or compel someone". This would be *iallach* or *iachall a chur ar* in GCh. PUL uses this phrase without an intervening *de*, but the phrase may be found as *cur d'fhéachaint ar dhuine rud a dhéanamh*.

feadar: "I know", usually found in negative or interrogative contexts, with *ní fheadar* meaning "I don't know; I wonder". While this verb is spelt *ní fheadair sé* in both the present- and past-tense meanings in GCh, there was traditionally a distinction between *ní fheadair sé*, present tense, and *ní fheidir sé*, past tense, pronounced /n′i: ed′ir′ ʃe:/.This distinction is found here, but *Scéalaíocht Amhlaoibh Í Luínse* (e.g. p23) shows that AÓL didn't have it. *Ní fheadraís a leath*, "you don't know the half of it", with *fheadraís* pronounced /n′i: adə'ri:ʃ/ and an epenthetic vowel in all similar forms (*ní fheadramair*, "we don't know", /n′i: 'adərəmir′/).

feadh: "fathom, extent", pronounced /er f′ag/. *Ar feadh*, "throughout, during".

feall: "deceit, evil, betrayal".

fearann: "land". *Fearann tailimh*, "a parcel of land". *Fearann tailimh saor*, or just *fearann saor*, "land free of tax obligations".

fearg: "anger", with *feirge* in the genitive and *feirg* in the dative, pronounced /f′arəg, f′er′ig′i, f′er′ig′/.

feargach: "angry", pronounced /f′arəgəx/.

feárr-de: "all the better". This is a 'second comparative' form, similar to *déine-de, usa-de, miste*, meaning "all the more X for it". *Nárbh fheárr-de Béibheann san* in chapter 46 here shows the syntax: "Béibheann would not be the better (off) for it/as a result of it".

feárr, fearra: "better". *Fearra*, /f′arə/, is a colloquial form of *feárr*, /f′a:r/. *Fearra* is more commonly used before *dhuit, dho* and related prepositional pronouns:

níorbh fhearra dho rud a dhéanfadh sé ná..., "the best thing he could do would be to..."

feidhm: "force, effect". Pronounced /f′əim′/. *Dlithe ' chur i bhfeidhm*, "to enforce laws". *Rud do dhul i bhfeidhm ar dhuine*, "for something to have an impact/make an impression on someone; to hit home".

féile: "generosity, hospitality".

feilmeanta: "elemental", and, by extension, "excellent, spendid", pronounced /f′el′im′əntə/.

féin: "self". This word is pronounced /f′e:n′~he:n′/ in WM Irish, although generally with an *h* elsewhere in Ireland. CFBB shows that the *h* pronunciation is more frequently used after prepositional pronouns, with examples including *doit hén* (p15), *air hén* (p34), and *ann hén* (p52), i.e. *duit féin, air féin* and *ann féin* respectively. Note PUL's comments on the use of *féin* in the notes to his *Cath Ruis na Rí for Bóinn*: "*Conchobhar féin*, Conchubhar himself. Never on any account, *Conchobhar é féin*. It is a very nice thing, is it not, to see rigid sticklers for certain forms of spelling make the most outrageous mistakes in syntax! The above is one of such mistakes" (p58).

féith: "sinew", with *féitheacha* in the plural. *Do ghluaiseadh an tsean-fhuil trí sna sean-fhéitheachaibh, 'na caisíbh tine*, "the old blood surged through their old sinews in torrents of fire".

feitheamh: "to wait", a verbal noun pronounced /f′ihəv/.

feóchaim, feóchadh: "to wither, decay", or *feoim, feo* in GCh. Pronounced /f′o:xim′, f′o:xə/. Note the past participle is *feóchta* here where *feoite* stands in GCh.

fiacal: "tooth", with *fiacla* in the plural. The historical dative, *fiacail*, is used in GCh. Pronounced /f′iəkəl, f′iəkələ/.

fiach: "hunt, hunting", with *fiaigh* in the genitive. See under *liú*.

fiach: *cur ' fhiachaibh ar*, "to force or compel someone". This would be *cur d'fhiacha ar* in GCh. PUL uses this phrase without an intervening *de*, but the phrase may also be found as *cur d'fhiachaibh ar dhuine rud a dhéanamh. Fiacha* literally means "debts", and the use of *fiacha* reflects some kind of confusion with the related phrase *cur d'fhéachaint*. PUL claimed (NIWU, p135) that there was a "manifest difference" between *d'fhiachaibh* and *fhéachaint*, with the former meaning "bound" to do something, and the latter "made" to do something.

fiafraí: "questioning". *An fiafraí* is adjusted here to *an fhiafrai*, in line with the correct feminine gender found in some other of PUL's works. Pronounced /f′iər'hi:/.

fiafraím, fiafraí: "to ask (a question of someone)", used with *de*. Pronounced /f′iər'hi:m′, f′iər'hi:/.

fiain: "wild". As the pronunciation is /f′ian′/, there seems no reason for the GCh spelling, *fiáin*; the classical spelling was *fiadhain*.

Fiann (an Fhiann): the roving band of warriors celebrated in the Fenian cycle of myths.

fiantas: "nonsense, wild folly", or *fiántas* in GCh. Pronounced /f′iəntəs/.

fiche: "twenty". The genitive has been adjusted here from *fichid*, which is found in all of PUL's works, to *fichead*.

ficheall: "chess", or more accurately the ancient Celtic boardgame, *fidchell*, similar to chess. *Ag imirt fichille*, "playing chess". Although PUL generally writes *ag imirt chártai*, with lenition, *ag imirt fichille* is regularly found without lenition, possibly because of a greater reluctance to lenite an *f*.

finne: "fairness", of hair colour.

finneóg: "window", or *fuinneog* in GCh. Pronounced /f′i'ŋ′o:g/.

fionn: "fair, fair-haired", pronounced /f′u:n/.

fionna-rua: "light-red, sandy", of hair colour. This was *fionn-ruadh* in the original, but PSD shows the epenthetic vowel. GCh has *fionnrua*. Pronounced /f′unə'ruə~f′unə'r′uə/.

fíor-uisce: "spring water".

fíoraim, fíoradh: "to fulfil, make true", or *fíoraím* and *fíorú* in GCh.

flaitheas: "heaven; kingdom". The original spelling here, *flathas*, has been adjusted to the accepted spelling, as it yields the same pronunciation.

fleasc: "rod". *Ar fleasc a dhroma*, "on the flat of his back".

flosc: "eagerness".

flúirse: "abundance, plenty".

focal: "word", with *foclaibh* in the dative plural. Pronounced /fokəl, fokəliv′/.

fochair: "proximity, presence". *I bhfochair*, "together with, in the presence of".

fód: "sod of earth". *Fén bhfód*, "six foot under (dead)".

foghail: "plundering, pillaging". *Lucht foghla*, "highwaymen, marauders". Pronounced /foul′/.

foghlamaím, foghlaim: "to study", or *foghlaimím, foghlaim* in GCh.

foighne: "patience", pronounced /fəiŋ′i/.

foighneach: "patient", pronounced /fəiŋ′əx/.

foighním, foighneamh: "to endure, have patience (with)", used with *le*; pronounced /fəi'ŋ′i:m′, fəiŋ′əv/.

folach: "act of hiding", pronounced /fə'lɑx/. *Rud do chur i bhfolach*, "to hide something".

folaím, folachadh: "to cover, conceal". Pronounced /fo'li:m′, fə'lɑxə/.

folaíocht: "breeding".

foláir: "excessive, superfluous". Pronounced /flɑ:r′/. *Ní foláir é ' dhéanamh*, "it must be done".

foláramh: "warning", or *foláireamh* in GCh. Pronounced /flɑ:rəv/.

folt: "a head of hair", with the plural given here as *foilt*, pronounced /fohl, fihl′/. PUL's *Eisirt* has *folta* in the plural (p55).

folús: "emptiness, vacuity".

fonn: "desire, urge", pronounced /fu:n/. *Níor chuid ba lú ná a fhonn a bheadh orthu*, "they would not be totally disclined"—literally, "their inclination would not be the smallest amount".

fóntacht: "goodness, something good".

fórlíonta: "complete". The *r* in the combination /rl′/ always resists palatalisation.

formad: "envy", pronounced /forəməd/.
formhór: "majority", pronounced /forə'vo:r/. *A bhformhór*, "most of them".
foth: "faugh!", an exclamation of scorn or disgust.
fothram: "noise, din", pronounced /fohərəm/.
freagra: "answer", pronounced /fr′agərə/.
freagraim, freagairt: "to answer", or *freagraím, freagairt* in GCh, pronounced /fr′agərim′, fr′agirt′/. While the verbal noun is normally *freagairt*, there is an example here of *freagradh* (/fr′agərə/) being used as the verbal noun of this verb.
friothálaim, friothálamh: "to serve, attend", or *friothálaim, friotháil* in GCh. *Friothálamh* also corresponds to the related GCh noun, *friotháileamh*, "reception, entertainment of guests". The genitive, spelt *frithálmha* in the original, is edited here as *friothála*, pronounced /fr′i'hɑ:lə/, in line with the pronunciation shown in CFBB (p113), but Osborn Bergin transcribed l*ucht friothálmha* as *locht frihálú* in *Eshirt* (e.g. p3). An addition meaning of *friothálamh* is "to prepare for": *bheadh fios na haimsire againn agus d'fhéadfaimís an aimsir d'fhriothálamh*, "we would know the time it was going to happen and we would be able to prepare for it". *Fear friothála*, "server, attendant".
frithghuin: "cut and thrust", as in a battle; *frithghoin* in GCh. This is glossed by PUL in NIWU (p54) as "the thick of the fight, i.e., where wounds are crowded thickly". FGB says that *thit sé i bhfrithghoin an chatha* means "he fell on the opposing side of the battle", which seems to be one of the most mistaken glosses in Ó Dónaill's dictionary. We find *i bhfrithghuin catha* in chapter 52 here, but *i bhfrithghuin chatha* in the original text of chapter 53. Lenition, or the lack of it, after a feminine noun is a problematic area in Irish grammar. As *i bhfrithghuin catha* is found in many of PUL's works (including *Eisirt*, p82; *Bricriu*, p93; *Sgéalaidheachta as an mBíobla Naomhtha*, Vol 4, p447; and *i bhfrithghuin mór-chatha* in *Táin Bó Cuailnge*, p127), the single identifiable instance of *i bhfrithghuin chatha* found here is amended. The LS version of PUL's *Eisirt* transcribes *i bhfrithghuin* as *a vriochuin* (*Eshirt*, p85), indicating the pronunciation is /ə vr′ixin′/.
fuadach: "plunder".
fuadar: "rush, hurry, activity". *Fuadar cuisíochta*, "the din of people walking". *Fuadar ná feadar*, "blind activity", given in PSD under *fuadar*. This phrase appears to mean, literally, "such a rush that I didn't know (what was going on)".
fuar-bhalaithe: "a dank, stale odour/smell". See also under *balaithe*.
fuar: "cold", but also "in vain".
fuaraim, fuaradh: "to cool (something) down", or *fuaraím, fuarú* in GCh.
fuasclaim, fuascailt: "to redeem, save", or *fuasclaím, fuascailt* in GCh, pronounced /fuəskəlim′, fuəskihl′/. *Fuascailt mic rí a braighdineas*, "a prince's ransom".
fuiligim, fulag: "to suffer, endure", or *fulaingím, fulaingt* in GCh. Pronounced /fil′ig′im′, foləg~fuləg/. Note devoicing of the g to *c* in the future and conditional: *fuiliceód*, /fil′i'k′o:d/; *fuiliceódh*, /fil′i'k′o:x/. The original spellings here included *fhuilingeóch'* and *fulang*, but some of PUL's other works show the pronunciation

better: see *fuiligimíd* in his *Lúcián* (p151) *fulag* in *Na Cheithre Soisgéil* (p6) and *folag* in *Lúcián* (p78).

fuilteach: "bloody". This word has a short vowel in the first syllable, /fil'həx/.

fuireann: "crew", or *foireann* in GCh. Pronounced /fir'ən/.

fuiriste: "easy", or *furasta* in GCh. *Uiriste* is also found in PUL's works and seems the more fundamental dialectal form, as *fuiriste* is generally found in PUL's works only where it is lenited.

fuirm: "form", or *foirm* in GCh. Pronounced /fir'im'/. *Aon ní i bhfuirm leabhair*, "anything that resembled a book".

ga: "spear", with *gathanna* in the plural. *Ga gréine*, "a ray of sunlight".

gabha: "smith". Note the plural here is *gaibhni*, but would be *gaibhne* in GCh. Pronounced /gou, gəi'ŋ'i:/.

gabhaim, gabháil: "to take; go" and a large range of other meanings, pronounced /goum', gvɑ:l'/. The preterite is *ghoibh* (adjusted from *ghaibh* in the original text) where there is *ghabh* in GCh, as the pronunciation is /ɣov'/ in WM Irish. Note the verbal adjective *gofa*, meaning "harnessed", of a chariot in chapter 42. The future and conditional forms resemble the absolute forms of the verb *gheibhim*, e.g. *go ngeóbhaidís de chosaibh i nGaelaibh*, "that they would trample on the Gaels". *Do geófí* in PUL's Irish is the conditional autonomous form of this verb (compare *do gheófí*, which is the conditional autonomous form of *gheibhim* in PUL's works), and so *aon chapall a geófí idir an dá chois sin* in chapter 28 means "a horse that would be caught/seized/taken between those two legs".

gach: "each, every". *Gach aon bhall*, "everywhere", pronounced /gə he:vəl/ (for /gəh/ as well as /gɑh~gɑx/, see IWM §377). *Gach aon rud*, "everything", pronounced /gə he:rəd/. *I ngach* is given three times here, in place of the dialectal *ins gach*.

gadhar: "dog", pronounced /gəir/.

gaidhrín: "lapdog", pronounced /gəi'r'i:n'/.

gáir: "cry, shout", with *gártha* in the plural. *Gáir mholta*, "cheer". *Gártha guil*, "cries of lament".

gáire: "a laugh", with both *gáir* and *gáire* found in GCh. This word is feminine here, but masculine in GCh. *Cúis gháire chúinn*, "that's a good joke! how funny!"

gáirí: a noun and verbal noun meaning "laughing, laughter", or *gáire* in GCh. *Gáirí um dhuine*, "to laugh at someone".

gairid: "short, near". This is pronounced /gɑr'id'/ or /g'ar'id'/ according to CFBB (p119).

gairíocht: "roughness, coarseness, ruggedness". This word is not given in FGB, which has only *gairbhe*.

gaisce: "heroism, exploits; arms". *Airm gaisce*, "weaponry".

gal: "valour", with *gaile* in the genitive. Pronounced /gɑl, gɑl'i/.

gallán: "pillar-stone".

gallda: "foreign; English"; pronounced /gaulə/.

gamhain: "calf". *A ghamhain!* "my dear!". Pronounced /gaun'/.

gan: "without". *Gan* often lenites *b, c, g, m* and *p* (i.e., lenitable consonants other than dentals and *f*). See O'Nolan's *New Era Grammar* (p113) for discussion of dynamic lenition "employed to mark certain psychological distinctions": *duine gan cos* means "a person without legs", whereas *duine gan chos* "someone deprived of a particular leg". PUL's commented as follows in NIWU (pp140-141): "*chuadar abhaile gan creach gan cath*, they went home without battle or spoils. In this form the words *creach* and *cath* are taken in a generic sense, and the English is 'without spoil, without battle'. Aspiration of the words would signify that they were used in an individual manner, and the English would be 'without a spoil, without a battle'. The use of the initial aspiration in the Irish has the effect which the use of the indefinite article has in English. It turns 'battle' in general to an individual 'battle'".

It is difficult to read this principle across in a way that would clarify every single use of *gan* in PUL's published works. For example in chapter 32 here, we read of someone who would gain *scolaíocht gan Creideamh*, yet in *Aithris ar Chríost* (p44) we read *a dhaoine gan mheabhair, gan chreideamh i nbhúr gcroídhe*. Logically, the distinction between generic and indefinite usages (*gan cos* vs. *gan chos*) is more clearly made with countable nouns. Usage with abstract nouns is particularly problematic, as *creideamh* is nearly always found in generic use (PUL nearly always writes *gan creideamh*), and yet *ciall* and *meabhair* are consistently found lenited (*gan chiall, gan mheabhair*), despite the fact that they appear generic too. If we glance at Eleanor Knott's explanation in the notes to PUL's *Lughaidh Mac Con* (p77) that lenited use often corresponds to an indefinite article "any" in English ("*gan chosdas*, 'without any expense', but *gan cosdas*, 'not under expense'"), it is possible to see that *gan chiall* and *gan mheabhair* regularly assume such an indefinite sense (*gan chiall = gan aon chiall; gan mheabhair = gan aon mheabhair*), but to a large extent this is also a matter of idiom and usage. In phrases such as *gan mheabhair, gan chreideamh*, where one noun is lenited, there is a strong tendency for the other to be so too. Where we read *gan Bhéarla, gan Ghaeluinn* in PUL's *Mo Sgéal Féin* (e.g. p54), we can also assume an indefinite sense ("without any English or Irish"), as PUL elsewhere writes *gan Gaeluinn* (e.g. *dá gcaithidís an chéad deich mbliana de d' shaoghal-sa, a Thaidhg, ag imirt na céirde ort chun na Gaeluinne mhúine dhuit bheidhfá gan Gaeluinn i n-aoís do dheich mblian duit agus bheidhfá ar bheagán Gaeluinne indiu* in *Sgothbhualadh*, p48). The comparison with English is not always helpful, as "any" can signify both generic and individual usage (*gan cos*, "without any legs", in the case of a countable noun; *gan chostas*, "without any cost", in the case of an uncountable noun).

Verbal nouns are not usually lenited after *gan* (cf. *gan briseadh, gan géilleadh, gan gluaiseacht, gan pósadh, gan bac, gan marú* and *gan corraí* here). *Gan chosnamh* (but see also under *cosnamh* elsewhere in this *Glossary*), *gan chosaint*, and the use of *chosc* in *gan chosc gan cheataí* and the use of *chodladh* in *gan chodladh gan suan* might appear to be exceptions, but it could be argued these are being used here as ordinary abstract nouns, and not as verbal nouns.

Personal names are not normally lenited after *gan* (cf. *gan Brian anso* here; *gan Bhrian anso* would mean "without any Brian here"). A further point worth noting is that nouns that are part of larger noun phrases are not lenited after *gan*: in an undated note to Shán Ó Cuív, held in the G1,276 collection of manuscripts held in the National Library of Ireland, PUL explained that in *gan {gáire dhéanamh}*, *gáire* is not lenited because *gan* governs the entire phrase. Relevant examples here where the nouns stand in longer phrases or are qualified include *gan {cead ó Mhurchadh}*, *gan {gearán a dhéanamh}*, *gan {cúrsaí an Árdrí do bhac}*, *gan {bua an chatha a bhí ag teacht do leogaint leis an namhaid}*, *gan {cuid acu ach ar éigin tosnaithe}* (cf. the phrase *duine gan chuid*, "one who has nothing" in *Papers on Irish Idiom*, p36), *gan {cómhairle agus teagasc agus stiúrú a bheith aige}*, *gan {cabhair ná cúnamh ó aon rí cúige eile}* (compare *gan chabhair gan chúnamh* elsewhere here), *gan {míle nú cúpla míle fear ollamh ann}*, *gan {culaith manaigh}*, *gan {grá don Mhaighdin Mhuire}*, *gan {céile eile}* (owing to qualification by *eile*) and *gan {priúnsa éigin}* (owing to qualification by *éigin*). Nevertheless, it is difficult to shoehorn this interpretation into every single instance of *gan* in PUL's published works: for example, we read *gan chead* in *Séadna* (p160), but *gan chead ó aoinne* in *An Cleasaidhe* (p3), where *gan cead ó aoinne* might have made more sense (alternatively, it could be argued that *gan chead ó aoinne* is less specific than *gan {cead ó Mhurchadh}*, as it essentially means the same thing as *gan chead* with no further qualification). See also under *i ganfhios*.

gann: "scarce". *Is gann do é*, "it's the least he can do", and so *ba lú ba ghann do ríthibh Éireann é*, "it was the very least the kings of Ireland could do".

gaobhar: "nearness, proximity", pronounced /ge:r/.

gaoth: "wind", with *gaoithe* in the genitive and *gaoith* in the dative.

gar: "nearness". *I ngar do*, "near to".

garbh: "rough, rugged, strong", pronounced /gɑrəv/.

gasra: "band, group of people", pronounced /gɑsərə/. *Gasra nár dhó*, "a warrior band not to be trifled with".

geal-chroíoch: "light-hearted".

geal-gháire: "a pleasant smile".

geal-gháirí: "pleasant laughter, cheerfulness".

geal-gháiriteach: "radiant, cheerful", or *gealgháireach* in GCh.

geal-gháiriteacht: "radiance, cheerfulness", or *gealgháireacht* in GCh.

gealaim, gealadh: "to whiten, brighten". *Ghealadh a croí dhóibh*, "she was fond of them, would show an inclination towards them".

geallaim, geallúint: "to promise", or *geallaim, gealladh* in GCh.

geallúint: "promise", with *geallúna* in the plural, or *gealltanas* in GCh.

geamhar: "corn in the blade", pronounced /g'aur/.

géaraím, géarú: "to sharpen; quicken". *Ghéaraíodar sa chómhrac*, "they stepped up their efforts in the fight".

gearán: "complaint", pronounced /g'i'rɑ:n/. Also refers to "medical complaints", i.e. "illnesses", as in chapter 42 here.

gearraim, gearradh: "to cut", but also "to backbite, make cutting remarks, run someone down".

gheibhim, fáil: "to get, find". *Gheibhim* is the absolute form of the verb *faighim*; the distinction is not observed in GCh, which has *faighim* alone. The future form found here, *gheóbhaidh*, is pronounced /jo:g′/. The past participle used here is *fálta*, /fɑ:lhə/ corresponding to *faighte* in GCh. *Fachta* is sometimes found in WM Irish with the same meaning (see, for example, *Aithris ar Chríost*, p177). The present autonomous form is found here both as *gheibhtear* and *fachtar*, whereas GCh has *faightear*; *faghtar* is also found in PUL's works (e.g. *Séadna*, p238). The use of *fachtar* in *ná fuil sa méid sin de thoradh an Chreidimh ach neamhní seochas an toradh a fachtar as ar an saol eile* is worth commenting on, as the direct relative pronoun should not entail use of the dependent form. PUL explained in a letter to Risteárd Pléimeann dated December 21st 1917, held in the National Library of Ireland in the G1,277 (1) collection of manuscripts, that the absolute form *gheibhtear* is used where there is more a sense of effort in getting something: "I feel that *fachtar* means that there was no *saothar* in the getting. *Gheibhtear* seems to be the result of the *saothar*. If I say *Is uaimse a gheibhtear gach nídh* I mean that, nevertheless there is some *saothar* in the getting. When I say *fachtar* the thing is got without *saothar*. It is simply 'found'". Consequently the contrast between *gheibhtear* and *fachtar* is not entirely one of an absolute/dependent contrast. The autonomous preterite form here is *do fuaradh*, where GCh has *fuarthas*. The imperative *faigh* found here is pronounced /fəig′/ or /fɑg′/.

giall "hostage, human pledge". The plural *géill* is used here, corresponding to *gialla* in GCh.

gileacht: "whiteness, brightness", pronounced /g′il′əxt/.

gínte: "nations". This word is the plural of *gin*, "birth, foetus", but is found in the plural in the meaning of "heathens, pagan peoples", thus corresponding to the Latin *gentes*.

giodam: "restlessness, liveliness", pronounced /g′idəm/.

giolla: "groom, guide, gillie", pronounced /g′ulə/. *Giolla turais*, "messenger, courier".

giorracht: "shortness", pronounced /g′i'rɑxt/. *Teacht i ngiorracht do rud*, "to get near to something".

giorrae: "hare", or *giorria* in GCh. The plural *giorraithe* is found here, where GCh has *giorriacha*. Pronounced /g′i're:, g′urihi/.

glacaim, glacadh: "to accept". This often takes a direct object (*rud do ghlacadh*), in addition to the more widely found use adopted in GCh, *glacadh le rud*. Note the past participle here, *glacaithe*, where GCh has *glactha*.

glaeim, glaoch: "to call", or *glaoim, glaoch* in GCh. This is one of a large number of words where the mid-20th century spelling change has produced a form that yields the incorrect pronunciation in WM Irish. The original spellings were *glaodhaim* and *glaodhach*, and the confluence of *aoi* in the new spelling—a combination that would be pronounced /i:/ in the dialect—means some other spelling system has to be adopted to show the dialectal pronunciations, /gle:m′, gle:x/.

glaine: "clarity, purity", pronounced /glin′i/.

glaise: "rivulet, stream", pronounced /glɑʃi/.
glanachar: "cleanliness", pronounced /glɑnəxər~glə'nɑxər/.
glao: "call, summons". Feminine here, but masculine in GCh.
glas: "green", but also sometimes "chilly"; with *glais* in the masculine singular genitive. Pronounced /glɑs, gliʃ/.
gleann: "glen, valley", with *gleanna* in the genitive. Pronounced /gl′aun, gl′anə/.
gléasaim, gléasadh: "to equip, make ready", e.g. of a body of men. IWM §283 indicated this verb was pronounced with /e:/, and not /ia/, whereas the cognate noun had /ia/ (compare IWM §130), but it seems this may have been a presumption made by Brian Ó Cuív based on a number of poetical forms found. The original spelling found in *Niamh* (e.g. *gleusan* for *gléasann*) shows the verb did have /ia/ in PUL's Irish.
gleic: "struggle, contest", pronounced /gl′ek′/.
gléigeal: "brilliant white; dear". *An Slánaitheóir Gléigeal,* "the fair Saviour". An original medial *-gh-* has become delenited in WM Irish (and in GCh too).
gléineach: "glittering; clear, lucid".
gleó: "noise".
gliocas: "cleverness, ingenuity", or *gliceas* in GCh.
glóire: "glory", or *glóir* in GCh.
gluaisim, gluaiseacht: "to proceed, move, go". In PUL's works, this verb is generally in the first conjugation in the present tense (*gluaisim, gluaiseann sé*) and the past tense (*do ghluaiseas, do ghluais sé*). The future (*gluaiseód, gluaiseóidh sé*), conditional (*do ghluaiseóinn, do ghluaiseódh sé*—the latter of which is found in the text of *Niamh* here), and the past habitual (*do ghluaisínn, do ghluaisíodh sé*) are in the second conjugation, with a mixture of forms (*gluais* in the singular and *gluaisidh/gluaisídh* in the plural) in the imperative. However, extraneous forms are also found, including *ghluaisighean* (*Sgothbhualadh,* p50), *ghluaisís* (*Na Cheithre Soisgéil,* p274) and *ghluaisidís* (*Séadna,* p50).
glúin: "generation". PUL uses the historical dative for the nominative here, but the historical nominative, *glún,* nevertheless reappears in his Irish for the genitive plural: *ar feadh seacht nglún.*
gnaoi: "beauty, comeliness".
gnáth-theaghlach: "permanent retinue; the household troops of a king".
gnó: "business, affair", with *gnótha* in the genitive. *Gnó súl,* "an ostensible business, something to keep up appearances". *Ba ró-bheag an gnó é,* "it would be a waste of time". *Gnótha stáit,* "affairs of state; politics".
gnúis: "face, countenance". PUL glossed this word in NIWU (p60) as "the face as giving expression to the mind and its passions or energies; the equivalent of the Latin *vultus*".
go leith: "and a half", pronounced /gil′i/.
goilim, gol: "to cry", pronounced /gol′im′, gol/.
goillim, goilliúint: "to harm, affect adversely", with a long vowel in the preterite, *ghoíll.*

gol: "crying". The genitive is given in the original text here as both *guil* and *goil*. *Guil* is used in the editing here, as it shows the pronunciation.

gorm: "blue", pronounced /gorəm/.

grá: "love." *Mo ghrá thu agus rud agat*, "I love you for what you've got".

gradam: "dignity, glory, grandeur".

gráinniúil: "abhorrent, hateful", or *gráiniúil* in GCh. Pronounced /grɑ:'ŋ′u:l′/.

grásaeir: "cattle-dealer". The original spelling *gráséir* was unclear as to the pronunciation but CFBB (p129) shows it to be /grɑ:'se:r′/, and the spelling *grásaeir* is found in PUL's other works, including *Ár nDóithin Araon* (p12).

grásta: "grace". PSD shows the nominative singular to be *grás*, but *grásta* is used as a nominative singular and plural (*an grásta, na grásta*) in PUL's works. *Flaitheas na ngrást*, with the genitive plural, "the kingdom of heaven".

greadaim, greadadh: 1. "to scorch". *Greadadh chuige!*, "confound him": this phrase is derived from *greadadh trí lár a scairt!*, "may his entrails be scorched!", but the authorised *Foclóir do Shéadna* (p66) explains that the force of this expression was much weakened. 2. "to strike, thump". *Ag greadadh a dhá bhas*, "slapping the two palms of his hands".

grean: "gravel, grit". *Chómh tiubh le grean*, "as numerous as grains of sand".

greann: "humour, pleasantry". *Greann a dhéanamh de rud*, "to make jokes about something".

greanta: "graven, polished, beautifully done", pronounced /gr′antə/.

greas: "a turn, a bout", or *dreas* in GCh. *Greas guil*, "a bout of weeping".

gréas: "ornamental work, decorative pattern".

gríosaim, gríosadh: "to inflame, spur, incite, urge on", corresponding to *gríosaím* and *gríosú* in GCh.

groí: "strong, spirited".

gruama: "glum, dejected". Traditionally spelt *gruamdha*, the pronunciation is, or can be, /gruəmhə/.

guala: "shoulder", or *gualainn* in GCh, where the historical dative has replaced the nominative. The dative plural here, *guaillibh*, is derived from a plural *guaille* (found in *Papers on Irish Idiom*, p47), where GCh has *guaillí*.

guí: "prayer", masculine here, but feminine in GCh. Some of PUL's works have this word as feminine, including the version of *An Teagasg Críostaidhe* edited by him (see p39 of that work for *an ghuídhe*).

guidim, guid: "to steal", or *goidim* and *goid* in GCh. The spelling of the original is retained here as showing the pronunciation better. *Ghuid sí amach é*: this is a rarer meaning of *guid*, "to take away, remove", i.e. "she stole him out, smuggled him out, got him out", a usage that possibly reflects the influence of the English phrase "to steal someone out". The past participle here is *guidithe*, where GCh has *goidte*.

guin galáin: "a victim of the running of the gauntlet". *Do deineadh guin galáin de*, "he was killed by being forced to run the gauntlet, i.e. with everyone present stabbing him". *Galán* is mentioned in PSD as a variant of an obscure word, *galann*, meaning "enemy". However, the true etymology of this phrase is unclear. The glossary to PUL's *Táin Bó Cuailnge* (p264) comments on this word, "this phrase, fairly common in Mid. Ir., is obscure, but in the recorded examples it is always used of the slaying of one man by a number".

guin: "wound". This word is found as both *guin* and *goin* in the original text here, and standardised on in this edition as *guin*, which shows the pronunciation, rather than the *goin* of GCh.

guinim, guin: "to wound", or *goinim, goin* in GCh. The only form of this word found here is the verbal adjective in *tar éis a ghunta*, "after his being wounded", where *gunta* corresponds to *gonta* in GCh.

guith: "reproach, censure". This is cognate with the word *guth*, "voice". In GCh, *guth* is found in both meanings. Generally found as *de ghuith*, "as a reproach".

gunta: "wounded", or *gonta* in GCh. Pronounced /guntə/.

gurb, gurbh: the combination of the conjunction *go* and the copula, pronounced /gurəb~gərb, gərv/.

gus: "vigour, spirit".

i ganfhios (do): "unbeknown, unawares". Pronounced /ə'gɑnis/. While FGB has *gan fhios* as two words, *gan* does not lenite an *f*, as shown by *gan fios* in chapter 37 here, and so *ganfhios* is properly a single word.

i gcian: *i gcian agus i gcóngar*, "far and near". It is worth noting that PUL did not use the traditional dative singular form *céin* here, although *i gcéin* is found in some of his other works. In GCh this would be *i gcéin agus i gcóngar*.

i gcómhair: "for, in store for". This phrase was uniformly spelt *i gcóir* in the original, in line with PUL's view (see NIWU, p24) that this phrase derives from *cóir*, "proper arrangement (among other meanings)" and not *cómhair*, "presence". He indicated he did not have a nasal vowel in this phrase, but the issue is complex, as his etymology seems faulty (*The Dictionary of the Irish Language* has *i gcomhair* under *comair*) and it is possible that *i gcómhair* has become conflated with a separate phrase *i gcóir*, "ready", in WM Irish. In any case, nasalisation is not a noted feature of modern-day WM Irish, and so the GCh form produces the correct pronunciation. *I gcómhair na hoíche*, "for the night", and so, by extension, "by nightfall".

i: "in". *I* becomes *ins* before the article (*insna*), and before *gach* in WM Irish, although the GCh form, *i ngach*, is also found here and is left unamended where found in the original. Note the combinations *'nár* for *inár* (found as *i n-ár* and *'n-ár* in the original text) and *'núr* for *in bhur* (found as *i nbhúr* in the original text). For a similar approach, see pp6-7 of *Aithris ar Chríost* (the LS edition, which was published in 1930 with LS and the normal spelling on opposite pages), where Shán Ó Cuív transcribes *i n-ár mbeatha* as *'nár meaha*, and pp106-107 of the same work, where Shán Ó Cuív transcribes *i nbhúr gcroidhe* as *'núr gry*.

iallait: "saddle", or *diallait* in GCh. Pronounced /iəlit'/.

iarmharán: "remnant; something worthless; dregs". *Ag cur na n-iarmharán i leataoibh*, "discarding the dregs".

Glossary

iarracht: "attempt, try", or "a bit or a touch of something". *Do baineadh iarracht de gheit as,* "he got a bit of a fright".

iarraidh: "request; asking". *Ar iarraidh,* "missing, being sought".

iarraim, iarraidh: "to ask; to attempt". This verbal noun is used, not as *ag iarraidh,* but *a d'iarraidh.*

íbirt: "sacrifice", or *íobairt* in GCh, used here frequently in *An Íbirt Naomh,* "the sacrifice of the Mass". Pronounced /i:birt′/ according to IWM (§57), with a broad *b*, but PUL consistently used a slender *b* in this word. The genitive here is *íbirte,* where GCh has *íobartha.*

idir: "between, among". This preposition, which traditionally took the accusative (see PSD), generally takes the dative in PUL's works, although *idir Éire agus crích Lochlann* is found in chapter 26 here (cf. *idir Éirinn agus tír Lochlann* in chapter 27). Note *eadrainn, eadraibh, eatarthu,* "between or among us, you, them", pronounced /ɑdəriŋ′, ɑdəriv′, ɑtərhə/. The first vowel of *idir* can be elided, as in *'dir dhá chómhairle* here, "in two minds (about something)".

ifreann: "hell", pronounced /if′ir′ən/.

imbriathar: "really! upon my word!" PUL used the spelling *ambriathar* in the original.

imigéiniúil: "remote".

imím, imeacht: "to go, go away". Note that the participle, *imithe,* is stressed on the second syllable: /i'm′ihi/.

imirt anama: "mortal combat".

ímpí: "intercession".

ímpire: "emperor".

ímpireacht: "empire".

imreas: "strife, discord", pronounced /im′ir′əs/.

imreasán: "constant discord, quarrelling", pronounced /im′ir′əsɑ:n/. Both *imreas* and *imreasán* are found in PUL's works, but FGB appears to recommend the use of *imreas* over *imreasán* in GCh. That there is a nuance of difference is indicated in the glossary to the 1910 edition of *Niamh,* which glosses *imreas* as "contention, fighting", but *imreasán* as "constant quarrelling".

imrim, imirt: "to play", or *imrím, imirt* in GCh, with *d'imir* in the preterite. This is a syncopating verb, with *imreóidh* and *imreódh* in the future and conditional. These forms are pronounced /im′ir′im′, im′irt′, im′i'r′o:g′, im′i'r′o:x/.

in: a form of the demonstrative pronoun *sin* used after the copula (*b'in, nách in,* etc). Often incorrectly written *shin*: as the *s* of *sin* derives from the present-tense copula, there should be no *s* when used with forms of the copula that do not end in *s*. Correct spelling of this word also yields the correct pronunciation. Often followed by *mar*: *b'in mar ba thúisce a dh'fhéadfaidís iad féin do leathadh isteach ar mhachairibh breátha míne na hÉireann,* "that way they could spread themselves over the fine, level plains of Ireland all the more quickly".

inead: "unit", or *ionad* in GCh. Pronounced /in′əd/. *In inead,* "instead of, in the place of".

iníon: "daughter", with *iníne* in the genitive and *inín* in the dative. The plural *iníona* is used here, in contradistinction to the *iníonacha* of GCh. *A 'níon ó*, "my dear girl, my dear woman". Note that the first syllable of *iníon* is elided in this phrase: /i 'n′i:n o:/ (or /i 'n′i:n′ o:/).

inis: "island". The genitive *ínse* is found here in a number of placenames.

iniúchaim, iniúchadh: "to scrutinise".

inné: "yesterday", /i'n′e:/. *Inné roimis sin*, "the day before that". This is one of a number of words (others include *inniu* and *coinníoll*) where *nn* (usually indicating tense slender *n*) does not yield /ŋ′/ in WM Irish. Elision of the initial vowel is sometimes indicated in *Niamh*, as in *tar éis an lae 'nné.*

inniu: "today", /i'n′uv/. The final consonant heard in the pronunciation is left untranscribed, as it was not indicated in the historical orthography, PUL did not spell it out and it is not indicated in the spelling adopted in GCh. The spelling *aniogh* was found in the works of Seathrún Céitinn, and so the development of /v/ from *-gh* is analogous to the way the word previously spelt *tiugh* is pronounced /t′uv/ (and nowadays spelt *tiubh*). This is one of a number of words (others include *inné* and *coinníoll*) where *nn* (usually indicating tense slender *n*) does not yield /ŋ′/ in WM Irish. Elision of the initial vowel is sometimes indicated in *Niamh*, as in *mí ó 'nniu.*

ínse: "inch, watermeadow".

ínsim, ínsint: "to tell", or *insím, insint* in GCh. *D'inis* is found in the preterite here, where *d'innis* is used in some of PUL's other works (see *Aithris ar Chríost*, p7). IWM (§238) shows that /(i)'n′iʃ/ and /iŋ′iʃ/ are both found. The future is *neósfaidh sé*, where GCh has *inseoidh sé.*

íntleacht: "intellect, intelligence". Pronounced /i:nt′il′əxt/.

íochtar: "the lower or more remote part". *In íochtar an tseómra*, "at the far end of the room", probably in the part of the room farthest from the hearth.

iomad: "much, too much; an exceedingly great amount", pronounced /uməd/.

iomaidh: "rivalry". *Ag iomaidh le chéile*, "vying with each other". Pronounced /umig′/.

iomarbháidh: "contention, contest", or *iomarbhá* in GCh. Pronounced /umər(ə)'vɑ:g′/.

íomhá: "image", pronounced /i:'vɑ:/. The plural found here is *íomhánna*; compare *íomhátha*, used in PUL's *Catilína* and *An Cleasaidhe.*

iomláine: "entirety", pronounced /umə'lɑ:n′i/.

iomlán: "full, whole, entire", pronounced /umə'lɑ:n/. *Go hiomlán*, "completely".

iomlascaim, iomlasc: "to roll, tumble", pronounced /umələskim′, umələsk/.

iompaím, iompáil: "to turn", or *iompaím, iompú* in GCh. Pronounced /u:m'pi:m′, u:m'pɑ:l′/.

iompraim, iompar: "to carry, bear", or *iompraím, iompar* in GCh. Pronounced /u:mpərim′, u:mpər/. *Beithíoch iompair*, "beast of burden". *Cóir iompair*, "transport, means of transport".

iomrascáil: "wrestling", pronounced /umərəskɑ:l′/.

íon: "weapon, spear, pike". *Íona fada,* "long weapons/pikes". *In íonaibh catha,* "in readiness for battle, in battle array". (*Íon* isn't listed in FGB.)

ionchas: "expection". Pronounced /unəxəs/. *Le hionchas go,* "in the expectation or likelihood that".

ionnuar: "cool", or *fionnuar* in GCh. Pronounced /u'nuər/. Spelt *ionfhuar* in the original.

iúir: "soil, earth". *San iúir,* "dead, in the grave". This word is *úir* in GCh, but the original spelling *iúir* is retained, as CFBB (p265) shows that *san iúir* is pronounced /sin′ u:r′/.

iúnadh: "wonder, surprise", or *ionadh* in GCh. Pronounced /u:nə/. This word slenderises the *n* of the article: *an iúnadh,* /in′ u:nə/ (see CFBB, p270). *Iúnadh* is consistently feminine in PUL's works, but masculine in GCh.

iúntach: "wonderful", or *iontach* in GCh. Pronounced /u:ntəx/.

iúntaoibh: "confidence, trust", or *iontaoibh* in GCh. *Iúntaoibh as duine,* "trust in someone". *Ní haon iúntaoibh tu,* "you are not to be trusted". Pronounced /u:n'ti:v′/. An apostrophe has been given in *oiread iúntaoibh'* in chapter 30 here, as the final *e* of the genitive was not given in the original text.

lá: "day", with *ló* in the dative in the phrase *de ló agus d'oíche,* "by day and by night", /də lo: gəs di:hi/. *Go minic sa ló,* "frequently/several times during the day".

labhraim, labhairt: "to speak", or *labhraím, labhairt* in GCh. Pronounced /lourim′, lourt′/.

lag: "weak". *Is lag an bheart é,* "it's a poor show; it's a poor way of going on". *Ba lag leat (a leithéid do dhéanamh),* "you would be loth to (do such a thing)".

lagachar: "weakness, faintness", pronounced /lɑgəxər~lə'gɑxər/.

láidir: "strong", with *láidre* in the comparative and plural. Pronounced /lɑ:d′ir′, lɑ:d′ir′i/.

laige: "weakness", pronounced /lig′i/.

laíghead: "smallness; fewness", or *laghad* in GCh, pronounced /li:d/ in WM Irish.

laígheadaím, laígheadú: "to lessen", or *laghdaím, laghdú* in GCh. Pronounced /li:'di:m′, li:'du:/. PUL's original spellings here, *luíghduigh* and *luigheadughadh* show the pronunciation clearly.

láimhseálaim, láimhseáil: "to handle, wield".

láithreach: "presently, without delay; present", pronounced /lɑ:r′həx/. *Láithreach bonn* /boun/, "on the spot, instantly".

lámh: "hand". Note that the nominative singular (and genitive plural) is pronounced /lɑ:v/ with the genitive singular (*lámha*) and the nominative plural (*lámha*) both pronounced /lɑ:/. PUL explained in NIWU (p70) that the genitive of this word should be *lámha* and not *láimhe,* and he generally adheres to this usage. Where, as in chapter 4 here, the original occasionally has *láimhe* for the genitive, this is edited as *lámha,* in line with PUL's stated preferences. The dative singular (*láimh*) and the dative plural (*lámhaibh*) are both pronounced /lɑ:v′/. PUL was insistent that this word had a nasal vowel, and thus was audibly distinct from *lá,* "day", but such nasalisation is not a feature of modern-day WM Irish. *Duine '* *thabhairt chun lámha*, "to capture/arrest someone, bring him to justice". *A láimh a chéile*, "in collusion, working together", also found here as *a lámhaibh a chéile. A lámhaibh a chéile* may be more likely to be used where many people are involved in the collaboration.

lámhach: "shooting", pronounced /lɑ:x/.

lann: "blade of a sword".

lánú: "married couple", or *lánúin* in GCh, where the historical dative has replaced the nominative.

laoch: "warrior, hero", with *laochra* in the plural. *Laochra* is, etymologically, a feminine collective singular, but is used as the plural of *laoch* (e.g. *laochra móra* in *Bricriu*, p1) in PUL's works. Pronounced /le:x, le:xərə/.

lár: "ground". *Ar lár*, "on the ground, laid low, fallen (as of a soldier)".

lasmu': "outside", or *lasmuigh* in GCh. Pronounced /lɑs'mu/, the spelling *lasmuich* was used in the original, probably to indicate that there is no slender *g* in this word. *Lasmu' dhe*, "apart from".

lathach: "mud, mire", with *lathaigh* in the dative. Pronounced /lɑhəx~lə'hɑx, lɑhig′/.

le: "with". Note the combination *lenúr*, or *le bhur* in GCh, pronounced /l′ə'nu:r/.

leabaidh: "bed", or *leaba* in GCh. The traditional dative has replaced the nominative in Cork Irish. Pronounced /l′abig′/. The genitive here is *leapan*, where GCh has *leapa. Scéalaíocht Amhlaoibh* (p19) shows that other speakers of the dialect, such as AÓL, also had *leapa* in the genitive.

leaca: "cheek". The dative/dual *leacain* is used here.

leagáid: "legate", spelt *legáid* in the original.

leagaim, leagadh: "to knock down, fell", or *leagaim, leagan* in GCh.

leanbaí: "childish", pronounced /l′anə'bi:/.

leanbh: "child", with *linbh* in the genitive, pronounced /l′anəv, l′in′iv′/.

léas: "ray, glimmer". *Léas meabhrach*, "a mental spark", pronounced /l′ias m′aurəx/: *níor fágadh léas meabhrach im cheann*, "my mind went blank". The pronunciation of this word contrasts with /l′e:s/ for the unrelated word *léas*, "lease", the pronunciation of which is explained by the fact that it is a loan-word.

léasaim, léasadh: "to beat, thrash".

leataoibh: *i leataoibh*, or *i leataobh* in GCh, "to one side". Pronounced /i l′a'ti:v′/. This word uses an old dative of *taobh, taoibh*, which is not often found with the noun *taobh* itself in PUL's works.

leath-lámh: "one hand", and, by extension, "a shortage of personnel". *Leath-lámh mór* was given in the original text in chapter 55, being adjusted here to *leath-lámh mhór*, on the assumption that the lack of lenition on *mór* was a typographical error.

leath: "side", with *leith* in the dative. *Rud do chur 'na leith*, "to accuse him of something". *Fé leith*, "separate, special, remarkable". *Dá mhéid leatha faoi* has the plural of this word, meaning "however extensive the territories under his control".

leathnaím, leathnú: "to spread out, widen", pronounced /l′ahə'ni:m′, l′ahə'nu:/.

leathscéal: "excuse", or *leithscéal* in GCh. Pronounced /l′a'ʃk′ial/.

leibhéalta: "level", pronounced /l′i'v′e:lhə/.

leicthe: "sickly, delicate", or *leice* in GCh. The LS version of PUL's *Mo Sgéal Féin* shows this word is just pronounced /l′ek′i/ (*Mo shgiàl fén*, p9), which matches the GCh spelling well. It may be that PUL spelt this word *leicthe* because it was originally the past participle of *leogaim* (or, more precisely, the past participle of the classical form *leigim*, with the *g* of *leigthe* devoiced by the *th*), meaning, fundamentally, "laid out", and so this word ought to have *-the* in the spelling.

leigheas: "remedy, cure", with the plural here *leighseanna*, where GCh has *leigheasanna*. Pronounced /l′əis, l′əiʃənə/.

leighim, leaghadh: "to melt, dissolve", *leáim, leá* in GCh. Pronounced /l′əim′, l′əi/. The future autonomous *leighfar*, /l′əifər/, or *leáfar* in GCh, is used here.

leighsim, leigheas: "to remedy, cure", *leigheasaim, leigheas* in GCh. Pronounced /l′əiʃim′, l′əis/.

léim, lé': "to read", or *léim, léamh* in GCh.

léimreach: "jumping", or *léimneach* in GCh. Pronounced /l′e:m′ir′əx/. *Léimreach* is a continuous act of leaping or jumping, as opposed to *léim*, the ordinary noun meaning "leaping, jumping" and *léimt*, the verbal noun meaning "leaping, jumping". *Léimreach* is a feminine verbal noun that is declined in the dative as *ag léimrigh*.

léine: "shirt". The plural used here is *léinteacha* where GCh has *léinte*, but PUL stated in NIWU (p73) that both plurals were found.

leithéid: "the like; something like it". *A leithéid seo*, "it's like this" as an introductory statement.

leitir: "letter", with *leitre* in the genitive and *leitreacha* in the plural, pronounced /l′et′ir′, l′et′ir′i, l′et′ir′əxə/. These would be *litir, litreach* and *litreacha* in GCh. In the older orthography there was a distinction between *litir*, "letter", and *leitir*, "the side of a hill", which have collapsed together in WM Irish.

leogaim, leogaint: "to let, allow", or *ligim, ligean* in GCh. PUL uses the spelling *leigim, leigint* in the original, influenced by classical norms, but the WM pronunciation is /l′ogim′, l′ogint′/. PUL's spelling varied over the years, but he used *leog* and *leogaint* in his *Don Cíochóté* (pp11, 20). *T'aigne a leogaint chun duine*, "to let someone know what you are thinking".

leómhaim: "I dare". The preterite/imperative form is *leómhaigh*, pronounced /l′o:g′/, corresponding to *leomh* in GCh. FGB lists a verbal noun *leomhadh*, but this is not attested in PUL's works, and it seems likely a verbal noun will rarely be needed.

leórghníomh: "restitution, amends" (*i rud*).

liag: "physician, healer", or *lia* in GCh. The plural is *liaga*, corresponding to *lianna* in GCh. The spellings found in the original text were *liagh, liaigh* (for the genitive singular) and *liaghaibh*. The classical forms were *liaigh* in the singular and *liagha* in the plural, but the notes to PUL's *Lúcián* show clearly that PUL had a broad *g*: "*liag* (not *liaig*,—P. O'L.), a doctor" (p176).

liath-ghorm: "steel-grey, grey-blue", pronounced /l′iə'ɣorəm/.

lín tí: "household", or *líon tí* in GCh, literally "the full number/complement of a house". This word is given as *lín-tíghe* in the original, with the *n* (potentially) slenderised in advance of the slender *t* that follows.

lín-éadach: "linen, linen cloth", the genitive of which, *lín-éadaigh*, is used adjectivally.

línn: "period", or *linn* in GCh. Note the long vowel here, /l'i:ŋ'/, whereas *linn*, "with us", has a short vowel, /l'iŋ'/.

línn: "pool", used in the sense of "harbour" here.

líon: "flax, linen". *Líon geal*, "white linen".

líth: "colour, complexion", or *lí* in GCh. *D'iompaigh a líth ann*, "he changed colour". The original text had *lith* with no long vowel indicated, but all other examples in PUL's works have *líth*, including *Séadna* (p166), and so a *síneadh fada* has been supplied in this edition.

liú: "shout". Note that *liú* is feminine in WM Irish, but masculine in GCh. *Liú fhiaigh*, "a hunter's shout, a wild cry", pronounced /l'u: iəg'/. *Liú mholta*, "a shout of praise, a cheer".

liúireach: "yelling, shouting". Note that as a feminine verbal noun, this becomes *ag liúirigh* in the dative, a distinction not observed in GCh.

Lochlannach: "Norseman, Viking".

lógóireacht: "an act of wailing or lamenting".

loilíoch: "milch cow".

loirgim, lorg: "to search, seek", or *lorgaím, lorg* in GCh. Pronounced /lor'ig'im', lorəg/. PUL replied to a query from Risteárd Pléimeann in a letter dated December 19th 1917, catalogued under G1,277 (1) in the Shán Ó Cuív papers held in the National Library of Ireland, on the pronunciation of *loirg*, stating the vowel is *o* and not *i*.

loiscim, loscadh: "to burn", with the participle *loiscithe*, where GCh has *loiscthe*.

loitim, lot: "to spoil, ruin", with the participle *loitithe*, where GCh has *loite*. Pronounced /lot'im', lot, lot'ihi/.

lom: "a chance, opportunity", pronounced /loum/.

lom: "bare", pronounced /loum/. *Lom dáiríribh*, "in dead earnest". *Lom díreach*, "directly, at once".

lómhar: "precious, brilliant (of gems)".

lón: "provisions, food". *Sáith lóin*, "enough food/sustenance".

long: "ship", with *luinge* in the genitive, *loíng* in the dative and *luingeas* in the plural. This word occurs as *an loingeas*, a collective word meaning "shipping" in GCh, but *na luingeas* is used as the plural of *long*, "ship", in WM Irish. PUL stated in NIWU (pp16, 74) "I have never heard any plural for *long* but *loingeas*" and "in some parts of the country the word is singular and means 'shipping'". The genitive plural is also *luingeas*, as in *ag déanamh luingeas*, "shipbuilding". Note the lenited adjective in *luingeas bhreátha mhóra*, as if *luingeas* were a plural noun ending in a slenderised consonant. These various forms are pronounced /lu:ŋg/, /liŋ'i/, /li:ŋg'/ and /liŋ'əs/ respectively.

longphort: "camp", or *longfort* in GCh, which appears to be an incorrect spelling. This word is believed to have originally referred to Viking ship enclosures (fortified camps where Viking ships could dock) in Ireland.

luacht saothair: "reward", or *luach saothair* in GCh. Both forms are found in PUL's works.

luaithreach: "ashes"; with *luaithrigh* in the dative. This word is stated in *Foclóir do Shéadna* (p76) to be masculine, and we read *a raibh de luaithreach* in PUL's novel *Séadna* (p257). The vocative is given in *Aithris ar Chríost* (p124): *Ꞁoghluim conus géilleadh, a luaithrigh.* The genitive is found both as *luaithrigh* (possibly calcified as such in *Céadaoin an Luaithrigh* in PUL's *Seanmóin is Trí Fichid,* Vol 1, p120) and as *luaithri* elsewhere in PUL's works (e.g. *os cionn luaithrighe na talmhan* in *Sgéalaidheachta as an mBíobla Naomhtha,* Vol 2, p12). These examples support the view this word is generally feminine in the genitive and dative cases.

luathacht: speed, especially in *dá luathacht,* "how fast". Note that this would be *dá luaithe* in GCh: *dá luaithe* is also used in WM Irish (e.g. *Séadna,* p119), but *dá luathacht* is many times more frequently encountered in PUL's works.

lúb: "loop, twist, bend". *Cor is lúb,* "twist and turn". *Cor is lúb 'na croí,* "wiles in her heart". Here *i lúib na finneóige* means "in the recess of the window".

lucht: "people". Pronounced /loxt/. *Lucht leanúna,* "followers (of the camp)".

luibh: "plant, herb", with the plural here *luíbhneacha,* where GCh has *luibheanna.* Pronounced /liv′, li:n′əxə/.

lúidín: "little finger".

luím, luí: "to lie". *Luí isteach,* "to get stuck in (to get stuck into the work)": *do luíodar isteach insna buínibh,* "they fell in line with/joined up with the troops". *Bhí (sé) ag dul 'na luí ar a n-aigne,* "they were beginning to realise".

lúireach: "breastplate; a hymn for protection". Especially in *Lúireach Phádraig,* "St. Patrick's Breastplate".

lúth-chleas: "athletic exercises".

machaire: "plain; battle". See *coímheascar.*

macshamhail: "copy", or *macasamhail* in GCh. Pronounced /mɑ'kaul′/. The entry in PUL's NIWU (p74) shows that he also accepted the form *macasamhail,* /mɑkə'saul′/, which is given in CFBB (p150). Note that *macshamhail don eochair,* "a copy of the key", spelt thus in the original, has been edited here as *macshamhail* <u>*den*</u> *eochair.*

mágh: "plain", with *mághaibh* in the dative plural in one passage here. *Bile Mór Mágha Adhair* seems to give one form of the genitive singular, although the genitive is found as *maighe* in PUL's other works (see *i gColáisde Mhaighe Nuadhat* in PUL's *Mo Sgéal Féin,* p61, transcribed on p25 of *Mo shgiàl fén* as *a Gláishdi Vy Nuat,* and *míol mhaíghe,* "hare", on p107 of *Mo Sgéal Féin,* transcribed as *míol vy* on p43 of *Mo Sghiàl Fén*). The vowel of *mágh* is generally long in the dialect—see *Magh Nuadhat,* transcribed as *Má Nuat* in the LS edition of *Mo Sgéal Féin* (*Mo shgiàl fén,* p38) and *an mágh so na h-Éamhna* in *Eisirt* (p65), transcribed as *an má so na Hâuna* in *Eshirt* (p67). Consequently, there is a long vowel in placenames such as *Mágh Adhair* and *Mágh Geirrghinn*; yet the vowel is short in *Magh Chromtha*, /mə 'xroumhə/, as shown in IWM (§148).

maidean: "morning", or *maidin* in GCh, where the historical dative has replaced the nominative.

maidrín: "little dog", pronounced /mɑd′i′r′i:n′/. *Im mhaidrín* in one passage here, "faithfully, obediently".

maighdean: "maiden, virgin", with *maighdine* in the genitive and *maighdin* in the dative. Pronounced /məid′ən, məid′in′i, məid′in′/.

maím, maíomh: "to boast" (*as rud*). *Cúis mhaíte*, "something to boast about".

mainistir: "monastery". With *mainistreach* in the genitive singular and *mainistreacha* in the nominative plural. Both *mainistreachaibh* and *mainistríbh/ mainistribh* are found here in the dative plural. Pronounced /mɑn′iʃt′ir′, mɑn′iʃt′(i)r′əx, mɑn′iʃt′(i)r′əxə, mɑn′iʃt′(i)r′əxiv′, mɑn′iʃt′ir′i:v′, mɑn′iʃt′ir′iv′/.

maíonach: "darling", or *maoineach* in GCh. *A mhaíonach*, "my dear". The vocative is not declined as this is a metaphorical use of a word originally meaning "treasured possession". The original spelling here, *a mhaoinach*, shows the *n* to be broad.

máireach: "morrow". *La-rna-mháireach*, "on the following day". Often found as *lar na mháireach* or *lá arna mháireach* [*lá* "day", *ar* "after", *n-a* "its", *mháireach* "morrow"]. Note that the *a* of *la* is pronounced short: /larnə vɑ:r′əx/.

mairg: "woe". *Is mairg a dh'fhéachfadh go dlúth in aghaidh mná*, "woe to him who would look intently in a woman's face". Pronounced /mɑr′ig′/. *Is mairg do Mh'leachlainn é*, "woe betide M'leachlainn".

mairim, maireachtaint: "to live", or *mairim, maireachtáil* in GCh. Pronounced /mɑr′im′, mə'r′axtint′/. *An dá lá 's 'n fhaid a mhairfead*, "for as long as I live".

mairineamh: "lament, elegy". This word is not given in this form in FGB, but is cognate with *mairgneach* and *marbhna* (/mɑrənə~mɑrhənə/). Various versions of *Mairineamh Phádraig*, the Lament of St. Patrick, were published by Pádraig Ua Siochfhradha as "Mairbhne Eithne Nó Mairbhne Phádraig" in *Béaloideas*, Volume 4, No. 3 (1934), pp. 264-276. The various versions there are variously entitled, including *Mairbhne Phádraig, Mairinn Phádraig, Mairneamh Phádraig, Marthain Phádhraic, Mairtheann Phádhraic, Mairbhne Áidhne.*

máirnéalach: "mariner, sailor", pronounced /mɑ:r'n′e:ləx/.

maisiúil: "beautiful, elegant, comely".

maithe: "goodness, good". *Ar mhaithe léi féin*, "bent on her own advantage". PUL explains in NIWU (p76) that the nuance is stronger than *mar mhaithe léi féin.* The latter is purely factual, whereas *ar mhaithe léi* shows clear purpose.

máithriúil: "like one's mother", pronounced /mɑ:r′'hu:l′/.

mala: "eyebrow". The dative *malainn* is used here. The plural here is *maili*, or *malaí* in GCh.

malairtím, malairtiú: "to exchange", or *malartaím, malartú* in GCh.

manach: "monk", pronounced /mə'nɑx/, with the plural *manaigh* pronounced /mɑnig′/.

Glossary

mangaireacht: "hawking, peddling". This word is believed to be ultimately derived from Old Norse, reflecting the trading role of the Vikings in early Ireland (see *Ireland before the Normans*, p106). Pronounced /maŋir′əxt/.

Maor Mór: "high steward, mormaer", a regional ruler in mediaeval Scotland. The etymology is disputed, meaning either "high steward" or "sea lord". PUL also uses the more conventional form, *mór-mhaor*.

mar a chéile: "identical, alike, just the same". *Mar a chéile i dtaobh arm*, "evenly matched in terms of arms".

mar atá: "namely, such as".

mar dhea: a phrase meaning "as if, supposedly, as it were". Probably derived from *mar bh'ea*. Pronounced /mɑr 'ja:/.

mar seo ná mar siúd: "in any case". *Níor tháinig sé mar seo ná mar siúd*, "he didn't come, whatever he did".

maraím, marú: "kill, slay". Note the preterite is *do mhairbh sé*, /vɑr′iv′/, where *mharaigh sé* would be found in GCh.

maraitheach: "deadly, lethal", or *marfach* in GCh, pronounced /mɑrəhəx/.

marbh: "dead", pronounced /mɑrəv/. This is both an adjective and a noun here. *Am mhairbh na hoíche*, "the dead of night".

marcach: "horseman, rider", pronounced /mər'kɑx/.

marcshlua: "cavalry". Pronounced /mɑrk'luə/. While PUL uses has a feminine *slua*, *marcshlua* is masculine here (as in GCh).

margadh: "bargain", pronounced /mɑrəgə/.

marthanach: "lasting, enduring, perpetual".

más fíor bréag: an sarcastic phrase meaning "I don't think!; I doubt it!; as if!", negating the previous phrase.

masla: "insult, abuse".

me: disjunctive form of the first-person pronoun, pronounced /m′e/ (or /m′i/ through the raising of the vowel in the vicinity of a nasal consonant). Always *mé* in GCh.

meáchaint: "weight", or *meáchan* in GCh.

méadaím, méadú: "to increase". Used impersonally with *ar*: *do mhéadaigh air*, "it increased".

meáim, meá: "to weigh", both in the literal sense and in the sense (found in chapter 51 here) of giving careful consideration to something. Pronounced /m′a:m′, m′a:/. *Meáigh é*, "consider it, weigh it up". It is worth noting that *meadh* (the noun, "balance, scales", /m′a/) and *meá* (the verbal noun) are both *meá* in GCh, but the former was *meadh* and the latter *meadhadh* in the older spelling.

meanmna: "good spirits, courage", or *meanma* in GCh. Pronounced /m′anəm(n)ə/. The form *meanma* is found in PUL's *Guaire* and *Bricriu*, showing that the second *n* may be omitted. In NIWU (pp77-78), PUL explains "the word includes courage and energy and spirits. It has sometimes a special signification—e.g. *m. na fáigeadóireachta* (*Sg*. IV. 384); the 'impulse' or 'influence' of the prophesying. Both the word and its meaning are well known in Irish thought, both ancient and modern. It is used to signify some sort of secret influence or 'wireless telegraphy' passing from the mind of one person to the mind of another when one or both are suffering or excited". Consequently, *meanmna ó Dhia inniu i gcroí gach fir* in chapter 54 here means "*energy infused* from God in the hearts of each man today".

méar: "finger", with *méar* in the genitive plural here too, where the weak plural *méireanna* could have stood.

mearaí: "bewilderment, distraction". See *meascán.*

mearathall: "confusion", or *mearbhall.* Pronounced /m′arəhəl/ in WM Irish.

meargach: "rusty-looking, crusty or irritable person", or *meirgeach* in GCh. While FGB cross-references *meargach* to *meirgeach,* implying the one word is a variant of the other, they are listed as separate words in PSD, with *meargach* meaning "wrinkled, creased", and *meirgeach* "rusty, freckled, pockmarked". PUL calls a blacksmith *Meargach* here, but uses *meirgeach* as an adjective later in the book. Pronounced /m′arəgəx/.

measa: "worse", the irregular comparative of *olc. Is measa liom,* "I prefer" or "I am concerned about": *is measa liom a lúidín ná dá n-imíodh sé siúd le fánaidh na habhann,* "I care more about his little finger than if that man fell into the river".

measaim, meas: "to estimate, judge". *Rud a mheas do dhuine,* "to think or expect something of someone". *Ní dócha gurb amhlaidh a mheasfá dhom gan mo dhícheall a dhéanamh,* "you probably wouldn't have expected me not to do my best".

meascaim, meascadh: "to mix". The past participle here is *meascaithe,* where GCh has *measctha.*

meascán: "muddle". *Meascán mearaí,* "bewilderment".

meata: "craven, cowardly".

méid: "amount". *Méid* resists lenition in PUL's works where the meaning is "amount", not "size": *sa méid sin,* "that, all that, that much, etc"; *tar éis an méid úd cainnte,* "after all that talk". PUL commented on this word in a letter to Risteárd Pléimeann dated November 29th 1917 and held in the G1,277 (1) collection of manuscripts in the National Library of Ireland: "*An mhéid* = 'the bigness' or 'the size', where *méid* is a definite thing. *An méid seo* = 'this much' or 'thus much', where *méid* expresses, not 'size' in itself, but the amount or degree of magnitude in something". However, *dá mhéid,* "however much", does have lenition. *Don mhéid a bhí beó dhíobh* in the original text of chapter 57 was adjusted here to *don méid.*

méinn: "mind, disposition", or *méin* in GCh. Pronounced /m′e:ŋ′/.

meirgeach: "pitted, pockmarked; irritable", pronounced /m′er′ig′əx/. See *meargach.*

méisín: "little plate".

meón: "disposition, temperament".

mí-fhoirtiún: "bad luck, misfortune", pronounced /m′iər′t′u:n/. This would be *mífhortún* in GCh.

mí: "month". This word is masculine in WM Irish, with the genitive also *mí.* The word is feminine in GCh with the genitive *míosa. Mí teástála,* "trial month", would be *mí tástála* in GCh.

mian: "desire, wish". IWM (§290) states this word is pronounced /m′ian/, in other words, without the /iə/ diphthong that the spelling might have indicated. The pronunciation given in IWM would suit a spelling of *méan.*

mileata: "martial, warlike", or *míleata* in GCh. This word is generally given with a short *i* in the original. The single case, in chapter 46, of *míleata* has been adjusted to *mileata* here. The explanation is given in the glossary to PUL's *An Cleasaidhe,* likely to have been compiled by Eleanor Knott: it is stated there that *mile,* "warrior", derives from an older *míle,* but "the word has apparently become confused with *bile,* 'forest tree', used poetically of a hero" (see p94 in that work). Yet where *mileata,* with no long vowel marked, is found in *Eisirt* (e.g. p5), Osborn Bergin transcribes this in *Eshirt* as *míleata* (p5).

míllteach: "destructive, pernicious, baleful", pronounced /m′i:l′həx/. Also often pronounced /m′e:l′həx/ according to NIWU (p79).

mineál: "neck". PUL had *muineál* in the original text of *Niamh,* but CFBB (p272) shows this word has a slender *m.* The slender *m* is also shown in LS editions of PUL's works (see *Shiàna,* p28).

minic: "often". Note the comparative here, *minici,* where GCh has *minice.*

míogarnach: "dozing off".

mion-duine: "a minor person", pronounced /m′undin′i/. Usually plural, with *mion-daoine* meaning "women and children; non-combatants".

mion-órd: "minor order". Note the plural *mion-úird,* "minor orders of clergy" (the orders below subdeacon, traditionally comprising acolytes, exorcists, lectors and porters), or *mionoird* in GCh. Pronounced /m′un'u:rd′/ in the plural.

míorúilt: "miracle", pronounced /m′i:'ru:hl′/.

mioscais: "malice, ill-will".

mísleán: "sweet", or *milseán* in GCh. Pronounced /m′i:ʃl′ɑ:n/.

misneach: "courage", pronounced /m′iʃn′ɑx/.

miste: "all the worse". This is a 'second comparative' form, similar to *feárr-de, usa-de, déine-de,* meaning "all the more X for it". *Ní miste dhom,* "I may as well". *Ar mhiste dhom?,* "might I?" *Ní miste a rá (go),* "you can bet your life, you can be sure, you may as well say (that)". *Ní miste gnó ' thabhairt do bheirt agaibh le déanamh* in chapter 43 has a sarcastic nuance, "what a great help you two were!"

miteal: "metal", or *miotal* in GCh. The genitive, *mitil,* is used with adjectival force.

mithid: "high time". *Is mithid duit é,* "it is high time for you (to do something)".

móide: "all the more, all the greater". This is a 'second comparative' form, similar to *feárr-de, usa-de, miste,* meaning "all the more X for it".

molt: "wether, castrated male sheep", pronounced /mohl/.

mór le rá: "important, significant". The comparative is *níos mó le rá.*

mór-chath: "great battle".

mór-iarracht: "great attempt". *D'aon mhór-iarracht amháin,* "in one big go".

mór-is-fiú: "self-esteem, self-regard, pride". This phrase is regularly hyphenated in PUL's works. Pronounced /'muərəs'f′u:/.

mór-mhaor: see under *Maor Mór.*

mór-shlua: "multitude", pronounced /muər'hluə/. This word is feminine here, but masculine in GCh.

mór: "big, large". This is pronounced /muər/ but as a common word has been left in its accepted spelling. *Is mór idir thu agus Brian, dá olcas é!*, "there is a big difference between you and Brian, however bad he is!" *Níor mhór di é*, "she had to do it".

móráil: "pride, vanity", pronounced /muə'rɑ:l'/.

mórálach: "proud; delighted", pronounced /muə'rɑ:ləx/.

mórán: "many". Usually pronounced /muə'rɑ:n/.

mórgacht: "majesty, magnificence, pomp", pronounced /muərgəxt/.

mórthímpall: "circuit; all around", or *mórthimpeall* in GCh. The broad *p* in WM Irish is preserved here: /muər'hi:m'pəl/. This is sometimes found as *mór-dtímpall* in the Irish of other writers of WM Irish.

mothaím, mothú: "to sense, feel, perceive", but often used to mean something close to "to realise". *Sara mothódh an namhaid go raibh an gnó á dhéanamh*, "before the enemy realised the thing was being done".

muin: "the upper back; the shoulders and neck". *Ar muin*, "on top of/riding", e.g. an animal. See under *bruach* for discussion of generic adverbial phrases such as *ar muin*.

muínteartha: "friendly, familiar", pronounced /mi:ntərhə/. *Daoine muínteartha*, means "relatives" or "friends"—and not just "relatives"—according to PUL's comments in NIWU (p81).

muíntearthas: "friendliness", or *muintearas* in GCh.

muiríon: "encumbrance", generally meaning "family", or *muirín* in GCh. This word is masculine (*an muiríon óg*). *Muiríon mo dhá lámh féin inti*, "as much as I could lift with both hands".

mullach: "summit", pronounced /mə'lɑx/. *Ar mhullach mo chínn sa lathaigh*, "with my head down in the mud".

mura: "if not, unless". *Mura* and *mara* are found in PUL's works, where GCh has *muna*. PUL uses h-prefixation here when *mura* is combined with the copula before a vowel: *mura héagóir*, "if it be no injustice". The concessive use of *mura* in *murar thárla, do thárla go* in *níor thárla an chainnt sin ná aon chainnt dá sórd, idir Bholingbroke agus Risteárd. Murar thárla, do thárla gur thóg Bolingbroke chuige ríocht Shasana, agus gur chuir sé Risteárd chun báis* can be translated "what did happen was that..."

músclaim, múiscilt: "to stir, arouse", or *músclaím, múscailt* in GCh. The present tense is found in PUL's works with a broad *sg* (*músglan sé* in *Mo Sgéal Féin*, p97), whereas the verbal noun is found invariably in PUL's works as *múisgilt*. The preterite is attested here is *do mhúisgil* (edited in this edition as *do mhúiscil*), where GCh would have *mhúscail*. The conditional tense is given here as *mhúisgileóchadh* (edited here as *mhúiscleódh*) where GCh has *mhúsclódh*. Pronounced /mu:skəlim', mu:ʃk'ihl'/.

mustairt: "white worsted".

nách: the negative subordinating or relative particle, or *nach* in GCh. Pronounced /nɑ:x/.

náire: "shame". This word, which is feminine in GCh, is found in both genders in PUL's works, and is masculine in *i dtaobh an náire a bhí uirthi* in chapter 31 here. Compare *an náire céadna* in *Táin Bó Cuailgne* (p133), and *an náire chéadna* in *Sgéalaidheacht na Macabéach* (Vol 1, p136).

namhaid: "enemy", pronounced /naud′/. Traditionally *námha*, the dative has replaced the historical nominative. *Namhaid* is also used in the plural (see *a namhaid go léir* in chapter 4 here), where *naimhde* would stand in GCh. With nominative singular and plural both *namhaid* and genitive singular and plural both *namhad*, it is only morphologically apparent when the plural is being used with the dative plural, *namhdaibh. A lár an namhad* in Ch55 shows this noun to be masculine.

naoi: "nine", pronounced /ne:/.

néal: "cloud", but also "mad rage". *Néal chun cogaidh i Lochlannachaibh na hÉireann* means "a mad rage for war among the Norse of Ireland" in chapter 43. *Néal codlata*, "a wink of sleep".

neamh-chorrabhuaiseach: "nonchalant, unperturbed", pronounced /'n′axorə -'vuəʃəx/.

neamh-eaglach: "fearless", pronounced /n′avɑgələx/.

neamh-ghus: "want of substance, flimsiness". Pronounced /n′aɣəs/.

neamh-iontach: "unconcerned, cool", pronounced /n′a'v′u:ntəx/.

neamh-thuairimeach: "light, casual". Pronounced /n′a'huər′im′əx/.

neamh-thuisceanach: "uncomprehending". Pronounced /n′a'hiʃk′ənəx/.

neamh-urramach: "disrespectful, insulting".

neart: "strength", but also used here for "forces" in the military sense.

neartaím, neartú: "to strengthen". Used impersonally with *ar*: *do neartaigh air*, "it strengthened".

neómat: "minute, moment", or *nóiméad* in GCh. The various words for "minute" in Irish are all corruptions of the original *móimeint*. Hence *nóiméad* is no more correct than *neómat*.

ní: "thing". *Is mórán nithe dhúinn é*, "it matters a great deal to us".

nimh: "poison". Note that this word is masculine here (with *an nímhe* in the genitive), but feminine in GCh. Compare *nimh dhearg* in Scéalaíocht Amhlaoibh (p169). The nominative is pronounced /n′iv′/, and the genitive, *nímhe*, /n′i:/.

nímhneach: "venomous, deadly", pronounced /n′i:n′əx/.

níos: "more". The form *níosa*, which lenites, is also found here. PUL claimed in NIWU (p82) that the use of *níosa* implied a progressive increase (*tá sé níos measa*, "it is worse"; *tá sé níosa mheasa*, "it has become worse"), but it does not always appear to carry this extra nuance (see for example the usage in the closing passage of chapter 33).

Nórmánach: "Norman; from Normandy", or *Normannach* in GCh. There may not have been an established form of this word in WM Irish, with *Nórmánach* being produced on an *ad hoc* basis here.

nós: "custom, manner", with *nósa* in the plural where GCh has *nósanna.*

nósmhaireacht: "civility, the customs of civilised life". This word is listed in FGB as meaning "customariness, formality, politeness". According to the glossary of words at the back of the 1910 edition of *Niamh*, this word means "civilisation". This word appears to be used in both meanings in the text of *Niamh* here.

nú: "or", or *nó* in GCh, pronounced /nu:/.

nua: "new", pronounced /no:/.

nuacht: "news", pronounced /no:xt/.

ó chiainibh: "just now", or *ó chianaibh* in GCh. Pronounced with a slender *n* in WM Irish, /o: x'iən'iv'/, which pronunciation was indicated in the original text of *Niamh.*

ó: "from". *Uathu féin*, "of their own accord". *Do chíodh sí uaithi*, "she saw in the distance (over from her)".

obair: "work", with *oibre* in the genitive and *oibreachaibh* in the dative plural here. Pronounced /obir', eb'ir'i, eb'ir'əxiv'/. *An obair* sometimes has the sense of "the real work" or "the real problem": *ansan is ea do chonacthas an obair*, "that was when they really got stuck in". *A leithéid d'obair*, "such a carry-on!".

obann: "sudden", or *tobann* in GCh.

ocras: "hunger", pronounced /okərəs/.

odhar: "dun-hued, khaki-coloured". Pronounced /our/. *Folt odhar*, "light-brown hair".

oibrím, oibriú: "to put to work, operate". Pronounced /eb'i'r'i:m', eb'i'r'u:/. CFBB (p270) indicates that *ag oibriú* is generally /ig' eb'i'r'u:/, although /əg ob'i'r'u:/ is also found. *Cómhachta ifrinn is iad atá dhá n-oibriú féin 'nár gcoinnibh*, "it is the powers of hell that are manipulating them against us". *Oibríodar an tua agus an tsleagh*, "they applied/put to use the axe and the spear". *Oibriú* is not a general Irish equivalent of the English "to work": in undated notes on Irish written for Shán Ó Cuív and included in the G1,276 manuscript collection held in the National Library of Ireland, PUL wrote "*ag oibiriúghadh* is not used for 'working', except in the case of a physic". This point is slightly overstated, as *oibriú* can be found in dialectal literature in the meaning of "to work".

oide: "tutor, teacher", pronounced /id'i/.

óig-bhean: "young woman", or *ógbhean* in GCh. The *g* is slender, /o:g'v'an/.

óig-fhear: "young man", or *ógfhear* in GCh. Pronounced /o:g'ar/.

óinseach: "a foolish woman", with *óinsigh* in the dative.

oiread: "amount", pronounced /ir'əd/. In the meaning of "as much as", generally found without the article: *oiread nirt agus d'fhéadadar*, "as many troops as they could".

óirnim, óirneadh: "to ordain", or *oirním, oirniú* in GCh. Pronounced /o:rn'im', o:rn'i/. The form *órdnuighthe* found in PUL's *Aithris ar Chríost* (p7) indicates that his usage varied between *óirnim* and *órnaím. Do hóirdneadh Donncha mac Briain in' Árdrí ar Éirinn* shows the meaning extends to the consecration of a monarch. PUL's NIWU (p84) has an entry on a form of this word: "*óirdniú*, the act of solemnly ordaining or consecrating a king". Compare the following referring to ordination as a priest in PUL's *Mo Sgéal Féin* (p106): *go dtí gur cuireadh fé ghrád sagairt mé.*

olagón: "wailing, lament". *Olagón a chasadh,* "to raise or begin a lament; to lament aloud".

olann: "wool", with *olla* in the genitive.

ollamh: "ready", or *ullamh* in GCh. Pronounced /oləv/. The original spelling here was *ollamh.*

ollmhaím, ollmhú: "to prepare", or *ullmhaím, ullmhú* in GCh. Pronounced /o'li:m', o'lu:/ in WM Irish.

ollmhúchán: "preparation", or *ullmhúchán* in GCh. Pronounced /o'lu:xɑ:n/.

onórach/onóireach: "honourable, honoured". Both forms were found in the original; GCh has *onórach,* which is also found in AÓL's Irish.

órd: "order", with *úird* in the plural. These would be *ord* and *oird* in GCh, but the pronunciation is /o:rd, u:rd'/. *Órd beannaithe,* "the sacrament of Holy Orders; ordination".

órd: "sledgehammer".

órdúchán: "act of giving orders".

órlach: "inch". *Sé hórla,* "six inches". Note that the plural of *órlach,* "inch", is *órlaí,* but *órla* is the plural used with numerals. *Sé hórla* found here corresponds to *sé horlaí* in GCh.

os cionn: "above". Pronounced /ɑʃ k'u:n/. Gerald O'Nolan commented in his *Studies in Modern Irish Part I* that the preposition *os* is "mostly pronounced *as,* except in *ós árd, ós íseal*" (p171).

os cómhair: "in front of". Pronounced /ɑs ko:r'/. See the comment on pronunciation under *os cionn.*

oscailte: "open", pronounced /oskil'hi/.

oscailteacht: "openness, open-heartedness".

oscall: "armpit", with the dative singular *oscaill. Fén' oscaill,* "under his arm". Note the nominative/dative distinction is not observed in GCh, where the word appears as *ascaill.*

osclaim, oscailt: "to open", or *osclaím, oscailt* in GCh. Pronounced /oskəlim', oskil'h/.

oth: found in the phrase *is oth liom,* "I regret".

othar: "patient, invalid".

págánach: "pagan". This is both an adjective and a noun in PUL's Irish; GCh has *págánach* for the noun and *págánta* for the adjective.

págánacht: "paganism", or *págántacht* in GCh. *An Phágánacht* is also used as a collective noun here, "heathenry; the entire forces of pagandom".

paidir: "prayer", with *paidre* in the genitive and *paidreacha* in the plural, pronounced /pɑd'ir', pɑd'ir'i, pɑd'ir'əxə/. *An Phaidir,* "the Lord's Prayer, the Paternoster".

páirteach: "participating". *Páirteach i rud,* "taking part in something".

paor: "grudge".

Pápa (an Pápa): "the Pope".

Glossary

pas: "a bit". *Pas beag*, "a little bit".

pé: "whichever, whoever, etc". *Pé* combines with the copula to produce *pé hé féin* in the present and *pérbh é féin* in the past.

pearsa: "person", but often by extension "appearance, features, bearing". *Pearsa* is ultimately derived, as with cognates in all European languages, from the ancient Etruscan *phersu*, "face mask". The genitive and dative here are *pearsan* and *pearsain* respectively.

peidléir: "peddlar", pronounced /p′e'dl′e:r′/.

péirse: "perch, rod", a unit of measurement. The Irish perch, at 21 ft, was longer than the English equivalent (16½ ft).

peocu: "whether", from *pé acu*, or *pé'cu*. Pronounced /p′ukə/. Often followed by a relative clause. Gerald O'Nolan explained in his *Studies in Modern Irish Part 1* the difference between *ceocu* and *peocu* (see p76). *Ceocu* is used with substantival clauses (*ní fheadar ceocu ' thiocfaidh sé nú ná tiocfaidh*), whereas *peocu* is used with adverbial clauses (*peocu ' thiocfaidh sé nú ná tiocfaidh, fanfad-sa*).

píopa: "pipe or butt", a measure of wine equivalent to 105 imperial gallons.

píoparnach: "piping, wheezing; the ringing of a harsh sound".

piseóg: "charm, spell", and in the plural, *piseóga*, "witchcraft, sorcery".

plaoiscín: the diminutive of *plaosc*, "skull", the WM form corresponding to the GCh *blaosc*. While *plaosc* has /e:/, the pronunciation of the diminutive is with /i:/ (i.e. /pli:ʃ′k′i:n′/).

poiblí: "public". Pronounced /pob′i'l′i:/.

poiblíocht: "public", as a noun. Pronounced /pob′i'l′i:xt/.

póirse: "porch, passage, corridor".

port: "port, bank", with *puirt* in the plural. *Baile puirt*, "a port town".

portach: "bog", pronounced /pər'tɑx/.

práinn: "hurry, rush, urgency". The glossary to the 1910 edition shows the meaning of this word extends to "mental stress from any kind of emotion".

praiseach: "porridge", pronounced /pri'ʃax~pir'ʃax/. *Bheadh gnó na hÉireann 'na phraisigh*, "Ireland would be in a right state".

prás: "brass".

preab: "start, bound", with *preib* in the dative. *De phreib*, "suddenly, with a bound" (found as *do phreib* in the original text).

priúnsa: "prince", or *prionsa* in GCh.

puball: "tent, pavilion". PUL states under *cábán* in NIWU that "the word *pubal* is not in the living speech" (p16).

púicín: "blindfold, mask; camouflage, deceit".

púnc: "a point", or *ponc* in GCh. Pronounced /pu:ŋk/. *Púnc dlí*, "a point of law".

puth: "puff, whiff".

rabairne: "extravagance, wealth".

raca: "comb".

radharc: "view, sight", pronounced /rəirk/.

rafar: "prosperous, fruitful".

ráfla: "rumour", pronounced /rɑ:fələ/.

rámhann: "spade", or *rámhainn* in GCh, where the historical dative is used. The only form of this word found here is the plural, *rámhainni* (spelt *ráinni* in the original text here). Pronounced /rɑ:n, rɑ:'ŋ'i:/. PUL commented on this word in NIWU (p87): "*rán*, a spade. The word is pronounced with a resounding nasal ring; hence it is often spelled *ramhan*".

ramhar: "fat", pronounced /raur/. It is worth pointing out that a distinction is made in the original text of *Niamh* between *ramhar* and *reamhar*. We read *trí mhíle bó ann de bhuaibh ramhara* (edited here as *ramhra*), but *trí chéad bó reamhar*. As a nominative singular, *bó* would lenite an adjective, thus producing *bó r(e)amhar*, pronounced /bo: r'aur/ by those native speakers who slenderised an *r* in leniting context. Here *bó* is genitive plural, which ought not to cause lenition of an adjective in the genitive plural, but clearly the phrase is influenced by the nominative singular. This is edited here as *trí chéad bó ramhar*.

raon: "range".

rás: "race", with the plural here *rásanna*, where *rásai* stands in GCh. A strong genitive plural, *rás*, is used here.

rástálaim, rástáil: "to stride, race", or *rásálaim, rásáil* in GCh.

ré: "interval, period". *Gach aon ré sholais*, "every minute of the day".

réabadh-reilige: "sacrilege, violation of a graveyard", pronounced /re:bə-rel'ig'i~ril'ig'i/. The spelling *raobadh-roilge* was used in the original text of *Niamh*.

réasún: "reason", pronounced /re:'su:n/. See under *cleas*.

réasúnta: "reasonable", pronounced /re:'su:ntə/.

réidh: "moorland, heather plain", or *ré* in GCh. Note the plural *réithe* here, in contradistinction to *réite* in GCh.

réidh: "smooth, even", with the comparative *ré* (spelt *réidhe* in GCh). Pronounced /re:g', re:/. *Go réidh*, "slowly, calmly, carefully".

réir: *de réir*, "according to", found as *do réir* in the original. This is pronounced /də re:r'/ in WM Irish, or /dr'e:r'/ when the words are run together.

rí-dhamhna: "heir to the throne", pronounced /ri:'ɣaunə/. Note that *damhna* means "matter, material", and so *rí-dhamhna* literally means "the material for a future king, the makings of a king".

rí-theaghlach: "royal household".

rí: "king". Note that *a rí!* was used as a term of address, not just for a king, but for noblemen too, as shown in *Niamh*. It is noted in IWM (§404) that *rí* retains its broad *r* in AÓL's Irish even after the vocative particle. Note PUL's use of *ríthe*, rather than *rithe* or *rite*, in the plural. Both *ríghthe* and *righthe* (and *ríghthibh* and *righthibh* in the dative plural) are found in PUL's printed works—although *ríghthe* and *ríghthibh* are used consistently in the original text of *Niamh*, and consequently these forms are edited as *ríthe* and *ríthibh* respectively in this edition. The various transcriptions used in the LS editions of PUL's works support the view that Osborn Bergin came to believe that there should be a short vowel in the dative plural (*ruíhi* vs. *ruihiv*; see p2 of the LS transcription of *Catilína*). In earlier works this principle was not adhered to: the LS edition of

Aesop a Tháinig go h-Éirinn, produced by Osborn Bergin in 1911, has *do ríhiv* (*Ésop*, p4), while *Eshirt* has *féna ruíhiv* (p32). *Rí cúige*, "provincial king", reflecting the division of ancient Ireland into small kingdoms, with a loose high kingship nominally over them.

riail: "rule, regulation", with *rial* in the genitive plural here. PUL generally uses *riail*, the historical dative, as the nominative of this word; the original nominative *riaghal* explains the occurrence of *rial* in the genitive plural.

rialta: "regular", but found in *bean rialta*, "nun". Pronounced /riəlhə/.

rialtas: "government". Note the plural *rialtaisí*, in contradistinction to the form used in GCh, *rialtais*. Pronounced /riəltəs/, with no medial /lh/, as this is a word revived in modern times and not fully aligned with the phonology of the traditional dialect.

riamh: "ever, never". *An uile dhuine riamh acu*, "every last one of them".

rian: "trace, sign, mark". *Fear cínn riain*, "leader, captain".

riaraim, riar/riaradh: "to arrange; distribute, allocate; administer", along with many other meanings. PUL uses here both the verbal noun *riar* found in GCh and a variant, *riaradh*. *Riar na sló*, "marshalling the forces, marshalling the army".

riasc: "marsh, bogland".

ríghe: "kingship, sovereignty". Note this is a rare, literary word, pronounced the same as the related noun, *rí*. PUL commented on this word in NIWU (p88): "*ríghe*, the function of government. *Rígheacht* is the object upon which that function is exercised. In modern speech *rígheacht* has come to be used in both senses".

ríghin: "slow", pronounced /ri:n'/.

ríghneas: "slowness, delay". Pronounced /ri:n'əs/.

rínn: "tip", with *reanna* in the plural. Pronounced /ri:ŋ', rɑnə/.

riocht: "guise". *I riocht*, "looking like, appearing on the verge of something, ready to": *i riocht titim*, "about to faint, looking as if you're about to faint". *I reachtaibh* is also found here with the same meaning. The original text of *Niamh* had *i rachtaibh*, reflecting the way in which an initial *r*, written slender, is generally broad in pronunciation. *Ceilt a chur air féin 'na lán de riochtaibh*, "to disguise himself in a number of ways", where a variant dative plural is used. *'Na riocht féin*, "back to his old appearance". *Sa riocht 'na raibh an chailís sin cúmtha*, "in the state in which that chalice had been made".

ríogan: "queen, princess, noble lady", or *ríon* in GCh. Pronounced /ri:gən/, with *ríogain* in the dative. Note that *a ríogan!* was a term of address, not just for a queen, but for noblewomen too, as shown in *Niamh*. Note *ríogana* in the plural.

ríogra: a collective word for "royalty, kings", or *ríora* in GCh. Pronounced /ri:gərə/.

rithim, rith: "to run". Impersonally, *ritheann leis*, "he succeeds". The original spelling often shows the quality of the *r*: in lenitable contexts, such as *do rith sé*, a slender *r* is shown; in non-lenitable contexts such as *ag ruith* (edited here as *ag rith*), a broad *r* is shown.

robálaim, robáil: "to rob".

roim ré: "in advance, beforehand". Pronounced /rim′ r′e:/.

roim: "before", or *roimh* in GCh, pronounced /rim′/. *Roime* is also found occasionally in this work. With the third-person pronoun, this becomes *roimis*, "before him" and *roimis sin*, "before that". *Roimis* is also the form used with the definite article. With the third-person possessive, this becomes *roimena*, "before her", /rim′inə/.

roinnt: "a share; some". Pronounced /rəint′/ in WM Irish. PUL does not use lenition after *roinnt* (see for example *roinnt ceisteanna* in chapter 14); AÓL had lenition in such cases (see *roint bhlianta* in *Scéalaíocht Amhlaoibh*, p20). PUL regularly spelt *roinnt* as *raint.*

Rómhánach: "Roman".

rosc: "rhapsodical chant, dithyramb". *Rosc catha,* "war cry; battle-chant".

roth: "wheel", with *rothanna* in the plural here, where GCh has *rothaí.*

ruag: "rout", or *ruaig* in GCh, where the historical dative has replaced the nominative.

ruagairt: "rout, expulsion". This word is cross-referenced to *ruaigeadh* in FGB, which therefore does service for both *ruagairt* and the verbal noun *ruagadh* in GCh.

ruaigim, ruagadh: "to expel, drive out", or *ruaigim, ruaigeadh* in GCh.

rud: "thing", pronounced /rod/. *Ba dhó' liom gurb in rud agus gur cheart d'fhearaibh Éireann féachaint chuige in am,* "I think that that is something the men of Ireland ought to attend to in time". *Dhein sé rud orthu,* "he did as he was told".

rún: "secret". *Fé rún,* "as a secret", pronounced /f′e: r′u:n/, as indicated by the original spelling here, *fé riún.*

sacraistí: "sacristy", an Anglophone word used by PUL.

saghas: "sort, type", pronounced /səis/. *Cad é an saghas í,* "what sort of person she was".

saibhreas: "wealth", pronounced /sev′ir′əs/.

saíghead: "arrow". This word is generally masculine here and in PUL's other works, whereas *saighead* is feminine in GCh. A dative *saíghid* is used in one passage here, reflecting the feminine usage, but *saíghead* is used in the dative elsewhere here. Pronounced /si:d/.

sáim, sá: "to thrust, plunge".

sáith: "sufficiency". *Sáith lóin,* "a sufficiency of provisions" and therefore "sustenance, food".

saithe: "swarm; multitude". Note this word is masculine here, but feminine in GCh. This word was spelt *satha* in the original text, showing the pronunciation /sɑhə/. However, the standard spelling of this word produces the same pronunciation, and so has been used in the editing here.

salach: "dirty", pronounced /slɑx/.

salachar: "dirt, waste", pronounced /slɑxər/.

san, sin: "that". *Air-sean* and *aige-sean* were found in the original. The normal WM forms *air sin* and *aige sin* have been used in the editing here.

saoirseacht: "craftsmanship, masonry".

saol: "life, world". The original spelling was *saoghal*, but the mid-20th century spelling change has introduced inconsistencies: the genitive is spelt *saoil* in GCh, which would give the wrong WM pronunciation, and so is edited as *saeil* here.
saolta: "worldly". *Do mheabhair shaolta*, "your normal state of mind, your wits".
saor-chead: "full permission".
saor: "craftsman, mason".
saoráideach: "easy", pronounced /səi'rɑ:d'əx/.
saothraím, saothrú: "to labour, cultivate". *An talamh a shaothrú*, "to till the soil". Pronounced /se:r'hi:m', se:r'hu:/.
sara: "before", or *sula* in GCh. Similarly, *sarar* is used in the past tense, where *sular* is found in GCh.
scáil: "shadow", but also "reflection, gleam". *Tháinig leis an gceárdaí scáil gnaoi éigin do chur san aghaidh*, "the craftsman managed to put some brightness of countenance into the face".
scairt: "entrails". By extension, "the nerve, 'the balls' to do something".
scannradh: "terror", or *scanradh* in GCh, pronounced /skaurə/ in WM.
scaraim, scarúint: "to part, separate", or *scaraim, scaradh* in GCh.
scárd: "terror, frightened look". The form used here, *scárd*, accords well with the *scard* used in GCh, but *scáird* is also found in the nominative, for example, in PUL's *Séadna* (p29).
scartálaim, scartáil: "to break up, scatter, demolish", or *cartaim, cartadh* in GCh. In NIWU (p96), PUL glosses this word as "to sack, plunder; primarily, the act of pulling the roof off a house". Note the verbal adjective *scartálta*, "broken up, scattered, demolished", pronounced /skər'tɑ:lhə/; the GCh equivalent is *carta*.
scáth: "shadow, veil". *Ar scáth*, "under the pretence (of); under the cover/veil of".
scáthúlacht: "nervousness, timidity", or *scáfaireacht* in GCh.
sceartaim, sceartadh: "to burst", or *scairtim, scairteadh* in GCh. Note that PUL's *Séadna* uses conjugated forms of both *sceartaim* and *scairtim* (compare pages 9 and 28 therein). *Sceartadh ar gháirí/ar gháiríbh*, "to burst out laughing". *Sceartadh gáire*, "a burst of laughter".
scéim, scéith: "to inform on", or *sceithim, sceitheadh* in GCh. Pronounced /ʃk'e:m', ʃk'e:(h)/, with the preterite *scéigh* (equivalent to *sceith* in GCh) pronounced /ʃk'e:g'/. *Scéim ar dhuine*, "I inform on someone".
scéimh: "facial beauty, appearance". The historical dative is used in the nominative here, which usage is also adopted in GCh; cf. PUL's novel *Séadna* (p60), which uses *sgiamh* in the nominative.
sceinnim, sceinnt: "to spring", used here of a button springing off a cloak.
sceón: "terror", or *scéin* in GCh.
scian: "knife", with *sciain* in the dative.
sciath: "shield".
sciathóg: "a shield-shaped wickerwork potato basket".
sciobaim, sciobadh: "to snatch".
sciomraim, sciomar: "to scour, scrub", or *scriomraím, sciomradh* in GCh. Pronounced /ʃk'umərim', ʃk'umər/.

scoil: "school". Interestingly, the dative plural, usually *scoileannaibh*, also appears as *scolaibh* in this work. *Scolaibh* appears to have been derived from a variant plural, *scola*, which is given in PSD.

scoilim, scoltadh: "to burst, split, break apart, cleave", or *scoiltim, scoilteadh* in GCh. This is often spelt without the historical *t* (*sgoiltim*), suggesting the pronunciation is /skol′him′~skol′im′, skolhə/. *Do scoilfeadh sé air*, "he would burst it out/reveal it", or literally "it would burst on him". The past participle is *scoilte*, /skol′hi/.

scólaim, scóladh: "to scald, torment". *Go loiscithe scólta 'na gcroí agus 'na n-aigne*, "tormented in their hearts and minds".

scoláirthe: "scholar". PUL uses the dative plural *sgoláirthíbh* (here edited as *scoláirthíbh*) in this work, but *sgoláiri* is found in some of PUL's other works, including *Mo Sgéal Féin* (p59). According to AÓL in *Seanachas Amhlaoibh Í Luínse* (p137), this word (both singular and plural) should have a *th* in it. Consequently, the pronunciation is /sklɑːr′hi, sklɑː'r′hiː/.

screadach: "screaming, shrieking", pronounced /ʃkr′ə'dɑx/.

scríbhinn: "writing". Pronounced /ʃkr′iːv′iŋ′/.

scrím, scrí': "to write", or *scríobhaim, scríobh* in GCh. All forms of this word are spelt here according to the pronunciation, eg *do scríodar* for *do scríobhadar*. The preterite has a slender *v* in the singular: *do scríbh*, /ʃkr′iːv′/. In an undated letter to Shán Ó Cuív held in the National Library of Ireland in the G1,276 collection of manuscripts, PUL wrote "what I heard was *do sgríbh*. In Waterford they say *do sgrĭgh*, short". PUL used the classical spellings *sgríobh, sgríobhadar* in the original. The past participle here is *scríofa*, where some other writers of Munster Irish have *scrite*.

scríob: "a scrape".

scriosaim, scrios: "to annihilate, blot out", or *scriosaim, scriosadh* in GCh.

scrúdaim, scrúdadh: "to examine", or *scrúdaím, scrúdú* in GCh. PUL uses *scrúdadh* here as the verbal noun (implying a first-conjugation *scrúdaim*) and *scrúdú* in some of his other works. *Aithris ar Chríost* has both *sgrúdann* (p192) and *sgrúdóchthar* (i.e. *scrúdófar*, p184). PUL's *Sgéalaidheacht na Macabéach* has *sgrúduigh sé* (Vol 2, p211).

scuab-bhuille: "sweeping blow".

scuirim, scor: "to break up", used here of breaking up camp. FGB has *scoirim, scor*, but PUL's original spelling here was *do sguireadh*, showing the pronunciation of the vowel in the first syllable.

seabhcaí: "hawk-like", or *seabhcúil* in GCh. Pronounced /ʃau'kiː/.

seachnaim, seachnadh/seachaint: "to avoid", or *seachnaím, seachaint* in GCh. Note that both *seachaint* and the older verbal noun, *seachnadh*, are found in *Niamh*. Pronounced /ʃaxənim′, ʃaxənə~ʃaxint′/.

seacht: "seven", used as an intensifier in *ní ba sheacht ndéine*, literally, "seven times harder".

sealbhaím, sealbhú: "to possess, gain possession of". Pronounced /ʃalə'viːm′, ʃalə'vuː/.

seamróg: "shamrock", pronounced /ʃamə'ro:g/. *Beidh an tseamróg ag an té a gheóbhaidh amach as mo láimh-se airís í!*, "it'll be a lucky man who manages to get it out of my hands again".

seanchas: "history, lore". PUL claimed in NIWU (p94) that this word means "history", whereas *stair*, usually used for "history", means only "recitation" (a more accurate statement would be that *stair*, a foreign borrowing in the meaning of "history", and *stáir*, a native word meaning "rush, gush", have become confused in WM Irish). Despite PUL's objections, *stair* is frequently found, among other writers of Irish at any rate, in the meaning of "history". As a verbal noun in chapter 44 here, *seanchas* means "to relate, to tell a story". Pronounced /ʃanəxəs/.

seang: "slender"; pronounced /ʃauŋg/.

seanmóin: a noun and verbal noun meaning "sermon; act of preaching", or *seanmóir* in GCh. Pronounced /ʃanə'mo:n′/.

seanndlí: "ancient law"; pronounced /ʃan-dl′i:~ʃaun-dl′i:/. I'm grateful to Dr Seán Ua Súilleabháin for informing me that Pádraig Ó Luínse of An Sliabh Riach (1907-1986) had the diphthong in this word.

seasaím, seasamh: "to stand", or *seasaim, seasamh* in GCh. Note the preterite *do sheasaimh sé*, where GCh has *sheas sé*, reflecting a general tendency for *-mh* to appear in the third-person singular preterite (and imperative) where the verbal noun ends in *-mh* in WM Irish. *An fód do sheasamh*, "to stand your ground".

seasamh: "standing", but also "reliance". *Mo sheasamh oraibh!*, "I'm relying on you!"

seasc: "barren, dry, not giving milk". *Ba seasca*, "dry cows".

seasmhach: "steady, constant", pronounced /ʃasəvəx/.

seilbh: "possession", pronounced /ʃel′iv′/.

séimhe: "gentleness, mildness", pronounced /ʃe:v′i/.

seinnim, seinnt: "to play (music); to ring out (of a sound)", or *seinnim, seinm* in GCh. Pronounced /ʃeŋ′im′, ʃəint′/.

seirbhíseach: "servant", pronounced /ʃer′i'v′i:ʃəx/. The plural is found here both as *seirbhísigh* and *seirbhíseacha*.

seirithean: "indignation", or *seirfean* in GCh. Pronounced /ʃer′ihən/.

seisean: "he", the emphatic pronoun. Pronounced /ʃiʃən/.

seochas: "besides", or *seachas*. Spelt *seachas* in the original, but pronounced /ʃoxəs/ (IWM §297).

seóid: "jewel, valuable object", with *seóide* in the plural where GCh has *seoda*.

seóigh: "wonderful, marvellous". Originally the genitive singular of the noun *seó*, "show", this is now used as an adjective in its own right. Pronounced /ʃo:g′/.

seólta: "graceful", a meaning derived from its literal sense of "well-directed".

seómra: "room", pronounced /ʃo:mərə/.

sí: "blast, gust". Note that *sí* is feminine here, but masculine in GCh. *Sí gaoithe*, "whirlwind". It is worth noting that PUL's use of *sí* as a feminine noun was noted as incorrect in "Séadna", *An Músgraigheach*, Uimhir 3, Nodlaig 1943, p8.

síbhialta: "civil, polite", or *sibhialta* in GCh. Pronounced /ʃi:'v′iəlhə/.

síbhialtacht: "civility", or *sibhialtacht* in GCh. Pronounced /ʃi:'v′iəlhəxt/.

sid é: "this is, here is", corresponding to *siod é* in GCh. Similarly, *sid í* and *sid iad* correspond to *siod í* and *siod iad*. The *d* may be pronounced either broad or slender; compare IWM §266 and §274 (line 128) for examples of both pronunciations in AÓL's Irish. As the *d* is consistently written slender in PUL's works, it seems likely that he had a slender *d* here.

silim, sileadh: "to droop, hang", and by extension, "to weep, shed tears", where *ag sileadh* is a contraction of *ag sileadh na ndeór*.

símplí: "simple", but also "simpleminded". *Beart shímplí*, "a stupid thing to do".

símplíocht: "simplemindedness".

singil: "single, unmarried", pronounced /ʃiŋ′il′/.

sínsear: "ancestor", or *sinsear* in GCh. The singular form can have collective meaning, "ancestors".

síntiús: "donation".

síoda: "silk", or as an adjective in the genitive, "silken, made of silk".

síolrach: "progeny, offspring, breed", pronounced /ʃi:rəx/ (see IWM, §400). Some speakers may have /ʃi:lrəx/ (see GCD, §27).

síolraim, síolradh: "to breed, propagate", or *síolraím, síolrú* in GCh. *Do shíolraigh sé ó (dhuine)*, "he is descended from (a certain person)". This verb is correctly given as *síolraim*, as forms such as *shíolradar* (e.g. *Mo Sgéal Féin*, p173) are found in PUL's works. Yet PUL has *shíolraigh* here and elsewhere in the singular of the preterite (and not **shíolair*). Pronounced /ʃi:lrim′, ʃi:lrə/. Although IWM shows the *l* in *síolrach* is not pronounced—and AÓL was the source for Brian Ó Cuív's phonetic transcriptions in that work—the *l* in the cognate word *shíolraidh* is shown in the transcription *híolruig* in *Mo shgiàl fén* (p42). It seems *síolraim, síolradh* is a literary word that has largely been replaced by *síolthaím, síolthú* in WM Irish, and so retains its historical pronunciation where the classical form is found. Compare *shíolthaíodar* in *Seanachas Amhlaoibh* (p3) and *go mbeidís 'n-a gclainn ag Ábraham chómh maith díreach agus dá mba ar a shliocht do shíoltóchaidís* in *Seanmóin is Trí Fichid* (Vol 1, p71).

síos: "down". Note *síos is suas*, "up and down", where the Irish leads with *síos*.

siúd, súd: "that", as an adjective qualifying a noun is often used "for the purpose of expressing strong contempt or disgust" for someone or something (see PUL's NIWU, pp120-121).

siúlaim, siúl: "to walk". While PUL tends to have *siúlaim* in the first conjugation in the present tense (cf. *siúbhlann sé* in *Na Cheithre Soisgéil*, p33) and the verbal adjective used here, *siúlta*, is also first-conjugation, the future, preterite and imperative forms found in his works are in the second conjugation, as with *shiúlaigh sé* here (cf. *shiúil sé* in GCh). *Siúl* can also be transitive, as with *scoileanna agus coláistí an domhain do shiúl* in chapter 42 here, "to go round the schools and colleges of the world". *Do shiúlaigh sé chuige*, "he wandered many lands in order to get it (the knowledge)".

slabhra: "chain", pronounced /slaurə/.

slachtmhar: "workmanlike, efficient".

slámaim, slámadh: "to tease, card (of wool); to tease out, examine in minute detail, in discussion".

slán: "healthy, safe". *Trí mhíle slán*, "three thousand and no less".

sleagh: "spear", or *sleá* in GCh. This word is consistently transcribed *shlea*, without a long vowel, in the LS editions of PUL's *Séadna* (see *Shiàna*, p82, and *Don Cíochóté* (see *Don Cíchóté*, p2). *Sleagh* is part of a class of nouns such as *cneadh* and *meadh* where *-adh* or *-agh* does not produce a long vowel in WM Irish (see the note to IWM §355). It is thus pronounced /ʃl′a(h)/. The plural is *sleánna*, pronounced /ʃl′a:nə/, the long vowel of which was given in the original spelling here.

sleamhain: "slippery; smooth, polished", pronounced /ʃl′aun′/.

slí: "way". Note that the plural is edited here as *slithe*, where *slite* stands in GCh. The single occurrence of the plural, in chapter 12, was given as *slíghthe* in the original, but this is likely to reflect the hand of an editor. A short vowel seems most likely, as given in the LS version of PUL's *Catilína* (*shlihi*, on p18). *Ar slí na fírinne*, "dead". *Teacht sa tslí ar*, "to get in the way of".

sloigisc: "riff-raff, rabble". Pronounced /slog′iʃk′/.

slua: "host, army". PUL normally forms the plural of this word, *sluaite* in GCh, with an *-ó-*. While IWM (§92) shows the local pronunciation as /sluət′i/, /slo:t′i/ is also found in verse. The medial *-ó-* is therefore retained wherever it was given in the original, including in the genitive plural *sló* (*slógh*). It is also worth noting this word, masculine in GCh and in the Irish of other writers of WM literature, is generally feminine in PUL's works (*an tslua* here), although *an tslóigh*, /ə 'tslo:g′/, is found in the genitive singular here. Note the phrase *ar shlua na marbh*, "among the great majority; i.e., among the ranks of the dead".

sluasad: "shovel", or *sluasaid* in GCh where the historical dative has replaced the nominative. The plural used here is *sluaiste*; *sluaisti* is found in GCh.

sméarabhán: "soot, lampblack".

sméidim, sméideadh: "to wink, nod".

smuta: "a bit", or *smiota* in GCh. *Smut* is generally the form found in the nominative in PUL's works, although PUL's *Séadna* shows that, when used with *gáire*, the form is either *smut de gháire* (p94 of that work) or *smuta gáire*. *Ag cur smuta gáire asat*, "to give a slight laugh".

snaidhmim, snadhmadh: "to knot, tie, join", or *snaidhmim, snaidhmeadh* in GCh. Pronounced /snim′im′, snɑmə/. While the balance of forms found in PUL's works —including *do shnaidhmeas* in *Bricriu* (p33), and *snaidhmighthe*, in *An Craos-Deamhan* (p87)—would support the view that an /im′/ (or /i:m′/ either finally or before a consonant, as in *do shnaídhm sé* and *snaídhmfidh sé*) would be preferable in the finite verb, conjugated forms replicating the /ɑm/ of the verbal noun can be found, including *shnadhmaigh* /hnɑmig′/ in the preterite here. *Do shnaidhmeas, do shnadhmuigh, snadhmadh* and *snaidhmighthe* are the only forms of this verb directly attested in PUL's works.

snap: "snatch, catch". *Snap a thabhairt ar rud*, "to snatch something, snatch at it".

snáthad: "needle", or *snáthaid* in GCh, which uses the dative. *Obair shnáthaide,* "needlework".
sneachta: "snow", with *sneachtaidh* in the genitive. Pronounced /ʃn′axtə, ʃn′axtig′/.
snua: "complexion, one's normal appearance". Pronounced /sno:/.
so-fheicse: "visible", or *sofheicthe* in GCh. Pronounced /so-ikʃi/.
sochar: "advantage, benefit", but also "produce, provisions".
sochraid: "procession". Pronounced /soxərid′/.
socraím, socrú: "to settle, place". Pronounced /sokə'ri:m′, sokə'ru:/. *Socrú ar rud a dhéanamh,* "to decide to do something".
sodar: "trot", of horses, a noun and a verbal noun.
sóil: "comfortable, luxurious", *sóúil* in GCh. The original spelling here was *sóghail,* a truncation of the traditional *sóghamhail,* showing the pronunciation is /so:l′/.
soilbhir: "pleasant, cheerful"; pronounced /sol′iv′ir′/.
soilbhreas: "pleasantness", pronounced /sol′iv′(i)r′əs/. *Marú le soilbhreas,* "killing with kindness".
soiléire: "plainness, clarity". *Dá shoiléire é,* "however clearly". FGB cross-references this word to *soiléireacht.*
soílse: "brightness". *A Shoílse,* "Your Excellency".
soir siar: "east and west, backwards and forwards", and, by extension, "upset, turned upside down", as in chapter 13 here.
soíscéal: "gospel". Pronounced /si:ʃk′e:l/.
sólaist: "delicacy; dessert". Usually plural (*sólaistí*), *sólaist* here appears to be a back-formation from *sólaistí*; the traditional singular, given in PSD, was *sólas* (*sómhlas*).
solaoid: "illustration, example, parable", pronounced /so'li:d′/.
soláthraím, soláthar: "to get, procure; to seek out (to search for and find)". Pronounced /slɑ:r'hi:m′, slɑ:hər/.
sop: "wisp". The plural *suip* tends to mean "stalks of grass or straw".
sórd: "sort", or *sórt* in GCh, pronounced /so:rd/.
sos: "rest, pause". *Gan sos,* "unceasingly".
speach: "kick".
speic: "a sidelong glance". *Níor chuir éinne aon speic air,* "no-one paid any attention to him".
spéirling: "violence, strife". *I spéirling catha,* "in the heat of battle".
spiaire: "spy".
spiaireacht: "espionage".
spídiúchán: "reviling, abusing".
spionnadh: "liveliness, animation".
splannc: "flash of lightning", with *splanncracha* in the plural. The double *n* is used in the editing here to show the diphthong: pronounced /splauŋk, splauŋkərəxə/.
spleáchas: "dependence". *Gan spleáchas do,* "in spite of".
spréacharnach: "sparkling, scintillating". As a feminine verbal noun, this becomes *ag spréacharnaigh* in the dative, although this distinction in not observed in GCh.

spreagaim, spreagadh: "to incite, inspire", although this is given in a musical context only here (*ceól do spreagadh suas*, "to strike up a tune, begin to play music"), the meaning of "to incite" being found here as *spriocaim*. Nevertheless, *spreagaim* is also found in the sense of "to incite, inspire" in PUL's other works (see *iad do spreagadh chun aithrighe* in *Críost Mac Dé*, Vol 1, p83*)*. See also under *spriocaim*.

spriocaim, spriocadh: "to incite, inspire". The verb *spriocaim* exists in GCh only in the meaning "to fix, arrange", but PUL uses this verb to mean "inspire" (as in chapter 40 here), a meaning that is covered by *spreagaim* in GCh. PUL also uses *spreagaim* in this meaning too, so the relationship between these forms is complex. *Spriocaim* results from the confusion of *priocaim* and *spreagaim* in WM Irish. See also under *spreagaim*.

spriúchaim, spriúchadh: "to fly into a rage".

spriúnlaitheacht: "stinginess, miserliness"; or *sprionlaitheacht* in GCh. As *beart spriúnlaithe* means "a mean or shabby trick", *spriúnlaitheacht* means "shabbiness" in chapter 57, when referring to the behaviour of Mac Giolla Phádraig.

sraith: "row, layer". *'Na sraitheannaibh*, "in rows".

srang: "string, cord", with *sraíng* in the dative. Pronounced /srauŋg, sri:ŋg'/.

srian: "reins of a horse", with *sriain* in the dative. Note that this word is feminine here, but masculine in GCh. *Srian a chimeád le t'fheirg*, "to hold your anger in check". *Tugadh a srian féin di*, "she was given her head of steam (i.e. given the latitude to proceed as she saw fit)".

sroisim, sroisiúint: "to reach", or *sroichim, sroicheadh* in GCh. Pronounced /sroʃim', sro'ʃu:nt'/.

sról: "satin". PUL speaks of soldiers wearing *léinteacha sróil*: PSD shows that *sról* can simply mean "white linen", and it is more likely that soldiers would be wearing white linen than satin; hence, "white linen shirts". But note that the 1910 edition of *Niamh* contained a glossary that claimed the meaning was "satin shirts". PUL probably didn't compile the glossary himself, so this appears to be an editorial error.

stáicín: "stake, post". *Stáicín áiféis*, "a laughing-stock", which phrase is regularly found in PUL's works without the genitive *áiféise*. See *Táin Bó Cuailgne* (p205) and *An Craos-Deamhan* (p56) for further examples. One possible explanation may be that PUL regarded *stáicín áiféis* as a single unit, rather than as a combination of two nouns that required the genitive on the second noun.

stail: "stallion". This is a feminine word, but note how it is referred to as *é* (and note also *ar a mhuin, ar a cheann*) in chapter 28 here. Compare *Scéalaíocht Amhlaoibh* (p194), where AÓL refers to a stallion as *í sin*, and *An Bhruinneall Bhán* (p13), where Diarmuid Ua Laoghaire refers to a stallion as *í*.

staithim, stathadh: "to pick, pluck", or *stoithim, stoitheadh* in GCh.

stálaithe: "seasoned, toughened".

stán: "tin". *Canna stáin*, "a tin can".

stangadh: "bend, sag, warp", pronounced /staŋə/.

steille-bheatha: found in the phrase *'na steille-bheathaidh*, pronounced /nə 'ʃt′el′i-v′ahig′/, "as large as life, in the flesh".
stíobhard: "steward". Also *fear tís.*
stiúraím, stiúrú: "to guide, direct", or *stiúraim, stiúradh* in GCh.
stiúrúchán: "act of giving directions", particularly in a constant fashion.
stoc: "stock, cattle", with *stuic* in the genitive.
stoirm: "storm". This word is transcribed *sdoirim* in *Eshirt* (p27), and so is pronounced /stor′im′/.
stollaim, stolladh: "to tear, rend", with *stollta*, /stoulhə/, as the past participle.
stracaim, stracadh: "to tear", or *sracaim, sracadh* in GCh.
stríocaim, stríocadh: "to yield, submit".
stuama: "level-headed; sensible", traditionally spelt *stuamdha.* The traditional WM pronunciation would be with a devoiced *m*, /stuəmhə/.
suaimhneas: "peace, quietness", pronounced /suən′əs/.
suairc: "pleasant, agreeable, gay".
suan: "sleep, slumber".
suas: "up", but also "alive, extant".
suím, suí: "to sit down; to place, locate". The verbal adjective *suite* has a short vowel, /sit′i/, in its most common meaning, "seated" (PSD states it is *suíte* where it means "certain").
suím: "sum, amount; interest". Masculine here, but feminine in GCh. Pronounced /si:m′/. The genitive *suime* has a short vowel, /sim′i/.
sult: "amusement", with *suilt* in the genitive. Pronounced /suhl, sihl′/.
sultmhar: "pleasant, enjoyable", pronounced /suhlfər/.
tabharthas: "gift", or *tabhartas* in GCh. The plural here is generally *tabharthaisti*, although *tabharthaisi* is found in one passage here (chapter 40). The GCh plural is *tabhartais.* Pronounced /tourhəs, tourhiʃt′i:~tourhiʃi:/.
taca: "peg, pin, nail; point of time, juncture". *Um an dtaca so*, "by this time".
tagaim/tigim, teacht: "to come". PUL used the classical spelling *tar* in the imperative, a spelling that has been adopted in GCh, whereas the form *tair* is more generally found in WM Irish, /tɑr′/. T. F. O'Rahilly used the spelling *tair* in *Papers on Irish Idiom* to transcribe an unpublished manuscript by PUL, *Measgra Cainte* (see p44). O'Rahilly was attempting in his editing to establish a more phonetically appropriate spelling system for WM Irish. It is not known for sure what pronunciation PUL had of this imperative, but the emphatic form of the imperative, *tar-sa* in the original of *Niamh* may indicate that PUL did have a broad *r* in this word. The autonomous form of the preterite is given here as *do tagadh*, a form not found in PUL's other works, which have *do tánathas*. The verbal adjective, found as *tagtha* in GCh, is *tagaithe* here, pronounced /tɑgihi/. *Do tháinig amach*, "it came out, it became known". *Teacht ar an obair*, "to set about the work". With *le*, "to be able to": *le heagla go mb'fhéidir go dtiocfadh le Risteárd a neart do chruinniú*, "lest Richard could gather his forces". Note *dá dtigeadh leis* in chapter 49, where *dtigeadh* is a past subjunctive formed from the older form of *tagaim*, namely, *tigim*.

taighdim, taighde: "to research into something", with *ar*. Pronounced /təid′im, təid′i/ according to CFBB (p254).

táim, bheith: "to be". The second-person singular form *taíonn tú* is found here, as well as an older form *taoi* (found in the relative here as *ataoi-se*) corresponding to *tá tú* (and *atá tú*) in GCh. Older second-person plural present-tense forms *atáthaoi* and *go bhfuiltí-se* are found here, corresponding *atá sibh* and *go bhfuil sibhse* in GCh. *Go raibh maith agat* is edited here as *go ra' maith agat*, as the *raibh* is not given in full in the pronunciation of this phrase. *Ní bheifá mar sin*, "you would not think that/say that in that case".

The use of the particle *a* with *bheith* is worth commenting on. PUL insisted there was no infinitival particle in Irish. In *Papers on Irish Idiom* (pp74-75), T. F. O'Rahilly transcribes an unpublished manuscript of PUL's explaining that *is maith lium do shiúl* (as it is spelt therein) means, not "I wish to walk", but "I like your walk". A particle is required where the verbal noun governs an object (*an bóthar do shiúl*): "when the object is expressed in the Irish there is a certain relation found to exist between it and the verb. That relation is expressed by *do*. The moment the object is dropped, that relation, of course, disappears, and as a consequence the *do* must disappear". As an intransitive verb, *bheith* does not govern an object, but a particle is required where a noun governs *bheith* as its subject. The particle *a* governing the verbal noun is a worn-down variant of *do*, and the same reasoning applies. Consequently, PUL's works do not combine *a* (or *do*) with the intransitive verbal noun *bheith* unless *bheith* is governed by a noun subject (*rud a bheith ann*) or there is some possessive or proleptic reason for the particle's being there. For example, in chapter 53, we read *ná fuil aon teip ná go mbuafaimíd sa chath so atá le troid. "Níl", arsa Maolmhórdha. "Ní fhéadfadh a bheith"*. Here *a bheith* is possessive in meaning ("its being"), with the sentence meaning "there couldn't be". Similarly, in *Don Cíochóté* (p10), we read *ba chuma cé'cu bhíodh 'fhios aici-sin a leithéid-sin do bheith ann i n-aon chor nó gan a bheith*, where *gan a bheith* is possessive, "without its being", i.e. "for it not to be/for there not to be". In chapter 17 here, we read *gan a bheith orm labhairt*, where *a bheith* is possessive with proleptic sense, anticipating *labhairt*. In chapter 56 here, *b'fheárr liom go mór a bheith ar chumas an tseanchais a rá gur chosain na fir é*, *a bheith* is also proleptic, as is *a rá* later in the sentence.

While *bheith* is not transitive, it can be followed by an adjectival complement (*bheith go maith*), and so *bheith* may be governed by such adjectival complements that precede it with the intervention of the particle *a* in a manner analogous to a verbal noun being governed a preceding object. For example, in chapter 31, we read *bhí sé groí cumasach láidir mar ba dhual athar do ' bheith*. While no particle (or apostrophe) is given in the original, there are many similar instances in PUL's works, such as *mar ba dhual athar agus seanathar dóibh a bheith* in *Sgéalaidheacht as an mBíobla Naomhtha*, Vol 5 (p589). Similarly, in *ad'shagart ba cheart duit a bheith* in *Cómhairle Ár Leasa* (p106), *ad'shagart* is a preceding complement governing *bheith*. By contrast, in *do leog sé air gur mhaith leis bheith 'na shagart* in chapter 30 here, there is nothing missed out, and a particle (or an apostrophe indicating the omission of a particle) has not been inserted in the editing process here.

The verbal noun is generally lenited in the modern language owing to the frequency with which it was found governed by a leniting particle, and GCD (§690, but for use of an unlenited *beith*, see also §531) shows there are Munster dialects or idiolects in which the particle *a* is regularly attached to *bheith* even where it is not governed by a noun or pronoun subject, or where there is no preceding complement, or where it is not found in a possessive or proleptic context (producing "ungrammatical" sentences like *tá sé chomh maith agam a bheith ag imeacht*), but such usages are absent in PUL's works. The only possible counterexample identified seems to be *pé cor a thabharfair dom ní féidir dó a bheith ach go maith* in *Aithris ar Chríost* (p131), although even here it could be argued that *a bheith* is possessive (or proleptic anticipating *go maith*), with the whole sentence meaning "whatever you do to me, it could not be anywise but good".

tairbhe: "benefit", pronounced /tɑr′if′i/.

tairbheach: "beneficial". Pronounced /tɑr′if′əx/.

tairgim, tairiscint: "to offer". Pronounced /tɑr′ig′im′, tɑr′iʃk′int′/. See also under *tarraigim, tarrac.*

taise naomh: "relics of the saints". *Taise* is plural in PUL's works (see NIWU, p102) and therefore equivalent to *taisí* in GCh. PUL seems to derive this plural from the variant singular, *tais*, glossed in PSD as "wraith".

taithneamh: "affection; shine, shimmer", or *taitneamh* in GCh. Pronounced /taŋ′həv/.

taithneann, taithneamh: "to please", or "to shine" (e.g. of the sun), or *taitníonn, taitneamh* in GCh. Generally in the first declension in PUL's works and pronounced /taŋ′hən, taŋ′həv/. The past is *do thaithn*, /də haŋ′/ and the conditional-tense form found in this work is *do thaithnfeadh*, /də haŋ′həx/.

talamh: "land". The genitive, *talaimh* in GCh, is found consistently with a slender *l* in PUL's works: *tailimh*, /tal′iv′/. The variant genitive, *talún*, is found in one passage here (*toradh talún*, "fruits of the earth", in chapter 57). It is worth noting that *talún* is found as *talúin* in the Irish of AÓL and DBÓC, and it is possible that this was also PUL's pronunciation too. The plural here is *talúintí*, where *tailte* stands in GCh. *Fé thalamh agus os cionn tailimh*, "overtly and covertly". *Tá ' fhios ag an dtalamh (go)*, "God knows, goodness knows; I swear".

taobh: "side". *Aon taobh acu*, "either of them".

taoide: "tide". This word is masculine in PUL's works. *Bhí an taoide lán*, "the tide was in".

taoiseach: "chieftain". Both *taoisigh* and *taoiseacha* are found in the plural here.

taom: "period of illness". The dative plural *taomaibh* here is formed from a nominative plural *taoma*, where GCh has *taomanna.*

tapaidh: "quick", or *tapa* in GCh. The comparative is *tapúla* (cf. the entry for *tapúil* in FGB). Pronounced /tɑpig′, tɑ'pu:lə/.

tapúlacht: "quickness, speediness".
tar n-ais: a delenited form of *thar n-ais*, "back". *Tar n-ais* is found more often after a dental, but, given the high incidence of typological errors in the original, *tar n-ais* is adjusted in this edition to *thar n-ais.*
tar, thar: "through, across, past". *Thorm, thort*, "past me, past you", spelt *tharam* and *tharat* in GCh; pronounced /horəm, horət/. *Tháirsi*, "beyond or across her", or *thairsti* in GCh; pronounced /hɑːrʃi/. *Teacht tháirsi*, "mention of her". *Thórsu*, /hoːrsə/, "beyond them", equivalent to *tharsta* in GCh. *Thar a bhfeacaís riamh!*, "exactly so!" (literally, "beyond everything you ever saw!").
tarna: "second", or *dara* in GCh.
tarraigim, tarrac: "to pull, draw", or *tarraingím, tarraingt* in GCh. Pronounced /tɑrig′im′, tɑrək/. The verbal adjective is *tarraicthe*, /tɑrik′i/, where *tarraingthe* is used in GCh. PUL used the classical spellings (*taraingim*, etc) in the original—albeit with a single *r*, reflecting his decision not to use double letters where the use of doubled letters had no significance in terms of the phonology of WM Irish—and these have been adjusted to *rr* in the editing process here. Shán Ó Cuív's LS edition of PUL's novel *Séadna* shows a slender *r* pronunciation, and GCD §522 also shows this to be the more general Munster pronunciation. However, Osborn Bergin's LS editions of PUL's *Catilína* and *Aesop a Tháinig go h-Éirinn* show a broad *r*, and Brian Ó Cuív also uses a broad *r* in the phonetic spellings he used in CFBB (e.g. p3). *Scéalaíocht Amhlaoibh* shows that forms with both broad and slender *r*'s were used by AÓL (cf. *tharraig* on p3 and *thairrig* on p5). As both forms exist (see Seán Ua Súilleabháin's comments in *Stair na Gaeilge*, p489), it seems best to edit here with the broad *r* that PUL himself used. It is interesting that *Foclóir do Shéadna*, the authorised vocabulary to PUL's novel *Séadna* probably drawn up by Norma Borthwick, confuses *tarraigim, tarrac* and *tairgim, tairiscint*, by glossing *taraingim* and *tarang* as "I offer; an act of offering", as well as "I draw, I pull; an act of drawing, pulling" (see p111). This entry in *Foclóir do Shéadna* reflects the spelling in the text of *Séadna*, which was also edited by Norma Borthwick: *b'fhuirisde dhuit a aithint, nuair taraingeadh trí fichid púnt duit ar do bhraimín giobalach, gorta, droich-mhianaigh, nár dhuine mhacánta tharaing riamh air a leithéid d' airgead* (*Séadna*, p146). Another piece of evidence that could be cited is the Irish of Diarmuid Ua Laoghaire, PUL's second cousin and professor at Coláiste na Múmhan in Ballingeary, who wrote *thairidh sé* with a slender *r* (*Cogar Mogar*, p20). *Tarrac anuas*, "to take up a topic for conversation": *do tarraigeadh anuas an uile fhocal den chainnt*, "every word of the conversation was discussed". *Tarrac chút*, "to bring up as a topic for conversation". *Beart a tharrac chút*, "to adopt a strategy, adopt a way of proceeding, take it up".
tásc: "report of someone's death". Generally found in collocation with *tuairisc.*
táthaím, táthú: "to weld, solder, unite".
tathant: "an act of urging or inciting".

te: "hot". Traditionally spelt *teith,* PUL is on record in NIWU (p127) as insisting this word has a "most distinct" final *-h* in the pronunciation. However, this is likely to be apparent only before a following vowel. Pronunciation /t′e~t′eh/.

té: a pronoun used with the article as *an té,* "he who". The *t* is calcified, and thus used in the genitive and dative of this word: *ar thuairisc an té, ag an té.*

téagartha: "substantial, bulky".

teaghlach: "household", pronounced /t′əiləx/.

téanam: "come along", part of a defective verb usually found only in the imperative. *Téanam* is derived from a first-person plural imperative, but is functionally a second-person imperative here in the phrase *téanam ort,* possibly analogous to the first-person singular imperative in English "let's be having you". Also note *téanaídh* here with the same meaning. Both *téanaídh* and *téanaidh* are found in PUL's works.

teanga: "tongue", with *teangan* in the genitive. *Fear teangan,* "interpreter".

teangmhaím, teangmháil: "to come into contact with something/someone", used with *le,* or *teagmhaím, teagmháil* in GCh. Pronounced /t′aŋə'vi:m′, t′aŋə'vɑ:l′/.

teangmhálaí: "a person one comes across", or *teagmhálai* in GCh. Pronounced /t′aŋə'vɑ:li:/.

teástáil: "trial", or *tástáil* in GCh. *Mí teástála,* "a month's trial, a month's probation".

teastaíonn, teastabháil: "to be wanted or needed", or *teastaíonn, teastáil* in GCh. The *bh* may be pronounced in WM Irish: /t′as'tɑ:l′~t′astə'vɑ:l′/. Used impersonally with *ó*: *rud a theastaíonn uaidh,* "something he wants/needs".

téim, dul: "to go". The dependent form is not always used after *go* in WM Irish in the past tense. PUL's usage is mixed; he normally writes *gur chuaigh,* although *go ndeigh* /n′əig′/ is also found in this work. *Sara ndeigh* is generally found with the dependent. In GCh, the absolute/dependent contrast is observed, as *go ndeachaigh. Ar chuais-se a choladh?* here has the same meaning as *an ndeachaigh tú a chodladh?* in GCh. Note the future tense here, *raghad,* /rəid/, where GCh has *rachaidh mé.*

Dul as, "to fail, decline". Impersonally, *dul de* means "to run out": *níor ghá do Cholla aon eagla ' bheith air go raghadh dá chuid lóin bídh ná dí,* "there was no need for Colla to be concerned that his food and wine would run out". The construction *dul de* was the subject of a letter by PUL published in *The Freeman's Journal* of March 17th, 1915, where he explained that Michael Sheehan in his *Gabha na Coille* had cited this construction as an example of "obscure and unintelligible construction" and inaccurately accounted for it. Despite Dr Sheehan's views, PUL insisted the construction was good Irish.

teinneas: "pain, soreness", or *tinneas* in GCh. Pronounced /t′eŋ′əs/ in WM Irish.

teipim, teip: "to fail". This verb is usually used impersonally: *do theip uirthi,* "she failed". Contrast the non-impersonal *bhí sé ag teip uirthi* in chapter 6: "she didn't manage to do it", literally, "it failed on her".

teithim, teitheadh: "to flee". Note the verbal adjective used here, *teithe,* "fled", corresponding to *teite* in GCh. In the classical spelling, the verb was *teichim,* with the participle *teichthe.* Other writers of WM Irish also preferred *teite* as the verbal adjective, thus clarifying the distinction between the verbal noun *teitheadh* and its genitive, the verbal adjective *teite/teithe. Teitheadh lena n-anam,* "to flee for their lives" (where *anam* is singular as each person has only one soul/life).

teóra: "boundary, limit", or *teorainn* in GCh, where the historical dative has replaced the nominative.

thíos: "down", but also note *thíos leis,* "suffering for it, bearing the consequences of it". The authorised *Foclóir do Shéadna* states (pp113-114) that the direction of the metropolis or capital is *thíos* in Irish, as with *thíos i dTeamhair* in chapter 9, which would probably be "up in Tara" in English. *Do crochfí me chómh luath agus ' bheinn thíos* in chapter 42, "I would have been hanged as soon as I was in Dublin".

thuaidh: "north". Note *ón gceann tuaidh* here, where the *th* is delenited after a dental.

tí: "point, mark". *Ar ti,* "on the point of, intending to".

tiarnas: "lordship". *Tiarnas ri,* "a king's domain".

tigh: "house", or *teach* in GCh. The historical dative has replaced the nominative in WM Irish.

tímpall: "around", or *timpeall* in GCh. The broad *p* in WM Irish is preserved in the editing system used here: /t′i:m′pəl/; PUL's original spelling was *tímpal.*

tionóisc: "accident". This is PUL's regular word for "accident"; *timpiste* in not found in his works.

tíoránach: "tyrant, bully".

tíos: "household, housekeeping". *Fear tís,* steward (also *stíobhard* here).

tirim: "dry", pronounced /tr′im′/.

tispeánaim, tispeáint: "to show", or *taispeánaim, taispeáint* in GCh. PUL consistently wrote this word with a broad *t,* but IWM (see the note to §368) shows the pronunciation is /t′is′p′ɑ:nim′, t′is′p′a:nt′/ (or /t′i′ʃa:nim′, t′i′ʃa:nt′/). A slender *t* is shown in the LS editions of PUL's works (e.g. *Shiàna,* p43).

tiubaisteach: "calamitous, disastrous", or *tubaisteach* in GCh. A slender initial *t* was used in the original text for this word. CFBB (p262) shows *tubaist* with a broad *t,* and *tubaisteach* is found in PUL's *Séadna* (e.g. p86). There are a number of words that are variously spelt with broad or slender *t* in PUL's Irish (see *tionóisg* in the original text here and *tonóisg* in his *Aesop a Tháinig go h-Éirinn,* 1903 edition, p4), reflecting a wider issue with the only slightly palatalised nature of slender *t* in Munster Irish.

tiubh: "quick", with the comparative *tiúbha,* pronounced /t′uv, t′u:/. The comparative would be *tibhe* in GCh.

tiúnlacaim, tiúnlacan: "to escort", or *tionlacaim, tionlacan* in GCh. *Tiúnlacan* is found in PUL's *Séadna,* (pp, 14, 278), and the transcriptions in the LS edition (see *Shiàna,* pp9, 112) variously indicate pronunciations of /t′unləkən/ and /t′u:nləkən/; GCD §576 has /tu:ləkən/, with a broad *t* and no medial *n.* It seems likely a pronunciation of /t′u:ləkim′, t′u:ləkən/ would be preferable here.

tiúnscal: "industry, project, plan", or *tionscal* in GCh, pronounced /t′u:skəl/ in WM Irish. This word was given as *tiúsgal* in the original text.
tiúnsclach: "industrious", or *tionsclach* in GCh, pronounced /t′u:skələx/ in WM Irish. This word was given as *tiúsgalach* in the original.
tnáithim, tnáitheadh: "to wear down, exhaust".
tocht: "silence".
tógaim, tógaint: "to lift, build", etc, or *tógaim, tógáil* in GCh. A variant verbal noun *tógáilt* is also found in PUL's works.
toghaim, toghadh: "to choose, select", pronounced /toum′, tou/. The preterite is *do thoibh sé*, /də hov′ s′e:/, but *thogh sé* in GCh. Brian Ó Cuív transcribed a note by PUL that accompanied his manuscript translation of the Old Testament that refers to his preferred spelling of the preterite of this word: "there is one other word and I think I must ask you to let me keep it. It is the past tense of *toghaim*, 'I choose'. *Do thoghas* is all right, 'I have chosen' or 'I did choose'. *Do thoghais* is all right. But for 'he chose' I have never heard any Irish but *do thoibh sé. Tá sé toghtha* = 'It is chosen' is quite manageable. It is easy to call it *toffa*. But *do thoibh sé* = 'He chose' must stand as it is or you will have nothing. I have seen it written *do thogh sé*. But that is not at all what is *said* and *heard*, so I find I must keep *thoibh*. It occurs also in the imperative *toibh é* = 'choose it'" ("An t-Athair Peadar Ua Laoghaire's translation of the Old Testament", p645].
toil: "wish", with the genitive *toile* here, in contradistinction to the *tola* of GCh. *Chun a thoile,* "to his liking".
toirmeasc: "mischief, row", pronounced /tor′im′əsk/.
tóirthneach: "thunder", with *tóirthní* in the genitive; corresponding to *toirneach* in GCh. Pronounced /to:rhn′əx/. PUL commented in NIWU (p107) that he had never heard this word pronounced without its medial *-th-*; nonetheless, the distinction in pronunciation is exceedingly slight, with /rh/ realised as a devoiced /r/.
toisc: "purpose, object; errand, expedition". *An toisc a thug sibh,* "the purpose that brought you here". *An toisc ar a raibh an bhuíon ag imeacht ó dheas,* "the errand that the group were going south to do".
tón: "bottom", or *tóin* in GCh, where the historical dative has replaced the nominative.
toradh: "product, fruit". *De thoradh aimsire,* "owing to the passage of time".
tórmach: "act of increasing or swelling". *Tórmach cogaidh,* "brewing of war".
torthúil: "fruitful, productive; something that 'pays off'".
tosach: "beginning, front", pronounced /tə'sɑx/.
tosnaím, tosnú: "to start", or *tosaím, tosú* in GCh.
tráigh: "strand, beach", or *trá* in GCh. The traditionally correct spelling of this word shows the pronunciation, /trɑ:g′/. The genitive has been edited here as *trá,* from *trágha* in the original, as the GCh form gives the correct pronunciation of the genitive.
traochaim, traochadh: "to wear out, exhaust; overcome, subdue".
tráthnóna: "evening", pronounced /trɑ:n'ho:nə/.
tráthúil: "timely".

treabhaim, treabhadh: "to plough", with *treafa* as the past participle. *Treafa* is pronounced /tr′afə~tr′ahə/; without clear evidence as to PUL's pronunciation, it is edited here with an *f*. *Páirc threafa*, "a ploughed field". Pronounced /tr′aum′, tr′au/.

treabhchas: "tribe". The plural *treabhchasai* is used here, where GCh has *treabhchais*. *Treabhchaisí* was the plural used by AÓL (see *Seanachas Amhlaoibh*, p3), and one that accords better with general declension patterns in WM Irish. Pronounced /tr′auxəs, tr′auxəsi:~tr′auxəʃi:/.

tréan: "strong". PUL uses both *treise* and *tréine* as comparatives here.

tréanas: "abstinence", e.g. from meat. Pronounced /tr′e:nəs~/tr′əinəs/.

treás go: "since, seeing as", or *tráth is go* in GCh. *Tráth 's go* is found in PUL's *Séadna* (*trá's go*, p50). PUL's forms point to a pronunciation of /tr′a:s gə~trɑ:s gə/, although other speakers of WM Irish also have /trɑ:h əs gə/.

treasna: "across" or *trasna* in GCh. Pronounced /tr′asnə/.

tréigim, tréigean: "to abandon".

tréith: "weak, feeble". *Fén bhfód go tréith*, "six foot under", i.e. "dead and buried".

trí chéile: "confusion". *Trí chéile aigne*, "mental confusion". *Trína chéile*, "mixed up, confused".

trí: "through". Note that this preposition is often lenited after a vowel or after an *r*. *Rud a chur thrí chéile*, "to discuss something". Also note *treasna thríom*, "through me".

trialaim, triail: "to try, test", or *triailim, triail* in GCh; pronounced /tr′ialim′, tr′ial′/. Note that in GCh the distinction between what in PUL's Irish is *trialaim*, "I try, test" and *triallaim*, "I journey" is a little clearer than in WM Irish: this verb has a slender *l* throughout in GCh, whereas in PUL's Irish a slender *l* appears only in the third-person preterite, the singular imperative and the verbal noun. The forms of this verb are: present, *trialaim, trialann sé*; preterite, *do thrialas, do thriail sé*; future, *trialfad, trialfaidh sé*; imperative and verbal noun, *triail*; past participle, *trialta*. The form *trialta* corresponds to *triailte* in GCh, and could be confused with *triallta*, the past participle of *triallaim*, "to journey". *Trialta* is theoretically pronounced /tr′ialhə/ and *triallta* /tr′iəlhə/, and so the quality of the diphthong provides a point of distinction; this was particularly the case in the speech of older speakers who maintained a regular distinction between /ia/ and /iə/ where younger speakers may have only /iə/. *Do trialadh i marú iad*, "they were tried for murder".

triallaim, triall: "to fare, journey"; pronounced /tr′iəlim′, tr′iəl/. *Ag triall ar*, "with recourse to" in various senses, including going to see someone, bringing something for someone and sending something to someone. See also under *trialaim*.

trínse: "trench".

trioblóid: "trouble", pronounced /tr′ubə'lo:d′/.

triúch: "district".

triúr: "three people", with *trír* in the genitive here where GCh has *triúir*.

troid: "quarrel, fighting". Pronounced /trod′/.

troidim, troid: "to quarrel, fight". Pronounced /trod′im′, trod′/.
trom: "heavy", with *truime* in the comparative here. Pronounced /troum, trim′i/.
troscadh: "fasting, abstinence".
truaill: "sheath".
trúig: "cause, occasion". *Trúig bháis*, "cause of death".
truime-de: "all the heavier". This is a 'second comparative' form, similar to *feárr-de, usa-de, miste*, meaning "all the more X for it".
truime: "heaviness", or *troime* in GCh. *Ag dul i dtruime*, "getting heavier".
tu, thu: disjunctive form of the second person pronoun, pronounced /tu, hu/. Always *tú* in GCh.
tua: "axe". Note the genitive *tua* and the dative *tuaigh* (pronounced /tuəg′/), forms that are more easily derived from the traditional spellings *tuagh, tuagha* and *tuaigh*. The plural is *tuanna* (originally *tuaghanna*).
tuairim: "opinion". *Tuairim do rud*, "an opinion on something, an idea of it". It seems the preposition is *do* and not *de* in this idiom, as we find *tá tuairim agam do* in chapter 46 here.
tuairisc: "account, description". *Tuairisc cruínn*, "a detailed account", is without lenition on the adjective, possibly because an /ʃkxr/ cluster would be hard to pronounce. This phrase is repeatedly so found in PUL's works.
tuath: "the countryside; rural district". Note the genitive here is given as *tuatha*, where GCh has *tuaithe*. Either spelling would yield the pronunciation /tuəhə/, but PSD shows that PUL's spelling was accepted.
tuathal: "blunder". *Fear is ea é nár theip an tuathal riamh air*, "he is a man who has never failed to do the wrong thing".
tugaim, tabhairt: "to give". *Tabhairt ar*, "to call". The present autonomous is given as *tugtar* here, but can be pronounced /tugtər/ or /tugəhər/. Note the past participle *tabhartha*, pronounced /tu:rhə/. *Tabhairt leat*, "to mentally grasp, to catch, to 'get' something": *thugais leat an chainnt cruínn go leór*, "you grasped the conversation entirely correctly". Note that *tabhair dhom*, "give me", is pronounced /trom/.
tugtha: "devoted". Equivalent to *tabhartha*, with the same meaning, which form is also found here and is the form more generally found in PUL's works. *Tugtha do rud, tugtha chun rud a dhéanamh*, "devoted to something, devoted to doing something". Pronounced /tukə~tugəhi/.
tuilleadh: "addition; more". PUL consistently used spellings (*tuille* in the original text here) indicating a pronunciation of /til′i/, where AÓL had *teilleadh*, /t′el′i/ (see *Scéalaíocht Amhlaoibh*, p8).
túirligim, túirleacan: "to descend", or *tuirlingím, tuirlingt* in GCh. IWM §395 show that /tu:rl′ik′/ is also found for the verbal noun, which form is found in PUL's *Na Cheithre Soisgéil* (e.g. p225), albeit spelt *túirling* in that work.
tuisle: "hinge". PUL uses *tuisleanna* in the plural here, where there would be *tuislí* in GCh. However, he wrote in NIWU (p110) that both forms of the plural were acceptable.
tur: "dry", but also "blunt, peremptory".

turas: "journey, round, occasion". Pronounced /trus/.
tús: "beginning". The dative is *túis* here (*ar dtúis*, "at first"), implying this word is feminine in the dative, although this word doesn't seem to be used in WM Irish outside of phrases such as *ar dtúis* and *ó thúis go deireadh*. Munster Irish seems to prefer *tosach* to *tús* in most contexts.
tútach: "crude, botched".
uabhar: "pride", pronounced /uər/. Note that sometimes, as in chapter 48 here, "wounded pride" would be a more appropriate translation.
uacht: "will, testament". *Fágaim le huacht (go)*, "I vouch, I swear", as an asseveration.
uachtar: "cream". *In uachtar*, "on top, having the upper hand".
uaigh: "grave". Note the genitive singular *uagha* and the plural *uaghanna* found here, in contradistinction to *uaighe* and *uaigheanna* in GCh. Pronounced /uəg', uə, uənə/.
uaigneach: "lonely, desolate", pronounced /uəg'in'əx/. *Seómra uaigneach*, "a private or secluded room".
uaigneas: "loneliness, grief", pronounced /uəg'in'əs/.
uair go leith: "an hour and a half", pronounced /uər' gil'i/.
uair: "time; hour". *Ocht n-uaire is daichead*, "forty-eight hours", illustrating the fact that *uair* can mean "hour", even when it does not stand as *uair a' chluig*.
uaisleacht: "nobility". *Dá uaisleacht é*, "however noble".
uan: "lamb", also *uan caeireach*.
uanaíocht: "alternation, rotation", or *uainíocht* in GCh. *Uanaíocht a dhéanamh ar a chéile*, "to take turns, take it in turns".
uathás: "horror; an astonishing amount of something", or *uafás* in GCh.
uathásach: "terrible", or *uafásach* in GCh. Pronounced /uə'hɑ:səx/ in WM Irish.
ubh: "egg", with *uíbhe* in the plural where GCh has *uibheacha*. Pronounced /ov, i:/.
uchtach: "spirit, vigour; the delivery of a speech". *Bhí rith cainnte aige agus uchtach láidir ceólmhar bínn*, "he had a way with words, and a strong, musical, melodious delivery". Pronounced /əx'tɑx/.
úil: "knowledge", or *iúl* in GCh. PUL used the spelling *i n-iúil*, but the *n* is broad in this word, /ə 'nu:l'/; cf. Brian Ó Cuív's spelling *i n-úil* in CFBB (p50). The word *úmhail*, "attention", appears to have become confused with the dative of *eól*, producing *úil*. *Rud a chur in úil do dhuine*, "to let someone know something, to make someone realise something".
uille: "elbow", or *uillinn* in GCh, where the dative has replaced the nominative. *Fé m'uillinn*, "under my elbow", referring here to the way one would hold a harp.
uisce-fé-thalamh: "intrigue", or *uisce faoi thalamh* in GCh. This is properly a single hyphenated noun, and not a noun phrase.
uise: "temple (of the head)". Usually plural, as in *uiseanna* here, corresponding to *uisinní* in GCh.
um: "about, round". PUL uses the traditional *do bhuail sé umam* in preference to *do bhuaileas leis* to mean "I met him, bumped into him". PUL stated in NIWU (p112) that *um* was not an obsolete word for him, and that he had always heard *cuir*

umat do chasóg for "put your coat on", and not *cuir ort do chasóg*. Note the combined forms: *umam* /ə'mum/, *umat* /ə'mut/, *uime* /im'i/, *uímpi* /i:mp'i/, *umainn* /ə'miŋ'/, *umaibh* /ə'miv'/, *úmpu* /u:mpə/. *Um a chéile* in the original text is adjusted in this edition to *um á chéile* /i'm'a: x'e:l'i/, which spelling is found in many of PUL's works, e.g. *Sgéalaidheachta as an mBíobla Naomhtha*, Vol 2, p6. See *Stair na Gaeilge, VI: Gaeilge na Mumhan*, §6.22, for discussion of the pronunciation of these forms.

úmhal: "submissive, obedient". Pronounced /u:l/.

úmhlaím, úmhlú: "to humble (e.g. yourself); to bow (to someone)". Pronounced /u:'li:m', u:'lu:/.

úmhlaíocht: "humility", pronounced /u:'li:xt/.

únthairt: "rolling, tossing about", or *únfairt* in GCh, which spelling was used in the original text of *Niamh*. That PUL used the pronunciation /u:nhirt'/ is shown by the spelling *únfhairt* used in his novel, *Séadna* (p69), and in his *An Craos-Deamhan* (pp63, 76) and *Eisirt* (p41).

úr: "your (plural)", or *bhur* in GCh. Pronounced /u:r/.

urchar: "shot". Usually pronounced /ruxər/ in WM Irish (see IWM, §421). PUL's classical spelling is retained, as *Scéalaíocht Amhlaoibh* (p346) shows that /urəxər/ is possible here too.

úrlár: "floor". Note the long *u* here.

urraíocht: "surety, guarantee".

urrús: "guarantee, assurance".

Proverbs

is feárr bheith díomhaoin ná droch-ghnóthach: "it's better to be idle than up to no good".

is feárr féachaint roim(e) dhuine ná dhá fhéachaint 'na dhiaidh: "look before you leap; look ahead and be circumspect lest you are left with regrets later".

is feárr teitheadh maith ná droch-sheasamh: "discretion is the better part of valour".

www.ingramcontent.com/pod-product-compliance
Lightning Source LLC
Chambersburg PA
CBHW020504310726
48979CB00016B/2782/J
* 9 7 8 1 7 3 9 8 8 7 2 0 9 *